W9-ACL-740

MADAME CASTEL'S LODGER

Pierre Gustave Toutant Beauregard, first brigadier general to be appointed in the Confederate States' Army. From a portrait painted at Charleston in the spring of 1861, Fort Sumter in the background. Courtesy of City Hall, Charleston, South Carolina, where the original hangs.

THE

Deas, from whose grandfather's house on the Battery Beauregard watched the bombardment.

WITHDRAWN
L. R. COLLEGE LIBRARY

Madame Castel's Lodger

Frances Parkinson Keyes

FARRAR, STRAUS AND CUDAHY

NEW YORK

CARL A. RUDISILL LIBRARY
LENOIR RHYNE COLLEGE

813.52
K52m
44,953

Copyright © 1962 by Frances Parkinson Keyes

July 1963

The drawings of the "Plantations of the Lower Mississippi," on pages 64–65 is the work of Boyd Cruise; the photograph of the Louisiana marsh scene following page 216 is reproduced by the courtesy of Elemore Morgan, Sr.; the print of the plantation bell on page 368 is from the collection of Leonard V. Huber.

Published simultaneously in Canada by
Ambassador Books, Ltd., Toronto

Manufactured in the United States of America

To

Laure Beauregard Larendon
this story inspired by her grandfather
Pierre Gustave Toutant Beauregard
is dedicated with admiration and affection

by

Frances Parkinson Keyes

ILLUSTRATIONS

Between pages 90 and 91

Between pages 218 and 219

Between pages 282 and 283

Between pages 378 and 379

William H. Russell, correspondent for the *London Times*.
Dr. Charles Turpin.
Slaves en route to Manassas.
General Beauregard at the Battle of Bull Run.
Farragut's fleet passing Forts Jackson and St. Philip.
Scene in New Orleans during the evacuation.
General Beauregard as he appeared after the Civil War.

MAPS AND CHARTS

GENEALOGIES

MADAME CASTEL'S LODGER

HE IS THE MOST COLORFUL OF ALL THE CONFEDERATE GEN-
erals. He had more glamor and drama in his Gallic-American
personality than any three of his Anglo-Saxon colleagues in
gray rolled into one. The people of the Confederacy idolized
him into a great popular hero, second not even to Lee. He
was chivalric and arrogant in the best Southern tradition, but
he was more. Something in his resounding name of Beauregard, in his Creole origin in south Louisiana, in his knightly
bearing suggested a more exotic environment than the South
of Jefferson Davis. A vague air of romance, reminiscent of an
older civilization, trailed after him wherever he went. When
he spoke and when he acted, people thought of Paris and
Napoleon and Austerlitz and French legions bursting from
the St. Bernard Pass onto the plains of Italy.

His military career was one of the most unique in the
Confederacy and in many ways is more significant to the
student of the Civil War than the record of any other Confederate general. It was not confined to one narrow area like
Lee's or interrupted by long periods of inactivity like Joseph
Johnston's or cut off before the end of the war like Braxton
Bragg's. Beauregard was in every important phase of the war
from its beginning to its conclusion. He fired the opening gun
of the great drama at Fort Sumter. He commanded the Confederate forces in the first great battle of the war at Manassas.
In 1862 he was second and then first in command in the West;
he planned and fought the first big battle in that theater at
Shiloh.

From the West he went to Charleston, and there he conducted the war's longest and most skillful defense of a land
point against attack from the sea. In 1864 he returned to Virginia to direct the defense of the southern approaches to
Richmond. Later in that year, the government assigned him
to command the Division of the West, a huge department
with an impressive title and few resources. In the waning
months of the war, he was in Georgia and the Carolinas as

3

first and then second in command trying to halt the onward rush of Sherman. He and Joe Johnston surrendered to Sherman in North Carolina the most formidable Confederate army left in the field after Lee yielded to Grant.

He saw most of the war to preserve the Old South. Then, after his cause crashed to defeat and the dream was ended, he was able to adapt himself to the ways of the New South.

—T. Harry Williams, *P. G. T. Beauregard: Napoleon in Gray*
(Louisiana State University Press)

❧

THERE WAS NO IMMEDIATE ANSWER WHEN HE RANG THE DOORBELL. This did not surprise the slight, elderly man, clad in a threadbare uniform, who had slowly ascended one of the twin curving staircases of wrought iron which led to the front gallery of the house on Chartres Street, where he sought admittance. Many of the doorbells in New Orleans were out of order these days—and why not? It would have been strange if they had functioned properly; indeed, it would have been almost unseemly.

He pulled at the bell a second time and then a third, listening attentively for the jangling sound which would have normally been the result. None came. At last he knocked, not demandingly but questingly, almost beseechingly. If there were anyone in either of the two front rooms—the *salle de compagnie* on the right of the long central hall, the master bedroom on the left—surely the knock would be heard and heeded. But, as a matter of fact, he had little hope that anyone *was* there. The batten shutters were closed, though it was late afternoon when, according to custom, they should have been open; the heat of the day was over and this was the time to admit, not to exclude, outside air. Since this had not been done, it was all too plain that the rooms were unoccupied.

It was not like him to abandon any undertaking, however slight and, besides, this had not seemed slight to him; he wanted very much to enter and for a definite reason. Perhaps, if he went around to the rear. . . . There was only a carriageway now, at the left, between this house and the two next door, which formed an insignificant block redeemed only by its wrought-iron balconies. The corner lot, where they stood, had originally been part of this same property, and successively the site of Joseph Le Carpentier's "jungle" of ferns, iris and ginger lilies, open for all to see, and the walled garden, planned and planted and greatly beloved by Aloïse Merle. He had never been in the jungle, but of course he had looked at it from the street over and over again; and though the Merles had left and Mme Andry had taken possession, when he and Caroline spent their honeymoon in the house as a result of Mme Andry's hospitality, the garden was still intact. He and Caroline had walked there together almost every evening. And now, no one would ever walk there again, because of this insignificant block, occupied by heaven knew whom. But the house—this house, which he always thought of as his and Caroline's, even though they had never owned it—still stood, virtually unchanged; except, of course, that its paint was peeling off and a pane or two missing from the glass of its classic doorway and the bell out of order. Somehow, he must get into it. Yes, probably it would be better to go around to the rear. It was not as if he did not know the way.

He had just come to this conclusion and was turning toward the curving stairway when the front door suddenly opened and a thin elderly woman came out and stopped short when she saw him. Obviously, she had not expected to find anyone there; she had not heard either his ring or his knock. Probably she was on her way to church across the street, for she had a lace scarf on her head and a rosary in her hand. She looked at him with an expression that was not only surprised, but slightly startled.

"Oh—" she said, and drew back a step, as if preparing to retreat into the house. At the same time, the would-be caller, who had turned quickly, took a step forward.

'Good evening, Madame," he said courteously. "Please pardon me if I'm intruding. Have I the honor of speaking to Madame Andry?"

"No, no," the woman said hastily. "Madame Andry doesn't live here any more. In fact, she has died. Her daughter, Madame Garidel, who is her heir, is negotiating for the sale of the property to Dominique Lanata. She's asked me to live here as caretaker until the deal is put through. My name is Simone Castel—Madame Castel. What was it you wanted?"

"Please pardon me," the stranger said again. "It's a long time since I've—I'd seen Madame Andry and, in the dim light, I couldn't be sure. But I wasn't planning to make a personal call on her—I mean a social call. I only wanted to see the present owner of this house on —on a matter of business and I didn't know it had changed hands again. I've been away from Louisiana four years and only got back a fortnight ago. Since then, I've been upriver in St. John the Baptist Parish and down in St. Bernard and Plaquemines, visiting my kinfolk. I didn't hear much New Orleans news. I wanted to inquire whether or not you'd consider taking a lodger."

"You're talking about yourself?"

"Yes. I lived in this house for a little while before the war, through the hospitality of the lady to whom it then belonged. I was very happy here. I've looked forward to coming back. I'd take it very kindly if you'd consider me."

"Why, I don't know." The woman, whose attitude had been at first defensive, almost antagonistic, was conscious of something disturbingly appealing about this shabby stranger. She could not see him very well, in the fading light, but she now began to wonder whether or not she had met him sometime, somewhere before; his face was vaguely familiar. Besides, it might be set down to her credit if she gave shelter to a veteran who was obviously in need of it. Of course, there was always a chance that Mme Garidel would object, but Simone did not think so. And she could use the money a lodger would bring in, provided he could pay enough to count. From the looks of his clothes, that seemed rather doubtful. But he was not asking for board, only a room. After all. . . .

"Well, if you'd care to come in, I'll show you what might be available," she said.

"Thank you, thank you very much, Madame."

He followed her down the long corridor, past the *salle de compagnie* and the great ballroom on the right and the two first bedrooms on the left. He had always liked a house with a central hall, such as this one. At the door of the third bedroom she stopped and threw it open.

"This would be it," she said. "I'd have to charge ten dollars a month for it—or maybe we could make that eight, if you could pay in advance. And, of course, I'd have to ask for references."

"Yes, of course." The man reached in his pocket, drew out a worn purse and removed the five-dollar gold piece from the tattered tissue paper in which it had been wrapped. Then he carefully counted out the rest of the first sum she had mentioned, most of it in small silver coins. She saw that the purse was almost empty when he replaced it. "I'd like to move in right away," he said, "that is, as soon as you'd let me. I'm looking for employment and, while I'm waiting to get a position, I have some papers I'd like to go over. They're not in very good order, and I want to sort them, spread them out, arrange them chronologically. I have reason to feel it might be worth while."

He glanced around the room, which had the standard minimum furnishings—a four-poster with a mosquito bar, an enormous *armoire*, a washstand with a china bowl and pitcher, a *coiffeuse* which doubled as a sewing table, two or three chairs. "Perhaps you could let me have a desk," he said hesitantly; and, as his prospective landlady seemed to hesitate also, he added, "Or a table, an ordinary table; a large kitchen table would be just the thing. Then I could put my papers in piles as I sort them."

"I reckon I could spare you a kitchen table," the woman said. "I do have a large one, the kind you're talking about. We don't use one that size much any more. We don't have enough to put on it." She gave a forced laugh and it crossed her mind that, if she were going to supply a table, she might charge a little more for the room. But, as she opened her mouth to say so, she changed her mind. Where *was* it she had seen her caller before? He certainly reminded her of some-one; but the man she was thinking of had jet-black hair, and a glow of red in his cheeks that seemed to come from underneath, for he was olive-skinned, and magnificent eyes, and there had been some-thing jaunty about him, something dashing. This poor old derelict was gray-skinned, as well as gray-haired, and his lids drooped as if he were very tired, and he walked with a stoop and there was a button missing from his coat. . . .

"I've only a few things I want to bring with me, besides the papers and an old family album," she heard him saying. "They're all at a friend's house. I'll go and get them." Then, as she murmured that perhaps he'd like to go out on the rear gallery, to have a look at the patio and the quarters, so he could get his bearings, he smiled for the first time and, again, that jaunty, black-haired young gallant came to the landlady's mind. "As I said, I lived here once before," he went on. "But, oh yes, the references. I'll ask the friend I've been staying with to give me a letter of recommendation and bring it with me when I return. I hope and believe you'll find it satisfactory. I'm afraid I haven't a visiting card with me, but I'll tell you my name and perhaps it will mean something to you. It's Beauregard—Pierre Gustave Toutant Beauregard."

❦ 2 ❧

[From a letter written by Polyxene Reynes to Emile Reynes, New Orleans.]

21 January 1864.

Nina vient de chez Mme Deslondes où je l'avais envoyée pour avoir des nouvelles de Mme Beauregard. La pauvre jeune Dame est atteunt d'une maladie due cerveau qui ne laisse aucun d'espoir de guérison; ne n'en parle pas, parceque je crois qu'on respecte sa volonté de cacher son état a son mari. Elle ne veut pas que tourmenté comme il est il dejà par ses graves occupations, il aie encore des inquiétudes à son sujet. Ces Dames ont toutes été si bonnes, si affecteuses pour ton pére et pour ta sour [sic] *qui nous partageons leur douleur.*

(Louisiana State University Archives)

[From a letter written by Polyxene Reynes to Emile Reynes, New Orleans.]

3 March 1865.

J'ai une triste nouvelle a t'apprendre, mais qui ne l'étonnera pas si tu as réçu nos dernieres lettres. La pauvre Caroline Deslondes a succombé hier à cette maladie qui la tourmentait depuis trois ans; je pense que les inquiétudes que lui causaient les dangers que pouvait courir le Général à Charleston ont dû hâter sa fin; car ces maladies sont habituellement fort longues. On va la transporter demain à St. J. Baptiste; j'éspère que son cortège sera nombreaux.

(Louisiana State University Archives)

DEATH OF MADAME BEAUREGARD

Our eyes filled with tears as we read, on receipt of the last mail from New Orleans, that Marguerite Caroline Deslonde, the wife of General Beauregard, is dead. It is not pity for her, who, we doubt not, is among the blessed in heaven—but admiration of her virtues, and a sense of the greatness of her sorrows, these years past, and of the fortitude with which she has borne them, that has moved us. Ten years ago *Major* Beauregard, an accomplished soldier, a perfect gentleman, and a sincere Christian, was, perhaps above every other man in New Orleans, the favored man. When the people of that city rallied to throw off the Yankee "Know Nothing" rule that had been sprung upon them by the intrigue of a political secret conspiracy, it was on the popularity of the name of Major Beauregard that they rallied, as their candidate for Mayor. Beauregard, ever self-sacrificing, though devoted to his military profession, agreed to resign, and be Mayor, if they decided he ought to do so.

But there was one thing Major Beauregard cherished above all others. It was the affection of a devoted and virtuous wife, who was proud of his abilities, of his fame, and, above all, of knowing that he deserved all that his fellow-men thought of him. Well we remember, in days of peace, when Beauregard chanced to be in New York with his wife, how he excused himself from the dinner *en garçon*, even with some of his cherished companions in arms in the old army, on the ground that he would not be away from his wife. They, only, who know the mystery of the affection created by *marriage*, in the bonds of the Church that treats it as a sacrament, and irrevocable, can know what the affection was between the truly Catholic Beauregard and his chosen wife. This was in the days of peace. Horrible war came. We have read letters from tender women of the first rank at the South, telling of husbands and sons gone out to the war of defence, and wondering whether the war would last till *younger* sons would be able to bear arms in the same cause! Marguerite Deslonde, the child of an honored family, and the wife of Beauregard, with a breaking heart, a resolute will, but an earthly tenement unequal to her soul, gave her husband to the cause of her country.

Well might General Beauregard, without vulgar trumpetings of his religion, as others have practiced, bow before the altar and receive the Sacrament of the Eucharist on the morning of battle, as at the first Bull Run and at Shiloh. The wife of his heart was prepaying, too, offering up for him sufferings that wore away her life—praying for him, and for the cause he was engaged in.

Years of separation from her husband, for that loving and suffering wife! Yet her letters to him, when able to write, were always cheerful. When too ill to write, she would not permit another pen to inflict on her spouse the anguish of knowing the cause.

It is all over now. Heroic and saintly in her character and her life, she is now watching from heaven over the husband she loved and was proud of. Fiery, for him too, is the ordeal of separation from his wife during illness, and at the hour of death. Other hands than his closed the beloved eyes—he was far away. But it is by such crucibles as these that men's souls are lifted above the throng of clever men. The path of the hero will, henceforth, be easier to the gallant Beauregard.

Madame Beauregard was so beloved for her personal virtues, and so well known, that her funeral was the occasion of a vast demonstration of public grief and respect. Over six thousand people attended her remains to the levee. The saintly Archbishop Odin, with numbers of his priests, was present at the house to bestow the accustomed absolutions. The affection of friends strewed her coffin with the richest of garlands. Sorrowing and orderly, vast crowds followed the cortege from her residence to the levee where the boat was waiting to carry her remains to the family burying ground in the Parish of St. John the Baptist. The pallbearers were of the first gentlemen of New Orleans, except one, who was the commander of the French war-steamer *Catinat*.

May thy rest, oh, tried and true woman, be sweet! May virtues such as thine atone for much that is not virtuous, and win the smiles of Providence, in *peace* to the land of thy birth!

—*Freeman's Journal* (New York), March 19, 1864

L'ENTERREMENT À ST-JEAN BAPTISTE

Le Nebraska, à bord duquel se trouvait le corps de Mme Beauregard, est arrivé à l'habitation Deslonde, le 4, à 4 heures et demie de l'après-midi. Là, attendait une foule immense d'habitants accourus de 18 à 20 milles, pour prendre part à l'enterrement. Ils ont été transportés sur la rive droite avec la députation de la ville. A ce point était aussi une foule de Loui-

*sianais, venant de très grandes distances pour rendre un dernier
hommage à la morte.*

*Le corps a été reçu sur la levée par le prêtre qui, après avoir
prononcé une courte prière sur le cercueil, l'a fait transporter
à l'église de la Paroisse, où la bénediction a eu lieu.*

*L'église était tendue de noir, depuis ses dalles jusqu'à sa
voûte—grand deuil dans la maison du Seigneur, comme dans
le coeur de ceux qui s'y pressaient et de tant d'autres.*

*Après le service mortuaire, le cortège a pris la route du cimi-
tière de St-Jean Baptiste. Lees coins du poële étaient tenus
par Mme Waggaman accompagnée de M. Lefort, 1er lieutenant du Catinat, Mme Millaudon, accompagnée de M. T.
Guyol; Mme Boudousquie, accompagnée de M. P. Maspero;
Mme Rouzan, accompagnée de M. Toledano.*

*Les porteurs du cercueil étaient: MM. André Deslonde,
frère de la défunte; P. Sauvé, Beauchef, chirurgien-major du
Catinat; L. Guyol; N. Vignié. Le corps a été déposé dans le
caveau de la famille Deslonde.*

*Là bas, comme ici, tout a été grave, imposant, de toutes
parts les sympathies ont éclaté.*

*La journée du 4 mars 1864, laissera un souvenir profond,
impérissable, à la paroisse St-Jean Baptiste, comme à la Nouvelle Orléans.*

—*Courrier Français*, March 6, 1864

◈

Before he went to bed, the clothing he had brought with him
was neatly stowed away in the drawers of the commode and on
the hooks of the *armoire*; it had not taken him long to do this, for
there was not much of it—his baggage, like that of several other
Confederate leaders, had been captured during the confusion following their surrender, and he had had neither time nor money to replenish his wardrobe.

When he returned to his new lodgings after going to fetch his belongings, the kitchen table for which he had asked had already been

A LA MÉMOIRE
DE MADAME
G.T. BEAUREGARD.
4 MARS.
SOUVENIR !!

PAR MLLE OCTAVIE ROMEY

Propriété de l'Auteur
EN VENTE GHEZ A. ELIE, Rue Royale 66.
N. ORLEANS

brought into the room and he had placed on it the japanned tin boxes containing his papers. But these he did not intend to attempt sorting that night; diaries, letters, notebooks, newspaper clippings, official records were still all jumbled together. But that did not trouble him; what counted was that somewhere in the hodgepodge was everything he really wanted and needed. He smiled slightly. Those papers that were with his baggage when it was seized had been confiscated, like his clothing, and his captors had felt confident that there would be incriminating evidence in them. Instead, there were only some harmless letters from female admirers—the kind that came in by the dozen, which he had either neglected or lacked time to destroy. The documents that really mattered had been left at Contreras or Upper Magnolia before the war, or put elsewhere by Caroline for safekeeping when she realized that her end was near. He had retrieved them all and, at the same time, had repossessed himself of the family album he had entrusted to the Villerés, containing the photographs and daguerreotypes of his family and friends, which he treasured most highly. That was what he had been doing much of the time while he "was visiting his kinfolk in St. Bernard and Plaquemines." He was relieved to realize how little had been lost. But now that he had practically everything in his possession again, he did not intend to do anything about the hodgepodge until the next morning—or rather, the next evening. The morning, of course, he must spend looking for work. Surely there must be something he could do in New Orleans, someone who would be willing and able to employ him.

When the naval transport on which he had come from Mobile docked a fortnight before, there had been an immense crowd at the wharf to welcome him; his married sister, Elodie Proctor, and his old friends had received him at their homes and entertained him as liberally as their reduced means would permit. But when he had spoken to them about securing a position, they had all looked grave. It was almost impossible, they said, for anyone to get employment who had not taken an oath of fealty to the United States. Was he prepared to do that? Certainly not! He would rather starve first—well, perhaps, not actually starve, but certainly go hungry. His friends shook their heads. He was in an even worse position than most, for generals like himself had been excluded from the amnesty proclamations of both Lincoln and Johnson. They could not hold office; they could not even vote. Indeed, they could not so much as feel confident that the paroles they had signed when they surrendered would protect them from prosecution as rebels. Such of his surviving relatives as he saw when he went to St. Bernard were not only pessimistic, like his New Orleans friends, they were also frightened. They thought he might be arrested as a traitor because he had resigned his post as Superintendent at West Point to join the rebels; they would not put it past the Yankees to send him into exile or order him shot. Indeed, they would not put anything past the Yankees, but then, that was nothing new; they never had. He tried to laugh away these fears, not very successfully. Of course, he was not frightened himself; but he did not feel much like laughing, either.

He felt less and less like it as the days went on. He could not stay at Contreras, trying to reassure such of his elderly kinfolk who still lived nearby. Besides, now that his father and mother, his brother Alfred and his sister Angele were all dead, his brother Augustin in Texas, his brother Armand in Honduras, his sister Elodie in New Orleans and his sister Judith in New York, the place did not seem the same any more; had it not been for the cemetery, he would hardly have felt he belonged there; and, visiting that, he grieved increasingly for the past and made no progress in solving the problems of the present. His feelings had been deeply hurt because Judith, whose husband was dead and whose children were grown, so that she had no more ties, had made it very clear to him that she did not want him to count on living with her. She had gone to New York to educate her daughters and had steadfastly refused to return to the South; she said quite frankly that she did not want to see its desolation. Elodie, on the contrary, had been kind and hospitable and no man could ask for a better brother-in-law than her husband. But their means were limited, their house small and their family large; Pierre could not impose on them. The Villerés made him welcome at Upper Magnolia and he tried to find consolation in Doucette, the lovely fifteen-year-old daughter whose birth had so long embittered him because it had cost her mother's life, but who had become dearer to him than anyone else on earth, now that he had lost Caroline—dearer even than his sons, René and Henri, who were now respectively twenty-two and twenty and who, despite their youth, had both been officers in the war: René first on Slocum's Battery, later on Ferguson's and finally as his own aide-de-camp; Henri, at first too young to enlist, eventually served on General Hardee's staff. They were still at Upper Magnolia and could stay with their Villeré grandparents as long as they wished; but whereas that was the logical place—the only place—for dear little Doucette, who grew more and more like her mother every day, and who must be shielded and protected and pampered, the boys would have to come to New Orleans as soon as feasible arrangements could be made for them and see about getting jobs themselves. But not until he had one of his own, not until he could provide some place for them to stay. . . .

Well, he thought, as he climbed into the creaking four-poster and arranged the mosquito bar for the best possible protection, no doubt the world would look better to him the next day. As far as that went, it looked better already than it had when he left Mobile. He had been royally received there by his great friend Octavia Walton Le Vert, who was not only the undisputed leader of society but a traveler and authoress of renown. She had told him, in the presence of a distinguished gathering, that she herself would go to Washington and plead his cause with President Johnson; he knew she meant what she said, and her influence might prove powerful. But he did not want to be dependent on Mme Le Vert or anyone else for his re-establishment; and now that he had seen his children and assured himself of their welfare, he was ready to begin his campaign—not a military campaign this time, a commercial campaign. Now that he had lodgings where he would no longer be dependent on the hospitality of his friends, or prevented from keeping his own hours without consulting their convenience, he would begin it intensively, the very next morning. But, meanwhile, he must get a good sleep.

This was easier said than done. He was very restless. Not that the bed was uncomfortable. Again he smiled to himself. It was certainly a great deal better than most of those in which he had slept during the last four years, even allowing for the perquisites of his headquarters at Charleston and the refinements available during his recent visit to Governor Pickens at Edgefield. There he had not only been luxuriously installed, but had found transient enjoyment in the azaleas which still provided the garden with a riot of color. He was going to miss the garden at this place. It had been charming in itself, and the open space it occupied had assured the house abundant sun and air all along its uptown side. Now that other houses had been built so close, the bedrooms were dark and gloomy. And the sound of the fountain had been so refreshing, so soothing, so altogether delightful, that it had been a happy memory all through the war years. Involuntarily he found himself listening for it and was ashamed because its absence proved such a disappointment. As if a mere fountain could matter, in the midst of the general wreckage!

Yet somehow it did matter. He was thankful that the clock, which formed part of the dilapidated *garniture de cheminée*, was not running, that he did not have to listen to its relentless ticking and the vibrant striking of the hours and half-hours telling him that dawn was approaching and still he had not gone to sleep. But the sound of the fountain would have been different. He continued to miss its soothing music, to feel that the room was hot and airless because the garden was gone and the houses next door too close to this one. Then he realized something more significant, something much worse, something he could not understand his failure to think of before. It was not really the fountain he was missing, at least not primarily. It was Caroline.

He had never slept in this room without her beside him; and though his marriage with her had lacked the ecstasy with which every moment he spent with Laure had been permeated, he had loved her dearly, she had loved him, they had been happy together—and they had been vouchsafed such a short time together! They had been married less than a year when he kissed her good-by, before starting off for Montgomery to see Jefferson Davis and he had told her he would be gone only two weeks. Not that he had willingly or even consciously deceived her; that was what he believed himself, but he had been gone four years. Meanwhile, she had sickened almost as soon as he left her, and her fears for his safety had aggravated her condition. She had grown steadily worse and had died while he was in Florida during the Spring of '64. Despite the Federal occupation of New Orleans, he had been able, for a long while, to correspond with her intermittently through an intermediary—a French seaman in the crew of a naval vessel which sometimes put in at New Orleans. But since the preceding December there had been no letters from her, and he had not been able to convince himself that this was wholly due to failure on the part of the seaman; he had feared for some time that she had tried to make light of the gravity of her illness, and subsequent letters had confirmed the suspicion. When the fatal telegram reached him, via Mobile, the news it contained was not a surprise, but the blow was a shattering one just the same. He knew she must often have asked herself if she would ever see him again and he had written her sister Julia that he knew, considering her beautiful soul, her generous and patriotic heart, that Caroline preferred the salvation of the country to the joy that such a meeting would have given her. At that time, he still believed that he might help to bring about the salvation of his country and he also believed that what he said about Caroline's preference was true. Nevertheless, he had visualized her as trying, in the fevered pain and confusion of her last days, to reach him on the battlefield with a message. The vision had caused him untold suffering.

Because this was so, nothing he could remember that had happened in the entire course of the war, except her death itself, had crushed him like the notice that had appeared in *The Era* and which, of course, had reached him without delay or difficulty. Why was it that bad news always came through safely, when good news got lost? And why did you always remember the bad news when you forgot so many pleasant things? He did not know, he could not understand why this should be. But it seemed to happen, over and over again. Half a dozen copies of that dreadful lying paper had reached him, and he did not need to look in a japanned box to refresh his memory of the way the article had been worded, though he had kept one copy of it because he had in mind making use of it later in refuting some of the charges that had been lodged against him.

DEATH OF MRS. BEAUREGARD [the caption read]: The morning papers announce the death of the wife of P. G. T. Beauregard. She died at her residence on Esplanade street on the evening of the second instant. This woman has, we learn, been in poor health for the past two or three years and has required, what has been denied her, the care and attention of the man who gave his word at the altar to cherish and protect her. He also swore at one time to support the Constitution of the United States. He does not hold his oaths in very high estimation, as we find him not only plotting for the destruction of his country, but deserting his invalid wife for years and leaving her dependent upon others for those acts of kindness and support that should be given by a husband. We know very little of the life or character of the deceased, further than that she was an invalid, neglected by her sworn protector and left by him under the powerful protection of the flag whose glory he is devoting his puny energies to destroy. But when he is called to his final accounting, he will have the mortification of knowing that the lustre of the stars and stripes is all the brighter and his betrayed country the more powerful for the treason of himself and his co-conspirators.

There had been some small consolation in the news—and, for a wonder, this had reached him, too—that this article had been a boomerang, that an angry mob had gathered around the office of *The Era* threatening to tear it down, and that even Northern papers had branded *The Era* "a disgrace to journalism." Ten thousand people had attended Caroline's funeral. The Slidells' house on Esplanade, where she had gone to live with her mother after Pierre's departure, had been filled to overflowing, enormous though it was, with mourners on the galleries and gathered on the grounds, besides those that filled the parlors, and the streets through which the cortege passed were thronged on either side with black-clad men and women, many of them kneeling, who represented every class of society and several nationalities. So greatly was a demonstration feared that the Federal authorities had felt it wise to call out troops and long lines of soldiers had stood at attention, with fixed bayonets. But the crowd, though defiant so far as the troops were concerned, was respectful to the dead wife of its hero. There was no riot and General Banks, who had succeeded the hated Butler as Federal commander in New Orleans, did what he could to mitigate the resentment caused by the presence of the armed troops in the streets: he ordered that a steamboat be provided to convey Caroline's bier upriver for burial in her native parish of St. John the Baptist. So, after the services, conducted by the great Archbishop Jean Marie Odin, who had successfully defied Butler during the latter's tenure of office, the personal friends who had filled the house and galleries—the elite of the city—and the heterogeneous crowds which had lined the streets accompanied the bier to the wharf. The commandant of the French warship *Catinat* —stationed in New Orleans by order of Napoleon III to protect French nationals—as well as several of its officers, were among the honorary pallbearers; so was the French consul, M. Fauconnet. Never in New Orleans had there been a cortege so significant and imposing; and finally Caroline's body was taken in state to Edgard and entombed in the lot of the Deslonde family. There was now a slab on her resting place with the inscription *The Country Comes Before Me.* The words were her own and Pierre had called them "sublime" and asked that they should be carved on the tombstone which marked her "hallowed grave." In the first violence of his grief, he had exclaimed that he wished he could rescue this from "the vandals amidst whom his wife had died," completely ignoring the conciliatory gesture of General Banks. Even now, he admitted only grudgingly that this had shown a proper spirit; he still found it as hard to forgive and forget as when he was a child.

He was less superstitious than most Creoles; he did not believe in ghosts. But he almost wished he did. If the gentle presence of the girl he had loved and lost had seemed to fill this room where he was now trying to sleep, it would not have been so desolate and, certainly, it would not have been disturbing. Caroline never disturbed anyone. It was not her presence, or any semblance of it, that caused his overpowering sadness. It was her absence.

Morning found him haggard from something more than mere loss of sleep. With a trace of his old impetuosity, he sought out his landlady.

"I'm very sorry to trouble you, Madame. But I'm afraid I shall have to move."

She dropped the worn sheet she was carefully mending—a sheet, he guessed, she had intended to put on his bed—and looked up at him with hurt surprise.

"*Move!* But General Beauregard, you've just come! I'm so honored to have you here! And I'm trying so hard to see that everything is just as you'd like it! Why, I had that kitchen table you wanted put in your room right away and I'd decided to ask you, as soon as I saw you today, if you wouldn't like the washstand moved into the *cabinet de toilette* back of your bedchamber. The closed door that you've probably noticed leads into one and I could clear out the odds and ends that are stored there and provide a sitz bath or a hat tub, whichever you'd prefer—there's plenty of space. I would have sent you hot water to shave with this morning, if you'd only rung—no, of course, you couldn't have done that, the bells are all broken. But you could have called."

"Yes, I could have. I didn't think of it. But the truth is——"

"And you've paid—you paid a whole month in advance!"

For a moment, they stared at each other without speaking. What she said was true—he had paid in advance. And he could not ask her to refund the money; he knew she needed it. Neither did he have any left to give someone else. Except for the hospitality of his friends, which he would be forced to accept, so far as meals were concerned, even if he did not stay in their houses, he would indeed go hungry.

Simone Castel had been on the rear gallery when he found her. Now, after that startled moment of silence, he turned and looked across the neglected patio toward the building which had once been the slave quarters and which was in a sad state of dilapidation. He had never been in it, but Caroline had; she had gone there to see a sick slave and she had described it to him. Now he asked a question, as surprising to himself as to his hearer.

"The quarters—they're empty now, aren't they?"

"Of course they're empty! Who would I put in them? I've no one working for me but a pert sixteen-year-old girl and a lazy old man, who only come here when they feel like it. Has anyone servants any more?"

"Very few people. But I thought, if the quarters were empty, perhaps you'd let me move out there."

"*General Beauregard—in the slave quarters!*"

"As we've just said, hardly anyone has servants any more. So there's space in the quarters, more than you could give me in the house without inconvenience to yourself, I'm sure. And I need space."

"But if you had the *cabinet de toilette*, as well as the big bedroom, you'd have plenty, wouldn't you?"

"Plenty for myself. However, I'm hoping that my sons or, at any rate, my elder son, will be joining me here soon. He'll need a room to himself, or perhaps it would be more accurate to say that *I'll* need a room to myself. As I've told you, I want to work on my papers, I want to sort them and spread them out, I want to make notes on them. If I were sharing a bedroom with René, it would be hard to do that, even with the *cabinet de toilette* added. My papers would be in his way and his books would be in mine. He's planning to study law, if we can arrange it, and he'll need a table or a desk for his own use. And if Henri came too—well, the place would be bedlam. I'm afraid Henri isn't very orderly in his habits."

Simone Castel picked up the sheet she had dropped and folded it with care. "Madame Garidel didn't put the *salle de compagnie* and the ballroom at my disposal," she said slowly. "She told me to keep them closed, except while I'm dusting them and airing them of course, until she's sure the deal with Mr. Lanata is closed. He may come here to live himself, after all. Or he may sell it to a wealthy family who'd want to use the whole of it. I suppose there are some wealthy families left. But I do have those two bedrooms in front of yours. One is mine and one is my mother's. I'm glad you didn't hear us moving around, that we didn't disturb you. I tried to be as quiet as I could and my mother doesn't talk much or leave her bed much any more. She's almost blind and she just lies and grieves. We don't have any papers we want to spread out or any books we need to study. If your son, or both of them should come, my mother and I could manage with just the front room, and you could have the middle one which connects with the one you have now. Your sons could use that."

She had not previously mentioned her mother or made any reference to another person in the house; he had assumed she lived there alone. It was quite true that he had been conscious of almost no sounds in the room next to his; doubtless the mother occupied the one in front and such conversation as there was took place in that. As a matter of fact, he would have supposed that Mme Castel was herself so old that she probably would not have a mother still living; but women had aged rapidly during the war years. He blamed himself for having been so preoccupied with his own affairs, his own problems, his own despondency, that he had considered no one else's. . . .

"Tell me about your mother," he said gently. "I am sorry to hear she is so afflicted and that she grieves so deeply. She is at least blessed in having a devoted daughter. But no doubt there have been losses—?"

"Her husband, her two brothers, all her sons and my husband, who was also like a son to her: Manassas, Fredericksburg, Richmond, The Wilderness. For a long time, she was very brave, both about her failing sight and about the messages that kept coming in. It wasn't until the messages stopped coming promptly, until she didn't know what had happened, for months on end, that her courage began to fail her. And the last uncertainty—the one that's still an unsolved mystery—it was that which finally broke her spirit."

"Yes?" he said. It was not a statement, it was a question, asking her to go on and still not insisting that she should.

"My only son. He was just a drummer boy, fourteen when he left. The last we heard, he was at Shiloh. We still don't know whether he's alive or dead. And that was three years ago."

"Yes, that was three years ago."

This time, the silence was a long one. His heart was full of compassion and still he could not speak to her, if it must be about Shiloh. He had been standing, all the while they were talking, but now he drew up a chair and seated himself, facing her, intending to take her hand, to press it in his and thus show his sympathy. However, as he leaned forward, he realized that the gesture might seem presumptuous. After all, they were almost complete strangers, they had met only the day before and their relationship was that of landlady and lodger, not of old friends who were entitled to share each other's sorrows.

Simone Castel began to pick up her sewing utensils—a gold thimble engraved with her initials, an emery shaped and colored like a strawberry, a pair of scissors simulating a tiny stork, a small fat pincushion. He saw that her hands were trembling as she did this and was glad he had not tried to take them. He sensed that she had been afraid he might and that this was why she was using them to gather her belongings together.

"Not that my mother's given up hope entirely," Simone Castel was saying. "She still believes Lance will come home. That's one reason why she keeps so still. She lies and listens for him. For a long while, she insisted on putting a light in the window every night; but Madame Garidel wants us to keep the batten shutters closed in front, so we can't do that any more. Besides, she says that she doesn't really need a light, that she'd recognize the boy's step. And do you know, I really believe she would? He limped a little—not enough to handicap him, but enough to make his step distinctive. When he was a very small boy, he broke a leg and that one was always slightly shorter than the other. Most people didn't notice it at all, either from his looks or from his movements, but she did. That's why she didn't pay any attention when you came to the front door. She didn't think it mattered, because Lance is the only one that matters to her. But she must have heard you, even though I didn't. I was busy in the rear of the house and she was lying, just as she always does, close to the windows—just as close as she can get to the iron stairway outside. I

wouldn't think of asking her to move. I know you wouldn't want me
to. But I could move in with her."

"No, no," he said. He still spoke gently, but there was a note of
authority in his voice, the voice of a man accustomed to giving orders
and of being obeyed. Simone Castel recognized it as such. "The confinement would be bad for you if you were with your mother all the
time," he went on. "You'd get terribly depressed and, if you and she
were both depressed——" He did not finish his sentence, but she
could guess his unspoken thought: "—that might affect you mentally,
which would be disastrous. One of you must keep on working, for
herself and for the other."

"You should be close to your mother, but not too close," he said
after a short pause. "You need privacy and probably she does also.
Those rooms are just right for you two. But if you'll let me go back to
the subject of the quarters again. Quite aside from the space needed
for the work on my papers, it isn't the sort of thing you can do if
you're subject to interruption all the time. And no one could interrupt
me if I were working in the quarters. It wouldn't occur to anyone to
look for me there."

"Of course it wouldn't. Because it wouldn't be fitting for General
Beauregard—for any general—to live in former slave quarters."

"Wouldn't it be more accurate to say 'any Confederate general?'
Perhaps some of the Federal officers would have felt it entirely appropriate."

Again that smile, the smile which had baffled her in so many ways
the evening before! He went on, still smiling, "Besides, aren't we all
doing any number of things now that many of us wouldn't have considered suitable ten years ago, even five years ago? Excuse me if I'm
being too personal, Madame, but would you have considered taking
a lodger then?"

Confused not so much by the question as by its inescapable logic,
she turned again to her workbasket. A button box had become un-
fastened and the buttons were scattered among the stockings that
needed darning. She began to put them back where they belonged,
one by one. But she could not avoid answering him when he asked
the question a second time.

"No, I suppose not. Just the same—"

"And I wouldn't have considered living in slave quarters. Is it any
stranger for me to do what I want to do now than for you to do what
you want to do now?"

She recognized the tact which had made him say "what you want to do," rather than "what you have to do." And this time he did not press her for an answer. He remembered hearing Lee define a gentleman as one who never consciously, much less willfully, caused anybody pain or even embarrassment. He was trying to avoid causing his hostess embarrassment and pain now.

"I know that downstairs the quarters have never had a proper finish. There's nothing but earth underfoot. But upstairs, there are board floors in all five rooms and there are two fireplaces. It shouldn't be hard to keep those five small rooms clean all the time and two of them warm in winter. I could have one for a sort of study and one for a bedroom, at the end where the fireplaces are. René and Henri could have the rooms at the further end, if one or both of them came to New Orleans. The fifth room, the one in the middle, we could use as a kitchen. That is, if there were anything to cook."

He did not say it sadly, he said it humorously. Simone, for all her distress, recognized the whimsical note in his voice and her troubled spirits underwent a change for the better. Then he began to speak gravely again, not regretfully, not complainingly, but gravely.

"I'd like to stay in your house, Madame, at least until I can afford one of my own or until my sons have one they can share with me. But I can't stay in that room you let me have first. I'll tell you why, if you'll let me. When I lived in this house before, I was on my honeymoon. I shared that room with my bride, Caroline Deslonde. And, in the garden outside, there was a fountain. We used to listen to it together, we used to say it spoke to us. All night long, I kept trying to feel Caroline's presence and I couldn't. If I could have, if I could have reached her in some way—for instance, if I could have felt she was trying to speak to me through the fountain, I could have borne it. But the fountain wasn't there, either. I can't stay in that room, listening for a fountain that isn't there, trying to take in my arms a woman who isn't there, either. It's different from the way your mother's listening. She's still hoping, still believing that some night she'll hear Lance's footsteps on the stairway outside her room. But the fountain's sealed and my wife is dead. I can't hope, I can't believe. . . ."

He stopped, his voice breaking. Simone bent over her workbasket again. But she was not sewing; the sheet was still folded, the buttons were all replaced in their box. She was trying to hide her tears.

"You see how it is, Madame?" he asked, when his voice was steady again.

"Yes," she said. "I see how it is. You may have the quarters."

❧ 3 ❧

Avec Approbation et Privilege du Roy.

1688

Memoire pour servir d'instruction au Sieur de Beauregard, capitaine de frégate choisy par le Roy pour commander la frégate "La Frippone," que sa Majesté envoye sur les costes de l'Acadie.

[No. 101]   [No. 301]

L'intention de Sa Majesté est que le dit Sieur de Beauregard mette a la voile le 20 de ce mois, au plus tard. Il recevra sur la dite frégate l'officier et les trente soldats que Sa Majesté envoye en ce pais, avec les hardes et celles des 60 autres soldats qui y sont desja, et les armes que le Sr de Monclert a aussy ordre d'y envoyer; et il recevra le Sieur de Pasquine, ingénieur, que sa Majesté y faict passer pour visiter les postes qui pourront estre fortifiez et le Sieur Goutin, qui doit faire les fonctions de juge et d'escrivain du Roy.

Il se rendra au Port Royal le plus promptement qu'il pourra et aussytot qu'il sera arrivé, il en donnera advis au Sr de Méneval, Gouverneur du dit pais, et après avoir pris de luy les instructions et les éclaircissemens nécessaires sur tout ce qui se passe sur les dites costes il appareillera pour il aller croiser, et particulierement dans les endroits que le dit Sieur de Méneval lui indiquera, pou chasser les batimens estrangers de quelque nation qu'ils soyent, qui viendront faire la pesche ou la traitte sur la dite coste.

Il visitra tous les batimens, à la reserve des Anglois, d'ou il en retirera tous les François qui s'y trouveront embarquez; et mesme il pourra visiter les petits batimens Anglois quand il aura quelque prétexte pour le faire sans les faire crier.

Sa Majesté a esté informée qu'un François habite à Amster-

dam *prépare une frégate de douze piece de canon pour aller
dans quelqu'un des postes de l'Acadie pour faire la pesche de
la molue et la traitte avec les Sauvages et les Anglois. Elle veut
qu'il fasse en sorte de descouvrir cette frégate, et s'il peut la
trouver, qu'il s'en rendre maistre et qu'il l'amène avec luy en
France lorsqu'il reviendra.*

*Sa Majesté luy recommande de donner souvent de ces nou-
velles au Sieur de Méneval et d'entretenir avec luy une exacte
correspondance et d'exécuter les ordres qu'il luy donnera pour
le service de Sa Majesté et le bien de la colonie.*

*Il croisera sur les costes jusques à ce qu'il ne luy reste que
les vivres nécessaires pour revenir en France, et après en avoir
donné advis au Sieur de Méneval et au dit Sieur de Pasquine
qu'il ramenera avec luy, il en partira et reviendra a Rochefort
ou il trouvera les ordres pour son désarmement.*

1688

[*Lettre du ministre a Mons. de Beauregard*]

[No. 102]   [No. 303]

A Versailles, le 13 Avril, 1688

*Vous avez vu par l'instruction que je vous ay envoyée que
l'intention du Roy est que vous empeschez les vaisseaux des
estrangers de venir pescher sur les costes de l'Acadie, et comme
j'ay appris depuis que les Anglois prétendent que sans contre-
venir au 5ᵉ article du traitté de neutralité, arresté à Londres,
le 16 Novembre, 1686, dont je vous envoye copie, ils peuvent
y venir pourvu qu'ils soyent à deux our trois lieues de terre.*

*J'en ay rendue compte à Sa Majesté et elle m'ordonne de
vous expliquer que, comme par ce traitté, il est dit que les
Anglois ne pourront faire la pesche sur les costes appartenant
aux François et que par ces terres on a pu entendre que les
endroits qui sont par le travers des terres des François, on a
coustume de pescher en quelque distance qu'ils soyent de ces
terres, elle veut que vous en chassiez tout les dits Anglois que
tous coulx des aultres nations que vous y trouverez, et que
vous conformiez pour le surplus à ce qui est porté par vostre
instruction.*

ANCESTRY AND DESCENDANTS OF JACQUES TOUTANT BEAUREGARD AND HELEN JUDITH DE REGGIO

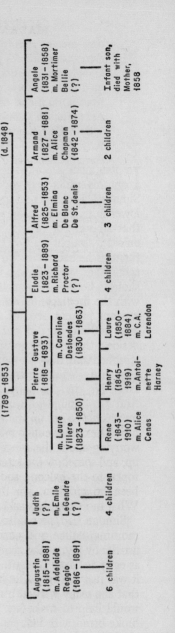

Caesar
(1562–1628)

Alphonso
(d. 1644)

Francis
De Reggio
(1610–1658)

Sieur Rinaldo
De Reggio
(1665–1737)

Dame Felicite
De Canopan
(?)

Francoise Marie
De Reggio
(1698–1780)

Helene
De Fleurian
(?)

Louis Charles
Emanuel De Reggio
(b. 1759)

Louise Judith
Olivier De Vezin
(?)

Helene Judith De Reggio
(d. 1848)

Jacques Toutant
Beauregard
(1684–1782)

Magdaleine
Cartier
(?)

Marie
Colon

Laurant
Conrad
Wiltz

Marguerite
Wiltz
(?)

Joseph
Ducros
(?)

Victoire Marie
Ducros
(?)

Louis Toutant
Beauregard
(1684–1782)

Jacques Toutant Beauregard
(1789–1853)

Judith
(?)
m. Emile
LeGendre
(?)

4 children

Augustin
(1815–1881)
m. Adelaide
Reggio
(1816–1891)

6 children

Pierre Gustave
(1818–1893)
m. Caroline
Deslondes
(1830–1863)

Rene
(1843–
1910)
m. Alice
Cenas

m. Laure
Villere
(1823–1850)

Henry
(1845–
1919)
m. Antoi-
nette
Harney

Laure
(1850–
1884)
m. C.A.
Larendon

Elodie
(1823–1889)
m. Richard
Proctor
(?)

4 children

Alfred
(1825–1853)
m. Elmina
De Blanc
De St. denis

3 children

Armand
(1827–1881)
m. Alice
Chapman
(1842–1874)

2 children

Angele
(1831–1858)
m. Mortimer
Bellie
(?)

Infant son,
died with
Mother,
1858

❧❦❧

IT HAD BEEN A LONG HARD DAY. IN THE MORNING, WHEN HE STARTED
out, his spirits were good. He was now settled in the quarters, where
Simone Castel had performed wonders. He had not even looked at the
lower story, in which there was only a dirt floor and in which he knew
that all sorts of rubbish must have accumulated; the stairway was
outside, straight and steep from the patio to the upper story; and
there, as he had reminded Simone, were five small rooms opening into
each other, without even a narrow corridor, like those in the so-called
shotgun houses. He had taken the two nearest the staircase, the ones
with the fireplaces, to use for his bedroom and study—not that there
was any present need of artificial heat or would be for months; but,
once settled, he did not want to move his belongings again and,
besides, these were the most convenient. They had been thoroughly
scrubbed and now, though sparsely equipped, their furnishings were
adequate. What did an old soldier need of carpets or ornaments, he
asked his kind landlady. He really preferred quarters without them.
And a cot suited him better than the four-poster they had found it
impossible to get up the narrow stairway; a cot was more like a camp
bed. The corner cupboard would hold all his clothes, so she must stop
worrying about the *armoire* which had also been impossible to move
up; and somehow the kitchen table had been hoisted, with the help of
ropes, to the balcony and then taken, still folded, inside. Chairs had
been no problem, nor the washstand. He even had the sitz bath.
What more could he ask?

Simone had persuaded him to let her give him his coffee every
morning, coffee and cornbread and grits. It was prepared anyway,
usually by her, as the sixteen-year-old mulattress, Bette, did not come
as early as Mme Cougot, Simone's mother, needed nourishment and
it was just as easy to fix breakfast for three as for two. He could see
that she really wanted him to share her frugal morning meal, that it
would help to make her feel he was her guest whereas, if he never
broke bread with her, she could not do this. So he consented on the
condition that she would permit him to help share the cost. He did
not feel too sure where the extra money was coming from, but he

decided it would be better to borrow it than to hurt her feelings. His sister Elodie's husband and some of his friends still had a reduced but dependable income, just as a few people still had houses of their own and continued to set tables where he was always welcome, even though these were not lavishly provided for any more. He would continue to accept his main meal from these sources until times were normal.

So he had started out, the better for strong coffee and well-cooked grits and hot cornbread, confident that, by dinnertime, he would have a favorable report. But business was still paralyzed; everywhere he was given a negative answer when he asked if there were an opening of any kind for him. In most cases, this was courteously, even regretfully, done; but twice a door was actually shut in his face and once there was a cutting remark about his personal appearance: he was no better than a beggar and he looked like one. Perhaps if he had some new clothes, civilian clothes. . . .

He turned away from the second door that had been slammed while he was still talking and walked slowly toward the shop kept by Louis Falk, the tailor who had always made his uniforms. Of course he had no money to pay for new clothes, but he thought Louis would trust him. He would explain the situation, say that as soon as he had a position he would begin to clear the account; he would take care of it gradually. He squared his drooping shoulders, quickened his pace and stepped into the shop with something of his old jauntiness.

"*Eh bien,* Falk," he said, "*me voici!*"

Falk, who had bowed and advanced as his customer entered, now stopped and looked blankly at the new arrival. The tailor's expression did not betoken welcome—in fact, his face was almost devoid of expression. For a moment Pierre thought bitterly, here's someone else who isn't glad to see me, who knows I'm not rich any more, who's forgotten I'm supposed to be Louisiana's greatest hero. Then he realized the truth: Falk did not recognize him, with his gray hair and his gray skin and his shabbiness and his stoop; Falk had seen in him only a would-be patron who, like most of his would-be patrons nowadays, could not afford to pay for what he meant to order. Pierre turned abruptly toward the door, without another word, but just as he did so Falk's expression changed from one of blankness to one of puzzlement, then to one of incredulity and, finally, to one of excitement. He took another step forward, cried out, "*Mais, c'est mon Général!*" and burst into tears.

The episode had been upsetting in every way. Of course, once recognized, Pierre had been treated like a demigod; he could have ordered a dozen suits on credit, instead of one, if he had cared to do so. But when he had chosen the least expensive material in the shop, stood to be measured and said he would return in two days for a fitting, he walked back to his lodgings without going anywhere for dinner. If he grew hungry later on, he would go over to the French Market and get some coffee and doughnuts at the *Café du Monde.*

The sun was still shining brightly when he climbed the steep stairway of the quarters, and he realized that he had at least two more hours of daylight before him. Well then, this was the time for him to start opening those boxes, to make a beginning of sorting his papers. If he did not do it now, he might never have a chance because, of course, presently he would have a position that would take up most of his time. He proposed to begin at the very beginning. That, logically, would be with his baptismal certificate. He had heard a great deal about his baptism: how his father and mother and his elder brother and sister, Augustin and Françoise Judith (François, the first-born, had died before Pierre was born) had all come up to New Orleans for it, accompanied by their body servants—and that, of course, included his wet nurse, Mamie Similien, who, like several of their other slaves, had been brought to the Toutant-Beauregard plantation from Santo Domingo. It was a regular cavalcade and increased in size as it went up the river. His father's great friend, Edward Livingston, was joint-owner, with Rezin Shepherd and Judah Touro, of the steamboat *Aetna,* Captain Anthony R. Gale, Master; and though the *Aetna's* regular run was between Natchez and New Orleans, Mr. Livingston thought nothing of diverting it from its course long enough to have it go south as far as Terre-aux-Boeufs in St. Bernard Parish to pick up the Toutant-Beauregards, the Bienvenues and the Ducros, then stop farther up the river for the Villerés and the de la Rondes. They were all great friends; they all took it for granted they would attend each other's christenings and weddings, and Mr. Livingston and Captain Gale took it for granted, too.

Pierre's maternal grandmother, Louise Judith Olivier de Vezin, had died several years before he was born; but her widower, Louis Charles Emmanuel de Reggio, had a house in New Orleans and was awaiting them all there; the christening party, which would be very gala, with champagne and *dragées* and all sorts of *bonnes bouches,* would be held at this house after the religious ceremony at the Cathedral, at which *Père* Antoine was to officiate.

The priest was getting to be an old man now; he was obliged to lean heavily on a cane when he walked and his once seemingly inexhaustible strength was failing him. There were those who urged him to spare himself, to let some of the younger clergy take over such

routine procedures as marriages and baptisms. But he had baptized
Pierre's uncle and father and both his elder brothers; for that matter,
he had officiated at the marriages which had been the natural forerunners of the later baptisms, so his association with the family was
one of long standing and, of course, he expected to baptize the new
baby, who was to bear such a grandiloquent name: Pierre Gustave
Toutant-Beauregard.

Père Antoine! Pierre could still remember him, for the good Father
had not died until the boy was eleven years old and, meanwhile, had
continued to administer the Sacraments. In 1824, he had baptized
Pierre's sister Elodie; in 1827, his brother Alfred and his cousin
Gabriel; and, in 1828, his brother Armand, though by then he was not
"getting old" any longer but was very old indeed, and this was an
exception to his general rule of taking life more easily. Pierre, with
all the rest of the Toutant-Beauregards and the de Reggios (not to
mention the Bienvenues and the Ducros, the Villerés and the de la
Rondes) had gone to these christenings, so he had a good idea of
what his own must have been like: the baby's long lacy dress, embroidered shawl, beribboned bonnet removed at the last moment; the
silver mug and *couvert* so ceremoniously presented to the somnolent
infant; the hugs and kisses, the cooings and compliments of the
feminine guests. All this had seemed to him rather silly at the other
family christenings, though he had enjoyed the *dragées* from the
beginning and had early learned to appreciate champagne; as for the
boat trips, when he and Charles Villeré had raced around the deck
together and, as a great treat, were allowed to go briefly to the pilot
house, those were always a source of sheer delight. And he had always been glad that it was *Père* Antoine who had given him the
name of which he was so proud. Like everyone else in New Orleans,
he dearly loved this priest.

He knew such had not always been the case, that when the man
whom he revered by that name first came to Louisiana, it was as Antonio de Sedella, a Spanish Capuchin who, shortly after his arrival,
had been made Commissary of the Inquisition. Everything and everybody connected with the Inquisition was hated by the French colo-
nists, who were seething with resentment anyway over the transfer of
their territory from France to Spain. As a matter of fact, Antonio
de Sedella had quickly run afoul of Governor Miro and of his own
ecclesiastical superior, Bishop Cirillo, and had been ordered to leave
for Spain. He had then invoked his personal authority as Commissary
and the controversy came to an end only when he was forcibly escorted by troops to a Cádiz-bound vessel. However, he may well have

said to himself, and doubtless did, that whoever laughs last laughs best: Miro was replaced as governor, Louisiana was ceded back to France, and the erstwhile Inquisitor returned as *Père* Antoine to become the fantastically popular pastor of St. Louis Cathedral. Part of this popularity was, no doubt, based on the legend of his tragic love story; Creoles reveled in romance, especially a romance in which duels and renunciation figured, as they did in this one—not to mention a palm tree which had grown and flourished on the grave of a loved one. Nevertheless, much of the affection and esteem with which he was surrounded could be laid to his own kindness and holiness of life. . . .

Yes, the baptismal certificate was the first document Pierre wanted to see—that and the family album. He had already located the keys he needed before he sat down at his kitchen table; now he drew one of the japanned boxes toward him, hoping that, by some fortunate coincidence, he would find the baptismal certificate on top of its contents, or at least near enough the top so that by laying aside a few inconsequential items, he could come to it quickly. Instead, after turning a rusty key in a refractory lock and prying open the lid, which creaked on its hinges as it rose jerkily, the first thing he saw was a document which no one could dismiss as inconsequential while searching for another, for its crackling parchment was stamped with heavy seals and its bold script revealed it as a royal decree, issued in 1688 by Louis XIV. It named *Sieur* de Beauregard commandant of the frigate *La Frippone* and ordered him to set sail not later than the twentieth of the current month, accompanied by the *Sieur* de Monclert, who had been ordered to supply him with arms, the *Sieur* de Pasquine, an engineer, and the *Sieur* Goutin, who would fulfill the functions of Judge and Royal Scribe. The *Sieur* de Beauregard would be in command of ninety soldiers; the purposes of the expedition, set forth in great detail, were to protect the colonies and obtain information regarding inimical encroachments on the waters surrounding their territories, besides taking proper measures to prevent further encroachments.

Jacques Toutant-Beauregard, the young captain entrusted with this important commission, had been Pierre's great-grandfather, the first of his paternal ancestors to come to Louisiana; and though he had gone briefly back to France and, indeed, had been decorated with the Cross of St. Louis in recognition of his valiant and useful service, he had returned to Louisiana, settled there and married there. Under the Spanish regime, he had become a *Regidor Perpetual*—that is to say, an alderman—and an *Alcalde Mayor Provincial*—that is to say, a judge—in short, a man of considerable consequence; one of his sons, Louis Michel Toutant-Beauregard, had succeeded his father in both positions, while his marriage to Victoire Marie Ducros had provided him with a father-in-law who was also a Perpetual Regidor as well as a Depository *Générale*. Their second son, named after Louis XIV's captain, who became a planter and married Judith Helene de Reggio, the daughter of another planter, was Pierre's father.

Over and over again, as a child, Pierre had listened to the recital of all the valiant deeds attributed to the Toutants and the Beauregards. Both families traced their illustrious lineages in an unbroken line all the way back to the thirteenth century; and when, toward the close of the sixteenth, the last male descendant of the Toutants died, leaving only a daughter who married the current *Sieur* de Beauregard, the names were hyphenated and had been so used by their descendants ever since, even if the King, in the royal decree which made the first Jacques Toutant-Beauregard commandant of the *Frippone*, had neglected to do so.

Pierre's father had talked on and on as they all sat around the fire on cold winter evenings, in the *salle* at Toutant, sometimes called Toutant Nord to distinguish it from the section of the property— all part of the original grant to the Toutant-Beauregard family—now held by his uncle Joseph, which was also called Toutant or Toutant Sud. When his uncle Joseph, as often happened, was present on these occasions, he added his reminiscences, for he had actually taken part in the Battle of New Orleans and had commanded a band of young Creole planters at Proctor's Point on Lake Borgne, and loved to talk about all this at great length. So, sometimes, Pierre grew drowsy while he was listening, partly because he had heard it all so many times that he knew it by heart anyhow and, consequently, did not find the repetition exciting; and partly because he had been outdoors all day, riding and shooting and trapping, which was what he really loved to do, rather than listen to stories; and now the warmth of the fire, after the crisp outdoor air, would have been conducive to sleep, even if he had not been so full of the wonderful food which loaded the dining-room table, partly as the result of Placide's prowess in the woods and marshes and partially as the result of Edné's superlative skill. Placide—the swift, lithe, powerful voodoo—was known as the best plantation hunter in Louisiana, despite the claims of several Indians who sought to dispute his right to this title; and Edné was the huge dusky goddess who presided over the kitchen, where she ruled with unquestioned and severe authority. If Placide were the best plantation hunter, then Edné was the best plantation cook and, when it came to that, no one dared to dispute *her* title!

So between the oft-told tales and the mingled effects of the day in the woods and the warm fire, and the wild-goose gumbo and other succulent dishes, Pierre often found his head nodding. But he was never so drowsy he did not notice that his beautiful mother was wide awake and that sometimes she opened her lips, as if she were about to say something, then closed them again, as if she thought better of it. But when Grandfather de Reggio was there, he did not hesitate long, for he was as opinionated as he was vigorous and handsome. He stood the stories for a while and then interrupted rudely.

"The Toutant-Beauregards!" he said with something very like a snort. "Very respectable people, I'm sure, dear Jacques. If they hadn't been, of course, I never would have permitted Judith to marry you. But don't forget who *her* ancestors were—mine and her mother's both. Why, the de Reggios are descended from the Dukes of Modena and Reggio—the illustrious House of Este! They were patrons of the arts and letters in the Renaissance. What patrons of arts and letters were there among the Toutants or the Beauregards, either? The de Reggios had a court of their own—several courts in fact. There were princes among them, not merely dukes, but *princes!* There were cardinals! And you brag about your captains and your judges! Besides, they made great alliances; Beatrice d'Este married Ludovico Sforza, Duke of Milan; her sister Isabella married Francesco Gonzaga, Marquis of Mantua. Beatrice lived in royal state, for her husband had one of the most luxurious establishments in all Europe; Isabella's portrait was painted by both Leonardo da Vinci and Titian. Who painted the early Toutant-Beauregard portraits, can you tell me? Beatrice and Isabella were both brilliant and beautiful, and their nephew Alfonso d'Este married the celebrated Lucretia Borgia."

"I believe he died, rather mysteriously, shortly thereafter, didn't he?" Pierre remembered that Jacques once had not been able to refrain from asking.

"He did not! That shows how little history you know, my friend! It was Lucretia's *second* husband, Alfonso of *Aragon*, who was murdered; her first marriage to Giovanni Sforza had been annulled to make possible a more brilliant alliance for her. But that was all her brother Cesare's doing, not hers. After she married Alfonso *d'Este*—her third husband—and escaped from the evil influence of her father, Rodrigo Borgia—"

"You mean the Pope, Alexander VI?"

"Yes, yes, I admit he was not one of the more estimable pontiffs.

But the Borgia family—*Borja* it was originally, of course—was one of the noblest in Spain. It has given the world a great saint, a great general, a great Viceroy of Peru. And, as I was about to say, when Lucretia escaped from the evil influence of her father and her brother, she showed herself worthy both of her own illustrious line and her new husband's. Many poets and artists were attracted to her brilliant court. She was learned, she was devout, she was kind, she was beautiful. All the stories you have heard about her are slanderous. There is not one word of truth in them."

At this point, Grandfather de Reggio would look about him as if defying anyone to contradict him. Then he would go on. "And my father, the Chevalier François Marie de Reggio, having distinguished himself under the Duc de Richelieu in the French Army, was given a captaincy by Louis XV and, shortly thereafter, sent with his command to Louisiana. When this was ceded to Spain, he became the Royal Standard-Bearer." After pausing a moment for breath, Grandfather de Reggio would continue, "As for my wife, Louise Judith Olivier de Vezin, she could trace her descent all the way from Adam and Eve to the present, via Alfred the Great, last King of the Saxons, and heaven knows how many other royal personages!"

It used to occur to Pierre, when he was a little boy, that if his maternal grandmother were still living, she would also be sitting with them, in that group gathered around the fire; in that case, undoubtedly, she would have started talking in detail about *her* ancestors and then the talk about the rival families would have gone on all night long. At such moments, he did not find it in his heart to be sorry that she was dead. But he knew that was very wicked of him. He tried to suppress such feelings, though he was not altogether successful. He was glad when his mother came and put her arm around his shoulders and smiled down at him, telling him it was bedtime for little boys and not to forget to say his prayers. . . .

Unless she had been loaned to one of the other plantations where there was a new baby, Mamie was always waiting to tuck him in and hear his prayers when he went to his room. No two women could have been more unlike than Edné, the infallible cook, and Mamie, the equally infallible nurse. Edné was almost as black as Placide and Tombie, Placide's son, but instead of being quick and lithe, she was thick and heavy and always seemed to be bursting out of her untidy clothes; Mamie, on the other hand, was much lighter in color, small and spry and very, very neat. She was barely five feet high and weighed a scant hundred pounds; but at least every other year she produced a bouncing baby, and she always had enough milk not only for her own pickaninnies but for a white baby, too. As there were five years between Pierre and his younger sister Elodie, Mamie had been sent away, since it was customary, when a slave was noteworthy for excellence in any particular direction, to lend such a slave to neighbors as a mark of special esteem. Mamie was a willing, active and diligent worker, and could get as many as a hundred pickets out of a swamp in a day, which was a record in Terre-aux-Boeufs; so sometimes she was loaned to do this. But it was as a wet nurse she was in most demand and Pierre was always sulkily resentful when he found she had been loaned again. As a very small child, he did not understand her disappearances—he only knew he missed her when she was gone, no matter how kind a substitute had been left in her place, and was overjoyed when she returned. But Elodie had only just been weaned when their cousin Gabriel was born and Mamie was hurried off to uncle Joseph's plantation. Pierre was old enough then to realize what had occurred and he was very unhappy about it. He did not often ask for any special thing in those prayers which were a nightly ritual; but now he did ask the Blessed Mother to send them another baby of their own, so that Mamie would come home; and She must have listened, for in little or no time after Mamie had taken charge of Gabriel, she was back at Toutant to take charge of Alfred!

Pierre not only loved to see her sitting in her rocker, with a baby in her arms; he loved to listen to the stories she could tell, if she could be persuaded to stop singing lullabies to the baby—stories much more exciting, to Pierre's way of thinking, than Grandfather de Reggio's. Mamie had been born in Santo Domingo; but in the terrible revolution of the black slaves, her parents' owners had escaped to Santiago de Cuba and had managed to take along their people, who were faithful to them. In Santiago, Mamie had been stolen by rival planters when she was only seven years old, and smuggled by her new owners to Savannah and thence to New Orleans, where Grandfather de Reggio had bought her while she was still a little girl. He had singled her out from the beginning as a slave of great promise, and his investment had certainly been a wise one. She had provided him, for free, seven husky young slaves and she had nourished his grandchildren so helpfully and abundantly that, after she began her services, there had not been a single infant death among them.

Pierre was glad that his father had married the daughter of a planter and not a princess, and that Jacques himself was a planter and not a Regidor or anything like that; for they had all been very happy there at Toutant, his father and mother, his brothers and sisters—two older and four younger than himself—his grandfather de Reggio, who was with them much of the time, his uncle Joseph and aunt Suzanne and their children, Louis, Gabriel, Marie Aimée and Paul, who lived nearby. With such a large and congenial family, they were not dependent on outsiders for diversion; and though they received and made friendly leisurely visits, after the manner of aristocrats to whom hospitality was second nature, and celebrated all anniversaries and feast days fittingly, they did not specialize in such an elaborate form of entertaining as some of the planters did. Toutant was not a grand house in comparison to many others where they went —in fact, it was not grand at all: a simple story-and-a-half building, with a sloping roof and wide galleries, all of wood, and a tall chimney rising above it at either end. But it was spacious and comfortable and Pierre's mother was the sort of woman who would give individuality and distinction and beauty to her surroundings whatever these were. She gave all, abundantly, to Toutant. Pierre was sure that she was the peer of her much-vaunted ancestresses, Isabella and Beatrice d'Este. She did not wear her hair in a big knot at the nape of her neck, like most of the ladies he saw, but in braids wound around her head to form a coronet which, in itself, gave her a queenly look; and, on great occasions, she wove pearls among the braids and wore a whole parure of seed pearls besides: earrings, necklace, bracelets, brooch. (She had declined, however, to have her portrait painted with this coiffure because she said it would look as though she were trying to copy the style effected by her aunt, Marie Lucie de Reggio.) She loved vivid colors, crimsons and emerald greens and royal purples, and had her dresses made from rich fabrics in styles to suit herself, whatever the fashion of the day might be; the effect was one of great elegance and originality. And as a chatelaine she had no equal; it was Edné who did the cooking, to be sure, but it was Judith de Reggio who knew what should be cooked to taste good with what and how it should be served to best advantage.

Nor was it only with the food served to her family and her friends that this incomparable chatelaine was concerned. Every day Tombie, or one of the other young slave boys, brought her a sample of each dish that had been prepared by Suzie, who cooked for the *atelier* which comprised the field hands of a planter. Judith de Reggio tasted the sample; if it was good, she praised it and this meant the dish could be served at once; if it did not come up to her standards she rejected it, and this meant that Suzie would have to try again. Not until it was satisfactory in every way could she turn her back on the huge kettles and ovens in which she cooked the corn soup and the

corn cakes, the meat which was sometimes salt and sometimes fresh
and the manifold vegetables which she must set before the hungry
workers. No sweets were included in this standard bill of fare, but
the Negroes had no scruples about helping themselves liberally to
figs, oranges and other fresh fruits in season, as well as to sugar cane,
of which they were inordinately fond; such pilfering was regarded
with a lenient eye, as was their catch from the bayous and rivers, and
the game that they shot or trapped, even if they went fishing and
hunting when they did not accompany their masters as part of their
routine duties. When it came to poultry, conditions were equally
favorable to the dusky residents of the quarters: they were permitted
to raise chickens, and their proprietary rights in these were respected
by the Boss Man. Indeed, ignoring his own legal title to whatever
belonged to his slaves, Jacques Toutant-Beauregard paid for the produce of their coops whenever he used it, though quite well aware
that the fowl in his own spacious barnyard seemed to stray rather
frequently to scratch and lay elsewhere.

Every cabin had its own coops, as well as its own garden, and
Pierre's mother, like his father, visited the quarters regularly. In fact,
she went not once, but twice a day to the slave hospital where a
capable old black nurse was in charge of the two wards, one for
men and one for women; both were under the careful direction and
supervision of Judith de Reggio. Once a week, Dr. Puisson came
down from New Orleans to check the health of the slaves, who regarded him with respect and awe; but it was their mistress to whom
they turned in times of greatest fear and suffering. She knew how to
comfort them and they believed she also knew how to cure them.
Certainly she never shrank from ministering to them, no matter how
repulsive a form their disease took; and, in like measure, she could
cajole them out of the plaintive "miseries" which she had reason to
believe were based largely on imagination or indolence.

In the late mornings, she went from the hospital to the communal
nursery, where another aged and capable Negress watched over the
welfare of the pickaninnies whose mothers were working in the fields.
In the case of babies, this watchfulness was supplemented by their
natural form of sustenance, for their mothers were free to visit the
nursery at regular intervals and, whether feeding their children or
not, to stay with them between the hours of eleven and one. By tim-
ing her visits as she did, the Boss Lady had a chance to judge if there
were any maternal neglect and to rectify this if she thought there
were; if her suspicions were in any way roused, she made a second

visit to the nursery in the afternoon, though this was not her invariable habit, as it was in the case of the hospital.

When he was a child, Pierre took all his mother's activities for
granted, without questioning how she could have performed so many
different functions, all with such uniform perfection. As he grew
older, he realized that often she must have been almost frantic with
fatigue, often deeply grieved or otherwise emotionally disturbed,
sometimes actually suffering. But none of this had ever been evident
and Pierre still remembered with what loving care and pride she had
supervised the preparations for the party on his tenth birthday and
how ill he had repaid her for all her forethought and her desire to provide him and his friends with an unusual treat. That morning, long
before the hour set for the feast, he had been presented with his first
musket. Enraptured, he had made for the woods with Placide and
the latter's son, Tombie, who was Pierre's preferred companion.
Pierre had never seen a live tiger, but he had seen pictures of them
and heard stories about them and he thought that, insofar as human
beings and animals could resemble each other, these two would have
much in common with panthers, being swift and strong and skillful
and black as night.

All day long Placide had guided the two boys through the wet
woods, skirting a *prairie tremblante* over which he did not permit the
boys to follow him. "Soon-soon you make enough years, yes, so you
can learn how to walk a marsh, but not till yet," he told them,
" 'special when you do carry a new gun, Pierre, dat you must got
to keep dry an' yo' powder horn, too."

He walked the quaking surface along a course paralleling the higher,
solid ground where the boys kept pace with him and, as he went, he
probed into the peaty soil with the long oak pole he carried, undisturbed by the coil of rope over one shoulder and under the other or by
the hatchet whose smoothly worn handle he had thrust through his
belt. At a shallow rivulet, little more than a trail of moist mud winding through the tussocks of roseau and *paille fine*, he turned and
followed the streamlet in their direction. He showed them tracks in
the mud, parallel paw-prints with an unbroken light furrow between
them.

"A she one done walk here," he said, "an' it ain't been too long
by. See how de water still a-dreenin' down in where she done put her
feets? She got a nes' not too far f'm yuh, you mark what I say."

Completely fascinated, the two boys followed Placide along the
bank of the narrow stream bed as it wound its way through the woods.
Neither had ever seen an alligator nest or, for that matter, a female

alligator. Most of the huge beasts who sunned themselves torpidly along the batture were big bulls, who could be heard roaring challenges in the springtime twilights, and who looked so much like stranded logs. Tame pigeons from the Toutant cotes and wild doves flew to the river's edge to drink just before sundown and, every now and then, one would fall victim to a log which slashed at it with a lightning-fast sweep of a great tail as it stooped to drink. Mostly, however, the birds were both alert and agile, and sprang into the air in time to let the swing of the tail pass scythelike beneath them.

The boys walked carefully, as Placide had taught them, keeping a sharp lookout for moccasins and for "congo snakes," as the swampmen, black and white alike, called the big conger eels. Pierre carried the new musket pointing back over his shoulder, as he had been instructed to do, so that no tough hanging vine or branch should snag the hammer, dragging it back and thus releasing it, so that it might fire a charge of fine shot accidentally and, perhaps, dangerously injure, blind or even kill a companion.

As they turned a bend in the rivulet's course, Placide stopped and pointed triumphantly at a conical mound of mashed vegetation, mostly cattail stems. It stood at the edge of the all-but-waterless stream, with a small muddy pool at its foot.

"Dah he!" chuckled Placide. "Dah de she-alligator's nes'. 'E got mo'n thirty eggs in 'em, I ga'ntee you."

"But where is she?" asked Pierre. "Don't they sit on their eggs like our hens do?"

"Deedy no, young marstuh! 'E watch de nes' so don't nothin' tear 'em up, but dat's de mostes' she do. Ol' flambeau yonnuh"—he pointed upward at the sun—"do all de settin' 'em eggs needs, an' when de young 'uns come out dey don' stay by dey mammy, no. Dey swim right off an' look fo' 'crevisse or pot-gut minnows an' starts to feed. But de mammy alligator close by now. Down in de bottom of yonnuh puddle 'e got a hole where 'e hidin'. You chillen res' quiet now an' watch."

He knelt by the bank and began to grunt, in tones not like those of the roaring bulls along the river batture, yet curiously reminding one of them—a low grunt which began at a higher pitch and then dropped abruptly. For minutes nothing happened, and the boys shifted nervously from one foot to another. A curt wave of Placide's hand bade them cease their movement.

Then there was a stirring in the murky pool. Twin knobs appeared above the surface of the water, sliding forward and finally followed by two other knobs, spaced farther apart. These became the nostrils and eyes of an alligator whose head gradually appeared in its entirety. Involuntarily, Pierre, who had cocked his musket, raised it to his shoulder and fired. The head snapped back out of sight as though a stretched spring to which it was attached had been released.

"Now look what you done," reproved Placide. "I had 'em almost in reach where I could crack down on 'em wid de hatchet, but now I got to dig 'em out."

"I'm sorry, Placide. I thought he was coming at you."

"All right, all right," chuckled the huge swampman, mollified, "long as you don' do such no mo'. Chillen's got to learn; young sheep follow like de ol' sheep show the way, ain'ty? An' load de gun right now, chile. What use a gun when it ain't been fed? Load 'em like you paw done showed you."

Carefully, and with an overweening sense of importance, Pierre poured a measured quantity of powder into the barrel of his weapon, tamped oil-soaked wadding above it with the ramrod, added a measured amount of birdshot, tamped that down, too, placed a percussion cap on the nipple, and cautiously lowered the hammer. While he was thus engaged and Tombie watched in round-eyed admiration and awe, not altogether unmixed with envy, Placide had uncoiled his rope and slipped from his belt the hatchet and a rusty iron hook, shaped like a long-shanked letter S with one bend much larger than the other. This he lashed to the end of the long oak pole he had been carrying.

"Now you chillens bes' stay back yonnuh," he warned. "Ol' Missy Gator li'ble to be cuttin' up big Jim by de acre, time I get 'em outen whe' 'e at."

Probingly, he pushed his pole, hook end foremost, into the murky puddle, moving it this way and that, to make certain he followed the tunnel that led from it. Before long they heard the iron hook grate along the horny-ridged hide of the big beast. Pierre was surprised by the clarity of the sound. He watched as Placide moved the invisible end of his pole this way and that, deftly manipulating it along the rough hide of his quarry. Suddenly the outer end of the pole surged violently to one side, almost out of the man's powerful grip. But he grasped it firmly and bore back with all his strength.

"Got 'em fo' true!" he exulted, unshipping the pole by cunning manipulation against the lashings which held it. Wrapping the rope about his hands, he began to pull, inchmeal, hand over hand. The heavy alligator struggled against him. But a bit at a time, the man won out, the head of the alligator reappeared, its lower jaw firmly held by the large bend of the iron hook. Then, with a rush, the big body followed as the beast strove for an opportunity to bring its mighty, flailing tail into play. But Placide remained always in front of it, where the alligator could not harm him and, finally, picking up the hatchet which he had laid on high ground when he unwrapped his rope, he sent the blade crashing into the alligator's neck, just back of the skull. Save for occasional twitchings, the great reptile lay still.

Pierre had watched in such complete absorption that he had not noticed the musky smell that pervaded the area.

"Gee gollies," he exclaimed, wrinkling his nose. "They sure enough stink, don't they? What you going to do with it, Placide?"

"Tote 'em home, skin 'em, salt de hide an' took it to town. Get me some argent to buy pindars fo' Tombie an' snuff and a seegar an' such." He strode to the nest. "Come look, chillens," he invited, and scooped away the rounded tip of the cone. "Look yonnuh de eggs."

Peering over the top in wide-eyed wonder, Pierre and Tombie gazed at the long cylindrical objects and felt the leathery texture of the shells. Pierre exclaimed, "Hey! It's alive! It wiggled inside!" as he dropped the one he held.

"Dey's about come to dey time," said Placide wisely, replacing the trashy material he had removed from the top of the nest. "I got all I kin say grace fo' in totin' de mammy now," he added. "But I'll be back soon in de mo'nin' an' get dem eggs, to let 'em hatch out by de cabin. Den I sell de young 'uns fo' mo' argent. 'Ey's a man in town what sells 'em to Yankee folks to show when 'ey gets home."

It was not until Pierre had finished telling the exciting story of this exploit that he realized something was strange about the way in which his hearers received it. Then suddenly he remembered—the promised birthday party! What had happened to it? Where were the guests? The party was over, the guests had gone home. His father had scolded him severely; but his mother, whose painstaking planning had gone for nothing, said she understood. That was the best thing about mothers; they might grieve, but they understood. . . .

Then there was the day when he had not come home with a full bag, but with only one measly little rabbit. A cousin, much older than he, who arrived to visit while he and Tombie were out for the day, had jeered at him and said that probably Pierre, who claimed to be such a mighty hunter, had not even killed that one poor old rabbit, that it had just died of fright! And this, though it lay torn and bleeding on the gallery! Enraged, Pierre had sprung at his tall kinsman, taking him completely by surprise and, with a short stick in his hand, had chased the offender off the gallery and pursued him until he took refuge in the nearest sanctuary he could find, which happened to be the outhouse. There the cousin had been obliged to stay, barricaded within, until Pierre's father had come to his rescue and told Pierre sternly to apologize. He did so, but with empty words. He never forgave this kinsman for casting aspersions on his integrity as a hunter. His mother had told him that she understood his anger and that time she had laughed when she said it. . . .

There had not been many bad days like that. Most of them were good and some of them were great. Those were the days when, instead of going hunting with Tombie, he went steaming off with his uncle Joseph and his cousin Gabriel in the boat that carried mail and supplies to the two forts farther down the river. To his great regret, Joseph had taken no part in the famous engagement when Fort St. Philip had held out for nine days and nine nights against the bombardment of the English fleet, because he had been with his company at Lake Borgne when the naval battle took place; but several of his close friends had been among the fort's defenders and they always made him and his young relatives welcome. Pierre found it thrilling beyond words to stand on the bastion, where ten pieces of eighteen caliber could cover all vessels in the open reach of the river, and to listen while these brave men revived every detail of the battle. Here, the war became real to him in a way it had never done when Uncle Joseph droned on about it, sitting in an easy chair by the fireside at Toutant. He listened eagerly to the story of the fort itself, whereas he had been rather bored by the recital of the magnificent Estes from whom, as he was so often reminded, the de Reggios were descended. Italy was a long way off, princes and potentates legendary figures; but the Deep Delta was his own country, its explorers and builders his own people. He asked eager questions and received willing answers. The bayou, which formed a natural moat on the lower side of the fort and served as its port, had been given its name by Iberville, who had camped there for the first time on Mardi Gras; it had been called Mardi Gras Bayou ever since, even though the Spanish changed the name of the fort itself to San Felipe when they took over from the French. The Spanish Governor, Carondelet, had enlarged and strengthened Fort San Felipe and had also thrown up a redoubt on the opposite shore, so that it would be possible to rake any enemy ship on that side of the river. Carondelet called this battery Fort Bourbon and, of course, the name suited the French when they took over again and San Felipe became St. Philippe. After the Spaniards and the French got through playing

battledore and shuttlecock and the *Americans* took over, General
Jackson ordered new emplacements and heavier armament for Fort
St. Philip and mounted two batteries on the west bank, one on the
site of Fort Bourbon and the other a half-mile upstream. But there
were no further fortifications on that side of the river until after the
glorious battle Pierre had been hearing about. Then the United States
Congress decided to honor the hero of New Orleans by building a
fort, to be named Jackson, quite close to the place where those two
batteries had stood. Work on it was now progressing famously. If
Pierre liked, they could row across the river and have a look around.
This new fort was really something to see. It was built in a most
curious shape, like a five-pointed star; it was immense; it had two
moats; eventually, it was to have a drawbridge that could be raised
and lowered with chain pulleys and weights. It would be possible
to quarter five hundred men there—a hundred more than at Fort St.
Philip. It covered eighty-two acres, that is to say, about sixty-nine
arpents. . . .

Of course, Pierre avidly accepted the invitation to cross the river.
Structurally, Fort Jackson was even more intriguing to him than
Fort St. Philip, which did not have such extraordinary attributes as
the shape of a star and two moats and a drawbridge; but it still
lacked the glamor of battle, and Pierre was conscious of this lack. He
returned to the bastion and clamored for more stories about the great
fight in which only two men had been killed and four wounded
out of the four hundred defenders, while the British fleet had been
decimated and burned. It was not until the mail boat gave a warning
whistle, and Uncle Joseph said they had stayed much too long and
seized him by the shoulder and hustled him down to the landing,
that Pierre was torn away from the bastion and his stories.

There were other great days, too, when he neither went hunting
with Tombie nor visited the forts with his uncle and cousin, but
took part in the greatest celebrations of the year on the plantation
itself. The first of these was the day the last cane was cut. It was
marked by ceremonies that must have survived some ancient barbaric
rite. When the cane-cutters came to the final row that was still standing in the fields, otherwise shorn and brown, the overseer surveyed
it carefully, looking for the longest stalk. When he located it, he
tied a colored ribbon around it. Then, after the pregnant pause that
marked his survey, the Negroes fell to again with their machetes,
working fast until they came to that tall beribboned stalk, at which
point they paused again. It was not for anyone's machete; together
with a present of clothing and money, it was the prize of the *meilleur*

couteau, the slave whose work had been outstanding for both diligence and skill throughout the year.

The overseer stepped forward and put his hand on the shoulder of the winner, and the other Negroes made a ring around him. They did not shout and jump; they stood quiet and silent. Then the ritual began: the winner touched the stalk with his forehead and next his forehead with his machete. Afterward, he began to sing and, as he sang, he moved around the stalk, swaying his body to the rhythm of his song. At last he leaped into the air, brandishing his machete; then, suddenly bringing this down, he plunged it into the stalk. As it fell to the ground, the women workers rushed forward to seize it and as many as could get hold of it raised it above their heads and, singing in their turn, carried it triumphantly to the Big House. The male workers climbed into the carts that had been brought beforehand into the field and formed a procession behind the singing women. In the first cart rode the winner. Sometimes Pierre was allowed to ride beside him, sometimes one of his brothers. Whichever boy was chosen talked about it for weeks afterward. The best harvest day of all was when a slave named Baptiste was chosen as *meilleur couteau.* He was a great storyteller, as famous for his tales as for his feats in the field. All the children loved him. Pierre did not think his stories were quite as exciting as Mamie's, but they were mighty tall tales, just the same.

The second great day was New Year's. Early in the morning, as the house servants went from room to room with the customary black coffee, they stopped to give a seasonal greeting. The Boss Man and the Boss Lady were saluted with becoming respect and gravity; but by the time they reached Pierre's room, they were chattering and giggling as they chanted: *"Mo souheite ké vou bon garçon, fé plein l'argent é ké vou bienheureux."*

In the afternoon came the distribution of gifts to the slaves. (The family had already exchanged theirs and eaten an enormous dinner.) Pierre's father stood by a huge table piled high with presents. Each slave received a quarter of beef, several pounds of flour, a new tin pan and a new spoon or, in the case of the children, toys and trinkets. More important, each man received a new suit of clothes, each woman a new *tignon* and a new dress. If a woman had given birth to a baby during the year, she received two new dresses, so Mamie often had two.

After the distribution of gifts came the bonfire, the music, the dancing. Pierre, with all the rest of the family, watched from the gallery. The tin covers of saucepans served as cymbals; a barrel, covered at one end with oxhide, served as a drum; the jawbone of a mule, with the teeth still in it, was a violin. The drummer did not use sticks; sitting astride the barrel, he beat it with his fists and fingers. The violinist drew a thin wooden bow across the teeth in the jawbone, threw it in the air, caught it behind his back with one hand.

Three singers took their places on either side of the drum. At first, there was only a faint murmur. Then the volume of sound increased. With a long eerie cry, the slaves began their song:

> Un, deux, trois
> Caroline qui fé com' sa ma chère
> Un, deux, trois
> Caroline qui fé com' sa ma chère.

This was the signal for the dance, the *counjeille*. At first, the slaves' movements were slow and restrained, marked by a strange dignity. Then they all began to sing and the music grew louder and faster and the steps more rapid, the gestures provocative; the elephantine Edné and the spry Mamie, the pantherlike Placide and Baptiste, the sweet singer, all took part in this dance, and Tombie and three of Mamie's brood were in the group of children who followed after them. As these dances became more and more lustful, the tom-toms sounded and Pierre's mother said it was time for the children to go into the house.

Long after he was in his own room, Pierre heard the tom-toms, vibrating through the night. Now, as he sat in the silent quarters, he seemed to hear them still. And he could still see that single, beribboned stalk, standing high above the shorn fields. That was the way he had visualized the Stars and Bars, waving above the wreckage the Yankees had wrought, but which his own people would redeem. Instead, the Yankees had struck the flag down, just as Baptiste had struck down the stalk, and there was something barbaric about both actions.

"General Beauregard, I thought I heard you come in several hours ago. Have you had any supper?"

He sprang up, startled, the crackling parchment—his great-grandfather's commission—still in his hand. He refolded it in its worn creases before he answered.

"Why yes, I must have! Why no, I don't believe I did! It doesn't matter."

"But it does. I have some gumbo left over. My mother couldn't seem to take anything tonight. Won't you come and sit on the gallery and eat it? I'd regard it as a favor if you would."

❦ 4 ❧

"Condemned to forced inaction and to wait the un-known results the victor had prepared for the vanquished, he began, while the facts were still fresh in his mind to write the historical outlines of the great drama in which he had played a leading part, primarily, to safeguard his reputation from the imputation of errors that he had not committed, the recollection of which rankled in his mind still suffering and sore from the after-war conditions. After much labor and time consumed in collecting and verifying the documentary evidence of what took place . . ." two compendious volumes were published.

—Grace King, *Creole Families of New Orleans*
Courtesy of Frederic D. and H. C. Miller King

He decided that he would make no further efforts to obtain a position until his new civilian clothes were ready. With the first fitting two days off, the second probably three days after that, he could not expect completion for nearly a week. This would give him an opportunity to go through a great many papers and to enjoy at his leisure the family album at which he had only glanced the evening before. It would also give him an opportunity to spend more time with Mme Castel's mother, Mme Cougot, and that was what he wanted to do, now that he knew it would be a comfort to both women.

It was while he was eating the gumbo on the back gallery that he had begun to realize this. The gumbo was surprisingly good; and there was a surprising—even a suspicious—amount of it, considering that the serving he had been offered was supposed to represent only the amount which failed to tempt the delicate appetite of an invalid. Mme Castel did not set a small, half-filled bowl before him, as he had expected she would. Instead, she ladled the steaming mixture of rice, shrimp and crabmeat, mingled in the broth of a savory *roux*, from a tureen; when he had done full justice to the first helping, she lifted the lid of the tureen and invitingly raised the ladle, which was dripping with more of the same delectable mixture. It had been a long time since he had eaten anything that tasted so good to him, perhaps because, at his sister's house and those of his friends, he had hesitated to eat his fill for fear of depriving them. Now it was obvious that there was more than enough for two persons in the tureen, and he ate with such evident relish that he suddenly began to fear he had betrayed the degree of his hunger. He forced himself to take more time between spoonfuls and to talk a little.

"I'm very sorry to hear that Madame Cougot is so poorly," he said with sincerity. "Is there anything I could do for her, do you think?"

Simone did not hesitate. "Yes. If you would go to see her, that would mean more to her than I can possibly tell you."

"You mean this evening?"

"Since you've offered—unless, of course, you had other plans."

"I had no other plans," he said slowly. "I'll be glad to go. But perhaps you'd better prepare me for the visit. You told me your mother was nearly blind, that she was so feeble she spent most of her time in bed. Is she handicapped in other ways? Should I raise my voice in speaking to her? I mean, will she have difficulty in hearing me, for instance?"

"She will not have the least difficulty. Her hearing is still very acute. You remember I told you that she listens all the time for footsteps on the stairway and that when she hears the ones she is waiting for, she will recognize them instantly."

"Yes, you did tell me," he said hurriedly, feeling his question had been a stupid one. At the same time, it had been prompted by consideration. After all, very few persons, as aged as Mme Cougot must be, were still "acute" when it came to hearing. As if she guessed what was passing in his mind, Simone smiled faintly and gave him some information of her own accord.

"Perhaps you are thinking of my mother as a very old woman," she said. "She is just sixty, and until the war she had exceptionally good health. She was what I believe is called 'well preserved'—a fine figure of a woman. In fact, she was quite handsome. Now all the color, all the animation are gone. But, to me, she seems even more beautiful, with her white hair and her white skin, than she did when she had glossy black ringlets and rosy cheeks."

He was glad that Mme Castel had gone on talking, so that he had time to recover from his surprise. So her mother was only sixty! And he had been thinking, all this time, that she must be at least that old herself! He tried, without seeming to stare, to observe her more closely as she sat opposite him at the small table which separated them. She was straight and slender and there was a trimness about her which indicated a sure sense of style. Her black muslin dress, sprigged with small white flowers and finished with a white collar and white cuffs, was certainly not new; but if it had lost its first crispness, the soft folds in which it fell were nevertheless graceful and her figure was the sort to which full sleeves and a full skirt were especially well adapted. The pallor of her face and its drawn expression had deceived him; now that he looked more closely, he saw there was not a line in it, and he guessed that its texture was fine, that it would be soft to the touch. Her hair, parted with precision in the middle, lay smooth above her forehead and temples and almost covered her ears; he could not see beyond those at the moment, but he remembered now that it was neatly arranged in a series of coils above the nape of her neck and confined with a net; there must be a great deal of it. In color it was lighter than that of most Creoles; once it might have had almost a golden sheen. Now it had lost its luster and, because of this drabness, it was hard to tell whether the color was dull grayish brown or dull brownish gray; but he could well have been mistaken in assuming the latter. Her nose and mouth both had a pinched look—another deceptive characteristic when it comes to judging a woman's age. As she looked him full in the face, he saw that her large eyes were her finest feature. This time, there was no mistaking the color; they were a clear and beautiful gray.

"Well, shall we go?" she was saying and she rose as she spoke. Apparently she had been aware of his covert scrutiny and felt it had lasted long enough. "I will put our dishes in the pantry, to wash later on, and join you in the hall."

"Couldn't I help you?"

"Yes, if you like. You may take the tureen and the ladle and I will take the spoons and the bowls."

The pantry was still where he remembered it, conveniently placed back of the great room which had served for either banqueting or dancing as the occasion arose. Originally, this pantry had been used only for serving and for keeping dishes hot; they were brought from the huge kitchen located at the foot of the stairway leading into the patio. Now he saw that Mme Castel used it for cooking, too—a sensible arrangement, since that saved her many steps and, after all, she could not have much to cook. He was pleased, perhaps not too rationally, both because she still called it the pantry and because she made no effort to hide its use as a kitchen. She set the remains of the gumbo in a small meat safe, rinsed the dishes and silver with water she poured from a pitcher, and placed them in a dishpan for later thorough washing. Then she dried her hands and opened the door into the banqueting room.

"Shall we go through to the front of the house this way? I like to, once in a while, even though I don't need to, because of keeping it in order. It's such a splendid apartment."

He nodded and followed her; it was an effort, but he could hardly decline. He had told Mme Castel how he and Caroline had listened to the fountain together from the bedroom they shared on the other side of the house; he had not told her about the party Caroline had planned to give when he returned, victorious, from the war. He was to wear his full-dress uniform and she her wedding dress, with pink roses substituted for the white ones which had originally caught up its lace flounces; and they were to stand and welcome the guests in the wide French doorway between the *salle de compagnie* and the room with the dual purpose, which that night, of course, would be used for dancing. One of the airs the orchestra would play would be the "Beauregard Manassas Quick Step," composed to celebrate his greatest victory; and he and Caroline would stop receiving long enough to dance it together. Later on, everyone would sing "Lorena" and "The Bonnie Blue Flag" and end up with "Dixie" before they went out on the gallery for champagne and cakes and ices; and then courting couples would begin wandering through the patio and the garden, arm in arm. He had often thought that if it were true houses *were* haunted, the ghosts in this one would be happy revenants, Caroline and himself and their guests. Of course, he did not believe in ghosts. But when he thought of this gay spectral scene, he almost wished he did.

While all this was going through his mind, he and Mme Castel had passed into the shrouded *salle de compagnie* and entered the hall; now she was opening the door into the front bedroom. It had already been first evening when he left the quarters and since then the short twilight had merged into darkness; only the slender flames

of three candles, one by the bed and two on the mantel, gleamed in
the engulfing gloom. If the dimly seen form of Mme Castel had not
been before him, it would have been hard for him to grope his way
to the chair toward which she was guiding him. But by the time he
reached it, he had adjusted himself to the dimness; and the almost
startling contrast of the white bed, with the white-clad, white-faced,
white-haired woman in it, to their somber surroundings, made this
easier. The outline of the frail figure betrayed its emaciation, for the
otherwise flat surface of the counterpane was raised only a few inches
in the place where she was lying; but her hands were visible, resting on
either side of her still form, and Pierre took the one nearest him
and raised it gently to his lips.

"Good evening, Madame," he said. "You are very kind to let me
come and see you. But I do so with a guilty feeling, because it seems
I have eaten the supper that was meant for you."

"No, it was meant for you all the time. I suggested to Simone
that she prepare some. I do not relish gumbo any more, but I hoped
you might. I have had a *tisane*, as usual."

"But you will not get strong on *tisane!* And you must build up
your strength, so that when better days come again you will be able
to enjoy them. Don't you agree with me, Madame Castel?"

"I do, and I have told her the same thing. But she will not pay any
attention to me."

"Then I shall insist that she must pay attention to me. After all,
I have been a general. I am used to having orders obeyed."

He spoke playfully, but the tone of authority, which Simone had
caught before, was noticeable again. Mme Cougot turned her head,
as if seeking to see him and, though failing to do so with any degree
of clarity, as if she were beginning to sense what manner of man he
was.

"Do you really believe there will be better days?" she whispered.

"Of course. They could hardly be any worse, so it stands to reason
that they must get better. And you believe it, too. Otherwise, you
would not keep on listening, as your daughter tells me you are doing,
for the footsteps you expect to hear."

She did not answer immediately and he realized that he had presented her with a new idea, one she had not evolved herself. When
she finally spoke, her words came clearly; they were not merely a murmur, as they had been before.

"Perhaps you are right in a way. But I do not dare say I *expect*. I
only say I hope."

"Then you must dare more greatly."

"How can I? We Southerners did not merely hope! You expected, I expected—we all expected that the South would win the war. What happened to those expectations?"

"They were unfulfilled, but that does not mean all our expectations will be. Certainly it does not mean that they must be."

"Is there anything you can do to help fulfill mine?"

"I don't know, Madame. But I will try. First, however, if it will not tire you, please tell me more than I know so far: the time and place of your grandson's enlistment. Where he saw service besides at Shiloh. The name of his commanding officer and the number of his regiment—or, if there were several, the names and numbers of all. What has already been done, and by whom, in an effort to find the boy."

"There was only one regiment. The Crescent, Colonel Marshall J. Smith commanding. My daughter will tell you all the other details gladly. You didn't ask before. We didn't want to impose on you."

It was true. He had not asked before. Again he blamed himself because he had been entirely preoccupied with his own troubles, because he had not given enough thought to the problems and troubles of others. Again he thought of his sons René and Henri, safe and well and at least comparatively happy at their ancestral home of Upper Magnolia, of his brothers Augustin and Nicolas, carving out new careers for themselves in Texas and Honduras, of his sister Elodie, happily married to Richard Proctor, of his nephews and nieces. And these two women had no one left but each other and the forlorn hope, which he probably had no right to fan into flame, that one long-lost boy might be returned to them.

"It was negligence on my part, but it was not willful negligence," he said. "It was—well, I won't try to explain, to find excuses. And the negligence will be rectified, right away. I'll get all that information from your daughter, as you suggest; I'll do it before I go to bed and act on it the first thing in the morning. I'm going to leave you now, Madame. I don't want to tire you on my first visit. If I did, you might not make me welcome again. And I'd like to come and see you often. We must get to know each other better and there are so many things we should enjoy telling each other—about our respective families, I mean, the places we have lived, the things we used to do before the war." He had continued to hold her hand all the time they had been talking; now he raised it and kissed it again. "I am so glad I moved to the quarters," he said. "I wouldn't like the bother of moving a second time. And Madame Castel must get that room I had first ready for Lance."

<figure>ଏୄ 5 ଽ</figure>

1830 CENSUS OF ST. BERNARD PARISH–
HOUSEHOLDS

BEAUREGARD

	White Males	White Females
Under 5 years	2	1
5–10 "		1
10–15 "	1	
20–30 "		1
30–40 "		1
40–50 "	2	

	Slaves	
Under 10	1	1
10–24	8	6
24–36	21	3
36–55	12	7
50–100	1	

No free persons of color.

ଏୄୖ

EARLY THE NEXT MORNING, WHILE HE WAS DRINKING HIS COFFEE and eating his corn bread and grits, he obtained the information from Simone for which he had asked and recorded it meticulously. Then he wrote several letters based on his notes and went out to post them. He also made several visits in the course of which he sought advice and information which might be useful in tracing the

Reggio

lost boy. He did not mind doing this while he was still wearing his shabby old uniform—that might in fact be an advantage; it was a reminder that he himself had been at Shiloh, which some persons, however well-intentioned, seemed almost to have forgotten; it gave substance to his search. Only when it was better that there should be no such reminder, when he was dealing with persons who were not so much forgetful as antagonistic, would it be wise to wear new neat civilian clothes, to speak only of his basic familiarity with the land, his training as an engineer, his abilities as a linguist and historian. He could take over a devastated plantation and make it productive again; he could rebuild a ruined railroad; he could teach French and Spanish in one of the new American schools.

Well, he would explain all that as soon as he could get someone to listen to him, and this should not be too hard, once he had made himself more presentable. Meanwhile, he would do some work on his papers, or rather, some *real* work, because what he had done the day before hardly counted. After he had posted his letters and made the round of calls which he thought might be helpful in locating Lance, dead or alive, he went to his sister Elodie's house and was, of course, invited to remain for dinner. As they lingered around the table, in the pleasant way to which they had always been accustomed when they were too replete for immediate activity, he began to tell Elodie and Richard about his landlady and, finding their interest awakened, went on and on. When he finally rose to leave, his sister and his brother-in-law both detained him.

"I have a little May haw jelly in the house," Elodie said. "Wait a minute, Pierre, I'll get it for you. That might taste good to Madame Cougot. So might some orange wine. I've two bottles of that I can spare. Give one to her and keep the other for yourself. I'll make you a few sandwiches and those, with a glass of wine, would take care of your supper tonight. Then you can wait until you've had it before you take Madame Cougot my little presents. It would save you embarrassment and explain why you couldn't possibly eat anything more if Madame Castel suggests that you should."

As Elodie left the room, Richard put his hand in his pocket and drew out a crumpled bill. "I got this just a few hours ago in long-overdue payment of some cotton I shipped to Cairo," he said. "It was a debt I never expected to collect, so I hadn't counted on the money. In fact, I don't really need it. You better have it. You needn't hesitate because you can just take over the other man's debt, don't you see?"

Pierre told himself he could not refuse the loan when it was so kindly made and then, more honestly, confessed to Richard that without it he would not have known how to pay Mme Castel for his share of the food she set before him. He had a feeling that, besides his breakfasts, which he had already agreed to accept from her, she *would* ask him to supper again, and not merely once—if not regularly, at least frequently—and would be hurt if he declined her hospitality. Besides, with increasing honesty, he admitted that, while he appreciated Elodie's tact in providing for him that night, he would, as a general rule, be glad to avail himself of whatever Mme Castel might offer him in the way of an evening meal. At the end of a hot day, it was pleasant on the rear gallery, and it would be much more convenient to take his supper there than to go out in search of it, when he had already tramped around all day hunting for a position, or when he was tired after prolonged research and writing.

Well, he should be getting back to the latter now and, as it was beginning to rain, the sooner he reached the quarters, the better, in any case, for he might get drenched. The afternoon showers, an almost daily occurrence during the summer, were often tropical in their violence and this one showed every indication of becoming so. Consequently he did not stop when he reached the house to speak to Mme Castel and give her the wine and May haw jelly for her mother, but went as quickly as possible across the patio and up the steep stairway. It was just as well; he barely escaped the deluge.

He had not even closed the japanned box the night before, so now it stood open, inviting his orderly inspection. He realized that the story he wanted eventually to tell, with the help of documentary evidence and before they could beat him to the draw, was his side of his differences with the Johnstons, Joseph and Albert Sidney both; of the mutual contempt and endless controversy between himself and Judah P. Benjamin, and of his enmity with Jefferson Davis. That was the story which would set the record straight, that the public would "read, mark, learn and inwardly digest." He needed to do this, not to gain greater glory for himself—what did that matter any more?—but to help the American people arrive at an intelligent and tolerant appraisal of all the reasons why a cause had been lost instead of won.

However, this was not the story that was pushing at the forefront of his consciousness at present. He wanted to get at the root of things, for roots had been significant; to begin at the beginning, to recapture his childhood, his youth, his education, his idyllic years with Laure, his brief months of tardy happiness with Caroline. And did his earlier public achievements count for nothing? He had done good work from the beginning, at Fort Adams, at Pensacola, at Barataria Bay. Even if no one else wanted a record of this, surely his children would! And what about the Mexican War, in which he had twice been brevetted for "gallant and meritorious service"? Well, he had kept a diary of sorts during that campaign, it must be among these papers somewhere. He would review it, enlarge it. But not yet.

He was not sorry that it was his great-grandfather's commission which had come first to hand after all. He had wanted to recreate his background, since background was important in his case. The commission would serve a useful purpose. It would help him to explain why he, a Catholic, an aristocrat and a Latin, had a set of values and standards—yes, and of honor—different from those of Protestant, middle-class Anglo-Saxons and Jews. (Of course, there had never been any quarrel between himself and Lee, only occasional misunderstandings, courteously handled on both sides, but then Lee, though a Protestant and an Anglo-Saxon, was also an aristocrat.) And the commission had also led, naturally and logically, to recollections of his carefree childhood at Toutant, where he had first heard his background discussed. But now he wanted to get away from Terre-aux-Boeufs, and go out into the world, step by step.

The first step had not taken him any great distance—only as far as the primary school of Victor Debouchel, which was located nearer New Orleans than Toutant, but still in Pierre's own world of plantation houses, fields of sugar cane, forests and swamps and bayous and, beyond them all, the great river. During term time, he and some of his fellow pupils, the sons of other planters in the parishes of St. Bernard and Plaquemines, lived with M. and Mme Debouchel in their unpretentious but pleasant house. Monsieur represented authority; he presided over the primitive schoolroom, supervised the games and administered discipline when it was called for. The boys recognized his intellect, his sportsmanship and his justice; they respected him and admired him; but it was Madame they loved. She realized that they might be homesick at first, she noticed what they liked best to eat and saw that they got it; she nursed them when they were ill. Pierre, subject to feverish colds and severe sore throats, more than once benefited by her tender care.

He had every reason to be contented and he was. The food at the Debouchels' was abundant, the atmosphere uniformly kind, the lessons surprisingly easy. He had learned how to read and print before beginning school, at the age of eight; now penmanship and arithmetic were stressed, but not to an extent that required much effort. He took readily enough to his books, though his real interests still lay in the woods and along the streams. He was always glad to get back to his pirogue and his gun; but more and more he associated his old musket not only with rabbits and squirrels to be hunted but with soldiers on parade to the accompaniment of flying flags and beating drums and all the paraphernalia of battle. It was only on rare occasions that he could see and hear any of this. But the thought of it captured his imagination and he longed for a time when such sights and sounds might become more frequent. Meanwhile, he liked his schoolmates, especially Charles Villeré, and his teachers, especially the one who taught him his catechism.

Religion was treated with respect at Toutant, feasts and fasts scrupulously observed; but it did not have a conspicuous influence on life there or really play an important part in it, at least as far as a boy could judge. At school, this was different; in fact, the greatest difference between life at home and life at the Debouchels' lay in the prominent place given to religion at school. Along with penmanship and arithmetic, Pierre had daily lessons in catechism; he found this as easy to master as he did all the other tasks set before him. He answered all the questions it contained so glibly that his parents and his teachers decided he was ready to make his First Holy Communion.

It did not occur to him then to question their judgment, though it had many times since. He always welcomed the prospect of a trip to New Orleans, whatever the reason. When a new suit of clothes was involved, so much the better; if a new prayer book, a new rosary and a huge white candle were now part of the picture, that was all right, too. When the great day came, he unquestioningly took his seat in a pew near the altar, accompanied by his mother, his favorite teacher and his elder brother Augustin. The cathedral was crowded with other children, boys and girls, about his age or slightly older, all dressed in new clothes, all carrying candles, all accompanied by fond elders. He had gone to Mass regularly ever since he could remember, he was thoroughly familiar with the ritual, even though, on the present occasion, the scene and the procedure had been formalized. He did not really need his mother's gentle touch on his shoulder to tell him when he should join the other candlebearers going up the aisle. But, as he slid out of his seat, he stood for a moment irresolute. Before him was the altar, ablaze with lights; but behind him, through the open door, came the sound of drums and marching feet.

This was what he had yearned for, months on end: to see soldiers, to hear their drums, to be near them as they marched, to feel the rhythm of their music beating in his own breast because of his closeness to them. He hesitated, but only for a moment; caught his mother's imploring glance, his teacher's expression of outrage and hurried the faster to forget them—but toward the open door.

He had never been allowed to forget his defection, even when, two years later, he actually did make his First Holy Communion, far better prepared for it spiritually than when he merely pattered off his catechism as he did the multiplication table. He supposed people would go talking about it as long as he lived—perhaps even after he was dead. But though he had, of course, apologized to his teacher and told his mother he regretted the embarrassment he had caused her, which was true, in his heart of hearts he had never been sorry for what he did that day. He had always felt sure it had been that impetuous action which was responsible for his father's decision to send him to a military school, and a military school in New York at that.

When this decision was made known in the family circle, Grandfather de Reggio was at first incredulous and then enraged. He argued vehemently with his son-in-law.

"If you feel the boy has learned all he can with Debouchel—and I admit he has done very well at that school, such as it is—then the place for him is Paris. Several of our friends are sending their sons abroad this year. The same competent person can take charge of them all, see to their installation in suitable *lycées*, supervise them when they make the Grand Tour."

"Yes, I know. I have considered it. And I have decided against it."

"But why?"

"Because if he spent the next few years in Paris and traveling about France and Spain and Italy, Pierre would become, to all intents and purposes, a Continental."

"Well, of course, he is not a Continental, but he *is* a Creole. And that—to use your own phraseology, my dear Jacques—is, to all intents and purposes, the same thing."

"I am sorry to disagree with you, but it is not the same thing. Pierre is an American."

"An *American!* Why, you just said yourself that he is a Creole! He is a Toutant-Beauregard, he is a de Reggio, a de Vezin, an Olivier, a Ducros, a ——"

"Yes, that is true. But he is also an American. We have all been Americans, whether we like it or not, since 1803—fifteen years before Pierre was born."

"How can you talk such nonsense? Sooner or later, the United States will cede us back to France, just as Spain ceded us back to France. We will become a French colony again."

"It does not look that way to me. I must remind you that Louisiana is already a state, a part of the Union, as much as New York or Virginia. The people from those states and others who have moved into New Orleans and settled above Canal Street are here to stay. They are our fellow Americans. We have got to learn to live with them."

"The next thing you will be saying we have all got to learn how to speak English!"

"That *is* the next thing I am going to say. Very well, not you, if you don't want to. But I am already beginning to find it inconvenient because I cannot do so fluently. Our new neighbors are not very good linguists and that makes it all the more important for us Creoles to be bilingual. Certainly Pierre must learn to be. At Debouchel's, all his lessons were in French, and of course they would be in Paris. I do not seem to find the right school for him in New Orleans. You have just referred, with disparagement, to the one where he has been so far. I believe you would have no higher opinion of others in this vicinity."

At this point, Grandfather de Reggio became almost incoherent with rage. Pierre's mother, as was her custom, had been silent during the heated discussion between her husband and her father; but Pierre, glancing at her, could not help seeing that her eyes were full of tears and sensed this was less because she did not want a son of hers to grow up an American than because she did not want him to be as far from her as New York. She was a woman who seldom wept and never to gain selfish ends; therefore, as a rule, her husband was greatly moved by her tears. This time they failed to alter his decision; he took Pierre to New Orleans and put him on the copper-fastened ship *Huntress*, Captain Shepherd, Master, bound for New York, which, having her cargo engaged and going aboard, would have quick dispatch. In New York, he would be met at the wharf by one of the teachers in the school run by the brothers Peugnet, the elder an ex-captain of artillery, the younger an ex-captain of cavalry. They had been exiled because of their alleged association with the *carbinieri*, but they had both distinguished themselves in the Napoleonic Wars. The educational institution over which they presided was located on Houston Street between Broadway and Crosby, and called itself "A Commercial and Mathematical School." Most people in the North merely called it "The French School." Pierre knew that his father had selected it not only for its wholly American setting, but because it was a military school.

❦ 6 ❧

IN 1815, THE ENGLISH ARMY INVADED LOUISIANA, COUNTING upon finding a divided State through the ill feeling of the Creoles to the American Government, and an easy and sure conquest of New Orleans. But the annals of military history do not contain a more striking example of miscalculation than the simple story of what ensued. It is too well known to repeat except in connection with Villeré. Offering himself at once to Governor Claiborne, he was made Major-General of the first Regiment of Louisiana Militia, and given a commission at one of the outposts of defense of the city.

The English plan of campaign was to secure a position on the river, whence they could strike at New Orleans before it had time to prepare adequate means of defense. Through the treachery of some Spanish fishermen, they were led from the lake where their ships lay, through a bayou, to the Villeré plantation canal, in full view of the river. But the story should be told in its full completeness:

At dawn the barges entered the bayou. The English sailors, standing to their oars, pushed their heavy loads through the tortuous shallow water. By nine o'clock the detachment was safe on shore. "The place," writes the English authority, an officer during the campaign, "was as wild as it is possible to imagine. Gaze where we might, nothing could be seen except a huge marsh covered with tall reeds. The marsh became gradually less and less continuous, being intersected by wide spots of firm ground; the reeds gave place by degrees to wood, the wood to enclosed fields.

"The troops landed, formed into columns, and pushing after the guides and engineers began their march. The advance was slow and toilsome enough to such novices in swamping. But cypresses, palmettoes, cane brakes, vines and mire were at last worried through; the sun began to brighten the ground and the front ranks, quickening their step, broke joyfully into an open field, near the expected canal. Beyond a distant orange grove, the buildings of the Villeré plantation could be seen. Advancing rapidly along the side of the canal, and under cover of the orange grove, a company gained the buildings and, spreading out, surrounded them. The surprise was absolute. Major Gabriel Villeré and his brother [Jules], sitting on the front gallery of their residence, jumped from their chairs at the sight of the redcoats before them; their rush to the other side of the house only showed them that they were bagged!

"Secured in one of his own apartments, under guard of British soldiers, the young Creole officer found in his reflections the spur to a desperate attempt to save himself and his race from a suspicion of disloyalty to the United States, which, under the circumstances, might easily be directed against them by the Americans. Springing suddenly through his guards, and leaping from a window, he made a rush for the high fence that enclosed the yard, throwing down the soldiers in his way. He cleared the fence at a bound and ran across the open field that separated him from the forest. A shower of musket balls fell about him. 'Catch or kill him!' was shouted behind him. But the light, agile Creole, with the Creole hunter's training from infancy, was more than a match for his pursuers in such a race as that! He gained the woods, a swamp, while they were crossing the field, spreading out as they ran to shut him in. He sprang over the boggy earth into the swamp, until his feet, sinking deeper and deeper, clogged and stuck. The Britons were gaining; had reached the swamp! He could hear them panting and blowing; and the orders which made his capture inevitable. There was but one chance; he sprang up a cypress tree, and strove for the thick moss and branches overhead. Half way up, he heard a whimpering below. It was the voice of his dog, his favorite setter, whining, fawning and looking up to him with all the pathos of brute fidelity. There was no choice; it was her life or his, perhaps the surprise and capture of the city! Dropping to the earth, he seized a billet of wood, and aimed one blow between the setter's devoted eyes—with tears in his own eyes, he used to relate. To throw the body to one side, snatch some brush over it, spring to the tree again, was the work of an instant. As he drew the moss around his crouching figure, and stilled his hard breathing, the British floundered past. When they abandoned their useless search, he slid from his covert, pushed through the swamp to the next plantation, and carried the alarm at full speed to the city!

"The British troops moved up the road along the levee to the upper line of the plantation, and took their position in three columns. Headquarters were established in the Villeré residence, in the yard of which a small battery was thrown up. They were eight miles from the city and separated from it by fifteen plantations, large and small. By pushing forward, General Keane in two hours could have reached the city, and the Battle of New Orleans would have taken place then and there; and most probably a different decision would have been wrested from victory. The British officers strongly urged this bold line of action, but Keane, believing the statement that General Jackson had an army of about fifteen thousand in New Orleans, a force double his own, feared being cut off from the fleet. He, therefore, concluded to delay his advance until the other divisions came up. This was on the twenty-third day of December. 'Gentlemen,' said Jackson, to his aides and secretaries at half past one o'clock, when Villeré had finished his report, 'the British are below; we must fight them to-night.' "

In the skirmishes that followed, and in the great battle of the eighth of January, Joseph Roy Villeré fought gallantly and brilliantly, when (so it is always repeated in the family tradition) he wielded the sword presented to him by Louis XVI. One of the trophies picked up from the field of battle was given to Villeré—a small, very pretty fowling-piece, said to have belonged to General Lambert. All the boys of the Villeré family learned to shoot upon it, calling it familiarly and tenderly "le petit Lambert." It is still a cherished heirloom in the family, having survived all the trials and tribulations possible to a gun during the Confederate War.

Pakenham, shot on the field of battle, was carried, dying or dead, to the Villeré house and there laid upon a bed in a front room. According to the slaves employed in the house, he was buried temporarily under a great pecan tree on the lawn; by the same token, the old slaves, more picturesquely than truthfully, aver the nuts from that tree, for years afterwards, always showed a red streak as of blood.

—Grace King, *Creole Families of New Orleans*
Courtesy of Frederic D. and H. C. Miller King

❦

WHEN HE ARRIVED IN NEW YORK, HE WAS STILL A LITTLE BOY FROM
the country; not, as the term would have suggested in the
North, a little boy brought up on a farm—there was a vast difference
between a farm in the North and a plantation in the South—but a
junior member of the landed gentry. As such, he had no hankering for
city life. He enjoyed the brief glimpses of it on some special occasion;
but he always gladly returned to his long days of hunting and fishing,
his long evenings in the family group seated around the fire, his
leisurely visits with his relatives and friends who lived on nearby
plantations in much the same way he did—that is, as if their own
realm were indeed a royal domain.

This was especially true of the two—the de la Rondes and the
Villerés—that his family made a point of visiting more or less ceremoniously. The Melicourt Bienvenues' place, Kenilworth, and the de
la Vergnes' place, Concorde, were so near their own that they dropped
in there at any time, as the Bienvenues and the de la Vergnes did at
theirs, in order that the children of the three families could play together while their elders sat in the grove or the *salle* and talked
companionably about the crops or the fashions, according to their sex.
Pierre did not count such visits or the houses where they took place
as important when he was young. It was only later that he valued the
friendship of these families, especially the Bienvenues, at its true
worth and recognized the charm of Kenilworth's sturdy style—the
massive square brick columns, the substantial outside stairways, the
great doors with their wrought-iron hinges—and the singular beauty of
its setting: the flagstone walks leading to the gateway and the garden,
the variety of the trees whose luxuriance embowered the house—oak,
pecan, fig, cedar, palm. Mamie told him that there were ghosts at
Kenilworth—a headless man who roamed the grounds, a white-clad
lady who not only appeared on the stairway the night of the full
moon, but who left footprints which could be seen there the following
morning. He and the Bienvenue children lay in wait for these revenants, but in vain; someone always came and said it was bedtime and
hustled the youngsters away; and when Pierre asked if there were not

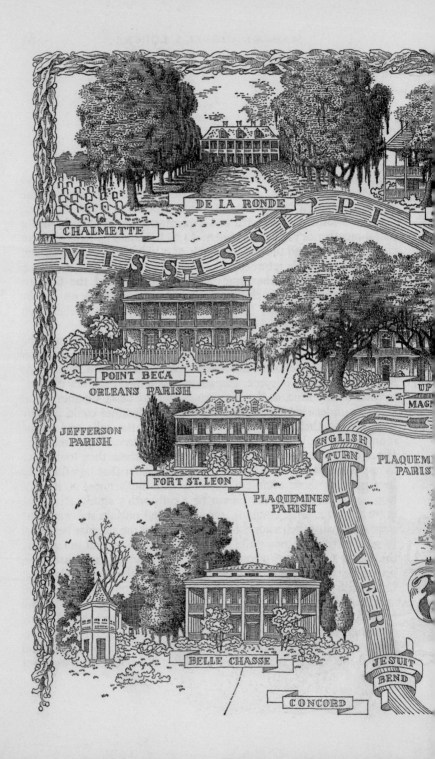

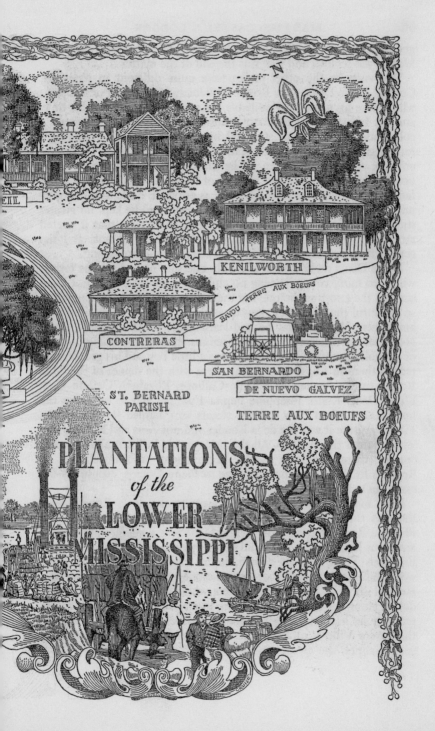

EIL

KENILWORTH

CONTRERAS

BAYOU TERRE AUX BOEUFS

SAN BERNARDO
DE NUEVO GALVEZ

ST. BERNARD
PARISH

TERRE AUX BOEUFS

PLANTATIONS
of the
LOWER
MISSISSIPPI

ghosts at Toutant, too, for which he *could* watch, he was hushed and Mamie was scolded and that was the end of the matter.

The visits to the other places were quite different in character. Colonel Pierre Denis de la Ronde, builder and first owner of the place which bore his name, was probably the wealthiest planter of his time; and his two-story, sixteen-room mansion, surrounded by a beautiful colonnade, was made of stuccoed brick and set in the center of a formal garden encircled with orange trees. He died when Pierre was only six years old, but even so, he made an impression on the boy, both by his personality and his way of living, so strong that it never faded; he was quite as forceful, quite as arrogant, quite as uncompromisingly aristocratic as Grandfather de Reggio and he kept far greater state. Besides, his family was so striking in many ways that it riveted attention upon itself whether it wished to do so or not, and the general impression prevailed that this was far from displeasing.

Pierre Denis de la Ronde had only one son, named for his father, who died fairly young, leaving no children at all; so he did not loom large on the arresting picture; but there were nine blooming daughters, so beautiful that they were known as the Muses. Pierre recalled with amusement the fact that he had learned the names of these Greek goddesses not when he began the serious study of mythology as part of a scholastic course but when he was a little boy and his grandfather recited them in singsong, coupling them with the names of the de la Ronde sisters: Madeleine Eulalie–Calliope; Elizabeth Celeste–Clio; Eloise Denis–Erato; Josephine Pepita–Euterpe; and so on down the line. (Later, when New Orleans streets were named for the Muses, Pierre was sure it was the de la Rondes and not Zeus and Mnemosyne who inspired the choice.) All the sisters made brilliant alliances and one of them, Adelaide Adele (Terpsichore on Grandfather de Reggio's list!) through her marriage to Pierre Ducros, eventually became kin to the Toutant-Beauregards.

Even more memorable than the visits to the de le Rondes were those to the Villerés, because the patriarch of this family, Jacques Philippe Roy, far from dying when Pierre was a small child, kept a tenacious hold on life, as he did on everything and everybody within his orbit. There was no danger, in his case, that his proud name would become extinct or that his fine estate would fall into desuetude. He had six sons and two daughters whom he encouraged or bulldozed, according to their disposition, to settle on the land close to the property he had originally acquired and develop it further. Presently there were Villerés on both sides of the river, more and more every year. Gabriel, the eldest son, who married the eldest Muse (Made-

leine Eulalie–Calliope) had five children; Jules, who married Perle
Olivier, had three; Delphin, Caliste, Felix and Anatole among them
sired twenty-four sons and daughters. Their sister Adele, as Madame
Hugues de la Vergne, added six; and though Jacques Philippe Roy
did not attach the same importance to these as he did to his sons'
children, since they did not bear his name and he could not control
Hugues, it pleased him to know that this daughter's fecundity was
comparable to his sons' virility. Only his other daughter, Léocadie, was
a disappointment in this respect; though she married twice, she remained a barren fig tree.

The fact that all of Jacques Philippe's progeny had reached ma-
turity by the time Pierre knew them had not altered the patriarchal
character of the Villeré clan. Every morning the old man seated himself in the shade of a great tree, situated in what seemed to him an
ideal meeting place, and awaited the arrival of his six sons. Only the
gravest type of emergency would excuse their absence and, as soon
as they were gathered around him, he gave his orders for the day;
not until he was sure these directions would be carried out did he
signify that the gathering could disperse. Not unnaturally, his plantation acquired the designation of Conseil, first as a jesting nickname
and then as a proud title. The prestige it enjoyed was enormous.

Despite its enviable social standing, the establishment at Conseil
was not a magnificent one, like the de la Rondes'; in general character
it was more like Toutant. Perhaps that was why Pierre enjoyed going
there more than he did to any of the other plantation houses. To be
sure, he had to sit and listen to tall tales about the Villerés, for
Jacques Philippe's father had been a victim of the Spanish Occupation under dramatic circumstances; and Jacques Philippe himself
had been a page at the Court of Louis XVI, had served as a lieutenant in Santo Domingo, as major on the staff of the Colonial
Prefect Laussat, as a major-general in the Third Regiment of the
Louisiana Militia, and as the first Creole governor of Louisiana. Interwoven with all these stories there were, of course, accounts of the
Battle of New Orleans, part of which had occurred on portions of the
de la Ronde and Villeré properties, and the thrilling escapes of
Gabriel and Jules from the British soldiers.

But, after all, these stories, this delight in dwelling on the glories
of the past, rather than on the pleasures of the moment, were another
characteristic of Conseil which made it seem akin to Toutant and
Pierre felt thoroughly at home there. Several of the young Villerés
were his contemporaries and Charles had been his schoolmate at
M. Debouchel's. He and Pierre became good companions, a relation-

ship which was all the easier to establish since Charles' little sister, Laure, was so shy that she ran and hid whenever a visitor appeared. The boys were therefore able to map out their days to suit themselves, and wonderful days these were.

So, on the whole Pierre preferred the country to the city and, whether in the city or the country, he had never been among strangers; the people he saw in New Orleans were always members of the same charmed circle he saw in St. Bernard and Plaquemines, living in much the same way, so far as their houses were concerned, even though these had only patios behind, instead of endless arpents all around them. They were well served by slaves, they spent long hours at laden tables, they dispensed bountiful hospitality, they celebrated family betrothals and weddings and baptisms with great ceremony, they were at home in the woods and fields and on the streams and they rode horseback as naturally as they walked. And no word of English was ever spoken by any one of them.

Pierre began to hear this and speak it a little in the course of his first ocean voyage on the sailing ship *Huntress* when he started for school in New York. As advertised, the extensive furnished accommodations were ably commanded and among the fifteen passengers were several he found especially congenial; but life on shipboard, as leisurely and as pleasant as life at home, did not prepare him for the different world he entered at his journey's end. Certainly, he was used to city ways—but city ways of New Orleans, not of New York. He was terribly homesick and terribly ashamed of this; it seemed to him a form of weakness. In his resolution not to betray it, he buried himself in his books. He had always been good at arithmetic; now he plunged quickly and easily into higher mathematics. He discovered the wonders of geography and reveled in them; and partly because he was burdened with the realization that he must be an American, whether he liked it or not, and partly because it bothered him not to chat readily with his schoolmates, he made rapid progress in English. His father was greatly impressed when he went home for his first vacation.

"Why, you speak it as if it were your native language, Pierre!" he said with mingled pride and astonishment.

"Well, isn't it supposed to be, if I'm an American?"

They laughed together and in that moment felt very close to each other. But Grandfather de Reggio, sitting on the farther side of the room, growled and swore and pounded on the floor with his cane. And Pierre's mother, still habitually silent in the midst of a storm, turned her head away.

In the autumn Pierre returned to school and, after that, throughout the next four years, he was at home only for the long summer vacations. Once, in 1830, he took the steamboat *Long Branch*, Captain Charles Walker, Master, for Mobile and made the rest of the journey by post coach through the Atlantic states. Mail was now regularly dispatched over this route, and not a few travelers preferred it to the lengthy coastwise voyage; the *Long Branch* had a sister steamboat, the *Mount Vernon*, John Queen, Master, and a triweekly service was established. But Pierre found the overland coach a "bruising" method of transportation and had no desire to repeat the experiment. He prided himself on being a good sailor and found that seafaring had rich rewards. He was deeply interested in the mechanics of navigation and improved every opportunity of learning more about them. Soon he numbered several of the masters among his friends; Captain Gaylord of the *Osprey*, Captain Fitten of the *Casten*, Captain Storey of the *Alexander*; they watched for his name on the passenger lists, spring and fall, with the same anticipation he felt in putting it there. There was always congenial company to be found among his fellow passengers, too: senators and representatives on their way to and from Washington were occasionally among them; more frequently merchants, brokers and outstanding planters. A few students, like himself, were sent north for their education, though the others were mostly "Americans"; once in a while a pretty young girl traveled with her mother to rejoin the head of the family who had preceded them in seeking a new home. Among all these there was always someone with whom Pierre could play games and carry on long conversations and he had the leisure for quiet reading, which was always such a delight to him and for which it was hard to find opportunities ashore. The voyage never seemed long and tedious—in fact, he was always sorry to have it end and to find himself again restricted to the discipline of institutional life.

But this, too, had its compensations. The Commercial and Mathematical School did not feature history to the same degree that it did subjects considered more practical; nevertheless, this was taught in a very effective way. Both the Peugnet brothers were born storytellers; and in the evening they gathered their pupils around them, much as the Toutant-Beauregards and the de Reggios gathered their children and grandchildren and nephews and nieces around them at the plantations which bore their names, and told them tall tales of Austerlitz and Jena and the St. Bernard Pass, of campfires and cavalry charges and guns dragged through snowdrifts on great sleds. The younger brother had been sought out personally by the Emperor, personally praised by him; Napoleon had even suggested that Peugnet should give him a namesake, in the person of the cavalry officer's son. Alas! he had no son. But looking at Pierre, he knew he had a disciple, another hero-worshiper at the shrine of the Little Corsican. After that exchange of understanding glances, the teacher and pupil grew closer together.

Besides, English was no longer a strange language, New York no longer a strange city. The school was so close to Broadway that almost every outing, of whatever kind, took him there, and the extraordinary width which gave the avenue its name ceased to be a source of surprise to him—the straightness of its course, more than two miles without a single turn, was more remarkable. So was the variety of buildings which lined the spacious sidewalks; the Merchants' Exchange and the Bank of the United States were large imposing structures, with white-marble façades; and there were numerous other handsome edifices, rising to the height of four or five stories; unpretentious wooden cottages, well shaded with poplar trees, were scattered among these.

Less accessible than Broadway, both from the viewpoint of location and of its desirability as a promenade for the young, was the Third Avenue Trotting Course; but occasionally, as a special treat or a reward for good behavior, a group of the Peugnet brothers' students was permitted to stroll over to it, under proper supervision, and watch the spectacle it afforded. Through the center ran a smoothly graded macadamized road and on either side was a well-beaten track; all were kept in perfect order, but it was the tracks which were preferred by the "knowing trotters" who came streaming into the city from all outlying districts. The horses themselves, to Pierre's critical and knowledgeable eye, did not bear comparison to those on the plantations of his family and friends; but he was willing to accept the verdict of his schoolmates that "there was no such road in the United States as Third Avenue for a trot," and to admit there was something stirring in the sight of so many fast-moving vehicles jumbled together, whatever the caliber of the steeds which drew them.

It took him longer to admit that New York could bear comparison with New Orleans when it came to the theater and the opera. In New Orleans, attendance at both was taken as a matter of course for both young and old, and there were any number of attractions among which to choose; New York restaurants, too, were subject to condescending appraisal. He and his schoolmates were permitted diversions which would take them to such places even less frequently than they were permitted to visit the Trotting Course. But for "cultural advancement" they were escorted to see Charles Keane in *Richard III*;

and during the first short holidays, the father of one of his newfound friends, Derek Vanderveer, a boy as fair, stocky and jovial as Pierre was dark, slim and serious, took Pierre and Derek to the Italian Opera House to hear *La Donna del Laco* and *Il Barbiere del Siviglia* and to the New American House, which was opening with *The Rivals*. These spectacles were seen after dinner at Delmonico's, which, as Pierre wrote his mother, was run by a "capable" French restaurateur, on William Street, and was very good. The Vanderveers had a town house on Hudson Square, and Pierre was made welcome there whenever the rigid schedule of the school permitted; and they also had a vast estate on the Hudson River, where they spent the summers and the longer winter holidays. When Derek suggested that Pierre come there with them, the prospective guest was puzzled by the way the invitation was worded.

"I'm sorry those old martinets won't give us a decent vacation at Thanksgiving, but what could you expect? They wouldn't even let us go to see the Siamese twins at Masonic Hall or Charles Durant trying out his balloon from Castle Garden! We'll have to make do with Thanksgiving in town. But you must spend Christmas with us in the country. We always bring in the Yule log and this year we're going to follow that new English custom—of course, it's German really—of setting up an evergreen tree in the drawing room and putting ornaments and candles on it."

"Thanksgiving? Yule log? Decorated tree in the drawing room?"

"You don't mean to tell me you don't celebrate Thanksgiving in Louisiana? Or Christmas?"

"I never heard of Thanksgiving. Christmas, certainly. We all go to Midnight Mass and afterward there's *Reveillon* and——"

Derek threw up his hands. "I'm not going to try to *explain* Thanksgiving. I'll let Father do that—about the Pilgrims and the Indians and everything. Just plan to come to dinner next Thursday and——"

"But the Peugnets will never let me off to dinner on a Thursday!"

"They will *this* Thursday and I'm willing to wager you'll have a bigger dinner than you ever had in Louisiana. At Christmas, too. Naturally, the Dutch Reformed don't go to Mass, midnight or any other time. But we'll see you get there if you want to. We'll see you do everything you want to."

Derek was as good as his word. Thanksgiving was not only explained, but celebrated; the dinner was stupendous, the company delightful, the house on Hudson Square elegant, spacious and supremely comfortable. But it was to the big estate on the Hudson that Pierre really lost his heart, after he had recovered from the first strangeness of white servants and high teas and Protestants who were actually Christians. Mrs. Vanderveer was of English descent and had contrived to mingle the best traditions of the landed gentry in her country with those which the Dutch settlers, from whom her husband was descended, had brought to Nieuw Amsterdam and, to a certain degree, left unchanged ever since. Both were tempered and mellowed by the American ways which the distinguished couple had also gladly adopted; and the whole gracious and expansive design for living was facilitated by substantial fortunes and impregnated with the refinements and enlightenment of long-developed cultures. Pierre had had no idea that, in the North, people lived in such stately and, at the same time, in such easy style, laying no stress on material possessions, taking integrity and breeding for granted, respecting scholarship and religion, but revealing this reverence, rather than discussing it. Derek was by no means the only one of his schoolmates to open new vistas to him; but he was the first and remained the most valued, the one to whom Pierre felt he owed the most.

As he approached New York Harbor by boat, after his last visit to the Vanderveers in the spring of 1833, he thought he had never seen the river look so beautiful. More than a thousand sloops were now employed on the Hudson, many of them painted brilliant colors; and the natural scenery of the river formed a verdant background for their white sails and variegated flags and streamers. The port itself was crowded with vessels of every description; and as the *Nashville*, Captain Rath, Master—the five-hundred-ton brigantine on which he had taken passage—pulled away from the wharf, Pierre realized for the first time that he was actually sorry to leave New York; and when he drove from the docks to Grandfather de Reggio's house, somehow it was New Orleans that had now begun to look unfamiliar, French the tongue which he spoke less instinctively; and at Toutant he had lost his boon hunting companion, for Tombie, now almost as tall and lithe and powerful as his father, the famous hunter Placide, had been put to work in the cane fields, since he was old enough for such labor. All this made it easier for Pierre to speak to his father on a certain subject which he was hugging to his heart, but which he knew would be alien to everyone else's. Fortunately, the Peugnets had given him a letter, which he believed would have great weight— the same letter which, thirty-five years later, he was hoping to find near the top of the japanned box on the kitchen table in the quarters.

This time he was not disappointed, as he had been about the baptismal certificate. A bundle of communications from the Peugnets, mostly term bills and reports, all penned in the same small precise writing and neatly tied together with string, came almost immediately to hand. He had no difficulty detaching from the other papers the one in which he was especially interested. He spread it out and read it in the fading light. The rain, which had brought him back in a hurry to the quarters, was falling in sheets now and there were frequent flashes of lightning; the thunder, no longer merely an ominous rumble, had become close and resounding. Every few seconds the shadowed room where he sat was illumined by a sudden zigzagging bolt. He smiled to himself. It was appropriate for him to reread the letter under such conditions. Its effect had certainly been electrifying when his father read it at Toutant.

"So it is the considered opinion of the Peugnets that you would make a name for yourself as a soldier. Well, that was not exactly the career I had in mind for you when I sent you to school in New York."

"But you knew it was a military school."

"Exactly. And I thought the amount of discipline you would undergo in a military school would dampen your enthusiasm for beating drums and flags waving in the breeze. You may recall that we have had one rather embarrassing experience because of the irresistible attraction these had for you. And a soldier's life is not all beating drums and waving flags, by any means."

Pierre was always annoyed by any reference to the fiasco of what should have been his First Holy Communion. He answered his father with more spirit and less respect than usual.

"I'm quite aware of that. And I don't need to be reminded of something that happened when I was ten years old, in order to prove or disprove a point. Now that I'm sixteen——"

"Yes, now that you have reached the advanced age of sixteen, you feel you could make a name for yourself as a soldier although, as I am glad to say, we are not at war and there is no prospect that we will be. How would you propose to go about making a name as a soldier?"

"The first step, of course, would be to enter the United States Military Academy at West Point."

This was the thunderbolt, and it took the family weeks to recover from its shock. Even Jacques, when he reminded Pierre that they were now Americans, whether or not that was what they wanted to be, had failed to visualize him as an officer in the United States Army and the prospect was displeasing to him. He wanted all his sons to be planters like himself, practically controlling a small empire. All right, Augustin and Alfred and Armand were welcome to the empire; all Pierre wanted was a uniform and a chance to wear it. The argument grew more and more heated and finally Jacques put an end to it by saying it had gone far enough, that he did not wish to listen to anything more, that talk was futile anyway, because he did not propose to give his consent to any such mad scheme.

Pierre excused himself politely and left the *salle*. Half an hour later, when his mother went to find him in his room, he was packing, opening and shutting drawers with such violence that he did not even hear her quiet entrance or look up long enough to see her standing behind him. It was only afterward that he learned she had been there, that she had turned without a word and gone back to the *salle*, or that it was she, who, despite her desolation at the thought of losing him, had persuaded her husband to write their friend Governor Roman and request his good offices in obtaining an appointment to the Military Academy for their son. The Governor, in turn, had written their Congressman, Mr. White, and Mr. White, in his turn, had written the Secretary of War, the Honorable Lewis Cass—a letter more laudatory than accurate, for it stressed the distinguished services of the Beauregards toward the patriots' cause during the American Revolution! Nevertheless, Mr. Cass was obviously impressed with it, since the appointment came through, even before it was time for Pierre to go back to Toutant for another vacation; and, for some unknown reason, it was sent to him direct, in care of the Peugnets, in New York, instead of in care of his father at Toutant. He did not so much as wait for Jacques' approval in writing—a legal formality. He decided it was wiser not to do so. His father might still change his mind, if given time to think things over; but if he, Pierre, were actually at West Point, the sternest parent would hardly humiliate his son by recalling him. The boy rushed off, ensconced himself at the desk allotted him by the astonished superintendent, and wrote to the Secretary of War. He had kept a copy of the letter, exactly as he had written it; it was attached to the one from Peugnet, extolling him as a prospective soldier:

I have written to my father to beg him to inform you weather he wished me to accept or not; I will submit myself to the answer you will receive from him.

(Of course, he had no idea of doing any such thing; and he was not as good at spelling as he was at mathematics; afterward, he wondered if he should not have written *whether* instead of *weather*. Not that it mattered much; and the last of the letter was at least sincere, even if he did leave out a word.)

I shall endeavor by my conduct during the period I remain here to merit in some manner the bounty which my country to bestow on me.

After he had dispatched this hastily written letter, he enrolled himself with the same degree of haste as Pierre Gustave Toutant Beauregard, thus giving the impression that Toutant was part of his baptismal name and not part of his surname. But haste was not responsible for his omission of the hyphen. For some time, he had been casting about in his mind for a way to abbreviate his signature, to make it seem less ostentatious; boys with signatures like John Jones and George Brown made fun of it. Of course, all his names had to be written out in full on his enrollment; but hereafter he proposed to sign himself merely P. G. T. Beauregard and do away with a lot of chaffing.

He felt slightly guilty about this decision, for he knew he should be just as proud of the Toutant as he was of the Beauregard and just as eager to retain it; but, as a matter of fact, he had begun to resent it, even before he came to West Point, not as a name for himself but as a name for the plantation. He wished it were named with more originality, as Kenilworth and Conseil and Concorde were. Of course many plantations, even the de la Rondes', were still known simply by the names of the families who owned them. But the trend was away from that custom; and when two families shared the same holdings, as in the case of his father and his uncle Joseph, it caused confusion. He had many times been tempted to ask them if they wouldn't make a change, but had refrained for fear of hurting their feelings. Perhaps he would hurt their feelings now, with his new signature, but he was having enough of a struggle with his Christian name, without having to struggle with his surname, too. He wished that Pierre did not come so hard to most of his schoolmates, because that was a fine strong plain name, one that he really loved, whereas Gustave was in the class with Algernon and Clarence among Anglo-Saxons. Well, perhaps he could think of some way to take care of that later. For the moment, it was enough to be rid of the hyphen and to know that, on roll calls, he would be called directly after the boys whose surnames began with A, instead of after all those whose surnames covered practically the whole alphabet. He was not so silly or so stupid as to suppose this position would actually affect his scholastic rank in the class, which naturally would be determined by the marks in his courses, and which he meant to make and keep as high as possible. At the same time, Beauregard certainly *sounded* nearer the top than Toutant!

With his marks he had no trouble; in fact, his knowledge of French

was a distinct advantage, for many of the best works on the art and
science of war were in that language, and his classmates either toiled
helplessly through these or made practically no pretense of reading
them, for French was not taught at all in most preparatory schools or
with any degree of thoroughness, even at the Academy, until he himself began to teach it in his second year. For the sake of salving the
feelings of a senior teacher, he was classified as an "assistant," both
then and in his first year. Mathematics continued to come easily;
military engineering became his new interest and an absorbing one.
He liked to draw, kept his "drawing instruments" in a rosewood box
and did not hesitate to try his hand at classical subjects, such as a head
of Andromache; but when he found this was considered a peculiar,
not to say effeminate, pastime, he did not indulge in it often and
missed the distraction which it gave him. But, on the whole, he was
happy, though he considered both the food and the climate appalling.
He was good at sports and took part in all for which there were
opportunities; it pleased him, then and later, to hear that his classmates said that he excelled in them and that his horsemanship was
extraordinary. (Of course, it seemed extraordinary to them; the under-
privileged lads had not started riding before they were weaned, as he
had!) But it pleased him still more to learn, by circuitous means later
on, that they were impressed by his marks. Of course, they never told
him so then. That is not the sort of thing schoolboys say to one
another.

Still less would they have commented to him favorably on his
personal appearance and, happily, they were not disposed to comment unfavorably. He was not so tall as most of his fellow cadets
and he was very slender; but he carried himself so well that he gave
an illusion of height and he was so wiry that there could be no
question of his strength; besides, he was so quick in all his movements
that speed made up for size when it came to contests of any kind. His
high cheekbones, his skin—olive, except for the red glow in his cheeks
—his thick black hair and big black eyes made him outstanding among
fairer companions. But the comparison was to his advantage; it put
him in a category of high class: the debonair, the jaunty and the
daring.

His father and mother were also pleased with his marks, so pleased
that they thought Grandfather de Reggio could not help being gratified also. When Pierre's class went on its furlough, in June 1836, and
he came home for his only vacation during the four-year course,
Jacques and Judith tried to talk to the old man about his grandson's
high scholastic standing, but he would not listen.

"Americans!" he growled, thumping with his cane. "*Yankees!* The next thing we know, the boy will imagine he's fallen in love with one of those Yankee girls, he'll be wanting to bring her here to Toutant! What will you say then, I'd like to know? You'll stop bragging about his marks when you find he expects you to welcome a daughter-in-law with a name like Smith, among the de Reggios and the de Vezins. Look me straight in the face, Pierre, and tell me that you haven't some such idea, that you haven't become infatuated with some Yankee!"

"I haven't any such idea," Pierre said, with unnecessary force, his mother thought, and she noticed that he blushed when he said it. Of course, he had always blushed easily. But still. . . .

As a matter of fact, he was telling the truth. He had no such idea—then. But it was because the parents of the girl with whom he had fallen in love—he scorned the word *infatuation*—had declared that he and she were both too young to enter into an engagement or even to have an "understanding." They had been forbidden to see each other and, from the day of their enforced parting, he had never heard from her; though he had, by then, partially recovered from the blow, he was still smarting at the thought of her inconstancy. He tried to avoid thinking about it. And now his grandfather had recalled it to him by those prying questions.

The worst of it was that the old man had hit very close to the mark. The girl's name was not Smith, to be sure, but it *was* Scott— Virginia Scott. And she was not a Yankee, for she came from the state for which she had been named; but she certainly was an American. And the fact that her father was a general, indeed, considered a very distinguished general, probably would not have made any difference to Grandfather de Reggio, either.

No, of course Pierre had not cared about her any more, when he said he had no idea of bringing Virginia Scott to Toutant. But it had hurt to be reminded of her, just the same. It still hurt a little, after all these years and after two happy marriages. He had never fully recovered from his resentment of the unfairness and duplicity which had separated him from Virginia. For Mrs. Scott had intercepted both Virginia's letters to him and his to her and the girl had believed him dishonorable, just as he had believed her inconstant. And then she had been whisked off to Europe, where there would not be the slightest danger that they could meet, and there she had taken refuge in religion; she had become a convert to Catholicism. And then she had gone a step further: she had joined the Order of the Visitation and entered its convent at Georgetown (where she had previously been a pupil) as a nun. Of course, he should have rejoiced because she had embraced the true faith, but he had never been able to do so; he had always felt that the Church and, even more, the convent had been a refuge for her, not a happy haven. How could he help it, after that letter she had written him on her deathbed? She was a cloistered nun by then and, theoretically, cloistered nuns were not allowed to write letters unsupervised by their superiors. But somehow this letter had been smuggled out of the Visitation Convent; or perhaps the Superior was an understanding woman, who realized that Virginia—now Sister Mary Emmanuel—would die more happily if she could write, just this once, to her lost love. Anyway, *that* letter he had received, and in it Virginia had told him the whole story and ended by saying her last thoughts would be of him.

It had moved him very much, though, as a matter of fact, by the time he finally heard from her, he had practically forgotten about her. He was ready to admit by then that he had "imagined" he was in love with Virginia, that his feeling for her, genuine enough at the time he experienced it, *had* actually been only an infatuation. For after that, he had fallen in love—really in love, deeply, tenderly, passionately in love—with Laure, and while she lived and long afterward, there had been room for no other love in his life. He had never told Laure about Virginia, because he had seen no point in it. If it had been a guilty secret, perhaps he would have felt that he should confess to it, though he would have shrunk from sullying her innocence with a sordid story; but since it was only a sad one, a wholly innocuous one, of a boy and girl, both still in their teens, who had been separated by Virginia's stern parents, he saw no reason for telling Laure she was not his very first, as well as his only real love. Besides, innocuous as it was, it did have dramatic overtones—the intercepted letters, the refuge in religion, the cloister instead of the bridal chamber, the deathbed letter! Too much drama was not good for delicate flowers like Laure; it upset them, it disturbed their peaceful thoughts, sometimes it even haunted them. Virginia's letter was not among those he would find in the japanned box. He had destroyed it as soon as he had read it—well, almost as soon. It had not immediately occurred to him that Laure might come upon it by chance and that, if she did, he would have to tell her the whole story. But when it did, he tore the letter into small pieces and burned them, doing so when Laure had just called to him from their bedroom that she thought it was cool enough to have a fire lighted in the *salle*. The bits of Virginia's letter were consumed with the rest of the great fire he built of cypress wood so that Laure should be warm and comfortable.

The rain was still falling steadily, though the thunder and lightning had ceased. He put aside the papers he had come across next: old sailing schedules, the copy of his letter to Cass, the program of a dance when Virginia had been his guest at West Point—after that he had found nothing of real importance. Then he opened one of the bottles of orange wine which Elodie had given him and undid the package of sandwiches. She had been most generous. He could indeed tell Mme Castel that he had already supped, and supped well, before he went over to the main house. He tidied the table where he had worked and eaten and, carefully carrying the jar of jelly and the other bottle of wine, went down the steep slippery staircase and across the wet patio.

A light was still burning in the gallery, but it was empty. Elodie was not the only one who had shown tact in dealing with the situation, he told himself; Mme Castel had made it evident that she would be glad to see him, if he felt like calling that evening, but she would not give the impression she was waiting supper for him. The door into the hallway stood open and, at the further end, another lamp was burning. He went on through the shadowy corridor and, as he approached Mme Cougot's room, called her name.

"It's Pierre Beauregard, Madame," he said. "I've brought you a little present from my sister. May I come in?"

The door of the bedchamber opened instantly and he had the feeling not only that he had been expected but that both women would have been disappointed if he had not come. There was more light in the room than there had been before and Mme Cougot, instead of lying prostrate, was propped up with pillows, and had already turned her head in his direction. Mme Castel, for the first time since he had met her, was not dressed in black; she was wearing a lavender-colored dress which also smelled faintly of lavender and he guessed that it had been put away for some time and had now been taken from some carefully packed chest in his honor. He was pleased and touched.

"We must drink some of the wine together," Mme Castel said. "Wait, I will get three glasses." When he protested, saying he had some of his own, she added, almost gaily, "Then the next time, we will drink some of yours." When she returned with the glasses, she also brought a plate of small fresh cookies which she said she had baked that afternoon, and Pierre could not decline to accept one of them, especially when she told him that her father had been a skilled confectioner, that her mother had always helped in his pleasant little shop and that, when she was a girl, they had both taken pride in teaching her all they could of their art. The cooking she did now, even if she had to do it in a makeshift way, was the result of their teaching. Without much to come and go on, it was a source of pride to her, seeing what she could concoct.

No previous mention had been made of her background; now, as he learned something of it, he began to understand her better, the care and precision with which she worked, her sense of style, her supreme neatness; to visualize the contented, industrious life of a prosperous and united family, not so frugal that it denied itself all the good things of life and yet provident for the future. And what had this providence availed it? Nothing, absolutely nothing.

"Did you find time to write any letters, General?" Mme Cougot was asking. "Please don't think me impatient. But I can't help asking."

"You have every reason to ask. Yes, I wrote three letters. One to General Sherman—"

"*General Sherman!*"

Her tone was one of uncontrolled horror. He forced himself to answer quietly.

"Yes. I was able to remember that, before he burned Atlanta and devastated all Georgia, he had been superintendent of the Military Academy at Alexandria, which my two sons attended. He was very kind to them. I believe he was fond of them both. Why, he even stopped in to bring me news of them when he came down from that seminary of learning, while I was still at the Customs House, just before I left for Montgomery. And when Bragg, the dirty old scoundrel, tried to prejudice him against me, he wouldn't listen. For all these reasons, I felt he might be more likely to grant me a favor than anyone else I know."

"It was very, very kind of you," Simone said quickly. "You were not asking a favor for yourself, you were asking a favor for us. But we know that it must have cost you a great effort to approach him. I am very grateful—and *maman* will be, too, when she thinks it over."

"I do not need to think it over. I am ashamed of my outburst. It was inexcusable."

"It was quite natural . . . I have also written Irvin McDowell. He, like Sherman, was a friend of mine at West Point. There was never the same sort of a tie with him as there was with Sherman; still, we were good friends once. He may remember that. He has been censured, as I have been, for defeat in cases where I believe someone else should have been blamed. That may be the bond in this case. At all events, I am under the impression he is fairly prosperous now. I hope so. I can afford to be generous in this instance. There has never been any question that I defeated him at Manassas."

"Of course not. How could there be?"

"Then I wrote a third letter," Pierre continued, without making a direct answer, "to a man who was a schoolmate of mine in New York at Peugnets', before I went to West Point. He belongs to a prominent old Dutch family and there have been outstanding figures in it ever since Henry Hudson sailed up the river that now bears his name. I spent many of my holidays with this family and, if I am not mistaken, my school friend now holds an important political position. As such, he may have many avenues of approach to the mystery which are closed to the others."

"That is true. Of course, it is true. You have thought of everything."

"I am sure I have not. But I hope I shall. When I went out to post my letters, I made several visits, in the course of which I mentioned Lance. However, I am afraid those were not very fruitful. I do not seem to have much luck, nowadays, when there is a question of trying to get help in New Orleans."

"But you are giving it. Sometimes it is better to give help than to get it."

"I haven't actually given any so far."

"Yes, you have—by trying. Just by being yourself. Just by coming to sit with us here, this evening, and telling us what you have tried to do. You have made us happier than we have been in a long, long while."

He knew that she was speaking the truth. As he went back to the quarters through the rain, which was now falling gently, he, too, was happier than he had been since he could remember.

❧ 7 ❧

PETER G. T. BEAUREGARD'S ACADEMIC RECORD
WHILE A CADET AT THE
UNITED STATES MILITARY ACADEMY
APPOINTED FROM LOUISIANA
ADMITTED 1 JULY 1834
AGE 16 YEARS 1 MONTH

FOURTH CLASS YEAR
Ending June 1835
Class of 57 members.

General Order of Merit   4*

In Conduct for the Fourth Class Year Cadet Beauregard
stood number 23 in a Corps of 240 Cadets, having received
11 demerits for the year.

THIRD CLASS YEAR
Ending June 1836
Class of 51 members.

General Order of Merit   2*

In Conduct for the Third Class Year Cadet Beauregard
stood number 13 in a Corps of 216 Cadets, having received
3 demerits for the year.
He served as a Corporal, United States Corps of Cadets,
1835–1836.

SECOND CLASS YEAR
Ending June 1837
Class of 46 members.

General Order of Merit   2*

In Conduct for Second Class Year Cadet Beauregard stood number 3 in a Corps of 211 Cadets, having received 0 demerits for the year. He served as Assistant Teacher of French during his Second Class Year, 1836–1837.

FIRST CLASS YEAR
Ending June 1838
Class of 45 members.

General Order of Merit   2*

In Conduct for First Class Year Cadet Beauregard stood number 2 in a Corps of 218 Cadets, having received 0 demerits for the year. He served as Assistant Teacher of French during his First Class Year, 1837–1838.

Peter G. T. Beauregard graduated number 2* in a Class of 45 members and was commissioned a 2nd Lieutenant in the 1st Artillery 1 July 1838.

* *Distinguished Cadet.* At that time the cadets who were among the first five in relative academic standing were so designated in the published *Official Register.*

WHEN HE WENT TO TRY ON HIS NEW SUIT, HE REALIZED THAT HE must make an effort to stand erect, or he would not do justice to the excellent tailoring. As he straightened up, Falk exclaimed with pleasure.

"*Merci, mon Général, merci!* I was longing to ask you to do that, but I was afraid you'd think me presumptuous. I have always thought of you slim and straight as a reed. And when I saw you coming into my shop, all stooped over, so—" he gave an exaggerated example of what he meant "—why, that is the reason I did not recognize you, even though you did make an effort to straighten up."

It was not true, of course, but Pierre smiled and let it stand. He did not want to start an argument with Falk, for the man could talk on and on, gesticulating more and more frantically the more excited he became. Pierre complimented Falk on the set of the sleeves, said he would return in three days for a final fitting, and went out into the street so pleased with the prospect of his new outfit that he hardly noticed the breathless heat of a summer day.

It would never have occurred to him that he would be glad to change a uniform for civilian clothes. Once he had been willing to give up an empire if he could only earn the right to dress like a soldier, and he had done it. For nearly thirty years he had not dressed otherwise, except during that brief interval after he had resigned from the United States Army and had not yet received his commission in the Confederate Army. And now he was ready to give up a uniform so that he might earn his daily bread.

Suddenly, the heat struck him like a blow and he felt unequal to going all the way home. He walked slowly from Bourbon Street to Royal and on to Chartres, seeking the comparative coolness of *Père* Antoine's Alley as he reached the Cathedral. Then he sought out a shaded bench in Jackson Square and rested, thinking about his first blue uniform—his first real Army uniform—and his pride in it the day he had been graduated from West Point.

He had never been prouder of his mother than he was that day, and he was sure it was not only because he looked at her with eyes of love that she seemed to him the most beautiful, the most elegant, the most distinguished woman among the visitors. As usual, she had contrived to achieve originality, as well as style, in her wardrobe and everything she wore was exquisitely fashioned of beautiful material in rich colors. She kept rather to herself, conscious of her imperfect command of English, but giving no sign of embarrassment because of this. She had, she told Pierre, been studying it at home—secretly, so that her father's feelings would not be hurt—and she had utilized every possible opportunity of speaking it on the *Alabama*, B. C. Merriman, Master, which she had taken for her voyage north. Her fellow passengers had been most kind and helpful, she said; and Pierre assured her, with sincerity, that she had made astonishing progress under the circumstances. She seemed perfectly self-possessed; in fact, her slight reserve added to her appearance of dignity. He was freer to devote time to her than if he had asked a girl to his graduation; he had, of course, expected to invite Virginia Scott but, in the absence of any reply to his letters, he had not done so and now he heard that, in any case, she could not have come, as she had just gone to Europe with her mother; so now he had a chance to talk more with his. She was especially interested in hearing about his friends, where they came from, what their preoccupations were, whether or not he had met their families.

"Most of them have at least one member of their family here to-day, just as I have, so you'll see them," he said, giving her hand a happy squeeze and indirectly answering her last question first. "They come from just about everywhere—McDowell from Ohio, A. J. Smith from Pennsylvania, Hardee from Georgia. Early, who was graduated last year, is a Virginian. He was a good sort, I'd like to see more of him."

"Is he the one you like best?"

"I reckon so. Otherwise, I like them all about equally. None of them as much as I did Derek Vanderveer, who didn't want to be a soldier—he's studying at Columbia College. The only one I really couldn't stand was a classmate of Early's from North Carolina—Bragg, his name was, and did he live up to it!"

"It isn't much of a name to live up to, is it, cher? Now, if his name were Toutant-Beauregard——" She hesitated and then summoned courage to go on. "We all feel rather badly, at Toutant, about the way you sign your name now, Pierre. Why do you do it?"

"I don't know that I can make you understand, but I'll try. You see, fellows with names like—well, like Bragg—thought Toutant-Beauregard was an affectation. I got a lot of ribbing about it. So I decided initials were the best way out." He hesitated in his turn, wondering if, to be really candid, he should not tell her about the willful omission of the hyphen, which had been his first step. Then he decided against this; it would probably only bewilder her. Instead, he would seize what might be a propitious moment to speak about Toutant in another connection. "As a matter of fact, I've been meaning to ask you and Father for some time if we couldn't change the name of the plantation. Our part of it, I mean. It's confusing to a great many people, because we call our section of the holdings Toutant and Uncle Joseph calls his section that, too. Of course, sometimes they remember that ours is Nord and his is Sud, but generally they don't; and, anyway, I think we should have a name of our own. Uncle will never change—you know that as well as I do. But is there any reason why we shouldn't?"

"Yes, Pierre. Sentiment."

"But we might think of something or find something for which we'd have more sentiment than just a family name. Other people do."

"For instance?"

"Well, Austerlitz on False River. Loche Breaux, who built and owns it, is a great admirer of Napoleon. The house is full of Napoleonic souvenirs and it was named for one of the Emperor's greatest victories."

"But you're a great admirer of Napoleon, too! You don't want to change the name of Toutant to Jena, do you?"

"Of course not. You asked me to suggest a name that was inspired by sentiment and I thought of that one. But the sentiment doesn't necessarily have to be about a victory—a victory wasn't what the de la Vergnes were thinking of when they named Concorde or the Villerés when they named Conseil. We ought to be able to do something like that. In fact, I'm afraid we'll have to, if we do change the name. I don't seem to remember that the Toutant-Beauregards are associated with any victory, for all their prestige."

He spoke almost sarcastically, which was not like him. But he did it intentionally. He wanted his mother to see that this question of a name was one he had taken to heart.

"Your Uncle Joseph served with distinction at the Battle of New Orleans," she reminded him gently. "And I am sure other members of the family have served with distinction, too, as occasion demanded. We should be thankful that there haven't been more occasions—war is such a terrible calamity! Thank God, there's no prospect of one at present!"

"Well, if there should be one, and you haven't thought up something else in the meantime, promise me you'll rename our part of Toutant Plantation for the first victory I figure in. We can't keep on letting such chances go by, the way Uncle Joseph did."

He spoke lightly and pleasantly again, but now it was evident that, in pressing his point, he had distressed her. A victory could mean many things besides glory—a battlefield on foreign soil, mutilating wounds, even hideous death. As the mother of a prospective soldier, these were the aspects of war that loomed large in her mind. He put his arm around her shoulders.

"All right, we won't talk about it any more. Instead, I'll go on telling you about my friends. I think we stopped with Bragg, whom I didn't like. As a matter of fact, the ones I like best at West Point, besides Early, are Sherman, who won't graduate until Forty, and Anderson, who got through before I came here and teaches artillery now. I'll present him to you. He's asked me to stay on for a little as his assistant and I was only too glad to accept, though of course engineering and not artillery is my department. Anyway, I don't know how long I'll be allowed to stay, before I get shipped off to my first post. Even if it's a dismal one, I won't care. The only thing that counts is that I'm really in the Army now."

It was not a dismal post, after all: Fort Adams, near Newport, Rhode Island. The salary was good, nine hundred a year; the assignment important since, next to Fortress Monroe, Fort Adams, now nearing completion, was the largest defensive works in the country. Moreover, it had great social prestige and, like most other young officers, Pierre would normally have enjoyed the pleasant diversions it offered. But his old enemy, tonsillitis, which miraculously he had managed to keep at bay practically all the time he was in New York City and at West Point, now laid him very low indeed; he was ill almost all winter and finally spent two months in a hospital, where he longed for the kindly care of Mme Debouchel. Under these circumstances, he was delighted when his doctors advised a milder climate and Colonel Totten, Chief of the Engineering Corps, lent a willing ear to this advice. With the rank of first lieutenant, Pierre was transferred to Pensacola for the construction of naval defenses there and, a few months later, still through the good graces of Colonel Totten, to Fort Livingston on Grande Terre Island—the old hideout of the Lafitte pirates—to make a topographic and hydrographic survey of Barataria Bay, which empties into the Gulf of Mexico at that point.

The sturdy old fort, surrounded by a moat and pentagonal in shape, was of curious construction, for large quantities of clam shells had been combined with brick in its building; but it had the character of individuality and even a certain degree of severe and rugged beauty. The steps which led from one elevation to another and the pediments crowning the windows were made of solid granite and the sequence of supporting arches represented a triumph of masonry, as harmonious as it was intriguing. Grande Terre itself was an island about nine miles long and about a mile wide and, from the sea side, the outlook was one of almost complete detachment from the world, with only open ocean in view; and on the west, it was separated from Grand Isle, which was about as large, merely by mile-wide Barataria Pass.

Pierre knew that very few of his former classmates, if any, would have been pleased to exchange the elegancies of Newport for such a location. Quite aside from what they would have considered its isolation, it was wholly lacking in prestige, from both a social and a military standpoint. Newport's smart set formed part of another and more glamorous world, and actual construction work on forts outranked soundings as an engineering project. Nevertheless, nothing could have made Pierre so happy as this new assignment. He was back in his own country, the country that he loved; he found both the young lieutenants who shared the Bachelor Officers' Quarters with him at the fort congenial company. Like himself, they were natural sportsmen, and they had only to cross the moat to find all the game they could use; wild doves and wild ducks flocked overhead, the open sea teemed with flounder, redfish and sea trout, the bays with oysters, shrimp and crab. Invariably, the young officers returned from even a short outing laden with all they could carry; and, after the bountiful supper provided by their bag or their catch, they sat around the huge fireplace, where much of their cooking was done and on which they were dependent for warmth during the long cold periods while the east wind blew incessantly. There they swapped stories about the Lafittes and the piratical loot of these infamous but intriguing brothers who had hardly withdrawn, to find more profitable fields from which to wrest their ill-gotten gains, when the fort was built; or else the lieutenants talked about the careers they intended to carve out for themselves, and where they would spend their next furlough, and whether or not Totten would ever get the appropriations to improve the fort, concerning which he continuously besieged the War Department to no avail. Until he did, they would be periodically short of supplies, and this meant they could not make the improvements on the fort, for which they were held responsible. It was bad enough to be half-devoured all summer by mosquitoes and green headflies while watching a brassy sky for hurricanes, without wondering whether or not they were going to get staple groceries, building materials and weapons.

As a matter of fact, they were not without some social life, even within the narrow confines of their small island. Sugar was raised there on a modest scale and the owners of three plantation houses, when in residence, made the young men welcome. Besides, whenever Pierre had a pass, he could turn his back on his swamps and his soundings and go to Toutant or any one of half a dozen plantations on the mainland; or he could go to New Orleans for the opera, the balls and the horse races. He often smiled at the misplaced expressions of sympathy for his hard lot that came in letters from his Northern friends. At first, they made a special effort to write him as often as they could, because they were so sorry for him. Then, after he had told them about the operas, the balls and the races he had attended, the letters came less and less frequently.

He did not much care. He certainly neither wanted nor merited their sympathy; and on one of his frequent visits to New Orleans, coming out of the bar of the St. Louis Hotel at his usual smart pace, he narrowly escaped collision with another young man who was hurrying in the opposite direction. In fact, the escape was so narrow that he stopped to apologize and found the apology cut short by a shout of welcome.

"*Pierre!* I heard you were back! I've been meaning to look you up."

"Charles Villeré, as I live and breathe! Am I ever glad to see you! Have you been hiding somewhere?"

"Have *I* been hiding! I like that! What have you been doing, I'd like to know."

"Well, don't let's stand here on the *banquette* and argue about it! Let's go in where it's cool or, at any rate, cooler, and have a drink!"

They sat for an hour, talking with the happy ease of old friends, so congenial that, even after a long separation, they can pick up the threads of their mutual interests as if these had never been dropped. It was Charles who finally pulled out his watch and rose hurriedly.

"Look, I've got to get back to Upper Magnolia! Mother's having some kind of a *soirée* tonight and I promised I'd be there. Why don't you come with me? Or have you promised *your* mother you'd be at Toutant?"

"No, as a matter of fact, I meant to stay in New Orleans and go to the theater."

"You can do that some other time. Of course, as far as that goes, you can come to Upper Magnolia some other time. But since you haven't done so of your own accord—"

"*Allons*, you can come to Toutant at any time and you haven't."

"*Cher*, we're getting right back where we started and that didn't take us any place! Let's be on our way. Is your horse at Cook's or at Preval's?"

"At Preval's."

"Good! So is mine. You know—or don't you? you're so out of touch since you went north!—that we have to cross over to the West Side?"

"I didn't know. Do you take the ferry or do you keep one of your own men waiting for you in a skiff?"

"Oh, I take the ferry," Charles answered, grinning at the oblique reference to John McDonogh, the rich miser who went back and forth between New Orleans and Algiers, where he lived, by the latter method, in order to save a nickel fare. "It's worth the price in more ways than one. Do you remember Conseil—and those conferences every morning under the favorite oak?" Charles paused as he asked the question and Pierre, understandingly, grinned in response as he nodded assent. "Well, I reckon Papa began to feel, after a while, that he'd had enough advice. Anyway, after Grandpapa died, Papa and Uncle Delphin, between them, bought Magnolia Plantation, in Plaquemines Parish, to add to some sugar lands the family already owned, just to the south of it and later, after Uncle Delphin died, Papa bought it lock, stock and barrel from the Delphin Villeré succession. So now we see various relatives in St. Bernard when we feel like it, but we and they don't actually live in each other's pockets any more. Uncle Caliste and Uncle Felix are the only ones near us."

"A much better arrangement, I should think."

"Right you are! Well, as I said before, let's be on our way."

They quickly covered the short distance between the hotel and Preval's and did not try to do much talking either during their walk or on the ferry crossing. But, as they started down the river road, on horseback, they resumed the conversation where it had broken off at the bar, speaking of inconsequential matters which were, nevertheless, of great interest to them both. It was a beautiful spring day and the white spider lilies, pink mallow and purple thistles formed a bright border to the roadside, while the low levee at its left was so thickly dotted with clover that the soft air was scented.

"I used to love to lie down and roll in that," Charles said, pointing with his crop to the flowering bank. "Just sniffing it from the road didn't get me close enough to it when it smells so good. In fact, I'd still like to do the same thing. But since I've now attained man's estate, which unfortunately means acting like an adult, I have to content myself with admiring our Chinese lilacs."

With a sweeping movement, he changed the direction of his crop and indicated the blossoming fences which separated the fields of Upper Magnolia, which they were now approaching, from the public road, and also from Caliste Villeré's field at Point Beca to the north. The same type of floral planting, Charles explained, separated Upper Magnolia from his uncle Felix's fields at Fort Leon to the south. Jules Villeré's property now consisted of about five hundred arpents of arable land, obviously in splendid condition. Pierre was able to appreciate both the exceptionally fine appearance and the immense material value of the fields before him and, for some minutes, he and Charles discussed crops, soil, labor and equipment, in the knowledgeable way natural to the sons of planters. Indeed, it was not until they turned in at the gate opening on the driveway that Pierre asked a question unrelated to anything that had been said before.

"Does your sister still run and hide whenever there's company? If she does, perhaps I ought to let you go ahead of me and warn her."

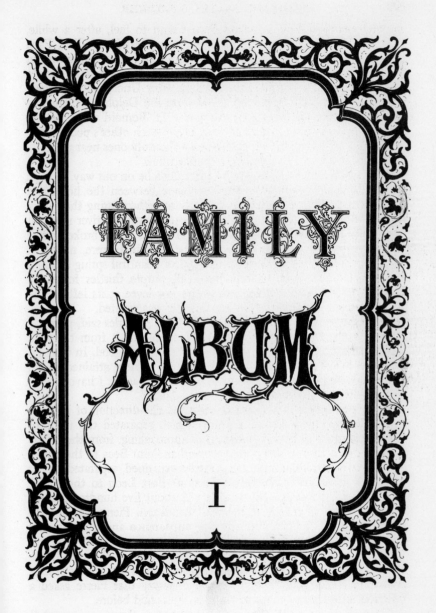

FAMILY
ALBUM

I

Michel Louis Toutant Beauregard

Paternal grandparents of General Beauregard. They were married in the St. Louis Cathedral in New Orleans on April 13, 1784. Reproduced by courtesy of Mrs. Porter F. Bedell (Elizabeth Toutant Beauregard), a

Victoire Ducros Beauregard

great-great-great-granddaughter of the couple pictured in these miniatures, and a great-great niece of General Beauregard.

Louis Charles Emmanuel de Reggio, son of Chevalier François Marie de Reggio and Helene de Fleuriau, husband of Louis Judith Olivier de Vezin, and grandfather of General Beauregard. Reproduced by courtesy of Sidney J. Villeré, his great-great-great nephew.

Lucie Marie de Reggio, great-aunt of General Beauregard. The original portrait is in the possession of Mrs. Charles Colomb, New Orleans, and is reproduced through the courtesy of the owner.

Jacques Elie Toutant-Beauregard, father of General Beauregard. From an original portrait owned by Mrs. Porter F. Bedell, reproduced by courtesy of the owner.

Judith Helene Antonia de Reggio, wife of Jacques Elie Toutant-Beauregard and mother of General Beauregard. From an original portrait owned by Mrs. Porter F. Bedell, reproduced by courtesy of the owner.

Don Pedro Marin y Argote, Marquis de Villa Lobos, treasurer of the Louisiana Province, godfather of General Beauregard. Reproduced by courtesy of Sidney L. Villere.

Charles laughed. "I told you, we have company already. You're just *more* company for a 'midnight gumbo supper.' And Laure doesn't actually run and hide any more. How funny that you should remember that! She is still very shy, though. Don't frighten her by acting the *beau sabreur*. If you do, she'll manage to retreat so effectively that, though she's still present in the flesh, you'll feel as if she weren't."

"Of course, I shan't act like a *beau sabreur* or anyone except myself."

"You look the part of a *beau sabreur* and very often you act it, too. You may not know it, but you do. I shouldn't wonder if you enjoyed playing the part, whatever you may say. Well, here we are."

The house was half-hidden by the great grove of live oaks and pecan trees with which it was encircled beyond a garden hedged in with orange trees and formally planted with tuberoses, grand dukes and jessamine and Pierre was fairly close to it before he realized that it was much more imposing, both in itself and in its setting, than either Toutant or Conseil, that it was in fact reminiscent of Versailles, as the de la Ronde plantation was now called. He had heard that Governor Villeré, who was self-willed and "absolute," had insisted, when he acquired the property, that a rickety old shanty, located behind two venerable oaks, which he called Philemon and Baucis, because their branches were intertwined, should be the seat of the plantation. Of course, Pierre understood that the "rickety old shanty" must have been remodeled and enlarged; still, he had not expected so much grandeur. There was no one on the gallery when they reached it, but, as they went up the steps, the front door opened and a young girl came out and glanced in their direction. When she saw that Charles was not alone, she turned to go in again. But he was too quick for her. He sprang forward, put his arm around her waist and drew her toward his friend.

"*Voyons*, Laure, is that the way to welcome a guest?" he asked reproachfully. "Pierre has just been asking me if you still hid when we had company and I told him you didn't. And then you try to do that very thing! You haven't forgotten Pierre Beauregard, have you? You shouldn't have; he visited us often enough when we were youngsters, even if he did desert us later on and spend eight long years among the Yankees, trying to become an American. But now, thank heaven, he's back in his own country at last, and I'm counting on you to help make it so pleasant for him that he'll say he never wants to leave us again."

With her brother's arm still around her waist, she came forward and gave her hand to Pierre, murmuring an indistinct greeting—or it might have been an apology. She was blushing and rosy color softly suffused the whitest skin he had ever seen. Her smoothly parted hair was very black and so were her eyebrows; her eyes were downcast and he was conscious, at first, only of translucent lids and long curling lashes, also very black. But presently, as if trying to make amends for her tardy and inadequate welcome, she raised her head, smiling and opening her eyes wide. Then he saw that they were not dark like the eyes of most Creoles, but the brightest possible blue: the blue of cornflowers, the blue of sapphires, the blue of the heavens. . . .

"I never want to leave you again," he said.

❧ 8 ❧

. . . . *Elle etait pale et blonde*
Jamais deux yeux plus doux n'ont du ciel le plus pur
Sondé la profondeur et réflechi l'azur.

—Alfred de Musset

Recipes (wording unchanged) for gumbo from Point Beca, Caliste Villeré's plantation, used at all Villeré plantations for "midnight gumboes" and also as designated below.

Gumbo filé aux huitres, jambon et la Poitrine de Veau
[Gumbo Filé with oysters, ham and veal brisket]
Iron kettle
Portions—for six

One large sliced onion, slice of raw ham (cut in small portions).
One pound of veal brisket.
Large tablespoonful of lard.
Fry above.
When fried, add one tablespoonful of loose flour and stir so as not to burn. When done, add lukewarm water (2 quarts or more).

Then add oysters (one dozen large).
Shallots, parsley, garlic, thyme (Powdered) ½ teaspoonful.
A pinch of cloves, and one large bayleaf.
Cook slowly (¾ to one hour).
Place salt and pepper only after tasting, i.e., it may be almost salty enough, as it is, without the addition of seasoning, being gumbo due to oysters and ham.

This recipe can be applied to crabs, shrimp or oysters.
For boiled shrimps (one boiling).
Use shrimp water for contents of gumbo.
Crabs must be fried first by pieces (hard shell retained).

Above recipe was served on Beca Plantation on Fridays and Sundays. Negroes when serving would invariably comment, *"Ça c'est qui chose qui bon!"* ("That is something that is good!")

Chicken Gumbo
Portions—for six

One young chicken cut in fricassee style.
No meat, but raw ham was added.
When with shrimp (mainly river shrimp for taste).
Served on Beca Plantation in large *"soupière."*
Master of the plantation served the gumbo.
Rice was served at each place by Negro domestics. ·
The children on the place loved gumbo so much, they would stamp their feet on the floor of the spacious dining room when waiting for helpings of heaping portions. For days of fast and abstinence, no ham or chicken was served in gumbo.

Okra Gumbo
Portions—for six

Wash one pound of okra thoroughly.
Cut heads and discard them. Cut balance of okra in very small pieces.
Add one slice of raw ham.
½ lb. of shrimp if desired for a better taste.
Use shrimp water after shrimp has had one boiling, and add gumbo.

Gumbo Z'herbes

Use spinach, lettuce, beets, turnips, cabbage, carrots and, if desired, water cress. Wash leaves of above vegetables thoroughly. Repeat process until water is clear. Use just leaves. Take away center sprig of leaves. One slice of pickled pork. Cut in pieces with one large onion. Add one pound of veal stew. Fry until well done. Add leaves to above, but hash them before. Add large soupspoon of table flour. Add water, and add a bit of garlic to water.

WHY WAS IT THAT PEOPLE WHO NEITHER KNEW NOR LOVED THE South spoke skeptically and sarcastically of "magnolias and moonlight," as if they thought either that these did not exist, that they were a vision rather than a reality; or that, existing, they were inconsequential and uncharacteristic, the rarity rather than the rule? Pierre did not understand, he could never understand, how people could talk like that, could feel that way. To him, and to anyone like him in heredity and environment, magnolias and moonlight were as real as sweet olive and vetivert; as pink buttercups, white clover, wild iris and spider lilies; as the cypresses and the swamps; the tangles of vine and palmetto; the lazy bayous and rushing river; as the levees and the battures, the cane fields and the cotton fields; as the blooded horses and patient mules; as the migrant wild geese, the white cranes and the crafty alligators; as the steamboat whistles and the street cries and the spirituals; as the Indians and the Negroes, the planters and the river captains, the proud ladies and the complacent quadroons; as the withering heat and violent storms of summer and the crisp coolness and mellow sunshine of winter; as Mardi Gras and All Saints' Day. . . . But then, it did no good to say so, because most of those wonders were not real either, or characteristic, so far as outsiders were concerned.

He knew they were all real and he thanked God that he did. Most fervently of all, he thanked God because, for him, magnolias and moonlight had been personified by Laure.

GENEALOGY OF MARIE LAURE VILLERÉ

Louis Rouer
De Villeray

Etienne Roy
De Villeré

Joseph Roy
De Villeré

Phillippe
Nepveu

Catherine
Sevestre

Jacques
Nepveu

Mary Catharine
Nepveu

Marie Denise
Sevestre

Pierre
Chauvin

Michelle
Chauvin

Marie
Antreul

George D'Aix,
son of Signeur
De La Choise,
(France)

Jacques
De La Choise
(d.1730)

Jacques
De La Choise

Marguerite
De La Choise

Governor Jacques
Phillippe
Roy De Villeré
(1761-1830)

Renee
Rochefort

Marguerite
LeCailly

Charles
Frederick,
Chevalier
D'Arensbourg
(1695-1779)

Catherine
Mextrine

Marguerite
D'Arensbourg

Jean Gabriel
DeFazende

Jules
Villeré
(1794-1866)

Mathurin
Dreux

Claudine
Hugot

Charlotte
Dreux

Henriette
De Fazende

Hughes
Olivier
De Vezin

Gotineau
Duplessis

Charles
Barromeo
Olivier De Vezin

Marie Perle
Olivier
De Vezin
(1800-1878)

Capt.
Charles
DeBlanc

Elizabeth
D'Erneville

Celeste Mathilde
DeBlanc

Marie Laure Villeré
(1823-1850)
m.
Pierre G. T. Beauregard
(1818-1893)

Charles Villeré
(1821-1899)
m.
Eugenie LaBranche
(1835-1874)

Rene
(1843-
1910)
m.
Alice
Cenas

Henri
(1845-
1915)
m.
Antoinette
Harney

Laure
(1850-
1884)
m.
C.A.
Larendon

Julie
(18__-1884)
m.
Walter S. Larendon

VILLERE

He had held her hand only for a moment, while he looked into those blue, blue eyes for the first time—or, at all events, the first time he really saw them—and said that he never wanted to leave again. But in that one moment he knew he had fallen in love, as deeply, as passionately, as hungrily as it was possible for any man to be in love. If he had not realized that Charles was right, that Laure would retreat within herself and become altogether inaccessible if she were shocked or startled, he would have told her so, that same night, when they strolled for a few minutes on the gallery in the magnolia-scented moonlight, after the evening's festivities were over. The stroll was, in itself, something of a triumph. The midnight gumbo supper—of which gumbo was actually only the first of numerous hearty dishes, all washed down with excellent wines—had been planned in honor of distinguished houseguests and other guests had come in for it from all the surrounding plantations; so considerable time was spent in the dining room. Then, after supper, there had been music in the drawing room. Several of the guests had good voices, several were gifted pianists. But Laure, seated at her golden harp, had over-shadowed all the others, not only because she sang so sweetly and touched the strings with such delicacy of feeling, but because she was such a vision of loveliness—her face, her figure, her neck, her arms. Surely she had the most beautiful arms in the world. Pierre could not be thankful enough that she had chosen to play the harp, instead of some more commonplace instrument, the piano or the guitar, for instance. Her soft white dress had very short sleeves and, as she sat at her harp, touching the strings, the full beauty of her arms was revealed.

When the musicale was over and the guests who lived on other plantations were preparing to leave, Charles and Laure had gone out on the gallery to join M. and Mme Villeré in bidding them good night. As the crowd thinned, Pierre approached Charles, who had stepped back in the hall with some of the houseguests.

Upper Magnolia was not built like Toutant and Conseil with a *salle*—what he had later learned was the equivalent to what the English called the Great Hall—which served as a general living room and which was entered direct from the gallery. An imposing white-paneled doorway, surmounted by an ogive arch which framed squares of varicolored glass and was flanked by matching glass, led to a central hall. This had formal double parlors on one side and a spacious dining room and a library, well stocked with French classics, on the other, and it was through this hall that company and family went—an arrangement which seemed to Pierre to possess great advantages, giving far more privacy and space than the other, though lacking its intimacy.

"It's very warm in the drawing room," Pierre said. "I'd like a breath of air myself. Is there any reason why I shouldn't join the others who are on the gallery?"

"None in the world."

So he stood beside Charles for a few minutes, exchanging banalities about the party and edging a little nearer the gallery—that is, to Laure—as he did so. Then Mme Villeré called her son to do some trifling errand for her and, after going off to perform her bidding, he had not returned immediately. Pierre had always been deeply grateful to him.

"Couldn't we walk around to the other side of the gallery? I believe there's more of a breeze than we're getting here," he said to

Laure. He mentioned only the breeze—not the magnolias and the moonlight. But he knew Laure was as conscious of them as he was.

She had hesitated, but she had not refused. She glanced toward her mother for directions, but Mme Villeré did not notice, whether purposely or not Pierre was left in doubt. Perhaps she thought it was time for her daughter to overcome her excessive shyness and Pierre believed that he enjoyed a good reputation. He might look like a *beau sabreur*, but there could have been no tales about undue boldness toward young ladies, since he had done nothing to give rise to such rumors, though he admitted to himself this was only because, until this moment, he had not been tempted to overstep the bounds of strict propriety in Creole circles. And now, resolutely keeping Charles' admonition in mind, he did not yield to temptation. When, after ten minutes of strolling and talking about nothing in particular, Laure said shyly that she thought she ought to go in, he did not try to detain her; he took her back to her mother and bade them both good night with the same formal courtesy.

Since the next day was Sunday, they all went to Mass and, though Pierre maneuvered to sit beside Laure and share her missal—having explained that he had forgotten his own—at the gargantuan meal served on their return from church—gumbo, roast chicken, roast beef, chicory and watercress salad and moulded creams—he was obliged to content himself with feasting his eyes on her from his seat on the opposite side of the table. However, when they went riding late in the afternoon, he kept his horse beside hers, though nothing about his manner or his conduct suggested ardor unbecoming such short acquaintance. But there were limits to his self-control—and to his leave. On Monday, he went to M. Villeré and asked to pay official court to Laure.

The older man listened to him courteously and answered him kindly. "You're both very young, Pierre," he said at last.

"For God's sake, don't put me off with that excuse!" Pierre burst out before he could stop himself. But if M. Villeré suspected that there was any special reason why Pierre should have recoiled from a seemingly inoffensive and certainly accurate statement, he did not betray it.

"Well, you are, you know," he said, still kindly. "But suppose we approach the situation from some other angle, if you'd rather. You've known Laure only three days—two days really. You didn't get here until quite late Saturday."

"Why Monsieur, we've known each other always!"

"Come, come! You've been a welcome guest at my house always, you and your whole family. But when you went to New York to school, Laure was just six years old, and so bashful it was almost impossible to get her into the parlor. You wouldn't have known who she was if you'd met her, instead of Charles, on the street last week."

Since Pierre could not think of a convincing denial to this, he tried another tack. "You've been good enough to say that we've always been welcome at your house, my whole family as well as myself. Doesn't that mean you regard us favorably?"

"Certainly it does. But it doesn't mean I can hastily decide you're the right husband for Laure, or that she'll do so."

"Then couldn't you think the matter over, Monsieur, and see if it doesn't? Couldn't you let me ask Laure to think it over?"

M. Villeré looked at Pierre, appraising him carefully. "I might," he said at last. "If you'd care to come back here, on your next leave, I'll let you know."

Never had a month seemed so long, before or since. Never had life on Barataria been so desolate, so futile, so lonely. When, out of a clear sky, an order came through from the War Department which would not only permit him to leave Camp Livingston earlier than he had expected, but which actually indicated that he should visit Upper Magnolia as promptly as possible in the performance of official duties, he saw in this the direct intervention of Providence. Pierre took the first available steamboat, which reached Upper Magnolia about noon, and went straight to M. Villeré's office, confident of finding him there. Even after a midnight gumbo supper, the planter was on horseback by nine the same morning after a breakfast of ham, potato stew, hominy, well-buttered biscuits, river shrimp and coffee with whipped cream; not a nook or corner of the fields escaped his vigilant attention; but, promptly at noon, he came to his *bureau* to read *Le Courrier des États-Unis* and *L'Abeille de la Nouvelle Orléans* before dinner. Pierre had already familiarized himself with these habits.

"I know you didn't expect to see me so soon, Monsieur," he said. "But I've been informed that there seems to be a shift in the channel of the Mississippi. A bar's building up, right opposite your landing. You may have to build a new one, in a different location. Of course, I hope not, but I've been told to make sure. I've taken the liberty of bringing my leadline with me and I thought maybe you'd be kind enough to lend me a skiff. If it isn't convenient to spare one of the field hands to row for me, I can send for an enlisted man. I

didn't like to take that much extra hospitality for granted. I thought
I'd better consult you first."

With the full realization that M. Villeré might receive this statement skeptically, Pierre handed the order from the War Department
to his reluctant host. The moment could hardly have been less propitious. The day before, Quabinen, a valuable field hand, had succumbed to sudden illness and had been laid out in the *purgerie*,
where the sugar was processed. An elderly Negro couple, who became drowsy after their long vigil, were the last to remain at the wake.
Suddenly, Quabinen sat up in his coffin and, after looking around
him with amazement, not unmixed with apprehension, straddled it
and confronted the terrified watch, who screamed, "*Mais li meuri!*"
In a deep voice, Quabinen denied the charge that he was dead, and
the elderly couple scrambled out of the *purgerie*, shouting at the top
of their lungs, "Quabinen, *li pas meuri!*" M. Villeré, who had just
begun the peaceful perusal of the day's news, was both disturbed and
displeased by the uproar. He laid down his paper and, after sternly
silencing the hysterical Negroes, went himself to the *purgerie* to in-
vestigate the situation. The discovery that Quabinen was, indeed,
alive was, in a sense, most reassuring; the suspicion that his supposed
demise might mark the onset of a greatly dreaded yellow fever epidemic was, obviously, unfounded; and, since the man had cost his
master more than one thousand dollars, his recovery was a distinct
financial advantage in a lean year. But M. Villeré was a man of
orderly habits; he did not like to have the pattern of his own days
disturbed; and he could not suppress the feeling that it was unseemly
for an alleged corpse, which had been favored with all the proper
rites, to cause such a commotion. When Pierre handed Laure's father
the order from the War Department, this meant that, for the second time that day, the planter's reading was abruptly interrupted.
However, he accepted the order courteously, if regretfully, inspected it
carefully and, to his even greater regret, found nothing apocryphal
about it.

"Have you thought things over, Monsieur?" Pierre asked without
further preamble, as soon as M. Villeré returned the document.

"About the plantation landing? I've hardly had time, with all this
hullabaloo about Quabinen. Of course, you're welcome to a skiff and
one of the field hands. Mealie's good in a boat, you'd better take him.
And I suppose I will have to follow whatever instructions result from
your soundings."

"Yes, I suppose so. But I wasn't referring to the landing when I
asked if you'd thought things over. I was referring to Laure."

"My dear boy, are you always in such a violent hurry?"

"No, Monsieur. But I am this time."

"Well, certainly no one can accuse you of being a laggard in love, whatever else they may say about you," M. Villeré remarked drily. "I confess that I should be a little better pleased if you would wait a year before saying anything to Laure, but—"

"*Wait a year!* Why, Monsieur, I've waited nearly a month already."

"You interrupted me, Pierre, and that is very discourteous."

"I'm sorry, Monsieur. I—"

"As I was about to say," M. Villeré remarked, interrupting in his turn. "*But,* realizing that even if you told me, meaning to tell the truth, that you would respect my wishes, I fear that in some moment of—ah—aberration, you might forget your promise. So I will permit you to speak to her if—"

"Oh thank you, Monsieur!"

"—*if* you will do so in the most measured terms," M. Villeré went on severely. "You interrupted me again, Pierre, and I greatly dislike interruptions. You are not to harass her. If she says she does not wish to listen, you must say nothing more. And, of course, there can be no official betrothal at present, no talk of marriage in the near future. No——"

But Pierre had already left the office. By what seemed to him another direct intervention of Providence, he found Laure in the summerhouse, busied with some fine needlework, and alone. She sprang up at the sight of him, the lovely rosy color coming into her white face. Her swift movement overturned her sewing basket, but she did not seem to be running away. He noticed that immediately and his heart leaped with joy.

"Why Pierre, I didn't expect you until tomorrow!" she said; and by the way she said it he knew she was glad it was today instead. He helped her pick up the things she had dropped and then sat down beside her. For a few minutes they talked of inconsequential matters, as they had before; but before long he said gravely, "I have your father's permission to speak to you."

"Why Pierre!" she exclaimed again. "You didn't need Papa's permission to speak to me! You are quite free to do that."

"I mean, on a special subject."

She clasped her hands lightly and looked down at them as they lay in her lap. Her color was deeper now. But she still did not move away from him.

"Aren't you going to ask me what the special subject is?"

"No-o-o. I'd rather you told me."

CARL A. RUDISILL LIBRARY
LENOIR RHYNE COLLEGE

"The subject of love."

This time, the lightly clasped hands fluttered a little. But when he leaned over and took them in his, she did not draw them away.

"He said I mustn't harass you, and God knows I don't want to. Does it harass you, Laure, to have me tell you that I love you?"

She shook her head.

"He said that if you did not wish to listen, I must say nothing more. Are you willing to listen, Laure?"

She nodded.

"To anything I may say?"

She nodded again.

"Then I'm going to forget what your father said after that. I'm going to tell you that I want our betrothal made official and announced, immediately, and that I want to marry you no later than September."

He heard her catch her breath, ever so slightly, and he drew her hands upward until they lay against his heart.

"Don't say yes right away, darling, if you'd rather not," he said. "But don't say no, either. And while you're deciding which you're going to say, I want you to put your beautiful arms around my neck and let me kiss you."

He smiled at her and waited. He did not have to wait long. Presently she unclasped her hands and he felt her arms stealing higher and higher while he put his around her yielding waist. When his mouth closed down on hers, it was quiescent, but he knew that the next time he kissed her those red lips would be warm with welcome.

❧ 9 ❧

1829–1853

Began weeding on March 30, 1830. Completed first weeding on April 30th, and the second on July 11th, 1830.

Began grinding on October 29th and finished on January 7th—230 hhds.

The grinding which was begun in 1832 was completed on

January 7, 1833. I had started on October 27th. Planting was completed on the 27th or 28th of March, began weeding on the 27th or 30th of the same month.

In the year 1833 I finished grinding on Dec. 21st, and I had begun on October 17th, I manufactured 170 hhds. of sugar that year.

In the year 1834 I finished grinding on Dec. 19th, and I had begun on October 17th. I manufactured 244 hhds. of sugar.

		Esc.*
Drew $100 in cash from Mr. Sarrat		
Gave to Mr. Albert	4	
To the carters	2	
—do—	1	
For 24 hampers	3	
For chickens	4	
Corded wood	4	7
Day laborers	2	
To an unfortunate	1	4
To the man from below for fresh fish	3	4
	$24	7

* An *Escalin* had a monetary value of 12½¢, and there are 8 Esc. in a dollar, hence the figures in the original text $24 and 7 Esc. ($24.875).

Notation:

J. Jacob owes me a Summer shirt.

In 1832 manufactured	200 hhds.	
Delivered to Tufts & Clarke	8,825 gals. syrup.	
" " Mr. Johnson	1,700 gals. syrup.	
" " Forstall's refinery	1,000 gals. syrup.	
Net weight of hhds.	11,525 gals.	
Mr. Forstall 75 hhds. net weight		67,000 lbs.
Mr. Johnson 24 " " "		25,000 "
Mr. Forstall 100 " " "		96,957 "
Various deliveries		188,957 Net.

Net result of the 1832 Crop:

Various syrup deliveries	11,520 gals.
" sugar "	18,895 lbs.

MAGNOLIA PLANTATION
DRAFTS DRAWN UPON THE FIRM OF
GORDON & FORSTALL
BY JULES VILLERÉ

1829

Jan.	16	Issued an order to the negro Jean Louis, to cover four barrels of meat, and additional cash required by him.			
"	19	Issued to a certain Nathan Robertson by name an order for	$	140	80
"	28	Issued an order to same for		285	00
Feb.	1	" " " to Mr. J. Miller		325	00
"	9	" " " " " " "		100	00
Feb.	7	Drawn by self		50	00
"	17	Drew		150	00
Mch.	4	Issued an order to J. Miller for		170	00
"	5	" " " " N. Robertson for		75	00
"	11	" " " " Wm. Goldering for		20	00
"	14	Drew		200	00
"	20	Issued an order to an American for		89	00
May	25	Issued an order to Dr. Allain for Magnolia and Concord Plantations, also for my own account		136	00
Apr.	9	Draft drawn by my father		40	00
Apr.	10	" " " Lavergne		60	00
Apr.	28	Drawn by self		50	00
Apr.	29	Ditto		200	00
		Notation: Jean Louis began working on Sept. 21, 1832.			

1832

Oct.	27	Paid Jean Louis for one month		45	00

1833

Jan.	3	Paid Jean Louis for two months		85	00
		Jean Louis was absent two weeks in the mo. of Feb. from the 10th to the 25th, and 4 days in the mos. of Nov. & Dec.			
Mch.	16	Pd. to Jean Louis for strayed horses		4	00
		Jean Louis was absent two weeks in the mo. of April			

1833

Apr. 24   Saturday, Jean Louis was absent this day. Jean Louis was absent three weeks in June, during Cholera period.
Mortality in 1832
    James, Jilly, Dick and Sambo
    Horse: Boto
Killed: Three young animals and one young two year old bull, which died on Aug. 3, 1833.

1836

Sept. 15   Delivered to Mr. Bonefil's boat 6 bbls. of sugar totaling 1450 lbs.

Nov. 25   To the order of G. & F. for certificates of stock required of all Magnolia proprietors   3,036   28

1837

Mch. 12   Renewed the note due Villeré, for $6,300 at sixty days.   6,300   00

Mch. 26   Renewed the note for $2,270 at sixty days.   2,270   00

Apr. 5   I gave Felix Forstall a note for $5,300 for supplies delivered to Magnolia Plantation, said note payable in one hundred and thirty days, dated Apr. 17, 1837.   5,300   00

MAGNOLIA PLANTATION
IN A/C WITH
JULES VILLERÉ

1829

Jan. 19   Pd. to a certan Nathan Robertson by name $140   80

" 28   " " same for a raft of squared timber   285   00

Feb. 1   " " J. Miller for posts, shingles and planks   325   00

" 9   " " same for a raft of rounded timber   100   00

" 15   " " the negroes for day labor   23   00

1829

Feb.	17	" for 3107 ft. of heavy boards @ \$2–2½ Esc.	74	71
"	17	" " the hauling of said boards	3	00
"	17	" " 15 bbls of lime @\$2½	37	50
"	17	Gave to Mr. Antoine	2	00
"	17	Pd. for nourishment of negroes while in the city	1	00
"	17	" " hauling of lime	2	00
"	17	" " an American barge	25	00
"	17	" " a book of accounts	1	00
"	18	" to obtain the release of the mulatto George from prison	2	00
Mch.	3	Pd. to J. Miller \$11, to Wm. Goldwing \$9 and to N. Robinson \$50	70	00
"	4	Paid to N. Robinson for posts & shingles	75	00
"	11	" " Mr. Wm. Goldwing, workman	20	00
"	12	Gave to Celestin Masson; Caliste's negro	1	25
"	15	" " Benj., workman, for one mo. of labor	35	00
"	15	Advanced to Jean Louis on a/c of his wages	10	00
"	15	Gave to Delphin for fence posts	20	00
"	20	Gave to eight negroes for having noticed Mr. Baker's pirogue	2	00
"	20	Gave to an American for 80 bbls. of corn & 4 bbls. potatoes	89	00
Mch.	22	Gave to the four sawyers	2	00
"	23	Fifi, workman, for 20½ days labor	20	4 Esc.
"	25	" " Dr. Allain for his fees	60	"
"	26	" " Francois for purchase of tins for his workman	2	5 Esc.

1829

Mch.	27	" " an American workman for two days' labor	1	4	"
"	27	" " the Manager for two days	1	2	"
"	28	" " the Coaster for a bbl of rice	7	"	"
Apr.	6	" " Mr. Francisque for hauling cypress	10	00	
"	6	Advanced to Antoine	20	00	
"	9	Gave for corn	40	00	
"	10	" " " and corn meal	60	00	
"	10	" " negro day labor	10	00	
"	10	Advanced to Benjamin, workman	10	00	
"	10	Gave to the Manager		4	Esc.
"	11	" for negro day labor	4	2	"
"	11	Advanced to Wm. Goldwing, workman	20	"	"
"	11	Gave to an American workman for his wages	2	00	
"	15	Advanced to Mr. Goldwing, workman	1	4	Esc.
"	19	" to Jean Louis, workman	5	"	"
"	19	Two chamber pots and 1 syringe for the hospital		4	"
"	19	For hooks and lines		4	"
"	19	Syrup of morphine and biscuits	1	1	"
"	24	Pd. Mr. Panier's workman Francois for eleven days at the rate of 40–	13	6	"
"	26	Pd. for 2 earthenware chamber pots and tinware for the Hospital	2	4	"
Apr.	29	Pd. for corn meal for the negroes at $2.25 a bbl.	27	4	Esc.
"	29	" " an American barge and oars	26	"	"
"	29	" " carting and feeding negroes while in the City	2	3½	"

1829

Apr.	29	Pd. for a bbl. of French flour for the workmen	7	4	"
"	30	Advanced to Jean Louis	5	00	
May	1	" " Benjamin	25	00	
"	1	Gave to Louis Duval for his day labor	10	00	
"	3	Advanced to Mr. William, workman	10	00	
"	3	Pd. a negro for 1 day's work		4	"
"	5	Gave to Desmasiliere for having worked at building the house	2	"	"
"	11	Pd. to the negroes for weeding the canes and to sawyers	13	"	"
"	16	Pd. for 7000 shingles @ $3.25 a M.	22	6	"
"	31	" to Neola for days at the house and for 4 spade and ax handles	4	00	
"	31	Three lbs. of seine twine	2	00	
June	11	Pd. to a laborer for a bbl. of rice	12	00	
July	12	Gave to Caliste's negro Moses for stopping a fugitive negro	2	00	
"	12	Gave to Mr. Antoine for going in search of a negro	1	00	
"	14	" " Fanchonnette for two iron tongs	3	00	
Sept.	24	" for a craft stolen by our negroes	8	00	
"	27	" to Hecta, workman, for carts for thread and white cotton cloth for the negroes	1	4	Esc.
Oct.	14	Pd. to Adat for mounting a plow	2	00	
Oct.	17	Gave to Mr. Morgan's negroes for helping to turn over large cypress-trees to make stave-wood	1	3	Esc.

1829

Oct.	27	Gave to the Descoteau Sisters for meat	7	4	"
Dec.	2	Gave for the lightning-rod	2	00	
June	4	To Mr. Villard for shoes	1	6	Esc.
"	4	" Lyons as a reward	2	00	
"	20	For staves and hogsheads	40	00	

1829

Jan.	16	Rec'd. from Messrs. Gordon Forstall & Co.	—	—	
Feb.	1	Rec'd. from Messrs. Gordon Forstall & Co.	140	80	
Apr.	29	Rec'd. from Messrs. Gordon Forstall & Co.	200	00	

1837

Dec.	24	Remitted to two Americans for additional horses; therefore $200 for Felix's a/c	130	20	Esc.
"	24	Gave to Felix Forstall's negro on a/c of the $100 which I got from Lanusse	16	00	

1829

July	6	Gave for red fish		1	Esc.
"	11	" to the negroes for cord wood	6	4	"
"	24	" for Honey and Oysters	1	00	
Aug.	1	Paid for 25 hampers	4	5½	"
"	7	To the Manager of the Hospital	2	1	"
"	17	Gave to the cooper on account	5	00	
Oct.	27	Gave for bread, meat and vermicelli	1	4	"
Sept.	15	" to Mr. Turpin for grapes and orgeat	2	00	
"	15	For purchase of dishes for the workman	1	6	"
Dec.	17	Gave for pepper		4	"
Dec.	18	Gave for onions and repairs to fret-work		7	Esc.

1829

Mch.	14	Gave to Delphin & Felix for my a/c	10	00	
May	10	Gave to a man for guiding the barge of corn, which sum I deducted from the cost of said corn.	1	4	Esc.
"	14	Gave to Louis Duval for brokerage	10	00	
"	20	Gave to a Spaniard for an American barge	14	00	
July	20	Gave for lilies	12	00	

1833

Nov.	—	Gave to an American for a horse	75	00	
Dec.	22	" " three Irishmen for their wages during grinding	85	00	

1834

Mch.	31	A draft for four pairs of oxen for a/c of Concord Plantation	200	00	
Aug.	31	To Mr. Alexis Martin for freight on bricks and various objects which he delivered for the a/c of Magnolia Plantation for the year 1834	194	68	
Dec.	14	To Mr. S. Simon for two cows, one each for Concord and Magnolia Plantations	24	00	
"	23	To Mrs. Jules Villeré for my personal a/c	100	00	

1835

Jan.	25	To Theophile Fazende for 250 fence posts	20	00	

1835

Mch. 27   Pd. to Miss Corinne Lambert
          for one-half of the
          salaries during the
          year 1834   209   75

1836

Nov. 28   Gave a draft upon the firm of
          Forstall & Bro., to
          Mr. Ponson, piano
          deliverer   42   75

1839

July 16   To Appolinaire Firmin in set-
          tlement   132   00
  "   16   To Mr. Adam, painter   10   00
  "   16   To Mr. Espiran by Perle   36   00
  "   24   To Mr. Marly O'Brien for Fe-
          lix and self, for dig-
          ging the Canal, re-
          tained from Mr. But-
          ler's a/c   100   00
Oct. 22   To Mr. Pinaut for one of my
          friends   15   00
Nov. 12   To Mr. Sidney Jenkins for a
          mule   70   00

1840

Jan. 21   To Perle   50   00
  "   21   To Mr. Dutuit for the making
          of robes   85   00
Apr. 3   To Mr. McLein, overseer, for
          year 1839   410   00
Mch. 3   Perle drew upon Lanusse   100   00
Apr. —   To the Dames Doubriere—mil-
          liners   38   00
Nov. 20   To Vlasin for mattresses   12   00

1841

Feb. 25   To Mr. White for having dug
          my road   173   25
Dec. 14   I finished grinding on Dec. 13
  "   14   Gave the negroes a holiday.

1841

Dec. 16   All negroes are cleaning the
                ditches, and a piece
                of ground comprising
                eight arpents; 4 men
                are making pickets
                and bars; 4 are squar-
                ing to build a stable;
                6 men are plowing.
                The work is contin-
                ued from the 16th to
                the 24th inclusive.

Dec. 26   Sunday.
"   28   It rained all day, nothing done.

Extracts from Jules Villeré's

BOOK OF ACCOUNTS OF THE MAGNOLIA PLANTATION.

[These extracts are from an important journal, dealing with
the management of a large ante-bellum plantation in Louisiana, written by Jules Villeré, owner of Upper Magnolia and
father of Laure Villeré, General Beauregard's first wife.

The journal, originally written in French, is now the property of the Cabildo Library of New Orleans. The translation
and compilation of this "Book of Accounts" were done under
the direction of the eminent genealogist Sidney Villeré, with
whose kind permission these extracts are used.]

THEY WENT BACK TO THE HOUSE TOGETHER. AS THEY STARTED ACROSS
the lawn they met Charles. After one swift glance at them, he
burst out laughing.

"Poor Papa!" he said mockingly.

"Why do you say 'poor Papa?'" they inquired simultaneously.

"Because he has just finished telling me that Pierre has asked him for permission to pay his addresses to Laure and that he said, of course, there could be no question of an official betrothal at present. From the look of you both, I'd say he wasted his breath. I never beheld such undisguised rapture."

"You might, incidentally, say you're very pleased," Pierre said reproachfully.

Charles laughed. "Well, I'm certainly not displeased. If I hadn't known something of the sort was likely to happen eventually, I wouldn't have invited you here when I met you on the street a month ago. But I confess I didn't expect it to happen quite so soon—considering that when you arrived, we had a hard time to keep Laure from following her usual custom of going into hiding. And now, obviously, she's been enjoying stolen sweets with you. . . . There, there, it's all right, Laure! I'm only teasing you. That's what brothers are for, didn't you know? Come along, I think perhaps I'd better stay with you while you break the news. Otherwise, Papa may order Pierre off the place tonight, with instructions not to come back for a year, if ever."

"He can't do that. I've got to stay and make my soundings."

"He'd be perfectly capable of asking the War Department to send someone else, if you get in his black book. And I don't want that to happen. I enjoy your company myself. Not that I'm likely to have much of it from now on, I'm afraid."

M. Villeré had finished reading his newspapers and had now turned to Lamartine. He was not quite so prompt in detecting the telltale signs of lovemaking as Charles had been, doubtless, Pierre told himself, because more time had elapsed since the poor old man had engaged in anything of the sort himself. Neither did the poor old man, who was all of forty-seven, order Pierre off the place. But his reception of the great news was undeniably stiff, not to say frosty, and he sent Laure in to see her mother while he detained the two young men, Pierre for admonition, Charles as a witness. He thought he had made himself quite clear, he told Pierre severely. Yes, Monsieur, that was true; and he had been very careful to follow instructions. He had asked Laure if he were harassing her when he spoke to her of love and she had assured him that he was not. Even then, he had gone ahead very slowly. He had asked her if she were willing to listen, and she had indicated that she was, though he took the further precaution of inquiring whether or not this would be true, no matter what he talked about. So, after that——

"After that, I am very much afraid you forgot I said there could be no betrothal at present, no question of a marriage in the near future."

"No, Monsieur, I didn't actually forget. I just did what seemed natural under the circumstances."

"*What seemed natural under the circumstances!* You come of a good family, none better, you've been well brought up, even though your father had this crazy idea, doubtless due to his association with Livingston, of making you into an American! You know that an innocent, modest, virtuous Creole girl never permits a suitor to embrace her until after their marriage. When they *are* officially betrothed, provided he has her parents' sanction, he may kiss her hand, perhaps even her brow, but there is never any more ardent demonstration."

"Yes, Monsieur, so I've heard, but I've often wondered whether or not it were true. Now I'm quite sure it isn't. For certainly no Creole girl could possibly be more innocent, modest and virtuous than Laure, and I'm proud to say she did permit me a—a slightly more ardent demonstration than what you've just described. I feel greatly honored because she did. But if *you* feel she should have waited until after we were married, then of course we ought to be married immediately."

Charles coughed slightly. M. Villeré glared, first at his son and then at his guest.

"I think, Pierre, you will find that, despite her—ah—temporary aberration this afternoon, Laure will not be in favor of such a rash step. Her mother is doubtless giving her wise counsel at this very moment. I will have a talk with her myself later on. Meanwhile, I want you to give me your word of honor that you will not try to see her alone until you have received permission to do so from either Madame Villeré or myself. There must be no further question of your doing what seems to you natural under the circumstances."

"Very well, Monsieur. You have my word of honor. At least, you have my word that I will not seek her out. Of course, if she should happen to seek me out, when I happen to be alone—"

"That is quite beyond the realm of possibility," M. Villeré said, even more stiffly than he had spoken before. "Since you are acting under official orders in coming here, you may proceed with what you have been sent to do. I suggest you begin your soundings the first thing in the morning. I have already given orders for the skiff and the helper. This interview is now at an end. I should like to resume my interrupted reading of *La Chute d'un Ange*; but I will talk to you again tomorrow after I have had a chance to confer with my wife. Meanwhile, I will see you at dinner."

The evening was not rapturous, like the afternoon, but it had its compensations. The dinner—soup, *daube à la sauce,* cowpeas, boiled corn, cucumber salad, tomatoes, frozen cream cheese eaten with sugar and *café noir* with whipped cream—was excellent and Pierre did it full justice. M. and Mme Villeré both treated him with cold politeness, but Charles was in high good humor and after dinner Laure, again a vision of loveliness, sat at her harp and sang one romantic, ecstatic song after another until her mother sent her to bed; just to sit and feast his eyes on her and listen to her voice was enough for Pierre at the moment, especially as he was sure M. Villeré would prove a poor prophet.

He was right. Underneath the sugar bowl, on the tray with his morning coffee, was a slip of paper, small to begin with, and folded and refolded until it was almost invisible against the white cloth. Pierre unfolded it and read the message penned on it with the most delicate of tracery.

I am going to the woods back of the grove to look for a locket I have lost. Papa rides through the fields every day, but he and Uncle Caliste meet on the edge of the woods, to go through these together only every three days, and they went yesterday. Perhaps, when you have finished your soundings, you would be kind enough to come and help me hunt for my locket.

He laughed aloud from sheer triumphant joy. Then he swallowed his coffee almost at a gulp, shaved, bathed and dressed in record time and bounded down the stairs. It was so early that only the house slaves were moving about in the big rooms on the ground floor, dusting and sweeping and polishing; M. Villeré's office was still closed and empty. Pierre went on to the river, whistling as he walked.

He did not shirk on his soundings; his work was thoroughly done, but it was done rapidly, for he knew beforehand exactly what he should do and, once that was established, he had the knack of moving fast and expertly. M. Villeré joined him briefly about nine, watched him with a scrutinizing gaze for a few minutes, as Mealie rowed him about in the skiff, and then departed, apparently well pleased with the procedure and with no mention of Laure—in fact, with little conversation of any kind. Matt Hawkins, the overseer, made a longer call, asked a few questions, assured himself that Mealie was satisfactory and then departed, in response to an urgent summons from the field. Charles, who was not a conspicuously early riser, sauntered into sight at a slightly later hour, but complained that it was too hot to stay.

"Do you expect it'll take you much longer?" he asked, as Pierre returned to the landing.

"To find out exactly what the situation is? No, I'm pretty sure of that already. There's no doubt at all that a bar is building up and, of course, that means you'll need a new landing."

"And that you'll need to supervise its construction?"

"Not necessarily its construction. But I'll certainly be required to approve its location."

"And that might require frequent visits here during the course of the summer?"

"It might require at least a few. In fact, it will—unless M. Villeré does not accept my report and asks for another opinion."

They looked at each other and laughed. "I hardly think he'll go as far as that," Charles said. "Actually, he rather likes you. But don't forget Laure's his one ewe lamb."

"I shan't."

Charles sauntered away, again complaining of the heat. Pierre told Mealie that he would not be going out on the river again until late afternoon, dismissed him and made a few final notes, assembling them neatly. Then, in his turn, he sauntered away from the landing, but not in the same direction his friend had taken. Instead of going toward the Big House, he took the levee path, heading downstream, the river on his left and the woods on his right. The formally planted grove, in which the Big House was so attractively located, merged gradually into a natural setting of palmetto and live oak, magnolia and cottonwood, which increased in density as it showed fewer and fewer signs of cultivation. But every now and then its tangled density parted to reveal a glade. As these were not characteristic of the thick undergrowth, Pierre, wise in the way of woods, felt it probable that they had been deliberately cleared to give added charm to their sylvan surroundings; to the uninitiated, they would have appeared entirely natural; and, if they owed their existence to artifice, there was nothing about their enclosed verdure which suggested this. Instead, they suggested beauty, tranquility and seclusion—ideal attributes for a trysting place. Pierre felt sure it was in one of these enclosures that he would find Laure waiting for him.

He was not mistaken or disappointed. He had gone through only two such clearings when he came almost abruptly upon another. He parted the clinging branches of a muscadine and saw her, seated on a log that had fallen slantwise across the greensward, her full white skirt spread fanlike around her, the broad-brimmed hat she had worn to protect her from the sun swinging at her side, suspended by the wide pink ribbons which normally secured it under her chin.

She must have heard him coming, for the branches which he parted and the undergrowth on which he trod had snapped and crackled as he went along. But though she had looked up and was gazing toward him with eyes of love when he caught sight of her, she did not leap to her feet and rush forward to meet him. Instead, she sat very still, apparently doing what seemed natural to *her* under the circumstances. She met his eyes steadily, without lowering her white, translucent lids and veiling them with her long lashes, and her gaze invited him to kiss her; this time he knew that the kiss would not only be welcome when it came, but that she had been yearning for it, if not with the same passionate desire that he had, at least with all the virginal longing of which she was capable. And when he had seated himself beside her, with his arm around her waist and her shoulder against his, she spoke to him without hesitation or shyness of everything that was burdening her heart.

"Of course my parents are very displeased. You know that, Pierre. Not only with you, but with me. They think my conduct is most unbecoming, and I'm afraid it's been doubly a shock to them, because I've always been so shy. But I don't seem to feel shy with you. I want to talk with you, I want to be with you. It seems the natural thing to do—the right thing to do."

"That's because you love me, darling. That's what makes everything different. You were never in love before."

"No, of course not. And now that I am, everything *is* different. You're right, Pierre. I'm sure you're always right about everything."

"I'm not, of course, darling. But I know I'm right in wanting to marry you and I hope I'm right in believing you want to marry me."

"Mother has been talking to me about that," Laure said, with a sigh. "She told me if I knew more about marriage, I'd be glad to put it off. And when I asked her to tell me more, to explain why, she wouldn't. She only said I'd find out all too soon. Can you explain, can you tell me why?"

They were on dangerous ground and he knew it. He chose his words cautiously and kept his voice low and gentle.

"I think perhaps I can guess. Most well-born Creole girls don't know the man they marry very well. They don't see him alone very much, if at all. They don't know whether they share his tastes, whether or not they'd find the same things amusing or sad that he does, whether or not he likes a great deal of diversion, dancing and gaming for instance, or hunting and fishing, or prefers a quiet studious life. They have no chance to talk with him confidentially. I think all that makes it hard for them sometimes. Especially because they're not used to having him touch them. I think perhaps that is one of the few ways in which American customs are better than ours are."

"And you learned about American customs when you were at West Point?"

There was no hint of disturbance in her voice, no indication that she felt such knowledge could have come only through experience with American girls and that she was jealous. She continued to gaze at him fondly and trustfully and, as he drew her closer, she raised her face so that he could kiss her again if he chose, which, of course, he did choose.

"It makes me very happy to have you touch me," she said eventually.

"Yes. But you've found that out now. If you hadn't found out before you were married that you welcomed the touch of the man who had become your husband, you might have been very much offended when he claimed you as his wife. No matter how much he loved you, no matter how hard he tried to see that this did not happen, you might have been startled and shocked—even frightened and hurt. And I'm afraid bridegrooms don't always try as hard as they might—not that they mean to offend, but they're men, they have a man's viewpoint and a man's experience. It's very different from a girl's viewpoint and a girl's—inexperience. I think your mother meant that you might resent an intimacy which was entirely new to you and which had been forced upon you. I don't know. Perhaps it happened in her case. I don't know that, either. But it must happen in lots of cases. I mean, when a girl finds herself alone for the first time with a man she hardly knows, and it's night, and she's been undressed by her mother and put to bed and told to wait for her bridegroom and not told anything else."

He paused, half expecting that she might draw away from him or say something that would show him he should not tell her anything more. But though she continued to look up at him, her beautiful blue eyes fixed steadily on his face, there was no fear in them, only questioning and wonder and the same unfaltering faith as before.

"I'm not supposed to talk to you like this, darling," he said. "I'm afraid your father and mother would think it was even worse than kissing you. But I'm glad I've had this chance, just the same. Because, when we're married, I don't want you to be offended or surprised or shocked or frightened. When I come into the room—our room—and find you waiting for me, I want you to be just as glad to receive me as I am to come. And I believe you will be."

"I believe it, too, because you say so and because I know you wouldn't tell me anything that wasn't true. Even so, Pierre, I wish you could explain a little more why *maman* thought——"

Probably he had said too much already, but if so, it was now too late to retreat. "I'll try," he said and searched, harder than ever, for the right words. "You've told me that it makes you happy to have me touch you and I can see that it does, which makes me very happy, too. You're glad to have me put my arm around your waist, and you didn't try to draw away, even the first time I kissed you. But you weren't ready to kiss me, of your own accord, until today, were you?"

"No-o-o."

"That's because everything was new and strange to you at first, but it isn't any more. So now you not only accept my caresses, you welcome them, you respond to them. And gradually you'll discover that the closer caresses are, the more joy they bring. Gradually they'll prepare you for the greatest joy of all—the perfect and complete embrace of lovers, no longer merely betrothed, but united in marriage. Don't ask me to tell you any more now, darling. Just keep on believing I wouldn't tell you anything that isn't true. I never shall."

They walked back through the woods and grove arm in arm and went straight to the office. At the sight of them, M. Villeré threw down his book and sprang up from his desk with an angry exclamation; but Laure ran forward and threw her arms around her father's neck, speaking before either he or Pierre could do so.

"Pierre didn't break his promise, Papa," she explained. "He told you he wouldn't try to see me alone unless I asked him to, and that's exactly what I did do. I wrote him a note and begged him to come and help me find a locket I had lost in the woods. He couldn't refuse to do that, could he? It would have been most unbecoming a *beau sabreur!*"

She looked up at M. Villeré fondly, and with the same touching confidence that she had shown in looking at Pierre—no, not the same, he told himself with a poignant feeling of triumph: the confidence which a cosseted girl child felt in her father was instinctive; the confidence which a modest maiden felt in the suitor who desired her must be earned and fostered; and though he had hardly begun to foster it, though as yet he had done nothing to deserve it, Laure trusted him, too. The thought was a solemn one. But as he glanced again at his beloved and her father, he saw that their faces were not grave; Laure was smiling and, little by little, the angry lines in M. Villeré's face faded from view, for he was smiling, too.

"And of course the *beau sabreur* found the locket!" he said jestingly.

It was only then that Pierre and Laure realized they had not given the locket a thought while they were in the glade.

Pierre was not surprised when M. Villeré told him the next day that, though he and his wife had decided to recognize the engagement, they would not announce it just yet, nor would they consider making any definite plans for a wedding. Despite this verdict, he went back to Barataria with undaunted spirits and discovered, even sooner than he had dared to hope, that his buoyancy was well founded. Laure's letters told him how much she missed him and how much she loved him and ended there, except for a few inconsequential remarks about how she was managing to pass the time while waiting for him to rejoin her; but Charles' letters told him that she had stopped playing the harp, that she merely toyed with her food, in short, that she seemed to be going into a decline; and before he had leisure to worry overmuch about these lovesick symptoms, another letter came, this time from M. Villeré: he and Mme Villeré had decided that, after all, there was not much to be gained by insisting on a long secret engagement; if Pierre would let him know the date when it would be convenient for him to inspect the new landing, arrangements could be made to have a ceremonious betrothal at the same time. As for the wedding, if Pierre felt September was the best month for it, arrangements for that could begin, too.

The "arrangements," as he soon learned, involved a great many details to which, had he been left to himself, he would never have given thought: the selection of a suitable setting for the wedding reception as well as the religious ceremony; the choice of official witnesses; the compilation of a guest list which would include the countless relatives of both the Toutant-Beauregards and the Villerés, and all the close friends of the two families, besides numerous distinguished acquaintances with whom they were on less intimate but still very cordial terms and whose social standing was such that they must certainly be invited; momentous decisions about a menu; and—of immediate importance, because time was so short—the preparation of a trousseau. They had not expected their daughter to be snatched away from them so soon, Mme Villeré told Pierre reproachfully; of course they had been collecting and embroidering linen for her marriage chest ever since she was born—sheets, towels, pillow slips, napkins, tablecloths; but practically nothing had been done about her clothes—chemises, petticoats, nightgowns. These involved mountains of handwork, without mentioning the wedding dress, the morning dresses, the walking dresses, the visiting dresses, the ball gowns. Didn't Pierre remember that, when his sister Judith was married to Emile Legendre, all these things had to be provided? No, he did not. He questioned his mother, who smiled and said that they had; but, after all, Judith had not been married on three months' notice. She had a more reasonable bridegroom; there had been more time for preparations. And then it appeared that although Judith had, indeed, been supplied with all these different varieties of dresses, probably there had not been so many of each kind or any so elaborate in style as what Mme Villeré considered suitable for Laure.

It seemed to Pierre that, whenever he went to Upper Magnolia, his fiancée was being fitted for something. He had to wait until she was through trying on dresses before he could see her. Apparently, it was hardly decent for a girl to be married unless her supply of body linen were almost limitless and unless it were covered with embroidery. The rear gallery was crowded with slaves who excelled as seamstresses and who plied their needles from morning until night. The older ones dozed a good deal and the younger ones giggled a good deal, but, between them, they managed to turn out an immense amount of work; and, every now and then, they began to chant a favorite song—one which seemed especially appropriate under the circumstances:

> "Ah wants to be ready,
> Ah wants to be ready,
> Goin' to Jerusalem,
> Jes' lak John."

Pierre did not see how one lady, in a lifetime, could use as many garments as were being made and ornamented at Upper Magnolia, and yet Mme Villeré and Laure sewed and embroidered all the time, too. Even when he escaped to the glade with his prospective bride, she took her needlework with her. Once he had accustomed himself to this preoccupation with fine raiment, however, Pierre did not find it altogether displeasing. Laure would not let him see her wedding dress—that would be bad luck, she said—or the simple muslins she was to wear at home "because those did not count." But he saw a rose taffeta with fluted ruffles, a sky-blue satin with a lace bertha, and a flowered brocade, trimmed only with bands of its own rich material, which especially pleased him, though he could not have told why. And he was not regretful of the excuse these gave him for going to Falk, the family tailor, and ordering a new dress uniform to be worn at his wedding. Falk did himself proud; the fit was faultless, the blue broadcloth the best England could offer, the style superb: enormous epaulettes, accenting sloping shoulders, glittering buttons running all the way from the neat collar to the shining buckle fastening the wide belt that encircled—and emphasized—a trim waist. As Pierre surveyed himself in the mirror at his final fitting, he told himself that his uniform would be worthy of Laure's dress, whatever she had chosen. No bridegroom could hope for more elegant apparel. He would have liked to show it to her at once, to hear her exclaim over its perfections.

Well, that was twenty-four years ago and now he had just come from his final fitting with Falk—not a uniform this time, but a sober civilian suit which he hoped would help him to present a good appearance as he went about looking for a job. He decided that after it came, he would put it on, for the first time, when he went to spend the evening with Mme Castel and Mme Cougot, and find out if the former were favorably impressed with it. Since the latter could not see, she naturally could not voice an opinion; and probably Mme Castel would not do so, either. But he would be able to guess her verdict, whether she mentioned the matter or not; there would be something in her manner which would tell him what he wanted to know. He was still not altogether without vanity.

However, he should not wait for the new suit before he went visiting again. He had not been to the main house in the evening for nearly a week, giving as his excuse that his sister had supplied him with sandwiches, and that he was so busy with his papers he felt he should continue to work on these without the interruption of a social call. He was trying to strike an even balance between intrusion and neglect, so far as these two nice women, who had unexpectedly entered his life, were concerned, and he was not sure that he was altogether successful. He continued to breakfast with Mme Castel on the gallery every morning, but he did not linger after he had finished his coffee; he started out immediately on his daily search for work; and he had not seen Mme Cougot since he told her that he had written three letters about Lance. Now the answer to one of them had come in. He must let her know.

He did not wait until suppertime, but went directly from his mid-afternoon fitting at Falk's. There was no light in the gallery, because it was too early for one. However, the door into the hallway was open, as it had been previously, and before he could call out to announce himself, Mme Castel emerged from the pantry, smiling her welcome.

"I heard your step on the stairs," she said; and it was on the tip of his tongue to ask if she, too, were listening for steps, not at the front of the house, like her mother, but at the rear. Wisely he refrained; they still did not know each other well enough for shared jests, even though they had now reached the point of shared sorrows. "I hope your sister didn't give you any sandwiches today," Simone went on, "because I've been making courtbouillon. Do you like that as well as gumbo?"

"Better, when it's as good as yours is sure to be. And I did mean to stay to supper with you tonight—that is, if you invited me. But I should like to see your mother first, provided she's ready to receive me so early. I haven't any definite news for her, I'm sorry to to say. But I do have a letter I'd like to share with her."

"Then come quickly. Of course, she's ready to receive you. She's been waiting to—hoping to."

"I know that sometimes a lady needs a little time to make preparations for a visit from a gentleman."

"You're very thoughtful. I'll go ahead of you. But I'm sure it's all right for you to come. I believe you'll find my mother much improved, that you'll see she's already made preparations. You can't imagine what your kindness has meant to her!"

It was certainly true that the atmosphere of Mme Cougot's room was more cheerful than when Pierre had gone there before. This might, of course, be due to the daylight. The gallery at the front of the house and the nearness of other buildings at the side prevented this light from being brilliant; still it streamed softly in through the long windows, giving lambency, if not radiance, to the room. Mme Cougot had left her bed for a large easy chair and was wearing a dove-colored dressing gown and a lace cap on her well-arranged hair. The change from the dead-whiteness of her clothing and coverings, which had so depressed him the first time he entered the room, was as encouraging as her willingness to lighten its general gloom.

"You've had some kind of an answer," she said without preamble, as he entered. Her face was turned toward him so eagerly that it was hard to believe she was not actually looking at him.

"Yes. Would you like to guess which of the men to whom I wrote replied first?"

"Your Dutch friend in New York?"

"No. General Sherman."

He paused, to add weight to the words. Simone gave a cry, half surprise, half happiness. Mme Cougot continued to look eagerly toward Pierre and her lips parted a little, but she did not speak again.

"The letter couldn't have been pleasanter. He said he would, at once, have all Federal prison and hospital records checked, to see if, by any chance, an oversight could have occurred in any of those and that he'd let me know the results. Meanwhile, he hoped I'd let *him* know if we found out anything from another source. He asked after my sons. He said he remembered them as very fine boys. He—he thanked me for thinking of him when it came to a question of doing me or any friend of mine a possible service. He signed his letter, 'Always your friend, William Tecumseh Sherman.' "

Pierre stopped again, not because he felt he needed to add weight to his words this time, but because he found he could not go on for a moment. Then he rose, cleared his throat and spoke huskily.

"I'll leave the letter with you, if you like," he said. "Then you two can talk it over together, while I take a turn around the patio before supper."

◦§ 10 §◦

PIERRE GUSTAVE TOUTANT BEAUREGARD WAS MARRIED IN ST. Bernard Parish, La. Saturday September 18, 1841 by Father L. Moni of St. Louis Cathedral to Marie Antoinette Laure Villeré (a native of Plaquemines Parish) daughter of Jules Villeré (son of Jacques Phillippe Villeré, second Governor of Louisiana and Jeanne Henriette de Fazenda) and Marie Perle Olivier. The witnesses were Evariste Marin, Mrs. Evariste Marin, Joseph Marcel Ducros, Pierre Reaud, Jules Villeré, Perle Villeré, J. Toutant, R. Toutant, Elizabeth Villeré, Caliste Villeré, H. Lavergne, Lucie Ducros, Laure Varret, Theodore Varret and Gabriel Villeré. Marie Antoinette Laure Villeré was born March 22, 1823.

—From *History of the Toutant-Beauregard Family*, compiled
by R. T. Beauregard

WHEN PIERRE RETURNED TO THE QUARTERS AFTER SUPPER, HE LEFT Sherman's letter with his landladies. If he did not mind, Mme Cougot had told him, she would like to keep it on her bedside table, where she could touch it from time to time during the night. She was afraid that would seem silly to him, she said; but when she still had her sight, she kept precious letters near her in that way, reading and rereading them if she were too excited to sleep or, if she did sleep fitfully, lighting her candle every time she woke, to gloat over them again. Now that she could no longer see, she did the next best thing, which was to feel. He did not think this was in the least silly, he told her; as a matter of fact, he himself had often kept letters that he valued on his bedside table.

"Then surely you will want this one there!"

"No, I was planning to put something else there. As you know, I'm going through old papers of all kinds—official documents, account books, army orders, family letters. When the letter from Sherman came, I set my work aside, in order to bring it to you promptly. I knew it would mean a lot to you. As far as that goes, of course it meant a lot to me, too. But I'd just reached a very important point in my research; the last document I'd found was my marriage certificate. I'd been thinking a good deal about the preparations for the wedding, about my fiancée's trousseau, about all the time it took for her to have fittings and embroider initials, when I'd so much rather have had her devoting herself entirely to me during my brief visits to Upper Magnolia—it wasn't easy for me to get away from Barataria. I was goaded, partly by resentment and partly by vanity, into getting myself a brand-new dress uniform, just to prove I was entitled to finery, too. I really didn't need it at all, I had a perfectly good dress uniform already. But I ordered another, from the same tailor who's making me a suit now, which I do need, and the bill for that uniform was one of the papers I came across yesterday. I sat brooding over it for a while, thinking what a conceited, extravagant young fool I'd been; and then, when I came across the marriage certificate next, I began to feel differently. I knew I'd wanted to show my bride, in every way I could, what a great occasion the wedding seemed to me, and wearing that new full-dress uniform was one of the ways. Of course, there were lots of others. . . ."

For a moment, he remained silent and motionless, his thoughts suddenly encompassing him with such force that he almost forgot where he was and what he had been doing and saying. Then he laid Sherman's letter down on Mme Cougot's bedside table, bade his land-ladies a courteous goodnight and returned to the quarters. He had failed to leave a lamp burning when he went out and, had it not been for the light of a full moon, it would have been hard for him to see as he made his way up the steep staircase. But he did not feel the need of a lamp inside, even now. A shaft of moonlight fell directly across the kitchen table which served him as a desk and he made his way straight to it, oblivious of shadows elsewhere. He could, had he so desired, have read by the radiance which seemed centered there. But, of course, every word inscribed on the document which lay before him was also enshrined in his heart; and, besides, like the blind woman whose presence he had so recently left, he felt it was enough just to touch the precious paper. He took it in his hand and held it as he sat on and on, thinking of his wedding day.

The arrangements for this had continued to appall him because they were so many and so complicated. The Villeré clan, assembling in full force for the betrothal, proclaimed almost with one voice that Upper Magnolia was no place for the wedding. Comparatively few of them lived on the west bank in Plaquemines Parish, now that Jules had brought out his brother Delphin in the Villeré succession; on the other hand, Gabriel, the eldest of the brothers, still lived at Conseil, which their father had built, and most of the others nearby. What could be more fitting than that Laure should be married from the first Villeré home? Perhaps Pierre's future mother-in-law might have prevailed, insisting that Upper Magnolia was, after all, the house of which she herself was mistress and that here she could do things in her own way, which Eulalie de la Ronde (Calliope!) Villeré could not be expected to let her do at Conseil. She might have added that this was Laure's home and that a girl should be married from her own home, not her uncle's, even if this had once been her grand-father's. But, at a crucial moment, the Toutant-Beauregards, with what Mme Jules Villeré considered great lack of tact, agreed that Conseil would be much more convenient for them. There were all the de Reggio and Ducros and de Vezin relatives to consider, too, besides the Bienvenues, who were such old friends that they, too, were almost like members of the family.

So the die was cast in favor of Conseil. So far as Pierre was concerned, it mattered very little to him where the marriage ceremony was held—if it took place promptly. Neither was he disturbed or disappointed when he heard that Laure's *dot* would be a modest one. He had not given the matter of a dowry a thought, when his future father-in-law spoke about it apologetically; he was not in a position, Jules said, to follow the custom of more opulent planters, like Zenon Ranson, for instance, who had given each of his daughters a hundred thousand dollars as a wedding present; and then Jules went on to speak of the wedding itself, one of the most important social events of the year in the plantation country. The two girls had been married at the same magnificent Mass, and the elaborate reception had been followed by a house party which lasted ten days.

Pierre told M. Villeré quite sincerely that he would have been glad and thankful to take Laure without a cent; and that if she were to have a dowry, besides all those mountains of household linen and *armoires* full of body linen and dresses, the preparation of which had so complicated the summer, he would really prefer that it should be a modest one. His own father was not numbered among the "opulent" planters, and he himself was one of seven living children, so that his patrimony would be small and army pay was always ridiculously low; it would have been a source of embarrassment, not of pleasure, for him to live on his wife's money and he was relieved to know he would not have to do it. As to a wedding reception, prolonged to include a ten days' house party, he could not imagine anything more objectionable, unless it were the more general Creole custom of having a newlywed pair remain at the bride's home and confining them in their nuptial chamber for a period of several days and sometimes even for a fortnight; that, in his opinion, was nothing short of barbarous.

This opinion was one of the "American" ideas which he had formed in the North and, indifferent as he was to the *dot*, he had a very definite viewpoint about the way the honeymoon should be spent. He gave the matter careful thought and eventually broached the subject to Laure.

"Since we're not going to be married at your parents' house, I don't suppose they expect us to go there afterward, do they?"

"Why—I hadn't asked them, *cher!* That might make a difference, mightn't it? But I'm sure we'd be welcome to stay at Conseil as long as we like."

"I don't want to stay there at all. I haven't said anything against having the wedding at Conseil, because I didn't care, one way or another. But I want us to spend our honeymoon in a house by ourselves."

"What house?"

"Any house. The point is, I want to be alone. Oh, of course, we'll have to let one or two of our people come in to look after us, cook our meals and so on. Mamie would be terribly proud if we'd let her do it and she's a fine cook. Now that she isn't having babies any more, I'm almost sure she'd be available. If that would be agreeable to you, I'll ask *maman*. But I don't want the whole family around, your family or mine, either. And I don't see why we should eat on trays all the time in our bedroom. It'll be fun having morning coffee together there and I should think a bedroom would be a good place for a cool drink in the evening, after a siesta. But the rest of the time, in this hot weather, it seems to me that it would be a lot pleasanter to eat in a dining room, under a punkah, or on a gallery. Don't you think so?"

"Why yes, I do. But do you suppose—"

"That our families will approve of our defying custom like this? Of course not! But then we've been defying custom all summer, haven't we?"

She blushed, enchantingly, and the blush made her so beautiful that he defied custom again, in the usual way. When he released her, he told her he had a plan.

"I know the Bienvenues aren't using their *garçonnière* right now. It's a large one—four rooms and two *cabinets*—and it's very attractive. It has a wide gallery running around it on three sides, with square brick columns like those on the Big House, and it's nicely located, too, at the back of that lovely grove. I haven't been in it lately, but when I was a boy, and the Toutant-Beauregards and the Bienvenues used to visit back and forth a lot, I often went there. I'm sure the Bienvenues would lend it to us for a couple of weeks and tuck Mamie and anyone else we'd need into their quarters. I really think it's ideal for our purposes. Is it all right if I ask for it?"

"Yes, of course. I want to do whatever you want to do, Pierre."

As might have been expected, Pierre was not able to put through his plan without considerable opposition from both families. But the Bienvenues, though amused and astonished, consented to it hospitably and Laure's insistence that she thought the idea was wonderful prevailed to the end. Pierre visited Kenilworth several times and found his prospective hosts most cooperative; when it came to detailed arrangements, he undertook the responsibility. Mamie, of course, would be present at the wedding, like all their people, but as soon as supper was over, he would send her ahead with the baggage, in Mealie's charge, so that she would be waiting at the garçonnière to give Laure maid service. Mealie would then return with the coach and wait at the back door of Conseil until Pierre and Laure could slip out.

Both slaves were delighted with the duties assigned to them; actually, they did not need the amount of drilling in these which Pierre insisted upon giving them; furthermore, Mamie hinted that she was fixing to surprise him and that he was going to be mighty proud when he found out about it. Mealie said nothing about a surprise; on the contrary, he showed Pierre exactly how he was planning to braid the horses' manes with white ribbon and decorate his whip with white bows.

Pierre was pleased and touched at these evidences of good will, as he had been by the Bienvenues' ready acceptance of his every suggestion; but all this did not wholly offset his annoyance when he found he was not supposed to see his bride on their wedding day until, escorted by her father, she entered the drawing room where the officiating priest and the entire assembled company, as well as Pierre, would already be waiting. But with the first glimpse of her, his annoyance was forgotten. Never, he was sure, in all the history of the world, had there been such a vision of loveliness as Laure in her wedding dress. It was made of the sheerest, softest muslin, exquisitely embroidered in tiny delicate figures from the wide hem, which barely cleared her dainty satin-shod feet, to the narrow belt which clasped her unbelievably small waist. The full transparent sleeves covered but did not conceal her beautiful arms, and her neck and shoulders were bare, except for the filmy veil, so soon to be lifted, which fell over them. In her hands she carried a white-bound prayer book—the book from which the priest would read the solemn words:

"I, Pierre, take you, Laure, for my lawful wife, to have and to hold, from this day forward, for better, for worse, for richer, for poorer, in sickness and in health, until death do us part.

"I, Laure, take you, Pierre, for my lawful husband, to have and to hold, from this day forward, for better, for worse, for richer, for poorer, in sickness and in health, until death do us part."

The solemnity, however, was of short duration—almost too short, Pierre thought. He would have been glad if he and Laure could simply have stood there, looking into each other's eyes, for one blissful moment after they had been pronounced man and wife and before everyone began crowding around to embrace them, when they wanted only to embrace each other. But, aside from this instant of frustration, he could not have asked to have everything suit him more perfectly:

he and Laure even manged the almost unbelievable feat of stealing away unobserved, while everyone else was dancing. The marriage ceremony took place at six and was followed by a bountiful supper and a seemingly inexhaustible supply of champagne. By the time everyone had toasted not only the bride and groom and their respective parents, but the Gabriel Villerés who had so kindly loaned Conseil for the occasion, and then all the uncles and aunts on both sides of the family who might feel there had been discrimination if such toasting ended with Gabriel and Eulalie; and then the Bienvenues, who were being so cooperative about the *garçonnière;* and all the distinguished guests who had been invited because they were too important to leave out—well, after all that it was not strange that when the dancing got well under way everyone was feeling full of good will to the world and no one was especially observant, so the bridal couple, who, naturally, had led the dancing to begin with, managed to get gradually closer to the rear of the room and then actually out of it before they were missed. Then came the quick flight down the hall, the dash through the back door, the leap into the coach; and this was rolling down the avenue of oaks, well along toward the high road, before the sudden cry went up that they were nowhere to be seen, that they must have escaped.

In the friendly darkness of the coach, they sat embraced, punctuating their conversation about the wedding with kisses; and when they came to the gate of Kenilworth, they found it had been left open to receive them and they rode on until Mealie reined in his horses at the entrance of the *garçonnière,* which was all alight to welcome them. Then Pierre stepped down and, turning toward Laure, lifted her bodily from her seat.

"Of course, I'm going to carry you over the threshold," he told her. "What if this isn't *really* our house? It's our house for now and we'll always think of it as our first home. Put your arms around my neck, darling, and shut your eyes. Then don't open them again until I tell you to."

She was so light that he could easily have carried her three times as far as he did, without feeling her weight. It seemed as if they had gone no distance at all when he set her down in a big chair and told her that now she might look; and, even before she spoke, he could see by her happy expression that she was delighted with the small parlor. It was not customary to place the most elegant furniture in the *garçonnière,* since this was normally used only by bachelor members of a family and their bachelor guests; but the Bienvenues had insisted that, for its present occupants, this one must be suitably equipped and adorned. The Empire furniture in the *salon* was upholstered in pale blue brocade, a crystal chandelier hung from the ceiling, an *étagère*, laden with miniatures and other small *objets d'art*, stood in one corner and, under a gilt-edged mirror, the mantel had its traditional *garniture de cheminée*. Laure's exclamation showed she felt that nothing was lacking to give it intimacy and charm.

"Very well. Now that you've approved the salon, we'll go on into the dining room," Pierre told her. "Right through this door to the left." He opened it to disclose a table decorated with flowers and attractively set with a cold supper. "Please be seated, Madame Beauregard," he said, making her a sweeping bow. "This is the first time you've presided at my board. Permit me to hold out your chair for you."

She laughed, entering into his mood, but shook her head as she sat down. "Pierre, I couldn't possibly eat anything! Have you forgotten so soon? We've had supper!"

"You mean there was supper at Conseil. But neither of us had much chance to eat. We were interrupted all the time by well-wishers. Not that I minded. I knew we'd have much more fun, eating here by ourselves and toasting each other. Just let me open the champagne and we'll begin."

He bent to lift a bottle from the silver ice cooler in which it was imbedded, drew the cork noiselessly and filled her glass and his with foaming golden liquid. Then he put cold meat, savory cheese and crisp rolls on two plates and sat down, not opposite her but beside her, daring her to keep up with him as he made a good meal and washed it down with sound wine. Again, she found his mood contagious; if she did not actually eat as heartily and drink as much as he did, she still found the food appetizing, the champagne exhilarating; and if she did not match him in badinage, she responded merrily to his.

At last he rose and put his arm around her shoulder. "You must see some more of the house now," he told her. "We'll go back to the parlor and have a look at the room that leads out of it on the other side." Then, he threw open the second door and stood with her on its threshold, she saw that beyond it towered the time-honored *lit à ciel* —the great canopied bed in which the Creole bride was always ceremoniously installed to await the coming of her bridegroom.

"I'm going now to find Mamie and send her to you," Pierre said. "I told her not to come until she was sent for. I didn't want anyone else around when I lifted you over the threshold and showed you our house. But she'll do anything for you that you need done—in fact, I think she'll do it better than your mother would have, because she'll do it your way, not hers. Then, when you're through with her, she'll go back to the quarters and you'll call me. I'll be listening for you while I get out of this uniform and put on a dressing gown. My things are in the other chamber—the one back of the dining room." He bent over her for another kiss. "Do you remember my telling you, the first time we met in the glade, that when I came to your room—our room—I wanted you to be just as glad to receive me as I would be to come? I said I believed you would be. Was I wrong?"

"You know you weren't. You know you've been right about everything."

It was nearly an hour later when she called him and he returned to find that several candles had been left burning, instead of merely the vigil light, as he had expected, Laure was sitting up in bed, propped by big square pillows, and she did not look in the least as he had expected, either. She was not clad in the conventional, high-necked, long-sleeved nightgown of the period and her hair had not been neatly plaited in braids. Instead, she had on a garment cut as low as a ball gown and soft and sheer as her wedding dress; her long black hair lay in soft waves about her face and neck. She was ten times more beautiful than he had ever seen her before, even earlier that same evening, in her wedding dress.

"Mamie made my nightgown," she said. "She said to tell you this is the surprise she told you about. She said it was all foolishness for a young lady to be taught to show her neck and arms when she went to a party and then be all buttoned up to her throat and wrists when she went to bed. I never thought of it before, but now I believe what she said makes sense. What do you think?"

"I think so, too. That's putting it very mildly. I don't know how I'll ever be able to thank Mamie enough for her surprise—or you either, for listening to her. Also, for leaving the candles burning, so that I could look at you."

"You can look at me as long as you like. That is, now that we're married, everything is perfectly proper, isn't it?"

"Yes, darling. Perfectly proper and wonderful. I'll never forget how you looked when I came into our room tonight."

"Mamie had a bath ready for me," Laure continued, "a perfumed bath. I told her that I'd had a bath already today, and she said that was before I'd been dancing and taken a long ride and eaten supper and, of course, it was. Besides, Mamie said this bath was different. It had all sorts of scents in it—magnolia and sweet olive and vetivert and I don't know what else. Mamie extracts the scents from the plants and mingles them herself. I never knew before that Mamie made perfume. Did you?"

"No, but I might have guessed it. There was always something sweet-smelling about the rooms where she worked. Nothing quite as sweet as this, though."

"It seems Mamie makes love philters, too, and voodoo charms and gris-gris. She's had great success with them. But she laughed and said we didn't need any of those."

"I don't think we do."

"I'm sorry I was so long getting ready. But the bath *was* wonderful! And I thought you'd want me to take it when Mamie had it all ready."

"Yes, I'm glad you did. But I was beginning to feel I'd waited quite a while for you to call me. I hoped you weren't going to change your mind and not do it after all."

"Why, Pierre, you know I wouldn't have done that!"

"I didn't think so, but I wanted to be sure. Is it all right if I blow out the candles now? Except for the vigil lamp?"

By the dim light that this gave, he could see that she was still smiling; and as he lay down beside her and took her in his arms, he was conscious of the same willing quiesence in her whole being that he had found in her lips when he first kissed her. He remembered how quickly those had warmed to welcome and he wanted to feel the same quickening now, the assurance that this compliance did not merely signify acceptance of the mysterious mastery to which her mother had told her she must submit, because it was an inevitable and predominant part of marriage. He had tried to prepare her differently. He had told her, in that secret glade which had been their first trysting place, that the closer caresses became, the more joy they brought, that when he and she could embrace as lovers united in marriage that would bring them the greatest joy of all; and he wanted, more than anything in the world, to make his words come true, for her as well as for himself. But this perfect and complete union of which he had spoken so blithely could not be achieved until she had yielded her maidenhood; for that, he had not known how to prepare her. No matter by what name, lovely or harsh, he called the act which would make her his, it would remain essentially the same and must so remain for all time, as it had been since the beginning of time. And she was so young, so trustful, so innocent, so defenseless.

She stirred ever so slightly and he drew her, still unresisting, still quiescent, closer to him. As he did so, she murmured his name and nestled in his embrace. The movement was so slight he told himself that, from very yearning for it, he might have imagined it. But as he drew her closer yet, she whispered, "Oh, I love you so!" and, as he murmured words of endearment in reply, he realized this was the perfect love that casts out all fear. She did not know his will with her, but, whatever it might be, it was hers also. It was not enough for her, any more than it was for him, that a priest had pronounced them man and wife, in the presence of witnesses; it was in this dark and silent room that she must earn the right to call her beloved her husband. This much, at least, she understood; and there was no dread in her heart of the moment which would make her wholly his and bring about her fulfillment. She was awaiting it. He locked her in his arms and with his lips against hers and his heart beating against hers took her with him into realms of rapture.

⋙ 11 ⋘

Comme la cloche du village
Mon coeur bat pour toi, Ninon,
don, don, don, don, don, don,
En songeant à notre ménage
Mon coeur fait un carillon,
A la fête du village,
La clochette fait din, din, din, din,
En songeant à notre ménage
Je sens mon coeur qui tinte aussi din, din,
comme la cloche du village don, don,
En songeant à notre ménage din
Mon coeur fait un carillon don
Fait un carillon, un carillon, un carillon.

—Dictionnaire lyrique portatif, Ariette 1766
(François Cali, Dictionnaire Pittoresque de La France)

❦

THE NEXT TWO YEARS FORMED AN IDYLLIC INTERLUDE: THEY WERE
not only a period of cloudless happiness, they were a period of
sustained rapture; every separation, however brief, became merely a
prelude to joyous reunion.

After making more than ten thousand soundings in Barataria Bay,
Pierre had been assigned to Fort St. Philip and Fort Jackson for repair
and construction work; the transfer was, in every way, a welcome one.
He had never outgrown the enthusiastic interest in Fort St. Philip
which had been awakened by his early visits there with his uncle
Joseph; and now that Fort Jackson was completed and garrisoned, it
was equally appealing to him. Moreover, these forts were much more
accessible than Livingston. As he and Laure were living at Upper
Magnolia with the Villerés, it was sometimes possible for him, by
leaving very early in the morning, to rejoin her late that same evening.
Even when the steamboat schedule did not make this feasible, he
assuaged his longing for her, as he lay alone in the barracks at night,
by dwelling on the ecstatic moments when he would again be at her
side; and he was able to perform his appointed tasks all the more
capably and conscientiously, because his working days were brightened
by the realization that every passing hour shortened the time that
divided them. Invariably, as soon as he came within sight of the
house, he caught a glimpse, through the trees, of Laure waiting for
him on the gallery; and when he reached the steps, he took them two
at a time, in order to hold her more quickly in his embrace. If he
had arrived early enough to take the evening meal with the family,
she went upstairs with him and remained in their chamber, so that
he could talk with her through the open door while he bathed and
changed his clothes in their dressing room. If, on the other hand, he
was so late that M. and Mme Villeré had already retired for the night,
he washed his hands in a *cabinet* on the ground floor, and he and
Laure had a cold supper together before they went upstairs. Then
came the wonderful hours when nothing from the outside world
intruded on their happiness. Laure's bounty, like Juliet's, was as

boundless as the sea; the more she gave, the more she had to give—and the more she wanted to give. As for him, his passion, far from slackening after its first fulfillment, became an increasingly vital force, as their mutual desire grew in scope and splendor.

He did not, like so many men he knew, crave prompt paternity, both as the outward and visible sign of virility and as the assurance, before there could be any anxiety on this score, that he would have an heir. As a matter of fact, he gave surprisingly little thought to the probable and natural consequences of his lovemaking. Indeed, it was not until Laure told him, with a whimsical little smile, that her mother had asked, rather anxiously, if she, Laure, were by any chance failing to fulfill her wifely duties, and they had laughed together over the question which revealed how imperfect was Mme Villerés visualization of her daughter's attitude in this important matter, that they themselves discussed the subject of childbearing.

"You know, Pierre, I'm almost afraid that she wouldn't wholly approve if she knew."

"Knew what?"

"That I don't submit to you; that I welcome you."

"I can't imagine anything worse than a submissive wife. I tried to make that clear to you in the beginning. If that's what your mother was, all I can say is your father must have missed a great deal."

"Hush, you shouldn't talk like that. It isn't respectful. Besides, I do more than welcome you; I invite you."

"Don't talk such nonsense, darling. You know I've never given you time to invite me. I want so much to come to you that I can't wait. I want so much to stay with you, I can hardly bear to tear myself away. But perhaps you'd better be more careful about doing anything to detain me when you see it's almost impossible for me to go. There's a sad story about one of my predecessors at Fort Jackson. He overstayed his leave and resented the kind of rebuke he got from his commanding officer on his return. The result was an argument and then a court-martial and then a firing squad. When the poor boy was dying he fell on ground where there were some orange seeds—well, of course he'd have hard work not to, down on the Delta. Anyway, the tree that sprang up bore fruit that looked as if it were streaked with blood. There's a tree near the fort that still bears that kind of fruit. I could bring you home one of those bloody oranges any day when they're in season, if you don't believe that story. Perhaps I'd better. It might be a warning to you not to make me so happy when I'm with you."

"Oh, Pierre, don't joke about it! It frightens me. I feel as if we ought to cling to every moment of possible happiness. Perhaps we won't have them always."

"Of course we'll have them always! What's the matter with you; has your mother upset you with her silly questions? It isn't like you to talk like this, to feel like this."

"No-o-o. She hasn't exactly upset me. But she has made me realize that we've been married over a year and that I'm not even expecting a baby yet."

"Did you expect to begin expecting one around the first of October, Forty-one, after we'd been married ten days?"

"I'm afraid I wasn't thinking about a baby ten days after we were married. I wasn't thinking of anyone in the world but you."

"And I wasn't thinking of anyone in the world but you. I'm still not doing so—in a way that counts. I wouldn't care if we never had a baby."

"How can you say a thing like that? I think it would be dreadful."

"You never thought of it at all until your mother upset you. I can see that she *did* upset you. She probably told you that a woman isn't complete until she's borne a child, all that sort of thing. Didn't she now?"

"Well——"

"Of course she did. I think you're perfect, darling, just as you are. I don't want to share you with anyone, even a child of our own. I hope it will be a long time before I have to."

It did not occur to either one of them that, unless they materially altered their way of life, this hope was not likely to be fulfilled, that the astonishing aspect of the case lay in the fact that Laure had not been "expecting" within ten days of their marriage rather than in the probability that such expectations should be indefinitely delayed. And presently the inevitable happened.

Pierre tried to give Laure the impression that he received the great news with the same overwhelming joy it was evident she felt. But if he failed to do so, he at least managed to conceal from her the fear which suddenly gripped him: women died in childbirth. It happened all the time, among people they knew, and Laure herself had said they should cling to every moment of happiness because these moments might not last. Did she have a presentiment which she was concealing from him? No, she must have merely been talking at random, for she did not betray the slightest fear, even the slightest anxiety about her condition, nothing but thankfulness because she was fulfilling her manifest destiny, that her passion had been productive. Apparently she was in perfect health, for she showed none of the symptoms that often made pregnancy unpleasant and even nauseous: vertigo, morning sickness, sudden fits of depression and tearfulness, abnormal craving for peculiar foodstuffs and an equally abnormal aversion to meals. She sat for hours on end, stitching away at exquisite baby clothes, the picture of peace and contentment. She "ate for two" with excellent appetite. She took leisurely strolls, arm in arm with Charles or Pierre, after the heat of the day was over. And she carried her child well: the increasing amplitude of her figure became her stature quite as much as the wasp-waist; and she actually gained in dignity of carriage as she lost her fleetness of foot. Observing all this, marveling and rejoicing in it, Pierre's fears were calmed; he told himself he had worried for nothing over a completely normal process; and he began to think of the women among their acquaintances who, far from dying in childbirth, had produced six, eight and ten children and were still in blooming health; why, his mother had borne seven! Not that he wanted six or eight children; he wanted only Laure. But the tragic cases were the exception, not the rule.

Rudely, his fears were awakened again. He had been old enough to be conscious of bustle around the house and a strain in the atmosphere when his younger brother and sisters were born; but he and Augustin and Judith had always been sent to his uncle Joseph's or to the Bienvenues for a brief visit at such times; and when they returned, there was a beautiful bouncing baby sleeping peacefully in its cradle beside their mother's bed, and their mother, propped up with pillows and wreathed in smiles, welcomed them back and told them how happy they should be that there was a new member of the family. Of course, the process of parturition had been no secret to him since he was a small boy, any more than it was to other boys brought up on a plantation where almost every sort of animal life abounded. And, with the awakened curiosity of adolescence, he had taken advantage of some births in the quarters in order to satisfy this. But somehow, nothing he had seen or heard had prepared him for what happened after Laure woke him with a kiss, one September morning just before dawn, to tell him that perhaps it was time to send for Mammy Louison. She had been having slight pains—oh, not bad at all!—for several hours and they seemed to be coming closer together. She had rather hoped this wouldn't happen until tomorrow, because she thought it would be so wonderful to become a mother on the anniversary of the day she had become a wife; and she was sorry to disturb him, but. . . .

He rose hurriedly and lit the candles; even though it did not take him long to dress and the light was dim, he could see that Laure was suffering. Then all through an endless day there was the bustle and strain which he remembered at Toutant. Madame Villeré, as well as Mammy Louison, had come immediately to the room that had been his and Laure's and now was only Laure's; and presently Mammy Louison had opened the door into the hall where he was sitting, inefficient and helpless and miserable, and said, please, Monsieur Pierre, would he go and get one of the young girls to help her. She thought probably Henriette would be best. She couldn't manage alone and she couldn't leave long enough to go herself.

He found Henriette in the pantry, with three or four of the other young slaves who were clustered together and giggling about something, probably how there happened to be babies; and he spoke to her sharply, which was rare for him, especially when he was speaking to one of their people. The girls looked at him in a startled way, their giggling suddenly hushed, and then they scuttled off, scattering in different directions. He made sure that the direction Henriette took was toward Laure's room, and then he went to the sideboard and poured himself a stiff drink, which was another unusual thing for him to do, at least before first evening.

As he passed the open door of the library, he saw that M. Villeré and Charles were both there and that they also had drinks in their hands. They called to him to come in, and said he would be much better off with them than in the upstairs hall, where he would hear everything. Hear what? he asked impatiently, and went along, but not before he had seen them exchange glances and heard them call after him to come back; and before he reached the top stair he knew what they had meant; a horrible scream came from Laure's room and then another and then another. Tardily, he remembered that one of the slaves, part of whose labor he had surreptitiously witnessed as an adolescent, had screamed before she brought forth her child; but she had sounded like a wounded animal rather than a human being and, though he had felt sorry for her, her pain had not affected him too much. This was different; it sounded like the wail of a doomed soul in Purgatory and it cut through him like a knife.

He braced himself and listened, hoping against hope that the cry he had heard had been wrung from Laure at that last terrible moment, the moment when the child forced itself into the world. If this was what had happened, there would be no more such sounds. She was both so brave and so self-controlled that she would not cry out unless she were in mortal agony, and this might now be over. But almost before the hope had become a reasoned thought, he heard the dreadful wail again and, this time, it rose to a shriek that seemed to rend the air. A moment later the door opened and Mme Villeré, white-faced and trembling, came rushing toward him.

"We'll have to get a second midwife. Mammy Louison can't manage alone and Henriette doesn't know how to help her. If it's possible to get a physician, we must do that, too. If only Dr. Piussan were here! But he came to see the slaves just yesterday and he won't be due back for another week."

"A physician!"

Pierre had never heard of calling in a doctor on a confinement case. As far as he knew, there was none nearer than New Orleans. He was trembling, too, as he answered.

"Where do you think I'd better go?"

"I don't think you'd better go anywhere. You must stay where you are in case—" She did not finish the sentence, but she was weeping now and he knew what the end of the sentence would have been if she could have gone on "—in case we're sure that Laure is dying and we can send for you, so that you can see her once more before she's gone."

"Go downstairs and tell my husband and Charles to start out at once," Mme Villeré continued, when she had controlled herself enough to speak. "I have heard that there's a good midwife at Belle Chasse. Charles can get there on horseback and Monsieur Villeré can go in the opposite direction. Tell Matt to stand at the plantation landing and watch for the steamboat to come in. There might be a doctor aboard. But after you've given these messages hurry back here as fast as you can."

It took him only a few minutes to act on Madame Villeré's instructions. All through the rest of the dreadful afternoon and evening, he sat in the upper hall, with nothing to do but listen. Luke, the old butler, came and brought him some dinner, all his favorite dishes, smoking hot, on a neatly set tray. He could not touch food and could not even bear the sight of it; he told Luke to take it away and bring him another drink. But when that came, it revolted him almost as much as the food. Charles returned from Belle Chasse, bringing with him a wrinkled, bent, old hag, ironically named Venus, whose dress was ragged and whose *tignon* and apron were both dirty. Pierre shuddered at the mere thought of having such a filthy creature touch anyone as dainty and fastidious as Laure. Charles' announcement, given almost jauntily as he ushered this monstrosity into Laure's room, that he had been positively assured at Belle Chasse that Venus was wonderful with this sort of thing, that she had practically never lost either a mother or child she delivered, did nothing to give him confidence or courage; and looking miserably and searchingly at Charles, he did not believe his brother-in-law felt any happier about the situation than he did. He saw Charles wince when the next cry came from the closed room, and a minute later Charles remarked that perhaps he'd better go down to the plantation landing himself. In case there were a doctor aboard the steamboat, it would be more effective if one of the family were there to explain and solicit help than if this mission were entrusted to an overseer.

Hours passed and still M. Villeré did not return. Pierre was suddenly conscious that it was growing dark, that night must be coming on; and shortly thereafter Luke came and lighted the candles and again vainly tried to persuade Pierre that he should eat. Once in a while Henriette came out of the closed room on some errand for the midwives; she scuttled past him, her head averted, giving an impression of fear, almost of flight; he felt sure that had she not thought that she would be whipped the next day, should she desert her post, she would have fled to the most distant cabin on the plantation.

Once, but only once, Mme Villeré returned to speak to him. Her face was stricken, but she was more controlled than when she had come before.

"Laure wanted me to give you her love and tell you it looks as if she were going to have her wish, after all."

"Her wish?"

"Yes—that the baby would be born on your anniversary."

"My God! You mean to tell me this is likely to go on until past midnight?"

Mme Villeré lips quivered. "It will unless—" Again, she did not finish her sentence and, again, he knew what the ending would have been if she had gone on: "—unless it stops because she has died."

"Laure wanted me to tell you she was sorry she could not seem to help screaming," Mme Villeré continued with a great effort. "She's afraid it must distress you to hear her. She asked where you were, and when we told her, she said she thought it would be better if you went downstairs."

So, in her agony, Laure was thinking of him, thinking of him lovingly, wishing he need not know what she was going through and still hoping the baby would be born on their anniversary! He was so greatly moved that he could make no adequate reply. Instead, he answered almost gruffly.

"I hope you didn't tell her why you thought I ought to stay near by!"

"No, of course not. And it hasn't occurred to her yet that there might be any reason—any special reason. We've told her that labor is usually very long with a first baby; we haven't told her that it isn't often as long as this before—well, before it's possible to tell that there's been some progress made toward getting the child into the world."

"Are you going to tell her?"

"Not unless she asks us. Of course, if we send for you, she'll know." Again Mme. Villeré's self-control deserted her. "Pierre, I've lost two children already, a boy and a girl, when they were very young. Laure is my only daughter. If I lose her, I'll have just Charles left. One out of four. I can't bear it."

"I suppose you'll have to bear it." He knew he was speaking brutally when he should have spoken consolingly, but he could not help it. "Just as I shall. That is, if it happens. You're not sure yet that it's going to. Or are you?"

"No—no. But I'm afraid, terribly afraid. And I can't do anything for her. That makes it worse. To have your daughter, your little girl, suffer like this."

"And how do you think I feel? I'm her husband, I brought her to this pass."

He turned away. He could not bear to look at Laure's mother, to look at anyone. He could not say any more. There was nothing left to say.

He did not know how much later it was when Charles came bounding up the stairs, followed by a handsome, portly man of imposing presence, who was carrying a small black bag.

"Pierre, we're in tremendous luck!" Charles exclaimed triumphantly. "This is Dr. Labatut of the New Orleans Medical College. He's been visiting the Bienvenues at Kenilworth, he was just on his way home. When the steamboat drew up at the landing and I called for a doctor, he immediately stepped forward and offered to come with me. He knows all about—I mean, he says he's had confinement cases before. If anyone can help Laure, he can."

"Of course she can be helped," Dr. Labatut said, speaking kindly and competently. But he stopped only long enough to make this reassuring statement and to wring Pierre's hand before he hurried on to the closed room.

As Pierre had long since lost all track of time, he had no idea how many hours elapsed before Dr. Labatut came out and spoke to him again. The physician's tone was still the same—kindly and competent. But his manner was grave.

"I wish I might have arrived sooner," he said. "If I had, I think I might have made things a little less hard for your wife, though I'm afraid this would not have gone easily with her in any case. And now there will be only one way of saving either her or the child— and that is with instruments. Fortunately, I have what I need with me. I have found even when I am on so-called vacations that it is always better to be prepared in a region where there is a scarcity of doctors. I believe I can do as much for Mme Beauregard as any physician you could find and, be that as it may, there is no time to wait for anyone else. But I must tell you that Mme Villeré is very opposed to the procedure I am suggesting. Therefore, I feel I must have your authority to act as I think best."

"What will happen if you don't operate?"

"Your wife will certainly die within a few hours."

"Good God! Then how can you hesitate?"

"Only because it is customary, in such cases, to respect the family's scruples, as far as possible. Perhaps, if I waited a little longer, I could convince Mme Villeré that she must choose between sacrificing her daughter to false modesty or saving your wife's life."

"And you're sure of saving her life?"

"No, I won't lie to you. But neither will I conceal from you that it is her only chance and I think it is an even one, if we don't delay any longer."

"Then, for the love of heaven, don't delay any longer!"

The doctor laid his hand on Pierre's arm. "I shan't. And I'll do everything I can to save your wife and your child. But I want you to do something for me. I want you to go out to the grove and walk as far as the woods. It is almost daylight, you won't have any trouble finding your way. Then stay in the woods until I send for you."

It was very still in the woods. Pierre sat on a log which had fallen slantwise in the green glade and listened to the stillness. He saw it was the same log on which he and Laure had sat when he told her not to listen to her mother, not to be afraid of marriage, because their embraces would bring her nothing but happiness; and he cursed himself for a liar. This is what their embraces had brought about— agony, manhandling, possibly death.

The deep stillness of the woods was broken by crackling branches. He looked up and saw Charles coming toward him and leaped up.

"It's a boy," Charles was shouting. "A strapping big boy. Laure sends you her love and wants to see you. Meanwhile, she says to remind you she hoped to give you a baby for an anniversary present and that she's delighted she's done it. I gather she's so pleased with herself that she's practically forgotten about yesterday already."

"It's more than I have," Pierre said brokenly. "More than I ever shall."

❧ 12 ☙

Lieblich in der Bräute Locken
Spielt der jungfräuliche Kranz,
Wenn die hellen Kirchenglocken
Laden zu des Festes Glanz.
Ach! Des Lebens schönste Feier
Endigt auch den Lebensmai,
Mit dem Gürtel, mit dem Schleier
Reisst der schöne Wahn entzwei.
Die Leidenschaft flieht,
Die Liebe muss bleiben;
Die Bjume Verblüht,
Die Frucht muss treiben.
Der Mann muss hinaus
Ins feindliche Leben,
Muss wirken und streben
Und pflanzen und schaffen,
Erlisten, erraffen,
Muss wetten und wagen,
Das Glück zu erjagen.

—From Schiller, *Lied von der Glocke*

❦

HER LIFE HAD BEEN SAVED, BUT IT DID NOT BELONG TO HIM ANY more. It belonged to the baby.

His presentiment had been accurate: she accepted maternity with the same intensity that she had accepted marriage. She would not listen to the suggestion of a wet nurse; she wanted to feed her baby herself, to feel that he was dependent on her for sustenance, to hold him in her arms for hours every day, to have his cradle beside her bed at night so that she would be sure to hear him if he cried. Dr. Labatut upheld her; she had plenty of milk, it would be better for both her and little René if she nursed him; if it prevented her from anxiety to have him close to her at night, that would be a wise plan, too. She must be saved strain of every sort—worry, fatigue, excitement. She had had a close call. It would be months before she would be strong and well again.

"Wouldn't she get her strength back faster if she didn't nurse the baby?"

Dr. Labatut shot a keen glance at the father and answered rather shortly. "I doubt it. She's got an abundant supply. If we try to dry it up artificially, she might have abscesses in her breasts or a bad case of milk fever. Either would drag her down more than nursing the baby. Besides, that's what she wants to do. And she's always been used to having pretty much her own way, hasn't she?"

"Yes," Pierre admitted, recalling her defiance of her parents in the early days of their engagement.

"Then I say you'd better let her go on having it. If she nurses the baby for a year—"

"A year!"

"Why yes, that's quite usual, as you know. And that will take him through next summer—not the second summer, which is proverbially so critical, but at least through the first. After that, we can talk about weaning him."

Laure was not the only person whose attention was riveted on the baby. Pierre would have expected this from his parents and from hers; but it never would have occurred to him that Charles would develop into a doting uncle, that all the innumerable Villeré relatives would come visiting at Upper Magnolia in order to see René and then prolong their visits indefinitely, or that his brothers and sisters and the Joseph Toutant-Beauregards would join in the general and extended homage. The christening was, of course, a logical occasion for the gathering of the clans; but after that he felt they should disperse and they showed no disposition to do so.

It was customary for a young couple to remain with the bride's parents for at least three years before setting up an independent establishment, and he had been quite prepared to do so, especially as there were two great advantages, from his viewpoint, in living at Upper Magnolia: it was conveniently situated, so far as his work was concerned and, financially, it was a godsend. But he began to wonder whether or not these advantages really outweighed those he might enjoy if he had more privacy. He liked to read, and he liked to do so in an atmosphere of peace and quiet impossible to achieve in the Big House of a plantation which was always overflowing with company. Increasingly, it was important for him to do a great deal of paperwork in connection with his engineering, to draw plans, to order supplies, to check on the receipt of equipment. That also was impossible in a place where he had no office or study. Before the birth of the baby, he had been able to work in his bedroom, which of course was also Laure's. Now there was no room for a desk; there was a cradle beside the four-poster, a small tub in front of the fireplace, a *bonnetière* for little dresses wedged close to the large *armoire* and, on the most comfortable chair in the room, a frilled, silk-lined basket, which accommodated a powder puff, a cake of Castile soap in a fancy box, a supply of olive oil in a tiny bottle and various other infantile necessities. Lack of space did not present the only handicap; Henriette, who had been promoted to the position of nursemaid, was constantly coming in and going out, fetching water, carrying it away, picking up clothes, tending the fire.

It was hard to find the time to talk things over with Laure. Even if she were not nursing the baby or bathing it or dressing it or undressing it, she seemed to be completely absorbed in it; and then there were all those interruptions from adoring relatives and Henriette. It was only at night that he could be sure that no one would come bursting in and at night, though Laure waked instantly if the baby so much as stirred, she sank into a deep, dreamless sleep as soon as her head touched the pillow. He knew she needed all the rest she could get, both because of the ordeal she had been through and because of the constant drain on her strength as a nursing mother.

He waited and waited for an opportune moment to consult her about a project he had in mind, and when no such moment came he acted without consulting her and told her afterward what he had done.

"Do you think you could spare me a few moments, Laure?"

"Why, *cher*, what a way to speak to me! As if I couldn't spare you all the time you want—that is, if the baby doesn't need me and I'm not showing him to guests."

"That's just it. The baby seems to need you all the time and we have guests all the time. I'm hoping the baby won't need you quite so much when his feedings come a little further apart and I'm also hoping we won't have as many guests in New Orleans as we do at Upper Magnolia."

"What on earth do you mean, in New Orleans?"

"I've taken a little house for us there. A very little house on St. Louis Street, just big enough for us to fit into ourselves without any room for company. Of course, we'll take Henriette with us for a nursemaid, and Mamie would be delighted to come as cook. I've already asked if she could be spared at Toutant. Between them, they should make things pretty easy for you. I've also taken an office just around the corner, on Bourbon Street. I don't need to be at the forts as much as I did when we were first married. A lot of my work now is just drawing plans and ordering and checking supplies, and I can do that more easily in a New Orleans office than in a crowded bedroom at Upper Magnolia."

"Oh, Pierre—"

He had hurt her feelings, he could see that, and he was sorry—not sorry for what he had done, because it seemed to him the only thing to do, but sorry for the way he had done it. Somehow, he should have managed to consult her. But he was proud of the way she stood by him when her parents were told; they would never have known from anything she said or did that the decision had been made by him alone. He was proud, too, of the efficiency with which she managed to share in the moving and of the way she ran the little house on St. Louis Street; she had never taken any share in domestic management, she had never lived in the city; but she adapted herself to both with grace and apparent ease. And Pierre's hope that she would have more time for him was fulfilled; the baby's feedings did come further apart; there were comparatively few guests and these largely in the evening. He and Laure strolled along the Esplanade together, they went to Mass at the Cathedral together, they saw all the best performances at the opera together; and he had long quiet days of work and reading in his office. He did not recapture the sense of satisfaction and achievement which his engineering activities at Barataria had given him, or the rapture of those two years with Laure before René was born; he would have welcomed a more exacting military assignment and a more sustained degree of romance in his personal life. However, he was glad he had made the break with Upper Magnolia and, on the whole, he was content until his new orders came through; then he learned that he was not to go, as he had kept hoping, to the Mexican border, where the atmosphere was already triggered to war because of boundary disputes. He was to go to Baltimore, where the atmosphere was triggered to nothing except parties and balls, to take charge of engineering at Fort McHenry.

This in itself was disappointing enough; what was worse, he could not possibly take Laure and René with him to share his Northern exile. (Of course he could not have taken them to Texas, either, but at this moment of disappointment he was not reasoning with any marked degree of logic.) He had already strained his resources to the limit by renting the house and office in New Orleans. Now his wife and child would have to return to Upper Magnolia and he would have to go into exile without them. In returning Laure to her parents he would, in a sense, be surrendering his claim to her; he was grieved and he was also chagrined which, in his case, was often more devastating.

Again, Laure rose nobly to the occasion. She had sometimes been homesick in New Orleans, she confessed; after all, she was a country girl, born and bred; she was used to the spaciousness of a large house, to fields and flowers, groves and bayous; she missed them, when Pierre was at his office and she was confined by four walls. Of course, the house which Pierre had chosen was most attractive; she would be glad to come back to it when he did and she would count the days until then. Perhaps their separation would not be very long—just long enough for René, who was already creeping everywhere, to learn how to stand sturdily on his own two feet and run from room to room. She and Pierre would have the greatest fun watching him together and, meanwhile, how much her parents would enjoy having him back! And, of course, when Pierre returned, René would be weaned, he would not need anywhere nearly as much of her attention. She would be able to give a great deal more to Pierre. She was afraid she had neglected him sometimes these last eleven months.

He often asked himself afterward, if it would have been easier to leave her if she had not been so cheerful, so sweet and loving, so solicitous about saving him from any sense of failure to provide for her adequately. He thought that if she had complained, if she had been mournful or censorious, perhaps the parting would not have been so hard. On the other hand, he occasionally experienced a brief sensation of resentment because he sensed that there was something almost maternal in her attitude now. He felt she was trying to save him from censure and disappointment, the way she would have tried to save a child, and that was not the way a wife should act toward her husband, or rather it was not the way she would act if she respected him and admired him for his strength. He had told her and told her truthfully that he did not want a submissive wife, much less a dutiful one; a marriage relationship which was not inspired by mutual love would have been abhorrent to him. But he longed, as he had never longed before, to know that she wanted and needed him as much as he wanted and needed her, to have her feel that nothing mattered if he could be the possessor and she the possessed.

He never told her of this desperate yearning. Perhaps she guessed it, as she guessed so many things of which he never spoke; at all events, he was convinced that this longing had been fulfilled, that something deep within her had demanded his dominance. Once he had taken her back to Upper Magnolia, once the reasons for this return had been explained to her parents, her attitude toward him ceased to be protective. In the presence of others, it was proud. When they were alone, it was passionate.

He did not know until he had been in Baltimore nearly five months that she was pregnant again.

~§ 13 §~

Pour un soldat
Qui veut avec éclat
Signaler son courage,
Le tapage, le carnage (bis)
Ont des appâts (bis)
Le tapage, le carnage (ter)
Le ta-pa . . . ge ont des appâts, ont des appâts.
Tranquille au milieu des combats (bis)

Malgré la bombe qui tombe (bis)
Et se brise en éclats (bis)
Les grenades,
Pétarades,
Carabines,
Couleuvrines,
Baïonnettes,
Escopettes,
Hallebardes et mousquetons,
Rien ne l'inquiète,
Comme au son d'une musette
Il danse au bruit du canon,
patapon, patapon, tapon, tapon, tapon, tapon.
Il danse au bruit du canon.

—*Dictionnaire Lyrique Portatif*, 1766
(François Cali, *Dictionnaire Pittoresque de La France*)

❧

T HE SAME MAIL WHICH BROUGHT A LETTER FROM MME VILLERÉ, telling him that Laure had been safely delivered of a second son, brought one from the War Department ordering him back to New Orleans.

He received both communications jubilantly. His mother-in-law said nothing about "complications" and he gathered that, this time, things had gone "easily" with Laure. He had frequently been told they were apt to with a second baby, especially when it came along fairly soon after the first; so he was greatly relieved. He tried, with a certain degree of success, to convince himself that his recall might be the prelude to a transfer which would enable him to see active service. However, when Charles questioned him on the subject, he was obliged to admit that there had been no definite assurance of this. He added that, despite this lack, he hoped he might be allowed to join General Taylor's "Army of Occupation" which was then encamped in Natchitoches. He intended to make every possible effort

OFFICIAL

ARMY REGISTER,

FOR

1847.

PUBLISHED BY ORDER OF THE SECRETARY OF WAR, IN COMPLIANCE
WITH THE RESOLUTION OF THE SENATE, DECEMBER 13,
1815, AND RESOLUTIONS OF THE HOUSE OF
REPRESENTATIVES, FEBRUARY 1, 1830,
AUGUST 30, 1842, AND FEB-
RUARY 16, 1843.

ADJUTANT GENERAL'S OFFICE,
Washington, January, 1847.

NAME.	Rank in the Corps.	Army.	Date of first appointment.		Born in.	Appointed from.

Colonel.

| Joseph G. Totten,* | 7 Dec. 38 | Bvt. 11 Sept. 24. | 2 lt. | 23 Feb. 08 | Conn. | Conn. |

Lieutenant Colonels.

| Sylvanus Thayer, | 7 July, 38 | Col. bvt. 3 Mar. 33. | 2 lt. | 23 Feb. 08 | Mass. | M. A. |
| René E. De Russy, · | 7 Dec. | Bvt. 30 June, 34. | 2 lt. | 10 June, 12 | N. Y. | M. A. |

Majors.

John L. Smith,	7 July, 38	Bvt. 29 Aug. 30.	2 lt.	16 Oct. 13	S. C.	N. Y.
William H. Chase,	7 July,		Bvt. 2 lt.	4 Mar. 15	Mass.	M. A.
Richard Delafield,	7 July,		2 lt.	24 July, 18	N. Y.	M. A.
Cornelius A. Ogden,	7 Dec.		2 lt.	1 July, 19	N. J.	M. A.

Captains.

Henry Brewerton,	21 Sept. 36		Bvt. 2 lt.	1 July, 19	N. Y.	M. A.
George Dutton,	7 July, 38		Bvt. 2 lt.	1 July, 22	Conn.	M. A.
Joseph K. F. Mansfield,	7 July,	M. bvt. 9 May, 46.	Bvt. 2 lt.	1 July,	Conn.	M. A.
Alexander H. Bowman,	7 July,		Bvt. 2 lt.	1 July, 25	Pa.	M. A.
Robert E. Lee,	7 July,		Bvt. 2 lt.	1 July, 29	Va.	M. A.
Alexander J. Swift,	7 July,		Bvt. 2 lt.	1 July, 30	N. C.	M. A.
Frederick A. Smith,	7 July,		Bvt. 2 lt.	1 July, 33	Mass.	M. A.
Jonathan G. Barnard,	7 July,		Bvt. 2 lt.	1 July,	Mass.	M. A.
George W. Cullum,	7 July,		3vt. 2 lt.	1 July,	N. Y.	M. A.
William D. Fraser,	7 July,		Bvt. 2 lt.	1 July, 34	N. Y.	M. A.
John Sanders,	7 Dec.		Bvt. 2 lt.	1 July,	Ky.	M. A.
George L. Welcker,	25 Apr. 46		Bvt. 2 lt.	1 July, 38	Tenn.	M. A.

First Lieutenants.

James L. Mason,	7 July, 38		Bvt. 2 lt.	1 July, 36	R. I.	M. A.
Henry W. Benham,	7 July,		Bvt. 2 lt.	1 July, 37	Conn.	M. A.
Danville Leadbetter,	7 July,		2 lt. 1 art.	1 July, 36	Me.	M. A.
Montgomery C. Meigs,	7 July,		2 lt. 1 art.	1 July,	Ga.	M. A.
Daniel P. Woodbury,	7 July,		2 lt. 3 art.	1 July,	N. H.	M. A.
P. G. T. Beauregard,	16 June, 39		2 lt. 1 art.	1 July, 38	La.	M. A.
James H. Trapier,	1 July,		2 lt. 1 art.	1 July,	S. C.	M. A.
Jeremiah M. Scarritt,	1 July,		2 lt. 6 inf.	1 July,	N. H.	M. A.
Isaac J. Stevens,	1 July, 40		2 lt.	1 July, 39	Mass.	M. A.
Henry W. Halleck,	1 Jan. 45		2 lt.	1 July,	N. Y.	M. A.
Jeremy F. Gilmer,	29 Dec.		2 lt.	1 July,	N. C.	M. A.
Henry L. Smith,	25 Apr. 46		2 lt.	1 July,	Me.	M. A.

Second Lieutenants.

Zealous B. Tower,	1 July, 41			1 July, 41	Mass.	M. A
Horatio G. Wright,	1 July,			1 July,	Conn.	M. A.
Masillon Harrison,	1 July,			1 July,	Md.	M. A.
Henry L. Eustis,	1 July, 42			1 July, 42	Mass.	M. A.
John Newton,	1 July,			1 July, ·	Va.	M. A.
John D. Kurtz,	1 July,			1 July,	D. C.	M. A.
William S. Rosecrans,	3 Apr. 43	Bvt. 1 July, 42.	Bvt.	1 July,	Ohio.	M. A.
Barton S. Alexander,	30 Sept.	Bvt. 1 July,	Bvt.	1 July,	Ky.	M. A.
Gustavus W. Smith,	1 Jan. 45	Bvt. 1 July,	Bvt.	1 July,	Ky.	M. A.
William H. C. Whiting,	1 July,			1 July, 45	Mis.	M. A.
Edward B. Hunt,	29 Dec.	Bvt. 1 July, 45.	Bvt	1 July,	N. Y.	M. A.
Charles S. Stewart,	1 July, 46			1 July, 46	At sea.	M. A.
George B. McClellan,	1 July,	Bvt.	Bvt.	1 July,	Pa.	M. A.
Charles E. Blunt,	1 July,	Bvt.	Bvt.	1 July,	N. H.	M. A.
John G. Foster,	1 July,	Bvt.	Bvt.	1 July,	N. H.	M. A.

2

to secure this permission; if he were unsuccessful, this would not be because he had failed to try.

He was as good as his word. Hardly a day—never a week—went by that he did not besiege the War Department with pleading letters. The answers, when they came, were anything but satisfactory: he was needed elsewhere. . . . And just where was elsewhere? . . . That was not yet decided. . . . Why not? . . . Silence.

He found this silence nerve-racking and, because of his emotionalism, often acted and spoke in ways that would not have been characteristic in his calmer moments. Although he could ill afford such a purchase, he sent to Kentucky for a thoroughbred stallion and, when it arrived on the packet *Grace Darling*, rode it bareback through the streets from the wharf to his little house, holding the two-year-old René precariously in front of him. It was a foolhardy thing to do, but it gave him satisfaction; it was proof to the public that he did not lack daring, that he was military material, even if the War Department declined to recognize this. He did not have a suitable stable for his new mount, much less a dependable stableboy; and he waited, almost defensively, for Laure, who had made no comment when he told her about the intended purchase, to make one now, possibly a caustic one. He would not have blamed her if she had. Instead, without saying anything at all to him, she asked Henriette if there were not a young slave, a brother or cousin of hers, at Upper Magnolia, who could be pressed into service and Henriette assured her that there was. Two days later, Mealie, the same boy who had helped with the soundings, appeared on the scene, grinning broadly, and quickly assumed full and competent charge of the stallion, even to the extent of locating a nearby stable.

Pierre had always heard that women who were too talkative were the bane of a man's existence; but he began to wonder whether or not their silence—like that of the War Department's!—might not sometimes be even more provocative; and, unjust though he realized he was in doing so, he thought of his mother's and wondered if this had irritated his father, as Laure's now irritated him. He knew very well it had not, that it had been a calming and stabilizing factor in controlling turmoil at Toutant; and his annoyance increased because he knew it was unfounded and unreasonable in the present instance. How could any man in his senses be irritated with an angel like Laure? He supposed the answer was that he was not in his senses.

Unfortunately, he did not always reason so logically: he took umbrage because he considered that a civilian employe whom he had sent to Fort Wood with a request for supplies had been refused help and ordered to leave. He wrote the temporary commander, Lieutenant Henshaw, an indignant letter, and pronounced the reply to this "insulting and abusive." His next step was to challenge Henshaw to a duel and announce that the latter had tried to avoid fighting—this as the preliminary of publicly denouncing him as a coward. By now, Henshaw was roused, too; he replied, with spirit, that he had never received the challenge; that he was willing to fight Beauregard at any time; and a meeting was accordingly arranged by the friends who were to act as seconds. The weapons were to be shotguns, the first blast fired at thirty yards, the second at twenty-five, if neither combatant was injured the first time, and so on until one or the other had received satisfaction. They had actually met in the chilly dawn of an April day and begun pacing off their distances under the dueling oaks, when a deputy sheriff arrived posthaste and arrested them both.

On returning to his house a few hours later, after the formalities of establishing bail had been met, Pierre found Laure kneeling at her prie-dieu, with only a light negligee thrown over her nightgown and her long hair still disordered and unbound. He realized that she must have been praying there ever since he left the house, before daybreak, and, for the first time—with regard to the duel—his conscience smote him. He had not been able to keep his preparations for it secret, though he had tried to do so, instead of telling her about it with a certain amount of braggadocio, as he had about the stallion. He knew that, whereas she would not have resented his extravagance, even though this meant further economies on her part, and had unshaken confidence in him as a horseman even when he rode wildly, she would have shuddered at the prospect of having him risk his life in a duel. She had, as a matter of fact, gone further than that: she had begged him not to do this so rashly, so unnecessarily; and when he had told her, speaking coldly to her for the first time, that his honor was involved, and that this was something he could not tolerate under any circumstances, they had been nearer a quarrel than ever before. She admitted that Henshaw had been unhelpful and discourteous, but she could not see that his attitude actually constituted an insult, that it justified him in taking the chance that he might leave her without a husband and their children without a father. That was because she did not want to see, Pierre told her shortly, and declined to discuss the matter with her again. As he lay rigid and wakeful beside her, the night before he left for the dueling grounds, he could feel her trembling and hear her suppressed sobs; but he did not draw her to him or try to comfort and reassure her, and he did not kiss her good-by when he rose in the darkness and left her; he told himself that it would only upset her further. Now he hastened to her and put his arms around her.

"Darling, everything's all right. There wasn't any duel—a nosy deputy sheriff stepped in and spoiled the fun. Why, you're chilled through and through! Come, let me help you back to bed and send for Henriette to bring us coffee! We'll drink it together. I haven't had any myself, thanks to that ill-timed interference. I even missed the traditional rite of 'coffee for one' after 'pistols for two.' "

She did not repulse him, but neither did she respond to him. When she was in bed again she pulled the covers up closely around her and turned away from him. He repeated his suggestion of shared coffee, but she shook her head and closed her eyes. Pierre stood for some minutes watching her and spoke to her again several times, softly and lovingly. She gave him no sign that she heard him, that she was so much as aware of his presence. Finally, he left the room, still baffled, more and more conscience-stricken. When he returned, she was either really asleep or so convincingly pretending to be that he did not dare risk disturbing her, and left for the office without speaking to her again. When he came home for dinner, she was waiting for him in the parlor, her appearance as soignée as usual, both children at her side. She did not seem in the least constrained, but on the other hand she did not welcome him with that gladness which, as a rule, she showed so openly and so naturally; and though she remained calm and amiable, he continued to be aware of reserve and gravity for some days. The duel was not mentioned between them again.

Eventually, a letter arrived from Colonel Totten, the same kindly and understanding officer who had managed to get Pierre transferred from Newport to Florida and from Florida to Louisiana. The Colonel desired to inform Lieutenant Beauregard, of course quite in confidence, that Congress might decide to increase the scope of military establishments; in this case, engineers could, if they wished, be transferred from one branch of the service to another and with higher rank. Should this come about, would Lieutenant Beauregard prefer the artillery or the infantry and what was the lowest rank he would accept? The touchy situation with Mexico was not mentioned in the letter, but Pierre had no difficulty in reading between the lines and lost not a moment in sending his reply: he would prefer the artillery; he wanted the rank of captain at the very least; and he wanted to be placed in an outfit which would immediately be sent into action, if action were indicated.

Perhaps the War Department considered that he wanted too much, too soon. At all events, there was another long period of silence and finally a letter, very curtly worded, to the effect that no more engineers were needed at present. There was no mention of a transfer. Again he made his headquarters in New Orleans, going back and forth, as the occasion arose, among the forts on Barataria Bay and near the mouth of the river. It was a tedious, disheartening business.

Laure and the children had been installed in the little house on St. Louis Street and, on the whole, conditions there were satisfactory. Laure was not so completely absorbed in the newborn Henri as she had been in René. This, of course, was partly because the latter, at sixteen months, still required a good deal of her attention. She could not give it all to one baby as she had before; necessarily, it was divided between two. But Pierre again felt that there was something maternal in her attitude toward him. She did not understand why he was not so happy to be at home as she was to have him; but since this was obviously the case, she did everything she could to make life easier and pleasanter for him. And he did not want her to shield him and save him; he wanted to shield and save her. She looked very delicate to him and, this time, she had been obliged to accept the services of a wet nurse, as her own supply of milk was not sufficiently abundant to satisfy the voracious appetite of a vigorous and demanding infant. However, when Pierre tried to ask her questions about herself, she changed the subject.

"Please, *cher*, let's talk about something else! I had to keep listening to *maman*'s worries and Dr. Labatut's advice all the time you were gone and I'm heartily sick of both. It has taken me a little longer to get my strength back than it did before, but that's not strange, under the circumstances."

"What circumstances?"

"Well, the babies came pretty close together, you know, and I suppose—nursing one as long as I possibly could while I was carrying another——"

"They shouldn't have come so close together. You shouldn't have had another baby for years, if ever. I'm very much to blame because you did."

"You're not to blame for anything. Why, Pierre, I wouldn't change a single moment of the time we had together before you went away! Change it! I thank the Blessed Mother every night when I say my prayers, because She's let me have you for a husband and because you're the father of my children. Oh darling, I do love you so!"

They had been sitting on either side of the hearth in their candle-lighted parlor and, as she spoke, she rose and came over to him. He drew her down on his knees and she nestled close to him. She had always been slender and lithesome, but now there was an element of fragility, almost of ethereality in her slimness.

"I want you to promise me something," she whispered.

"What?"

"You won't promise unless I tell you?"

"Certainly not."

"I want you to promise that you'll never stop loving me."

"That's easy. I never could."

"What I mean is—don't ever stop *making* love to me because you're afraid I might have another baby if you did."

"Look here, *chère*, I can't promise that! You've reminded me that René and Henri came along mighty close together and—"

"I didn't mean to *remind* you. I was only trying to explain that might be the reason why I'm not getting my strength back fast. It seems to worry you because I don't. It doesn't worry me at all. I don't need to be strong as long as I have you to lean on."

"I'm not much of a support and you do need one. I'm no earthly use to you. In fact, I'm no earthly use to anyone. What does the work I'm doing now amount to? Any good bricklayer ought to be able to reconstruct obsolete forts with just a modicum of supervision. But if I could join the Army of Occupation and we went to war with Mexico——"

"But why should we go to war with Mexico?"

"I'll try again to explain that to you, darling. But not while you're sitting on my lap. I couldn't possibly make myself clear under those conditions."

"All right. What about dinner tomorrow, when we're on opposite sides of the table and Henriette keeps coming in and out of the room?"

"That might do. If you really want me to attempt another explanation."

"I really do. But right now, I want that promise. These conditions ought to be propitious for that."

"They are. They're almost perfect and therefore extremely dangerous. Stop putting temptation in my way and run along to the nursery. I'm sure the boys need you."

He told himself he should be thankful that he still had some strength of mind, that his will had prevailed against Laure's; but somehow this did not make him as happy as he had hoped. In fact, nothing happened that made him especially happy; he realized that he was becoming increasingly resentful of the War Department's silence, increasingly restless in New Orleans, increasingly eager to be with fighting men wherever a fight was likely to occur. He had begun to hug his grievances to his heart, but he felt no inclination to talk about them. Actually, if Laure had not reminded him, the next day at dinner, that he had said he would explain the war situation to her, he would not have tried to do so.

"It began with a boundary dispute," he said and stopped.

"Yes?" Her tone was attentive and eager and he realized she expected him to go on.

"Mexico claims that the Nueces is the southern boundary of Texas and Texas claims it's the Rio Grande. Therefore, the strip of land between them is disputed territory."

"And a strip of land is worth going to war over?"

He suppressed a sigh. "It's a good-sized strip of land. Besides, the trouble really goes back a long way. There was an uprising in Texas against Mexico while I was still at West Point. After this revolution, a treaty of peace was signed and Texas was declared an independent state, though Mexico did not recognize it officially as such. Then Texas decided it would prefer to be part of the United States, rather than an independent country, and Mexico protested. So diplomatic relations were severed."

"What are diplomatic relations?"

"Official *entente cordiale*. Each government maintains a Minister—"

"A *minister!* Are they all Protestants?"

"No, most of them—most of the Mexicans anyway—are Catholics. The kind of Minister I am talking about is a representative of one government in the capital of another. He has a good deal of power and he's supposed to see to it that nothing happens to the *entente cordiale*. But he isn't always successful. So when that happens, his country recalls him and then diplomatic relations with the other country are severed."

"Oh! I see."

"Are you sure? And are you sure you want me to go on trying to explain something you should never bother your pretty little head about?"

"Yes, I'm sure. Sure I see and sure I want to bother my pretty little head."

"All right. Just remember you brought it on yourself. It was next decided that we—I mean, the United States—must have troops ready to defend our territory, if necessary, and the so-called Army of Occupation was formed, with General Taylor at its head. You've heard about that already."

"Yes, of course. But I didn't know what it meant. And I thought the Army of Occupation was at Natchitoches, where you've been clamoring to go."

"It is. But it's in readiness to advance any time. I want to be around when it does. There must be some way to get there."

But apparently there was not. Eventually, the Army of Occupation was ordered to leave Natchitoches and proceed to Corpus Christi, via New Orleans—an order which, as far as Pierre was concerned, turned the knife in the wound. The troops arrived in New Orleans and departed from there amid scenes of tumultuous excitement. War was in the air—or rather those aspects of war which had so enthralled him when he was a boy that he had dashed out of the Cathedral at the sound of marching feet and martial music. Now he constantly heard the same sounds and someone had even written a silly song about the drums, which everybody was singing:

> "The drums, the drums, the busy, busy drums,
> The drums, the drums, the rattling, battling drums
> The drums, the drums, the merry, merry drums."

All day and every day he listened to this song and, at night, it seemed to echo through his dreams. No matter where he went, he found waving flags and cheering people. Through correspondence with them, Pierre knew that several men who had been friends at West Point were in the detachment at Natchitoches. But he did not want to see them. No matter how hard they tried, he felt sure they would not be able to conceal the fact that they were secretly gloating over him. So he made no effort to get in touch with them. They sought him out of their own accord, surprised and a little hurt because he had not been the first to welcome them in New Orleans. Laure was charming to them when they called at the house and they all told him how lucky he was to have such a beautiful wife and such fine husky children. But when the troopship, bound for Corpus Christi, pulled away from the wharf, he knew that not a single man was jealous of him.

He was still in New Orleans when the news reached there, eight months later, that Taylor had advanced his army to the Rio Grande, because a lawless band of Mexicans, venturing into the disputed territory, had attacked and killed a few Americans. For the next two months he, like everyone else, waited breathlessly to hear that the two armies, encamped in sight of each other, had actually met in combat; and, in common with his fellow citizens, glowed with pride because New Orleans was receiving the news of developments more rapidly and more directly than any other place in the country. A pony express, run by two venturesome entrepreneurs—Lumsden and Kendall—enabled the *Picayune* to print such news even before the official dispatches reached Washington; it repeatedly scooped the world. Finally, the great tidings came through: a battle had taken place at Palo Alto; the Mexicans had been completely routed and had retired, in wild confusion, to Resaca de la Palma; Taylor had routed them and followed them again; President Polk had declared that a state of war existed between the United States and Mexico.

So far, Pierre's inability to accept the situation had made him silent and morose, but he had not actually raged against it; he had merely felt chagrined and disappointed because he was not taking part in a gay adventure which called for waving flags and beating drums. Now the feeling went much deeper. It no longer resembled the childish enthusiasm for gay trappings that had turned him from the altar and precipitated his flight from the Cathedral at ten; it was like the sense of destiny which had made him ready to foreswear his heritage of rich acres in order to become a soldier. Had he, after all, sold his birthright for a mess of red pottage? It certainly looked that way to him. Apparently, it did no good to badger the War Department. Well, there were other means to an end. He seized his pen and wrote demandingly, presumptuously and angrily to his Congressman.

When his orders came through, he cursed himself because he had not done so before. He was transferred to the port city of Tampico, on Mexico's eastern coast, which was among the points already captured by American troops and now occupied by them. This was to be used as a base from which to supply Taylor's army and to protect it against possible attack; fortifications were to be built about it on the land side; Pierre was to assume charge of these fortifications. He had missed the first excitement, the first glory of conquest and he would never forgive the War Department for cheating him of that. But at least he felt like a soldier again. He had not, after all, sold his birthright for a mess of red pottage.

This had been his triumphant conviction when he finally started for Mexico. Now, nearly twenty years later, he was again beginning to question it.

His first doubts had arisen because he was given no chance to prove his mettle, because he was stuck in New Orleans when every other able-bodied man he knew—or so it seemed to him—was starting off to fight the Mexicans. But now that he had proved his mettle over and over again, now that he had fought not only the Mexicans but the Yankees, he was no better off than when he had traded an empire for a uniform. Better! He was a thousand times worse off. Aging, obscure, penniless, powerless, he was of no use to himself or anyone else. He was nearly fifty years old and the glory of his name was so dim that once, when he introduced himself, in his vain search for work, the man before whom he stood hardly seemed to identify him. "Beauregard, did you say? Any relation to Augustin Beauregard who went to Texas a while back? Oh, his brother! Why don't you join him there? I hear lots of jobs are opening up in Texas. Sorry, but there doesn't seem to be much of anything in New Orleans these days."

Day after day, the verdict was the same, and he was warned that it would continue to be the same until he had taken an oath of loyalty to the United States and applied for a pardon. Desperate as he was, he had not been able to bring himself to do this. Somehow, he would struggle on a little longer. . . .

His new suit had been delivered, and again he tried to buoy himself up with the hope that when he made a more presentable appearance, the results would be favorable. Meanwhile, he had not changed his mind about putting it on when he went up to the main house for supper. As he took off the shirt which he had been wearing all day, while he tramped from one discouraging interview to another, he noticed that the fresh shirt that he drew from his meager supply had not only been capably laundered, but carefully mended, the frayed cuffs carefully turned. Bette did the washing with the aptitude for it that seemed to be almost instinctive in women of her race, like the care of the very young and the very sick and the inspired seasoning of foods; but fine needlework was not among these gifts. Mme Castel must have done that stitchery. Pierre looked at the shirt which had been lying underneath the one he had just lifted out and then at the others in the small pile. Every one was in the same impeccable condition.

How was he ever to make the gentle, bereft woman, who was showing him so much kindness, realize his sense of indebtedness and gratitude to her? Of course there was only one way—by restoring her son. And the power to do that did not lie with him. He could only persevere in his efforts to secure information; the rest was in the hands of God.

Another letter had come in, but that really did not help much. McDowell, like Sherman, had replied courteously and cordially. He reminded Pierre that nearly a thousand Confederates had been reported missing after the Battle of Shiloh. (A third of the number reported missing from the Union forces, Pierre said to himself, not without grim satisfaction; but naturally McDowell did not mention that.) It was quite possible that many of them were still alive, that these would turn up yet. In fact, McDowell had heard of a man in the Army of Tennessee, who was missing after the Battle of New Hope Church. His twin brother, who had been in the same company with him, went out on the field, with a lantern, looking for him. His search was not successful, but he wrote his mother not to lose heart; there was still a good chance that his brother might turn up; and, sure enough, a year or so later, he did! Then there was another case McDowell remembered of a young officer who had received a bad head wound at Chancellorsville and who still couldn't be identified at the hospital where he had been taken; but, physically, he was now all right and, mentally, he seemed to be slowly improving. The authorities felt reasonably sure that, some day, he would be able to tell them who he was. McDowell mentioned these cases, thinking they might possibly prove encouraging to Beauregard's friends; but he had no suggestions to make as to how their young relative might be traced, other than through the usual channels. He did not, like Sherman, himself suggest checking the prisons and hospitals; however, he did say that if any helpful information came to his attention, he would be glad to pass it along.

This letter had seemed like such an anticlimax to Sherman's, which had moved them all so deeply, that Pierre had not even taken it to show his landladies. Now he decided to do so, after all. It would at least prove to them that his appeal had not been ignored. And McDowell could be right in believing that the examples he cited might be of some encouragement.

As Pierre had foreseen, he was instantly aware that Mme Castel had quickly observed and as heartily approved his new suit. But, contrary to his expectation, she did mention it.

"Won't you let my mother feel the cloth?" she asked. "She always took so much interest in nice materials and it's a long time since she's had a chance to touch any. If it wouldn't annoy you——"

"Of course, it wouldn't annoy me," Pierre said. And as he stood before Mme Cougot and she ran her fingers lightly, but knowingly, over the fine fabric that Falk had managed to get, heaven knew how, at the price Pierre had stipulated, he found his own pride and pleasure in it doubled. He was careful not to hurry her delighted appraisal; and it was only when she sighed and folded her hands in her lap, smiling as she did so, that he took McDowell's letter from his pocket.

"I'm afraid you will not think this amounts to much," he said. "But, after all, perhaps the reminder of the number missing after Shiloh should give us encouragement. As McDowell says, a great many of those men must still be alive."

"Yes, and it wouldn't be any stranger if Lance came home than that this other boy—the one whose brother went looking for him with a lantern—finally turned up. Would it, General?"

"No, except—" He stopped abruptly.

"Except that he turned up in a year and that Lance has been missing for three. That's what you started to say, isn't it?"

"Yes, but I shouldn't have. I should have reminded you instead about this other boy—the one who still can't remember who he is. But he will some day. Something like what happened to him may have happened to Lance. If it has, he'll remember some day, too."

"Yes. Of course he'll remember some day if that was what happened. You're right, it probably was."

It was Mme Castel who had spoken, but her mother was nodding in agreement and her fine old face, which had seemed to him so parchmentlike in texture when he had first seen her, was now more like alabaster, lighted from within. He drew a little closer to her and, in the way that now seemed so natural to him, took her hand.

"Tell me a little more about Lance," he said. "So far, I've been thinking of him only as a son and grandson of two wonderful women whom I admire very much. I'd like to begin to think of him more as a person, as an individual in his own right. What did he look like? What were his tastes—his talents? Was there anything special he enjoyed doing or disliked doing?"

"He was a good-looking boy," Simone said quickly. "Well, naturally, you'd expect me to say that, because I'm his mother, but he really was. He was well built and he had clear fair skin and brown hair and big gray eyes."

"In short, he looked a good deal like you."

Simone blushed and the blush was very becoming. Pierre wondered, for the hundredth time, how he could possibly have mistaken her for an old woman the first time he saw her. She was not old at all and she was extremely attractive.

"I think he did, a little," she went on hurriedly. "Only he was better looking—that is, he would have been, except for his limp. And he liked all the things most boys do—sports and games, I mean. He was crazy about music—military music. If he so much as heard a drum—"

Pierre laughed. He could not remember when he had laughed before. "I can see that Lance and I are going to be kindred spirits," he said. And, for the first time in his life, with spontaneity and without shame, he told the story of the abortive incident when he had failed to make his First Holy Communion. "And so Lance decided to be a drummer boy, in order to beat a drum himself," he added.

"Yes. I think that really did have a lot to do with his wanting to enlist. I mean, at first. But afterward, he thought things through more seriously. As one man after another in the family was killed, Lance said, undoubtedly someone would have to take his place. And finally he was the only male member of the family left. And as he was just fourteen, the one way in which he could enlist was as a drummer boy. But he could have waited another two years. No one was trying to make him go to war. In fact, I'm afraid we were trying to hold him back, Mother and I both. Because he *was* the only one left, and it was hard, very hard."

Silence fell on the room, as it so frequently had when Pierre first began going there. The happy mood he had succeeded in creating by his story about his own early passion for drums had been engulfed in a somber one. I should not have said what I did about the boy's reason for enlisting, he told himself bitterly. Of course, I meant it as a jest and I've been reminded before that it's still too soon for these women to jest about anything; it will never be possible for them to jest about the patriotism of a beloved, sacrificial boy. Now I must try to do something to recapture some of the previous feeling we all had about happy companionship. Perhaps some inconsequential question might be helpful, a question similar to those I asked to make Lance seem more of a person in his own right.

"You haven't said anything about Lance's scholastic record," he reminded Mme Castel, without attempting a labored preamble. "Was he a good student?"

"He loved history and he was a good mathematician, but—"

"More and more you're convincing me that Lance and I are kindred spirits, Madame!"

"*But* he was a very poor linguist and you're a remarkable one. That is, you're trilingual, aren't you?"

"Yes, but that's not remarkable, under the circumstances. Almost everyone spoke some Spanish in Terre-aux-Boeufs when I was a boy. Why even the old cemetery is still called San Bernardo de Nuevo Galvez! That's what it was named by the Isleños, who were brought over from the Canary Islands when Galvez was governor and who settled south of New Orleans as trappers and fishermen." He paused, involuntarily thinking about the old cemetery. But he must not allow himself to dwell on that. If he did, they would be back where they were a few minutes earlier, in the depths of a depression from which he was trying to rescue them. "And then, of course, it came in handy during the Mexican War," he went on. "I was called on, quite often, to interpret for others when I was the only Spanish-speaking officer around. As far as that went, not many of the officers spoke French, either—not in Mexico or at West Point or anywhere I've been in the last four years. I was enrolled at West Point as Peter G. T. Beauregard and how I hated it! Then when I went to Montgomery in Sixty-one, to offer my services to Jefferson Davis, Leroy Walker, the Secretary of War, referred to me in the same way, even when he wrote to Governor Pickens that I had been appointed to command the provisional forces at Charleston. That was the last straw. I couldn't stomach the Peter! I started signing myself G. T. Beauregard and I've done it ever since. But, naturally, I still think of myself as Pierre, that's what my good friends still call me." He leaned closer to the blind woman's chair. "It's what I'd like to have you call me," he told her. "Not now, if you'd rather not. But when Lance comes home, as part of the celebration." He stopped again, struck by a sudden thought. "You said Lance wasn't a good linguist," he said, turning toward Simone. "Just what did you mean? That he wasn't fluent in French or that he wasn't fluent in English?"

"That he wasn't fluent in English. You see, we never spoke it at home. . . . Oh, General Beauregard, what have I said wrong? Why do you look at me like that?"

"You haven't said anything wrong!" Without realizing it, he was almost shouting in his excitement. "We never spoke English in my home, either—not at Contreras, not at Upper Magnolia. But don't you *see?* If no one in the military circles where I moved could master enough French to call me Pierre, instead of Peter, why should we think for a moment that anyone who picked up Lance—either as a prisoner or as a casualty—would understand a word he was saying to them? The reason he hasn't been found yet is probably because he fell in with an outfit of worse linguists than he is himself!"

❧ 14 ❧

First reconnaissances showed singularly difficult terrain around San Augustin [about twenty-five miles from
Mexico City]. The Acapulco road to Mexico City led northward to a hacienda known as San Antonio, distant about three
miles. Although quite practicable for the wagon train and the
artillery, this highway was swept for a long distance by gunfire
from San Antonio, which was found to be heavily fortified. It
was not possible to avoid this road by marching to the east of
it, because there the ground was so soft that wheeled vehicles
would be mired. Nor did it seem possible to turn San Antonio
from the west, because the most conspicuous feature of the
landscape was on that side—a great field of lava, more than
five miles wide on its east-and-west axis and three miles long,
from north to south, broken into great blocks and fissures—a
hopeless barrier to the advance of the guns or the trains.
Such a tract of volcanic scoria was known locally as pedregal
and bore an evil name. Furthermore, even if a way for the infantry could be found through the pedregal, so that they
could turn San Antonio without artillery support, their advance would be halted in another two miles at the town and
river Churubusco, which had not been reconnoitred but were
believed to be heavily fortified. In short, an advance up the
Acapulco road seemed an almost hopeless undertaking. . . .

Never, perhaps, in American history did a force of such
limited numbers include so many men of future eminence as
the column that filed westward from San Augustin on the
morning of August 19. Twiggs and Pillow, the commanders,
are now mere names, but some of their subordinates will long
be remembered. Lee was in general charge of the reconnaissance; Lieutenant P. G. T. Beauregard was one of his assist-
ants. Lieutenant G. B. McClellan of the engineer company
was there with his captain, Gustavus W. Smith, who was sub-
sequently a major general in the Confederate armies. Captain
Joseph Hooker was assistant adjutant general to General Pil-

low. One of the two light batteries that accompanied the infantry was commanded by J. Bankhead Magruder, who, in the early spring of 1862, opposed McClellan on the peninsula of Virginia. Magruder's lieutenant was an awkward young man who had been transferred from the dismounted 1st Artillery, when Magruder had received his guns. That morning, perhaps for the first time, Lee saw this quiet "Mr. Jackson" who was to be his own most trusted lieutenant fifteen years thereafter, the "Stonewall" of the Army of Northern Virginia.

Under the direction of these men the troops slowly advanced, covering the working party engaged in the difficult work of turning a mule path into a road fit for artillery and wagons.

—Douglas Southall Freeman, *R. E. Lee: A Biography*, Vol. I
(Scribner's)

"The castle was completely torn to pieces; nearly every part was riddled by our shot, while the pavements and fortifications were completely torn up by the shells. In it were crowds of prisoners of every rank and color; among whom were fifty general officers, and about a hundred cadets of the Mexican military academy. The latter were pretty little fellows, from ten to sixteen years of age. Several of them were killed fighting like demons, and indeed they showed an example of courage worthy of imitation by some of their superiors in rank."

Thus was Chapultepec taken. Its rocky heights—its strong batteries—its military college—its mines—its succoring army— were all in vain. The heroes who had stormed the hill of Contreras, the intrenchments of Churubusco, and the King's Mill, failed not here. Chapultepec is taken, and the great causeways to Mexico are no longer defended by fortresses. The gates alone remain.

—Edward D. Mansfield, *The Mexican War: A History of Its
Origin* (A. S. Barnes)

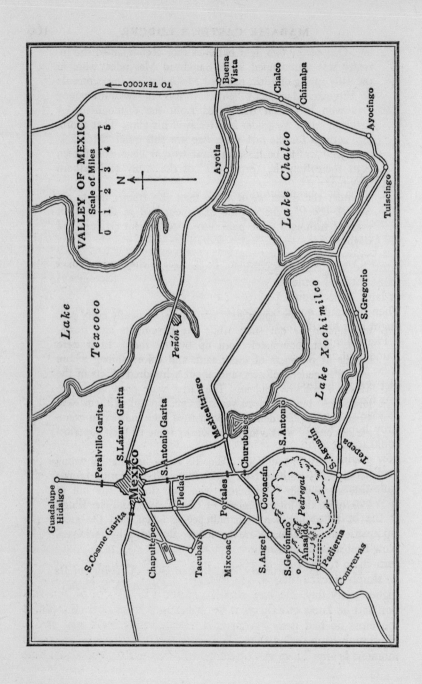

❧

HIS EXCITEMENT WAS CONTAGIOUS. FOR A FEW MOMENTS THE ROOM, which had been so oppressively silent, actually rang with jubilation. Of course, of course, that was why they hadn't heard from Lance! He might have been wounded, he might have been in prison, but surely he was still alive! The reason they had not heard from him was because he had not been able to make himself understood, because he was still unidentified by his rescuers or his captors. But sooner or later someone would come along who knew French, sooner or later Lance would pick up enough English to tell his own story. Then he would come home safe and sound. Why, any day now they might hear his step on the stairs.

Pierre did not have the heart to tell the two women that their new-found confidence was without firm foundation; as a matter of fact, he knew they would realize this only too well themselves, as soon as this first ecstasy had passed; and he did not want to be with them when this happened. Tomorrow would be time enough; by then he would be able to frame appropriate words which would temper, but not destroy hope. Meanwhile, without being selfish or seeming abrupt, he could return to his own work. He told Mme Cougot and Mme Castel how gratified he was that he had thought of possible language difficulties as a partial solution of the mystery surrounding Lance and bade them a courteous good night.

When he reached the quarters, Pierre sat for some moments staring at the bulky script which he had just lifted from the first of the japanned boxes on his worktable, the one that was almost empty. Now that he was sure no one would touch his papers, he did not return them to the original places every night as he had done at first; he simply stacked them to one side in a neat pile, which grew a little higher every day. He had almost reached the bottom of this first box and he knew exactly what he would find there next: the pitiful souvenirs he had gathered together after Laure's death and burial. He shrank from seeing them, but, after all, this might be as good a moment as any. There was no reason why he should spend much time on the script he was now holding; he could use it again, just as it was, for the same purpose that he had used it originally: that is, to set the records straight. He had written every word of that script himself, in 1852, and had seen to it that copies of it were circulated among his friends, both civilian and military, and widely disseminated elsewhere. It bore a lengthy title: *Personal Reminiscences of an Engineer Officer During the Campaign in Mexico Under General Winfield Scott in 1846–48*, which would deal with the war in its entirety, rather than the part he had played in it; he thought the scope of this subject might even justify a book instead of a slim pamphlet. He had always read history avidly; as things were in 1852, he felt in a position to write it. But, unfortunately, the personal memoirs were so casually and unfruitfully viewed that the idea of supplementing these died aborning. It was only now, after all these years, that he began again to visualize a book. And, this time, the Mexican War was playing only an incidental part in it; the script that lay before him would make two or three chapters at most; by and by, he would insert them in their proper place, chronologically speaking. For the moment, he would not even read them through.

But, in the very act of putting the script aside, atop the growing pile of papers, he changed his mind, and began leafing through it. This was not, he tried to tell himself, in order that he might postpone taking the last things from the first box. It was because, both as a middle-aged man and as a high-ranking officer who had led great armies into battle, he would have a better perspective on the Mexican War than a man still in his twenties, who was a mere lieutenant and who had been smelling gunpowder for the first time. To be sure, he had been brevetted captain and major before he left Mexico; but, as far as his salary went, he was still only a first lieutenant when he wrote those *Personal Reminiscences*, the script of which now lay before him. That was part of the trouble. He had penned those lines when he was smarting with a sense of injustice. Others, who had done less than he, had been *really promoted*; moreover, nowhere had proper credit been given him for having shown General Scott how to capture Mexico City.

General Scott! "Old Fuss and Feathers!" Pierre saw him as he was at the beginning of the War Between the States—a red-faced, obese man, soon to be retired for incompetency—not as he had been at the beginning of the Mexican War, when he was in the prime of life and at the height of his considerable powers. It was not an accurate visualization, it was not even a reasonably fair one. But however hard he might try—and he confessed to himself that he did not try very hard—he could not see otherwise the man he had once thought he wanted for his father-in-law. The first disappointment in the Mexican War for Pierre had come when the troops sailed from New Orleans for Corpus Christi without him. The second had come when Winfield Scott and not Zachary Taylor was to be his commanding officer. He knew that the original plan had been to invade Mexico via Vera Cruz; but this had been temporarily abandoned in favor of a land attack; and the brilliant victory at Palo Alto and subsequent successful skirmishes with Taylor in command had led to the general and logical conclusion that the disputed territory would be the main theater of military operations. Zachary Taylor was the hero of the day and, like everyone else, Pierre worshiped him as such. Taylor's son-in-law, Colonel Jefferson Davis, was sharing some of the spotlight. If memory served and rumor were well founded, General and Mrs. Taylor had opposed the marriage of their daughter, Sarah Knox, to Jefferson Davis, with just as much determination as General and Mrs. Scott had opposed the marriage of their daughter, Virginia, to Pierre Gustave Toutant Beauregard. But, somehow, Sarah Knox and Jefferson Davis had prevailed; and, once the alliance was a *fait accompli*, the Taylors not only accepted it with good grace, but had smiled upon it. Even the untimely death of Sarah Knox had not affected the closeness of the bond between the Taylors and their son-in-law; they had mourned together and now the two men were going forward together with a background of mutual esteem. Neither one begrudged the other his success; affection and respect were proof against jealousy.

Rather wryly, Pierre wondered whether or not his relations with Scott and, consequently, the reports sent in by Scott and the importance given these by his fellow officers might have been different if his first ill-starred romance had not been thwarted. He rather thought they would have. And this was exactly the sort of thing he could say now, if he chose, though, of course, nowhere was there any hint of it in those personal reminiscences which, after all, were not in the least personal, as far as any intimate disclosures were concerned. So perhaps there were other reasons, which had not at first occurred to him, why it would be well for him to read the memoirs carefully, with a view to expanding them, though, for the moment, he continued merely to leaf through them, pausing from time to time before some entry that especially arrested his attention.

By the time he was on his tardy way to Mexico, a third plan of action had been developed in the higher echelons, for President Polk did not share the popular rejoicing over Taylor's victories, which

made the general a formidable political rival. It was therefore decided that Taylor was to be left where he was, with a greatly reduced
force, but that the major part of his troops was to proceed to Tampico—the supply base already in occupied territory—where they would
be joined by forces taken from other theaters. When all arrangements were complete, the Navy would transport the combined forces
first to the Lobos Islands and thence to the nearby port of Vera
Cruz. From Vera Cruz, the national highway led straight to the
capital city of Mexico. The main point of difference between this and
the original plan was that Winfield Scott and not Zachary Taylor
was to be commander-in-chief.

For the first few months of his service in Mexico, this difference
did not much affect Pierre. Taylor was still on the defensive at Mon-
terey and destined to remain there; Scott had not yet arrived in Mexico. Pierre was delighted with his work, with his associates and with
his post. Tampico was a pleasant city, beautifully located and well
provided with amenities. Pierre's predecessor in charge of defenses,
Captain Barnard, remained long enough to familiarize his relief with
the plans of fortification and they became fast friends; the other
young engineers were all congenial, especially Lieutenant Smith and
Captain Lee. When Colonel Totten arrived to make a visit of inspection, he pronounced himself greatly pleased with what had been
done; in his report to the War Department, he sang Pierre's praises
and announced that he was ordering that Lieutenant Beauregard
should be prepared to join the first big offensive of the war, which was
then imminent. Scott's arrival was hailed with flying flags, martial
music and booming guns—all the trappings of war that Pierre loved.
When he left Tampico aboard the *Alabama*, to join Scott's army, he
was still in the highest spirits, and so was everyone else. The sailors
were singing:

"We are now bound for the shores of Mexico
And there Uncle Sam's soldiers we will land-oh!"

and the young officers took up the refrain.

Spirits were still high when the troops landed at Vera Cruz. Beauregard was not immediately aware of friction or favoritism. Scott, who
was without formal military training himself, far from resenting it in
others, welcomed it warmly. The Engineer Company, of which Pierre
was a member, was one to which he kept close, working with it effectively and, like Totten, praising it in his reports. Pierre was thrilled
because he had been briefly under fire when Scott, taking his principal
generals and the engineering corps with him, went in a small steamer

to inspect the place which Commodore Conner considered most suitable for landing. The Mexicans' scattered shots were all wide of the mark and, when the landing actually did take place, none were fired. The proceedings were almost theatrical. The first contingents went ashore in surf boats, while mosquito gunboats shelled the beach to cover them, and the regimental bands played patriotic airs. The initial landing party planted the flag on a sandhill and a tremendous shout arose to be drowned by saluting guns. Ships of several nationalities—English, French, Spanish—were anchored in the harbor and their officers lined up on deck and watched the progress of events with eagerness and attention; so did the inhabitants of Vera Cruz, who thronged the city walls. By night, the army, ten thousand strong, was ashore without a single untoward incident. Pierre had never known such exaltation of spirit.

In the course of the next few weeks some of the glamour wore off. Scott decided to take the city by siege, rather than by assault, basing his procedure on teachings by Vauban, a great French engineer. This involved the digging of trenches, completely encircling their objective, and working as much as possible within this protection, and the construction of platforms on which siege cannon could be mounted. The platforms, in turn, were shielded by massive earthworks thrown up before them, most of the labor on these being done under cover of darkness.

The work itself was thrilling; the conditions under which it had to be done were something else again. The days were terribly hot, the nights terribly cold, and the seasonal winds wrought havoc with tents and filled the trenches with debris. But if the weather were a torment, the insects were a plague. In desperation, Pierre and his companions greased themselves all over with lumps of fat salt pork and slept, or tried to sleep, in canvas bags.

As it became evident that some of the large cannon from the warships would have to be brought ashore to replace the smaller siege guns, the larger weapons had to be dismounted, ferried to the beaches and dragged by main strength to the platforms from which they would be directed against the fortress walls. The continuous, unremitting labor of a hundred men and twenty horses for nearly twenty-four hours was needed to put the guns of even a single battery into position; but, overcoming all such obstacles, preparations for the siege were finally completed. The bombardment which followed was beyond the endurance of both the civilian population and the military forces in Vera Cruz. Within a matter of days, the garrison com-

mander surrendered the city and its defenders formally laid down
their arms.

The heat, the cold, the winds, the insects, the hard work, the long
hours—none of these had affected Pierre's spirits in the least. But he
had been running a fever for several days before the surrender and
after it and, as there was nothing more to demand his attention and
his services or to buoy him up, he was persuaded, without much difficulty, to stay in bed. He was still there when news of Totten's report
about the siege reached him. The colonel stated that the engineers
were responsible for the position, form and arrangement of the
trenches and batteries and commended each officer by name. But he
commended them equally. He made no mention of the fact that
Pierre had located most of the batteries which reduced the city; he
failed to recommend promotion on this score.

Pierre had written quite frankly about his resentment of this in the
Personal Reminiscences and now, nearly thirteen years later, the para-
graphs he was reviewing were among those which outlined this resentment: "Out of the five batteries which reduced the city of Vera Cruz,
I had the honor (with Lieutenant G. W. Smith) to select the position of three of them! During the siege, one or two other batteries
were established along our parallel, but they never opened. Now, in
his report of that siege, what does the Chief Engineer, who ought,
above all, to be extremely jealous of the reputation of his subordinate
officers, say? 'That all his officers behaved so well and did their duty
so faithfully and zealously that it would be invidious to distinguish
between them.' Without wishing to detract one iota from the reputation of my brother officers, who during that siege displayed constantly that activity, intelligence and gallantry for which they are so
well renowned (conspicuous amongst them, however, were Captain
Lee and Lieutenant McClellan), have I not the right, if not to complain, at any rate to feel surprised and pained at his lack of memory
in this instance? If the thing was not very important in itself, yet to
me, it was 'more than my all'; for I had done there more than my
legitimate duty, not only in selecting the position of those batteries,
but especially in condemning one *which I had received orders to mark
out!*

"History tells us that on one occasion, the establishment of a battery stamped a young officer of artillery as a very promising one in the
eyes of his superiors! and although far from pretending to such a high
aspiration and not wishing in the least to establish a comparison
between us, I was certainly entitled on that occasion, if not to a

brevet, at any rate, to at least a passing notice in the official reports of the Chief Engineer!"

This was not the first, nor was it to be the last, entry in which he presumed to suggest that he was worthy of comparison with his idol, Napoleon Bonaparte; and, much as he admired Lee, he had begun to feel touchy because so much emphasis was laid on the young Virginian's perfections, and because the narrow escape which the latter had had from a serious wound was creating so much excitement. Robert and Pierre had started back to the lines from the position of a working party, along a narrow path cut through the brush, when, at a turn in this path, they were suddenly challenged by one of their own men. Robert called out, "Friends!" and, in the same breath, Pierre shouted, "Officers!" But quick as the answer had come it was not swift enough; the sentry, convinced that Mexicans were upon him, had already fired. The bullet passed between Robert's left arm and his body, singeing his uniform; a very slight deviation in aim would certainly have been serious and might have been fatal. General Scott, enraged, declined to overlook the sentinel's recklessness and insisted on the severest discipline.

The episode was the talk of the camp and, in the course of it, there were occasional comments to the effect that the way the two engineers had answered the challenge was characteristic: Robert would always instinctively say that he was a friend; Pierre would always instinctively say that he was an officer. The comments were not ill-natured, but sometimes they became tinged with slight sarcasm at Pierre's expense. A few weeks later, he himself had a narrow escape from a serious accident and, instead of being dramatic, it was humiliating: as he was getting ready to mount, his horse reared and then came down hard on his foot, tearing off a nail. This time the camp comments were definitely jesting; did the loss of a toenail enter the category of military wounds, Pierre's friends wanted to know, clapping him on the shoulder. He limped away from them, almost as angry as Scott had been over the sentinel and, still seething with rage, recorded the incident in his diary. He was pleased when, later on, he could record two more standard and less humiliating wounds.

After the capture of Vera Cruz, Scott had kept the main body of his forces at the port long enough to consolidate it as a base of supplies for future operations, meanwhile sending a field force under General Twiggs and General Patterson up the road to the interior to open the way for the final assault on Mexico City itself. Pierre, attached to this force as senior Engineer Officer, was put in charge of reconnaissance and Santa Anna's hacienda, Mango de Clavo, from which the general had prudently retreated, lay directly on the way to the American Army's first major objective. "Stopped there one hour," Pierre wrote in his diary. "Drank Santa Anna's health with his own champagne and fought his own gamecocks." In his letter to Laure, he was somewhat more expansive.

> Mango de Clavo is situated about halfway between Vera Cruz and Jalapa and comprises about twelve square leagues—that is, it's about four times the size of Upper Magnolia—and there are herds of cattle and flocks of sheep roaming all over it. There isn't a garden, I mean, not what we would call one—I understand Santa Anna boasts that the whole country is a garden and that, therefore, he doesn't need to enclose a special section for one. I can see what he means, for the place is a regular riot of acacia, ferns and fruit trees, with tangled masses of roses—such roses as you never saw—sprawling in the most unexpected places and morning glories climbing over the tree trunks. The house itself isn't large, but it's very elegant, and it's said the banquets Santa Anna gives there are regular Lucullan feasts. We'd all been looking forward to seeing a unique and rather bizarre attraction—the tomb where Santa Anna buried the leg he lost in the so-called Pastry War with France. But he'd had it put in a crystal urn and transferred to the Santa Paula Cemetery in Mexico City, where it was placed in a very fanciful monument at a ceremony with all sorts of speeches, &c. I wish I could have seen it. Well, anyway, I'll go and have a look at the monument when we get to Mexico City and write you all about it then. Meanwhile, I certainly enjoyed our brief stay at the hacienda.

There were not many such diversions, however. Santa Anna had disposed his forces to command the valley along which the Americans must advance, dominating this from the heights of Cerro Gordo—Fat Hill. Scouting, Pierre discovered a trail which indicated the existence of a road by which Cerro Gordo might be bypassed and attacked from the rear, while its defenders' attention was held by a frontal feint. Before he could fully explore this route, he was felled by a recurrence of the intermittent fever to which he was subject and confined to his tent. Completion of the reconnaissance was assigned to Captain Robert E. Lee, who later received equal commendation with Beauregard for their share in Santa Anna's subsequent rout; and thus another faggot was added to the smoldering fuel of Pierre's resentment.

As a matter of fact, there was plenty of glory to go around, regardless of its division. Santa Anna, who had been the victor of the Alamo's bloody massacre and the vanquished captive of Sam Houston at San Jacinto, failed lamentably in his defense of Cerro Gordo; and, after a smashing victory, the American forces pushed forward to Puebla, where they remained for nearly three months, while Scott engaged in petty quarrels with Nicholas Trist, Chief Clerk of the State Department, who had been sent—without previous notice to the general—to pave the way for negotiations that might presumably lead to peace. Nothing could have been better calculated to spur Scott on to further war efforts. But he bided his time, organizing his forces for his final push and waiting for reinforcements, which arrived under the command of Franklin Pierce, in whom Pierre almost immediately thought he discovered great qualities, though his opinion was not a universal one among the junior officers. Meanwhile, Scott had been collecting information, through his own engineers and through Mexican spies, regarding the roads leading to the capital and its defenses. Pierre had taken an active part in this reconnoitering, except while totally incapacitated by his injured foot; but most of the time he had managed to persevere, despite this handicap, for in the clear air of the highlands he had shaken off his fever. By the time the troops had been reorganized to include the additional numbers and marching orders issued—namely by the seventh of August—he was himself again.

The march lasted five days and brought the army to Ayotla, on the northern shore of Lake Chalco, at the very rim of the heights where they could look down on the Valley of Mexico. The sight which met their astonished eyes was one of beauty as extraordinary as it was unforgettable; it included ten crumbling volcanoes, six sparkling lakes, and countless expanses of emerald-green terrain dotted with quaint villages whose steeples pierced a cloudless sky of turquoise blue. But from the military standpoint, the scene presented many obstacles, though there were three ways by which Mexico City could be reached from this point: a direct road, which ran on a causeway between lakes and marshes and was crowned by a high hill, El Peñon; a long circuitous road to the north around Lake Texcoco; and a somewhat shorter route, which skirted the southern shores of both Lake Chalco and Lake Xochimilco, and which was said to be in very bad condition.

Though Scott had often found flank movements useful, he naturally wanted to take the shortest route if he could; but reports had already reached him that Santa Anna, who had not fought since Cerro Gordo, was now strongly entrenched at El Peñon, and the northern route would necessitate a long march. It therefore behooved Scott to find out first whether or not the reports about Santa Anna were correct; second, whether or not the northern route was so good as to justify the extra marching time and, third, whether or not the southern route was actually impassable. Again, the Engineering Corps had its work cut out for it.

Lee with his group was sent in one direction—toward El Peñon; Pierre with his group in another—around Lake Texcoco; the afternoon of the same day—August 12—both groups worked along Lake Chalco and ascertained that the route south of the lake was rough but passable. The following day they combined forces to reconnoiter El Peñon at close range. They returned with the news there was no doubt that the reports about the fortification of the hill were true. It could be taken, they thought, but with heavy losses, because the army would be confined to the narrow causeway for its stand. Scott lost no time in reaching his decision: he would proceed by the southern route.

Pierre was assigned as Engineer Officer to the advance division commanded by General Worth, and was consequently in the vanguard of the army as it entered the town of San Agustín, just beyond the western extremity of Lake Xochimilco. This seemed on the face of it an excellent position, for Mexico City lay due north. But Santa Anna had also been active. He had withdrawn his forces from El Peñon and was now at San Antonio, in the direct line of the Americans' intended march. They would be at the same disadvantage in a battle there as they were before, because they would have to fight from a causeway. Once again a detour seemed the only solution. But, this time, a detour involved more of a handicap than the previous one: crossing a huge lava bed called the Pedregal, where a raging molten mass had hardened into alternating sharp rocks, treacherous fissures and deep pits. Lee and Pierre were promptly dispatched to cross it. If the report they brought back was to the effect that at least part of the army could get over it, and reach the so-called San Angel road on the other side, running north, Scott could flank Santa Anna out of San Antonio.

The young engineers returned with the assurance that they had found a path which could be developed into a road. Scott did not lose a moment, either in making up his mind or getting the work started; the next day the engineers began to build the road. But, as the work progressed, Mexican pickets stationed at Padierna hacienda, near the village of Contreras, attacked the work party and Captain Lee reported that operations would have to be suspended until the Mexican force was driven off. As a result of this report, Scott sent forward artillery to engage the Mexican batteries, but the American guns were not sufficiently heavy to silence these, though they did serve the useful purpose of keeping the enemy occupied while Scott dispatched infantry to make a wide circle across the Pedregal and come down on the enemy's rear.

These additional troops required guiding, which Pierre was detailed to undertake. He led them over the rocky ground to the village of San Geronimo; once safely there, General Cadwalader, who was among the new arrivals, ordered his guide back to Scott's headquarters for still more help. Pierre was deeply disappointed. By this time, it was plain that a real battle was imminent and the smell of powder seemed sweet. However, he had no choice and doggedly started to retrace his steps. But luck at last was with him: as he was crossing a ravine, he met General Percival Smith, the ranking officer on the field, and pled with him for permission to return to San Geronimo, whither Smith was headed. The general, who needed a guide himself, agreed that, under the circumstances, the orders could be changed; he would take Lieutenant Beauregard with him to reconnoiter the Mexicans' position.

This reconnaissance revealed the startling fact that Santa Anna had moved about three thousand men to San Angel, a few miles to the north of Smith's forces, which consisted of about thirty-five hundred, without artillery or cavalry. This meant that the Americans were now caught between two forces, the one at Padierna and the one at San Angel. The position was perilous. Smith called his officers together and, in spite of some dissenting opinions, decided to attack that night. Pierre was among those who had not looked with favor on this plan and was relieved when the coming of darkness made it impractical. The night would have to be spent at San Geronimo after all, Smith conceded, but they would attack the first thing in the morning. He was a slight, stoop-shouldered, sandy haired man who did not look as if he had enough will-power to be so stubborn. Pierre had never come across more convincing proof that appearances are deceptive.

If the first sight of the Valley of Mexico had been unforgettable, the vigil of that night was no less so—in a much different way. Rain fell in torrents and most of the men were without shelter. When they were too tired to stand any longer, they simply lay down on the muddy ground wherever exhaustion overcame them. Pierre and some of his young fellow officers were more fortunate; they had noticed the white spire of the village church, glimmering through the dusk and, finding the building unlocked, sought asylum there. It was in darkness, except for the Sanctuary lamp and the votive candles burning before some of the altars. But, as their eyes became adjusted to the dim light, the young men could see statues adorned with glittering ornaments and the stiff brocade and velvet robes, trimmed with gold lace, in which they were clothed, as well as other images, ashen of face and emaciated of body, which were realistically gory, the better to emphasize their sufferings and martyrdom. These figures awakened no reverence in many of the strangers; on the contrary, they were considered offensive. But Pierre, born and bred in Catholicism, recognized in the Saviour and saints thus represented the glories and the agonies which the humble worshipers in this massive church, cold and forbidding except for its shining altars and striking statues, could visualize in no other way.

At first he joined in the general desultory talk. Then he left the others and went to kneel at the rail of the main altar. Perhaps, he thought, the parish priest, seeing that his church had been entered by the enemy, might come there, if only to protect it from possible vandalism. In this case, Pierre would assure him that the intruders meant no harm, and ask if it were not possible to confess and communicate. But the night wore on and he continued to kneel, alone with his troubled thoughts and his incoherent prayers, while the rain, thudding down with greater and greater force on the roof, muted the hushed voices of his companions; and from time to time, as the rain slackened, from a distance came the sound of music and cheering in the enemy camp.

It was only two-thirty in the morning when Smith's troops were quietly alerted; but in the comparatively brief time Pierre and his fellow officers had been in the church, there had been several significant developments. Around midnight, a division commanded by General Shields, hastily dispatched across the Pedregal by Scott, had moved in to increase Smith's forces, which now numbered about four thousand men. More important still, additional scouts, reconnoitering after darkness descended, had discovered another possible route to Contreras, which would permit a flank movement instead of the frontal attack which Smith had originally planned; and Lee, who alone of seven engineers sent out, had succeeded over and over again in carrying messages between Scott and Smith, had informed the General-in-Chief of Smith's change of strategy, and had received the assurance that a simultaneous frontal attack would be made over the Pedregal.

Pierre was now placed with General Smith at the head of Cadwalader's lead brigade—a position which he rightly felt to be one of great honor and danger. This, at last, was war as he had wanted it, and all its drama, all its alarums and excursions, all its blood and thunder. When they reached their chosen position for attack from the rear, Smith had already heard the opening guns of Scott's frontal assault. He took out his watch. "Are you ready?" he asked cheerily. "Ready!" came the swift answer. "Then forward!" he ordered. The command flew down the ranks. Firing volleys, the troops rushed forward with fixed bayonets into the midst of the startled Mexicans, who were caught between two fires, not in prospect, but in reality. Taken completely by surprise and finding that bullets were coming at them from every direction, the confused infantry was soon mingled with horses, mules, artillery, ranch laborers and women in a riotous mob. Some of the gunners remained at their places, but, like the infantry, they did little aiming. Scattering, they fled northward, as Smith's forces, joined by the troops which continued to cross the Pedregal, pursued them up the San Angel road. The general took out his watch again. "The battle has lasted just seventeen minutes," he said. It was unbelievable, but it was true. Pierre had stolen a look at his own watch when Smith made the first announcement. Now he did so again. Though the pursuit to Churubusco lasted for hours, the Battle of Contreras was over.

This time, Pierre had no reason to complain that recognition of his services was lacking. The skillful scouting from Puebla and Ayotla, the painful crossing and recrossing of the Pedregal, had pointed the way to the triumph at Contreras and through his gallant conduct there he had earned his share in its glory. He was brevetted captain on the spot and given the honor of bearing the great news of the victory to Scott. Still intoxicated with triumph, he borrowed a horse from a Mexican prisoner and set off; but before he reached San Agustín, he met the general and his staff riding toward him and galloped forward with his triumphant story. Scott answered him with exuberance equal to his own: "Young man, if I were not on horseback, I would embrace you!" he exclaimed. Then, turning to his staff, he added, "Gentlemen, if West Point had produced only the Corps of Engineers, the country should be proud of that institution."

By this time, Pierre's cup of joy was filled to the brim and running over; forgotten were the insects, the *vómito*, the chills and fever, the torn toenail, the sharp rocks of the Pedregal. But, with the diffidence that marked most of the entries in his diary, Pierre failed to record this glowing praise, though he never forgot it. "I was sent to announce the victory to General Scott," he stated simply after noting, "The battle was terminated in a complete victory—the enemy having lost 800 killed and a 1,000 w. and 900 pris.—4 generals and 22 p. artillery."

The victors were not allowed to rest on their laurels. The general surged forward with his whole army to Churubusco, won another smashing victory and stood at the gates—the so-called *garitas*—of Mexico City itself. His first idea was to enter these from the south, and Lee was among the junior officers who agreed that this would be the best plan. Nevertheless, Scott sent the engineers to reconnoiter every possible approach and, after a series of such inspections, called a conference at Piedad to settle the issue. Pierre also had decided views on the subject of attack and unhesitatingly rose to express these; it should, he felt very strongly, be made from the western *garitas*, via Chapultepec, "and as much as possible be one of surprise, assisted by strong batteries of heavy pieces." It was his viewpoint which prevailed, seconded, though not proposed—as he proudly recalled—by General Pierce. His own account of the attack—less terse than the others—bore witness to his strategy.

The attack lasted only 1 h when at about 9 h the star spangled banner waved on top of the castle. During the attack I fired one of M howitzers until all ammunition was out. I then took the rifles of five or 6 volunteers & fired at 75 or 100 yards until the storming party rushed forward when I joined them and got in the 2nd or 3rd officer with about 12 or 20 men. After taking & saving some prisoners from our soldiers (amongst the former Lt. Ximenes of the Engrs) I went down the east side of the building by one of the windows & the steep slope with Lt. Rogers, U.S.N. & joined Gen'l Quitman's column moving on the Tacubaya road to the Guerita—& finding that Lt. Tower, Engr., was wounded I kept with him. We moved along both sides of the acqueduct & drove the enemy before us until we came to their first battery ½ way to the Guerita. There they fired upon us grape & canister and musketry, until Capt. Dunn and Lt. Benjamin came with 1.24 p how and 1-18 pdr sending them, the rifles, from arch to arch. . . . I was wounded slightly in the right arm by a spent m ball & smartly in the left thigh also by a spent m ball. We pursued them hotly and in attempting to reconnoitre their left at the Guerita, I fell into the canal but soon got out. . . . I received another wound from a spent grape in my life side, the ball remaining in my pocket, but I still kept on & after a severe struggle & the most terrific fire of ball, grape, cannister & musketry I ever witnessed we took the guerita & waited until night to erect our batteries and defences against the citidel. . . . Gen'l Quitman and myself whilst reconnoitering again fell into a canal and although I had been up one whole night & the whole day I commenced the batteries at about 9 p.m. & they were completed before daylight. . . . At daylight a white flag appeared from the citadel for its surrender. I went with gen'l aid Lt. Lovell to see about it & the troops shortly after marched in. . . . The U.S. flag was hoisted on the Palace of the Montezumas at 7 h. a.m. on fourteenth. Gen'l Quitman & myself were the first officers that entered the palace & I was sent to report the facts to Gen'l Scott. . . . A short while after reaching the palace, I was taken down with a violent attack of fever and ague which kept me in bed for several days and from the effects of which I did not entirely recover for several weeks.

It was probably because of this fever, Pierre decided, that there was one phase of the victory at Chapultepec which made him wince whenever he thought of it; there had been no such revulsion after the Battle of Contreras: the panic of the unarmed Mexican laborers caught in the melee, the carnage of the unalerted Mexican troops, had made no impression on him because he himself was charging gloriously forward in the thick of the fight, realizing his battle ideal at last. But the hopeless, resolute stand made by the cadets of the National Military School, housed in the ancient castle fortress of Chapultepec, had affected him differently. When first seen, at a relatively safe distance, these cadets, in their jaunty uniforms and tasseled caps, looked like small boys who had dressed up for fun. As a matter of fact, they were practically children, some of them barely in their teens, none of them as old as twenty. But with the American troops closing in on them from every side, they had stood their ground and fought to the finish. Six of them were killed, then and there, two of these in hand-to-hand combat; afterward, the survivors —a hundred in all—were taken prisoner. It was more than ironic, it was tragic, that these brave little fellows, who had fought with such gallantry and determination, should have learned about war through actual experience, in the very school where they were studying its theory. One boy had stood so defiantly at his gun during the height of the attack, daring the onrushing Americans to shoot him, that not one of them had the heart to do so. He was among those hundred prisoners and Pierre heard it said the boy's mother had told him, beforehand, that she would rather see him dead with honor than alive with disgrace. Well, she would see him alive, when the exchange of prisoners was effected, and Pierre hoped she would recognize his heroism and not his failure. But you could never tell. Wasn't there some story about the mother of a Greek warrior who had told her son to return with his shield or on it? This boy would be doing neither.

As the fever dropped and the pain of his wounds abated, Pierre thought less and less about the cadets, except when he was reminded of them by some reference to the *niños héroes* (child heroes), as they were already called; there were rumors that statues would be erected on the parapet they had defended, to immortalize those who were killed. But other impressions, other experiences, came crowding in upon Pierre to dim the memories that had so disturbed his fevered dreams. He himself was now hailed as a hero; and he basked in the satisfaction and pride this gave him, to the exclusion of less pleasurable reflections. His convalescence was far from unpleasant. The officers of the various services had formed a society they called the Aztec Club and Pierre spent a good deal of time at its headquarters, while he and his companions rehashed the war which, to all intents and purposes, had ended with the capture of Chapultepec. Much of the time, while he was still abed, he lay listening to praise of his exploits—music to his ears. There were no more half-smothered sarcastic remarks, as there had been in Vera Cruz, when he proclaimed himself an officer to a sentry while Lee was mildly describing himself as a friend. Everyone was talking about his magnificent triumph at Contreras, the sagacity of the plan for attack on Mexico City that he had outlined at Piedad, of the well-merited honor he had received when he was chosen as the official messenger of victory. And, after he had recovered, one day when out riding with some of his fellow engineers, he met Scott, also out riding, and for the second time on such an occasion enjoyed a moment of signal recognition. The general reined in his horse and addressed Pierre with mock severity:

"Young man, I wish to reprimand you and I wish the whole army were present; but these generals represent it. Why did you advise me to attack by the western gates? You now see the consequences! We have taken this great city and the Halls of Montezuma after a few hours' fighting and a loss of only eight hundred men. Be careful in future, sir, to give such bad advice to your seniors."

It was unfortunate for Pierre's sake that the war could not have ended on this glorious note. For some time, he believed that it had; then he discovered, through the Register of Officers and Graduates of the United States Military Academy, that there were two officers in the Engineering Corps who had received three brevets, whereas he had received only two and had supposed, up to then, that no one except Lee had exceeded him in recognition. This he would have accepted; this he would have understood, even though it was he and not Lee who had done the most noteworthy reconnoitering and had expedited and facilitated the capture of Mexico City and who had twice been chosen to take the news of victory to the Commander-in-

Chief; he realized that Lee, rather than himself, had all the traditional attributes of a hero. But he could not tolerate the idea that any other junior officer had so exceeded him. The sense of slight and injustice which, throughout his career, was so often to rankle in his breast, had never been stronger than it was then.

Or was that quite true? Was it not even stronger now, years later? When he closed the copy of *Personal Reminiscences* through which he had been leafing, while he dwelt on other plans and events not therein recorded, he realized that his mood was more bitter than it had been in a long while. The brief feeling of exaltation which he had experienced early in the evening, because he had been able to fill the aching hearts of two lonely women with hope and joy, had long since evaporated. He was again the prey of the deep discouragement which pervaded most of his waking hours and to this was now added the corroding resentment his reading had reawakened.

❧ 15 ❧

THE STEAMSHIP PORTLAND, WHICH SAILED FROM VERA CRUZ on the 9th inst to the U. S. Quartermaster, arrived this morning. The following persons came passengers in the *Portland:*
Col. Bankhead, 2d. Artillery; Lieut. Bankhead, U.S.N.; Maj. Maingault, 13th Infantry; Quartermaster J. R. Page, do; H. H. Higgins, do; H. C. Clarke; E. J. Jones. Lieutenants —R. S. Heywood; J. C. Manasle; J. N. Perkins; S. S. Fahnestock; E. J. Dunnett, 13th Infantry; D. J. Wilds, do; S. H. Camps, do; W. F. Renes, do; E. F. Bayley, do; J. M. Ingle, do; Reynolds, do; Custis, do; Dr. Vanderburden and family; Dr. Banks; Captain Bernard, Captain Lee, Lieut. Beauregard, Engineers Corps; three hundred and fifty men of the 13th Infantry, Mr. Alex B. Forbes, with the bodies of the following persons: Lieut. Col. Baxter, Captain Pierson, Lieut. Chandler, Lieut. Gallagher, and Captains Van Olende and Barclay, of the New York Regiment.

—*Daily Crescent,* June 16, 1848

Lieut. Beauregard. We are glad to see that the services of this talented young Louisianian have been properly appreciated by the inhabitants of San Bernard and Plaquemine. A meeting of the inhabitants of those parishes was held on the 25th at the Station House of the Mexican Gulf railway for the purpose of celebrating the return of Lieut. Beauregard. A committee appointed to draft resolutions, reported in favor of presenting him a sword as a token of admiration.

—*Daily Crescent*, June 28, 1848

THE NEXT MORNING, WHEN HE WENT UP THE STEPS OF THE REAR gallery, his black and bitter mood had not changed. But Simone Castel, who was waiting for him, was still beaming, as she had been when he left her and her mother the evening before. Contrary to his expectations, their hopefulness had not been short-lived; it had survived the night, it was still strong in the morning hours; and when Pierre did not respond to her expressions of rejoicing, and she saw that he no longer shared it, a shadow fell on her own and she asked him, anxiously, if he still believed in the contingency they had discussed.

"Oh yes, I believe in it," he said, trying to speak heartily. And, seeing that his words did not carry conviction, he added, "As a matter of fact, I'll have to confess I didn't think much about Lance after I went back to the quarters. I started reading something I wrote a good many years ago and it depressed me."

"Could you tell me about it?"

"Why yes, I could, if you'd be interested."

"Of course I'd be interested."

She listened attentively to everything he told her, and he found himself speaking so freely and fluently that he talked for a long while. She did not stir until he had finished. Then she went to fetch fresh coffee and, after she had refilled both his cup and hers, she asked a pertinent question.

"It wasn't until you read the Register, some time after your home-coming from Mexico, that you began to feel bitter, was it?"

"No. I didn't realize that I had any reason to, until then. The homecoming itself was a period of triumph and joy."

"Well, while you were reminiscing, didn't you think at all about that? Wasn't it worth remembering, much more than the other?"

"Perhaps—yes, you're right, it was."

"Then couldn't you start thinking about that—right away?"

She smiled as she asked the question and suddenly his black mood lifted.

"I think perhaps I could. In fact, I shall."

That evening, he again failed to reach the bottom of the first japanned box. It was not because he consciously shrank from doing so, but because he was dwelling on that glorious homecoming and leaving papers which did not concern it undisturbed where they lay. Pierre was in the first detachment of troops to be returned from Mexico; and when the *Portland* steamed up the river toward New Orleans on a beautiful June day, the levee was crowded with throngs of cheering spectators. At the dockside, the crowds were even greater, the cheering even louder; as Pierre walked down the gangplank, his waiting friends quickly caught sight of him and called out to him; the cry was taken up by hundreds: "*Beauregard! Beauregard! Beauregard!*"

The sonorous name rang out above the music of the band and the uproar of the multitude; when he stepped ashore, so many surged forward to greet him, so many pressed closely around him, that he could not free himself and stride ahead, though he had caught a glimpse of Laure in the background and was determined to reach her side. After all, she was the only one he really wanted to see—that is, the boys, too, of course, but even they did not count beside Laure— or so he felt until he felt a different pressure against his knees and looked down to see that René was hugging them. The little boy had managed to break away from his mother and wriggle through the crowd, and here he was, fettering his father. His small happy cry of welcome had been drowned by the louder, more forceful voices, but his small arms were strong enough to prevail. Pierre leaned over and picked him up, swinging him shoulder high and sitting him down above the epaulettes. The crowd cheered more loudly than ever and parted now, so that Pierre could forge his way ahead to the place where Laure was waiting. Henri, holding fast to her hand, looked bewildered and not altogether happy. After all, he had been only a baby when his father went away; as far as that went, he was only three years old now, he could not be expected to remember, to understand, to rejoice. Pierre kissed him, of course, and Henri did not resist; but neither did he respond to this strange man in a blue uniform, though Laure came straight into his arms as naturally as if she had never left them and as if they were not surrounded by strangers in a public place. In the gladness of holding her to him after months and months of separation, he forgot to present the fellow officer who had followed him down the gangplank, and who was now standing quietly aside, unnoticed and unacclaimed, at the edge of the small space which the crowd had cleared around the reunited couple. Just in time to escape actual discourtesy, Pierre remembered.

"Laure, darling—" his voice was not quite steady, he was choked by emotion, but still he forced himself to go on. "I have a great friend here with me. You must welcome him, too. Captain Lee, this is my wife."

"I thought perhaps it might be." The second young engineer came forward, a slight twinkle in his eyes. But, as he bowed over Laure's hand, his manner was grave and courtly. Strikingly handsome though he was, he had the reserve of the Anglo-Saxon rather than the exuberance of the Latin. He was an alien in this tumultuous, vociferous crowd.

"I am so very happy to see you," Laure said sincerely. She was somewhat shaken and there were tears in her eyes—tears of joy, to be sure, but still tears. It was not altogether easy for her to give this outstanding young officer the welcome which was his due, because, for her, there was only one hero that day. But the courtesy which was almost as instinctive with her as breathing and loving came to her rescue. "You'll come home with us, of course? You must be our guest as long as you stay in Louisiana—that is, if your military duties permit."

"Thank you. But I must start north as soon as those obligations are discharged. I have a rather special welcome waiting for me in Virginia. I'm sure you'll understand."

"Captain Lee's wife is a direct descendant of Martha Washington," Pierre interposed. "They live at Arlington, the estate she inherited from George Washington Parke Custis."

"Where you must come to see us some time soon," Captain Lee said, bowing again.

"Not unless you will visit us first. Surely——"

But the impatient crowd was surging around them again and a minute later Captain Lee was lost to sight in it. Beauregards and

Villerés began to appear in large numbers, to be edged aside by the welcoming committee which, so far, had not been able to reach Pierre. He was separated from Laure and the boys and escorted to a waiting carriage, gaily decorated; it seemed he was to ride with the mayor, bowing and smiling right and left as he progressed through the streets, which were as crowded as the levee had been; and though he was able to rejoin his family later, he and Laure had very little time to themselves in the course of the next few weeks. Military duties were, indeed, largely suspended; but festivities, planned to celebrate his return, followed each other in quick succession. He was the idol of the state, of the city, of the two parishes—St. Bernard and Plaquemines—which both claimed him as theirs, though when it was decided to present him with a golden sword, Kenilworth, the home of his old friends the Bienvenues, and which had formed the charmed setting for his honeymoon, was chosen as the scene of the celebration.

Pierre was pleased at the selection; it would not have been suitable, of course, to have the celebration at Toutant, to make it appear that his immediate family was responsible for the presentation. But he was glad that it could take place in his own country, with lifelong friends as hosts, and not at City Hall or some such place in New Orleans, with municipal officials in charge. There was a great gathering of the clans at Kenilworth and his pride of race had never been stronger than when he saw them foregathered to do him honor—so many that the drawing rooms, spacious as these were, would not hold them all, and the ceremony took place on the lawn, under the shade of the great trees. He felt no embarrassment as one speaker after another extolled his prowess; praise had always encouraged and elated him, just as slights and criticism had always distressed and embittered him; but when he tried to reply, to thank his well-wishers and admirers, he was so greatly moved that he found he could not go on. As he accepted his golden sword, he stammered something totally inadequate, blushed deeply and sat down, without even fastening the sword in its proper place.

He and Laure were to spend the night in the *garçonnière* at Kenilworth before going on to Toutant to stay with his parents, and Pierre's mother had asked him to visit the old Spanish cemetery of San Bernardo de Nuevo Galvez, where his grandmother de Reggio was buried, and which Mme Jacques Toutant-Beauregard herself had been prevented from visiting lately, for one reason or another. It was diagonally across the road from Kenilworth on the further side of Bayou de Boeufs, which was narrow at this point and spanned by a little bridge; and, after breakfast, Pierre and Laure gathered some flowers and strolled over there together, taking the children with them. The boys ran about among the graves, chasing butterflies, playing ball with each other, and stopping now and then to examine one of the quaint shadow-boxes with which many tombs were ornamented. They had been taken, from infancy, not only to the family celebrations at *Toussaint*, but on frequent excursions when a cemetery was the objective, by no means always for a mournful reason; and it did not occur to them, or to their parents, that they should not play here. The lettering of the simple gray marble slab which marked the resting place of Louise Judith Olivier de Reggio needed to be sharpened a little, Pierre and Laure decided, as they placed their flowers in front of it. The inscription must not be permitted to become obscure. They traced it with their fingers as they had many times before:

LOUISE JUDITH OLIVIER

EPOUSE DE

LOUIS DE REGGIO

DECEDE

LE 21 Sept. 1811

A l'AGE

DE 48 ANS

QUE SES VIRTUES FASSENT

SOUVENIR

QU'EN VIVANT BIEN ON

NE CRAINT l'AVENIR

"Undoubtedly, she was very virtuous," Pierre said. "But of course she died before I was born, so I can't say that she set *me* a good example! And I remember how often Grandfather de Reggio said she could trace her line of descent all the way back to Adam and Eve, and I couldn't help being thankful she wasn't there to do it—we were treated to enough family history as it was! Also, I've often wondered . . . is it just leading a good life that saves us from fear of the future? Yes, I suppose so, when you're thinking of the future simply in terms of hellfire!"

"I don't think of it that way. I think of it as heaven. I believe our spirits come from there and that they return there. I've never been afraid of the future."

"There's never been any reason why you should, darling. And I believe you're right—I believe spirits do come from heaven and return there—spirits like yours, anyway. But perhaps Judith Olivier de Reggio needed more assurance on that score than you do, whatever they put on her tombstone about her virtues. . . . Well, we can report to *maman* that everything seems in order here, except that the inscription needs sharpening. There aren't any other tombs we're supposed to visit, are there?"

"No. But it's such a lovely peaceful place, I don't feel in a hurry to leave it. I'd like to think—"

"What, *chère?*"

"Well, that I'd be buried in a place like this when I die."

"Then remind me—fifty years or so from now. But don't talk about it today. Here I am, just back from war, alive, to find you and everyone else dear to me alive. . . . Why, what's the matter, Laure?"

"Nothing. Except that I couldn't help wondering. . . . You know when your mother said she hadn't been here lately, she told us it was 'for one reason or another.' Do you happen to know what the reasons are?"

"No, except that she's always very busy. Did you think there might be some other reason?"

"I didn't think she looked as well as usual and I thought she seemed very tired—very quiet. Of course, she never chatters. Just the same, without saying much, she usually gives the effect of enjoying herself and of adding to everyone else's enjoyment. Yesterday must have been one of the proudest occasions of her life and still—"

"It's no wonder she's tired. She's been going to party after party ever since I got home, and she isn't young any more. As far as that goes, I'm tired myself. But I'll have a good rest at Toutant."

"Yes, after the party to celebrate your homecoming."

"That's so. There is one more party, isn't there? But that's going to be just a family gathering, as I understand it, not a ceremonial like the one here at Kenilworth."

"Your mother hasn't told me exactly what she was planning. I think maybe something in the nature of a surprise. I noticed several times yesterday that people got off by themselves in small groups and laughed and whispered and then seemed to separate and stop talking whenever I went near them. I had the impression they were sharing some sort of a pleasant secret and that they didn't want me to know what it was. Of course, I could be mistaken. But when you talk about 'just a family gathering,' doesn't that include a good many people? Why, I've been to Toutant when there were twenty grown persons and twelve children at table and your mother said that was the *immediate* family! When you count all the Ducros and all the de Vezins and all the de Reggios, how many do you end up with? And I suppose at least a few Villerés will be invited at a time like this, don't you? Not to mention friends like the Bienvenues and the de la Vergnes and——"

"You needn't go on, Laure. I reckon it will be quite a gathering. So perhaps we'd better get started."

Not until after dinner, the Bienvenues insisted. Yes, they were coming, too, and they were quite sure no one was expected until evening. It was that kind of a party. What kind of a party, Pierre wanted to know. Why, the kind where carriagefuls and boatloads of people began to arrive about five and kept on arriving until supper-time and then danced afterward. No, there wasn't going to be any sort of presentation. On the other hand, there was something quite special about it. He would see. . . .

Even with Mme Bienvenue's warning, he was not in the least pre-pared for what he did see: the first extraordinary sight to meet their astonished eyes, as he and Laure and the children approached the driveway, was a triumphal arch curving above the entrance gates, on which the words VITOR BIENVENIDO A CONTRERAS were mounted in giant letters formed of roses. On either side of the driveway was lined up the personnel of the *atelier*, dressed in fresh white cotton. The women and children held baskets, heaped with roses, into which they dipped to throw flowers in the conqueror's path as he advanced; many of the male field hands were playing musical instruments—the same primitive substitutes for cymbals and drums and violins that they used in their New Year's dances. The men who were not playing were keeping time with their feet, some by shuffling, some by tapping; all were singing or chanting or shouting in welcome.

The gallery presented an abrupt change. At the top of the steps stood Pierre's father and mother, both magnificently clad; on either side of them were his brothers and sisters, his brothers-in-law and sisters-in-law, his nephews and nieces; beyond them were the aunts and uncles and cousins, all likewise clothed in splendor. From among them one of the younger boys, dressed like a medieval herald, stepped out and blew three times on a golden trumpet. Then he called, "Hear ye! Hear ye! Hear ye!" and bowed low before presenting, with a flourish, a scroll of parchment to Pierre's father. Jacques Toutant-Beauregard accepted it ceremoniously and read from it in a loud clear voice:

Whereas, our well-beloved son, PIERRE GUSTAVE TOUTANT-BEAURE-GARD, has now returned safe and victorious from a great war in which he was three times wounded and, over and over again, proved his prowess on the field of battle; and whereas, in one of these battles, to wit, that which took place in and around the village of CONTRERAS, in the volcanic region known as the PEDREGAL, he displayed qualities of such outstanding courage that he was then and there brevetted captain and selected to announce the complete victory to GENERAL SCOTT: be it resolved that this plantation, hitherto known as TOUTANT NORD, shall henceforth be known as CONTRERAS, in recognition of the signal serv-ice that PIERRE GUSTAVE TOUTANT-BEAUREGARD has rendered his country and the luster he has added to the family name. That thus the scene of his brave deeds and his privileged birthplace may be linked together and alike become familiar to his countrymen and honored from this time forth from one generation to another.

As he finished speaking, a great cry went up from all sides. "Con-treras! Contreras! Beauregard! Beauregard! Viva! Viva!" Jacques was motioning to Pierre that he must now descend from the carriage, with Laure and the boys, that he must stand on the gallery between his parents and fittingly respond to the tribute of all his kith and kin. But if he had been so moved by the presentation of the golden sword that words failed him when he tried to acknowledge it, he was now completely overwhelmed. His mother leaned forward and, kissing him on the cheek, murmured, "Voyons, cher! This is only what you asked me for years ago, at West Point! And what I promised you should have when you figured in a victory!" It was not until she finished speaking that he managed to steady himself and find his voice. After all, it did not matter much what he said, only that he should say something and, presently, he was interrupted anyway, for a band began to play, "See the conquering hero comes!" and all his family crowded around to embrace him and tell him how much they loved him and how proud they were of him and how delighted they were that, henceforth, Toutant Nord was to be called Contreras, which of course was the perfect name for it.

The orchestra which was playing now was a famous one; it had come down from New Orleans on purpose to supplement the home-made music; and there was a caterer from New Orleans, also, to supplement the masterpieces which Edné and her minions had made for the occasion. In the dining room, ropes of flowers trailed from the tall silver *epergne* in the center of the table to the smaller bouquets scattered among the pyramids of nougat, the towers of blancmange dotted with red cherry stars, the jellies and creams quivering in little baskets woven of candied orange peel and topped with sugared rose leaves and sugared violets. On a separate side table, less elaborately decorated, were cold meats, salads, salmis and galantines in seemingly endless profusion; and on the sideboard were vintage wines in cut glass decanters and champagne in silver buckets. Waiters passed to and fro between the dining room and the rear gallery, where the guests were seated at small tables from which they periodically rose and returned to dance in the *salle,* where the mantel was banked with roses; and roses in brackets lined the walls and formed the letters of CONTRERAS to surmount the doorways. First came the minuet, which was led by M. and Mme Jacques Toutant-Beauregard, then the waltz, the polka, the schottische, the mazurka. When the New Orleans orchestra stopped to rest, the plantation band took over again and, presently, there was another minuet, this time led by Pierre and Laure; then more waltzes, more polkas, more schottisches, more mazurkas.

Neither the feasting nor the dancing had shown any signs of coming to an end at sunrise, when the warning sound of a steamboat whistle sent a large contingent of the guests hurrying to the plantation landing. Those who had come by carriage or on horseback took a more leisurely departure, after a final dish of gumbo and a cup of strong black coffee; and they shared these refreshments with those who were staying on, as many were, either with the Joseph Toutant-Beauregards or the Jacques Toutant-Beauregards. Though neither house was built on the baronial lines of Upper Magnolia, both usually managed to accommodate as many guests as needed sleeping quarters. This time, however, it had been necessary to resort to extraordinary measures: thirty unattached young men, for whom no space could be found indoors, had retired, under the direction of their host, to the grove beyond the flower garden and there had managed to prepare for the party. House servants had supplied buckets of water in which to wash and had held up mirrors for shaving. And though there had not been much time to spare, the young men had all managed to reach the gallery, looking spick and span, before Pierre made his triumphal entry!

Jacques told the story of this episode, which lost nothing in the telling, as the "immediate" family ate the early morning gumbo and drank the early morning coffee and talked over the party, which Laure maintained was always the best part of it. René and Henri had long since fallen asleep at the table and had been carried off to bed by Mamie, just as she had so often carried off Pierre and his brothers and sisters. Now, gradually, the older guests drifted away, in the direction of the rooms allotted to them. But Pierre's mother still sat at the head of her table and would sit there, he knew, until she heard him say she had made him very happy and that he would always try to deserve the honor which she and his father had shown him. And, this time, the words came readily enough. It was a great moment for them both. Afterward, Pierre thought that, perhaps, next to the moment when he had first claimed Laure, it was the greatest in his life.

❦ 16 ❦

AT FORT LIVINGSTON, WHICH IS SITUATED ON BONNE TERRE Island, and which defends Barataria Grand Pass against marauders and smugglers, is a fort of very little importance. The work is constructed of brick, with a lighthouse, to prevent its being surprised at night in its loneliness and isolation. It has no garrison; a lieutenant and a sergeant compose the whole military force; and this is considered sufficient to hold it against any enemy, at least in time of peace. This and the adjoining islands were the headquarters of the pirate Lafitte and his robber crew. . . .

There are a great number of small islands in the vicinity inhabited by fishermen, oystermen and duck hunters, for these waters supply the New Orleans market with the best oysters, fish and crab the sea affords, and also with wild ducks, which resort to the marsh prairies by thousands, feeding on the grain of the marsh grasses.

—Excerpt from a report made to the President of Louisiana State University by Americus Featherman, Lecturer on Botany and Professor of Modern Languages, Louisiana State University

The engineers, P. G. T. Beauregard and Godfrey Weitzel, were impeded in building the fort by floods and rains which caused much damage to the foundation, as the land was low and marshy. Reports on progress to the war department said that for months at a time no work could be accomplished. In 1825 the rainfall was 107 inches. Many times the funds appropriated for a single year were not used and were carried over to the next. Apparently the delay in expending funds already appropriated was the reason why no money was voted in the years 1830 and 1831.

Brigadier-General C. Gratiot of the Engineering Department reported, on March 8, 1830, that the Fort Jackson would be completed that year; another report of November 19 said that it would be ready to receive a garrison within a few months. However, it was not completed and occupied until a year later. The fort was a regular star-shaped pentagon, with walls twenty-five feet above the water line of the wet ditch or moat which surrounded it. The walls were made of brick and the gun foundations were of grey and red granite. The two curtains bearing on the river were casemated for eight guns each. Guns could also be mounted on the parapets. In the center of the fort was a defensive barrack of decagonal shape. It was intended as a bombproof building, having a roof of heavy timbers with a covering of earth one foot thick. The building would accommodate four or five hundred men, and there was still the bombproof shelter of the casemates, where the garrison was well protected from bombardment. A drawbridge which was lifted by huge weights and chains, provided entrance over the moat. Outside of the moat another brick wall was constructed, facing a second low ditch. A bridge over the second ditch led southward to a water battery whose guns faced the lower part of the river.

Fort Jackson was thirty-two nautical miles from the Gulf of Mexico, twenty-two miles from the lighthouse at the head of the passes, and sixty-five miles in a southeasterly direction below New Orleans. The flagstaff of the fort was located in latitude 20 degrees 21 minutes 30.68 seconds north and longitude 90 degrees 26 minutes 21.46 seconds west. The altitude of the post above sea level was but a few feet.

During the construction of Fort Jackson, Fort St. Philip was garrisoned except for periods of floods and rains. It was abandoned in February, 1828, and regarrisoned a year later.

Again in June, 1829, it was abandoned. Upon the completion
of Jackson, the garrison of St. Philip was removed. Estimates
were presented to Congress in 1834 to build a first class defense for St. Philip at a cost of $77,810.79, but the work was
postponed.

—Excerpt from a thesis written by Ernest A. Landry

ALMOST IMMEDIATELY AFTER HIS RETURN, PIERRE HAD APPLIED FOR
leave with pay until November, on the ground of his health,
and it had been granted him. Except for the fact that the round
of festivities planned in his honor prevented him from having as much
time alone with Laure as he would have liked, he reveled in them.
It might be true, as a general rule, that a prophet was without honor
in his own country; he was proving that he was the exception to that
rule and this was extremely gratifying. Physically, however, he was
finding all these parties something of a strain; it was quite true that
he had not yet recovered from the Mexican Campaign and the
frequent illnesses which had interrupted his active service. He was
still subject to chills and fever and the quiet which settled over
Contreras after the great gala, that marked the change of its name
from Toutant, was especially welcome to him.

But he soon saw, with concern, that Laure had not imagined all
was not well with his mother; she did look very tired much of the
time, she was more silent than usual. She declined to discuss her
malaise with anyone, or even to admit that it existed. She continued
to weave pearls in her hair, to wear beautiful jewel-colored dresses and
to preside expertly and serenely over a large heterogeneous household,
which, without her firm control, would have been chaotic. She never
raised her voice, she never gave the slightest sign of strain or haste,
and she maintained the pleasant orderly pattern of life which had
always been habitual to her and which Pierre now found so suited
to his mood. But one bright October morning, when Mamie took in
her morning coffee, she did not respond to her faithful servant's

greeting. She had died in her sleep, as quietly as she had always lived.

Her death was an overwhelming blow to everyone in her family. Coupled with the sense of great personal loss, was the consciousness that no one would ever be able to take her place at Contreras, that nothing would ever be the same there again. Pierre was so shattered it was obvious that he must not remain in a house permeated with poignant memories; and when, by late autumn, he had still failed to regain his strength, Dr. Piussan suggested that he should try the "water cure" at Biloxi and he and Laure went there together. Living accommodations were primitive, treatments for baffling ailments hardly less so; but the reunited couple was happy there and gradually Pierre pulled himself together.

When they returned to Louisiana, it was to make their headquarters once more at Upper Magnolia. Pierre had been reassigned to the forts: "Mississippi and lake defenses in Louisiana" the order read; but that meant St. Philip and Jackson again—routine work which would have seemed dull after the glories of Contreras and Churubusco and Chapultepec were it not for his lifelong interest in the old forts. And now, though he was not disappointed in the assignment, it was a constant source of discouragement. He did not worry greatly over Livingston, about which he had never had much sentiment anyway; the network of bayous by which it was surrounded would make it impracticable as an approach to New Orleans, because these bayous could be successfully navigated only by native fishermen and it was unlikely that these would give traitorous assistance to an enemy. But Pierre did not believe that St. Philip and Jackson could be made effective without further fortification. True, St. Philip had withstood nine days and nights of bombardment in the War of 1812; but that was in the days of sailing vessels, not steamships. He continually hammered away on this subject in writing to his superiors, all to little avail. He began to have the same feeling that had obsessed him before the war, that no one in Washington was reading his reports. But his discouragement did not prevent him from working hard and getting results. The decrepit old buildings achieved a new sturdiness, a new soundness; he built batteries and mounted guns and the forts began to look menacing again. As their appearance became increasingly warlike, he tried to persuade himself that they might deceive an enemy to the extent of making him believe they represented a real obstacle. He had given up trying to persuade the War Department that they did not and could not.

If he had not been obliged to spend so much time away from

Laure and the children, he might have been better able to shake off the depression which was threatening to engulf him again. Life at Upper Magnolia was pleasant and his paternal instinct, so long dormant, was at last aroused. René and Henri were both fine, active, intelligent children, of whom any father could well be proud. They had been bred to the saddle, as he had been, and had ponies of their own now; they rode with him daily when he was at home, watched eagerly for his return from the forts and tagged at his heels all day long. When he left, they cried bitterly at the prospect of losing him, until he told them they were too big to cry now, that only girls did that. He read aloud to them, encouraged René to read to him in return, taught Henri his letters, often joined the little group when Laure was hearing the boys' prayers and said these with them. Laure was delighted. It had troubled her, though she had never told Pierre so, because he had not longed for a son from the beginning and had resented the change which babies necessarily made in their way of life. She knew that his love for her and his fears for her welfare had been primarily responsible for his attitude and she was touched that this was so; she believed that few husbands were so solicitous of their wives. But she had not wanted this solicitude to overshadow his parenthood and, as she watched him romping with the boys and heard all three shouting with laughter, she hoped that it never would do so again.

It was this hope that caused her to delay telling him that she was once more pregnant.

She had thought that, perhaps, she would not have to tell him, that he would guess. But, as before, her condition brought with it no vertigo, no fainting spells, no morning sickness; she seemed in radiant health and he had never been one to notice what they jestingly and euphemistically called "the inconveniences of women." The tardiness or absence of such inconveniences went unobserved; so did the first swelling of her breasts, the first thickening of her waist. It was not until after a longer absence than usual at the forts that, as he watched her moving about the drawing room, he wondered if she were putting on weight and later, when the impression persisted, despite the dim light of their chamber, decided that she was.

"It's very becoming, darling," he said. "I mean, you're growing a little heavier, aren't you? I've told you, over and over again, you could do with ten pounds more."

"I'm glad you think it's becoming. And I can promise you the ten pounds—at least."

Fear suddenly clutched him, fear such as he had never known in
Mexico. "You don't mean—"

"Yes, and I'm truly happy about it. Why Pierre, it would never do
for the boys to grow up without a sister!"

"It would be a thousand times better than to have them grow up
without a mother!" he said to himself. But, fortunately, he did not
say the words aloud; he only asked a question.

"When is this going to happen?"

"In April."

"April! Then you've kept this from me for months already!"

"Not so many months—no longer than when I was expecting
Henri. And this time, as you were home, I thought you'd notice—
that you'd ask—"

"And so I would have, if I hadn't been the world's worst simpleton,
if I hadn't been blind as a bat! If I hadn't been worrying about those
obsolete old forts when I ought to have been worrying about you!"

"You weren't so very blind. You just said it was becoming to me
to be a little heavier, so I can't be too unsightly, even yet. And
there's nothing to worry about. It's only first babies that come hard."

She might be telling him the truth. He clung to the hope that she
was. He had still been in Baltimore when Henri was born and he had
never been able to persuade her to talk about her second confinement.
But he had not forgotten that she was unable to nurse the second
baby and that she had been a long time in getting back her strength.
He was badly shaken, he cursed himself for a selfish and sensuous
fool. He would not have blamed himself so much if this had happened when he first returned from Mexico. After all, he was a
normal man and for a year and a half he had lived continently, when
all around him he saw most of his fellow officers—with the signal exception of Lee—following the promptings of their natural instincts
when and where they could; if he had begotten a child while he and
Laure were at Contreras or Biloxi, he would have said that though he
would have been glad if he could have saved Laure from the curse of
Eve, this time he had not been able to do it; something stronger than
his will, something primeval in its power, had forced him to seek
constant proof that he and the woman God had given him were one
flesh. But God had been merciful to Laure; and, as the months had
gone by and Pierre's first hunger had been appeased, he had been
lulled into a false sense of security. What a fool, what a wicked fool
he had been!

"Don't you remember," Laure was saying gently, "that once I asked
you to promise me you'd never let your fear that I might have another

child keep you from making love to me? You refused to promise and I was afraid—I mean afraid you would let it make a difference! I was so glad, when you came back from Mexico, to find that it hadn't! Why, we had a second honeymoon—I think, in some ways, it was even more wonderful than the first! We'd been separated for so long, I'd missed you so dreadfully—and of course, before we were married, I couldn't miss you in the same way! And since we came back from Biloxi—well, that's been wonderful, too. A feeling of belonging so completely that we don't need constant proof of it, just the same way that you don't need to say, 'I love you,' all the time to a person who knows it and yet being glad whenever you hear it said. I've told you before that I wouldn't change a single minute of the time we've had together. I'm going to tell you that again and again and again until I make you believe it. Because it's true. Oh darling, please tell me *now* that you believe it!"

He knew it was true, he could not refuse to say what she asked; but this did not still the fear in his heart. And he was not only afraid, he was angry, angry with himself, angrier still with his mother-in-law, who seemed to him positively smug over the prospect of another grandchild. How could she have forgotten those awful hours when he had sat helplessly in the upper hall, listening to Laure's anguished cries, and had finally been sent out to the woods, so that he would not hear them, but where he had been conscious of them all the same? Goaded to exasperation by her attitude, he finally voiced the question he had long suppressed.

"Well, you forgot those awful hours yourself, didn't you, Pierre?" she asked ironically. "That is, you didn't keep thinking about them, did you, before you left for Baltimore and after you returned from Mexico?" Then, as he burst into vehement speech, all the more violent because it was mingled with shame, she said more kindly, "I'm sorry I said that, Pierre. You did nothing, either then or at any other time, for which you should blame yourself. You've made Laure very happy and she's never been happier than she is now. I assure you that *she* has forgotten all about the time you still dwell upon. There's a saying in the Bible which is as true now as when it was written. I'm not sure just how it goes, but it's something about a woman in travail who grieves because her hour has come, but who forgets the pain, as soon as she has been delivered, 'for joy that a man is born into the world.' "

"Laure has two sons already. She certainly doesn't need a third one."

"No, but she hasn't a daughter. She'll be delighted with a daughter. And so will you."

It was so evident that she was telling the truth, insofar as she could, that his anger cooled and did not again flare up. Life flowed on in its usual calm, productive way at Upper Magnolia and the spring was very beautiful. Pierre felt justified in spending less time than previously at Fort Jackson and Fort St. Philip because he had already done everything that was humanly possible to strengthen their defenses, until more money became available, through awakened realization in the higher echelons, of how much it was needed. From now on until summer, routine inspection would suffice to satisfy his conscience that he was not neglecting his work. Unless, of course, some emergency arose. . . .

In March, as usual, the river began its spring rise, but there was no menace in this, for no reports of unusually heavy rains had been made from stations along the upper valleys of the Mississippi River's watershed. The brief January rise had been anything but threatening and it was never really destructive; only the spring floods, fed by the run-off of water from melting snows on the western Alleghenies, the eastern shed of the Rockies and all the vast area between them ever brought dangerous floods into the lowlands. Like most of the plantations along the riverbank, Upper Magnolia was leveed, as were the two forts; and every evening Pierre walked down to the river at "just dark"—the half-light that preceded "good dark"—to check on the steady increase of the water's height against the embankment and assure himself that this was normal. When the weather was fair, Laure went with him; but a protracted spell of rainy days and unseasonable chill kept her indoors for a time. When she questioned him anxiously about the possibility of a flood, he smilingly brushed aside her forebodings.

"A Louisiana planter's daughter should know that the rains here are of no consequence, *chère*," he reminded her teasingly. "We live in the midst of the lowlands. Actually, your father's land runs uphill to the river bank, since the overflows of every spring for hundreds of years have deposited their silt right at that point. So no rain that falls on the countryside hereabouts ever reaches the river. It is not as though we were surrounded by hills from which the water would come rushing down in freshets. What might bring us a flood would be heavy rains higher up along the Mississippi and along the Missouri and Ohio and Red rivers and, so far, nothing of the sort has been reported. Of course, if a sudden warm spring in the North melted all the snow on the mountains, the situation would change rapidly. . . . Would you care for a round or two of cribbage?"

The subject of a flood was not raised again, though the inclement weather continued. After Pierre had made his routine visits to the levee, he and Laure spent their evenings quietly in the drawing room together. M. and Mme Villeré retired early, and Pierre buried himself in official documents, while Laure sat near him, contentedly sewing on baby clothes. Before they went to bed, he nearly always asked her to play for him; now that there were no "midnight gumboes" with amateur concerts afterward, because her time was so near, he was wholly dependent on her for music, he told her, speaking in the same jesting way as when he had teased her because she was worrying about floods. She did not need to have him add, in a more tender tone, that he would rather see her sitting at her harp and listen as she touched its strings than to have the room filled with boisterous company. He spoke little when he was engrossed with his reports and their companionship was not dependent on speech to be complete. The silence was so profound that both looked up quickly, Pierre from his papers and Laure from her sewing, when a distant sound, which they could not immediately identify, disturbed the quietude of the night; as it came closer, they realized it was made by the drumming splash of hoofbeats over the muddy driveway. Pierre shoved aside his papers and, pausing only long enough to put his arm around Laure's shoulders and tell her not to be frightened, strode out on the gallery, reaching there just as a man in uniform flung himself out of the saddle and saluted hurriedly.

"Sergeant Trent from Fort Jackson, Sir," he gasped, as he came up the steps. "Captain Tanner, Sir, instructed me to report to the Major that the levee in front of Fort Jackson has been damaged considerably by recent heavy rain and erosion gullies have appeared. He feels the river may overtop the levee and if it does. . . ."

"Never mind what would happen then. I know. How bad is it already?"

"Captain Tanner's orders were to tell the Major that the way the river's rising, it won't be but a day or two before the wave wash from passing steamboats will threaten a crevasse at the eroded part of the levee if it isn't strengthened immediately."

"Damn! That means Fort Jackson would be flooded!"

"Yes, Sir."

"And if the road from the landing to the drawbridge is flooded, we couldn't unload supplies anyhow. Haven't they started sandbagging the levee, for God's sake?"

"Sir, the supply's running out and the Major knows that if we can't sandbag the whole crest. . . ."

"Naturally I know it. They might as well sandbag none of it as leave a gap. . . . You rode up all the way from the fort?"

"Yes, Sir. There was no other way to get here, Sir. I changed horses at Myrtle Grove Plantation."

"Then take your horse to the overseer's house and tell him you need a fresh one and that I want one saddled for me, too. Better let him give you a drink and some food, but don't lose any time. We'll ride to New Orleans and I'll commandeer a boat there."

"Yes, Sir. Thank you, Sir."

Pierre turned on his heel and strode back into the house. Laure was already standing at the open door of the drawing room, facing him, a startled question in her eyes.

"Is it very bad, *cher?*" she asked. "I couldn't help hearing what the sergeant said."

"Nothing we can't handle, at least not yet." He gripped her shoulders hard. "That's not what's troubling me, darling. But I want you to tell me the truth. That baby isn't due until April?"

"No. I wouldn't lie to you, Pierre. I never have."

"And neither of the others came early?"

"No. René was just on time. Don't you remember how I hoped he'd be born on our anniversary—and he was? Henri was a few days late."

"All right. I believe you. If I didn't, I'd be tempted not to go to the damned old fort. It'd be no good anyway, under heavy attack. I've told the War Department so a dozen times. But it *is* my responsibility. As long as everything was normal there, I felt justified in staying with you until the baby was born. Now there's a possibility that it might be badly damaged—the powder magazine or medical stores could be flooded. And, since you're sure you don't need me——"

"I am sure. Good-by, darling. Don't think you even have to take time telling me how hard it is for you to leave. Just go quickly, so you can come back quickly!"

He swept her into his arms and held her close until he heard the men coming with the horses. Then, without another word, he swung out of the house and into the saddle.

Pierre encountered no difficulties in commandeering a sternwheel packet at the Bienville Street levee. In fact, during this slack season, a number of captains bid against one another for the commission of a short government charter. He found far more opposition at the refineries and at the hardware establishments where he swept up quantities of sugar sacks, spades and shovels, signing government due bills in return. It took considerable time to procure a large quantity of river sand and have it put aboard, but by 10 A.M. the *Douce Malou* was dropping downstream past Chalmette, heading toward Violet and Jesuit Bend, and Negro roustabouts were filling the sugar sacks with sand. The steamboat signaled her approach to the Fort Jackson landing with piercing blasts of her whistle and had barely edged up to it when Pierre leaped off, returned Captain Tanner's salute and asked where the levee was threatened. The captain pointed toward a spot a dozen yards away. Even from this distance, Pierre could see the evidences of erosion.

"We noticed it day before yesterday after a downpour," the captain informed him. "That's when I sent Sergeant Trent for you, Sir. I don't think it can stand another rain."

Pierre looked first at the sky, where a few cloud banks, low on the horizon, suggested a squall out of the Gulf, then glanced at the flagpole to see which way the wind was blowing. Fortunately, he told himself, there was little chance of another rainstorm from the south.

"I'll want a work party of fifty men or so at once," he said tersely. "Send out to the nearest plantations and hire some Negroes. We haven't any time to lose."

"I've arranged for extra help already, Sir. I detailed a dozen of our men to stand to your orders and have rounded up about half a hundred slaves. They're over by the barracks—ready for work."

"Good," Pierre said approvingly. "Send twenty-five aboard the *Douce Malou.* I brought a quantity of river sand and several thousand sugar bags; some of them were filled by roustabouts on the way down. Get your men to work at once filling the rest of the bags. I'll want ten to come with me to the levee. The others can carry the loaded bags from the ship to the threatened area."

Having thus set the wheels turning, Pierre himself went straight to the levee to inspect the area of danger. Glancing at his watch on the way, he saw that it was not quite four. Unfortunately, not much could be done before sunset, he realized, and he saw immediately that Captain Tanner had not been an alarmist. The river, in its normal spring rise, was lapping dangerously at the base of the three-foot levee where the heavy rainfall had, indeed, cut little gullies on both sides. Should there be even a slight rise in the river, it would complete the work of the weather, break the levee and flood Fort Jackson and its area. The first thing to do was to fill in those eroded gullies.

He had hardly reached this decision when he saw Sergeant Trent approaching with ten strapping slaves, with a soldier in charge.

"Everything is under way, Sir," the sergeant told him with pardonable pride.

"Fine," Pierre said, looking back in the direction of the steamboat, where some of the slaves were holding bags open, while others shoveled river sand into them and packed it firm. A third group was speedily stitching the end of the sacks as fast as they were filled. In a few minutes, the first of the bags would be carried to the danger zone; and while the immediate threat was confined to a grassless strip of levee about twenty yards long, Pierre decided to double that distance in strengthening it. When the first contingent arrived at the place where he was standing. Pierre instructed them to open some of the bags, fill the gullies with sand and stamp it down with their feet until there was no longer any gully in sight.

"Can you get me several hundred fenceposts or pales from the nearby plantations?" Pierre next asked the sergeant while this work was progressing.

"I think so, Major."

"Well, go and find out."

Darkness was already closing in before all the sandbags had been brought ashore and, despite the use of flares, it was impossible to continue directing the placement on either side of the levee. That would have to go over until the next day, he realized, since he had to build a "rampart" at the base of the levee on each side, to support the bags and there he would overlap them, like shingles on a roof, to provide stability. But, after all, considerable progress had been made; though not permanently placed, hundreds of bags had been packed and carried to the levee by dusk and Pierre called off work for the night and went into the fort, where he readily accepted the wild-goose gumbo and sound red wine Captain Tanner offered him.

While they were eating their supper, Sergeant Trent returned with the report that he had rounded up the necessary fence palings and posts from neighboring plantations. So, after a few hours' sleep, Pierre returned to the levee, where the crew immediately reported to him and, while the work of packing, stitching and carrying the bags continued, he supervised the men who were driving posts and pales halfway into the ground on each side of the levee's base. On the river side, the posts were sunk into the water until Pierre's rampart covered the threatened area and continued on each side of it for about ten yards. It took practically all day to get this part of the job finished, but when it was done Pierre looked with satisfaction on the work.

The posts would serve as an extra barricade against the lapping of the river, in addition to providing a base for piling up the sandbags, some of which were already in place when he called off work for the night and, now that all of them were filled, he estimated that the whole job would be completed by noon the next day and that he could leave immediately thereafter.

When the *Douce Malou* stopped at the Upper Magnolia landing, something about the stillness struck Pierre as uncanny. He had lost track of the days, but it must be Sunday, as no one was working in the field; since he had been unable to send any message about the probable time of his return, he did not really expect anyone to be on the lookout for him, though Laure had never given up her habit of patiently watching and waiting when there was any chance that he might come. Well, this was the hour of siesta and he had been insistent that she should not neglect her daily rest. So far as the other members of the family were concerned, no such insistence was necessary. And yet, his feeling persisted that there was something uncanny about this utter stillness.

As he walked hurriedly through the grove, he saw that all the shades had been drawn on the side of the house that he faced. The day was pleasantly warm, but it was not hot enough to warrant shutting out the spring breezes. He would remind Laure of that. Usually, they did not darken the house in the daytime until May and then they did it with shutters. This was only March—March twenty-fourth. April was still a week off, even the first of April.

He dashed up the steps of the gallery, calling to Laure as he mounted them. There was no answer and he called again. This time, a small shrill cry pierced the stillness—the cry of a newborn child.

At the same moment that he heard it, he saw the mourning wreath of white flowers fastened to the closed door.

❦ 17 ❦

TRADITIONALLY, CREOLE WIDOWERS OBSERVED TWO YEARS OF DEEP mourning. Often, they would have been quite content to shorten the period. Before it ended, their tears no longer dampened the black-bordered stationery on which they replied to letters of condolence, or the black-bordered handkerchiefs which supplemented the rest of their sable attire. And, to tell the truth, they were rather weary of crepe armbands on their black suits and crepe scarves on their tall hats; likewise of weekly visits to the cemetery, armed with floral offerings; also of social contacts limited to the sympathetic visits of their friends and to gatherings of immediate families whose members were similarly clad and similarly restricted in their activities, and whose outlook on life was almost inevitably lugubrious, because they did and heard nothing to relieve the general gloom.

But rebels against such customs were regarded with so much disapproval and, often, with so much suspicion (Had they really loved their wives? Were they seeking surreptitious consolation in unhallowed quarters? Were they perhaps actually thinking of remarriage *already?*) that, for the most part, they accepted the established pattern and, even after two years, walked warily for a time. The habiliments of woe were discarded only gradually. The black borders on the stationery and the handkerchiefs, at least half an inch wide to begin with, grew narrower and narrower, but did not disappear entirely for a long while; the crepe armbands and the crepe scarves were removed, but not the black suits and the black neckties. (In the case of a widow, crepe veils told the story: at first these were all-enveloping, but eventually the one which covered her face was discarded, and the one which still hung down her back grew shorter and shorter; and after the crepe trimming was removed from her dresses, she might, if she wished, begin to give thought to some which had a touch of white at the throat and wrists, or—if these dresses were made of muslin— to some sprigged with white flowers. But though she might yearn for gray or lavender, the really estimable widow never wore anything but

CRESCENT CITY BUSINESS DIRECTORY

FLORVILLE FOY,

MARBLE CUTTER

AND

SCULPTOR,

TOMBS, MONUMENTS,

TOMB SLABS,

GRAVE STONES & MARBLE WORK,

OF ALL DESCRIPTIONS EXECUTED AND MADE TO ORDER.

Grave Yard Work of all Kinds Done.

NO. 81 RAMPART ST.,

NEW-ORLEANS.

black, no matter how long she survived her husband; and of course she dressed her children in black, too, for a long, long while, and even draped her baby carriage with it.) The visits to the cemetery began to be monthly instead of weekly, the floral offerings less elaborate; and finally both were limited to *Toussaint* and the anniversary of the dear departed's death. If a *loge grillée* were occupied, and there were no visiting back and forth between this and open *loges*, attendance at the opera was no longer frowned upon; and it was not only correct, but commendable, to visit friends—afflicted like oneself—who sat secluded in other *loges grillées*. Chess and quiet games of cards became permissible distractions and, also, soirées which intimate friends as well as members of the family attended. Of course, there was still a long way to go before attendance at balls or races could form part of the program; but at least a start had been made in that direction.

In Pierre's case, no disapproval of his behavior was expressed or even felt, much less were any suspicions entertained on the usual grounds. Quite the contrary. The general opinion was that he did not show enough Christian resignation to his loss, and that he blamed himself unreasonably for a fatality which could not, with logic, be laid at his door. After all, Laure's death should be attributed to the Will of God, which gave life and took it away and, as such, should be acknowledged and respected by all true believers. The fact that she had died in childbirth did not alter this obligation; and certainly his vehement insistence that her third pregnancy represented nothing short of a crime on his part, since he knew the anguish and peril of her previous confinements, was a sign of morbidity. Nearly all women suffered bringing children into the world, many of them to the point of endangering or even losing their lives, but that was the curse of Eve. How was the race to go on unless they fulfilled their manifest destiny? For that matter, how was normal marriage to go on? Passion was part of it, at least for the husband; and even if his wife did not share his desire for union, she should not fail in her duty to him, for in that case who could blame him if he sought assuagement elsewhere?

Even Laure's parents tried to reason with Pierre that his abandonment to grief would overwhelm him and undo him, if he did not make some effort to rise above it, and that it would not help anyone else. He refused to listen to them, he refused to listen to anyone, and he declined to stay either at Upper Magnolia or Contreras. Nothing would induce him to sleep in a room which he and Laure had shared and, at Contreras, there were not only all the reminders of her, particularly on their last joyful visit there, but also the reminders of his mother, whose final heroic efforts for the enjoyment and welfare of others had undoubtedly hastened her end. How could anyone expect him to lie where he would wake from some dreadful dream that Laure was not beside him and reach out to draw her closer to him—only to find that the dream was true? For years they had slept locked in each other's arms and now his arms were empty; must he be reminded of it, night after night? And must he enter the great *salle* at Contreras, instinctively glancing toward the chimneypiece, where his mother had always sat in a great carved chair, with the firelight playing on the sheen of her brocade dress and the pearls twined among her coronet of braids—only to see the chair was empty and the embers gray? No, nothing that anyone could say to him would persuade him to do either one!

Nor would Pierre stay with the Bienvenues, who had immediately offered hospitality when it became evident that he intended to visit Laure's grave not weekly but daily. Kenilworth was close to the old cemetery of San Bernardo de Nuevo Galvez; all he would have to do was to cross the road and the little bridge spanning Bayou des Boeufs, which was so narrow at that point, and there he would be at her tomb! Didn't he know that? He asked the question almost savagely. Hadn't he and Laure gone there together, the last time he had stayed with the Bienvenues? And didn't everything about Kenilworth remind him of her? Their rapturous honeymoon at the *garçonnière*, her lovely presence when the golden sword was bestowed upon him, a thousand other things. . . .

Fortunately, his uncle Joseph's plantation, which was still known as Toutant and adjoined his father's, since both had formed a part of the original Toutant-Beauregard holdings, had no poignant associations for Pierre, and here a vacant cottage, formerly occupied by the overseer, whose increasing family had necessitated the move to a larger house, proved the answer to the problem of shelter, at least temporarily. It was near Contreras, so his father could and did come to visit him, since he would not visit his father; and it was a scant three miles from the cemetery, so that it was a simple matter to go there every day. Neither was there any lack of proper household arrangements, since it was the most natural thing in the world for Mamie to install herself in the cottage without any argument on the subject, keep the place clean, do the laundry and cook and serve as much food as she could persuade Pierre to eat. This was little enough, for a long while; but Mamie could coax him when everyone else failed; and it was actually Mamie who succeeded in persuading him to surmount his sorrow by means of reasoning which no one else had attempted—which, indeed, had not occurred to anyone else.

"*M'sieu* Pierre, you got to stop mournin' disaway. *Mademoiselle* Laure, it grieve her to have you."

"*Grieve Mademoiselle Laure!* You talk as if she were alive!"

"Sure 'nuf, she alive, *M'sieu* Pierre. Angels am alive, ain't dey? An' you know well's I do, dat's what she now, a angel. Only dif'rence, she alive in dat beautiful heav'n up yonner, 'stead o' down here on dis sinful earth. She waitin' for you up dere. Ain't she never done tol' you, iffen she die de firstest, dat's what she do?"

He did not answer immediately; he could not. He sat, with bent head and wet cheeks, thinking, as he had so many times before, of that day when he and Laure and René and Henri had all gone to the old Spanish cemetery together and that, while the boys played among the tombs and chased butterflies, Laure had said she wanted to be buried there. Now, for the first time, he found himself able to dwell not only on the fact that she had said this, but also on the fact she had said she believed spirits came from heaven and returned there and that, in answering, he had said he believed this, too. Until now, since her death, his faith had been submerged in his grief, so deeply that it had seemed to him it was gone forever. At last, he felt it stirring within him again and he managed an answer.

"Something like that, Mamie."

"Den ain't you never goin' do nothin' make her feel you gettin' ready to join her? You ain't done nothin' since de funeral, *M'sieu* Pierre, 'ceptin' sit an' mourn an' weep an' put flowers on her grave. Ain't even no fittin' stone markin' de place where her poor li'l body restin' an' words written on dat tomb tellin' strangers come to Terre-aux-Boeufs who she were an' where she gone."

What Mamie said was true. He had not even given thought to a suitable sepulcher, much less to an appropriate inscription. Laure had been laid to rest, temporarily, in the great family tomb of the de Reggios, since, of course, her funeral could not be delayed until one could be designed especially for her. He would go the next day to New Orleans to see Florville Foy, who had been trained in France as a marble cutter and sculptor and who was generally regarded as superior to all his fellow craftsmen. Foy would design a tomb which Gillous, the local mason, could construct in brick and mortar and the marble tomb tablet would be executed in Foy's establishment. As to the inscription, that would be ready to give Foy at the same time the order was given for the tablet. Pierre walked over to the plantation desk and, drawing a sheet of paper from a pigeonhole, wrote without a moment's hesitation.

Ici repose

M. A. Laure Villeré

épouse de Major G. T. Beauregard

officier de l'armée des Etats Unis

née 22 mai 1823

decedée le 21 mars 1850

Esprit descendu du ciel tu y es remonté

Dors en paix, fille, épouse et mère chérie

Foy's "establishment" was only a long open shed, piled helter-skelter with slabs and blocks of marble and blocks of rough or semi-finished granite. There were always eight or ten workmen on the place, one at least using, as an abrasive, a mixture of sand and water, to smooth the stone on which he was grinding. Others were cutting marble by striking stone chisels with wooden mallets and still others, who worked in granite, used heavier steel chisels and metal hammers. All this grinding and chiseling created an atmosphere of intensive industry, but the noise it made was deafening.

As Pierre walked into the shed, Foy looked up quickly from a design on which he was working and hastened forward to greet the visitor with grave respect. "I have been hoping you would come to me, Major Beauregard, under the sad circumstances, on the occasion of which I have already sent expressions of condolence," he said. "Would you have the kindness to let me lead you to my little office, where we can talk more quietly than we could here in all the din? This way, if you please, *M'sieu le Majeur.*"

He would be honored to accept the commission, Foy assured Pierre when the latter explained what he had in mind. The inscription was beautiful, most appropriate, most moving; he would take charge of presenting it in the most suitable and artistic way; and, as soon as he could complete drawings for the tomb, he would come to St. Bernard and show them to Gillous in the Major's presence. Then there would be no question as to satisfactory results. Two days later the proposed meeting took place in the cemetery and from then on, until the brickwork was finished, Pierre continued his daily visits there; but now that Gillous was always present and the parish priest and Foy very frequently also, it was necessary for him to talk with them, instead of standing silently with bowed head before Laure's temporary resting place. Every now and then he went in town to visit Foy's establishment, to see how the marble tablet was progressing; the noise of grinding and chiseling which, at first, he had found so nervewracking ceased to irritate him; the friendly greetings of the workmen, the atmosphere of industry and accomplishment were a helpful tonic. Gradually, it became easier for him to meet other people, to accept their services and their sympathy. The day of the removal of the coffin from the de Reggio tomb to the new one was, inevitably, one of great strain and sorrow. But once the tomb tablet made by Foy was in place and Pierre could feel that the last fitting step had been taken to honor his beloved, he wanted to get back to his normal work, to fill his days so full of endeavor and achievement that at night he would be exhausted, both physically and mentally, and able to sleep because he could not drive his body or his mind any further. He gathered together a few sad souvenirs: a lock of Laure's hair, which some day he would have made into a brooch for her daughter; the notes of condolence in which he had pressed the flowers that had adorned her casket; the locket whose alleged loss had given them the excuse for their first tryst; one of the black-bordered notices which had been tacked on the trees in the parishes of Orleans, St. Bernard and Plaquemines; a lace-trimmed handkerchief, still delicately scented, which had been his last gift to her; the painted fan with mother-of-pearl sticks which had been his first present to her. These he placed in a japanned box for safekeeping, but the intervals between the times he took them out to view them became farther and farther apart.

The fortification of St. Philip and Jackson had become an obsession with him. Hitherto, those who had been with him, either as fellow officers or enlisted men, had not found him unduly demanding as a superior officer; now, he tried to drive everyone else as hard as he drove himself. There must be more guns and they must all be mounted in the casements or on the parapets; the powder magazines must be similarly enlarged. But he had come to the conclusion that guns and powder would not suffice; steam vessels could move so fast that many of the enemy would escape fire, unless the river were obstructed in such a way as to prevent their rapid passage; unremittingly, he sought a way to provide such obstruction. He was having the same difficulties he had experienced before in getting a hearing at Washington; but the Engineering Department marveled at the speed with which he got things done and he made some progress with the guns, though he made none about the obstruction of the river.

He spent weeks on end at one fort or the other and, since he took no time off himself, claimed there was no reason why anyone else should do so. Neither did he see any reason why living conditions at the fort should have more amenities. He no longer occupied officers' quarters in the barracks outside the inner moat at Jackson, but a room in the tall decagonal citadel that towered above the great star-shaped structure from its center. He did not care what kind of a bed he slept in, he did not care what he had to eat, so why should anyone else? He did not mind mosquitoes, so why should a few bites cause complaint? It was not strange that, in the face of such an attitude, his former popularity quickly waned.

The two years' mourning period was just coming to an end when the National Government appointed a board of Army and Navy Engineers to survey the problem of how best to deepen the mouth of the Mississippi River. The necessity for doing so was twofold: ocean-going vessels were increasing in size all the time and required more draft; it was imperative that this need should be met, for the railroads were beginning to threaten the preëminence of river traffic; but bars of silt and clay kept piling up and preventing the passage of the larger ships. Moreover, "mud lumps" had begun to appear mysteriously from underneath the surface, sometimes rising to a height of not less than fifteen feet and changing the channel of the river overnight; no satisfactory explanation of their origin had been found, though all sorts of fantastic reasons for it had been given, and no remedy for the dangerous nuisance had been found, either.

Pierre was among those chosen to serve on the new Board and nothing could have proved a more welcome challenge. He was fascinated by the "mud lumps" and worked out a device that he thought would explain them as underwater clay formations, escaping from the pressure of the river sediment which rested on them. The plan for this device he finally submitted to the authorities under the title of "Self-Acting Bar Excavator." He did so with the highest hopes. The experiment of using towboats to dredge a channel at Southwest Pass had proved, as he had expected after long observation, to be only temporary in its good results; and though earlier he had recommended jetties, or artificial banks on the sides of the bars, which would result in a stronger current, he knew these would take so long to build that it was doubtful if anyone on the present Board would be able to make a successful attempt to do so. Surely the Engineering Corps would welcome his latest suggestion, since it offered not only more lasting results than the towboats, but faster results than the jetties!

He received a courteous letter of thanks for his "device" from his old friend Totten, now a general. Then he waited for the letter which would authorize him to put it into practice. He had not forgotten how long it took for an official communication, which might be the bearer of good news, to reach him—probably he was destined to another period of hope deferred, like the one he had endured before he was finally ordered to Mexico. He hoped he had learned, since then, to be patient. . . .

His original draft of the plan for the Self-Acting Bar Excavator was the first document that he lifted from his second japanned box. The revised draft, the one he had sent to Totten, he had never seen or heard of again. When the Commission of Army and Navy Engineers disbanded, the futile little towboats were still chugging up and down the channel of Southwest Pass.

He could not have explained, beforehand, why he felt impelled to take this dogeared document with him when he went up to the rear gallery for breakfast the next morning. But as he handed it across the table, inviting Simone Castel to look at it, he understood the reason.

"You told me, day before yesterday, that I ought to stop thinking about the Register and think, instead, about the wonderful reception I had when I returned from Mexico."

"So I did. I hope you followed my advice."

"Yes and it helped—for an hour or so. But those thoughts led, inevitably, to sad memories of my mother and my wife. They both died within the next year."

"Then my suggestion, instead of being helpful, was just the opposite?"

"In one way, I'm afraid it was. But in another, perhaps it did help. I'd been dreading to look at the souvenirs of those two deaths that came so close together—and yet, I knew I must, sometime, if I were to empty one of the boxes I've been working on and get along to another. And it was necessary I should do so, in order to make the record I'm trying to compile a complete one, so I read everything in the bottom of the box, including my draft for the inscription on Laure's tomb. And then I opened the second box, hoping that I'd find something to give me courage to go on. And, instead, I found this."

He handed her the original draft for the Self-Acting Bar Excavator and, as she fingered it uncomprehendingly, he told her how it happened to be prepared, and how deep his disappointment had been because his device had never even been given a trial.

"I'd long since ceased to be a hero by that time," he said, and checked himself from saying "not quite as quickly, though, as I did after the War Between the States." Then he added, "In fact, a good many people were beginning to think I was a sort of crackpot, always coming up with some kind of an impractical scheme. Maybe they were right. I'd had an earlier one for building jetties—artificial banks on the sides of the bars—but the objection to those was that they'd take too long to construct. And I had a later one: a rock and lever for artillery chassis; I thought it would result in more accurate firing at moving objects; but the Ordnance Department rejected the idea. And then I had some others that didn't have any military significance. Perhaps they were all on the fantastic side."

"I don't believe so. You say you recommended the jetties, you believed they'd be the permanent answer to channel clearance. And the only reason your suggestion wasn't adopted was because there wasn't either time or money to build them just then. So then you suggested a possible temporary solution that might be better than the towboats that *were* used. I can remember hearing about those. I don't see anything fantastic about that recommendation. Don't you think that by-and-by someone will build the jetties?"

"Without doubt."

"Well, then——"

"Simone, isn't that rather far-fetched? That I should take heart merely because, at some distant date, a person unknown to me will profit because I believed in something?"

He had never before called her by her Christian name. To be sure, he had asked Mme Cougot to call him Pierre, but that was different. It had happened when he was telling her how much he had resented the Anglo-Saxon insistence that he, a Latin, should be called Peter; and thereby he had come to a logical explanation of the sad mystery surrounding Lance. Under those circumstances, it was logical that, on impulse, he should have made a gesture that seemed to unite him with the missing drummer boy and at the same time establish a semblance of social equality between him and the elderly mother of his landlady. He had not really expected her to act on his suggestion— in fact, he had said that she probably would not wish to, at least until Lance came home; and he had not made the same suggestion to the daughter. To be quite honest with himself, he knew he would have considered anything of the sort forward on his part and lacking in delicacy on hers if she had followed through. But now "Simone" had

come naturally to his lips, just as it was becoming increasingly natural, all the time, to talk to her about his troubles, both past and
present. As soon as he had addressed her so spontaneously, he wondered if he had not made a mistake, if she would not feel he had
been presumptuous or that he had failed in respect. However, there
was nothing in the way she answered to make him feel so.

"I don't think it's far-fetched at all. I think you *should* take heart
over that and a great many other things. What happened next—after
the Commission was disbanded, after your 'device' was overlooked?"

"Well, for a time I was very much interested in trying to further
Franklin Pierce's candidacy for President. That didn't meet with any
more local approval—my undertaking, I mean—than my inventions
had. I believe my detractors thought I was trying to feather my own
nest—that it might be an advantage to me, in a military sense, if
Pierce were in the White House. There wasn't any advantage and that
wasn't what I had in mind. I'd admired what I'd seen of him in
Mexico and I thought he'd make as good a President as he had a
general. I still think he did, in spite of *his* detractors. He was a firm
friend of the South. But I'll admit that one reason I was for him was
because I wanted to see him beat Scott."

"You didn't like Scott?"

"No, and the feeling was mutual—though he did praise me publicly
twice!" Pierre hesitated, almost ready to tell Simone the whole story
of his first thwarted romance and of the resentment that had persisted, unappeased, all these years. But he had just been talking to
her about Laure, and to mention the loss of Virginia almost in the
same breath would seem to belittle the shattering blow dealt him by
the death of his dearly loved wife. "I went on writing letters to the
papers and doing everything else I thought might be helpful to
Pierce in one small way or another," Pierre went on. "I continued to
do so even though I realized I was jeopardizing my chances of getting
an appointment that I wanted very much indeed."

"Which was?"

"Superintending Engineer of the New Orleans Customs House."

"But you did get that appointment after all!"

"Yes, Simone, I did."

There, he had called her Simone again and, if she resented it, there
was nothing to indicate this. On the contrary, she not only seemed
deeply interested in what he was saying, she seemed more friendly
than ever. She leaned forward and spoke eagerly.

"Tell me about it!" she said.

FAMILY ALBUM II

View of West Point, U.S. Military Academy. From an old painting re-produced in "The Spirit of West Point."

Pierre G. T. Beauregard

At the time of their marriage.

Laure Villere Beauregard

St. Louis Cathedral, New Orleans. Engraving by Ch. Colin from a drawing by K. Fichot. Press of Ch. Chandon, Paris. Collection of Leonard V. Huber.

General Winfield Scott as an old man. From a picture in *Old Fuss and Feathers* by Arthur D. Howden Smith, published by Greystone Press, New York, 1937.

Storming of Contreras. From an old print in *The Mexican War* by
Edward D. Mansfield, published in 1848.

Silver epergne owned by the parents of General Beauregard. Reproduced by courtesy of the owner, Mrs. Porter F. Bedell.

Typical Louisiana marsh scene.

❧ 18 ☙

1854.

July 21—Having occasion to go to Court this morning I was quite surprised and pleased at the cleanly, orderly appearance of everything in the heart of the French quarter, so different from its condition in former years. The beautiful square opposite the Cathedral is kept with scrupulous attention. I walked thru it after finishing my business at Court—the flower beds are in excellent order and stocked with choice varieties—The grassy circle in the center, which is used in the evening as a play ground for little children and their nurses, is surrounded with a hedge of orange trees, well clipped, and of the lovliest green. The streets around and in fact all Royal, Chartres & Levee streets paved with square granite blocks, and the delipedated relics of ancient times giving place to substantial modern constructions.

Sept. 20—Major Beauregard has been called upon by the Department to superintend the repairs of the "Branch Mint" here and accepted the appointment.

Dec. 18—The annexed plan and elevation show the effect of a change in the Collectors Room at the New Custom House N. O. proposed by Major Beauregard and sanctioned by the Department. It consists in substituting full columns in the place of square pilasters at B B.

1855.

Ap. 2—Major Beauregard returned from a visit of inspection to Proctor's Landing to select a site for the proposed Fort.

1856.

Mar. 28—Went with Major Beauregard to Jacob's Daguerretype establishment—Mr. Jacobs kindly initiated us into all the mysteries of the Photograph—explained the details of his ample laboratory Sc. The Major had his photograph taken with great success.

Sept 6—Major Beauregard has had one of the marble capitals unboxed and set up complete on a base and a piece of shaft—in a good conspicuous situation—Each capital consists of four pieces—The effect of the whole is exceedingly fine and the bold innovations on the classic model quite successful—

—Excerpts from the diary of T. K. Wharton

᪥

THERE WAS NO POSSIBLE DOUBT THAT SHE REALLY WANTED HIM TO tell her the story. Her eyes were shining and her cheeks were faintly flushed. Nothing he had told her about his frustrations and defeats had made her feel that he had been a failure as a young engineer, any more than she felt he was a failure now, as an impoverished and humiliated old campaigner. She not only respected him, she admired him and her admiration was tinged with warmth. They were not landlady and lodger any more; they were companions and confidantes.

"What do you want me to tell you about it?" he asked.

"Everything. Why you wanted the position and how you got it after all and what you accomplished when you did get it."

"That would make rather a long story."

"Well, is there anything else—I mean, anything else special—that you wanted to do this morning?"

He could not pretend that there was. He was only too glad of an excuse for a respite from his fruitless search for work. He shrugged his shoulders and shook his head.

"Well then! . . . Am I mistaken or wasn't there dissatisfaction, almost from the beginning, with the way the Customs House was built?"

"Yes, and there was every reason why there should have been. It was planned by people who knew nothing about our soil and climatic conditions and whose one idea was to make it impressive. As you know, it's enormous and it's constructed of granite. When it began to settle, the outer walls cracked and sank faster than the interior walls—at one end, they were actually twenty feet deeper! So the government appointed a board to determine why the building should be so unstable. That seems to be the government's answer to everything—appoint a board!"

"At least it put you on the boards!"

"Yes, and that's usually as far as it does go. But, this time, it listened to what I said—probably because this was something that other board members said, too: that the groined brick arches which formed part of its foundation bore down too heavily on the soft soil and that iron girder arches, smaller ones, should be used instead. I still don't know how the Secretary of the Treasury happened to single me out among all the other so-called experts."

"It was the Secretary of the Treasury who singled you out?"

"Yes, the Customs House comes under his jurisdiction. There wasn't any personal compliment involved. Very likely it was because he reckoned it would be more convenient to blame a local man, rather than an outsider, for anything that went wrong."

"Perhaps it wasn't a personal compliment exactly. But couldn't it have been because he thought a local man would understand local conditions better than an outsider? Apparently, that was the trouble in the beginning—they didn't have enough local advice."

"I won't argue that point with you, Simone."

"But you'll admit I have a point?"

"Yes, I'll do that . . . anyway, the Secretary of the Treasury asked the War Department to lend me to him as Superintending Engineer. At first, I refused. I couldn't believe that, this time, the powers that be in Washington would really listen to reason. Then I changed my mind in the hope that they might. I decided to accept the appointment after all. But I made it very clear that, in changing my mind, I hadn't changed my position about what needed to be done and I wouldn't accept the blame for any of the original mistakes."

"And they gave you a free hand?"

"Well, fairly free. They couldn't very well help it when they found that practically everything I tried was successful. I couldn't stop the settling completely, but at least I could equalize it and slow it down. You wouldn't be interested in all that."

"I'm interested in everything."

"Well, perhaps I could explain better if I made a sketch, showing how I bound the exterior walls to the interior walls with iron plates and piled weights on the higher part of the building."

He drew from his pocket a letter written on one side of a single sheet and sketched rapidly on the blank side. Simone pushed her coffee cup aside and leaned closer, in order to watch more attentively and, as he explained what he was pointing out and why, she nodded her understanding. After he had finished, he drew the paper to him and began to tear it up. She stretched out a detaining hand.

"Oh, please don't do that! I want to keep it! Unless you want to keep the letter yourself—after all, that *is* a letter you're starting to destroy! Had you forgotten?"

"I had, for a moment. As a matter of fact, I was glad to. It's just another of those communications telling me there was no opening for me in a place where I hoped there might be one."

"All right. Go on forgetting about it and let me have the sketch. I'll treasure it."

"You're welcome to it. But it's nothing to treasure."

"Haven't you learned by now that women treasure all sorts of things when men don't see any reason why they should?"

He tried to answer her question lightly and found himself unable to frame such an answer. Then he realized this was just as well; it was wiser not to do so in words. The answer she wanted was the gift of the sketch, nothing else. If he gave it to her silently, she would know that he recognized the truth of what she had said, but that he would not try to probe into the past to find out how she had learned the lesson which she thought he should have learned, too. He handed her the paper and, as she took it, he saw that her fingers shook, ever so slightly, and that she had bowed her head, as if to prevent him from seeing that there were tears in her eyes. But when she spoke again her voice was quite steady and something in her manner made her remark seem wholly impersonal.

"You must have found your position at the Customs House very rewarding."

"In many ways, I did—among them, financially. As soon as I accepted the superintendency, I began to get the normal pay for a captain, the first rank I had been given by brevet in Mexico. I never did get the pay for major, the second rank I had been given by brevet. Sometimes people referred to me as captain and sometimes as major, but I didn't mind that. At least, I had a living wage again, for I also drew eight dollars a day as superintendent. And I had so much work at the Customs House that it was soon obvious I couldn't do justice to that if I were to travel about much, though I was instructed to examine the Branch Mint Building and give a detailed estimate of the remodeling and repairs which should be undertaken there. So, except for occasional tours of inspection, I was relieved of duty at the forts and the passes; that was a relief, in the literal sense of the word, too! And I made one very good friend, Thomas Wharton, a prominent architect. He was an Englishman by birth and, originally, an artist by vocation. But, after spending a certain amount of time in Pittsburgh and studying architecture, he came to New Orleans and settled here. He rose rapidly in his profession and he was the type that made friends quickly and easily. I'm glad to say I was one of them. He was of immense help to me, in every way. But I was restless. My father died the same year I got my new job and though that wasn't as shattering a grief as the loss of my mother, it did hit me pretty hard. I not only loved him very much as a father, I admired and respected him greatly as a man. He wasn't a spirited, spectacular figure like the first Jacques Toutant-Beauregard for whom he'd been named, the commander of a flotilla that set out for parts unknown by order of his sovereign and was decorated with the Cross of St. Louis for his valiant and useful services; and he wasn't an alderman and a judge like his father, Michael Louis Toutant-Beauregard. He often said of himself he was just a planter. But a good planter needed to be as successful a disciplinarian as a commander-in-chief; he needed to have at least a rudimentary knowledge of surgery and medicine and the awareness of when this knowledge should be put into practice; he needed to excel as an engineer and a husbandman. My father qualified for all of that. He was a mighty good planter, and when I say good, I don't mean merely that he ran a plantation very profitably and expansively, even though it never achieved the proud estate of the de la Rondes! I mean that though he was an exacting taskmaster, in the sense that he wouldn't permit shirking or slipshod work, he treated his people —of course he never called them his slaves—humanely and understandingly; he was tolerant with their limitations and their welfare and happiness were important to him. They all loved him, they all vied with one another to deserve his approval and his praise. I don't believe there was a single place in Terre-aux-Boeufs—I'll go further than that, I'll say I don't believe there was a single place on the River —where such harmony existed between the Boss Man and the men under him."

"You could hardly pay him a higher tribute than that."

"No higher perhaps, but for even more reasons. It wasn't only his fairness to the men who worked for him that gave the plantation its tone and its standing. It was also his attitude toward the women who worked for him. He didn't consider them his lawful prey, he didn't clutter the quarters with a pack of half-breeds. Of course that was partly because he adored my mother, because he wouldn't consciously or willingly have caused her a moment of suffering or shame that he could have spared her; but it was also because his code as a gentleman and a Christian wouldn't allow him to dishonor any woman or sire a child he couldn't acknowledge as his. I don't need to tell you that not every aristocratic planter had such a code, or if he had one, he didn't live up to it. My father did both."

"And thereby set an example to his sons."

"Yes and, on the whole, I think we followed it fairly faithfully, despite some rather lurid stories to the contrary." Briefly, Pierre wondered if she had heard the slanderous rumors about a bevy of concubines that, along with wagonloads of champagne, were alleged by his enemies to have followed his line of march during the war. But he decided that probably she had not. Though such tales had been circulated, even in Louisiana, this had been in alien circles, not among Creoles like herself, who would have disdained to listen to anything of the sort, much less to repeat it. And, in any case, he did not want to discuss that sort of thing with her; he wanted to go on talking about other aspects of Jacques Toutant-Beauregard's nature and what these had meant to him.

"I spoke about my father's code as a gentleman and a Christian," Pierre continued. "I'd always been impressed with him as a great gentleman, as well as a great planter. But it wasn't until I saw how he accepted my mother's death and the prospect of his own that I was impressed by him as a Christian, even though I couldn't follow his example. I was crushed and rebellious, you see, about Laure's. It wasn't until my old nurse, Mamie, made me visualize Laure as an angel, waiting for me above, that I even made an effort to surmount my grief to the extent of living a more or less normal life. Even then, I couldn't see death as a law of nature, a normal change of conditions, until my father also helped me to do so. I couldn't make a conscious effort to be ready, through my own worthiness, to appear before my Maker, to rejoin my wife and my parents in heaven."

"Yes, it takes a long while to make that conscious effort—unless one has help, the kind of help you had from your father. You must be very grateful to him."

Silence fell between them, but it was the silence of understanding and sympathy, untinged by any sense of strain. When Pierre finally broke it, he took up his narrative where he had digressed from it to talk about the great qualities of Jacques Toutant-Beauregard.

"I hadn't any reason left for wanting to stay at Contreras or even to go there—my brother Alfred died the same year as my father, and after that the place was just an empty shell. Of course, I did go to Upper Magnolia to see my children, but I may as well confess I didn't do it any oftener than I could help. I mean, I realized that, as their father, I ought to keep in touch with them, but I knew the Villerés were giving them the best of care and *that* place wasn't an empty shell —it was still permeated by associations with Laure."

"Yes, I can see how it would have been."

"So I thought that, perhaps, if I could get away from New Orleans altogether, I would be more contented. The superintendency was rewarding, as you've said; but it wasn't rewarding *enough*, in the ways that mattered. I considered returning to Mexico—it looked as if there could be an opening for me in Tampico. The city was greatly in need of a municipal water system and I might possibly have been selected to introduce it. But I thought even more favorably of Nicaragua."

"Nicaragua! Was there some question of a water system there, too?"

"No, but it was just exotic enough to be especially appealing to me at that stage, considering my frame of mind—particularly as my friend, William Walker, had recently staged a *coup d'état* there and offered to make me his second-in-command. I didn't visualize him as a filibuster or a revolutionist at first; I thought of him as a liberator. I felt very strongly I'd like to have a share in his splendid adventure. I'm still not sure I wouldn't have been happier if I had—for a while, anyway. You know—'one crowded hour of glorious life' and so on——"

Something in her expression made him realize that she had not recognized the quotation; and she was plainly puzzled that he should have entertained so fantastic an idea as to take part in William Walker's opera-bouffe performance, of which she must have heard, unfavorably if vaguely. That he should have become involved in impractical engineering schemes, she could comprehend and countenance; but that he should have considered leaving his home and abandoning an honorable position to play the role of a flashy adventurer, she could neither comprehend nor countenance.

"Sober second thought prevailed," he said with a slight smile. "Sober second thought, jogged into realistic channels by several high-ranking generals, Scott among them. Yes, Scott actually wrote me that he was 'deeply concerned' at the rumors which had reached him about my possible retirement. He remembered the 'distinction' with which I had served in Mexico. He was sure a 'brilliant future' was before me still. After all, it's a truism that blessings brighten as they take their flight. But what he and other dignitaries who wrote me were really worrying about wasn't that I was damaging my chances for a brilliant future. They'd actually begun to notice that a good many first-class men were leaving the Army for more promising careers, and that if many more did so, it wouldn't be too good for military prestige. Even the departure of one mere Creole captain would dim it even more than they wanted to risk just then."

"Don't you ever give anyone the credit for being really disinterested, General Beauregard?"

"Not very often. I've very little reason to—even less now than ten years ago."

"I'm sorry you feel that way. Because it seems to me you've had a great many wonderful friends, very loyal friends, and yet you hardly ever speak or seem to think of those."

"I told you about Wharton."

"Yes, but that's the exception which proves the rule. It's the ones who disappointed you that you dwell on all the time."

He attempted to deny the charge, but as in the case of the light answer which he had tried to make half an hour earlier, he found that the right words did not come. He shrugged his shoulders a second time.

"Anyway, I allowed the generals to overpersuade me. I stayed on the job that I was finding duller and duller all the time. Then I thought maybe politics might be the answer to my ennui. Whatever else you might say about them, they're seldom characterized by dullness. In New Orleans, they certainly weren't just then."

"I seem to remember. Wasn't that the time Conservative Reform elements selected you to run against the Know-Nothings for mayor?"

"It was indeed. And no one can claim that the Whigs and Democrats—the ones who were supposed to represent conservatism and reform—acted as if they were doing so. They organized a Vigilance Committee consisting of over a thousand armed men, appropriated artillery from the State Arsenal and seized the Cabildo; then they threatened to take even more violent measures 'to ensure an honest election.' Why they thought it would help matters to install me in office by force, I can't see now. There certainly wouldn't have been anything honest, much less legal, about that. But sober second thought is always a good deal more sober than first impulse. And while we were resorting to violent measures, the Know-Nothings' thugs and cutthroats, of whom they had plenty available, ranged the city and terrorized the populace; one of their less criminal actions was to invade the Registrar's Office and confiscate the voting lists; and on top of that they had the supreme effrontery to demand arms from the city government to fight the Vigilantes!"

"And, in the end, they won!"

"Yes, in the end, they won, after they had been drawn up in battle array on one side of Canal Street and we had been similarly drawn up on the other. In the last analysis, it was a battle between the Creoles—the old established order—and the Americans, the newcomers who called themselves Know-Nothings. The latter were violently anti-Catholic and that part we tried to understand; but we

couldn't understand how we fitted into their anti-foreign policy because, of course, from our point of view, *they* were the foreigners!"

"Afterward—I mean, during the War—didn't you sometimes think
of that dividing line, I mean, Canal Street, as being, in a small way,
something like the Mason-Dixon line?"

"Of course I did! Over and over again. But no one except you ever
guessed it or, anyway, ever mentioned it to me before."

He looked at her with increasing appreciation. This woman was
not only kindly and personable, she was intuitive and intelligent. He
was still acutely conscious of failure and humiliation, but suddenly
he realized that he was not lonely any more.

"So I was defeated," he went on, "another defeat—a minor one,
compared to most of the others, but still a defeat. I didn't take it too
hard, partly because politics had been just a stop-gap and partly because, very soon after I lost the election, I had a far greater loss—
my youngest sister, Angele, died."

"In the yellow fever epidemic of that year?"

"It was during the epidemic. But that wasn't actually the cause of
her death. She died in childbirth. She was young, she was beautiful,
she'd been married only a little over a year. Since our father was
dead, I'd given her away myself at a magnificent ceremony in the
cathedral. It was a glorious moonlit night and I thought, as I kissed
her good-by on the gallery of my sister Elodie's house, after the reception, that I'd never seen but one bride who looked so radiantly
happy, and that was Laure. And then, Angele had to die in the same
way. All my bitterness, all my defiance of Divine Will was revived. I
couldn't reconcile myself to such waste, to such sacrifice. And of
course it didn't help that every day or so I went to another funeral,
that I couldn't leave my house to walk a block without seeing two or
three more. I believe nearly five thousand people died in that
epidemic."

"Yes, I believe so. I lost a sister in it, too. And of course a great
many other relatives and some very dear friends."

Simone spoke so quietly that, in the face of such self-control, he
was both ashamed of his outburst and at a loss for the right words of
condolence. She was not the sort of woman who could be comforted
by mawkish sympathy or who could find release from sorrow by talking about it; her sad and simple statement invited neither commisera-
tion nor questioning. The rejoinder he managed to make seemed to
him wholly inadequate. It would be safer, he decided, to change the
subject.

"We were still in the midst of the epidemic when Wharton took me out to the new Marine Hospital and kept me with him while he examined the work there—perhaps he already knew, or guessed, though I didn't, that this and the Quarantine buildings were to be transferred the following year from Captain Duncan's superintendency to mine. We made a day of it, driving out to the new Square on the Metairie Ridge and coming back to town by the Bienville Street shell road. And very soon after that, plans were underway to give General Scott, who was coming here for the anniversary celebration of the Battle of New Orleans, a royal welcome. I wasn't particularly pleased—that won't surprise you after what I've already said about Scott!—when I found I was detailed to ride with him in an open carriage drawn by four white horses. But I'm bound to say he was genial to me personally, bowed this way and that as the parade progressed, and looked hale and hearty. It wasn't as much of an ordeal as I had expected. And after that major celebration was over, I found I'd been drawn into a number of minor ones; almost before I was aware of it, I'd begun to go out in society again—to the opera, to dinner parties, to the races, eventually, even to balls. At first, I didn't get much out of it. But by and by—"

"By and by, you realized you were such a general favorite that you couldn't help feeling flattered and pleased. Why, it was impossible for you to accept all the invitations you received to dinners and dances! And you knew you were a dashing figure in your full dress uniform."

"You speak as if you remembered all about it!"

"Of course I remember all about it! Not that I went to any of those dinners and dances—I don't need to tell you that I never moved in the same social circles that you did. But I heard about you all the time. You were the talk of the town. And then there was that wonderful likeness Mr. Jacobs made of you at his Daguerreotype Establishment. He put it in his show window. And I did see you in person once in a while, at the opera. We were prosperous in those days and we were all very fond of music, so Papa didn't consider it an extravagance for us to have reserved seats on the parquet. And I used to see you at the Cathedral, too. We had our own pew there and went regularly to Mass."

Pierre had completely forgotten, in these last weeks, that he and Simone did not, as she put it, belong to the same social circles. Of course, the daughter of a confectioner would not have been included in the select milieu which a Beauregard frequented; but he was relieved that she made the statement simply and without the slightest trace of resentment. Creoles, he reflected, accepted class distinctions as a matter of course; it was one of the many ways in which they differed from Yankees, who loved to keep insisting that they were just as good as you were, especially when this was not actually true. But in this case, it *was* true. Simone was every bit as good as he was. Whether or not this would apply to all the Cougots and Castels, of course he could not know, but it did apply to both the mother and daughter with whom his lot in life was now so unexpectedly interwoven.

"I'm sorry I never met you in those days," he said, again feeling that he was expressing himself rather inadequately. "But I'm glad you had such glowing reports of me, though I'm not sure I deserve them. What I was going to say wasn't that I was a general favorite—I've often been accused of egotism, but I trust I'm not as egotistic as all that. I was going to say that, by and by—"

He paused and again Simone took up his narrative for him. "I think I know what you were going to say—that the last thing you thought could possibly happen did happen. For years, you'd been called the most eligible widower in New Orleans and you'd smiled and shrugged it off, just as you've been smiling and shrugging this morning. You were sure there could never be another woman in your life, after Laure."

"No, that's not quite accurate; women have always played an important part in my life. I mean, I have always enjoyed feminine companionship. In fact, I have never felt a social gathering was complete, unless it included both men and women, because they bring out the best in each other or, at any rate, they should, and I think usually they do. And, of course, among all the women I've known, there have been a few who were outstanding. There was one, in the very period we've been talking about. . . ."

"Yes?" questioned Simone, encouraging him to go on.

"She was very beautiful—in fact, I am sure she was the most beautiful woman in New Orleans, and I told her so. I wasn't by any means alone in that. Almost every man who looked at her must have been impelled to say the same thing. She was an American, the wife of a tremendously rich banker who was here for just a few years, and then moved his family back to New York, which is where he came from. He was old enough to be her father and, though he was devoted to her, he liked a quiet evening at home once in a while, which was the last thing on earth she wanted. So he was pleased, rather than otherwise, to have her go to soirées, balls and operas with some other suitable escort. Strange as it may seem to you, after what I have told you about her beauty, it never occurred to him that he might be putting temptation in her way, or in the way of some man, younger and more virile than he was. He had complete confidence in her and, as far as she was concerned, his confidence was not misplaced. She craved constant entertainment, but she did not crave anything else. She was beautiful, but she was what is sometimes defined as *une peu statue.*"

"Yes, I know the type," Simone said.

"Well, for a time I was very much at her disposal. I was mingling in society again, as I have said, and I was enjoying it, but it wasn't providing me with any major interest, much less anything essential to my happiness. I thought the role of *cavaliere servente* would suit me, better than any other. I found out that it didn't, possibly because it's more in character for an Italian than for a Creole. The lady's husband always made me most welcome at their home, which was noted for its elegance and its fine table, and I was greatly envied by all my male friends for the entree I had there. But, even if the family hadn't moved away, I know now that the association wouldn't have lasted. I decided that Alfred de Musset was probably right when he said, 'On ne badine pas avec l'amour.' "

For the second time Pierre gathered that he had used a quotation which was not familiar to Simone and, also for the second time, decided to let it pass rather than to run the risk of seeming to assume superior culture by explaining. "More and more I realized that, subconsciously, I was *searching* for a major interest, for essential happiness," he went on, "and that I would not find these by paying discreet attentions to another man's wife. I wanted a wife of my own."

"So at last you really fell in love again."

"Yes," he said, "you're right. At least, in a sense you're right. It wasn't the way it was before—magnolias and moonlight." Almost reverently he pronounced the words he had so often defended. "It wasn't high romance, hot young blood, irresistible yearning, passionate compulsion. But it was contentment after bitterness, communion after loneliness, quietude after restlessness, fulfillment after futility, peace after strife, haven after storm. It was tenderness, it was loveliness. In a word, it was Caroline Deslonde."

❧ 19 ❧

FORESTS COVERING THE LAND ON BOTH SIDES OF THE MISSIS-
sippi extended from the banks of the river to very great
depths, the boundaries of which were determined by French
and by Spanish surveyors and by natural limits. This is the
origin of what were called "simple" or "double" concessions;
the "simple" concessions being 40 (forty) arpents and the
"double" 80 (eighty) arpents in depth.

—René Toutant Beauregard, *Magnolia*
(Privately printed)

RECEPTION OF GENERAL SCOTT

General Winfield Scott arrived on yesterday's mailboat
from Mobile. Early in the morning the Mayor and a number
of the members of the Common Council went down to the
lake to give him a fitting reception as the city's guest. With
the above gentlemen were also a number of military officers—
General Lewis, General Forstall, and others—who felt that as
military men it was their privilege and duty to properly welcome the oldest and greatest military chieftain of the United
States and of the age. The Orleans Artillery were out with
their guns; Captain Lamothe and a squadron of men being
down at the lake with a cannon, and another squadron of the
company with another cannon stationed at the Pontchartrain
Railroad Depot in the city.

At about 8:00 o'clock the Mayor and the aldermen, with
the military participating in the reception, boarded the
steamer *California* and greeted General Scott in due form.
The Mayor addressed him as follows:

"General, it is my pleasing duty to inform you that the
Council of our city has invited you to accept its hospitality.

"In tendering you this token of popular regard, I can but
briefly refer to your distinguished public service since, unheralded by fame, as a young captain of light artillery you first

visited New Orleans. The recollection of the soldierly bearing
and patriotic conduct of the young officer is revived by the
presence of the veteran in years and fame. From that period
of promise to the present ripeness in honors, your path has
been illuminated by deeds which make a nation illustrious.
Queenstown, Fort George, Chippewa and Lundy's Lane are
lasting monuments of your early chivalry, valor and military
skill; Chicago and Rock Island to your self-denial and humanity; and Fort Moultrie of your discretion and prudence.
The hero of the battle in 1812 became the hero of humanity
in 1832 and of Union in 1834.

"To you, Sir, we owe the preservation of the peace of the
country on more than one memorable occasion, achievements
more honorable than triumphs on well-contested fields.

"The people of your city recognize your military energy and
daring, combined with the spirit of Christian philanthropist.
Your fame in war is equalled by your success as a benefactor
and a friend of mankind.

"In the ripeness of your renown, we welcome you to the
city where you first commenced your career of usefulness and
honor. To you, who by purity of private life and by singular
fidelity and success in the administration of public duties, deserve the commendation of the good; who by the glory shed
upon our arms through a long succession of bright victories
from the capture of Fort George to the capitulation of Mexico,
have given us a character among the nations as a people of
military prowess, who by a rare moderation and generosity
of character, united with prudence and wisdom in action, have
achieved moral influence as rich in benefits as the victories
on the battlefield, the people of New Orleans tender this testi-
monial of their respect and appreciation."

General Scott made a response, brief but feeling and to the
point. He accepted the honor paid him as one for which he
was sincerely grateful—a reception that he did not expect—
and alluded in pleasant style to his past experiences in this
city; the city in which, for the most part, he had fitted out
the expedition with which he landed at Vera Cruz during the
Mexican War. He spoke of the pleasure it would give him to
be present during the celebration of the Eighth of January
and alluded to something about the Battle of Chalmette,
which he said was more curious than otherwise, he having
had but a remote connection with it, adding that he would

reserve the relation of this circumstance to a more fitting
time. He expressed the pleasure he felt in recognizing Mayor
Stith and General Lewis as men whose parents and ancestral
families had been his friends in years gone by, and again returned his thanks for the honor tendered him, stating that he
accepted that honor and would place himself a willing captive
in the hands of those who had so generously come forward to
receive him.

The General was then escorted from the steamer to the
cars on the wharf, preceded by Old Jordan and his drum and
fifers, who had been brought down for the occasion. As the
cars left the long wharf for *terra firma*, Captain Lamothe and
his men began thundering off a salute with the cannon. Before
the salute was well finished, the distinguished visitor and the
crowd who had him in charge were at the Washington Hotel,
where a breakfast had been ordered to suit the occasion.

The breakfast was as superb an affair as fish, fowl, and the
French market, with French cookery, could make it. The
meal was unusually long for a breakfast; genial converse retarding its first part, and champagne, toasts and other pleas-
antries lengthening out the last. Mayor Stith sat at the head,
with the guest at his right, and General Lewis sat at the other
end, with another guest, Colonel Leigh (the companion of
General Scott) at his right. Captain Lamothe and his Artillery
were ranged on one side of the table; and from the quantity
of champagne and compliments that lengthened out the meal,
and the late hour at which that meal was finished, it was entitled rather to the name of a dinner than that of breakfast.
General Scott, upon whom age was visible—his hair being
scanty and quite white, and his manly face plentifully marked
with the creases of time—still appeared stout, healthy and
hearty, and enjoyed his meal as well as the youngest man at
the table. Time, though it has furrowed his face and whitened
his hair, has made no inroad upon the size of General Scott.
Over all the men we saw him among yesterday, he was a head
the tallest and portly in proportion.

There were some pleasant incidents at the Hotel before the
General and his entertainers left for the city. Old Jordan,
the drummer of Chalmette, and of the War with Mexico, was
introduced to him, and in his modest way, said some right
pretty things. With the latest train of cars arrived that veteran
citizen, Bernard Marigny. His reception of the General had

no music of cannon or breakfast about it; but there was so much of the human in it, that none could fail to feel the force of it. He took the General by both hands and after coming to an understanding with him about some meetings of theirs forty or fifty years ago, threw himself upon his breast and embraced him as he might have embraced one of his own children. In their conversation, the General asked him how old he was. "Seventy-four years," was his answer. The General then told him that he (Mr. Marigny) was just a few years his senior.

Several rough, hard-working men that we saw rushed up to the General and took his hand without ceremony, introducing themselves by saying that they had served under him in Mexico. But for the numerous little incidents of the day we have no further room.

A special car of the train was reserved for the guest and his companions; and with flags flying and Old Jordan and his men giving out their choicest field music, the train came whizzing into town. Great crowds of people had gathered along the railroad, and at the depot the crowd was a perfect crush. Meantime the artillery near the depot were thundering forth a second welcome for the General. As he left the cars, the crowding to see him amounted to the insane; a dense mass of struggling people on every side. When he was seen, however,—for it is not much trouble to see General Scott where the ground is level—he was saluted with a number of cheers, given with a will. With the Mayor, in an open carriage drawn by four white horses, he came uptown, followed by a train of other carriages, filled with the aldermen and other parties to the reception. We may add that so distinguished a visitor would never have been able to get from car to carriage but for the hard and rather rough labors of the Third District police, who were on hand for the occasion.

The line of march uptown was crowded with spectators, the men in some places fairly breaking their necks to get a glimpse of "Old Lundy's Lane," and the ladies waving their kerchiefs to him from window and balcony as he passed along. A halt was made opposite Jackson Square to enable "Old Lundy" to take a good look at the equestrian statue of "Old Hickory," whom he knew in the old fighting times. Nearing Canal Street the General was saluted with a third cannonade, given by the Washington Artillery at the foot of that street. The procession passed up from Chartres through Camp and around Lafayette Square to the City Hall, where a halt was made and a blast of martial music given by Jordan and his men, with another round of cheers from the multitude. Then the procession went on and in a few minutes, General Scott was rushed through another insane jam of cheering and shouting people and safely lodged in the St. Charles Hotel.

With the firing of the cannon and flying of flags from public buildings and a crowd of people about the streets, the arrival of General Scott fairly gave New Orleans the appearance and atmosphere of a holiday.

The General will not appear in public or take part in any public proceedings until the day after tomorrow, the Glorious Eighth.

—*Daily Crescent*, January 6, 1859

❧

THAT WAS THE WAY HE HAD ALWAYS FELT ABOUT CAROLINE. TO HIM, she represented quietude, contentment, communion, fulfillment. She was the embodiment of serene loveliness and deep tenderness. He was supremely thankful for what she had given him and been to him, and when he told Simone Castel what the second blooming of love in his life had meant to him, he had described it as he had felt and seen it from the beginning.

Of course, there were many other ways in which he might have felt about it, many other aspects in which he might have seen it. Caroline, like himself—and for that matter like Laure—had a patrician plantation background, though the Deslondes did not, like the Toutant-Beauregards and the Villerés, belong to the aristocracy of St. Bernard. Their ancestral plantation, Belle Pointe, was in St. John the Baptist Parish, opposite the little town of Edgard, on the River Road some ninety miles north of New Orleans. Caroline's father, Major André Deslonde, was the son of a certain Jacques Deslonde who, in the latter part of the eighteenth century, had come from Normandy, via Santo Domingo, to Louisiana, where members of his family had al-

Baltimore 25 June 1852

My dearest Beauty

"It is an ill wind that blows
no good", & but for this unwished for breeze that is
driving one towards W.P. I fear I should never
have heard from you. The reception of your letter has
been the only pleasurable emotion produced by the order,
which is the first I ever rec'd that I did not at once
commence to obey. — I have been wanting to hear
from you badly, & have not yet got over my disappoint-
at missing you when in Mobile. I am glad to find
that you are well & hearty. Long may you remain so.
You are right in your conjecture of my not being
pleased at being ordered to W.P. I know too well
the thanklessness of the duty, & the impossibility of either
giving or rec'd satisfaction. I have been behind the
Scenes too long. I know exactly how it works. The
Supt: can do nothing right & must father every wrong.
I acquiesce, if I was allowed any option in the
matter, that I prefer some other in my place. I have
been told it cannot be done. I shall therefore have
to go & am to relieve Capt B. on the first day of September.
I shall endeavour to do my duty, & to consult the
interests of the Academy in every particular. Any
aversion to the Service shall make no difference
in my wishes or efforts, for the maintenance & advance—
ment of an Institution upon which I believe the standing
of the Army, & military success of the Country, in mainly
depends. But I shall get away from it as soon as I can.
I agree with you entirely in the advantages to be derived
from giving the Professors an opportunity to visit foreign
Institutions, & of enlarging & liberalizing their sentiments
on the wide subject of education & instruction. I have
advocated it for years. But the narrow policy of our people
& government forbids it. As soon as it was found that, a
Prof: was sent off on such an errand, the appt. for his
maintenance at the Academy, would be stricken off. Neither
would they meet the expenses of such a mission without
a proper allowance, & where could that be obtained from?
It is also difficult to get the proper officers to go there as

as'l. teachers. The Service is not sought for by those best qualified in general to perform it, nor will they do anything to make it attractive. To get them at all, you must catch them young, before they have gained experience in their profession, or to enable them to leave a more disagreeable position. Bad alternatives both. But we must take it as we find it Beaury & make the best of it. If you were with me I should hope to succeed. But you must come in & see one.

There is a great assemblage of Engr officers in Washington at this time. The whole Pacific Board to commence with, Col. Smith at their head. Newton & Wright of the Florida reefs, & the Engineer of Pensacola Harbor. G. W. Smith passed through here on his way from there, a few days since. Stevens Foster & others of the Coast Survey, & those in the Engr Bureau, make a goodly show. Congress will be alarmed to see so many fine officers idle. Look out for retrenchment when the Appn Bill comes up. I have not been to W. since the Christmas Holydays. Can therefore tell you nothing of the future. I shall work up the little balance of the former Appn by the time I leave. The Sub-marine work goes on well. The foundation piles are driven, sawed off & prepared with ease & precision by steam Machinery, for the reception of the stone work. The stone is laid by a diving bell in 15 ft water, at the rate of 100 rectilineal feet of wall, 8 ft high, a day, after the bottom Course is laid. If we had have had sufficient funds, the whole wall would have been up to low water level this season. As it is two faces are brought to that point, & we have turned on the third. Beauveton takes my place here. I wish they had have left us as we were.

That young Cadet of mine is with me now. This is his furlough year. Several of his Comrades are also in Baltimore. Young Jerome Bonaparte, grd. Assistant to the Empress, graduates this year, & has brought with him 3 of his Classmates. Casey, 1 Son of Capt C. of the Army 1st of his Class, Ives & Polk. We had them all with us last night, together with the young officers on the Station, & all the pretty *young girls of about 16 — They were a merry set & talked so much they could hardly find time to eat like Raspberries & Ices. They did contrive to swallow a little Champagne?*

— I don't know how any One will come out this examination. The standing was not published when he left. He thinks he will not be below 2nd. His Comrades say 1st. Either will do, if he desires it. I am glad to hear Barnard is improving. Remember me to him. Also to your handsome boys, & believe me always your friend RBlee

Major P G T Beauregard
U. S. Engrs

ready settled fifty years earlier. He had left the West Indies somewhat precipitately, during the insurrection of the blacks and the massacre of the whites; his brother-in-law, Baron Gravier, had accompanied him and his wife, Magdeleine Picou, in their flight and had become a member of their household. Although their first home was in New Orleans, they had soon acquired extensive holdings on the River Road and, from the beginning, had prospered there, originally raising cotton and indigo, but later concentrating on the cultivation of sugar. Meanwhile, André had been an officer on General Jackson's staff and had brought his slaves with him to Chalmette, so that they might help in the making of ramparts with cotton bales; he was now a member of the State Legislature. He had first met his future wife, nee Rosine Chastant, when this charming young girl had been selected to crown the General with laurel leaves at a ceremony which took place shortly after the battle. Their marriage had been a happy one and a fruitful one. Nine children were born to them and not infrequently these were called the Muses, though the reference was not nearly as applicable to them as to the de la Rondes, since five were sons! However, the four daughters were all attractive enough to de-

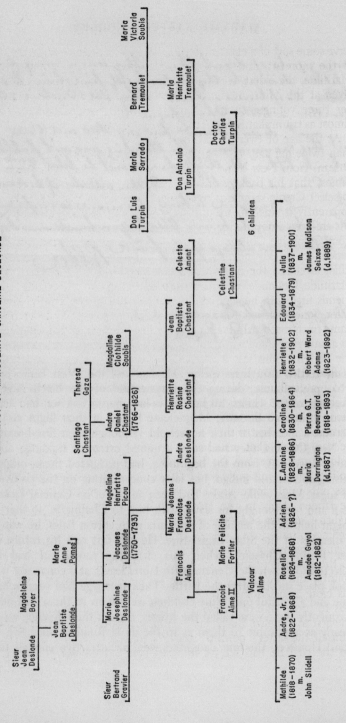

GENEALOGY OF MARGUERITE CAROLINE DESLONDE

serve some sort of a classical designation, in accordance with the mode of the moment, and no other came readily to the popular mind. Mathilde, the eldest, created a sensation when she appeared at a ball, given at the Mint, in the elaborate costume of a French marquise; her three younger sisters, Henriette, Juliette and Caroline, scored almost as triumphantly in French peasant dresses.

At the age of twenty, Mathilde insisted on marrying a man more than twice her age, who had arrived, comparatively recently, in New Orleans from New York. His name was John Slidell, and there were rumors that his background left something to be desired, according to select Creole standards. Undeniably, his father was "in trade"; but apparently it was not only a respectable but also a profitable trade. His children enjoyed every educational advantage. John was graduated from Columbia College and afterward studied law, in the practice of which he quickly made a name for himself. John's younger sister, Julia, attended the celebrated school of Madame Chegaray, where Mathilde Deslonde, who had been sent north for "finishing," made friends first with her and then with the rest of the family. Another sister, Jane, married Matthew Perry, who also very quickly made a name for himself. All in all, even the most carping critics were obliged to admit that there was nothing really *deplorable* in an alliance with the Slidells. John was a personable man, pleasant of manner, florid of face; and, though he was slightly inclined to embonpoint, he carried his portliness well and gave the impression that it was due to exuberant good health, expansive good nature, and a zestful enjoyment of the good things of life, rather than to indolence or gourmandizing. Almost from the moment of his arrival in New Orleans, he had proved that, in addition to his legal gifts, especially in the field of maritime law, he had equally great gifts as a financier. In politics, which intrigued him to the point of fascination, he had been less unfailingly fortunate; but, after a succession of ups and downs, he landed safely in the House of Representatives in the Twenty-eighth Congress and remained ensconced there for twelve years, resigning to undertake a special mission to Mexico. Again, this did not seem to be one of his happier ventures, but that could easily be laid to the strained relations, so soon to break out in war, between this country and the United States; and the friendship which grew out of his close association with the Secretary of State, James Buchanan, was to prove one of dazzling advantage to both. Slidell was one of the first to visualize Buchanan as presidential timber and, constituting himself the latter's political manager, he kept his eyes fixed steadily on the goal he had set for himself—the United States Senate. His former law partner, Judah P. Benjamin, was already firmly entrenched there and the two made a potent pair. With Buchanan in the White House, Slidell became very generally recognized as "the power behind the throne." Louisiana basked in his benefits.

To be sure, up to the year 1858, Pierre was not among those who had done so. It was not until Wharton brought the Senator to the Customs House, to cast his vigilant eye on the improvements which had been made there, that Slidell had given any signs of special interest in the Superintending Engineer. But after the tour of inspection was over and Slidell had expressed himself as being "much gratified—especially with the splendid marble capitals," he issued a casual but cordial invitation.

"I suppose you've already a dozen invitations for this evening, Major?"

"No, Sir. I go out very little. I mean, at any time and, just now, I'm in mourning for my sister."

"Of course, of course, I should have remembered. You must accept my expressions of sympathy and forgive my lack of delicacy. But, as a matter of fact, I wasn't about to suggest a formal entertainment of any sort—just a quiet family supper—potluck, you understand. Mr. Wharton has already told me that he'd come and bring that charming wife of his. There won't be any other guests. But I'd like to talk with you a little further about the work here."

"Under those circumstances, of course I'd be very glad to come, Sir."

So he had gone, for the first time, to the Slidells' elegant house on Esplanade Avenue and in one respect the Senator had told the truth —it was just a family supper, though if what they ate and drank constituted potluck, Pierre could not help wondering of what a feast in that dining room would consist; and, though he did not usually notice such details, he could not help observing the elegance of the gold-initialed porcelain on which the meal was served and the massiveness of the crested silverware. However, besides the Whartons and himself, there were no other guests, except Mrs. Slidell's younger sister, Caroline, who had come down from Belle Pointe Plantation to make a short visit; of course, she did not really count, any more than the Slidells' three children, because she was one of the family. She was very quiet, taking little part in the general conversation; but when she did speak, it was pleasantly and intelligently; and though, compared to the coloring of her sister Mathilde, whose beauty was of the vivid type, her smooth brown hair and clear hazel eyes did not seem striking, Pierre realized before the evening was over that she had a charm all her own. She seemed so gentle, her hesitant smile was so sweet, her face so calm in repose. She carried herself with dignity and moved with grace, but he thought she was even more attractive when she was sitting still and the folds of her dress fell into place around her. The dress was made of some soft material, cashmere, he believed it was called, and it was soft in color, too—pale green tinged with silver. She wore a small cluster of moss roses at her belt and a smaller one at the fastening of her bodice, but no jewelry, not even a ring or a brooch. However, she did not seem to require such adornment.

After supper, Mrs. Slidell left the room for a few minutes to supervise her children's bedtime prayers; and, as Mr. Slidell seemed to be directing most of his questions to Wharton for the time being, Pierre changed his seat, instead of resuming the one he had occupied before he rose, as courtesy demanded, when Mrs. Slidell did so. The chair he now took brought him to Caroline's side.

"Are you planning to make a long visit in New Orleans, *Mademoiselle?*" he inquired.

"No, just a few weeks. John and Mathilde and the children are coming to spend the holidays at Belle Pointe and, even if they weren't, I'd be going home before then. I love to have Christmas and New Year's on the plantation."

"I can understand that. I always loved the grand celebrations at Contreras when my father and mother were alive." He might in justice have said that Christmas and New Year's were still suitably, not to say lavishly, celebrated at Upper Magnolia, but somehow he did not want to. "Now I almost never go to Contreras any more," he added. "In fact, I haven't any special plans for the holidays this year."

This was not strictly true. He would, of course, go to Midnight Mass and observe *Réveillon* with the Villerés; he would provide gifts for René and Henri and their little sister both on New Year's Day and on Three Kings' Day. And he probably would take the children these presents himself. Despite his resistance, the little sister, whom he called Doucette though she had been named for her mother, was finding her way into his heart. But he had no idea of staying a whole week at Upper Magnolia—much less twelve days, so what he said was at least *partly* true.

"Have you ever spent them in St. John the Baptist Parish? I don't know whether or not the Negroes in St. Bernard and Plaquemines have the same quaint custom ours do of utilizing driftwood and roseau reeds."

"I don't believe so. Tell me about it."

"Why, early in December, they start piling up huge stacks of drift-wood and roseau reeds along the levee for Christmas Eve bonfires. The tall poles in the center make them look like trees, and when the roseau reeds begin to burn, the joints explode and give the effect of firecrackers. The whole family goes out to see them. I've been doing it ever since I can remember—ever since I was a very little girl—and I still find it all just as exciting as I did the first time. I wouldn't miss it for anything."

"I can understand just how you feel about it. I felt just the same way about our people's dances on New Year's Day, the way they used to do them when all our family was together."

"We do something else at Belle Pointe, too, Major Beauregard, that perhaps would be new to you. We cut down a big evergreen tree and trim it with colored balls and light it with candles and pile presents around it. It seems lots of people do that in New York now and, after John and Mathilde were married, he wanted to keep up the custom, as it's observed in the Slidell family—and many other families, too, I understand."

"Yes, I know it is. When I went to school in New York, one of my classmates was a boy by the name of Derek Vanderveer. His father was Dutch by descent and his mother English, and they always had a Christmas tree. Quite often I spent the holidays with them, because there wasn't time for me to come home, except in the summer. I always enjoyed these celebrations very much. But I've never seen a Christmas tree since then, and I've never seen the lighted roseau reeds on the levee."

Why, that was practically asking for an invitation! He hadn't meant to do so, but the words were out of his mouth almost before he knew it; in his fear that Caroline would think him forward, he wished he could bite them back. But she answered so cordially that he knew she was not offended after all.

"Of course we'd all be very much pleased, Major Beauregard, if you could spare the time to make us a little visit at Belle Pointe during the holidays, so that you could see our tree and our people's roseau reeds."

"You know how gratefully I'd accept after what I've just said so impulsively. I hope you didn't feel it was presumptuous as well as impulsive."

"Not at all. You spoke as it is natural for friends to speak to each other."

So she had already accepted him as a friend! He would have liked to tell her how much this meant to him, but quickly decided that he must not risk impetuosity a second time. Instead, he asked a question which he hoped he had succeeded in making sound casual.

"And after the holidays won't you be coming back to New Orleans?"

"I think not. John and Mathilde will be returning to Washington then."

"So you'll visit them there, instead?"

"No, I think I'll just stay at Belle Pointe. Of course, while I was at the Visitation in Georgetown—"

"You went to school at the Georgetown Visitation Convent! Did you know a Sister Mary Emmanuel there?"

"No, she died before I entered. But I often went to visit her grave, on the Convent grounds, with other students and we talked about her a great deal. We thought she was a very romantic figure. It was rumored that she entered the Visitation on account of a disappointment in love. Of course, that is the reason given, over and over again, when, actually, it has no foundation in fact, but, schoolgirl fashion, we reveled in believing the story was true."

"In this case, I think it may have been. I knew Sister Mary Emmanuel when she was Virginia Scott and I was also—well, acquainted with the man who wanted to marry her and whom she wanted to marry. Her mother took her to Europe to break up the match. It was there she was converted to Catholicism and then that she decided to become a nun."

"Oh, I'm glad! No, I don't mean that exactly. Of course, it's a sad story. But I'm glad to know that all the sympathy my classmates and I felt for her was justified, that we weren't sorrowing over a myth. I must write and tell them what you've told me—that is, if you don't mind."

"No, I don't mind—as long as you don't think that will start them guessing who the unhappy man was."

"It might, I suppose—and you'd rather I didn't?"

She looked at him thoughtfully and he had the feeling that she herself had already guessed. "I'm afraid Sister Mary Emmanuel was very unhappy," she said gently. "I can understand that. I know I should be if I cared for some man and wasn't allowed to marry him. It was probably partly her mourning for her lost love that affected her health. Though she was only twenty-three years old, she was delicate, so delicate that after she entered the Convent, the nuns feared she might not live the required year before being allowed to take her vows. Actually, she was on her deathbed when she was granted the privilege of doing so, not quite a year after her clothing."

Before Pierre could answer, Mrs. Slidell re-entered the room and all
the gentlemen sprang to their feet again. For a few minutes, conversation once more became general. Then Wharton glanced first
at his wife and, afterward, at Pierre, who caught the signal. But, as
they were saying good night, Slidell detained Pierre for a moment.

"I'll be coming over to the Customs House again, Major, before I
leave for Washington. Still a few little points I'd like to check over
with you. And now you've found your way here, I hope you'll come
again—there might be something you'd like to ask *me*. If there
should be, don't stand on ceremony. You'd be welcome any time.
Wouldn't he, Mathilde?"

"Of course. Make it 'soon and often,' as our people say."

"Thank you very much. I'd like to."

He glanced toward Caroline, hoping that she would also echo her
brother-in-law's invitation. But though she did not do so in words,
he thought he read the second invitation in her face.

So this was the way it had begun, as simply as all that. He had
gone frequently to the Slidells' house, to talk about matters which
came up at the Customs House, for he found that he did want to
take the initiative in discussing these with John Slidell; and when he
went there, he was always invited to share what was called potluck,
and Caroline was always in the dining room and, afterward, in the
drawing room with the rest of the family. And he had gone to Belle
Pointe for part of the holidays and had enjoyed the way these were
celebrated in St. John the Baptist Parish, which was, indeed, quite
different from the way they were celebrated in St. Bernard and
Plaquemines, except that the same spirit and show of conviviality was
as great not only at Belle Pointe, but at Bon Sejour and Armant, San
Francisco and Mount Airy and half a dozen other plantations in the
vicinity, as it was at Contreras and Kenilworth, Conseil and Upper
Magnolia. Now that the Deslondes' neighbor, Valcour Aime, "the
Louis XIV of Louisiana," had gone into perpetual mourning for his
only son, who had died several years earlier of yellow fever, his
plantation, "the little Versailles," was no longer the scene of the
most magnificent entertaining in Louisiana; and, with his withdrawal
and that of his wife, the daughter of Governor Roman, from the
closely knit social circle, the Deslondes became their natural suc-
cessors as its leaders. They did not possess, as he did, a dinner service
of solid gold or a steamboat operated like a private yacht, to convey
his family and guests between his plantation and New Orleans; but
they had a race track and, if they chose, they could have boasted, as

he once had, that they could serve a perfect dinner while using only the produce of their own property—fish, game, fruits, vegetables, nuts and coffee. Belle Pointe, like Upper Magnolia, represented a "simple concession," a plantation forty arpents in depth. Instead of the hedges of Chinese lilacs, which were such a feature at the Villerés, the Deslondes had fences twelve feet high, surmounted with a patterned border of fleurs-de-lis; and their plantation bell, engraved with the date 1792 and the words *J'appartiens à Monsieur Jacques Deslonde*, was one of the largest and most imposing Pierre had ever seen. The plantation house, built foursquare with walls of extraordinary thickness, was surrounded by fifteen-foot galleries and contained forty rooms; it could house any number of guests without seeming overcrowded. And the great drawing room, decorated completely in white from its lofty ceiling's sculptured plaster cornices and rosettes to its enameled floor, made a dazzling setting for the tall lighted Christmas tree, the garlands of yupon and the gaily packaged gifts. In this opulent and hospitable atmosphere, Pierre's mind had been diverted, for the first time, from morbid thoughts of Angele and the tragedy of her death. The welcome given him by Captain and Mme Deslonde was most heartening; and, under its benign influence, he was more and more easily persuaded to join his hosts and his fellow guests in their celebration of the holidays.

Among these at Belle Pointe were three of Captain and Mme Deslonde's four sons: André, Jr., Adrien and Edmond Antoine, with his wife Maria; and all of the Deslonde daughters: Mathilde, Rosella and Henriette—with their husbands, John Slidell, Amedée Guyol and Robert Adams—Julia, still unmarried, to whom James Madison Seixas of Charleston was paying assiduous court; and Caroline; and at the nearby Armant Plantation, Mme Deslonde's nephew, Jean Marie Chastant, was entertaining a bevy of his relatives, among them his sister Celestine and her husband, a prominent young physician by the name of Charles Turpin. Turpin was invariably dressed with great formality, whereas all the other young men affected carefree country dress, suitable for hunting and other sports. In fact, Charles' white tie became a subject of much good-natured raillery; the others all insisted that he wore it even with his nightshirt!

The fact that Caroline had welcomed him as warmly as the rest of the family had, of course, not a little to do with Pierre's change of mood. But he never saw her alone or tried to do so and, presently, the Slidells returned to Washington for the opening of Congress and he became engulfed in the elaborate preparations to celebrate the anniversary of the Battle of New Orleans, when he was to ride with

General Scott in an open carriage. The procession moved, to the music of a military band, from Lafayette Square to the Cathedral, where a *Te Deum* was sung by the full choir, accompanied by instrumental music; and an address was delivered, in French, by the Reverend Napoleon Leon Perche; after the Mass, the General and his entourage, including Pierre, returned via Royal Street to the St. Charles Hotel, where Scott was staying and where his arrival was heralded with the strains of "See the Conquering Hero Comes!" But the pause in the gala proceedings was a brief one; in the evening there were fireworks on Canal Street, and a military and fancy-dress ball, at which Pierre danced every dance—but, mindful of the proprieties, only three of these with Caroline—was given at the Armory Hall by the Louisiana Grays. After that, as Pierre had told Simone, he found that this major celebration led to various minor ones and that he was involved in all of them.

Though the Slidells had left for the winter, occasionally Caroline came down from the plantation to visit friends, briefly, and, when she did, he saw her, off and on, since they moved in much the same circles, though she did not do so at the same hectic pace he did; and eventually he gathered that not only disinclination for ceaseless gaiety, but lack of strength to pursue an endless round of parties was responsible for this. Not that she seemed sickly in an unattractive sense, or that she gave the impression of "enjoying" poor health like many silly, vapid women he had met. When he first heard allusions to her "delicacy," he thought these referred to the fineness of feeling and exquisite sensitivity which he had so admired in her from the beginning. Later, he began to wonder whether or not they might also refer to her physical condition, though obviously, whatever her indisposition might be, it did not cause her much pain, if any, and she certainly was not wasting away. She never could have achieved or maintained such serenity if she were suffering; and her color was fresh, her figure stately. Probably nothing serious was the matter with her.

She never made a point of telling him whom she would be visiting or when, and he did not ask her. He was content, for a long time, to see her only when chance brought them together. He was busier than ever, now that he had the Marine Hospital and the Quarantine buildings on his hands, as well as the Customs House; and though he made a second visit to Belle Pointe at Easter and went boating with Caroline on Lake Maurepas, it was not until the Slidells returned to New Orleans later in the spring, and she came to stay with them again, that he began to recognize the degree of attraction she held for him. He called more and more frequently and occasionally he took her a discreet present: some sheet music, a box of bonbons, a book especially designed as an ornament to the center table in a drawing room. Among the latter was a volume of Shakespeare's *Sonnets*, and he permitted himself to put a ribbon bookmark in the one beginning:

> "Shall I compare thee to a summer's day?
> Thou art more lovely and more temperate. . . ."

Caroline did not refer, specifically, to the bookmark. But she did tell him, when next he called, that she was more pleased with the present of this book than with any other he had given her.

Even then, it did not occur to him that he might ask her to marry him, and this was not only because he was still convinced that Laure was his only true love. It was also because his dread of childbirth had become almost a phobia with him. Marriage, to be normal, even if it were not ecstatic, must involve union; and such union involved the probability of offspring, the contingency which he was determined to avoid at all costs. He was now persuaded that Caroline needed to be treated with supreme tenderness; how then could he willfully shut his eyes to this special need, in order to gratify his own increasing ardor? He did not blame himself for falling in love; he was only human, he had lived continently for a long while and many times had wondered if he could continue to endure celibacy. But there were other answers to passion, long dormant through grief and finally re-awakened. Perhaps it would be better, after all, if he chose a less honorable way than marriage of finding assuagement.

He had almost decided that it would be, when John Slidell spoke to him on a subject seldom, if ever, mentioned among gentlemen, especially when their own womankind was concerned. But one evening Caroline did not appear at the supper table and, as soon as the bountiful meal was over, Mathilde excused herself to go and stay with her sister. The children were in a small sitting room where they kept their games and books and, when John and his guest were left alone in the library, Pierre asked a hesitant question.

"Caroline isn't seriously ill, is she?"

"No." The answer was not really hesitant, too, but it lacked the immediacy and force with which Slidell usually spoke. "You've realized, I suppose, before this, that her health isn't robust," he continued after a minute. "Nothing to cause us real anxiety—I mean no indication of a decline or anything like that. She hasn't Mathilde's boundless energy—in fact, she tires more easily than any of the

Deslonde sisters. But that doesn't mean anything, except that she isn't as strong as they are. At least, that's what we've always supposed. But lately there have been some disquieting symptoms. I wouldn't know just what they are—I believe what are generally called 'female troubles.' Our old friend, Dr. Charles Turpin, came to see her today—I mean professionally. He quite often stops in just for a social call—as you know, his wife Celestine is the daughter of Jean Baptiste Chastant, Madame Deslonde's brother, so she and Caroline are own cousins. It seems that, in the course of his professional visit, Dr. Turpin told Caroline something that upset her very much. That's why she didn't come down tonight—because she's mentally upset, I mean, greatly distressed. Nothing worse than that. She'll be all right in the morning, when she's had a good sleep. She'll put what he's told her out of her mind, and then she'll be all right again, as long as she doesn't overdo."

"Is it—could you tell me what he said that upset her? I mean, is that a proper question for me to ask? If it isn't, of course——"

John Slidell laid down the cigar he had been smoking and looked searchingly at his guest. Pierre was conscious of the scrutiny with which he was being studied.

"Why yes," Slidell said at last. "I think it's a proper question for you to ask, unless I've misread a lot of the signs I've seen lately. I'll tell you exactly what Dr. Turpin told Caroline: he said she must never hope to have any children. He said he was practically sure she couldn't."

The next day, Pierre went to Belle Pointe and asked Captain Deslonde for Caroline's hand in marriage. The planter not only gave his immediate consent, he gave it with obvious approval; and Mme Deslonde, who was promptly asked by her husband to join him and their daughter's suitor in the drawing room, seemed equally pleased. No one, they assured him, could have been more welcome to them for a son-in-law as far as background, breeding, position, character and religion were concerned. His candid statement regarding his limited finances was brushed aside: what was mere wealth compared to all these other qualifications? They insisted that he must take a glass of champagne with them, that he must stay to supper, that he must spend the night. They would not take no for an answer. Why, he was already one of the family!

As he lay wakeful in the pleasant chamber that had been assigned to him, he could not help thinking of the difference between this reception and the one the Villerés had given him when he made the precipitate announcement that he had fallen in love with Laure and wanted to marry her immediately. He tried to dismiss such thoughts as lacking in loyalty to the past. The situation was entirely different, he told himself. No one could say that a man in his early forties and a woman in her middle twenties were too young to marry. No one could say he had made his bold demand on a few days' acquaintance. No one could say that he was too inexperienced to know his own mind and, evidently, no one intended to warn Caroline against shock and disillusionment. Her sisters were all happily married; and Robert Adams, Henriette's husband, though not so conspicuous a figure as John Slidell, was one of the largest wholesale grocers in the city, had several times been appointed Bank Director by the state and, of late, had developed important steamboat interests. Rosella's husband, Amadée Guyol, was Street Commissioner of New Orleans, and this position carried with it a good salary. The Deslondes, for the third time, had been obliged to overcome their aversion to trade; but there was no doubt that Henriette, as well as Mathilde, had done very well for herself financially; and it seemed likely that Julia was soon to make a similar match, for her ardent suitor, James Madison Seixas, was a partner in one of the leading cotton firms in the city. So perhaps the elder Deslondes were actually gratified that, this time, there would be no question of trade and that Pierre's unassailable social standing would more than make up for his lack of wealth. Moreover, the Captain and his wife might well have wondered, rather wistfully, if Caroline were not to have the same fulfillment of love three of her sisters had enjoyed, why no man had realized what a treasure he would find in their middle daughter. This was no case of one ewe lamb, like Laure. Pierre told himself all this over and over, and still the feeling that he was somehow being disloyal to the Villerés persisted.

Morning brought with it a more reasonable viewpoint and better cheer. After an early but bountiful breakfast, eaten in the same atmosphere of cordiality as supper the night before, he took the steamboat *Lafourche*, Captain A. Dugas, Master, enjoyed the trip downstream and, reaching New Orleans in midafternoon, went straight to the Slidells' house. Chance had favored him. Mathilde was out, paying visits, the children were in their game room, Caroline was resting. There was no one to interrupt a quiet talk with John.

"I've been to Belle Pointe," he said without preamble.

"I know. I went to your office to see you about a matter of importance, but—"

"I went to Belle Pointe about a matter of importance. I wanted to ask Captain Deslonde for permission to pay my addresses to Caroline. After what you told me, night before last, I knew there wasn't any reason why I should hesitate any longer."

John Slidell looked at Pierre gravely and no less searchingly than he had done two nights earlier. "I see," he said at last. "What would have frightened most men off was just what you needed to give you courage. And—yes, I understand why. I'll have Mathilde talk to Caroline and—well, explain your attitude. So suppose you don't ask her to marry you until tomorrow. But when you do, I think she'll say yes."

Pierre did not even inquire what the matter of importance about which John wished to see him might be, and it was not until after the happy betrothal had been duly celebrated that the secondary subject came up again. John had reason to believe that Colonel Richard Delafield, Superintendent of the Military Academy at West Point, would like to retire. After all, he was getting to be an old man and he had served several times already, beginning as far back as '38, retiring in favor of Henry Brewerton in '45, and then getting back on the job again after Barnard succeeded Lee in '56. If Delafield's wish became an actuality, John would be in a position to recommend a successor. He had long felt that the Customs House and the Marine Hospital should not be allowed to absorb all Pierre's talents or restrict his horizon. It had occurred to John that Pierre might be interested in the position at West Point and he had meant to suggest his name anyway. Now that he knew—instead of merely hoping—that Pierre was to be his brother-in-law, the suggestion would be all the more natural.

There was not the slightest hesitation on Pierre's part in answering John Slidell. He would be very much interested in the position, even though he had not forgotten that Lee felt differently about the matter when it was offered to him. But then, Pierre thought, as he had many times before and was to think many times again, Lee had been so favored by fortune that the only opportunities which appealed to him were those of exceptional brilliance and spectacular advancement and, apparently, the superintendency of the Military Academy did not fall within those categories, in his opinion. Pierre had kept the letter Lee wrote, in answer to the one he had written, congratulating his old friend on the appointment and, when he went home, after the festive evening when his engagement to Caroline was announced, he took it from the pigeonhole in his desk where it had long laid unnoticed and reread it.

Baltimore 25, June 1852

My dearest Beaury,

"It is an ill wind that blows no good" & but for this unwished for breeze that is driving me toward W. P., I fear I should never have heard from you. The reception of your letter has been the only pleasurable emotion produced by the order, which is the first I ever rec'd that I did not at once commence to obey. I have been wanting to hear from you badly, & have not yet got over my disappointment at missing you when in Mobile. I am glad to find that you are well & hearty. Long may you remain so. You are right in your conjecture of my not being pleased at being ordered to W. P. I know too well the thanklessness of the duty & the impossibility of either giving or rec'ing satisfaction. I have been behind the scenes too long. I know exactly how it works. The Supt. can do nothing right & must father every wrong. I requested, if I was allowed any option in the matter, that some other be app'd in my place. I have been told it cannot be done. I shall therefore have to go and am to relieve Capt. B. on the first day of September. I shall endeavor to do my duty and to consult the interests of the Academy in every particular. My reluctance to the service shall make no difference in my wishes or efforts for the maintenance & advancement of an Institution upon which I believe the standing of the Army and military success of the country mainly depends. But I shall get away from it as soon as I can. I agree with you entirely in the advantages to be derived from giving the Professors an opportunity to visit foreign Institutions & of enlarging & liberalizing their sentiments on the wide subject of education and instruction. I have advocated it for years. But the narrow policy of our people & government forbids it. As soon as it was found that a Prof'r was sent off on such an errand, the app'n for his maintenance at the Academy would be stricken off. Neither could they meet the expenses of such a mission without a proper allowance & where could that be obtained from? It is also difficult to get the proper officers to go there as ass't. teachers. The service is not sought for by those best qualified in general to perform it, nor will they do anything to make it attractive. To get them at all, you must catch them young, before they have gained experience in their profession, or enable them to leave a more disagreeable position. Bad alternatives both. But we must take it as we find it, Beaury, & make the best of it. If you were with me I should hope to succeed. But you must come on & see me.

There is a great assemblage of Engr. officers in Washington at this time. The whole Pacific Board to commence with, Col. Smith at their head. Dutton & Wright of the Florida reef, & the Engineer of Pensacola Harbour. G. W. Smith passed through here on his way from there a few days since. Stevens Foster & Hunt of the Coast Survey & others in the Engr. Bureau make a goodly show. Congress will be alarmed to see so many fine officers idle. Look out for retrenchment when the App'n. Bill comes up. I have not been to W. since the Christmas Holidays. Can therefore tell you nothing of the future. I shall work up the little balance of the former App'n. by the time I leave. The submarine work goes on well. The foundation piles are driven sawed off & prepared with ease & precision by steam machinery, for the reception of the stone work. The stone is laid by a diving bell, in 15 ft. water, at the rate of 10 rectilineal feet of wall, 9 ft. high, a day after the bottom course is laid. If we had have had sufficient funds, the whole wall would have been up to low water level this season. As it is, two faces are brought to that point & we have turned on the third. Brewerton takes my place here. I wish they had have left us as we were.

That young cadet of mine is with me now. This is his furlough year. Several of his comrades are also in Baltimore. Young Jerome Bonaparte, G'nd nephew to the Emperor, graduates this year & has brought with him 3 of his classmates. Casey (son of Capt. C. of the Army & 1st of his class), Ives & Polk. We had them all with us last night, together with the young officers on the Station & all the pretty young girls of Sweet 16. They were amusing, but talked so much they could hardly find time to eat raspberries & ices. They did contrive to swallow a little champagne.

I do not know how my son will come out this examination. The standing was not published when he left. He thinks he will not be below 2nd. His comrades say 1st. Either will do, if he deserves it.

I am glad to hear Barnard is improving. Remember me to him. Also to your handsome boys & believe me always your friend.

R. E. Lee

Major P. G. T. Beauregard
    U. S. Engrs.

Evidently, when he wrote Lee, he himself had not thought the position was so desirable or he would not have suggested that Lee might not be pleased with it. Well, that was nearly eight years ago and his own viewpoint had changed since then. He put the letter back in its pigeonhole and forgot about it.

⊷§ 20 §⊶

CONGRESS CONTINUED ITS SESSION INTO JUNE OF 1860. BUT the momentous convention to nominate a new President drew Slidell for a space in April away from his seat in the senate into the political storm center at Charleston. Of Slidell at this convention a pen picture survives, drawn by a skilful hand, for Murat Halstead, its author, was worthy of the occasion which brought him to Charleston, a master journalist, one of the outstanding figures of his profession. He describes Slidell in action:

Within, seated at a round table on which books, newspapers and writing material is scattered about, is a gentleman with long, thin white hair. . . . The gentleman has also a cherry-red face, the color being that produced by good health, and good living joined to a florid temperament. His features are well cut, and the expression is that of a thoughtful, hardworking, resolute man of the world. He is a New Yorker by birth, but has made a princely fortune at the New Orleans bar. He is not a very eloquent man in the Senate, but his ability is unquestioned; and it is universally known that he is with the present Administration, the power behind the throne greater than the throne itself. Mr. Buchanan is as wax in his fingers. The name of this gentleman is John Slidell. His special mission here is to see that Stephen A. Douglas is not nominated for the Presidency. If I am not much mistaken, he just now manipulated a few Northeastern men with such marvelous art, that they will presently find that they are exceedingly anxious to defeat the nomination of Douglas, and they will believe that they arrived at the conclusion now coming uppermost in their minds in their own way.

I have quoted the description first, but on the previous day Halstead had paid even higher tribute to the political influence of Slidell when he wrote that only the arrogance of the Douglas men induced Slidell to meddle in what was felt to be certain victory. "He will be here this evening, and will operate against Douglas. He is a matchless wire-worker, and the news of his approach causes a flutter. His appearance here means war to the knife. It means also, that the Administration is uneasy on the Douglas question—and feel constrained to use every influence against the Squatty Giant of Illinois, whose nomination would be perdition to Buchanan, Slidell & Co." Two more allusions to Slidell find place in Halstead's account of these critical days. On April 29 he opines that the enemies of Douglas are making little headway. "Slidell and all the rest, have been, as it were, but taking up arms against a sea of troubles, and they have not made much progress toward ending them." On the thirtieth he begins to see results gained by methods which he does not scruple to characterize. Not all followers of Douglas were trustworthy; some were leaky "and whenever the Convention adjourned they were found together buzzing and busy as green flies. It was known that Slidell & Co. were willing to buy all such fellows, and there was alarm in the camp of Douglas on the platform question." Testimony like this of Halstead's, however uncomplimentary to the political methods of Slidell, betokens a political influence which marked him as one of the great figures of the day. The man who divided his party in 1860, whatever his methods or motives, assumed no mean responsibility for the vast consequences determined by that event.

—Louis Martin Sears, *John Slidell*
(Duke University Press)

THE MONTHS THAT ELAPSED BETWEEN THE ANNOUNCEMENT OF THEIR engagement in the autumn, and their quiet wedding, which took place the following May, was a period of great happiness to both Pierre and Caroline. The question of precipitate marriage was never raised by him; he realized that she felt entitled to the prerogatives of an orderly and leisurely betrothal, just as he had realized that his courtship must be conducted on conventional and conservative lines. When she was in New Orleans he visited her daily, unless some unforeseen emergency arose at the Customs House; in that case, he sent her, by special messenger, a loving note attached to a little nosegay; when she was at Belle Pointe, he managed to get there every week, sometimes for over Sunday, sometimes only for one evening, since he still went regularly and conscientiously to Upper Magnolia to see his little daughter Doucette. René and Henri had now gone to the State Seminary of Learning at Alexandria, of which Pierre's old friend, Major William Tecumseh Sherman, was superintendent—in fact, Pierre had recommended him for the post; the boys would therefore be home, hereafter, only for the longer vacation periods. Pierre had consulted M. and Mme Villeré as to the advisability of having Doucette come to school in New Orleans after his marriage to Caroline, but they were unalterably opposed to this. They did not resent his engagement—in fact, they considered it highly suitable under all the circumstances. But Doucette was essentially a Villeré and they wanted her raised like one, meaning by that the way her mother had been raised. Pierre could think of no valid objection. Doucette was only ten years old, she had never known her mother and had known her father only as a visitor; it would be nothing short of refined cruelty to take her from her grandparents, with whom she had always lived. Of course, when she was old enough to make her debut, the situation would be different. But that was looking too far into the future, and probably the governess and tutors who would take charge of her studies would do so quite adequately. Personally, he was enjoying the results of a more comprehensive education, as embodied in Caroline, than would be possible on a plantation; but he could hardly suggest that Doucette should be sent to the Visitation Convent in Georgetown.

When he was at Belle Pointe, he and Caroline spent happy quiet hours in the drawing room; she played the piano while he turned the pages of the sheet music he had given her—the "Poet and Peasant Overture," "Listen to the Mocking Bird," "A Maiden's Prayer." At other times, he read aloud to her while she embroidered; he was again discovering that needlework played an important part in a trousseau, but now it did not constitute a preoccupation from which he was excluded. Caroline had a greater appreciation of *belles lettres* than any woman he had ever known; and listened, with appreciation, to chapter after chapter in Mr. Nathaniel Hawthorne's recently published *Life of Franklin Pierce*, which, Pierre pointed out to her, fully corroborated everything he had said in defense of the General. She agreed that this was a very fine book; she understood its value from both a literary and an historic viewpoint. But she was fonder of poetry than she was of biography. The marked copy of Shakespeare's *Sonnets* which he had given her was the first of many similar offerings. Robert Browning's *Men and Women* had recently reached New Orleans and, after leafing through it by herself, Caroline insisted that the book had so many beauties that these must be shared, not read in solitude. Pierre had always been a great reader himself, though he had concentrated largely on books devoted to military matters in general and the Napoleonic Wars in particular. But he adapted himself readily to Caroline's tastes, for he, too, was a romanticist at heart, and he frequently paused at passages which seemed to him especially significant in relation to his fiancée and himself.

> " 'All is silver gray,
> Placid and perfect in my art' "—

He read and stopped. Then, before going on to the next lines of *Andrea del Sarto*, he said slowly, "Those words describe you perfectly, Caroline, 'placid and perfect,' I mean. And there is something silvery about you, too—about the atmosphere you create. It's so untouched by anything garish or tawdry."

Besides the tranquil hours in the drawing room, there were many when they went walking and boating together and sometimes riding, though Caroline was not essentially a horsewoman. It was in the quieter pursuits that she excelled, and he was content to have it that way. Early in the new year, they began to speak of a tentative date for their marriage and Pierre suggested an Easter wedding, but John Slidell made a countersuggestion.

"I expect to be in Charleston most of April," he told the assembled family, "as much of it, anyway, as I can get away from Washington. In Louisiana, people don't seem to be much concerned with the national situation, but I'm here to tell you it's chaotic. Unless it can be stopped before it begins, I look for trouble at the national convention that's going to assemble the latter part of the month. And that's what I aim to do, if I can. At all costs, the Cotton States have got to prevent the nomination of Douglas and in the struggle to do it they'll have the support of the President. Buchanan doesn't want the nomination—in fact, he'd decline to accept it if it were offered to him. But he doesn't intend to have it go to Douglas."

The Deslondes were accustomed to thinking of John Slidell primarily as a thoroughly satisfactory son-in-law, who saw to it that their darling Mathilde was lapped in luxury and who had made possible her proud position as an outstanding official hostess. Only Pierre, among those who sat listening to him as he talked about the Charleston convention, recognized him as a great political power, who managed to mold the President in any way he chose while adroitly giving the impression that he was scrupulously carrying out Buchanan's wishes. If Slidell were preparing to campaign against Douglas, the Little Giant was as good as doomed already. But John had spoken the truth when he said that Louisiana was not yet thoroughly aroused to the gravity of the national situation; indeed, like most of his acquaintances, Pierre felt that John was inclined to exaggerate this. He had every reason to hope so. He was on the threshold of marriage and the thought that he might be wrested from his bride to see active service again was anything but welcome. Moreover, there was that question of the Superintendency at West Point, dormant for the moment, but by no means abandoned. Never in his life had he felt less like a fire-eater.

"Now if May—late May—would suit our courting couple," John went on, "that would be much better for me. Even if Congress doesn't adjourn until June, I could probably get a pair long enough to justify me in coming south. After all, I did that when I went to Charleston and the political situation in Louisiana bears watching, too. Mind you, I'm not promising I can come, but it's a possibility and there's no possibility that I could be here in April, none whatever."

"Of course we want you at our wedding, John," Caroline said, cordially and sincerely. "You wouldn't mind, would you, Pierre, if we decided on May instead of April?"

As a matter of fact, he really did not mind very much. Like Caroline, he was enjoying the betrothal period. Besides—though he hoped and believed he was not allowing this to become a major consideration —he realized that it was to his best interest to go along, as far as possible, with almost any suggestion John Slidell chose to make. The realization was strengthened by his future brother-in-law's next proposal.

"All right. We've decided now on the date of the wedding. Late May. Have you made up your mind where you and your bride are going to live, Pierre?"

"Why no! At least—"

"At least, you must have known you and she couldn't live in the haphazard way you've been doing these last few years," John Slidell said rather sarcastically. It was true that, since Laure's death, Pierre had taken little interest in what kind of a place served him for an abode in New Orleans. He did not have a permanent *pied-à-terre* of his own, but for a time had usually made his headquarters with one of his married sisters. Since Angele's tragic and sudden death, instead of staying all the time with Elodie, he had often visited friends, including Charles and Celestine Turpin, whom he now numbered as such, except while on his regular stays at Upper Magnolia, his less frequent sojourns at Contreras and the tours of inspection which still took him, occasionally, to the forts. It had not occurred to him that he could not go on drifting aimlessly like this, because, until so recently, there had been no reason why he should give that matter much thought. But John Slidell was quite right, as usual. It was high time he did.

"I had rather a special reason for asking," John continued. "A certain client of mine, a Madame Andry, is looking for a temporary tenant. She's going to be absent from New Orleans for a time and she doesn't want to leave her house unoccupied. On the other hand, she doesn't want to sell it or have it tied up on a long lease. She asked me the other day if I could suggest someone who might take it over under those conditions at a very reasonable rental, really a nominal one. I thought of you and Caroline right away, Pierre, but naturally I waited for a chance to consult you before saying anything definite. I didn't mention your names at all. I only said I had some friends who were going to be married before long and that I'd speak to them about the house, that I had an idea it might suit them."

"Where is the house?" Pierre inquired. "What's it like?"

"It's on Chartres Street, directly opposite the former Ursuline Convent, which is now the Archbishopric. It's a very fine house—or rather, it was when it was built. It's changed hands twice since then and it hasn't been kept up as well as it should have been—not that it's in bad condition, I don't mean that, but it isn't the showplace it once was. You must know the one I have in mind. It's a raised cottage type, built by the famous Spanish architect Francisco Correjolles for the rich auctioneer Joseph Le Carpentier, whose daughter Telcide married Judge Alonzo Morphy. Most people associate it with the Morphys, particularly Paul, that wizard of a chess player, though the family moved to Royal Street years ago and still lives there. Le Carpentier sold the place to John and Aloïse Merle and Aloïse did wonders with it. Le Carpentier had a sort of jungle in the side garden, wild but effective, and Aloïse followed a formal French pattern, also with very good results. By the way, it's the only house in the Quarter that has both a patio and a side garden. All the fostering care that's been put on the place still shows, even though it hasn't had so much lately. I believe Caroline might be glad to undertake that."

"Why yes, I should, if Pierre likes the place," she said readily, glancing at her fiancé. Then, seeing that his expression was alert and receptive, she went on, "When could we see it, John?"

"Right after Twelfth Night. I'll make an appointment for you."

There was no doubt in the mind of either one that this was the house for them. They fell in love with it almost as soon as they were inside the front door, and their feeling of enthusiasm increased as Mme Andry took them down the long central corridor and invited them to inspect the great rooms that led out of it on either side. What spaciousness! What elegance! What ornamentation! What harmony! The cornices and rosettes represented masterpieces of a plasterer's art; the wide-columned opening between the *salle de compagnie* and the banqueting hall would facilitate the joint use of the two for entertaining, and given such a setting of course they would wish to invite their friends to share it with them as often as possible. The outlook from the bedrooms, which gave on the garden, was delightful, and so was the sound of the fountain which formed the garden's central ornament. When the visitors reached the rear gallery, facing the ample slave quarters and looking out on the patio, which was flanked by the kitchen on one side and the carriage house on the other, they were beginning to feel that their praise might sound fulsome, because it was so all-embracing; however, Mme Andry beamed on them, obviously not only relieved but overjoyed at the prospect of such appreciative tenants.

"And I understand your marriage is planned for late May?" she asked. It was half a statement, half a question. "That would suit me perfectly. I do not want to leave before June at the earliest, but it is really imperative that I should do so then. You see, my married daughter——" She embarked on a detailed description of family problems and obligations. "I may wish to be absent as much as two years," she said finally. "But I cannot be certain. That would not deter you?"

They assured her that nothing would deter them. As they went down the winding stone steps leading from the front gallery to the street, they turned back several times to look at the classic entrance. When next they went through it together, it would lead to their bridal home.

◄§ 21 §►

The ordering of divers sorts of herbes for the pot; for meat;
and for the table

TIME, SAVORY AND HYSSOPE, ARE USUALLY SOWEN IN THE
Spring on beds by themselves, every one a part; but they that
make a gaine by selling to others the young rootes, to set the
knots or borders of Gardens, do for the most part sow
them in July and August, that so being sprung up before
Winter, they will be the fitter to be taken up in the Spring
following, to serve any mans use that would have them. Sage,
Lavender and Rosemary, are altogether set in the Spring, by
slipping the old stalkes, and taking the youngest and likeliest
of them, thrusting them either twined or otherwise halfe a
foot deep into the ground, and well watered upon the setting;
if any seasonable weather do follow, there is no doubt of their
well thriving: the hot Sunne and piercing drying windes are
the greatest hinderances to them; and therefore I do advise
none to set too soone in the Spring, nor yet in Autumne, as
many do practice: for I could never see such come to good,
for the extremity of the Winter coming upon them so soon
after their setting, will not suffer their young rhootes to abide,
not having taken sufficient strength in the ground, to maintain themselves against such violence, which doth often pierce
the strongest plants. Marjerome and Bassil are sowen in the
Spring, yet not too early; for they are tender plants, and do
not spring until the weather be somewhat warme: but Bassil
would be sowen dry, and not have any water of two or three
dayes after the sowing, else the seed will turne to a gelly in
the ground. Some use to sow the seed of Rosemary, but it seldom abideth the first Winter, because the young plants being
small, and not of sufficient strength, cannot abide the sharp-
nesse of some Winters, notwithstanding the covering of them,
which killeth many old plants, but the usual way is to slippe
and set, and so they thrive well. Many do use to sowe all or

the most sorts of Pot-herbes together on one plot of ground, that they need not to go farre to gather all the sorts they would use. There are many sorts of them, well known unto all, yet few or none do use all sorts, but as every one liketh; some use those that others refuse, and some esteem those not to be wholesome, and of a good rellish, which others make no scruple of. The names of them are as followeth, and a short relation of their sowing or planting.

—John Parkinson, Apothecary of London, and the Kings Herbarist, *Paradisi in Sole Paradisus Terrestris*

'Ting to Fix, Madam?

A common sight in the streets of old New Orleans . . . was the perambulating tinsmith or " 'Ting To Fix Man." Armed with a charcoal furnace, a soldering iron, a bar of solder, a pair of snips, a small bottle of acid, and a few scraps of tinned sheet metal in a carrying case slung over his shoulder, men of this craft, usually Lombardians, scorched the English language as well as the French, in announcing their presence in the neighborhood, and their readiness to render first aid to sheet metal utensils in need of repair.

" 'Ting Ta Fix," he would yell at the top of his voice at every ten paces. And if a woman showed her head at the door, " 'Ting to fix, madam?" he would entreat; meaning, "Anything to fix, madame, any clothes boilers, milk pails, tin dippers, tin pails needing repair?" And any such which were brought out for the ministrations of the tinsmith, were usually repaired on the spot. On those occasions when an utensil required a major overhauling, the smith would be entrusted to take it to his shop. . . .

It was not unusual for the " 'Ting To Fix Man" to double as an organ grinder doing a stint of two tunes for a nickel, late afternoons and evenings before the ragtime era impelled Negroes to take over and jazz up the tunes with a rhythmic turning of the organ handle. The same tune ground out by the Italian and the Negro were entirely different things. Both races are said to have music in their souls. Granted. But they certainly have different techniques.

—Leon H. Grandjean, *Crayon Reproductions of Leon J. Fremaux' New Orleans Characters and Additional Sketches*

Supt's Office N. C. Semie
New Orleans Jany 12th/60

Dear Major —
Your favor of the 8th inst
has just been received — I suppose
under the present circumstances the
supervisors may get larger appropriations from the Legislature for
the Seminary as a State Institution.
Hence I would not oppose them — let
them go ahead. With regard to the
bedstead question I do not attach
much importance to it: but if the
rooms are large enough — I think they
will & ought to come to it — The public
system at West Point seems to work
beautifully — the Cadets bed them, always
looking, until night; like an old maid's
bed.
I have received a long letter from my
son Rhea; he appears to be highly pleased
with all that he sees all this entirely
novel to him — Rhea has never been
even to a boarding school — but he says
he has made up his mind to stand
this world whatever it may be —
By the by, I attach not much importance
to his Latin & Greek — indeed I do not
care about his learning the latter — but
I do about his English, Spanish. In the

matics, history & Geography but the
latter I think he has got better with as
well as with his French —

He is a good gymnast & boxer — &
might if you desire instruct in both
during spare moments —

My desire is to have been to give him
a thoroughly practical & matter of fact
education —

I understand you are giving yourself
some concern about political matters
if I was in your place I would pay
not attention whatever to them — When
& where necessary I would clearly & strongly
state my views & position — & if those
with whom you are acting are not satisfied I would quietly put my resignation in their hands but I do hope
for the sake of the State & of myself
that you will not have to come to
such a pass — With a little patience
& time everything will no doubt
work smoothly & to the advantage
of all concerned —

         Yours truly
         G. T. Beauregard

Major Wm H. Thomas
   State Secretary of Living
     Alexandria
       La

Pierre and Caroline were married, very quietly, by Father Claude Maistre, Pastor of St. Rose of Lima, at the Slidells' house on Esplanade. John succeeded, as he had hoped he might, in getting a pair which would permit a brief absence from his duties at the Senate Chamber; but this proved difficult to arrange and gave almost no leeway as to time. When a deal was finally made with Senator Sumner of Massachusetts, the telegram, announcing that John and Mathilde were starting immediately for New Orleans, further stated that it would be almost impossible for the Senator to be absent from Washington long enough to allow a trip to Belle Pointe. Personally, Pierre was pleased rather than otherwise by this arrangement; he wanted nothing about his marriage to Caroline—except, of course, the element of happiness, and even that of a different happiness—to remind him of his marriage to Laure. A huge plantation house wedding, with relatives and friends flocking to it from near and far, feasting, dancing and general merrymaking over a long period, would inevitably bring back recollections which could only be painful. He hoped and believed that Caroline was not disappointed, that she did not feel she had too readily agreed that, of course, John must be present at her wedding, first by consenting to postpone it for a month and now by consenting to have it in her sister's house instead of her parents'. He knew that young ladies generally had fixed ideas about their bridal plans and that, often, these plans were made long in advance; certainly, Caroline must have visualized a bevy of bridesmaids, a sumptuous spread and the great white ballroom at Belle Pointe transformed for a marriage ceremony in a way that would make it more beautiful than ever. But if she had any regrets, she gave not the slightest sign of it; quite the contrary.

"A big wedding is a terrible strain," she told him. "All of us at Belle Pointe were exhausted after Mathilde's marriage to John, and Rosella's to Amedée and Henriette's to Robert, and I'm sure I'd have been even more exhausted if I'd been the bride, instead of merely a bridesmaid. I tire so much more easily than any of the others that it's a relief to know I won't have to pretend it isn't an effort to keep up with them. This will be much simpler for my mother, too. Mathilde will take everything off *maman*'s shoulders—she's a natural-born hostess and, besides, she's had no end of experience. It won't seem any harder for her to prepare for a small wedding, on short notice, than it would to give a dinner party. Remember how astonished you were at first by the elegance of what she and John called potluck suppers? I'm really delighted at the way things have turned out. I'm going to wear a very beautiful dress, though, unless you feel that wouldn't be appropriate for such an unpretentious occasion. We have a great deal of old family lace and we felt—after all, I'm well along in my twenties now; we thought it would be more suitable than something a young girl would wear for her wedding."

There was no question that it was both suitable and elegant. The priceless lace, tinted ivory with age, its deep fichu and wide flounces mounted on creamy satin and caught up with white roses, and a great length of it serving as a veil, made superb bridal attire; a parure of topazes gave it added brilliance. Thus robed, Caroline was transfigured. Hitherto, in a family gathering her sisters had outshone her. She was lovely, but she was so retiring that her essential dignity and grace were obscured by the resplendence of the others. Now, theirs were obscured by hers. There was a new note, a note of intense pride and satisfaction in Pierre's happiness as he stood beside her for the exchange of vows. Because of him, Caroline was at last magnificently revealed.

No question of a wedding journey had been raised, and neither had that of the time-honored round of family visits, long considered the logical sequence to nuptial seclusion. Both were eliminated by Pierre's inability to get prolonged leave of absence from his duties at the Customs House and the forts. After the marriage ceremony, he and his bride drove quietly from the Slidells' house to the one they already looked upon as their own, which had been put in complete readiness for them by Mme Andry before her departure. She had left her capable domestic staff behind her and the household ran smoothly and unobtrusively. Pierre was able, almost every day, to come home for dinner and, in his absence, Caroline spent much of her time outdoors. She took immense pride in restoring Aloïse Merle's garden to its original charming and orderly pattern, and great pleasure in the herb garden of the old Ursuline Convent, now the Archbishopric, which she had only to cross the street to visit. A section of the kitchen garden at Belle Pointe was devoted to the herbs regularly used for seasoning in everyday cooking—sage, basil, chives, mint, rosemary

and tarragon; but Caroline had not previously seen a far greater variety planted in a spacious design which achieved a delightful harmony
of color and scent. The first Ursuline nuns had brought with them
from France booklets in which were carefully inscribed directions for
the nurture and administration of these herbs for medicinal purposes, as well as drawings intended to serve as guides for the pattern
of a formal garden; and these booklets were still carefully preserved
in the Archbishopric. Caroline was permitted to see them and, mindful of the privilege, pored over them and made meticulous plans and
sketches for a herb garden of her own.

From the front gallery of the house, she watched the traditional
Corpus Christi procession as it wound its way from the old convent
to the Cathedral—the white-clad children scattering flowers, the
priests in gorgeous vestments, the glittering monstrance displayed
beneath a splendid canopy supported by four poles and carried by
stalwart bearers. A few weeks later, as it followed the same route, she
watched the magnificent funeral cortege of the great Archbishop Antoine Blanc, who had been her kindly neighbor, and who had died
suddenly in an upper chamber of the historic building. Very often,
too, she lingered on this gallery, not to see some extraordinary spectacle, but to make closer acquaintance with the picturesque itinerant
vendors who went up and down the street hawking their wares.
Earliest in the morning came the fruit-and-vegetable man calling,
"Redder de beets, yellow de bananas, redder de strawberries." Then
came the bottle man, pushing a cart and calling out, "Bottles for
candy!" which meant hard candy in glass jars; and soon thereafter
the Switzer candy man, who did not have a cart, but came dancing
along the street, calling, "Candy five cents a stick!" Next, in rhythmic
succession came the old rag man, who made new hats out of tattered
scraps; the " 'ting to fix" man, who mended pots and pans; the chimney sweeps, always frolicking along two by two, wearing tall hats
and carrying brushes and chains; and finally the organ grinder, who
would play three tunes for a nickel. Caroline was careful to save a coin
for him after buying her stick of candy.

She could while away half a day contentedly looking at sights and
listening to sounds like these—or as much of a day as she was not
either in Aloïse Merle's garden or in the Archbishop's; at night, she
drifted off to sleep still thinking happily of these simple pleasures
and, in the morning, she woke conscious that she was facing another
day of similar joys. Meanwhile, when it was time for Pierre to come
home from the office, she never failed to listen for his footsteps and
run to greet him at the front door. Then there were quiet hours de-

voted to reading and music, as there had been at Belle Pointe; and there were other quiet hours, later in the evening, when they sat on the rear gallery or in the garden, enjoying the cool breeze which rustled the leaves after the heat of the day and listening to the music of the fountain.

They were so happily self-sufficient by themselves that they craved no other company; but, wisely, they did not shun this when it seemed natural and fitting to welcome family and friends to their new home or, in their turn, to make visits. Far from resenting Pierre's second marriage, the Villerés had been pleased with it; there was always a welcome waiting the bridal pair at Upper Magnolia and, from time to time, they took advantage of it. The boys and Doucette were shy of Caroline at first, and she of them, but it was a shyness from which they all quickly recovered. At Belle Pointe, the family gatherings were as expansive and lavish as ever; all the various branches of the Deslonde family vied with each other in hospitality. In town, Charles and Celestine Turpin lived in a tall, handsome house with multiple ironwork galleries on Royal Street, just around the corner from Chartres; visiting between the two *jeunes ménages* was constant and congenial. Then there were Pierre's sister Elodie and her husband Richard Proctor, almost as near at hand, and Caroline's sister Henriette and her husband Robert Adams, also easily accessible. All these establishments were well staffed and well run; open house was the rule rather than the exception; and they harbored a circle so closely knit that it needed no added members to make it festive. However, all social New Orleans wanted to show its approval of the match between two of its prime favorites; one gala occasion succeeded another.

In July, Pierre was called on to make one of his periodic routine visits to the forts, and Caroline went to Belle Pointe for a few days; after that, nothing again interrupted the even tenor of their life until October. Then a prolonged drought, threatening the water supply at both Jackson and St. Philip, indicated the necessity of his return there. It was not merely a question of insufficient rainwater, he explained to Caroline; it was also a question of salt water, coming so far upstream from the Gulf when the water in the river was low, that this was undrinkable, too. Additional gutters and pipes must be built and cisterns enlarged or supplemented to make sure that every drop which fell from the skies could be turned to profitable account; and, though wells had never been successfully utilized in the area of the forts, he decided to have some dug, as an emergency measure. It might do no good, but it certainly could do no harm. He wished that so many episodes in his life, apparently trivial enough in themselves, would not serve to revive such poignant memories. The last time he had been called to the forts in an emergency it had been on account of a flood and not on account of a drought; instead of dwelling on what happened before, he should be thankful that no element of danger was now involved, either for himself or for the woman he loved. His leave-taking of Caroline was as untroubled as when he set out for his daily duties at the Customs House; he would miss her and she would miss him, but after all they must expect occasional brief separations. Another cause for thankfulness lay in the fact that there was no prospect of a long absence.

"The funny thing about this is," he said, as he kissed her good-by, "that I have a feeling the drought's about over. In fact, I shouldn't wonder if a storm blew up before the end of the day, though there's no sign of it yet and the glass hasn't begun to fall. Well, if rain does come right away, so much the better! Then I won't have to stay long to see whether or not the measures I've advocated are working out all right or come home still wondering and worrying about them."

He made the trip downriver comfortably and quickly on a supply ship opportunely starting early that morning for Jackson. Once there, he promptly made his tour of inspection, gave directions for supplementing the pipes, gutters and cisterns with materials he had brought with him and set fourteen colored enlisted men to digging a well under the supervision of a lieutenant. Then, as first dark had still not set in, he decided to cross the river to St. Philip in a rowboat and spend the night there after sizing up the situation. He had hardly left Jackson when he saw that the prophecy he had made early that morning was on the point of being fulfilled. The wind was already blowing upstream against the current, and soon the first drops, forerunners of a brief but violent southeaster, came pelting down. The conflict between opposing current and wind made navigation difficult and Pierre realized that, even without the increasingly heavy downpour, the waves slapping against the bow would soon have drenched him with their spray had it not been for the poncho he had had the foresight to bring with him. The powerful rowing of his two Negro boatmen was aided by the wind, but impeded by the current, as they crossed on a long diagonal, which kept their small unsteady craft on a reasonably direct course; and, as they neared the opposite bank, a curling brown eddy swept them a bit downstream, enabling the rowers to approach the entrance to the St. Philip landing bow on, with just enough headway to keep the craft in the channel leading to the plank wharf. Pierre rose unsteadily and stood for a moment, teetering and balancing against the sluggish but unpredictable roll of the skiff. Then he attempted to get one foot on the slippery planks of the dock, just as a sudden quirk of the current swung the boat fore and outward; he tried to straddle the widening rift, lost his foothold and pitched headlong into the swirling water.

He was a powerful swimmer, but his poncho, uniform and boots weighed him down and, moreover, he had the current against him. He sank quickly and came to the surface, struggling to rid himself of his poncho, only to sink a second time before he succeeded in doing so. Once freed, he desperately fought his way to safety, though it was all of five minutes before he managed to get close enough to the landing to muscle himself up onto the slippery planks, where the boatmen, terrified lest they be blamed for the mishap, helped to pull him to his feet.

"Fo' God, Mist' Major," one of them began, "it weren't none of us fault, we done de bestes'. . . ."

"I know that," he said ungrudgingly. "Tomorrow, we'll hope for better luck. Meanwhile, I must go ahead and do what I came here for—after I've seen if anyone can lend me some dry clothes."

He nodded and strode off toward the fort. A week later, he made light of the incident in describing it to Caroline.

"While I was thrashing around in the water, I saw the face of God. He was not very pleased with me."

"Darling, don't jest. If you had lost your life, it would have killed me, too. I'd have had nothing left to live for. And here you are home, safe and sound." She clung to Pierre, still shaken with sobs, momentarily wordless. Then, as he stroked her hair and murmured to her soothingly, she became calmer and finally looked up at him with a smile. "I don't know why He shouldn't have been pleased," she said. "I believe you're mistaken. I believe He was. And Pierre—if you really did look into His face—don't you know that in itself shows He loves you? Don't you remember what the Bible says about those who shall see God? They are among the blessed."

⌬ 22 ⌬

Special Order, No. 238.

War Department, Adjutant-General's Office,
Washington, *November 8th,* 1860.

By direction of the President, brevet Major Peter G. T. Beauregard, Corps of Engineers, is appointed superintendent of the Military Academy, and will relieve the present superintendent at the close of the approaching semi-annual examination of cadets.

By order of the Secretary of War.

S. Cooper, Adjutant-General.

7th.   MAJOR G. T. BEAUREGARD

Took leave of us all today, he having been appointed as Commander at the Military Academy at West Point. Since his appointment as Superintendent of the New Custom House, he has always conducted himself with dignity, and treated all with that respect that was their due. In regard to myself I have received at his hand many favours and although I have tried to serve him in return by obeying his orders and carrying them out to the letter, many a man in his situation would have considered that my duty, without the many kindnesses that he has shown me from time to time, and I and every person employed upon the works wish him Godspeed and pray that his sicknesses may be no worse.

—Private Memorandum Book of John Roy, January, 1861

Jan. 7, 1861.

Major Beauregard formally turned over to me today the Superintendence of the New Custom House, and the new Marine Hospital, which was duly communicated to the Treasury Department, and to the Collector of the Port. . . . The Major leaves for West Point tomorrow.

Jan. 8, 1861.

The vote yesterday was in favor of the candidates who advocate the withdrawal of this State from the Union, and then the construction of a Southern Confederacy.

Jan. 9, 1861.

Major Beauregard got off this morning at 7 in the Jackson R. R. cars.

Jan. 14, 1861.

Very busy at the office trying to keep the operations at the Customs House in unbroken progress until the wounds that afflict the country are healed or a permanent settlement of the "questio vexata" determined upon.

Jan. 26, 1861.

The "Ordinance of Secession" of Louisiana was passed at 12½ P.M. and announced to the city by the simultaneous ringing of the Fire Alarm Telegraphs, and the booming of cannon. The weather cleared up, and the sun shone out with special brilliance at noon much to the revival of depressed spirits, and the general vivification of street life in New Orleans.

Jan. 28, 1861.

Everything financially, politically, and socially is resolved into an aggregate of utter incertitude.

—Excerpts from the diary of T. K. Wharton

IT WAS, PERHAPS, BECAUSE HE AGREED WITH CAROLINE, BECAUSE HE felt himself truly blessed, especially in his life with her, that Pierre continued to be either oblivious of the mounting peril in the national situation or untroubled by it. True, he recognized the menace to peace presented by the election of Lincoln and went so far as to ex-

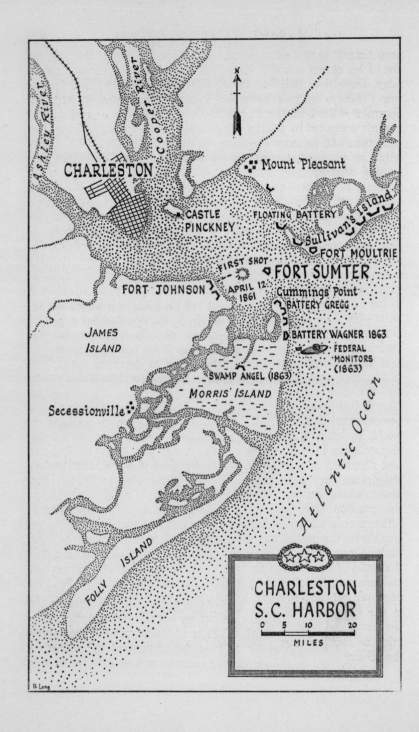

CHARLESTON
S.C. HARBOR

0   5   10   20
MILES

press himself to that effect in writing to Captain Charles Barnard, still one of his closest friends. "Everyone seems bent on beating Breckinridge, Douglas or Bell," he said. "They never trouble about Lincoln who I think is our most dangerous enemy." But, writing to his friend Sherman at the Louisana State Seminary of Learning, he belittled the hazards presented by political problems; he said he felt confident that with time and patience the crisis would probably pass. In the same letter, he discussed the question of bedsteads, which were apparently causing dissatisfaction at the school. "I do not attach much importance to it, but if the rooms are large enough, I think they will & ought to come to it—the present system at West Point seems to work beautifully—the Cadets' beds there, always looking, until night, like an old maid's bed." Further along, Pierre dwelt on his son René's general situation. "He appears to be highly pleased with all that he sees altho' entirely novel to him—for he has never been even to a boarding school—but he says he has made up his mind to stand the worst, whatever it may be. By the by, I attach not much importance to his Latin & Greek—indeed, I do not care about his learning the latter—but I do about his English, Spanish, Mathematics, history & Geography, but the latter I think he has got thru' with as well as with his French."

If he had been really troubled about the national situation, Pierre told himself later, he could hardly have written about old maids' beds and the comparative importance of Greek and English to a young Creole. But perhaps, he also admitted later, he was neither oblivious nor untroubled, but willfully blind. More than anything else in the world, he desired the superintendency at West Point. A year had now elapsed since John Slidell first spoke to him on the subject and they had discussed it together many times since; but Delafield, whose resignation they had hopefully awaited, seemed inordinately slow about taking action; and, meanwhile, various other aspirants for the position were appearing on the horizon. Moreover, though hitherto only officers of the Engineering Corps had been considered eligible for the post, it was rumored that Jefferson Davis, now United States Senator from Mississippi, was ready to advocate that, hereafter, it should be opened to officers in other branches of the service. Several senators, Slidell among them, could be counted on to fight the proposal; but the power and prestige of Davis, founded on his prowess in the Mexican War, were increasing by leaps and bounds. Were the power and prestige of Slidell—and of Benjamin, on whose cooperation he could of course count—still strong enough to prevail against the others?

Pierre believed that they were, Caroline believed that they were; her confidence in her brother-in-law was exceeded only by her conviction that no one, absolutely no one, could possess the same supreme qualifications for the position as did her idolized husband. When the orders finally came through, appointing him Superintendent of the Academy as of January, 1861, she told him, between tears and laughter, that of course she had known all along John would manage, that Pierre would get his just reward.

"If you were so certain, why all this excitement now?" he asked her teasingly.

"Why, it's one thing to believe you're certain and another thing to have it proved!" she told him. "You know that as well as I do, *cher!*" And she added, still speaking joyously, "We'll have to leave right after New Year's, won't we? That is, so there'll be time to make Mathilde and John a short visit in Washington on our way to New York—Washington's such a good place to break the trip! And we'll have to send Madame Andry word, won't we, that we're giving up her lovely house? That will be my one regret in leaving New Orleans. I'll start hunting right away for someone who'll come here and stay until she can get back. I wouldn't feel easy if the place were left without anyone to take care of it."

"Well, darling, I don't know. . . ." He spoke reluctantly. She was so full of happy excitement that he dreaded to say anything that would dampen this; but he knew there was no way to avoid telling her what he must. "I'd hate a separation as much as you would. But I think perhaps it would be better if you didn't come with me," he went on slowly. "I'm not at all sure what shape the Superintendent's house is in, for one thing. Perhaps you couldn't be comfortable in it until it's undergone some renovation. I'd like to be sure."

"Why, Pierre, you know I wouldn't mind some discomforts, if I could only be with you!"

"Perhaps you wouldn't mind them for yourself. But I'd mind them for you. It can be terribly cold at West Point in midwinter. Do you think I'd let you risk contracting pneumonia?"

"Is it so much colder than Washington? I never contracted pneumonia there!"

"It's a great deal colder. Besides, when you were in Washington, you were either in a well-organized school or in your brother-in-law's luxurious house. This would be entirely different."

"Pierre, isn't there something you're not telling me? Something besides the possible condition of the Superintendent's house or the rigorous climate at West Point that makes you hesitate to take me with you?"

"It's just a feeling that it isn't best, Caroline."

"Aren't you going to say anything more than that?"

"I can't. I'm sorry, terribly sorry, but I can't."

He had hurt her, he knew, and for the first time. But still he was not ready to put into words his unwelcome consciousness that the country was seething with unrest, that almost anything might happen at almost any moment, that though the coveted appointment had at last come through, forces stronger than any that either Jefferson Davis or John Slidell could summon might prevent him from filling it.

She did not bring up the subject of going with him again nor, even when the news of South Carolina's secession reached them just before Christmas, did he discuss with her the crisis which he was still trying to pretend would pass, given time and patience. Charlestonians were proverbially hot-headed; when they had cooled off they would see reason. *Reason!* Did anyone recognize reason at a time like this? Whatever it might be, no one in the Deep South seemed to see it, Charlestonians even less. They had been fussing about their old forts for nearly a month before they seceded and, so far as Pierre could see, they had had nothing to worry about—then. Of course, some people might say he was a poor one to criticize anyone else for fussing about old forts, because that was what he was doing all the time himself. But, in his opinion, the circumstances had been entirely different. Of Charleston's four forts, only Moultrie was garrisoned when the Secessionists began their clamor, and the entire staff, headed by a gouty old colonel, reportedly consisted of only eight officers, sixty men and thirteen musicians! Besides, it was half-smothered with the beach sand that had drifted all over it on the sea side, and was so easy of access, on the land side, that not only did the inhabitants of Moultrieville—from which it was separated only by a wide street—enter it and leave it at their pleasure; cattle also wandered in and out at will. What sort of military menace had that represented? As to the other forts, there was Johnson, on James Island, which had been built during the Revolution and completely abandoned afterward; to all intents and purposes it was now a ruin. Castle Pinckney, occupied only by an ordnance sergeant and his family, was located on Folly Island which, in Pierre's opinion, was well named. Of course, there was Sumter, which did have a commanding position at the entrance to the harbor; but Sumter was still unfinished, after thirty years of desultory work on it. If the United States Government had not cared enough about these forts to see that they were kept in some semblance of order all this time, why should Charlestonians have been so quick to assume that its so-called defenses were to be reactivated?

Pierre was bound to admit that, since November, there had been signs of radical change. Captain John Gray Foster, an able engineer of whom Beauregard had seen a good deal in the Mexican War and whom he had liked, arrived on the scene, opened an office, hired a small army of stonemasons and mechanics, and set to work to rid Moultrie of intruders, both two-legged and four-legged, and prepare Sumter to mount guns. Indeed, he was so determined to make up for previous slackness that he brought energetic workmen down from Baltimore, to swell the ranks he could not fill with easy-going Charlestonians. But this in itself did not signify too much: Foster was a New Englander; he disliked slovenly habits on general principles.

Then there was all that hubbub about the arsenal. Colonel Gardner had finally asked the Secretary of War, John Floyd, for reinforcements: fifty drilled recruits for Moultrie and two companies to occupy Sumter and Pinckney. The Secretary, characteristically, took no action and, in the absence of more men, Gardner was finally persuaded by two of his officers, Abner Doubleday and Truman Seymour, that those who were already in the fort must be better armed; so he detailed Seymour to replenish their stock of ammunition, hand grenades and maintenance supplies from the United States Arsenal. This would, ordinarily, have been tolerantly regarded; after all, it was routine procedure. But Gardner endeavored to cloak it in secrecy, ordering that the enlisted men in the squad should wear civilian clothes and that the entire project should be carried through under cover of darkness. Seymour had hardly tied up at the wharf customarily used and begun operations when he was tapped on the shoulder by an individual who informed him that the wharf was private property and could not be used for such a purpose. A hostile crowd gathered, there were shouts and threats, and Seymour decided that his wisest course was to retreat. But he went straight to the City Hall with a bitter complaint, and the Mayor apologized for his fellow citizens and assured the Captain that he would have no more trouble. The tempest in a teapot might easily have subsided then and there if Gardner, nursing what he considered an insult to his authority, had not declined to take advantage of the Mayor's conciliatory gesture. Very well, he would do without the arms! Floyd was unconcerned as to whether or not Gardner had arms, just as he had been unconcerned about reinforcements; but he did not like the way things were being handled and decided it was time for a change all around. He put Brevet Colonel Benjamin Huger, a scion of one of Charleston's most distinguished families, in charge of the arsenal; and he ordered Major Robert Anderson, First Artillery, to proceed to Fort Moultrie and immediately relieve Brevet Colonel John L. Gardner, who was to repair without delay to San Antonio, Texas.

All this, Pierre felt, was to the good. Certainly no one could be more acceptable to the Charlestonians than one of their own, who was also one of their best—Huger. He saw no reason why Anderson should not be equally acceptable. Though it was years since he had seen his friend and fellow teacher, later his companion in arms during the Mexican War, the two had kept in touch with each other, both directly and indirectly, and the early admiration Pierre had felt for Anderson never waned. A Kentuckian of Virginian ancestry, married to a Georgian, there was certainly nothing of the Yankee about him. Moreover, he was one of the few American officers Pierre knew whose knowledge of French was comprehensive; he had not only taught it capably at West Point, he had translated various French texts on artillery which were used as manuals of instruction. He was profoundly religious; somewhat on the strait-laced and scholarly side, possibly overcautious; but, in the present situation, that would be a good thing. It would serve to counterbalance the impetuosity of the Charlestonians.

No one was more surprised than Pierre when the news was flashed over the wires that, on the night of December twenty-sixth, Anderson had moved his entire garrison—except for a small rear guard which followed the next morning—from Moultrie to Sumter!

This was not the act of an overcautious man; it was the act of a bold and determined one. And—since it was Anderson who executed it—Pierre felt sure it had been done with no violation of official orders and with the firm conviction that it was the right thing to do, in an ethical as well as a military sense. But its reverberations were nothing short of thunderous. In Charleston, sirens wailed from guard ships and rockets soared from lookout stations; Fort Moultrie, Castle Pinckney and the arsenal, the Customs House and the Post Office were quickly taken over by South Carolina authorities; every Federal officer in the state resigned. In Washington, charges and countercharges were hurled back and forth between the President and his Cabinet and the President and the South Carolina Commissioners who had been sent to negotiate with him.

Winfield Scott, who had removed his headquarters to New York when his arch-enemy, Franklin Pierce, beat him to the draw by his election to the Presidency, began sending memoranda to the Secretary of War. He expressed the hope "1. That orders may not be given for the evacuation of Fort Sumter. 2. That one hundred and fifty recruits may instantly be sent from Governor's Island to re-enforce that garrison, with ample supplies of ammunition, subsistence, including fresh vegetables, as potatoes, onions, turnips; and 3. That one or two armed vessels be sent to support the said fort." Buchanan replied that the time had not yet come for that—if it were to come at all. Official assurances that it never would were freely and publicly made. Pierre was inclined to credit them. He was sorry for Anderson, who had become the whipping boy of politicians. But Anderson was resourceful as well as upright; he would find a way out of his difficulties, a peaceful way. He had spoken sincerely when he said he believed the step he had taken was necessary to prevent "the effusion of blood"—and that it would do so. Pierre believed this, too.

However, on the ninth of January, just as he was taking the train for Washington, he received the news that Mississippi had followed the example of South Carolina, and it was useless to try to explain this action away by merely saying that Jacksonians were hot-headed. The station platform was seething with excitement and the coaches fairly crackled with it. Indeed, the trip which Pierre had expected to find almost unbearably tedious was, instead, almost unbearably tense. Not only did the news that Florida and Alabama had followed the example of South Carolina and Mississippi add fuel to the flame; a rumor that the *Star of the West*, carrying supplies from Brooklyn to Fort Sumter, had been cannonaded from the batteries of Morris Island and Fort Moultrie sent the conflagration of spirits roaring still higher.

Pierre was, at first, inclined to scoff at these rumors and spoke on the subject as one having authority, though with less conviction than he might have wished. "The *Star of the West!*" he exclaimed. "Why, that's nothing but a merchant steamer, a sidewheeler! Old Fuss and Feathers started his voyage to the West Coast in her, two years ago, when he went to mediate between the British and American Commissioners, who were disputing over the boundary line affecting San Juan Island in Puget Sound. Of course, he had to make the Panama transit and take another ship northward; but he chose the *Star* for the first part of his voyage. She's a comfortable old vessel, just the type he'd like. Her regular run's between New York and New Orleans. I've been on her dozens of times. Her master's John McGowan, almost the only Irishman I've ever known who wasn't always looking around for an excuse to start a fight; and even if he were the other kind, he's no more fitted to deal with actual hostilities than a scrappy street urchin! If the Secretary of War really meant business, he'd have sent something like the *Brooklyn*, a twenty-five-gun sloop, to Charleston."

Some of Pierre's fellow passengers were inclined to agree with him; certainly Major Beauregard should know what he was talking about; but the next time the train stopped, the rumors were confirmed by the newspapers on sale at the depot. It was, indeed, the *Star of the West* that had been sent to Charleston and fired on there; but she had headed back to sea without returning fire and was now on her inglorious way to New York. Meanwhile, Charleston was in a state of wild jubilation; she had proved not only her mettle but her inviolability.

Pierre was chagrined because he had spoken so positively, for he was not slow to realize that he had lost face by so doing; it would have been better to remain silent. He was also genuinely puzzled at his mistake; what he had told the excited group on the cars was based on both experience and reason; well, experience did not seem to count as much as it once had—it was only a few days since he had told himself that no one recognized reason any more. He had learned what had happened, but now he wanted to know why, when and how and this he could not do until he reached Washington. His impatience to see his journey end mounted hour by hour, while it seemed to him that the train was going on aimlessly forever.

When he finally arrived at the Slidells' house, travelworn, weary and anxious, he found John in a state approaching explosion and only too glad to let off steam. On December twenty-first, Buchanan had told the three Commissioners from South Carolina—Adams, Barnwell and Orr—who had been chosen to negotiate for the cession of Federal property that he would not parley with them any more on the subject of Sumter, but that he would give them a little leeway to retreat from their belligerent position before himself taking any action which might be considered belligerent. However, the Secretary of the Navy, Isaac Toucey, wired the Commandant of the Gosport Navy Yard, near Norfolk, to ready the *Brooklyn* for immediate service; at the same time, General Scott, at the President's direction, drafted orders for two hundred regulars with sustenance for at least ninety days to be prepared to embark; and by January third, the *Brooklyn* was anchored off Fortress Monroe and equipped to start at a moment's notice. All this was common knowledge; unfortunately, something else had been going on that was not common knowledge: Scott had begun to worry about the *Brooklyn,* which was a deep-draft vessel; he was afraid it might have trouble getting over the bar in Charleston. Besides, he did not want to weaken Fortress Monroe by reducing its force. He therefore came to the conclusion that it would be better to send recruits from New York on a merchant vessel; and though he did not actually convince the President of this, Buchanan yielded to his judgment. The orders to Fortress Monroe were canceled and the *Star of the West* was secretly chartered by the government for twelve hundred and fifty dollars a day.

Pierre exploded in his turn. "So it was Scott's idea to do this stupid, sneaky thing! If he weren't in his dotage, he'd have known it was doomed to failure from the beginning! He ought to be in a home for imbecile old men, not pretending to function as General-in-Chief of the Army. Even so, I wouldn't have dreamed he'd stoop to such criminal folly as this! Go on, John. When was the dastard found out?"

"Well, the *Star* sailed late on the fifth and anchored off Staten Island. The recruits got on board during the night. Your friend McGowan was provided with good help in the person of a lieutenant, named Woods, to command the troops, and a New York pilot to navigate the Charleston Harbor. The getaway was kept dark. But on January seventh, the *New York Tribune* printed a piece about the *Star* and hinted at what was happening. Do you mean to say rumors hadn't already reached New Orleans when you left? The ninth, wasn't it?"

"Yes—I mean, that was the day I left. And no, the *Picayune* hadn't printed anything about the *Star* then. I heard the first rumors the next day when the train stopped at a depot. The same day we heard Florida had seceded."

"Well, by then, the shooting was over—and that's not a figure of speech. No one in Charleston was surprised to see the *Star* steaming into the harbor. Thompson, the Secretary of the Interior, had been doing the hare-and-hounds act, first wiring his crony, Judge Longstreet—on the very day the *Star* sailed—that no additional troops would be sent to Sumter at present, then following this up by two more telegrams saying they were on their way. Wigfall had sent the same message to Pickens. Of course, Wigfall is still United States Senator from Texas, but it doesn't seem to have occurred to him that this makes it improper for him to give vital information to the enemy."

"Hasn't anyone any sense of loyalty left? Or common decency?" Pierre asked hotly.

Working drawing of the New Orleans Customs House, used to construct the beautiful "Marble Hall." Approved and signed, June 20th, 1855, by "G. T. Beauregard, Capt. & Brevet Major of Engineers, Supt., etc." Collection of Leonard V. Huber.

John Slidell, commissioner of the Confederate States to France.

Mrs. John Slidell (Mathilde Deslonde). From the painting by George
Healy.

Ursuline Convent, New Orleans, La.

The firing on the *Star of the West*. From a contemporary engraving (January, 1861).

Pierre G. T. Beauregard in the uniform of a major in the Army of the
United States. From a portrait painted probably in 1860 by Jaume, and
now on display at the Cabildo in New Orleans. Photograph courtesy of
the City Hall, Charleston, S.C.

Caroline Deslondes Beauregard. Reproduced by the courtesy of Miss
Laure Beauregard Larendon.

The Battery at Charleston, S.C., during the bombardment of Fort Sumter. A contemporary print reproduced from *Harper's Weekly*.

"Well, Thompson has at least—and at last—resigned," John Slidell answered drily. "But, as I've said, he and Wigfall between them had Charleston pretty well alerted. McGowan, of course, didn't know this; and what's more, Anderson didn't know it, either. The day before the *Star* entered the harbor, at dawn, some workmen, rowing out to Fort Sumter, had brought a copy of the *Mercury* with them and that said the *Star* was on the way, carrying reinforcements. But the *Mercury*'s more or less specialized in false rumors and Anderson didn't take any stock in this one, or so the story goes. Said Scott wouldn't send troops, except on a war vessel."

"Poor Robert! Of course that's what he'd say. Because, if he'd been in Scott's place, it never would have entered his honest old head to do such a thing. As a matter of fact, much as I hate Scott, it wouldn't have entered *my* head that *he* would do it."

"Well, the upshot of all this misunderstanding and disbelief and mystery was a general mix-up. McGowan didn't know anyone was watching eagerly for his approach, didn't see how what he thought was a well-kept secret could have leaked out, was taken completely by surprise when the first shots were fired from Morris Island. And Anderson, who wasn't expecting any reinforcements and who had been ordered, as we understand it, to act 'strictly on the offensive' was also taken by surprise. And after all, no one was firing on Sumter. So Anderson gave no orders to return the fire and McGowan, when he got farther into the harbor and realized he'd soon be within range of Fort Moultrie, turned and headed out to sea. The *Star* got one more shot from Morris Island as she fled. Now she's limping back to New York. The *Brooklyn* was finally sent after her, but that was too late to do any good. It's a sorry story all around."

Pierre's stay with the Slidells was not a happy one. He tried to tell himself that this was because Caroline was not with him, that he could not dismiss from his mind the wistfulness of her voice when she asked, "You will send for me just as soon as you can, won't you, Pierre?" But though he did miss her greatly and though he could not rid himself of remorse because he had wounded her, he knew there were many other reasons why the visit was not a success. The story of the *Star* was on everyone's lips because its implications were on everyone's minds. John and Mathilde had issued invitations to a dinner complimentary to John Floyd, the Secretary of War, and on the day that it took place the President asked Mr. Floyd for his resignation. It was not surprising, of course, that under these circumstances the guest of honor sent word to Mathilde he had been taken suddenly ill, and that the resulting party was uncomfortably reminiscent of *Hamlet* without the Prince of Denmark. The evening was a dismal one.

The morning Pierre spent in General Totten's office was no less so. He found his old friend absorbed in the examination of some drawings which proved to be plans for the defense of Charleston; he was "endeavoring to describe the circles of fire of Sumter and Moultrie." He shoved the papers aside and jumped up, greeting his visitor with affection and congratulating him on his appointment. For the first time, Pierre put into words the doubts he had tried so hard to suppress.

"I don't know, General, I don't know. Perhaps I shouldn't go on to West Point."

"How can you say such a thing? It's what you've wanted above everything else, what all your friends in Washington, myself included, have worked hard to help you get."

"Yes, but that was before South Carolina and Mississippi and Florida and Alabama seceded. There's a well-founded rumor that Georgia is seceding today. If it has, Louisiana will be next."

"That doesn't necessarily follow."

"Perhaps it doesn't necessarily follow, but it *will* follow. And when it does, I'll have to resign my commission in the United States Army. So maybe I ought to do that now. Perhaps I should give the War Department full opportunity to rescind the order assigning me to West Point and take whatever action it deems proper under the circumstances."

"You shouldn't do anything of the sort. You should go ahead with the schedule as it stands—that is, take over at the close of the January examinations."

"But suppose that before then. . . . After all, hostilities started when that cadet from The Citadel, Haynsworth, fired on the *Star* from Morris Island. That was the first shot in a civil war. And I hear a good many South Carolina cadets have resigned already."

"You're making a mountain out of a molehill, and I'm not supposing anything. I'm issuing an order, Major Beauregard."

The sincere approbation, the friendly warmth were lacking in his voice now. He looked steadily at Pierre for a moment and then picked up his drawings again. What he had given was more than an order; it was a signal of dismissal. As Pierre went down the steps of the War Department, he felt an unwelcome moisture on his cheeks and took out his handkerchief. He could not guess and did not learn until long afterward that Totten had been equally moved, that he had taken the only way he knew to hide his feelings.

Pierre next went to pay the official call, required by etiquette, on Scott, General-in-Chief of the Army; but he was not at his headquarters and though Pierre had intended to submit his resignation there, also, he did not feel impelled to do so during the General's absence in New York. He was still seething over Scott's behavior about the *Star of the West*, and the very idea of coming into personal contact with Scott was revolting to Pierre. Indeed, there seemed no reason why he should prolong his stay in Washington and he had no wish to do so, especially as the gloom of the Slidells' house was now permeated with electricity. John was feuding with the President (who, for so long, had been "wax in his hands"!) over the appointment of Joshua Holt of Kentucky as Secretary of War. This appointment had been made without senatorial confirmation and, strictly speaking, was therefore unconstitutional. Action of this sort, Slidell maintained, "if suffered to pass by without expressed dissent, would establish a precedent alike dangerous to the principles on which our system of government was established, and in derogation of the constitutional rights and privileges of the Senate."

Technically there was, of course, no question that Slidell was right. But with so many apparently graver problems at stake, the Senate was not disposed to make an issue of this one. Pierre left for New York realizing that his brother-in-law's days of supremacy were over and that, possibly in the very near future, even his seat in the Senate would be insecure. This was no time for him to be dispensing hospitality to his wife's relatives.

The welcome given Pierre in New York by his old friends of Mexican days—Gustavus Smith, a Kentuckian now acting as Street Commissioner, and his classmate, Mansfield Lovell, a Washingtonian who had resigned from the Army to act as Smith's deputy—did a great deal to raise his spirits. Both of them had Southern leanings. When he told them that if Louisiana seceded he would follow it out of the Union, both approved his proposed course and told him that, if they were similarly situated, they would act in the same way. Other military cronies were rounded up, and the days passed in an atmosphere of far greater conviviality than those in Washington. But when he reached West Point, Pierre found that several cadets from the seceded states had already resigned, and that several others were undecided whether or not they should do so. Word had come to the Military Academy that commissions in the Confederate Army awaited all boys from the South. With some hesitation, he advised those who consulted him that he felt they could properly remain as long as he did. But he had no delusions about the probable length of his tenure. Almost from the moment of his arrival at West Point, Pierre could read the handwriting on the wall, and within five days the words he had visualized were no longer merely symbolic. He received a letter from Totten telling him that his orders were revoked and that he was to turn over the office of Superintendent to the previous incumbent, Colonel Richard Delafield, who was still at West Point. This letter was promptly followed by one from Holt, the new Secretary of War, himself, written to the same effect, but couched in even stiffer language; and the following day a communication arrived from John Slidell which shed further light on the situation: John had protested against the removal; in fact, he had written a formal note to Buchanan, asking whether or not it met with the President's approval. Buchanan had replied, with equal formality, that he upheld the Secretary of War in all things, and that the latter's official acts were his own. The question had ceased to revolve exclusively around loyalty or disloyalty to the Union; instead, "a serious disagreement" between Mr. Holt and Mr. Slidell, which had its source in the alleged unconstitutionality of the former's appointment, had caused the Secretary of War to "indulge his private pique." Slidell did not propose to tolerate such flouting of senatorial prerogatives; he was resigning his seat and retiring to Louisiana, where he proposed to put his services at the disposal of his adopted state.

Pierre's friends in New York City were again waiting to welcome him and he was showered with invitations to remain there indefinitely; the feeling that he had been shabbily treated and that amends must be made for this was prevalent; Derek Vanderveer was especially urgent in his efforts to detain the visitor. But a telegram had already come in from Governor Moore of Louisiana and it carried the long-expected tidings: his native state had seceded; he was badly needed at home; how quickly could he return? The sidewheeler steamboat *Bienville* was leaving the next day and, thankful that this provided an alternative to another grueling trip by train, Pierre immediately engaged passage on her.

When he reached the wharf, he found it in a state of tumult: the *Star of the West* had come limping in from Charleston, her hull and chimney stack perforated with shot holes; a huge, excited crowd had rushed up to look at her and to learn as much as possible about the hostile episode which had brought her to this pass. Pierre elbowed his way through the mob, managed to get aboard the damaged vessel and was warmly welcomed by McGowan.

"Major Beauregard! I'd been hoping you'd drop in! That is, I read in yesterday's papers that Louisiana had seceded and in this morning's papers that you'd left West Point. So I knew you'd be hurrying back to New Orleans, possibly on the *Bienville*, and I thought if you happened to catch sight of this poor battered old hulk on your way to board your ship, you might steal a few minutes for a visit with me. I can't wait to hear your latest news and perhaps you'd like to hear mine. Come along to my cabin. We'll have a drink while we talk and if you can stay to dinner, too, so much the better."

The captain's cabin on the *Star of the West* was a large, comfortable room which Pierre had occasionally visited before, when the ship was in port at New Orleans, and which gave him a sense of ease and friendliness which were very welcome. He sank down into one of the well-upholstered armchairs, accepted the proffered drink and took a couple of long refreshing swallows before shifting to more leisurely sips while he answered McGowan's questions about his plans.

"Well, obviously, I can't make any until I get home and I must do that as soon as possible. As a matter of fact, I've begun to wonder if I shouldn't go by train, instead of by ship—it's a horrible trip, but it is faster. I think perhaps I ought to cancel my cabin and see if I can get space on one of Mr. Pullman's new sleeping cars or, rather, see if Derek Vanderveer can get it for me. Could you send someone out with a message while we're talking?"

"Nothing easier. Write out your directions and I'll have them on the way in five minutes. I hate to see you deserting the sea, but you're right, it's quicker the other way. . . . You think there'll be a war?"

Pierre did not answer immediately. He set down his glass and, taking a notebook from his pocket, walked over to the round felt-covered table on the far side of the room, drew up a straight-backed chair, and began to write hurriedly, by the light of the large whale-oil lamp that hung suspended from the ceiling. Then he tore off two sheets, one addressed to the purser of the *Bienville* and the other to Derek Vanderveer and, before he returned to his drink and resumed the conversation, handed them to the steward who was already waiting for them.

"I still hope not," he said slowly. "I'm sure you do, too. But I'm afraid it's a forlorn hope. To all practical purposes, the war started when the first shot was fired on you from Morris Island. Didn't it?"

"Yes, if the powers that be decide to interpret it that way. But I doubt if they will. After all, the *Star* wasn't seriously damaged, much less sunk. If it had been, of course the situation would be entirely different. However, I don't think anyone, in either the North or the South, really wants war, except for a few Carolina hotheads and a few New England Abolitionists. Between them, they could touch one off, of course, with the help of a few fire-eaters in the military high command. For instance, if troops were sent to Louisiana, wouldn't your state resist?"

"I'm afraid so. No, I don't mean that. Of course it would. Of course it should."

"Well, there you have it. You Creoles are a touchy lot. Incidentally, how do you feel about what's just happened at West Point—or would you rather not talk about it?"

Again Pierre made no immediate answer. He turned his glass around several times without drinking from it, and then he set it down for good, shaking his head when McGowan suggested a refill. "Naturally, it's a rather sore subject," he said at last. "But I know I'll be asked that question, again and again, and I'll have to answer it. Perhaps it will help me to decide how I can best do that if I practice on you." He managed to smile and went on. "The superintendency at West Point is something I'd wanted for years. At first, though I yearned for it secretly, it never occurred to me that I might actually get it. Later, when my brother-in-law, John Slidell, told me he thought I could, with his help, I began to look on it as a probability and then as a certainty. After I heard about the quarrel—it *was* a quarrel—over the appointment between Holt, the new Secretary of War, and John, and the position President Buchanan was taking, I began to have doubts about the propriety of my acceptance. However, General Totten insisted I must go ahead and it was too late then to say I wouldn't."

He paused and looked across at McGowan, who nodded. "Everyone at West Point was very polite to me," Pierre said. "Painfully polite. Delafield and all the teachers and all the cadets. Delafield isn't much to look at—a pudgy man with heavy eyebrows and a beaklike nose. But he's a very good sort. He's done a great deal to improve the Academy. He's an excellent administrator and he'll pick up again just where he left off last week. Kendrick, the Professor of Chemistry, invited me to one of his famous Saturday-afternoon parties and it was a good one. He and the others showed me all the respect due the Superintendent of West Point, but I couldn't help feeling they knew, even beforehand, that I wouldn't last, that I couldn't. After all, my classmate Hardee had resigned as Commandant just a week before when Georgia seceded and Louisiana was bound to come next. Every time a new message was delivered to me, my equivocal position became more evident to them and to me. We all did our best to play up to each other. I hope I succeeded as well as the rest."

He paused again and then continued. "Late last night I went out and walked around the Plain, alone. Of course, it was bitter cold, the elms all stark and bare. I always thought, when they were in leaf, they were the most beautiful trees I ever saw. The lights had been turned out in the library and the chapel, so I could barely see their outline and I was sorry. I'd wanted a last look at them while no one was watching to see how it affected me. Lights did show through the windows of some houses, but the Superintendent's was dark. I'd never had time to move in there. Not that it's much of a house, nothing like as pleasant as the one I'm living in at New Orleans. I'd told my wife I didn't want her to come to West Point until I was sure she could be comfortable there. Of course, that was only part of the truth. I knew before I left home that I probably wouldn't be at the Academy long. But I confess I didn't think it would be only five days. I'd hoped I'd live in that house for a short time—say a month or so. It would have given me the feeling of belonging again. Now I'll never have that. I stood and looked at that dark house a long while and I knew for the first time what some old Spanish saint meant when he talked about the dark night of the soul. A man's soul can't help being dark when he's ordered away from the place where he's been taught to serve his country and where he thought he was going to serve it again, because he's considered a traitor to it, even if he's followed his conscience in changing his allegiance."

There was a long silence which neither man attempted to break. Then Pierre went on again. "I went back to the grim old West Point Hotel on the brink of the bluff and got the key to my room. The night clerk didn't say anything when he gave it to me, but after a minute he followed me and put out his hand. He didn't say anything then, either. I knew he couldn't. And I couldn't. But that was the real good-by. The official farewells this morning were just a form."

McGowan rose and crossed the stretch of carpeting between him and his visitor, refilling Pierre's glass himself. "I shouldn't have asked you about West Point," he said. "Let's talk about something else for a while. I know you've always been interested in the defenses of the Mississippi River forts, St. Philip and Jackson especially. Well, so have I. And I'd been curious about their ability to stop an ascending fleet of steam vessels if there weren't any artificial obstruction in the river. I decided to experiment and find out for myself just how long a steamer would be exposed to the forts' fire. So the last time the

Star went to New Orleans, I timed the passage from the moment the first gun of Fort Jackson could be brought to bear on the ship until she passed beyond the range of Fort St. Philip. It took exactly twenty-five minutes. On the trip down, aided by the strong current, it took the *Star* only fifteen minutes to get in and out of range. I don't know whether or not the Navy has bothered to make the experiment, but I think it's important. Anyway, I pass it on to you for what it's worth."

"And I'm very grateful to you. *I'll* pass on the information to the quarters where it ought to do some good, though I doubt if it will."

"Look, you're depressed, and no wonder. But it doesn't do any good to take the worst for granted until it actually happens. I don't suppose you've had much of anything to eat all day. You'll feel better after a good dinner. Why shouldn't you stay and have it with me? After all, you've got to wait for an answer to those messages you sent."

"Thank you. If the answer hasn't come before your dinner's ready, I'll stay with pleasure. But I know you'll understand if I find I have to hurry off to catch a train. While we're waiting to be served, tell me how the recruits on the *Star* stood up under fire. They were pretty raw material."

"Yes, but they stood up well. Of course, I wasn't in charge of the troops—that was Lieutenant Woods' job. But I think he'd say the same."

A steward had replaced the felt tablecloth with one of linen and was putting carafes, cruets, china and silverware in place, when Vanderveer was announced. As usual, he was the personification of efficiency, stability and dependability; the fair, stocky, good-natured boy had developed into a man of considerable substance, both physically and materially. He had decided it would save time, he said, if he came in person to answer Pierre's message. As a matter of fact, they had none to lose. If Pierre wanted to get on the southbound train, they must be on their way to the depot at once. He had taken the liberty of getting Pierre's luggage off the *Bienville*, where the purser, who had already received Pierre's message, saying he would cancel his passage if he could get on a train, had facilitated its removal; it was piled in a waiting hack outside. He would go to the depot with Pierre. Bad luck that they had to hurry so with dinner—which he was, of course, immediately invited to share—just ready to be served. Such were the fortunes of war and rumors of war.

"And it is only rumors, so far, remember," Derek told his friend as they went clattering along over the cobblestones to the depot.

"And don't you ever forget, you sadistic old slave-holder, you, that there's one Black Republican who's always thought the world of you, ever since you and he refought the battles of Jena and Austerlitz under the expert direction of those great Napoleonic heroes, the brothers Peugnet. What's more, he always will think the world of you, whatever you and your fellow traitors do next. And, Pierre, you listen here—"

"I'm listening."

"If things shouldn't go too well with you sometime, don't forget that Napoleonic motto hanging on the wall of our dear old school-room: *'If it's possible, it can be done; if it's impossible, it must be done.'* If you want or need something everyone else tells you it is impossible to get, let me show you and them that it must be done."

✠§ 23 §✠

AND NOW TO YOU, MR. PRESIDENT, AND TO MY BROTHER SENA-tors, on all sides of this Chamber, I bid a respectful farewell; with many of those from whom I have been radically separated in political sentiment, my personal relations have been kindly and have inspired me with a respect and esteem that I shall not willingly forget; with those around me from the Southern States, I part as men part from brothers on the eve of a temporary absence, with a cordial pressure of the hand and a smiling assurance of the speedy renewal of sweet inter-course around the family hearth. But to you, noble and gener-ous friends, who, born beneath other skies, possess hearts that beat in sympathy with ours; to you, who solicited and assailed by motives the most powerful that could appeal to selfish na-tures, have nobly spurned them all; to you who, on our be-half, have bared your breast to the fierce beatings of the storm, and made willing sacrifice of life's most glittering prizes in your devotion to constitutional liberty; to you, who have made our cause your cause, and from many of whom I feel I part forever, what shall I, can I say? Naught, I know and feel, is needed for myself; but this I will say for the people in whose name I speak today; whether prosperous or adverse fortunes await you, one priceless treasure is yours—the assurance that an entire people honor your names, and hold them in grateful and affectionate memory.

But with still sweeter and more touching return shall your unselfish devotion be rewarded. When, in after days, the story of the present shall be written; when history shall have passed her stern sentence on the erring men who have driven their unoffending brethren from the shelter of their common home, your names will derive fresh lustre from the contrast; and when your children shall hear repeated the familiar tale, it will be with glowing cheek and kindling eye, their very souls will stand a-tiptoe as their sires are named, and they will glory in their lineage from men of spirit as generous and of patriotism as high-hearted as ever illustrated or adorned the American Senate.

—Robert Douthat Meade, *Judah P. Benjamin: Confederate Statesman* (Oxford University Press)

Feb. 9, 1861.

Letter from Col. Beauregard, at New York: two hours after he himself was at my office. My letter has taken *5 days* longer on the way than he! No infrequent event in these troublous times of tempest, and political storms. . . . The Colonel then sat down in my office, and wrote his resignation of his commission in the U. S. Corps of Engineers. . . .

—Excerpt from the diary of T. K. Wharton

11th.

Called to see Major G. T. Beauregard. He proposed to throw three wire ropes 5″ in diameter across the river at Fort St. Philip the cost of which on calculation was found to be too high—$88,000 dollars. Then a raft was proposed; this was also abandoned and I proposed the following plate with kelsons set at an angle with the front of the plate, say 60°, so as to shear the plate into the proper position so as to make them meet so and to have water-tight compartments every three hundred feet to prevent sinking.

—Private Memorandum Book of John Roy, February, 1861

❦

THE FRIENDLY VISIT WITH MCGOWAN AND THE FRESH EVIDENCE OF Derek's affection and loyalty did much to mitigate the mournful memories of the five days at West Point and the apprehension about the days to come in Louisiana. Pierre started his journey in good spirits; but his train missed its connection in Washington for Richmond, which meant he would miss a connection in Richmond for Lynchburg, in Lynchburg for Chattanooga, in Chattanooga for Memphis, in Memphis for Jackson and in Jackson for New Orleans. Even so, he would halve the time it would have taken him to reach his destination on the *Bienville* and, in any case, he was not sorry to have a valid excuse for stopping over in the capital long enough to give his brother-in-law his version of his dismissal as Superintendent of the Military Academy. He realized, from his visit on his way north, that the atmosphere of the Slidells' house, so long a center of the most distinguished society and the most brilliant conversation in Washington, had undergone a sobering change since John's quarrel with Holt and his break with Buchanan. It was not until he reached there this time, however, that he knew how great the change could be. He had been so preoccupied with events in New York, as these affected his own career, that he had neglected to pay the same amount of attention to events in New Orleans and Washington. It had actually slipped his mind that the State Convention called by Governor Moore which, among other activities, would elect delegates to represent Louisiana at the General Convention of Southern States in Montgomery on February fourth, had opened in Baton Rouge on January twenty-third, passed the Ordinance of Secession on the twenty-sixth and reassembled in New Orleans on the twenty-ninth. Even if it had not, he would have taken it for granted that Judah P. Benjamin and John Slidell, who had so long and so ably represented Louisiana in the United States Senate, would almost automatically be chosen, and this had certainly been the assumption of both these gentlemen. When Pierre finally waked from the long refreshing sleep which had followed his wearisome night on the train and his predawn arrival in Washington, it was to learn that telegrams had arrived, saying both had been overwhelmingly defeated, Benjamin by John Perkins of Madison Parish and Slidell by Alexandre de Clouet of St. Martin Parish.

The blow to the losers' pride was terrific, and neither was of the temperament that stood up well under such humiliation. Moreover, both were absorbed in preparing the speeches they were to deliver when they formally resigned from the United States Senate the following week. If Pierre's position at West Point had been equivocal, theirs was certainly more so now that Louisiana had seceded; but if they felt the same embarrassment on this score that he had, it was not evident. On the contrary, he had the impression they were actually reveling in the sensation caused by their continued presence in the Senate Chamber, and that this notoriety helped, in some degree, to take their minds off their grievance at the Convention's amazing lack of appreciation for their great qualities. It did not astonish Pierre that John was not disposed to listen to another man's story at such a crucial time; but it left him with the feeling of having had a rug pulled from underneath him.

This was the way he expressed it to himself, perhaps because the subject of rugs was one on which Mathilde—suddenly confronted with the necessity of tearing her orderly and elegant establishment to pieces—was persistently dwelling. What on earth was she to do with all the Oriental rugs? Not to mention all the brocade and velvet draperies? And all the massive furniture for which there would be no room in the house on Esplanade, since that was already well appointed? They could always use the silver, the china, the crystal, the bric-a-brac and the linen somewhere else. But what about the rest of the equipment? Above all, what about those huge rugs? Overnight, she had ceased to be a poised and gracious official hostess and had become a petulant and harassed housekeeper.

It was as great a relief to be rid of her complaints as it was to be spared the necessity of listening any longer to Benjamin's grandiloquent peroration, which he insisted on declaiming in advance for Pierre's benefit, since the latter would not be present when the retiring senior Senator from Louisiana, a pistol at his side, would take his majestic farewell of the greatest deliberative body in the world. The next lap of Pierre's journey was comparatively brief and comfortable and, though in some respects the trip south had become pretty tedious before it was finished, he found, as he had on the trip north so short a time earlier, that the exchange of views with his fellow passengers about the current situation was stimulating and provocative. At first, he was kept busy parrying questions; that was inevitable, in view of his uniform. But his reluctance to talk about himself was respected and the conversation drifted to the secession of Texas, which had just taken place over the opposition of Governor Sam Houston; to borrow the expression of Mr. Horace Greeley of the *New York Tribune,* she was the latest of the erring sisters to depart. The probable policies of Mr. Buchanan during his last month as President furnished another topic; so did the cautious pronouncements of Mr. Lincoln during this preinauguration period.

Governor Moore headed the welcoming committee that was waiting for Pierre at the depot in New Orleans. The Governor had a copy of the Secession Ordinance in his hand and they were hardly seated in their carriage when he voiced an urgent request that Pierre would immediately resume work on the defenses of New Orleans.

"I'd better resign from the United States Army first, you know," he told the Governor, attempting to speak lightly.

"Very well. Send in your resignation today."

"I'll try to get it written. But first of all, I have to get home and see my wife."

Caroline had not come to the depot to meet him, as Laure had come to the wharf on his return from Mexico; but he knew this was not because she was not waiting eagerly to see him. Her welcome would be both warm and tender; but it was not her way to show her feelings in public—nor was she able, as Laure had been, to forget the public entirely and feel that there was no one in the world except Pierre and herself. He excused himself from the Governor and the committee of welcome as quickly as he could without discourtesy and was driven through streets crowded with troops and echoing with martial music to the house on Chartres Street. According to her custom, Caroline was watching for him, as he had known she would be, and as soon as the front door closed behind him, she was in his arms.

"So this is why you wouldn't take me with you," she whispered. "Because you knew you were coming straight back again! Oh Pierre, why didn't you tell me? Then I wouldn't have minded being left behind at all."

It was too late for explanations now and, anyway, these did not seem to matter much any more. What mattered was that they were together again and, if other separations were ahead of them, they need not think of those, for there was no prospect that they would come immediately. Pierre had promptly begun work on the plans for the defense of Fort St. Philip and Fort Jackson which, as he had long insisted, were inadequately prepared to repel an armed attack. These plans would take him some time to perfect, but that did not greatly matter for, though Louisiana had seceded, she had not yet entered the new Confederacy, but was functioning as an independent republic, celebrating her status with flag-raising, dancing, parades and illuminations. Carnival had never been celebrated with such joyous abandon. On Washington's Birthday there was a tremendous parade, well calculated to impress the public with the might of Louisiana's armed forces. New military companies were formed almost daily, and these vied with each other in selecting the most flamboyant and ferocious names possible and in flaunting the gaudiest of uniforms. Pierre and Caroline, like everyone they knew, were swept along in the rising tide of excitement, and he again became the dazzling figure that had dominated the social scene before his second marriage. He had welcomed the interval of quiet domesticity which had followed and had been supremely happy in it until it had been disrupted by his departure for West Point; but now he was reveling in the limelight again and Caroline was, at last, willing to share it with him, not insisting that she must retreat into the background as she had done at first. It was not for some days that she realized that the glitter which surrounded them was not all gold, so far as her beloved was concerned.

The legislature had authorized the establishment of a state army. Pierre had taken it for granted, from the Governor's urgent and enthusiastic approach to him, that he would be put in charge of it. In fact, he had been so sure of it that he could not believe his ears when he learned that the appointment had not gone to him, but to Braxton Bragg.

Bragg, the only man he had really disliked when he was a cadet at West Point! Bragg, who had been given the derisive nickname of "Captain-Throw-'em-More-Grape" in the Mexican War! Bragg, who had resigned from the army five years earlier to take his ease as a planter! Bragg, who was not even a Louisianian, except by tardy self-adoption, much less a Creole! A man of no presence and no manners, thin to the point of emaciation, round-shouldered, stooping and, what was worse, brusque, surly, perpetually ill-tempered. Whatever military qualifications he might have possessed, which would have entitled him to the honor conferred upon him, Pierre stubbornly overlooked. Nor was he in the least mollified because Bragg promptly called on him to offer him a colonelcy. He was out when the call was made and, though Caroline had received the visitor and he had done his best to show her every respect and courtesy, Pierre immediately sent a curt note to him, declining the commission. He smarted with a sense of injustice. He, a native son, an officer who had only just resigned an important position in the United States Army and had never relinquished active service, had been passed over for an outsider, a constitutional quitter, a boor! He made no secret of his feelings; Caroline had no sooner discovered them than she realized he had expressed himself to the Governor, to John Slidell and, indeed, to all his friends, in much the same way that he had to her. Of course his services were at the command of his state "even unto death"—he used the expression again and again. But it would be with suitable rank or none at all. To prove that he meant what he said, he enlisted as a private in the aristocratic Orleans Guard, a battalion recently formed by his friend, Colonel Numa Augustin. The colonel was, like himself, a patriot, a gentleman and a Creole. It would be an honor to serve under him in the humblest capacity.

The appointment of Bragg was not the only thorn in Pierre's admittedly sensitive flesh. He had received the thanks of Governor Moore for his plan of floating booms to be stretched across the river. The Chief Executive seemed to recognize the importance of the information Pierre had given about inadequate defenses in the event of a possible naval attack, and the feasibility of his suggested remedy for these. But the members of the Military Board, to whom such questions were automatically referred, failed to visualize the extent of damage which might result if they made no move. Their indifference was bad enough; their inaction was insult added to injury. Pierre brooded over this, just as he had exploded over the appointment of Bragg.

But he did not have to sit idly by, nursing his grievances, for long. He had been home only a few weeks when he was summoned to Montgomery, the capital of the new Confederacy which Louisiana had finally joined, by a letter from the Secretary of War, Leroy Pope Walker. The provisional President, Jefferson Davis, had expressed a desire for a special and immediate meeting with Major Peter Beauregard.

He was packing his bags to leave when a visitor was announced: Major Sherman was passing through the city and had called to bring Pierre news of René and Henri; he was happy to say they were both in good health, both seemed contented and both were doing well in their studies. Pierre appreciated the thoughtfulness that had prompted the call and was genuinely glad to see his old friend. Under ordinary circumstances, he would have urged Sherman to stay for a few days, so that they could talk over old times, as well as the current state of upheaval in the country, but he was in a hurry, he had barely time to catch his train. He hoped the visitor would understand. Sherman assured Pierre that he did and took his departure. Pierre closed the bags and glanced out of the window to make certain the hack he had sent for was awaiting him. Reassured, he turned back to Caroline, who had been helping him with his preparations.

"This is another time when I won't be gone long," he told her as he kissed her good-by. "I've only been asked to attend a conference."

"I've been gone four years. I never saw her again," he heard himself telling Simone Castel, as he finished the story she had invited when she said, "You fell in love again."

ᒪᔆ 24 ᕉᔊ

IT WAS A MOMENT WHEN OLD DREAMS RETURNED, WHEN NEW freshets of ambition welled within him. From that day onward there is to be a new impulse in his life, a driving urge. Possibly, at times, it became a little like madness. It was the will to be great. It will thenceforth modify all his acts, color all his thoughts. Now was his eye indeed turned toward posterity. He was determined to send his name, like the blast of a trumpet, down the whirling cycles of time.

—Hamilton Basso, *Beauregard: The Great Creole*
(Scribner's)

꧁ꕥ꧂

NEITHER PIERRE NOR SIMONE WAS CONSCIOUS OF HOW MANY HOURS they had sat there. The coffee cups, which had been pushed aside when he made his sketch showing how he had bound the exterior walls to the interior walls of the Customs House, were standing forgotten near the edge of the table; their contents had been only partly consumed when he began to draw, and what was left had long since cooled. On the plate which had held the batch of cornbread still lay a few broken pieces, surrounded with crumbs. These unappetizing remnants of a good breakfast were not disturbing because they were unnoticed; like the passage of time, they had ceased to have any meaning; what mattered was the story Pierre was telling. During the first part of his recital, Simone had glanced, occasionally, at the sketch she was holding and had fingered it as if she enjoyed touching it; but eventually she put it down and it now lay, neatly folded, beneath her clasped hands. Her eyes were fixed on Pierre's face. As he said, "I never saw Caroline again," he bowed his head and there was a long silence.

The cathedral bells, ringing for the noon Angelus, roused them both. Pierre sprang up, horror stricken at the thought Mme Cougot might have been neglected because he and Simone had become so absorbed in his story. But, as he tried to voice his apologies and his anxiety, she shook her head and smiled.

"If *maman* had wanted me, I should have known it," she said, quietly gathering together the dishes and rising at the same time Pierre did, though less hastily. "You may think that's fantastic, but it's true. Of course she has a bell and the doors are all open; but even if she didn't or if the doors were shut, I'd have sensed her need. If you don't believe me, come in to the drawing room and wait, while I go and speak to her. I'll leave these dishes in the pantry as I pass by."

He followed her into the house, still troubled and contrite; but he had hardly seated himself in the dim shrouded drawing room when she called to him, almost gaily, that Mme Cougot would like to see him, too; and, as he entered her chamber, he instantly realized that she, also, was in unusually good spirits. She was still in bed, but that, she explained, was because her daughter had not come bustling up to her, insisting that she must have her face washed and her hair combed before her coffee was really settled in her stomach; as it was, she had been able to drift peacefully off to sleep again and had had a nice long nap. She would be very grateful to General Beauregard if he could manage to detain Simone for a time every morning. The notion that elderly persons did not need as much sleep as young persons was a fallacy, for her at least; she needed more and more all the time.

"Then I hope you will have it," he said, genuinely relieved. "But as to detaining Madame Castel every morning, of course I mustn't do that. Not only because I should be wasting her time, but because I should be out looking for work, all the more diligently, considering that I haven't done so today."

"Oh, General Beauregard, how can you say you wasted my time! *Maman*, you must persuade him to tell you everything he's told me —about how he met that lovely Caroline Deslonde, his courtship, his marriage, his happy honeymoon here in this house. It's a beautiful story."

"I'm sure it is, *chère*. And I hope he will tell it to me some time. But not now. You couldn't expect him to tell it twice in one day."

"No, of course not. Especially as he's told me about all sorts of others things, too—his plans for channel clearance in the Mississippi River, and his championship of Pierce when the President was unjustly accused of cowardice and his campaign for the mayoralty and all the wonderful things he did when he was Superintendent of the Customs House! Why, even long before the War, I mean the War Between the States, he'd proved that he was a great and gifted man! And that without going into his record in the Mexican War at all! I don't think we began to realize how great and how gifted!"

"I realized it, Simone, and so did your father. But in those days you were more interested in other people and other things and quite naturally—your husband, the first home which you and he owned, the little son who was doubly dear to you because you had lost two children before he was born. And then, when Lance met with an accident——"

Pierre was thankful that the conversation had taken a different turn; though he reveled in praise and loved to dwell on it alone after it had been given him, he had never outgrown the embarrassment he felt while it was being voiced.

"Speaking of Lance," he said, "I have at last had a letter from the third old friend who I thought might be of help to us—Derek Vanderveer. I couldn't imagine why I didn't get a letter from him as promptly as I did from Sherman and McDowell. It seems that he's in Europe and though my letter was sent to him, it had to undergo several forwardings before it finally reached him. He's not returning to the United States until autumn—he was sent abroad on some kind of an official mission and, to his regret, he can't do as much for us as if he were in this country. However, he immediately began to correspond with several highly placed persons of his acquaintance about Lance and he is hopeful that these letters may bear fruit. If they do, we will be hearing direct from the persons he has approached and, of course, from him as soon as he gets back."

"Well, after all, autumn will be here before we know it now," Simone said, with a valiant attempt at hopefulness. "That is not long to wait."

"But we do not know that autumn will bring an encouraging answer," her mother reminded her. "Mr. Vanderveer does not promise anything, any more than General Sherman and General McDowell have done. They have all only said they would be glad to help if they could."

"I suppose that's all they can say, *maman*. Isn't it, General Beauregard?"

"Yes, I'm afraid so."

He could see that Mme Cougot's mood was already less buoyant than when he had come into the room and he was loath to make such an admission. But there seemed no help for it. Besides, he himself was feeling a letdown from the exaltation of the morning. He spoke despondently.

"I think perhaps my wisest course would be to go to City Hall and seek amnesty by swearing fealty to the United States. But I hate to do so. It's hard to ask for pardon from an adversary you despise."

"When you speak of the wisest course, do you mean as far as you yourself are concerned or as far as Lance is concerned?" Mme Cougot asked.

"Why—both. If my citizenship were restored, I could move about freely; then I'd have a better chance of getting a job as an engineer and that would mean I could support my family properly again. It also means I'd be in a better position to ask favors."

"Of course you must do what you think best about mending your own fortunes, General Beauregard. But I'd rather never hear Lance's step again than to have you go and forswear yourself at City Hall. Wouldn't you, Simone?"

"I—I don't know, *maman*."

Without answering, Mme Cougot turned her face to the wall and did not turn back again. Simone stood very still and tried, several times, to speak before she succeeded.

"My mother's a better patriot than I am," she said at last. "I ought to be able to say that, too, if she can. I wouldn't have supposed she could. That's all she's lived for, years now—to hear Lance's footsteps again. It's all I lived for, too—until just lately. Knowing you has made a difference. But still I'm not brave enough to feel it would be better to give up all hope of seeing Lance than to have you commit perjury."

"It wouldn't be committing perjury exactly. There isn't any Confederate Government for me to support any more. If I took an oath to support the United States Government, I'd do it. And there must be some way in which I could make such a promise without saying I was sorry I hadn't done it in the past. Anyway, I'll try to think of one. And I'll ask Lee's advice. I won't do anything until I find out what he thinks. I'll write him this very afternoon."

Pierre returned to the quarters to write the letter and, when he went out to post it, he stopped at the French Market and bought himself some coffee and a doughnut. His sensation of letdown persisted. He did not want any dinner, he did not want to see any of his family or friends, and certainly he did not have the heart to resume his thankless search for work. On the other hand, he did not feel like tackling the second japanned box again.

He told himself that he really did not need to do this, at the moment anyway, in order to continue reviewing the events which he meant, eventually, to record at length in his own way, and not as someone else—prejudiced, ignorant or pedantic, as the case might be —had done already and would do again. He had taken Simone, verbally, all the way from the days of the "Self-Acting Bar Excavator" and his championship of Pierce in 1852 to his departure for Montgomery in 1861. He could take himself mentally—and lay the foundations for taking his readers on paper—from Montgomery to Charleston and possibly beyond there. He found an empty bench in Jackson Square, eased himself into a comfortable position as he had done once before when overcome with the heat, and closed his eyes. If he should fall asleep, it would not matter. No one would bother a shabby but seemingly respectable man with grizzled hair, who was drowsing through a warm summer afternoon.

Subconsciously, he put up his hand and smoothed the crisp graying

locks, smiling to himself as he did so. His welcome in Charleston
had been so unquestioning, so spontaneous, so adulatory as to be
almost overwhelming. Everything he said and did met with paeans
of praise. Yet, inevitably, the gossips sought for some flaw in his
perfection and, after saying that his background was one of which
even Charlestonians could be proud, that his manners were impeccable, that he carried himself with an air and gave dash and distinction to any gathering he attended, they whispered that he dyed his
hair. It was jet-black, the same jet black as the hair of his brothers
and sisters, of his cousins and of nearly all the Creoles he knew, including Laure. (Caroline's soft brown hair had been the exception.)
But such hair was unusual as you went farther north and was, admittedly, often the result of artifice. The whispers should not have
annoyed him, because they were so insignificant, compared to everything else that was being said about him; but he had felt they reflected on his masculinity: a vain woman might dye her hair in a
futile attempt to look younger than she was, but such petty tricks
were beneath the dignity of an officer and a gentleman. He resented
the rumors and rejoiced, rather than otherwise, when the first gray
hairs appeared. He had heard the rumors about those, too: the supply
of dye had been reduced, because of the war; he had not been able
to get it any more. It was only after Shiloh that the gossips began
to admit there might be reasons for his graying hair other than a lack
of dye.

Well, it would soon be snow-white now and he did not mind in the
least. Snow-white hair was distinguished; it was this half-and-half
that was not so good; and since he could not seem to get a job anyway, probably the snow-white hair, which was generally associated
with old age rather than with the later forties, would not make any
difference. As he sat on his park bench, he could look back with
amusement he had not felt, when he went to Charleston, on the
stories about his dyed hair.

He had been glad for all sorts of reasons that his stay in Montgomery was so brief. The erstwhile quiet pleasant little city was
bursting at its seams with the crowds of patriots and politicians and
the hangers-on of both groups which had poured into it. Some of
these were the duly chosen delegates to the convention which was
seeking to form a stable government from a provisional one; others
were enthusiasts and office-seekers who had come of their own voli-
tion, and who were now milling aimlessly but vociferously about the
streets and the lobby of the hotel. Montgomery could not decently
accommodate such hordes; it was not adaptable to noise and confu-

sion. Pierre, who had always enjoyed a well-ordered existence, and whose predilection for it had increased since his marriage to Caroline, was appalled by such a state of hurly-burly. He breathed a sigh of relief when he was out of it, though—all things being equal—he would have preferred heading back to New Orleans rather than onward to Charleston.

He had not willfully deceived Caroline when he told her he thought he would be away only a few weeks. Though he had been passed over for Bragg when Louisiana was organizing its forces as an independent state, he believed that the principal powers in the new Confederacy would recognize his special fitness to supervise the defense of New Orleans and the approaches to it, both by land and by sea, and that he would be permanently stationed at home. Instead, Leroy Walker, the Secretary of War, had greeted him in Montgomery with the exclamation, "Just in time to help me out of a great dilemma!" when Pierre walked into his office; and after inviting suggestions as to the availability and suitability of certain friends of his visitor for ordnance duty, he passed on to the subject of Charleston's defenses. The interview with the President followed much the same pattern; Mr. Davis wanted information about the temper of people and the condition of affairs in New Orleans and Mobile; and when Pierre had answered these to the President's satisfaction, Davis read aloud a letter which had just reached him from Governor Pickens of South Carolina, describing the situation in Charleston as he saw it, and asking that an experienced officer should be sent there at once to take charge of operations.

Exactly what these operations should be was not yet determined, but the *status quo* was delicate and might at any moment become dangerous. Fort Sumter was still held by Anderson, who obviously did not intend to leave it unless he were forced to do so; Pickens was threatening to use the indicated force, with the help of state troops, unless the Confederacy showed signs of preparing for prompt action against the intruders. Therefore, the Confederacy felt it had no choice; the demand for evacuation of the fort must be made by a duly authorized representative of the central government, and he must be a military man, preferably an engineer, so that, if the demands were refused, he would know how best to proceed against the fort. The inference was plain: Davis recognized Pierre's fitness for the task at hand and needed him in Charleston.

However, at midnight, when the two men wearily said good night to each other, the inference had still not been put into words. Davis saw Beauregard to the Exchange Hotel, shook him by the hand, thanked him for coming to the new capital. He was courteous, he was complimentary, but he was also cautious; even in this hour of emergency, when delay might well be disastrous, it was not in him to follow instinct rather than prudence, to act with impetuosity. Well, that was all right with Pierre. He had always enjoyed the limelight and he visualized quite clearly the dramatic role he might play at Charleston; a few years earlier, he would not only have welcomed the opportunity to fill it, he would have snatched at it; but that was when life had seemed so futile and meaningless, when nothing came his way more important than reconstructing the Mint and the Customs House, when he was defeated for mayor, when his plans for clearing the river channels and strengthening the forts were rejected or disregarded. It was before he had married Caroline. He now wrote her a loving letter, reiterating that he would be home almost before she had time to miss him; then he went to bed, slept soundly until nearly noon and, descending to the dining room, ate a leisurely breakfast. None of the other guests in the hotel paid any attention to him, for they were all absorbed in their own petty plans, and no further word came to him from either the Secretary of War or the President. He finally decided not to wait around for one; there was no telling how long it would take Davis to make up his mind. Meantime, he, Pierre, might as well go for a stroll.

As he made his way along a crowded dusty street, where raw recruits were drilling, he was suddenly surrounded by an excited group of gentlemen who were all talking at once. It appeared that they were delegates to the convention from Georgia and South Carolina and they wanted to be the first to congratulate him on his appointment. What appointment? Pierre wanted to know, speaking more calmly than he felt. Why, as the first Brigadier General in the Provisional Army of the Confederate States! He was to proceed immediately to Charleston, where he would assume command and direct operations against Fort Sumter. He expressed surprise; it was an honor he had neither expected nor desired. He feared it might prevent him from returning to New Orleans, which he wished to do for both personal and professional reasons. He was not acquainted with the defenses of Charleston or with the temper of its people. On the other hand, he had intimate knowledge of both in New Orleans. He had been especially eager to see the recommendations he had made regarding the fortification of St. Philip and Jackson put into effect; if he were *sur place*, he believed they would be, for the Confederates had already seized both forts. Of course, he was always at the service of his country, which was now the Confederacy, wherever he might be stationed, but, in that connection, it would be a source of great embarrassment, even of great grief, to find himself face to face, as an enemy, with Robert Anderson, whose friend and fellow teacher he had been at West Point. Moreover, there might be another handicap: he was not certain that his resignation from the United States Army had been accepted. To be sure, he had sent it in on the eighth of February and this was the twenty-sixth, so it must have been received long since; but until he was officially notified that he had been relieved of his former fealty, he could not take up arms under another flag. Well, he could discuss that with Davis, his new-found friends assured him; probably a telegram would settle that question quickly—the lines were still open. And the President was waiting to see him. They hurried him along to the Capitol. . . .

Everything had been resolved without delay. The telegram had been sent and the reply had come through promptly: his resignation from the United States Army had been officially accepted by President Buchanan. Governor Pickens had been advised by Leroy Walker that Brigadier General Peter G. T. Beauregard was on his way to Charleston, where he would assume command of all military operations. Less formally, the Governor was assured that, in addition to his supreme fitness for these, because of his engineering skill and experience, General Beauregard's background and personality were such that they could not help but be satisfactory to Charlestonians; and now Pierre, armed with all these recommendations, was on the train headed for his new post.

He was displeased with his designation as *Peter* Beauregard and decided that, rather than submit to it, he would drop his first name entirely. His old friends would, of course, continue to call him Pierre —heaven forbid that they should call him Gustave! But henceforth, he would sign himself merely with the initials G. T. Did these Anglo-Saxons think they could turn him into one of their own? If so, they would discover their mistake; he was a Latin to the very marrow of his bones—his new associates might as well try to turn him into a Protestant! No doubt, they would try to do this, too; although many Charlestonians were of French descent, he understood that most of these were Huguenots, that is to say, heretics. Moreover, he would have felt it more fitting to hear of the appointment from the President personally, and not from strangers on the street. He was meticulous himself about such matters and he preferred that all others with whom he dealt should observe the same rules of law and order. In addition to the slight feeling of dissatisfaction which he experienced on these two scores, he was suffering twinges of conscience.

Perhaps he had not been wholly sincere in telling those Georgia and Carolina delegates that he would have preferred to return to New Orleans, that the assignment to Charleston had come as a surprise; it would have been more accurate to say that it *would* have come as a surprise before his talks with Walker and Davis. But, after all, that was an insignificant detail, just as the misuse of *Peter* for his real name and the manner in which the great news had been broken to him were insignificant details compared to the fact that he was now, indisputably, the first Brigadier General in the Confederate Army.

When it came to meeting Robert Anderson as an enemy, he supposed he would have to get used to experiences like that. Why, even Sherman—who had gone out of his way just the week before to come and tell Pierre that all was well with his sons—must be classified as an enemy now! It hurt, but there would be hundreds of other hurts like it. And so far as his hopes and expectations went—if those had changed, too, was not that still another detail that did not need to be explained to outsiders? To himself he would admit that the more he thought about this new assignment, the better it pleased him. True, Charleston and its defenses, its people and its ways, were all strange to him; but it was a strangeness that he would quickly overcome; and whereas a return to New Orleans would have represented personal happiness and professional honor, the road to Charleston might very well be the one so long sought and so long elusive—the way to glory. He would have to take it alone now, but later Caroline would share it with him. She would be willing to wait and he would be willing to have her wait, under all the circumstances.

He wrote her again, putting this feeling into words and then he dashed off another letter. The President had told him that Captain Raphael Semmes, who had been dispatched to New York for the purpose of buying arms and, if possible, ships for the new Confederacy, had been informed that Captain G. W. Smith and Captain Mansfield Lovell, late of the United States Army, might aid him in his task; he was to assure them that they would be very welcome in the Confederate Army. It would do no harm, Pierre decided, to follow up this statement from the President with a letter of his own. He wanted, in any case, to enlist Smith's assistance in some purchasing; so he concluded his letter by asking, "When shall we have the benefit of your services and those of Lovell?"

He sealed, stamped and posted both letters before leaving for the depot. As the train carried him closer and closer to his destination, he became more and more convinced that this was, indeed, the road to glory; and, with the surge of exultation which the assurance carried, came the consciousness that, instead of feeling jealousy toward the President or a grudge against him, he now felt gratitude tinged with sympathy. His jealousy went all the way back to the Mexican War, when he had felt that Davis' much-heralded prowess on the battlefield was closely allied to the fact that he was Zachary Taylor's son-in-law, whereas he, Pierre, had not attained a similar position in regard to Scott; for fifteen years, this green-eyed monster had obsessed him. The grudge was of a much later period: it dated only from the time when he had learned that Davis, then the powerful United States Senator from Mississippi, advocated a measure which would make the superintendency of West Point available to officers other than those of the Engineering Corps; but if this feeling were not so ancient as that of jealousy, it had, if anything, been stronger. And how could he continue to hold it, now that Davis had given him this supreme opportunity? He told himself that it was unthinkable, that he would never again permit his mind to be corroded by such a sensation. Moreover, Davis, he knew, still imagined himself a great militarist; he would vastly have preferred being General-in-Chief of the new Confederate Army than President of the provisional government; but he had been marked for the role of Chief Executive and he had bowed to the will of his people. It must have been a great disappointment for him to do this, it must have required a great effort of will. Pierre paid him the tribute of admiration for his self-sacrifice. It did not occur to him until much later that Davis might try to resume the abandoned role without resigning from the one he had accepted and that, when this happened, what had once been only jealousy and resentment might flare into open enmity. When Pierre remembered Davis, as the train moved along through the night, it was to think of him as a friend to whom he owed much and who well might envy him; but his thoughts were chiefly centered on himself and the destiny toward which he was traveling.

"Look here, you, it's dark. Loafers aren't allowed on the park benches after dark. You better get a move on and go home. That is, if you got any home. Looks to me as if you might be one of them vagrants back from the war. New *Orleens* is crawling with them. Still and all, I might remind you there's such a thing as a curfew."

Pierre rose slowly and found he needed to steady himself against the back of the bench as he did so. He had been sitting still for so long that he was cramped, and it was hard for him to straighten himself up. This, he knew, would give the Union police officer who had shaken him the impression that he was drunk, as well as disorderly, but he did not care. Perhaps he had dozed a little and, if he had, his drowsiness would help to explain his unsteadiness to himself, while confirming the policeman's belief that he was intoxicated. And to his relief, when he began to speak, he found his voice was quite clear.

"You're right, officer, it is time I went home. Yes, I do have one to go to—a good one. And I didn't intentionally break the rules. When I came here, the sun was still shining. I seem to have lost track of time. And that makes twice in the same day."

He turned away and found, to his further relief, that he could walk with a firm step and with no hesitation as to direction. Although it was too dark to see the man's features clearly, he was conscious that the policeman, who was muttering something under his breath, was also watching him. Pierre left the Square and went on down Chartres Street without looking back. He could see a light in Mme Cougot's chamber as he passed it going along the carriageway and, though the other rooms on that side of the house were in darkness, there was a second light on the rear gallery and a third one in his quarters. Simone must have lighted these for him, he realized, and he also felt sure he would find something to eat spread out on his work table, but with due care not to disturb his papers or move the japanned boxes and the family album. He stopped for a moment, reflecting that perhaps he should go up on the gallery and put out the light, which had obviously been left so that he could see his way across the patio; but he could manage very well without it, and there was no sense in leaving it there all night to burn up precious oil. However, just as he started up the steps, Simone came out of the house, wearing a long violet-colored dressing gown and carrying a candle, which she shaded with one hand.

"I'll put it out," she said, answering his unspoken question. "I'm certainly glad you're back. It's so late, *maman* and I have been worried about you. Where have you been all this while?"

"Most of the time I was in Montgomery," he said, "and then I was on a train going to Charleston. But I think it's reached there now."

~§ 25 §~

PICKENS HAD BEEN HOWLING TO MONTGOMERY FOR AN ENGI-
neering officer and a "commander-in-chief," and late in February he got the engineer in the person of Captain William
Whiting, an able West Pointer from Mississippi. Whiting,
the first representative in Charleston of the fledgling Confederate army, was perhaps not as diplomatic as he should
have been. He made an inspection of the harbor armament
and criticized much that was done. In his judgment there
were too many guns aimed at the reduction of Sumter and
too few placed to prevent naval entrance into the harbor—an
attitude that so wounded the sensitive Charlestonians that
some demanded his removal.

On March 1st, Pickens got his commander-in-chief. He was
Pierre Beauregard, the Louisiana Creole who had skyrocketed
from major in the federal army to brigadier general in the
Confederate army since his removal from command at the
Military Academy. Beauregard, West Point '38, was a hero of
the Mexican War, in which he had been twice wounded. A
skillful man with artillery, he agreed entirely with Whiting's
criticism of the gun concentration. Much as he respected
Major Anderson, he saw instantly that there would be no
problem in overpowering Sumter's meager garrison, or starving it into submission. The only problem was to make certain
that no reinforcements or supplies could reach the fort, an
end to which he bent immediate efforts. But he was tactful,
careful not to offend these touchy people. Beauregard soon
became a social lion in Charleston, an ambassador of good
will who persuaded the chivalry that the Confederacy was
worthy of their support.

From Sumter, Anderson watched these developments
thoughtfully. He knew Major—or rather *General* Beauregard
very well. Back in 1837 when Anderson was instructor in
artillery at West Point, one of his students had been Cadet
Beauregard, such a keen young fellow that Anderson had
marked him as a comer. When Beauregard graduated in 1838,

he had been given at Anderson's request the post of assistant instructor of artillery and the two had worked together in imparting the lore of cannon to undergraduates. Yes, he knew Beauregard—vain as a peacock but generous, brilliant, magnetic—knew he would be a formidable adversary. Anderson reported to Washington:

> The presence here, as commander, of General Beauregard recently of the U. S. Engineers, insures, I think, in a great measure the exercise of skill and sound judgment in all operations of the South Carolinians in this harbor. God grant that our country may be saved from the horrors of a fratricidal war! . . .

Former Senator Wigfall, himself a one-man example of secession, ready to secede from anything and everything, had quit the Senate and spent a busy fortnight establishing a secret Confederate recruiting station in Baltimore. He had sent sixty-four recruits to Charleston when the trend of events warned him there might be war over Sumter after all. A native Carolinian and a combative man drawn irresistibly to any scene of strife, Wigfall dropped his Baltimore enterprise, went to Charleston and registered April 3rd at the Mills House, where he strode out on the balcony and gave a fighting speech to a crowd of serenaders.

"Whether Major Anderson shall be shelled out or starved out," he said, "is a question merely of expediency. The honor of South Carolina was vindicated when the flag of the United States was fired at, and it has remained vindicated, because they have never resented that shot . . . that flag was never fired at with impunity until it covered a crew of Black Republicans."

Then Wigfall spoke sense: "We have a new flag; that flag has not yet been baptized in blood. I hear someone say, God forbid.

"I tell you, fellow citizens . . . South Carolina became a nation, South Carolina became a people and declared their independence before the 4th of July, 1776. But it was not acknowledged until after seven years of suffering and shedding of blood, and if you suppose this is going to be gained without blood, I think you are mistaken."

—W. A. Swanberg, *First Blood: The Story of Fort Sumter*
(Scribner's)

So many despatches and letters, public and private, had been forwarded to the South by influential Southern statesmen then in Washington, to the effect that, despite heavy outside pressure, the President could be induced to settle the question at issue without a resort to arms, if sufficient time were allowed him, that up to the very last hour the Confederate authorities at Montgomery, and many high officials in Charleston, really hoped that the Federal troops would yet be withdrawn from Sumter, and the impending danger of war be averted. General Crawford, United States Army, in his essay, "The First Shot Against the Flag," speaking of this impression, says distinctly, "and they had at one time reason for the belief." General Doubleday expresses himself with no less certainty when he states that "Anderson now had no doubt that we would be withdrawn, and the papers all gave out the same idea."

Not until Captain G. V. Fox, of the United States Navy, had obtained introduction into Sumter, under the plea of "pacific purposes," though in reality to concert a plan for its reinforcement; not until Colonel Lamon, representing himself as a confidential agent of President Lincoln, had gained access to the fort, under the pretence of arranging matters for the removal of the troops, but "in reality to confer with Major Anderson, and ascertain the amount of provisions on hand"; not until, on the 8th of April, Mr. Chew, from the State Department at Washington, had notified both Governor Pickens and General Beauregard "that the government intended to provision Fort Sumter peaceably, if possible, forcibly, if necessary"; not until then was the last expectation of an amicable settlement of our difficulties dismissed from the minds of those who, though vigorously preparing for war, cherished none the less the delusive hope of peace. . . .

Major Anderson's letter to Colonel L. Thomas, Adjutant-General United States Army, dated April 8th, 1861, and the telegrams from Messrs. Crawford, Roman, and Forsyth, from Washington, establish the fact that the object of the Federal government in delaying its final answer to the Southern Commissioners was to gain time for the reinforcement of Sumter before it could be reduced by the South Carolina troops under General Beauregard. The following is an extract from Major Anderson's letter. It explains itself, and clears him from all participation in that act of duplicity:

Fort Sumter, S. C., April 8th, 1861.

To Colonel L. Thomas, etc.:

Colonel,—

I had the honor to receive by yesterday's mail the letter of the Honorable Secretary of War, dated April 4th, and confess that what he here states surprises me very greatly, following, as it does, and contradicting so positively, the assurance Mr. Crawford telegraphed he was "authorized" to make. I trust that this matter will be at once put in a correct light, as a movement made now, when the South has been erroneously informed that none such would be attempted, would produce most disastrous results throughout our country. It is, of course, now too late for me to give any advice in reference to the proposed scheme of Captain Fox. I fear that its result cannot fail to be disastrous to all concerned. Even with his boat at our walls, the loss of life (as I think I mentioned to Mr. Fox) in unloading her will more than pay for the good to be accomplished by the expedition, which keeps us, if I can maintain possession of this work, out of position, surrounded by strong works, which must be carried to make this fort of the least value to the United States government.

We have not oil enough to keep a light in the lantern for one night. The boats will have to, therefore, rely at night entirely upon other marks. I ought to have been informed that this expedition was to come. Colonel Lamon's remark convinced me that the idea, merely hinted at to me by Captain Fox, would not be carried out.

We shall strive to do our duty, though I frankly say that my heart is not in this war, which, I see, is to be thus commenced. That God will still avert it, and cause us to resort to pacific means to maintain our rights, is my ardent prayer.

I am, Colonel, very respectfully, your obedient servant,

Robert Anderson, Major 1st Artillery Commanding.

—Alfred Roman, *The Military Operations of General Beauregard* (Harper & Row)

❦

HE HAD NOT BEEN MISTAKEN; A SIMPLE BUT APPETIZING SUPPER, carefully covered with a white napkin, was set out on his work-table: salad, cheese, crusty bread and a thin slice of meat loaf. The bottle of wine his sister had given him, still half full, had been placed beside it, and a carafe of water. Gratefully, he sat down to eat and drink, suddenly conscious that he had not had a real meal that day, just coffee and cornbread in the morning and coffee and a doughnut at noon. Well, he had often gone for days at a time on less than that; but perhaps a man needed more substantial food and needed it more often as he grew older. He realized that he was beginning to think of himself as an old man, which was, of course, absurd. At forty-seven, he was really just approaching the prime of life, or would have been, had the events of the last few years not aged him prematurely. Be-sides, it was not only hunger that made him grateful for this food; it was the fact that Simone had thoughtfully provided it for him. It was a long time since a woman had ministered to his needs, until this one had begun to do so, and no man's life was complete without such ministrations. He had ceased to feel that he must not be obligated to Simone, for he had come to believe it was equally true that no woman's life was equally complete unless she could so minister to a man. Why, Simone had said that knowing him "had made a differ-ence," that the sound of Lance's footsteps was no longer all she lived for! He had filled a void in her life, just as she had filled one in his and she revealed this in many touching ways. It had not only seemed natural to her to keep a light burning and prepare supper for him; she had worried because he was so late, and when she heard him walking down the carriageway, she had come out on the gallery to tell him she was relieved, even though she had already retired for the night. She had no false modesty about letting him see her in her negligee. Of course, it covered her completely, quite as completely as a dress; but there was something about a negligee that bespoke greater informality than a dress. The same was true about the way a woman's hair was arranged; gathered into a knot at the back of her head and confined with a net, it did not give at all the same casual effect as when it fell in two long braids over her shoulders, even though, in both cases, it was neatly parted in the middle and smoothed down over her ears. Simone's hair had been braided and the braids were hanging over her breasts when she came out on the gallery to speak to him, clad in the violet dressing gown. He had realized before that she had a great deal of hair, but not how much. The braids reached well below her waist.

He finished his supper and cleared it away, still thinking of Simone and not of Charleston. But it was true that he had almost reached there, in his dreams, and he decided to continue the research which he had not resumed after writing to Lee. The first letter which came to his hand when he opened the second japanned box was the one Gus Smith had written in answer to the hasty note Pierre had dashed off at the Exchange Hotel in Montgomery, asking when Smith's services and Lovell's would be available to the Confederacy. It had not seemed very significant when he received it, but in the light of later events it had become so and he now reread it with interest.

> You ask in your joint letter to Lovell and myself, "When may we expect your services?" &c. Neither he or I are citizens of the seceded states, but you know well what our views, opinions and sympathies are. . . . In a word, propositions from either Mr. Davis or his military representative, his Secretary of War, would, if up to our standard (as we understand it) be favorably considered and in all probability accepted. . . . But if L. and I are wanted we take for granted we will be invited.

Pierre laid the letter aside, with bitter memories of all that the "invitation" to Lovell had eventually entailed in misery for his friend. Then he drew from the box the rough sketch he had made when he first went to Charleston, showing the way in which he felt the city should be defended and be prepared to attack—in a continuous circle of fortifications and not merely with the strengthening of individual strongholds, which the Charlestonians had already done. As he looked at the brittle piece of paper with its dimmed drawings, he felt a momentary surge of triumph, reminiscent of the one he had experienced when he first realized that his plan was acceptable to his hosts. They were a proud lot, unaccustomed to taking orders or even heeding advice from an outsider; and rich and poor, high and low, black and white, they had already thrown themselves into the work of fortification when he arrived. To convince them that their plan of action was not practical, to persuade them to try one that was—

this required all the intuition, all the tact, all the finesse which he could command. And he had convinced them, he had persuaded them and, far from antagonizing them while he was so doing, he had won their confidence and their admiration. More than that: he had become almost a superman in their eyes, a being endowed with all social and spiritual graces, in addition to his military skill, wisdom and experience. Never before, in Charleston's long and glorious history, had a stranger penetrated to the inner circle and dominated it. His desk was adorned with fresh flowers and littered with invitations. When he walked through the streets he was constantly stopped by devotees eager to shake his hand. When he went out to dinner, the loveliest ladies, the most distinguished men, hung on every word he uttered. The fact that he spoke English with a slight accent was considered "fascinating" by the ladies; the fact that he had a comprehensive knowledge of a great many subjects and could discuss them in an interesting as well as an informative way gave him added stature among the gentlemen. When he attended the theater, the press reported that he was "the cynosure of all eyes." He glowed with gratification and, because it was in just such an atmosphere that he operated most effectively, his ring of fortifications grew apace. This was broken only by Sumter itself; and that could be attacked—reduced, to use the current term—successfully at any minute. Its only hope of survival would have to come from a fleet, steaming up toward the harbor from the open sea. The only question was whether it should be reduced with or without provocation.

For a time, the former policy seemed the wiser. All the amenities were duly observed, so far as Anderson and his garrison were concerned. Their mail was delivered to them regularly and so were fresh vegetables and fresh meat. As a further *beau geste*, these staples were augmented by Havana cigars and vintage wines, sent with the compliments—or at least with the connivance—of General Beauregard. Inevitably, such a *guerre de dentelles* was too frail a fabric to stand any strain. Regretfully, he was obliged to inform his old friend Anderson that staples could no longer be delivered. He did not immediately realize that if this new order were carried out literally, Sumter would soon be short of food. The realization came when he learned that the Federal Government was preparing a fleet to reprovision it.

He had kept his sketches, but he had not kept a complete record of dates, pinpointing each one as to what made it uniquely significant. But there were, inevitably, a few which stood out. It was on April eighth that Pickens sent for him, to come and confer with the Governor and "an emissary from Washington." When he responded

promptly to the summons, he found a nervous little man who introduced himself as Robert Chew, a clerk from the Department of State.
Chew was fingering a sheet of paper which he had already shown to
the Governor, who had informed him that General Beauregard was
in charge of all military operations and must therefore be consulted.
"I am directed by the President of the United States," Chew now
read aloud, "to notify you to expect an attempt will be made to
supply Fort Sumter with provisions only, and that if such an attempt
is not resisted, no effort to throw in men, arms or ammunition will be
made without further notice, or in case of attack."

Pierre felt sorry for the poor little man, whose nervousness increased
visibly when he realized that a crowd was gathering outside; he was
sure its mood was menacing. Not at all, Pierre assured him; there
was naturally widespread curiosity about his message, but no violence
was intended; would he care to step outside and tell these people what
he had just told the civil and military authorities? They would be very
much interested. Chew replied, in an agitated way, that he would
really feel easier if he could leave by the back door and he would be
grateful for a military escort to the depot. Of course, he would
also like to see Sumter, if he could do so with suitable safeguards. The
latter, Pierre said gravely, was unfortunately impossible; but the back
door and the escort to the depot could be easily arranged. . . .

The train did not leave on time, which worried Chew; every moment that he spent in Charleston seemed to him fraught with danger.
He would have been still more worried if he had known that the telegrams he had written to Washington were not sent promptly, either.
But Pierre's conscience did not trouble him about these delays, which
he had instigated. As a matter of fact, he had hardly given the necessary orders when he dismissed them from his mind. His desk was
already cluttered with telegrams inferring that the relief expedition
was on its way; and as soon as he reported Chew's visit to Montgomery, a fresh batch came in: he was on no account to allow provisions
to reach Sumter. He was to demand its immediate evacuation. If the
demand were disregarded or refused, he was to reduce the fort.

The next date that stood out clearly in Pierre's mind, after all
these years was, of course, the twelfth; but this was less because of
what had actually happened then than because he had aroused so
much curiosity, which he could not satisfy, when he replied to the
order, saying he would make the demand on that day. Secretary Leroy
Walker saw no reason why General Peter Beauregard should delay
as long as this, now that the die was actually cast and the South had
taken the responsibility for firing the shot that was sure to start a

war. Pierre, on the contrary, saw a very good reason: his supply of ammunition was insufficient for a bombardment of any length; but he was momentarily awaiting the arrival of a shipment from Atlanta. It reached Charleston on schedule and early on the afternoon of the eleventh, he sent three of his aides—Colonel James Chestnut, Captain S. D. Lee and Lieutenant A. R. Chisolm—to Anderson with a written demand for the surrender of the fort.

The report which they brought back did not surprise Pierre in some respects. He had expected the demand to be rejected, formally and in writing, following the pattern in which it had been made; he had also expected that Anderson would confer for some time with his officers before making the answer which would wring his heart, and that he would show the emissaries every courtesy, even going so far as to see them off himself when they took their departure. But he had not expected the verbal admission with which Anderson supplemented the official rejection and which Colonel Chestnut duly relayed to Pierre. "Gentlemen, if you do not batter the fort to pieces about us, we shall be starved out in a few days."

So his old friend Robert was hungry already and would soon be worse than hungry: famished. It was a grueling thought. If Anderson had spoken the truth—and of course he must have—would it not be better to let the inevitable capitulation come through want than through force? Nothing had been seen of the relief fleet; if it were delayed, perhaps Anderson would be driven to asking for food on any terms and of course the terms would be unconditional surrender. But then there would be no shot fired, no bloodshed; what was more important still, the South would be exonerated from having committed the first warlike act. Pierre could hardly wait to establish communication with Montgomery, and Montgomery reacted as he expected: Anderson had only to indicate when he would evacuate voluntarily; he had only to agree that before doing so he would not fire on the Confederates without provocation; if he would meet those conditions, there would be no bombardment. Late at night, the same emissaries who had gone to the fort early in the afternoon returned to it, bearing another official communication, which was couched in terms very different from the previous one.

This time Anderson's conference with his officers lasted even longer than before. It was three in the morning before he handed his reply to Colonel Chestnut and, this time, Chestnut did not wait to consult Pierre before answering. If he had. . . . Well, it was certainly too late to speculate on that now, more than four years afterward. It was already too late on the morning of April 12, 1861. But Anderson had done his best to be conciliatory: he would evacuate on the fifteenth; he would not fire on the Confederates in the meantime if they revealed no hostile intentions and committed no hostile acts; that is, unless he received new instructions or additional supplies. It was that one word *unless* that caused Chestnut to act with such precipitation. But after all, the Confederates had no idea of revealing hostile intentions or committing hostile acts; they had welcomed the loopholes of escape from these which the fort's starving condition permitted. As to new instructions, all those sent out were so contradictory, as far as Pierre could make out, what with Seward wiring that the fort would not be revictualed and Lincoln wiring that it would, Anderson could easily get confused and his confusion would be a godsend to all concerned, because not knowing what he should do, he would do nothing, as in the case of the *Star of the West*. As for the additional supplies, there was no sign of those yet, so why not assume they would not arrive before the fifteenth? It was a safe enough assumption, as safety went these days.

But Chestnut had not seen it that way. He had made a lightning decision to the effect that Anderson had not met Beauregard's terms and, standing in a casemate, had written that firing would begin in one hour. The previous afternoon Anderson had asked for the assurance that Beauregard would not open fire without further warning; this time, he asked for no such assurance; he did not quibble over Chestnut's revolt against the word *unless*. He shook hands courteously with all three aides and remarked gravely that if they were fated not to meet again in this world, he hoped they might do so in the next.

Pierre did not see them or hear their report until after he had heard the first shot and seen the "arching shell" which curved over the bay, followed by clouds of white smoke, and which appeared to land in the center of Sumter. His emissaries had stopped at Johnson —no longer an antiquated ruin as it had been in November, but a well-repaired and well-equipped fort—and ordered the commander, Captain George S. James, to start firing; and the arching shell which Pierre had seen was the signal for all the batteries which he had so carefully constructed to start firing and, presently, the noise was deafening. At first, Sumter did not return this fire. But presently Pierre saw its flag go up and heard its guns open. The noise became more deafening still.

The firing went on all that day and all the next with increasing sound and fury, but with surprisingly little damage. Most of Pierre's guns, with the exception of the latest shipment he had received, were smooth bores. He had a heavy Dahlgren, which he had succeeded in placing at the western end of Sullivan's Island, and a rifled Blakely which threw shot of shell with deadly accuracy and which had been promptly shipped to Cummings Point. But, despite the added assurance these fine pieces gave him, reluctantly he began to believe that though he could easily pepper and injure the fort, it would be difficult for him to destroy it. It was not until he saw flames shooting from the barracks and realized that the fire would soon spread to the magazines, because of the strong wind blowing, that he felt the elements were contributing to his cause. Watching developments with an eager and vigilant eye, he next saw the flagstaff topple over; obviously, the garrison must be in desperate straits. He summoned three aides—Stephen Lee again, Porcher Miles and Roger Pryor—and ordered them to proceed at once to Sumter; they were to offer Major Anderson help in extinguishing the flames.

Pierre saw nothing inconsistent about such an offer. True, he was bombarding the fort, but that was a normal act of routine warfare. Its defenders must not be hampered in their gallant efforts to resist attack by an accidental fire which had nothing to do with hostilities. Once he had sped his emissaries on their way, he resumed his watch and almost instantly saw an astonishing sight; the Stars and Stripes were floating again; then they were hauled down and a white flag raised in their stead. True, in sending his emissaries, he had hoped that the moment might be propitious for suggesting that the flag, which had not been voluntarily lowered, but had toppled over, should not be raised again. However, he had not empowered his aides to offer terms for surrender and he quickly sent out three more. Then, with what show of composure he could command, he awaited their return. Patience had never been his forte and, having made what he considered a generous gesture, he felt justified in hoping and expecting an early response. Hours passed and still nothing visible happened and no one came to him. By nightfall, he was almost beside himself, not only with excitement, but with bewilderment. The explanation of the delay, when it came, was not calculated to soothe him:

When Lee, Miles and Pryor arrived at the fort, they found they had been forestalled by the unheralded and unauthorized arrival of Louis T. Wigfall, formerly United States Senator from Texas and now a colonel on General Beauregard's staff. Pierre had consented to the appointment with his usual courtesy, but with no real cordiality. He had not forgotten that Wigfall was among those senators who agreed with Jefferson Davis that the superintendency of West Point should be available to officers who were not members of the Engineering Corps; and he had considered the Texan's conduct highly improper, when the latter had continued to hold his Senate seat for weeks on end, meanwhile sneering at the Union and dispatching messages to Charleston, urging that supplies should be cut off from Sumter. But he had finally resigned and the pressure to put him on the General's staff had been so strong from the Carolinians whom he had favored that Pierre finally yielded to it. Now the happenings of the day were certainly not calculated to increase his admiration for his insistent aide, who did not take his duties very seriously—indeed, Pierre had not seen him for two days. But Wigfall had observed the fall of the flag from a vantage point at some distance from the General's head-quarters—Cummings Point, on Morris Island. Thereupon, he im-mediately commandeered a rowboat and two Negro oarsmen and, accompanied by two privates, made for the fort.

Wigfall was a huge, red-faced, black-bearded man of ferocious aspect who delighted in duels and who had equipped himself for his voluntary mission in a fantastic manner: a red sash and a sword belt encircled his substantial middle and in one powerful hand he carried an unsheathed sword with a white flag tied to its blade. The terrified gunner, who first caught sight of this formidable visitor glaring through an embrasure, was about to fire when Wigfall waved a handkerchief, bellowed that his mission was both peaceful and urgent and demanded to be taken to the commander. As he was able to identify himself to a nearby lieutenant, he was ushered into Ander-son's presence. There he assured the Major that the latter could name his own terms for surrender and it was then that the white flag had gone up; but hardly was this in place when Lee, Miles and Pryor arrived with their offer to help put out the fire and their amazed statement neither they nor Wigfall had been authorized to agree on terms for a surrender. In that case, Anderson replied, with some chagrin, he would raise the Stars and Stripes again and resume fire. Would he not at least wait until they could return and advise the General of the situation? Lee inquired. Yes, Anderson agreed, he would willingly do that, provided no undue delay was involved.

They had hardly departed with the written document setting forth the terms of an agreement with Wigfall, when the second group of aides, headed by Major David R. Jones, Pierre's Chief of Staff, arrived bearing the official message from the General. Since, to all intents and purposes, Anderson had already surrendered twice that day, the whole episode had begun to assume the characteristics of an opera bouffe, despite the tragic circumstances under which it took place. But it was not until long afterward that Pierre was able to see it in that light and certainly Anderson did not, either then or later.

He and his men had subsisted for days on spoiled pork and moldy rice and the rice was suspect. A window had broken in the room where it had been spread out to dry and bits of shattered glass were mixed in with it; considerable caution was indicated in its consumption, even by the hungriest men. After forty-eight hours of fighting, they were so exhausted they could not continue the struggle. The supply fleet, represented in the Southern press as comprising eleven vessels, two hundred and eighty-five guns and two thousand four hundred men, had never come to their rescue, though after the surrender it was sighted still well out to sea and making no effort to advance.

Pierre was not present at the ceremony of capitulation for which he had dictated the terms; he had no wish to witness his old friend in defeat and tried to spare him all possible humiliation. Anderson was allowed to parade his men and salute his flag before it was lowered; ironically enough, it was during the course of this ceremony that the only casualties occurred: Private Daniel Hough was accidentally killed by the premature discharge of the piece he was loading and five other members of the garrison were wounded when a pile of cartridges exploded; so, instead of battle carnage, there were only accidental injuries. Pierre remembered his chagrin when his first "wound" during the Mexican War had been a mangled foot caused by a trampling horse and not by enemy fire. Of course these casualties at Sumter, which included a fatality, were much graver than that; still the comparison lingered in his mind. He knew that these men and their commander must wish that, if harm were coming to them, it might have been in another way.

The entire garrison took its departure aboard the steamer *Isabel*, which had been put at Anderson's disposal, and the Confederates stood with uncovered heads along the waterfront until it had passed Cummings Point. It was only after the vessel was out of sight that Pierre joined the official party which went to take possession of Sumter. But the celebration of the victory was not confined to this favored group. Except for that brief respectful pause while the *Isabel* steamed out of sight, Charleston had been in holiday mood from the time the bombardment began. People had poured into the city from every part of the state, jamming the roads, crowding the trains, filling the hotels and descending on their relatives, secure in the knowledge that, with characteristic expansive hospitality, somehow room would be found for them. If they had been going to a cockfight, a picnic, a circus or the races, their mood could hardly have been more jocund. When the flags of the Confederacy and South Carolina were raised and the guns from all the fortifications surrounding the city fired a salute, the Battery was lined with cheering crowds, the harbor was filled with small craft loaded with merrymakers and bands were parading through the streets to the tunes of the new popular airs. Elegant ladies, dressed as if to attend a St. Cecilia Ball, foregathered on balconies and took up the refrain. So this was war! This was victory! This was glory! It was a day in which to rejoice and be glad!

Pierre did not feel so sure. He went to the cathedral where a *Te Deum* was sung with great pomp and ceremony. He mapped out a plan for repairing Fort Sumter and saw it put into action. He authorized the painting of a full-length portrait of himself. He accepted with graciousness the role of paladin and played it superbly. But in his heart of hearts he knew that the triumph had come too easily and the rejoicing was too great. One victory was not enough to win a war or immortalize a man.

❧ 26 ❧

Bruges, September 25th, 1880.

My dear General,—The facts with reference to the proposed fleet of armed vessels for the service of the Confederacy were briefly as follows:

I had, from the very beginning of the struggle, been more impressed with the vital importance of the seaports than with anything else. I regarded them as the lungs of the country, which, once really closed, asphyxia must follow. I therefore took an early occasion to go to London to see what could be had in the shape of vessels fit to take and keep the sea, for a lengthened period, and strong enough to carry an armament which would render them efficient war-vessels, or, at all events, equal to cope with those of the enemy engaged in the blockade of the coast.

I was fortunate in finding exactly what was wanted. A fleet of first-class East-Indiamen was lying there idle, under circumstances of a financial nature which made them available to a buyer at less than half their cost. They had been built with a view of being armed if required, and also to be used as transports for troops, as well as to carry valuable cargoes and treasure in time of peace. Four of them were vessels of great size and power, and of the very first class, and there were six others which, although smaller, were scarcely inferior for the required purpose. Having, with the assistance of an expert, thoroughly inspected them all, I at once entered into negotiations for their purchase, and having secured them for the reply of the Confederate authorities, I submitted the proposal, in a letter to the Hon. G. A. Trenholm, who referred it, as I believe, to Montgomery. The total cost of buying, arming, and fitting-out the ten ships was estimated at two millions of pounds, to put the fleet on the coast ready for action; a sum which would have been covered by forty thousand bales of cotton, out of the three or four millions of bales which the government had, at that time, under their hand, and which would not have cost them, at 6d. in their own currency, more than two millions of dollars. There would have been little or no difficulty in getting the ships to sea. The Foreign Enlistment Act had not then—and, indeed, never has been—authoritatively interpreted to mean that a neutral may not sell an unarmed ship to a belligerent; all that was required was commercial caution and coolness, and naval skill and address; all these were at hand, and there is no room for reasonable doubt that, within six months at furthest of the acceptance of the offer being received on this side, the fleet would have appeared off Boston and swept the coast thence to the Gulf, an achievement which would have compelled the prompt recognition of our government on this side, and the speedy triumph of our cause. I have always understood that the proposition was considered and rejected by the Confederate government, but I never had any communication from them on the subject. Although much disappointed at this result, so convinced was I of the value of the ships that I determined to retain my hold upon them as long as possible, to prevent their being sold elsewhere, and in hope that other counsels would prevail at home before it was too late. By means of negotiations which it is not necessary to detail here, I did succeed in retaining control of them until the occurrence of the "*Trent* outrage"; when the British government, requiring immediately ships of this class for transportation of troops and war-material to Canada, the owners broke off the negotiations with me, and got the ships, or many of them, employed in this service, in which they remained until there was no further need of them.

This is a correct and simple statement of the facts which are (as far as regards this side of the water) necessarily known better to myself than to any other living person, and concerning which my memory is perfectly clear and reliable. It occupied my mind almost exclusively for some time, and I built the highest hopes upon the success of the scheme. It is true many of the ships were of too great draught of water to enter some of our ports, but that was a matter of comparatively little importance. What was wanted, in my view, was the moral effect which would have been produced everywhere by such a blow as could have been struck by even half of the whole number; an effect which I have always, and will always believe, would have gone very far towards determining, if it had not entirely reversed, the result of the struggle.

I am, dear General,
Yours very truly,
C. K. Prioleau

General G. T. Beauregard.

(The writer of this letter was a member of the firm of John Frazer & Co. of Liverpool, through whose hands passed the negotiations relative to the purchase of the ten vessels released by the East India Company. The *"Trent* outrage" to which the letter refers was the halting, by means of a shell fired across her bow by Captain Wilkes of the United States sloop *San Jacinto,* of a ship belonging to the British Merchant Marine, on which Slidell, with his family and his staff, was traveling to Europe.)

—Alfred Roman, *The Military Operations of General Beauregard* (Harper & Row)

WEEKS WENT BY AND THE AURA OF GLORY WITH WHICH PIERRE WAS surrounded grew brighter. Wigfall was by no means the only prominent official who insisted on joining his staff; it was overweighted with the great and the near-great. His attention to his own appearance, always meticulous and discerning, became fastidious; his new gray uniforms, made of the finest fabrics and tailored by the most expert hands, were increasingly elegant. He had never cut so striking a figure, even in the days when he dominated the social scene of New Orleans; and it was the easier for him to do so, as the care of his clothes was not his personal responsibility; he had only to wear them. Straitened circumstances no longer entered the picture; he had both a quadroon body servant and a Spanish valet. Yet, because of his untiring energy, his enormous executive ability and his devotion to duty, he escaped the attributes of a fashionable fop; Beau Brummel had been transformed into a military man.

He kept long hours, rising early and spending some time at his office before going out to the fort, where he supervised every detail of reconstruction. His correspondence was enormous, and he discovered that the best way to keep abreast of this was to open and answer letters and telegrams as they arrived, before he did anything else. The task of replying to the messages of congratulation which poured in from all over the Confederacy was monumental; yet lack of response would have been not only ungracious but unwise. Davis wired, requesting that "if occasion offered" his friendly remembrances should be tendered Major Anderson. Walker wired, saying Pierre "had won his spurs" and asking how many guns could be spared for Pensacola. Benjamin wrote and said that though a triumphant general would probably put little value on the tribute of a poor civilian who knew nothing of war, he—Benjamin—could not refrain from joining in the universal voice of their fellow citizens and offering congratulations on the signal success which had crowned the first blow struck in defense of Southern rights. The Congress of the Confederacy and the Legislature of South Carolina tendered formal expressions of appreciation and gratitude; military leaders, civil officers and influential editors wrote by the score; private citizens, both male and female, by the hundred. Some of the latter were rather silly and gushing; these were better disregarded. All the others were extremely gratifying; the least Pierre could do was to say so.

He made a point of writing daily to Caroline, before he wrote to anyone else; in that way he was sure that the inevitable interruptions to correspondence in the form of official visits, the issuance of orders, interviews and so on would not make it possible to wedge her letter in, before he started for Sumter. He was worried about her. Something about the chattiness and cheerfulness of her letters seemed to him rather forced. She was enjoying the new streetcars, the first in the city, which were apparently causing quite a sensation; but did she and her friends really find it as thrilling as she said to ride about in these mule-drawn vehicles? More and more volunteer companies were being formed and the uniforms were getting gaudier all the time. The latest was the Tiger Rifles, captained by a man who called himself Alex White; they wore scarlet skull caps, red shirts, open brown jackets and baggy Turkish trousers of blue-and-white bed ticking, tucked into white leggings. They were said to be the lowest scrapings of the city, mostly wharf rats, but since they feared neither God, man nor the devil, the general opinion in New Orleans was that they would make wonderful fighters. For once, Pierre told himself, general opinion was correct. He would have use for those Tigers, unless he were very much mistaken, in the not-too-distant future. Caroline wanted him to know that every morning when the roll was called in the Orleans Guard, and his name was reached on the muster, the color sergeant stepped forward and announced, "Absent on duty." Well, that, of course, was as it should be. He was glad she was gratified, but he felt she was perhaps attaching too much importance to a mere matter of form. (Or did she perhaps feel there was something a little theatrical about the announcement, but hesitated to say so and therefore said something else instead?) She was very lonely, she missed him very much; doubtless this was why she was not quite herself these days. Well, actually, he would have been rather sorry, in a way, if that had not been the case. But though she did not say, in so many words, that she was feeling ill, he gathered this was so. He wrote to her kinsman and physician, Dr. Charles Turpin, and asked the kindly doctor to tell him candidly whether or not his anxiety was justified. Though Turpin replied guardedly, Pierre feared that it was. Nothing serious, according to the report; just a certain malaise, lack of appetite, a constant feeling of languor, severe headaches. Pierre's next letter to Caroline was couched in terms of special tenderness. "And remember, darling," he said at the end, "that our separation won't be long. I know I was mistaken when I said I'd be gone only two weeks, but I can't keep on being mistaken. The general feeling seems to be that ninety days will see the end. I wouldn't set quite such a definite time limit, but I do believe that one decisive battle— in which the South would, of course, be victorious—is all we need. From my point of view, that battle could not possibly come too soon. Join your prayers to mine in asking that it may be."

He worried not only about Caroline, but about his younger son Henri. The elder, René, who had promptly enlisted as a private in the Washington Artillery of New Orleans, was now offered by Governor Pickens a commission in the First Carolina Battalion of Light Infantry. That would mean father and son could see each other from time to time. Also, that was fitting, that was as it should be, just as it was fitting that Pierre's little daughter, Doucette, should remain at Upper Magnolia with her maternal grandparents. But Henri was restless, as a letter written at Upper Magnolia early in May plainly revealed.

Magnolia, May 8, 1861

Dear Father:

I have just arrived from the seminary. on the 4th uncle Charles sent us our resignation on account of the disorganization of the college; they made us stop our english studies for two months and learn latin every day and from one hundred cadets that were there there is only thirty-four remaining, they are all starting off for war and I believe that if you go in Virginia you will meet up with some of them as most of them have high offices, as, those of lieutenants orderly sergeants and sergents. We are here waiting to know what you intend to do with us. I am very willing to join a regiment if you will allow me to do so.

Adieu dear father,

Your affectionate son,

H. T. Beauregard

This was one of the letters Pierre had managed to keep, the letter he lifted from the second japanned box after he had laid aside the rough drawing of his first plan for the defense of Charleston; and remembering how troubled he had been about Henri, the other worries which had so riddled the glories of that long-ago spring came crowding back to his consciousness, as he sat at the wooden table from which he had cleared away the remains of his frugal supper. True, his concern for his younger son had been assuaged the following fall, when the South Carolina Legislature, "in grateful recognition of his distinguished services," tendered him the privilege of sending two pupils to be educated at the military school of the state. Henri and his cousin, James Proctor—the son of Elodie and Richard Proctor, who were so unfailingly kind to Pierre now—had been sent to the Military Academy of South Carolina and, for the next two years, Pierre was able to dismiss all question of the boy's welfare from his mind. But the other worries which began at Charleston lasted far longer than that.

Chief among these was his continued anxiety about Fort Jackson and Fort St. Philip. He wrote urgently to Leroy Walker. "I am surprised that we are not yet prepared on the Mississippi River, when we have had ample time to do so. Could you not find someone to take hold of matters with energy while waiting that I may be sent there?" He clung to the hope that he would go home. Much as he longed for that "one decisive battle," he did not want it to occur anywhere near New Orleans; and he was convinced that it would not do so, were he only empowered with authority to take the steps he felt necessary to prevent it. But when he went briefly to Montgomery, accompanied by William H. Russell, the gifted and agreeable representative of the London *Times,* and saw both Davis and Walker officially in the course of his stay, they brushed off the subject of his return to Louisiana; and this despite the recent visit of a deputation from New Orleans, which had come to the capital for the express purpose of calling the President's attention to the unprotected condition of their city. Pierre had to take what comfort he could in the fact that he himself successfully brushed off the subject of an assignment to Pensacola, now under the command of Bragg, and for that and several other reasons extremely distasteful to him. He was obliged to content himself with reassignment to Charleston.

Not that this lacked interest to him or failed to furnish a challenge to his experience and resourcefulness. He especially enjoyed a reconnaissance of the South Carolina coast, made at the request of Governor Pickens for the purpose of adopting a widespread system of defense. The memoir which he prepared as a result of this trip was, he believed, one of his most important contributions to the war effort. In it, he advised fieldworks at the mouths of the Stono and the two Edistos and at Georgetown, but stated he feared similar construction at Port Royal would be a waste of time, money and effort. The Governor's insistence that he should modify his original plan was a source of disappointment to him. And a much more serious one followed.

His journey to Montgomery had been rendered enjoyable by the presence of Mr. Russell as his traveling companion and, during the course of it, he made an acquaintance who seemed even more important to him than that of the London *Times* correspondent: a certain W. L. Trenholm, whose father—later to become Secretary of the Treasury—was a partner in the firm of John Frazer and Company, which operated from both Charleston and Liverpool. According to the son, he himself was on his way to offer the Confederate Government ten steamers, originally built for the East India Company, which no longer required them. These ships could be made available immediately, and could be used to export the surplus cotton with which the South was amply provided at the moment; this cargo would serve to finance the project. As yet, there was no effective blockade, and it did not look as if the North could achieve one in short order, since its fleet was admittedly inadequate; and after a certain number of voyages with large cargoes of cotton, the ships under discussion could be converted into cruisers. What did General Beauregard think of this proposition?

He thought so well of it that he dwelt on it with excitement all night and could hardly wait to see it laid before Davis. His astonishment was equaled only by his dismay when Davis declined to consider it. Never had he argued more eloquently or vehemently for any expedient. Such steamers, under the command of available officers—Semmes, Huger, Pegram and Reid, to mention only a few—could not only raise any blockade but become a menace to United States commerce. As a matter of fact, what blockade was there to raise—as yet? Later, of course the situation would be different. This offer was providential, it might easily be the answer to all their problems—well, if not all of them, a great many. He could find no words adequate to express his conviction that the government must accept it without delay.

His oratory was entirely without effect. To Davis—even cooler, even more cautious than Pierre had found him in February—the whole idea was impractical if not actually fantastic. The contrast between the Anglo-Saxon and the Latin temperaments was close to becoming a clash. Pierre pressed his lips together and withdrew from the chilling presence, all too conscious that if he remained where he was, harsh words would be exchanged which could never be forgiven or forgotten. Eventually, he was to characterize Davis' failure to adopt the scheme proposed by the house of John Frazer and Company as "the first of a long series of irremediable errors committed by the administration"; at the moment he fortunately saw it only as an isolated mistake. But when, a few days later, he learned that Mr.

Davis had sent a "special emissary" abroad on a "secret mission" and that this mission was the purchase of ten thousand rifles, he was sorry he had not exploded, after all, when conferring with Davis.

"A special emissary to get ten thousand rifles!" he raged to William Russell, who was in his office at the time. "As if I couldn't have got that many through John Frazer and Company without even lifting a hand myself! The President calls a trifling errand like that a secret mission! What we need is a hundred thousand rifles and it's futile folly to pretend there's anything secret about it. A *hundred thousand right now!* What we're going to need later on, alas! is something else!"

Mr. Russell shook his head and smiled wryly as he reached for his notebook.

Pierre was still the hero of Charleston. He had been gone only a few days, but his return from Montgomery was hailed with as much delight as if his absence had been a matter of long regret. He resumed his interrupted schedule: several hours for correspondence and interviews at the office in the early morning; supervision of work at the fort from nine to two; return to the office for more routine work. Pierre prided himself that none of these activities was interrupted by a long leisurely luncheon—a glass of water sipped, a few biscuits nibbled while he walked around the fort; that was quite enough at midday. But he consented to interrupt his schedule by dining with friends and, though he always drank sparingly, he did justice to the dishes which comprised his dinner. Charlestonians knew how to entertain; he praised their she-crab soup; their benne-seed and beaten biscuits; their shad roe; their Lady Baltimore cake. He told them their cuisine was comparable to that of Orleanians; he could pay it no higher compliment. And, as he walked back to his office, he was sure to hear gay groups of young folk singing the latest ditty:

> "Flashing, flashing, along the wires,
> The glorious news each heart inspires,
> The war in Charleston was begun,
> Its smoke obscured the morning sun,
> As with cannon, mortar and petard
> We saluted the North with our Beauregard."

He might be tired, he might be discouraged, he might be worried, but this song never failed to raise his spirits. And he had a sense of work well done, quite aside from the glory it had brought him. When, in mid-May, he wrote Davis he felt there was nothing more for which he was needed in Charleston and that he would be ready for duty elsewhere whenever the President saw fit to give him a new assignment, he spoke with complete sincerity. He had come to feel very much at home in Charleston; so far as he was personally concerned, he would leave it with regret; but as a professional soldier, he felt he should be on his way to a more active field.

His first orders were to go to Corinth, Mississippi, to take command of the Great River's defenses from Vicksburg to the Kentucky and Tennessee borders. But before he could get ready to leave—in fact, only two days later—the orders were changed: he was to go to Richmond instead of Corinth.

He had expected that this would prove an anticlimax to his previous triumphs, but he was quickly reassured on that score. His fellow passengers in the cars, Benjamin among them, could not make enough of him. Every time the train stopped, he was importuned to address the eager crowds who were waiting to hear his voice or even to catch a glimpse of him. When he reached Richmond, he was met by an official delegation of dignitaries and a brass band; a coach and four were waiting to take him to the suite which had been reserved for him at the Spottswood Hotel. Now that Montgomery was no longer the Confederate capital, that was where Davis was making his headquarters. It was partly because of this and partly because the journey had proved something of an ordeal and he was momentarily tired of hero-worship that Pierre asked if he might be excused; he would prefer to go quietly with two members of his staff, in an ordinary hired hack, to some less pretentious hotel. Afterward, he was afraid he might have given offense by a seeming lack of appreciation, but he found he need not have worried about this, either. His withdrawal was considered a token of modesty.

When he reported to Davis the following morning, he had a pleasant surprise: his old friend Robert Lee was with the President and, in the warmth of the former's greeting, Pierre was hardly conscious of Davis' coolness and entirely oblivious of any actual antagonism. The three talked for several hours and, throughout this time, it was Lee, now Commander of the Virgina State Troops and acting Commander of all the Confederate Forces in Virginia, who dominated the scene, in Pierre's eyes. It was at Lee's suggestion, not on Davis' initiative, that Pierre was given command of the so-called Alexandria Line, replacing General Bonham. Lee had just come from Manassas, a small railroad junction less than thirty miles south of Alexandria, which the Federals were already occupying. He believed this junction to be the point of greatest danger, and he also believed General Beauregard was the man best fitted to cope with it.

Davis agreed. If he did so grudgingly, he gave no sign of it. But he imposed a drastic condition: General Beauregard was to act "only on the defensive." Pierre tried to argue against this. If an immediate attack were made before the Federal forces advanced any farther toward Manassas and they were defeated, operations could begin against the second Union Army at Harper's Ferry. Then would come the invasion of Maryland—the capture of Washington—victory and peace! Pierre believed with all his heart that this would take place and, with fiery conviction, he outlined the campaign to Davis, step by step. The President remained as unmoved as he had been when Pierre pleaded for the ten ships released by the East India Company. His policy was one of defense. He repeated this again and again— only defense, only defense. From this position Lee had no more success than Pierre in moving him. The orders Lee had written, at Davis' direction, for Pierre's predecessor, General Bonham, were now referred to him.

The policy of the State, at present, is strictly defensive. No attack or provocation for attack will therefore be given, but every attack resisted to the extent of your means. Great reliance is placed on your discretion and judgment in the application of your force, and I must urge upon you the importance of organizing and instructing the troops as rapidly as possible, and preparing them for active service. For this purpose it will be necessary to post them where their services may be needed and where they can be concentrated at the point threatened. The Manassas Junction is a very important point on your line, as it commands the communication with Harper's Ferry, and must be firmly held. Intrenchments at that point would add to its security; and in connection with its defence, you must watch the approaches from either flank, particularly towards Occoquan. Alexandria, in its front, will of course claim your attention as the first point of attack, and as soon as your force is sufficient, in your opinion, to resist successfully its occupation, you will so dispose it as to effect this object, if possible, without appearing to threaten Washington city. The navigation of the Potomac being closed to us, and the United States armed vessels being able to take a position in front of the town, you will perceive the hazard of its destruction unless your measures are such as to prevent it. This subject being one of great delicacy, is left to your judgment. The railroad communications must be secured, however, and their use by the enemy prevented. . . .

                    R. E. *Lee*, Maj.-Gen. Comdg.

Pierre read these orders with a heavy heart. Very well then, defense it must be. Three days after his conference with Davis and Lee, he assumed command at Manassas. When the South Carolina troops who had served under him in Charleston learned of his arrival, a great cry went up—"Old Bory's come! Old Bory's come! Old Bory's come!" In the force and warmth of that welcome, his depression had lifted. Perhaps, after all, Manassas would be the site of the "decisive battle" for which he and Caroline were hoping and praying.

A copy of these orders was still another document Pierre had managed to keep. He lifted it out of its box and reread it before placing it beside the rough sketch of the fortifications for Charleston and the badly spelled, smudgy letter from Henri. His heart was very heavy as he did so, even heavier than it had been when he first saw those orders. The belief was still strong within him that if the plan of campaign he had urged so vehemently and with such conviction had only been adopted, the war would have been over within the limits of the ninety days the optimists had predicted. The Confederacy would have been a nation among nations and he himself would not be a penniless has-been, but a great international figure. Fate or providence or whatever it was that ruled the destinies of men and countries had ruled it otherwise. The President had decided that the strategy of the South should be one of defense, so defense it had to be.

Pierre had been all night at his work table and now dawn was stealing into the little room he had chosen for his study. He rose and went to the door. The trees in the patio were stirring slightly and there was a freshness in the air at this hour which did not come at any other time of day. He stepped out on his balcony and drew in deep breaths of it. Then he continued to stand there as narrow streaks of light, faintly rose in color, began to stream across the sky and, growing gradually wider and wider, suddenly suffused it with radiance. At the same moment, Simone appeared on the gallery and called to him.

"It's going to be a beautiful day. Isn't there something in the Bible that says, 'Weeping endureth but a night, joy cometh in the morning'? Anyway, I feel very joyful for some reason. *Maman* woke early, so I've already made coffee and biscuits. Come over and share them with us both."

❧ 27 ❧

HE WAS FRUGAL . . . HE ATE SPARELY . . . HE COMPLETELY abstained from drink in societies and at a time when drinking was universal; General Beauregard's courtesy, his correctness toward women, was as absolute as all the traditions of chivalry descended in him."

—Joseph Hergesheimer, *Swords and Roses*
(Knopf)

Dr. Charles Cyprien Turpin was born in New Orleans, September 9, 1816. At the age of 17 years he went to Paris, where he studied at the college of Louis-le-Grand, having as fellow students Doctors Alfred and Armand Mercier, also of New Orleans. Upon completion of his literary education, Dr. Turpin returned to New Orleans, intent upon being a sculptor, but to please his mother returned to Paris and studied medicine. He received his degree in 1843. Dr. Turpin was distinguished as a skillful physician, soon acquiring a very large clientele among the best class of people in New Orleans.

As a scholar, and in attainments in French literature, he had no superior in this city. He was the best conversationalist in his mother tongue to whom we have ever listened, knowing how to make his subject, however modest, interesting, and adapting himself always to the intelligence of his auditors. Modest and retiring, he always shrank from notoriety, and occupied no public office, except once when he acted for a short time as member of the Board of Health. To his clients he was not only a physician, but a true friend and adviser. In the family circle he displayed that tenderness and sympathy which springs from a generous and loving heart.

Dr. Turpin was a charter member of the Orleans Parish Medical Society, a member of its organization committee which drew up the constitution and by-laws, and its first president. He accepted the presidency after much persuasion. . . .

Modest and retiring in disposition, he never sought prominence, but his ability was so conspicuous that it was publicly recognized. . . .

Dr. Turpin was all his life a close student of science and literature and was a man of profound erudition and varied accomplishments in *belles lettres*. A graceful and vigorous writer, and entirely familiar with the refinements of the French language, he was a brilliant member of the Athénée Louisianais.

He loved poetry and sculpture. He had to choose between the latter, against medicine . . . but his mother swayed his thoughts to that of medicine.

He was small and thin, fastidiously dressed, and wore always a white tie. He was very brief in his manners, sometimes brusque, but had a sense of subtle humor, and was very charitable. He lived on Royal Street, between St. Philip and Ursuline Streets.

La nature avait doué Charles Turpin d'un caractère doux, sympathique, expansif, d'une intelligence apte à tout saisir. Le sentiment du devoir et l'amour de la justice étaient les deux grands ressorts de ses actes. Il n'hesitait jamais entre le sacrifice de ses satisfactions personelles et ce que reclamait de lui la prévoyance paternelle, ou son dévoument à ses amis et à son pays.

—Excerpts from a letter of Dr. Rudolph Matas, quoting
The Louisiana Medical and Surgical Journal;
and from family papers

EVEN IF MME COUGOT HAD WAKED EARLIER THAN USUAL, SHE HAD apparently slept long enough to refresh her for, like her daughter, she looked unusually well and seemed in unusually good spirits. The biscuits were made from white flour and there was butter and jam with which to spread them; the coffee unquestionably came from beans, with only a normal admixture of chicory, and there was sugar and hot milk to put in it. Although only the day before Mme Cougot had been unable to take heart from the suggestion that autumn was not far off, she had since begun to do so; and she had also decided that her uncompromising attitude in regard to the City Hall might be a mistake. In fact, of the three, Pierre was now admittedly the most depressed.

"I'm ashamed to confess it," he said, "especially when both of you are setting me such a good example by your cheerfulness; but I simply haven't the courage to start out looking for work today when I know there isn't any to be had, for me, at any rate. I'm whipped down, as they say in Virginia."

"You're tired, that's all," Simone contradicted. "You sat up all night, didn't you, going through your papers?"

"Yes, that's true. But I'd slept in the afternoon, on a park bench— and been treated like a vagrant, which I am, of course."

"You're nothing of the sort," Simone retorted, contradicting again. "Contreras could still be your home if you wanted it to be. I understand all the reasons why you don't, but there's land there just the same, land and a house. Oh, I know the land's unproductive now, I know the house is empty. But they exist, you can lay claim to them any time you choose. And what about Upper Magnolia? That's your second home, isn't it? Your children are there, aren't they?"

"Naturally, yes is the answer to both questions."

"And your brother-in-law, Captain Charles Villeré, of whom you're so fond, is running the plantation, isn't he?"

"If you can call it that."

"I do call it that. Why don't you go down and stay with your family a few days? I believe the change would do you good."

"It hasn't lately. I always return from Upper Magnolia even more depressed than before I started."

"This time it might be different. Leave your papers behind you. I promise they won't be disturbed while you're gone. What were you reading last night?"

"My orders for Manassas—that I was to act only on the defensive."

"And you still believe that if you could have acted on the offensive the outcome of the war would have been different?"

"I'm convinced of it, just as I was then. If only Davis—if only Benjamin——"

Simone did not interrupt him, but he let his sentence trail away into silence which neither she nor her mother attempted to break. At last, he rose.

"Perhaps you're right," he said. "Perhaps if I got out in the country for a few days, I'd feel better. It would be a change. It would be a break. And it's true I haven't seen my children in several weeks. It's time I did."

"It certainly is. It's right and proper that you should go whether you want to or not," Mme Cougot told him. "But I'll miss you. I can't tell you how much your visit yesterday afternoon meant to me and how greatly I've enjoyed our breakfast this morning. I hope when you return, you'll do me the honor of giving me your company at meals. Of course, I realize it's much pleasanter for you to have them on the gallery than in an invalid's room. But I'm selfish enough to wish that you would."

"Wouldn't it do you good to get out on the gallery, too? It wouldn't be any effort at all for me to carry you, and I'm sure Simone could improvise a *lit de repos* for you close to the table."

"It's very kind of you. But I couldn't dream of letting you carry me."

"If we only had a wheelchair—" Simone began.

"My poor child, are you dreaming? Where on earth could we get a wheelchair?"

"I think I know where it might be possible," Pierre said suddenly. "Anyway, I'll find out. I've heard that my wife's kinsman, Dr. Charles Turpin, has never been molested, that his surgery's been kept open all through the war. He was even allowed to keep five of his own slaves, until slavery was abolished, and I believe they've stayed on with him, voluntarily, ever since. He must have all kinds of equipment left, or if there's something he hasn't got himself, he must know where he could get it. I'll go straight around to his house and find out."

"But you're going to Upper Magnolia!"

"I can go to Upper Magnolia afterward. It won't take me any time at all to go to the Turpins' first—after all, they live practically around the corner on Royal Street. As a matter of fact, I ought to have gone long ago, to thank them for their kindness to Caroline. Celestine Turpin nursed her through her last illness and Charles, as her personal physician, did everything humanly possible to cure her. But of course the case was hopeless." Pierre sighed and looked away and, once again, neither Simone nor her mother broke the silence that followed. "It's so painful for me to speak about it, even briefly, to anyone," he said at last, "that I've shrunk from a visit where I know the talk wouldn't be of anything else. And then, I was afraid of seeming to ask for favors, even tacitly. Since the Turpins are still comparatively prosperous, they might easily have thought I had ulterior motives, that I was trying to take advantage of our kinship."

"I don't believe they'd have thought anything of the sort," Simone
said with spirit. "I think they must be wondering why you never have
gone to see them, feeling a little hurt because you didn't. Of course
I know you must have written them after—after your great bereave-
ment. But that isn't like a personal visit."

"Simone, you are forgetting yourself. You have contradicted the
General twice and now you are arguing with him. This is not the
proper way for you to speak to him."

"I'm sorry, *maman*—that is, I'm sorry you feel it isn't. But we're
such good friends now that I forget he's a general and I'm his landlady."

"You should never forget it."

"I'm glad she does," Pierre said hastily. "Please don't rebuke her,
Madame Cougot. I forget it, too. And it makes me very happy to do
so. Let's all forget it in the future. And now let me hurry over to the
Turpins' and see about that wheelchair."

He left the room almost abruptly, conscious of electricity in the
atmosphere and startled at the sudden realization that Mme Cougot
seemed to be taking exception to something in Simone's attitude toward him. Was it possible that her expressed desire to have him take
his meals in her room, rather than on the gallery, was based not only
on her own pleasure in his company, but on her feeling that he and
her daughter were spending too much time together unsupervised?
He found it impossible to dismiss the question from his mind as he
walked toward the Turpins' house, though at first the idea seemed to
him far-fetched. He was in his later forties, twice a widower, and still
unreconciled to the death of his second wife; it was fantastic to
imagine that he would form a romantic attachment for anyone.
Moreover, he was a gentleman of the old school, which, as he interpreted the term, was to say that he was scrupulously correct in his
behavior toward virtuous women; and there could be no question in
his mind or in anyone's, least of all in her mother's, that Simone was
a virtuous woman. Besides, she was a widow of middle age and,
though her appearance and her manner were pleasing, she gave no
illusion of youth—in fact, when he first saw her, he had mistaken her
for a faded, elderly woman; only later he had discovered that she was
trim and comely. Even so, she had none of the attributes belonging to
a conscious charmer. To be sure, there was a certain gentleness about
her which had its own charm, as it had in the case of Caroline. Not,
of course, that anyone would suppose that Simone Castel, a confectioner's daughter, who acted as caretaker for an absentee owner and

as a hostess to a lodger, could be compared with a great lady like Caroline Deslonde. . . .

And yet, he was forced to remind himself hastily, it was he who had involuntarily but instinctively made the comparison. Perhaps, after all, it was not illogical for Mme Cougot to wonder if he had been attracted to Simone and to feel some concern on that score. Doubtless, she had heard those absurd stories about trains of concubines and, without actually believing them, had wondered if something in his conduct had not given rise to rumors which, though exaggerated, were based on truth. She could hardly be expected to know how faithfully he had tried to observe the precepts and example of his father. And of course she would never connect such a suspected attraction with an honorable courtship. The consciousness of caste was too strong. A Beauregard, even though he were now a pauper, was still a *grand seigneur*, as far as she was concerned; he might have his distractions, but they would never lead to marriage outside of his own social circle. . . .

Then there was another side to this troubling question. If Mme Cougot were worrying lest he were attracted to Simone, she might also be worrying lest Simone were attracted to him. This was another idea which he was inclined to dismiss as far-fetched—only to find that he could not successfully do so. A woman might see to it that a man were properly fed and comfortably lodged, even if it were an effort for her to do so, merely from a sense of duty and of the fitness of things; but she would not eagerly ask him to tell her all the details about the dullest period of his life and then sit, seemingly entranced, as he did so. She would not ask him to give her a silly sketch he had made, so that she could treasure it. She would not stay up until all hours, after a long day, to make sure he had come safely home, and light his way across a dark patio with her own candle. Above all, she would not say, in the way Simone had said it, that for years all she had lived for had been the return of her only son, but that now the presence and friendship of another man "had made a difference." Pierre had become wise in the ways of women. That was inevitable, considering not only the ardor of Laure and the devotion of Caroline, but the widespread adulation shown him by the fair—and sometimes frail—ladies of the Confederacy; and what he had learned had made him skeptical of so-called Platonic friendships. He should have recognized these symptoms of deepening interest on Simone's part as danger signals. He should have remembered that it was impossible for a virile man and a vital woman, neither one of whom had passed beyond the stage where their senses, however dormant, could not be stirred through pleasant and close companionship, to discount the element of sex and its possible danger in their relation to each other. Yet that was what he had done and what, obviously, Simone had done, too, though neither one had realized it.

Of course there could be no question of courtship. Even if he could support a wife, which he certainly could not, since he could not even support himself, he was sure nothing would ever induce him to marry again. He had had his years of glowing rapture and his years of complete communion and now there was nothing left for him in the holy estate of matrimony. Certainly he would never risk the disillusionment of a marriage of convenience—a term which might and generally did mean money, but which also might mean nothing but the assuagement of some physical urge. An affair was equally unthinkable. Simone was not the sort of woman with whom one had an affair. As he had already reminded himself, a gentleman treated virtuous women with respect; they did not invite illicit relationships. And since neither marriage nor an affair was indicated, the question now was, what should he and Simone do next—or rather, what should he do next? Simone's plan of action would, necessarily, be dependent on his and he must give careful thought to it. Of course, there would be ample time for this while he was at Upper Magnolia, and he was going there this afternoon. Meanwhile, he must get a wheelchair, if one were available. That was what he had started out to do, not to lose himself in disturbing problems. He quickened his pace and took his way to the Turpins' house on Royal Street.

It was still outstanding for its size and the beauty of its tiered galleries framed in wrought iron, even though the other houses in the same block had much the same arresting attributes; and he was relieved to see that closer inspection than he had recently given it revealed no signs of deterioration or even of shabbiness. The brass knocker and door handle at the entrance were well polished, the panels gleaming with fresh paint. The door was opened for him by Celestine Turpin herself, who looked at him for a moment with startled unbelief. Then, exclaiming, "Pierre! I thought you would never never come!" she welcomed him with the warmth she would have shown a long-lost brother. "Charles is out making sick calls," she went on, drawing her visitor with her into the well-remembered parlor. "But his office hours begin at eleven, so he won't be gone long. And he'll be just as glad to see you as I am! We heard you were in town, that you'd taken lodgings in the old Le Carpentier–Morphy house— of course that's the way we always think of it! We don't know the people who live there now—caretakers for Madame Garidel, aren't they? We thought if you wanted to see us, you'd let us know. Please tell me all about yourself. Just what are you doing? How are the boys and Doucette?"

"I'm sorry to say I'm not doing anything," he said, taking the chair she indicated. "I've tried and tried, for nearly two months now, to find some kind of work and I haven't succeeded. As far as I know, the boys and Doucette are well. I haven't seen them lately, but I'm planning to go to Upper Magnolia this afternoon. Perhaps when I come back I'll have some news for you, but I haven't any now. You must have some, though. Tell me about yourself and Charles. I've heard you've never been molested and from the looks of your house, I'd say that was true."

He glanced about the handsomely furnished room, noting, with the same relief he had felt in looking at the intricate ironwork outside, that the gold inlay on the black marble mantel was undimmed and the bronze statuette of a slave boy smoking a cigarette was still in its accustomed place. Charles Turpin had renounced his chosen vocation as a sculptor to study medicine, at the instigation of his mother, but he had done so with regret, and he had continued to amuse himself by modeling from time to time, until the war had put an end to such diversions. Pierre did not especially admire the slave boy as a work of art, but as an example of his friend's perseverance and devotion to his ideal, it was a symbol.

"No, we've been very fortunate in that way," Celestine was saying. "Of course it's meant that Charles has had to care for anyone the Federalists wanted to send here. He hasn't minded in the cases of those who were badly wounded or very ill—in fact, like any doctor worthy of the name, a sick man or an injured man is one who needs help and that's all there is to it. But there have been some of the occupying troops who've abused their privileges and that's been harder to accept, especially for me. You see, I work in the surgery with Charles. I didn't think I could possibly learn to, I'd always been so helpless. I mean, there'd always been someone to wait on me hand and foot, just as there was for all of us. I'd never done up my own hair or even put on my own stockings. But when Charles couldn't get anyone else, he said I'd have to be his assistant! And I am! I'd had some experience in nursing—well, you know that; the kind of nursing where you just sit by a patient's bed, speaking sympathetically, and bathe her face and give her spoonfuls of broth and jelly and watch the time to see that she gets her medicine when the doctor's ordered it. But now I've learned what to do with broken limbs and festering wounds and how to hold down a man who's got to have his leg amputated."

She spoke proudly and Pierre felt that she had good reason to do so. He had always liked her, but he had considered her rather frivolous and when she described herself as helpless he recognized what she meant: the typical petted and pampered Creole young lady of happier times, served and adored not only by her slaves, but by all the male members of her family and by the man she married. She had only to express the slightest wish to have it fulfilled. Her black hair had framed her dimpled face with clustering ringlets; her dark eyes had flashed both fun and fire; her rosebud mouth had lent itself equally well to arch smiles and pretty pouting; her tiny white hands were satin-soft. Now her simply dressed hair was snow-white; there were wrinkles instead of dimples in her cheeks; her mouth closed in a firm line except when she smiled; and though her eyes were still wonderfully expressive, the expression was now one of determination and courage. But the greatest difference of all was in her hands; they were scrubbed clean, but they were red and rough and some of the nails were broken. All these changes testified to far more than the passage of time; they testified to unremitting labor and complete dedication. That from a coddled plaything of a girl a woman of such purpose, courage and skill had developed to become a helpmeet of her husband in every sense of the word was one of those miracles which could be put down on the credit side of war. There were, alas! few enough such items.

"I knew you'd been wonderful," he said with deep feeling, "but I didn't realize *how* wonderful until now. And I'm sorry—I'm ashamed —that I haven't been here before. There were several reasons. I won't try to go into those just now. But if you'll give me a chance, I'll tell you some other time how mistaken I know I've been in thinking it was better I should stay away. And I will tell you why I came this morning. The caretaker in Madame Garidel's house is a widow whose husband was killed in the war, a Madame Castel. Her mother, Madame Cougot, who is blind, lives there with her. She'd been bedridden I don't know how long when I went there in June. But now she sits up in an easy chair once in a while. She says I'm helping her to recover, which only means I've been able to cheer her up a little. I gather there isn't much organically wrong with her, except the blindness. But she's completely lost heart. Her husband, her two brothers, all her sons and her son-in-law, who was also like a son to her, were killed in the war. Her daughter says she was very brave as long as the messages came in. It was when they stopped that her courage and her health failed her. Now she just lies in a dark room listening for footsteps she'll probably never hear—the footsteps of a grandson who's been missing ever since the Battle of Shiloh. He was only fourteen when he left home—a drummer boy."

"Oh, how sad—how very sad!" Celestine's dark eyes instantly glowed with sympathy and understanding. "If only there were something we could do to help! Do you think there is? Of course Charles would come to see her willingly, but you say you think there's nothing organically wrong."

"That's so. But perhaps he'd come to see her anyway. Perhaps you would. More than anything else she needs cheering, and you could do that, just by telling her what you've done here. It would give her something new and different to think about. Her daughter's devoted to her, takes every care of her, but she's doing the same thing as her mother—just listening for footsteps." That was not the whole truth. He knew this now, but it was as much of the truth as he needed to tell Celestine Turpin at the moment. "They both feel very friendly toward me," he went on, "and Madame Castel's been wonderfully kind. She insists on feeding me and she feeds me well, though how she manages I can't imagine. We've been eating together on the gallery lately. But this morning we had breakfast in Madame Cougot's room instead, and she enjoyed it so much she said she hoped we'd always have our meals with her, though she realized it was pleasanter on the gallery than in a sickroom. So I told her I'd be glad to carry her out there and she wouldn't hear of it. But she did listen to the suggestion of a wheelchair—except that she didn't think it would be possible to get one."

"And you thought that it might?"

"I knew that if anyone could get one for her Charles could."

"Yes, I believe that's true. We did have one here, but it's been loaned to a very needy case." Celestine hesitated a moment and then went on, "If there really isn't anything wrong with Madame Cougot, except her eyes, couldn't she *walk* to the rear gallery? I mean, with you to support her? If she's got as far as an easy chair, she must have taken a few steps already and, little by little, she'd get the strength to take more. As I understand it, she's bedridden because she wants to be—no, I don't mean that exactly, but because she's got this *idée fixe* that she must listen for that poor boy's footsteps, day and night. Perhaps she wouldn't use the wheelchair even if we could get it for her. Perhaps she only said she'd consider the suggestion because she thought it was one that couldn't come to anything."

"I hadn't thought of it that way. You're probably right. Coming here has been futile, just like everything else I try to do—almost everything I've ever tried to do!"

"Pierre, please don't talk like that! Please don't feel like that! You're a great man, you'll go down in history as one."

"I shan't do anything of the kind. Lee's the one who'll go down in history as a great man. Lee and maybe Stonewall Jackson and Albert Sidney Johnston and Jeb Stuart, because those three were killed before they had time to be defeated."

"Pierre, I'm ashamed of you! What about Kirby Smith? What about Joe Wheeler? What about James Longstreet? What about—"

"Never mind. I'll grant you those to get rid of an argument, but I don't want to hear any more. Because, no matter how long you make the roster, Beauregard won't be on it a hundred years from now."

"I wish there were some way of proving you wrong," Celestine said earnestly. And, as he rose, obviously preparing to leave, she added, "Don't go, Pierre. Wait to see Charles and talk to him about the wheelchair. Stay and have dinner with us. In fact, we'd be delighted if you'd dine with us every day."

"I knew you'd say that. It was one of the reasons I didn't come sooner. I find it hard to accept charity—and sympathy. Our next topic of conversation would have been Caroline."

There, he had said it, after resolving that he would not. He was conscious of the grief in Celestine's eyes as she looked at him—grief not because of his defeat in the war and the loss of his wife, but because of another and still greater defeat and loss, that of the dashing spirit which had made him the first idol of the Confederacy. He tried to meet the gaze of this valiant woman, who had risen so nobly to meet the emergencies with which she was faced, and found he could not. The comparison with himself was unendurable.

"Please forgive me, Celestine," he said harshly. "I'll come again some day, if you'll let me. But now I think I'd better go, before I say something I *know* you won't be able to forgive."

❦ 28 ❧

CHARLES JULES VILLERÉ, SON OF JULES GABRIEL VILLERÉ AND Marie Perle Olivier de Vezin, was born on Magnolia Plantation in 1821. This estate, located in Plaquemines Parish, Louisiana, was the joint property of his father and uncle, Delphin Villeré, at the time of his birth. . . . In July, 1836, Jules Villeré became the sole owner of the plantation. It is there that Charles spent his childhood. Nothing is known of his formal education other than he practiced law.

His name first appears in June of 1853, in the family papers . . . when he was visited by the Honorable Casimir Lacoste so as to prevail upon him to run for the State House of Representatives. In a letter to Governor P. O. Hébert, Lacoste complained that the "blind young man wanted to run for Congress."

With his homeland in peril, he enlisted on October 1, 1861 in the Confederate Army and was appointed a 2nd Lieutenant of Company I, 1st Louisiana Cavalry, but resigned on February 16, 1862, so as to enter the Confederate House of Representatives. His name is accordingly found in that roster on February 18, 1862. He served in that capacity until the adjournment of the Second Congress on March 18, 1865.

—Excerpts from family papers in the possession of
Sidney L. Villeré

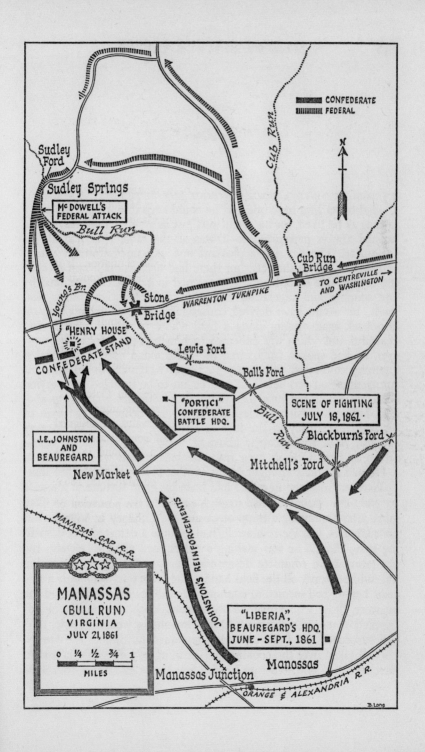

CONFEDERATE
FEDERAL

Cub Run

N

Sudley
Ford

Sudley Springs

McDOWELL'S
FEDERAL ATTACK

Bull Run

Cub Run
Bridge

Young's Br.

Stone
Bridge

WARRENTON TURNPIKE

TO CENTREVILLE
AND WASHINGTON

"HENRY HOUSE"

CONFEDERATE STAND

Lewis Ford

Ball's Ford

"PORTICI"
CONFEDERATE
BATTLE HDQ.

Bull

Run

SCENE OF FIGHTING
JULY 18, 1861 ·

Blackburn's Ford

J.E. JOHNSTON
AND
BEAUREGARD

New Market

Mitchell's Ford

MANASSAS GAP R.R.

JOHNSTON'S REINFORCEMENTS

MANASSAS
(BULL RUN)
VIRGINIA
JULY 21, 1861

0   ¼   ½   ¾   1

MILES

"LIBERIA",
BEAUREGARD'S HDQ.
JUNE–SEPT., 1861

Manassas

Manassas Junction

ORANGE & ALEXANDRIA R.R.

B. Long

ఴఄఴ

PIERRE OBTAINED A HORSE WITHOUT ANY DIFFICULTY; PREVAL WAS glad to let him have one and he could keep it at Upper Magnolia as long as he liked, for his credit was just as good at the livery stable he had always patronized as it was at the tailor's he had always patronized. The day was a pleasant one, not uncomfortably warm, and there were no showers; but there had been enough rain to keep the countryside from having the parched look it often developed by late summer and vegetation was at its most luxuriant stage. Normally, he would have derived considerable pleasure from being on horseback again, riding along a road whose natural attributes were beautiful and which was endeared to him by long association; however, he had spoken truly when he told Simone he was doubtful if anything connected with a trip to Upper Magnolia would raise his spirits; and that was before he had begun to be troubled by worrying thoughts about the turn his relationship with her was taking and, also, before his visit to Celestine Turpin had deepened his sense of his own inadequacy in the face of adversity, compared to the way she had risen triumphantly above it. Now he was sure he would return to New Orleans even more depressed than when he left it.

He had formerly thought of his brother-in-law as one of the most brilliant and dashing figures it had been his good fortune to know: a natural-born orator who had made his mark in the Confederate Congress, after organizing a troop of cavalry with himself as captain. But poor Charles, like Pierre himself, had become a defeated and despairing man; though he was making a determined effort to reclaim the plantation from complete desuetude, he was meeting with nothing but failure. Nearly all the field hands—the same ones who, only a few years before, had seemed so contented and devoted—had deserted the quarters; those who remained were mostly either extremely old or crippled or mentally deficient. Only Theophilus, who in happier days had succeeded old Luke as butler, remained faithful to the family. He had taken over the cooking and cleaning and also did his best to serve as stable boy, and care for the few horses and mules that were still left on the place. His wife, Manette, had been among the deserters; but when he went to New Orleans in search of her, expecting a struggle to get her back, he had found her only too willing to come. Freedom had not proved so glorious—or so carefree—as she had expected, and the same was true of a few others who gradually drifted home. With this insufficient and ineffectual staff, Charles was trying to repair the buildings and free the land from weeds. The spring had been promising; the weather was good, the land all the more fertile because of the time it had lain fallow, and hopes for a good harvest seemed well founded, though the river was high and threatening. Then the currents burst their bounds, water came rushing through a crevasse and the fields were flooded; now only a few tufts of cane showed here and there on some acres that had been above the level of the water. The beautiful hedges of Chinese lilacs had, of course, long since disappeared. All the money spent to reclaim the plantation had been borrowed and Charles' creditors were clamoring for full and immediate repayment; unless he could get credit somewhere, Upper Magnolia would have to be sacrificed to meet the debt.

He had not given up hope of salvage and his parents declined to so much as discuss the possibility of removal, so Pierre did not discuss it, either; but as he rode slowly up the driveway, which had once looked as if it were freshly raked every morning and which was now overgrown with weeds, he did not see how the day of doom could long be postponed. Everything about the place displayed the need of renovation. Much of the paint on the house was peeling and, where it remained intact, it had turned a dingy gray; the railing of the gallery lacked several spindles and several more were broken; the roof seemed to be sagging in places; two or three shutters were hanging askew. It was now midafternoon, a time when there was seldom anyone on the gallery, for it was the hour of siesta and, in any case, Pierre had not expected anyone to be watching for him, as he had given no advance notice of his coming. However, as he fastened his horse beside the iron figure of a small colored jockey which served as a hitching post, the front door opened and his daughter came out on the gallery.

Pierre had often told himself he was thankful that, except for coloring, the resemblance between Doucette and her mother was so slight; a constant reminder of Laure, in the form and features of another, would have been more than he could bear. Somewhat reluctantly, he had already begun to realize that Doucette had ceased to be just another pretty child and was fast becoming an attractive young girl; now he also admitted to himself, with less pain that he would have supposed possible, that it was chiefly in manner that she

differed from Laure. She had none of her mother's shyness and therefore lacked the elusiveness that had been one of Laure's most subtle
charms, in Pierre's opinion. Despite the fact that his visit to Upper
Magnolia was unannounced, Doucette did not seem in the least
startled or even greatly surprised to see him, though she did seem
very much pleased. She waved gaily, called, *"Oh, papa! Quel plaisir
inattendu!"* and ran across the gallery and down the steps to throw
her arms around him.

"Aren't they encouraging you to speak English, even yet?" he
asked, as he smiled and returned her kiss. He knew perfectly well that
they—her grandparents—were not and that they never would and,
truth to tell, he did not much care. But he felt it his duty to protest
that times had changed, as, alas! they had and that English should be
in general use at Upper Magnolia.

"Pepère and *memère* don't speak it themselves, so how can they en-
courage me?" Doucette asked merrily. "I do speak it sometimes with
René and Henri—they don't mind since they got used to it in school
and in the Army; in fact, they rather like it. And I do speak it once
in a while with Uncle Charles, who never did get used to it and
doesn't like it, as you very well know, even though he's so eloquent in
it. You're not going to start out by scolding me, are you, Papa? When
you haven't been to see me in such a long time and when I've missed
you so terribly?"

"No, I didn't mean to scold you. Is it a long time? Have you really
missed me?"

"It's a *very* long time and you don't *know* how much. . . . Are
you going straight back to New Orleans?"

"No, but what makes you ask?"

"Because you hitched your horse outside, instead of taking him
around to the stable."

"Force of old habit. I still keep forgetting that, presently, a grinning little colored boy won't come tearing up to take him around to
the stables for me."

"Well, leave him where he is—the horse, I mean. Let René or
Henri take him to the stables. They ought to wait on you by inches
when you're here."

"I suppose they're napping?"

"Oh no—they don't do that any more, didn't you know? But they
wander off, generally without saying where they're going. Probably
they don't know themselves beforehand. Everything they do seems so
aimless."

"Yes, I'm afraid it is. What about you? Were you planning to wander off somewhere, too, when I came along?"

"Not really. And not far. Just a little way down the *allée*. But sometimes I wish I were a boy, too, so that I could leave the house whenever I felt like it, the way my brothers can, without having anyone worry about me. Of course, it's a very nice house—at least it must have been before the War. But once in a while it seems to close in on me. It did this afternoon. Oh, Papa, I'm so glad you've come!"

She kissed him again and linked her arm in his as they went up the steps together. Then she insisted that he must sit quietly on the gallery in an easy chair, while she went into the house and fetched him a cool drink. Of course, it wasn't a terribly hot day, but just the same he must be tired and thirsty after his ride. It pleased him to see her so solicitous for his comfort; and it pleased him still more to realize how genuinely glad she was to see him, even though that was probably not all due to filial affection. It must, indeed, be terribly dull for a young girl at Upper Magnolia these days. There were no house-parties, no dances, no impromptu concerts, no midnight gumbo suppers, as there had been when Laure was young; the arrival of anyone from the outside world, even such a prosaic figure as a father, would serve to break the monotony. Doucette was probably hopeful that he would bring her news of what was going on in New Orleans, exciting news; and if there were any exciting news which was also good news, he did not know what it was. There was nothing he could tell her except that he had still found no work, that he could not buy her pretty clothes and send her to a good school, and see that she met some pleasant girls and boys in her own age group. Of course she was now nearly old enough to meet young men who would not be merely companions but beaux. *Fifteen!* In another year or so, she should make her debut, she should be a queen or at least a maid in a Carnival ball. And what prospect was there of that? The next thing he knew, she would be of marriageable age. How was he to see that she met someone eligible, several persons who were eligible, so that she could take her choice among them?

Doucette returned, bringing a pitcher filled with dewberry shrub and two glasses. She was sorry that there was no ice, but she had discovered that if you put napkin rings in a drink and jangled them around, this made the shrub *sound* cool anyway and that helped a lot, just as it helped a lot to wear a white dress, because that *looked* cool. She prattled on, cheerfully, while he sipped his drink. *Memère* had a migraine, not badly, but she was going to lie down the whole afternoon in a darkened room, with a handkerchief dampened in vinegar over her forehead. Of course, she would have preferred *eau de Cologne*, but she had used up the very last she had and, really, vinegar did very well as a substitute. *Pepère* had not returned from his office since he went there at nine in the morning; he spent more and more time there, perhaps because he, too, felt he wanted to get out of the house; Doucette did not know of any other reason, because he did not seem to be very busy. Theophilus said that M'*sieu* Charles had gone to Belle Chasse for the day and the two young gentlemen had gone with him, so that accounted for René and Henri; Theophilus had overheard them saying it was something to do with more credit; he did not know what that meant and Doucette did not know, either. Doucette had spoken to Manette about dinner, which was to be delayed until Uncle Charles and the boys came home, and she thought it would be pretty good, though they would have tried to make it better if they had known Papa was coming. Anyway, there were plenty of vegetables and a chicken had already been killed. One chicken was really enough for seven, wasn't it, when you had cream gravy and rice to go with it? They were not short of milk just now, so Manette had made blancmange the day before. That wasn't a very exciting dessert for a general, was it? But it was quite filling and tomorrow they would have a dewberry pie. There had been a fine crop of dewberries, so they had preserved as many as they could for both pies and shrubs. Of course, sugar was not very plentiful, and the jam was not so rich as Manette said it should be, but it was good that way, too. . . .

As he sat sipping his lukewarm drink and listening to her, Pierre found her cheerful chatter pleasant. When at last she paused, having evidently exhausted her slender stock of subjects, he knew he ought to respond in some way that would be interesting to her. To his surprise and relief, she helped him out.

"You're writing your memoirs, aren't you, Papa? I think that's what René said you were doing."

"I haven't actually done any writing yet. I'm just going through some old papers I've found, refreshing my memory, making some notes, getting ready to write, later on."

"Couldn't you tell me something about it? I mean, about what you've found in the old papers that refreshed your memory. Was there anything about Fort Sumter?"

"What made you ask, Doucette?"

"Why—because if there was, I wish you'd tell me about it. I've never heard half enough! Only that you were a great hero and—"

"I wasn't a great hero. I ordered the bombardment of a fort which one of the best friends I ever had was commanding—a fort where the garrison was close to starvation because the navy of its own government had twice failed to revictual it. The men there hadn't had anything to eat for days except some spoiled pork—and some rice with broken glass in it. The latter was the kind of fare the Borgias gave their enemies when they wanted to make short work of them. After I ordered the bombardment, I watched it through a telescope, from the front parlor of a handsome house on the Battery—one of the finest houses in Charleston. I didn't have a single moment of discomfort, much less of danger."

"Oh, Papa, that wasn't all there was to such a great victory! It couldn't have been!"

"Well, it was, very nearly. Of course I'd shown the Charlestonians, before that, how they could defend their city by a continuous circular fortification, which they hadn't thought of before and which they hadn't any idea how to construct. But any experienced engineer could have done that. And, after the bombardment and the surrender, I showed them how to repair the fort—any experienced engineer could have done that, too. I didn't say I wasn't a good engineer. I was. I am."

"But you weren't just a good engineer! You meant a lot more to the Charlestonians than that!"

"Yes, I was socially acceptable to them. They set great store by good birth and good breeding, just as we Creoles do, and they were agreeably surprised to find that I could meet all their standards, that I was just as steeped in tradition as they were. So they plied me with invitations and I accepted. They swamped me with flowers and I put them on my desk. They wrote me bushel-loads of letters and I answered them. They composed flattering songs about me and I listened. All that requires a certain amount of patience and a certain amount of endurance. But it doesn't require heroism."

He had begun by speaking vehemently, setting down his empty glass with unnecessary force as he did so. Then his tone had changed to one of bitterness and sarcasm. At first, he had hardly noticed his daughter's reaction to his violent speech. Then he became aware that she was looking at him with astonishment and that the astonishment was gradually more and more permeated with distress. Tardily, he saw that her beautiful blue eyes—the eyes which were so much like her mother's—were brimming with tears; but it was not until she covered her face with her hands and began to sob, that he realized the outburst which, for him, had been a release from long pent-up emotion, had been to her not only a source of disillusionment, but of grief. He rose hastily and put his arms around her.

"Don't cry, darling," he said remorsefully. "I shouldn't have said all that—at least, I shouldn't have said it in that way. Not that it isn't true. But I should have broken it to you more gently that your father isn't a hero."

"But you *must* have been! Everyone says so. Pepère and memère and Uncle Charles and the boys and—*everyone!* They can't all be mistaken."

"I'm afraid they are—about Sumter."

"Well, there were lots of other places besides Sumter! What about the Battle of Manassas? You didn't watch that through a telescope, did you?"

"No."

"Then tell me what you did do. At the very beginning and next after that and next after that, until you'd put all the Yankees to flight and everything was all over. Not looking at any old papers, but just the way you remember it. If you'll only do that, I'm sure I'll be able to keep on believing that you're a hero."

❦ 29 ❧

LOUISIANA—FORGETFUL OF THE SPANISH OCCUPATION—REmained French in spirit until it was finally absorbed into the United States. It was bound to the Confederacy by situation and sentiment; but its Latin traditions, its formal civilization, were foreign to the nationality and laws and temper of Missouri and Alabama, Georgia and Mississippi. Pierre Beauregard, principally French in blood, was reared upon French institutions and habits of thought and ideals. His conception of perfect glory was Napoleon. He was, accordingly, sustained with an insensate pride, a fantastic serious vanity. He regarded his birth and position and talents without an atom of compensating humor.

The deep South, a landed and slave-owning society, was at the same time peculiarly American; it had acquired its freedom too lately, Thomas Jefferson had not been long enough dead, for it to have become aristocratic at heart. A feeling of equality, of the integrity of the individual, was still strong. The American character, especially American humor, was fundamentally realistic; it was sceptical; hard circumstance colored it rather than dreams. General Washington in nothing resembled the Emperor Napoleon. Pierre Gustave Toutant Beauregard had a spirit different from the actualities around him; he never, it was clear, understood them; he remained to the end, as handsome as possible, a soldier in bronze. This was not evident in his contact with the men under him; he was—a good general—always careful of their needs; his democracy where they were concerned was easy and complete.

His difficulties were created by his attitude toward equals, toward his superiors. It was not invariably plain to his equals that he held them in equality; his superiors were permitted to doubt his allowance of their superiority. Beauregard spoke and wrote valiantly, his words had the ring of metal, the touch of formal greatness that was in him. He wrote and spoke, because of this, with frequency and with zest—he was forever addressing his troops and the Confederate Congress and Jefferson Davis. He was full of visions and elaborate plans for the immediate ending of the war, the complete destruction of the North. They were all dramatic, remarkable, and none was quite possible.

The Congress at Richmond and Mr. Davis, in return, met him with an increasing coldness; they rapidly lost confidence in him and the President's feeling, characteristically, advanced to an acute dislike. A soldier in the mould and form of the First Napoleon, in bronze, had little place in the harassed consciousness of the Confederate government. His courage and devotion were admitted, but his ability—even his proved skill in military engineering—was worse than questioned. He was, incontestably, treated very badly. . . .

At Manassas—the tributes of South Carolina repeated—Beauregard was enormously popular. His dignity mitigated an invariable reticence—no individual knew his plans, the movement of a regiment, until they were put into execution, and then the colonels alone received an explanation. His headquarters was at a small farmhouse on the Alexandria road, it had two lower rooms—the front was filled with desks, with clerks and orderlies and dispatch riders, the back room was a kitchen and place for stores. The general's room above was hung with maps of the state and surrounding country. There was a plain pine table with neatly folded dockets, a pervading air of order and coolness, of exact calculation. Hour upon hour Beauregard sat solitary over his maps and specifications and projections. In Charleston the correspondent of the London Times remembered, the maps and plans were supported by two vases of flowers and for paper weight a little bouquet of roses, geraniums and sweet scented flowers lay on an incompleted letter.

His relations with Jefferson Davis grew steadily more difficult.

—Joseph Hergesheimer, *Swords and Roses*
(Knopf)

"Rob" Wheat was universally liked in the army and by those who knew him well he was genuinely beloved. All his life he had the gift of making friends. A Cuban associate called him "a noble fellow, young and ardent in dangerous enterprise." To one who filibustered with him in Nicaragua, he was a "warmhearted and chivalrous gentleman . . . brave as the bravest." He was "dear, affectionate, tender Major Wheat," to an impressionable girl in New Orleans. He was "gallant, big hearted," to one of Stonewall Jackson's staff, and General Jackson himself said Wheat was "too brave ever to think of himself." To Dick Taylor, his immediate commander, he was a "gallant spirit."

It remained, however, for a lady of wartime Richmond to depict Wheat and his men with graphic accuracy: "The battalion of 'Tigers' from New Orleans, commanded by the intrepid Wheat, were, as their name denotes, men of desperate courage but questionable morals. They were well suited to the shock of battle, but wholly unfitted for the more important details of the campaign. Among them were many of lawless character, whose fierce passions were kept in abeyance by the superior discipline of their accomplished commander. . . . Educated under influences the most pious and refining, he was gentle, easy, graceful and dignified in society; toward the men under his command he was kind, but grave and reserved, and exacting in the performance of duty; in battle he was fiery, impetuous and resolute."

Of Major Wheat and his Louisiana Tigers, a fellow officer wrote after the war: "It required the iron hand of discipline tempered with fatherly kindness, to make soldiers of them. Wheat had these two good qualities of a commander in a remarkable degree. His men loved him—and they feared him —the power or spell he had over his men was truly wonderful."

—Charles L. Dufour, *Gentle Tiger: The Gallant Life of Roberdeau Wheat* (Louisiana State University Press)

HE MUST DO IT, HE SAW THAT ALL TOO PLAINLY. IF DOUCETTE COULD not go on believing he was a hero, she would lose faith not only in him, but in everyone and everything—perhaps even her religion, for he was practically a demigod in her eyes. She had not known him intimately as a person, because he had not spent enough time with her to make that possible; if he only had, she might not have built up this image of him which he had been so close to destroying. Now, some way, the image must be restored—and immediately. But he had no idea how to go about it, how to tell her what happened first and then next and then next after that at Manassas, in terms that she would understand.

"Well, the day after President Davis assigned me to the command of the troops on the Alexandria line, I left Richmond for Manassas," he began rather haltingly. "That was June first, Sixty-one. Manassas is about twenty-seven miles south of Alexandria, about seventy-five miles north of Richmond. It's just a small place, but it was important as a railroad junction. There were about five or six thousand men of all arms there already, under the command of General Bonham, whom I was sent to relieve. The location had been chosen on the advice of Colonel Thomas Jordan, who became my chief of staff, and who had written a careful memoir, showing that it was essential to occupy this junction because its seizure by the enemy

Oct. 21. 1861

Dear General,

I send you here-
with two despatches I found
at Iwelli. How true they are
I am unable to tell. but
I should not be surprised if
there was some truth in them.
espicially in reference to that
battery on the Maryland Shore.
probably a mortar battery. —
Bomb proofs ought to be provided at once for the garrison
& part of the reserves —
I think they ought to be telegraphed to know if they want Fire
Tele. Co. from Camp Pickens
or it might be sent there
any how for a few days — &
should they wish to keep it

they could return another Co.
in its place –

I return you the flag, I
think it will do first rate
they ought to be made to
on its be easily attached
to the staff – when will
the others be back? –

I send a despatch just
recd from Evans – I should
not be surprised if he whipped the whole of Banks army –
Yours truly
T. T. Flanagan

Gn. J. S. Johnston
Presr –

(over)

I think it would be well to
attack them wherever the
opportunity presents itself –
G. T. B.

would mean that the lower part of Virginia would be cut off from the upper part. You can understand that, can't you, Doucette?"

"Ye-e-s, I think so. Of course, I don't know much about railroads, because we never use them or even see them at Upper Magnolia. But it doesn't matter, does it, if I don't understand *everything*? I do understand that for some reason it was very important that the Yankees shouldn't get hold of Manassas."

"I'm afraid I was talking to you as if I were giving a military report. Let's see if I can't find a way to put it more clearly. Do you think you could find the toy trains your brothers used to play with when they were little boys? And the lead soldiers?"

"Why, of course I can! Sometimes I played with them, too! They've been put away for a long while, but I know exactly where they are—in an old chest in the nursery. I'll go and get them."

"Wouldn't it be better if we went to the nursery? It isn't used for storage or anything else now, is it? We wouldn't be in anyone's way there. We could set up our battlefield and move the lead soldiers around. Of course, they don't have the right uniforms, but we can decide which ones we want for Confederates and which ones for Federals."

"Yes, of course we could. And maybe we can find a little paint somewhere on the place and paint them over. But if we can't, we'll just remember which is which. Oh, Papa, I think that's a grand idea! Let's go up to the nursery right now. But we'd better be just as quiet as we can. We don't want to wake *memère*."

"That's right. We'll tiptoe."

The nursery, at the rear of the second story, was musty and dusty from long disuse, but Doucette did not seem to mind this in the least. She flung open the chest and handed out the tiny track and cars and engine as fast as Pierre could take them. There was even a little depot, which he promised to label MANASSAS JUNCTION the next day; and there was another set of old toys, representing a village, provided with a church, houses, barns and domestic animals. Doucette was entranced with the set-up when her father had completed it, using the top of the table where the nursery meals had formerly been served.

"We'll say this is where I had my headquarters," he said, as he placed a nondescript building on the outskirts of the "village." "They really were in a small farmhouse, something the shape of this. That's where I ate and slept and worked when I wasn't in the field. During the day, I was riding about most of the time, inspecting my forces and improving the defenses. I was with my men a good deal. Nights, too. I used to join them around their campfires, to smoke and talk with them. They liked me and I liked them. When the troops who were with me in Charleston heard I'd arrived, they set up a great shout, 'Old Bory's come! Old Bory's come!' and broke ranks and rushed out to meet me."

"There, you see! You were their hero—just as you are mine."

"Darling, those were my men. Besides, I never said the Charleston people didn't think I was a hero. I know they did and I'm very grateful for their admiration and their confidence, which later I did more to deserve. I shouldn't have given you the impression I didn't appreciate it. That was wrong of me."

"We don't have to talk about that any more, do we, Papa?"

"No, except there's one thing I ought to add, to be completely honest. I fitted readily into the role of a hero the Charlestonians were disposed to give me, posing for my portrait, appearing often in full-dress uniform, making oratorical flourishes in public statements, leading cotillions, taking part in all sorts of other social activities."

"Don't let's talk about Charleston any more. Please go on and tell me what happened after you got to Manassas."

"Well, I soon began to realize I didn't have anywhere nearly enough men. In order to defend Manassas, I had to put my army between the Junction and the advancing Federals. The best place for my line was behind a small stream called Bull Run, which had any number of fords in it, and which ran north and east of the Junction."

"Can't we make a river out of my blue hair ribbon, to show exactly where Bull Run was?"

She whipped it off, releasing her black curls, and handed it to him. Then, as her hair fell over her face, obscuring her view of his operations, she fished a piece of string from the chest and tied the unruly locks back with it as Pierre began arranging the lead soldiers among the buildings and along the "stream" on the nursery table.

"So I wrote the President and asked for more men," he said. "I told him I must either have reinforcements at once or be prepared to retire in the direction of Richmond. I got the reinforcements, but I had other causes for worry. There weren't enough earthworks and some of the recruits objected to building them; they said that kind of manual labor wasn't fit for gentlemen, that they had only enlisted to fight. I was deeply annoyed at their attitude. It was different from what I'd encountered at Charleston, where *everyone* was willing to help with fortifications."

"You couldn't always expect to have everyone willing to help, could you, Papa?"

"No, I couldn't—at least, I shouldn't. But this amazing behavior was a great handicap, until some of the planters in the vicinity lent me their slaves and the work went ahead. The next difficulty was about supplies. There was plenty of food to be had around Manassas and that was the logical place to get it. But I was ordered not to use it; all supplies would be sent me from Richmond. Nothing I could say or do made any difference, because the Commissary General of the army, a man by the name of Northrop, was a creature beneath contempt. He was arbitrary, he was inept, he was mean, he was callous. Sometimes I felt as if he wouldn't have cared if the entire Confederate Army had starved to death! I was the first to have trouble with him, but sooner or later, almost every other general had the same difficulty."

"Couldn't you just go ahead and buy the food you needed, where you wanted to?"

"No, I didn't have the purchasing powers—those lay with Northrop."

"But the poor men didn't go hungry, did they, Papa?"

"Not seriously or not for long. That came later. We'll talk about it some other time perhaps. Now let's stick to Manassas—remember that's what you wanted to do. I had still another worry though, which the authorities in Richmond treated like a minor matter, but which didn't seem that way to me. Hardly any of the men had proper uniforms. Probably I wouldn't have had them myself, if it hadn't been for that gorgeous interlude in Charleston. And, as a matter of fact, most of the time I was riding around, I wore a shabby old blue army coat that I'd had I don't know how long. But I was afraid, when we had a battle, that a good many of my men would be killed for the simple reason that they'd be mistaken for Union soldiers. So I suggested that, perhaps, the ladies of the Confederacy would make scarves for us, red on one side and yellow on the other, that could be worn crosswise from shoulder to waist. Davis thought scarves would be too large, so he directed that rosettes should be worn, instead. As if anyone could stop to notice something as small as a rosette when a battle was going on! The ones that came weren't much bigger than the buttons on your dress."

Doucette looked thoughtfully down at the fastenings of her bodice, which was closed in the front by a series of pearl buttons.

"Didn't you have anything bigger than that by the time there was a battle?" she asked with anxiety.

"Not much. However, about the middle of June things improved when reinforcements began to arrive. Among these were the Washington Artillery and several Louisiana infantry regiments. Also the Louisiana Tigers, commanded by a famous soldier-of-fortune, Virginia-born Major Roberdeau Wheat, whom I had known in New Orleans. One of Wheat's companies, the Tiger Rifles, gave their name and character to the whole battalion. And what a rough lot they were! But Wheat could handle them. And it was as natural for them to fight as it was to breathe; so when a battle was brewing, as it was by that time, they were just what I wanted and needed. I knew they'd rush gaily into a fight under their absurd standard—the picture of a lamb with the legend 'As Gentle As' streaming over it. They got the nickname Gentle Tigers and it stuck, perhaps because it was so completely inappropriate that it actually seemed to fit, if you know what I mean. The Tigers thought nothing of going after the enemy with knives if their rifles gave out. And they *had* their uniforms, gaudy fantastic ones, which we thought nobody could possibly mistake. I've got pictures of them somewhere; I'll hunt them up and show them to you."

"Don't forget, will you, Papa?"

"No, I won't forget. Well, to go on with my story—that is, if you're sure you want me to. . . . There, don't get so excited, I believe you. . . . By the time the Tigers arrived, I had a plan of strategy—a program which I thought would be effective in driving the enemy from northern Virginia. But to carry this plan through, I needed the assistance of General Joseph Johnston, who was commanding the Confederate forces in the Shenandoah Valley. I suggested to the President that Johnston's army and mine should be combined at Manassas. I thought that great general was needed more there than he was in the Valley. The situation called for some kind of action and I gave the best advice I could. But it wasn't until a month later that the President agreed the suggestion was a good one and acted on it."

"And what happened then?"

"Well, meanwhile, the Federal position had been growing stronger by the minute. General Irvin McDowell, an Ohioan who had been a classmate of mine at West Point and a fellow officer in the Mexican War, was making plans, too. This was the second time a good friend of mine had become an opponent and I hated it. But it didn't hurt as much as it had in the case of Anderson at Sumter. I still think Anderson's one of the finest men I ever knew. Mind you, I'm not saying McDowell isn't a fine man, too—according to his lights. But he doesn't compare with Anderson. . . . Well, anyway, I found out that McDowell intended to advance toward Manassas on July sixteenth."

"How did you find out?"

"A girl told me."

"A *girl* told *you!*"

"Yes, a very beautiful girl named Betty Duval, who was just a little older than you are. She got her information from a friend of ours in Washington, a Mrs. Greenhow, who had promised Captain Jordan she would keep us informed. Betty succeeded in getting a ride out of Washington in a farm wagon. She didn't attract any attention or arouse any suspicion, because she had put on a sunbonnet and a calico dress—in fact, she looked exactly like any farmer's daughter. But when she got into Virginia, she went to a friend's house, changed into a riding habit and galloped off to Fairfax Courthouse, where General Bonham had his headquarters. Actually, it was he who got the news first. Betty jumped off her horse, took the pins out of her long hair, to let it down, and shook out Mrs. Greenhow's message, which was made into a little roll."

"I wish I could have done something like that!"

"My dear child, I'm thankful that you couldn't. I had enough troubles at Manassas without worrying whether or not you were safe. It was a great comfort to me to know that you were—you and your brother Henri. It was quite enough to worry about René, who was already in the Army."

"As soon as you had Mrs. Greenhow's message, did you know you were all right—that is, did you know you had time to prepare for the Yankees?"

"No, I knew I didn't have time to prepare. But when her message had been confirmed from several other quarters, I at least knew what to expect from the enemy. President Davis still hadn't ordered General Johnston to join me and, after my outposts were driven in, I telegraphed again and asked him to rush reinforcements. That was on July seventeenth. This final appeal resulted in orders which started General Johnston on his way, but I was informed there would be still further delay. When the telegram came, saying that he actually had started, I was afraid it was too late to do any good and I was angrier than I'd ever been in my life. I threw the telegram down on the table and pounded with my fist and told the officers who were in the room with me that McDowell would be upon us the next day and that we had better all get ready to sell our lives as dearly as possible."

"But it wasn't too late, after all!"

"No, not really. There was fighting on the nineteenth at Blackburn's Ford, on the center of my line, and the enemy, who had been feeling me out, was repulsed by Virginia troops commanded by a formidable Georgian, General James Longstreet, who'd been Paymaster in the Union Army. He made a favorable impression on me by his calm soldierly bearing and his victory at Blackburn's Ford put new heart into me. Besides, I knew that Johnston was on his way by this time. His army came up in one piece on the Manassas Gap Railroad. The first troops arrived at about noon on the twentieth and Johnston was with them. He told us the rest should reach us that night."

"And did they?"

"Yes, and before that Johnston and I had a long conference and I explained to him how the two opposing armies were arrayed. It was like this," Pierre went on, indicating first one group of lead soldiers and then another. "Here's McDowell's army, around Centerville, five miles away. And here's Bull Run. Thanks to your hair ribbon, we can see how it goes winding along in dozens of twists and turns, but you'll have to imagine its steep banks and its innumerable fords. My front is eight miles long and I've got six and a half brigades on it, like this. On my extreme left is Colonel Evans—he was called 'Shanks' at West Point because of his extremely skinny legs—with Wheat's Louisiana Tigers, the Fourth South Carolina Regiment and a few pieces of artillery. They are protecting Stone Bridge, where the Warrenton Pike crosses Bull Run. And here, next to Evans' force of about thirteen hundred men, is Philip St. George Cocke's brigade, which covers three fords: Island, here; Ball's, here; and Lewis's, here. At Mitchell's Ford is General Bonham and at Blackburn's Ford, here, where he defeated the Yankees previously, is Longstreet. General Jones is at McLean's Ford, the next down Bull Run, here; and at the extreme right of my line, here at Union Mills, is Dick Ewell with Jubal Early in reserve."

Doucette glanced, enraptured, at the placement of the lead soldiers and then looked up quickly at her father, entreating him to go on.

"I showed all this to General Johnston on the map, just as I've shown it to you with our lead soldiers and toy village and your blue hair ribbon. After the situation was clear to him, he agreed to a plan which I had prepared and instructed me to direct the battle. This was all the more of a compliment because, of course, he outranked me—he was a full general and I was still only a brigadier. He told me to draft the battle orders for the next day and then he went to bed, exhausted. I was mighty tired myself, but I assigned positions to Johnston's troops as they arrived and then I worked on the orders and took them to Johnston at four-thirty the next morning. I signed them myself, as I thought that was what he meant me to do, once he had approved my plan and told me to go ahead with it. I didn't realize until afterward that he was irritated at what I had done. He approved the document without discussion or much of any comment—then."

"But, Papa, what was your plan?"

"I intended to move out in great force with my right wing and fall on McDowell's left flank at Centerville. Like this—a sort of encircling movement." Pierre paused and smiled at his daughter. "It really didn't matter whether Johnston approved it or not or who signed it," he said. "Firing had already begun before there was time to distribute the orders. The Yankees were very disobliging. They fired before we got around to it."

❧ 30 ❧

GENERAL JOHNSTON WAS NOW THE RANKING OFFICER AT
Manassas; nevertheless, as General Beauregard had already
made all his plans and arrangements for the maintenance of
the position, of which General Johnston was, as yet, completely uninformed, he declined assuming the responsibilities
of the command until after the impending battle, but offered
General Beauregard his personal services on the field, which
were cordially accepted. General Beauregard thereupon explained his plan of operations, which was agreed to, and he
continued his active preparations for the hourly expected
conflict.

−Alfred Roman, *The Military Operations of General
Beauregard* (Harper & Row)

❧

"DOUCETTE! DOUCETTE! WHERE IN HEAVEN'S NAME ARE YOU?"
The call rang out and echoed through the long corridor. Doucette put her finger on her lips and shook her head, signaling to her
father that she did not want their "battle" interrupted. But he shook
his head, too.

"They'll be worried about you, honey, if they can't find you," he
reminded her. "Probably they are already. Besides, I want to see the
rest of the family and I hope they want to see me. We can come
back here later."

"Directly after dinner?"

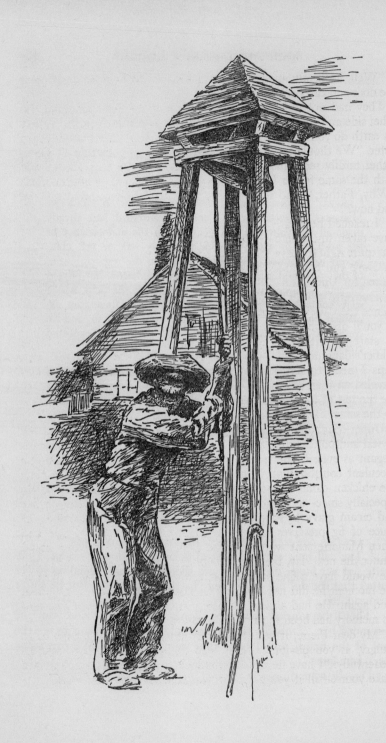

"Well, we'll talk about that by and by. Right now we must open the door and call back."

They had not quite reached it when it was flung open from the other side and René, flushed and breathless, confronted them. "What on earth do you mean, hiding out on us like that?" he shouted at his sister. "We thought you'd fallen into the river or something!" Then, rather tardily recognizing his father's presence, he embraced Pierre with the same fervor Doucette had shown a couple of hours earlier. "Why, Father, I had no idea you were here! When did you come and how?"

"I reached here early this afternoon, on horseback. Someone must have taken my superb steed to the stables. So you see, Doucette, I was quite right to leave it hitched so trustfully!"

"Have you had anything to eat? You must be half-starved, if you waited for Uncle and Henri and me to get back from Belle Chasse."

"Doucette gave me some dewberry shrub," Pierre said, smiling. "Since then, we've been setting the scene for the Battle of Manassas, as you'll observe if you'll take a look at the nursery table. She wants to start in with the fight right now—a suitable attitude for a soldier's daughter. But I confess I could do with some food first. Perhaps I need to remind her that Napoleon always insisted armies traveled on their stomachs. And I've already reminded her I'd like to see the rest of the family. Go wash your hands, Doucette, and let me do the same. I'll meet you in the dining room."

Upper Magnolia had escaped molestation during the war and the crystal and porcelain on which Theophilus served the dinner were as elegant as ever. Manette had contrived an extra course by making a succulent courtbouillon from a fresh-caught catfish, so by the time the chicken came on no one minded that the portions were small, especially since—as Doucette had predicted—there was plenty of rice and cream gravy to supplement the abundant garden vegetables. A sauce of fig preserves had done wonders for the blancmange; and when Manette sent word that the General was not to worry about dinner the next day, because Theophilus had "cotched" a turtle and she would have a fine stew, Pierre could say, in all honesty, that at the moment he did not feel as if he would ever have to worry about food again. He had almost forgotten what a real meal was like; now his memory had been most happily refreshed.

"My dear Pierre, if you would stay here, you wouldn't have to go hungry, as you obviously have been doing," Mme Villeré said reproachfully. "I have never seen you look so thin and drawn. You will make yourself ill if you persist in this fruitless search for work."

"But *chère* Madame, I must persist in the hope that it will not always be fruitless. I cannot be a drone—a burden on others—all the rest of my life." He very nearly added, "When it comes to that, I have never seen you look so badly, either." He remembered what Doucette had said about her grandmother's migraine, and wondered if it did not have its source in a condition more serious than the girl realized; Mme Villeré seemed to him much more frail than at the time of his last visit and Charles was obviously harassed and anxious; it was a relief to find M. Villeré still hale and hearty and the youngsters blooming with health. "At all events, I'm going to remain here for the next few days," he said, cutting short her protests. "Doucette and I are going to fight the Battle of Manassas all over again."

"In that case, make sure Father tells you all the more important facts," René said warningly to his sister. "For instance, that he went charging ahead at full gallop under furious fire to reform a line, while riding a headless horse."

"*A headless horse!*"

"Don't listen to your brother, honey. Of course I didn't ride a headless horse—that was just one of the legends that sprang up. My horse was killed. He was struck by a shell which exploded just as it passed under him. A splinter from it cut an artery and blood gushed out all over him, but he plunged ahead for another fifty yards or so before he fell—with his head still on his shoulders. A second splinter hit one of my boots, but I wasn't hurt at all and I shifted quickly to another mount— a small, dingy, white-faced horse that I took from a prisoner. I remember it distinctly. It closely resembled the one on which I came here today."

"Well, anyway, you'll admit the rest of the story was true—that you charged ahead at full gallop under furious fire and completely reformed a wavering line," René insisted. "At least I suppose it really was you, Father, and not Napoleon, miraculously resurrected. Wasn't there some talk about that, too?"

"There was some talk, some very foolish talk, about a *reincarnation* of Napoleon, not a resurrection. You know I did everything I could to discourage it, René. And I'd rather you didn't tell these silly stories to your sister, especially when she seems to be taking an intelligent interest in what really did happen."

"Can't we go back to the nursery now, Papa?" she asked, glancing reproachfully at her brother and tugging at her father's sleeve.

"No, darling. I want to spend the rest of the evening *en famille*. But we can go back tomorrow morning as early as you like."

She tried to tease him into changing his mind and he realized that he was close to letting her do so. She certainly was becoming more and more beguiling, and he suddenly recalled, with the poignancy that such memories always gave him, the insistence her mother had shown when she determined that he must explain the causes of the Mexican War. But he managed to remain firm. He wanted to hear whether or not Charles had succeeded in getting more credit and whether or not René and Henri were becoming restless with prolonged inactivity; a series of more or less private talks seemed to be indicated for the evening and he succeeded in wedging them in—not that they gave him much satisfaction. It was as he had feared: Charles had been unable to get additional loans anywhere and he was concerned about his mother's failing health; he felt it was no exaggeration to say that it would kill her to lose the plantation. René, on the other hand, was hell-bent to leave it and begged Pierre to take him to New Orleans; he was impatient to begin the study of law. It took all the patience and tact his father could summon to convince him that the problem of board and lodging was so acute that, for the time being, no such move was practicable; at Upper Magnolia there was at least food and shelter and Pierre was hopeful that, in the autumn . . . The argument closed on that note. He was relieved that Henri seemed content to drift along.

It was something, also, to Pierre that he was finding new companionship, new congeniality with Doucette. When he had told her they could return to Manassas as early in the morning as she liked, he had not expected her to come bounding into his bedroom, fully dressed, before Manette brought him his coffee; and the young girl was already seated, looking intently at the set-up on the old table, when he joined her in the nursery an hour later. He had taken time to label the little depot MANASSAS JUNCTION, but the paint was still wet; he had to warn her not to touch it. The soldiers' uniforms were still unchanged, to Doucette's increased regret, now that she had heard about the Gentle Tigers.

"Half of them are blue, anyway," she said resignedly. "The Yankees always had plenty of uniforms, didn't they?"

"Yes, they were kept mighty well supplied."

"But I hate having the Confederates in red."

"Never mind. I've found some gray paint, I'll try to have those done over by tomorrow—unless you keep me here the whole day. Are we all set? It is just before daybreak on July twenty-first, 1861. The Yankees have fired first, very inconsiderately. McDowell is attacking our left and Shanks Evans' demi-brigade is engaged. Major Wheat, on orders from Evans, has formed his command to the left of Stone

Bridge and has sent forward the Tiger Rifles under Captain White as skirmishers in the woods near Bull Run. So the Tigers actually opened the fight for us—right here. Wheat himself, with typical daring and recklessness, rode across Bull Run at Red House Ford, about a mile upstream from Stone Bridge, to reconnoiter. Unfortunately, he encountered some Union scouts on the far bank. I say unfortunately, because this moved him to shout at them defiantly and then wheel his horse and recross the stream. Such a bit of bravado was a costly mistake. It showed General Sherman a place where *he* could cross Bull Run and he promptly sent forward a company of skirmishers followed by a whole brigade."

While he was talking, Pierre had indicated some of the red-coated lead soldiers to represent the Tigers and then singled out one of them, which he lifted across Doucette's hair ribbon and, with a flourish, put him back again in his original position. Doucette nodded, understandingly and excitedly.

"Meanwhile, the Federal cannon were still bombarding Stone Bridge, but Major Wheat pointed out, and Evans agreed, that the noisy attack was not pushed with vigor. Then Evans learned that he was seriously menaced from another direction. A young captain by the name of Alexander, at the signal station on Wilcoxen Hill—right here —was surveying the field through his glasses, when he suddenly saw flashes in the distance and recognized them as the reflection of the sun on a brass field piece; presently he was able to pick out the glitter of bayonets and rifle barrels. McDowell was making a wide sweep around my left flank—like this. Without losing a moment, Alexander wigwagged Evans, 'Look out for your left; you are turned,' and sent a similar message to me. Almost simultaneously, a courier from the picket at Sudley's Ford reported that a large Federal force was crossing Bull Run—right here. Having decided to turn around and face the threat from his rear, Evans conferred quickly with Wheat and then acted with great boldness. He ordered Wheat, who was at Carter House with the bulk of his command, to advance as skirmishers, covering his—Evans'—new front. Then, leaving four companies to defend Stone Bridge, he took the rest of his command and marched off to join the Tigers. . . . Still with me, Doucette?"

"Yes, I'm still with you."

"Good! Meanwhile, Wheat had deployed one of his companies— the Catahoula Guerillas, commanded by Captain Buhoup—as skirmishers in the direction of Sudley's Ford, to meet the Union advance: over here. The rest of his command he moved into position on the extreme right of the new battle line. After he had done this, he moved by the left flank to an open field with a wood beside it. There he was surprised by a volley of musketry—Confederate musketry. Through error, Captain Hawthorne's company of Sloan's Fourth South Carolina Regiment had fired on the Tigers. Of course, the Tigers fired back. As I told you before, Doucette, they'd fire at anything or anybody, any time. Wheat called out to them to cease fire and some of them—the ones close enough to hear him—did as they were told, but those out of range of his voice went right on firing."

"What time was it by then? A lot seems to have happened already."

"A lot had happened already, but it was only about ten in the morning. While the South Carolinians and the Louisianians were doing their best to destroy each other, the leading Union brigade, commanded by General Burnside—the one who gave his name to those queer sidewhiskers—came out of the woods that parallel the Sudley-Manassas road and opened on Wheat's battalion with musketry, grape, canister, round shot and shells. In the face of this heavy firing, the gallant Wheat charged on the enemy and drove him back. He did that three times. The enemy was so galled and staggered that three additional regiments were hastened up, and Wheat sent a message to Evans, asking him to rush reinforcements, as he was now faced by a force of probably ten or twelve thousand. He ordered his men to seek the cover of the hills, but some of them crossed an open field and suffered heavily from enemy fire. However, Wheat succeeded in reaching some haystacks with a portion of his command and, with the protection of these, he did the enemy considerable damage. He would have done a good deal more if he hadn't been put *hors de combat* while he was bringing the rest of his command up to this advantageous position."

"You mean he was wounded?"

"Yes, very badly. He had dismounted and was holding his bridle with one hand while he waved his sword with the other. He was a huge man and, standing there like that, he was a conspicuous mark. He was struck down by a rifle ball that passed straight through his body, from one side to the other, and pierced one of his lungs."

"But he wasn't killed!"

"No, he wasn't killed, though most of his battalion thought he was when he fell and for a while there was general confusion. The various companies went on fighting under their respective captains, but it was highly disorganized fighting. Fortunately, Captain Buhoup crossed the field where Wheat had fallen and found him lying on the ground, bleeding profusely but still alive. He rallied his men around Wheat and the Catahoula Guerillas made a litter out of muskets and, under heavy fire, carried their commander through lanes of dead and wounded. He was conscious and kept telling them to put him down and save themselves. Of course they didn't listen to him for a minute. They managed to carry him all the way to a field hospital on the Manassas Road, half a mile above the New Market crossroads."

"So he was safe after all!"

"Well, he was safe from gunfire, but it still looked as if he would die from his wound. And, of course, his battalion was left without a field officer to hold it together. But the separate companies kept on fighting all day, in the face of an enemy that far outnumbered them. The rest of Evans' thousand-odd rifles fought just as valiantly and stemmed the Federal advance for more than an hour; but, by the end of that time, Evans was sorely pressed; and, though General Bee and Colonel Bartow were turning their brigades in his direction, they were on the other side of the Confederate lines and had a long way to go in order to reach him. Evans continued to fight furiously on the hills north of the Warrenton Turnpike, but the Union pressure soon became overwhelming. Remember Wheat's needless bravado in exposing Red House Ford and taunting the Yankees early that morning? Well, Sherman crossed Bull Run at that exact spot and struck Evans on the flank. This was more than our men could stand up under. They began to break ranks and flee in disorder across Young's Branch and the Warrenton Turnpike. If it hadn't been for one man, we could have lost the battle then and there. Do you know who the one man was and what he did?"

"Was it—did it have something to do with a nickname?"

Pierre laughed, not very heartily. "Yes, it did, and I suppose that's the way it's going to be remembered. General Bee was vainly trying to reorganize his men, who were scurrying up Henry Hill, right here, when, as a last resort, he waved his sword at them and shouted, 'Look at Jackson, standing there like a stone wall! Rally around the Virginians!' "

"What was General Jackson doing on Henry Hill? You didn't tell me about him before!"

"No, he had just moved up with his troops. He had been in the Shenandoah Valley with General Johnston and had not yet even been engaged in the battle. It was his stone wall stand that saved the day."

"And after that he was always called Stonewall Jackson! Wasn't his real name anything like that?"

"Nothing at all like that. It was Thomas Jonathan Jackson, which really seemed to suit him. He was a huge, awkward man with a big bushy beard and enormous hands and feet. He was a West Point graduate, won commendation at the Battle of Chapultepec and had been professor of mathematics at Virginia Military Institute. He was humorless and strait-laced, almost fanatically religious; it was against his principles to fight on a Sunday. But this was a Sunday and did he fight! Did he set an example that made other men fight, too, like grim death! That wasn't just a figure of speech, either, at Manassas, any more than Stonewall was just an ordinary nickname."

Earlier in the morning, Pierre had kept moving his lead soldiers from place to place as he talked; but as he became more and more absorbed in his story, he forgot to do so, except when Doucette nudged him slightly to remind him. Now he leaned back in his chair, gazing fixedly ahead of him, though there was nothing to see in the direction toward which he was looking, except a blank wall. Doucette glanced toward the wall, too, and then back at her father, puzzled by his expression and his silence, until she realized that he had forgotten about their game, because he was lost in his memories of a severe, awkward man who had helped to save an army from defeat by the sheer force of his steadfastness.

"He was a very great general, wasn't he?" she asked at length, rather shyly, because she was uncertain whether or not she should break in on his revery.

"Yes, one of our greatest. He was only a brigadier when the Battle of Manassas was fought, but he became a lieutenant general and General Lee called him 'my right arm.' If he'd lived, perhaps we wouldn't have lost the war, after all—in spite of Davis. But Jackson was killed at Chancellorsville—another of our great victories."

"Were you there when it happened?"

"No, by that time, I was back in Charleston."

Again, he was lost in revery and it seemed to Doucette that a shadow had fallen across his face. She sat very still, not wanting to disturb him and, at the same time, she was anxious, because he seemed so sad, and impatient to have him go on and tell her what happened after General Bee's men rallied behind Jackson and his Virginians.

"Did you realize right off that General Jackson might have saved the day?" she asked, even more shyly than before.

"What? Oh, I'm sorry, Doucette, I seem to have been woolgathering. No, because there was no evidence that it actually was saved yet. It would have been more accurate if I'd said that Jackson's action at a crucial moment was an important factor in making later victory possible. It was about one in the afternoon when Jackson took his stand. After that, there was a lull in the fighting while the Union forces, which had crossed the valley at Young's Branch, regrouped for a final assault. They thought at this point that they'd won. But Johnston and I recognized by then that the battle wasn't developing the way I'd planned and we ordered up the brigades from the fords farther down Bull Run. These reinforcements formed on either side of Jackson; and they were all in line when McDowell opened his attack at two. For an hour there was furious fighting, all the time at close range, part of the time actually hand-to-hand. Neither side was winning or losing; at one moment the odds would seem to be in our favor and the next in favor of the Yankees. Then Jeb Stuart came sweeping along with his plumes and his cavalry and charged Ricketts' and Griffin's advance batteries. That was when the tide definitely began to turn. The last of Johnston's troops had arrived at Manassas Junction from the Valley, and with good old Kirby Smith at their head, they had marched on the field; and next, as Jubal Early's brigade came up from McLean's Ford, a great shout rang out from one of the regiments, 'Hurrah for the Tiger Rifles, charge for the Tigers and Louisiana!' "

"Who was shouting?" Doucette asked, jumping up excitedly.

"Colonel Harry Hays' Seventh Louisiana Infantry, which was part of Early's brigade. The Seventh had marched eight or nine miles on the double, but it charged the Federals with a vengeance and the New York Fire Zouaves fled, throwing down their equipment as they ran. The Tigers, not satisfied merely to see the Zouaves in flight from the Seventh Infantry, dropped their rifles and rushed in among the enemy with Bowie knives. Wheat's men, believing him dead or dying, took their revenge as they pitched into Sherman's battery. And, at last, we were able to switch from defense to attack. The most glorious moment of my life! The rout of McDowell's army had begun and the whole Confederate line plunged forward to the charge, shouting the rebel yell!"

❧ 31 ❧

Despatch to the War Department

Manassas, July 21st, 1861.

Night has closed upon a hard-fought field. Our forces have won a glorious victory. The enemy was routed, and fled precipitately, abandoning a very large amount of arms, munitions, knapsacks, and baggage. The ground was strewn for miles with those killed, and the farm-houses and the ground around were filled with his wounded. The pursuit was continued along several routes towards Leesburg and Centerville, until darkness covered the fugitives. We have captured several field-batteries and regimental standards and one United States flag. Many prisoners have been taken. Too high praise cannot be bestowed, whether for the skill of the principal officers, or for the gallantry of all the troops. The battle was mainly fought on our left, several miles from our field works. Our force engaged them not exceeding fifteen thousand; that of the enemy estimated at thirty-five thousand.

Jefferson Davis

Appointment of Beauregard to full general

Manassas, Va., July 21st, 1861.

Sir,—Appreciating your services in the battle of Manassas and on several other occasions during the existing war, as affording the highest evidence of your skill as a commander, your gallantry as a soldier, and your zeal as a patriot, you are appointed to be "General" in the army of the Confederate States of America, and, with the consent of the Congress, will be duly commissioned accordingly.

Yours, etc.,

Jefferson Davis

General G. T. Beauregard

—Alfred Roman, *The Military Operations of General Beauregard* (Harper & Row)

From a letter written by Frank Shober to his wife, the sister of Roberdeau Wheat

Friday night, eight-thirty o'clock, July 26, 1861, Manassas.

This evening as I was walking around the entrenchment, looking among other things, at the perfect weldings of guns and camp equipment taken from the enemy, whom should I encounter but Beauregard with a brilliant staff, all splendidly mounted. They were examining the guns of Sherman's battery. I stood looking at them for a long time. His face stamps him at once [as a] modest, quiet, unassuming man, but the great victor in the greatest of all victories could have borne himself with such quiet simplicity under the gaze of hundreds who surrounded him. After riding around the entrenchments and inspecting the various points, the whole party halted at Rob's quarters and called in to see him. Rob presented me to Beauregard and I was charmed with his graceful easy manner. He spoke a few words of the most soothing and tender character to Rob, and when he went away, it seemed as if the influence of his presence had left a charm in the room. Rob seemed to feel it and he has been in good spirits ever since.

—Wheat-Shober Papers, University of North Carolina

HE WAS ON HIS FEET, SHOUTING AS DOUCETTE HAD NEVER HEARD HIM shout before and, instantly she was standing beside him, shouting, too. When she had come hurrying into the nursery early that morning, she had left the door ajar. Now, as she and her father gave the rebel yell, the sound reverberated through the silent house and, a moment later, it rang out again from another room, not once, but over and over again. Then it came nearer and nearer above the tread of rapid footsteps. Charles, René and Henri tore into the room together, all yelling at the top of their lungs. They rushed across the floor and locked arms with Pierre and Doucette and the five danced around the room, which resounded with the rebel yell as all five joined in the clamor. When at last, breathless and perspiring, they sank into chairs, Pierre was the first to start up again, somewhat guiltily.

"If your mother heard this racket, Charles, she must be wondering what on earth's going on. You'd better go and tell her that it was nothing but a family celebration. Otherwise, she may think war's broken out again." And, as Charles, wiping his dripping face, rose reluctantly and left the room, Pierre glanced with smiling satisfaction from his two tall sons to his young daughter.

"It isn't often we four get together," he said. "In fact, it isn't anywhere nearly often enough. We'll have to do something about that.

Doucette, daughter of Pierre and Laure Beauregard.

Dr. Charles Turpin as a young man. Reproduced by the courtesy of Mrs. C. G. Alba, Mrs. R. M. Boland and Mrs. Herbert H. Bleuler.

Left: William H. Russell, correspondent of the *London Times*.

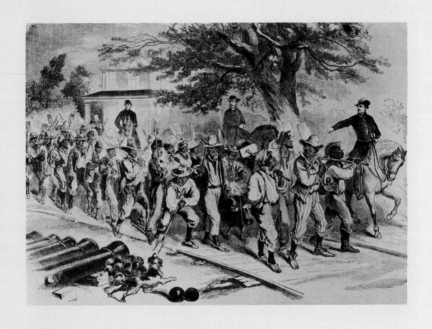

Print showing slaves en route to Manassas to work on the fortifications. From *L'Illustration des Dames*, Paris. Collection of Leonard V. Huber.

General Beauregard at the Battle of Bull Run. Reproduction of an original sketch, used by courtesy of the owner, Mrs. Porter F. Bedell.

Farragut's fleet passing Forts Jackson and St. Philip. From *Le Monde Illustre*, Paris. Original print in collection of Leonard V. Huber.

Scene in New Orleans during the evacuation. From *L'Illustration des Dames*, Paris. Original print in collection of Leonard V. Huber.

General P. G. T. Beauregard as he appeared after the Civil War.

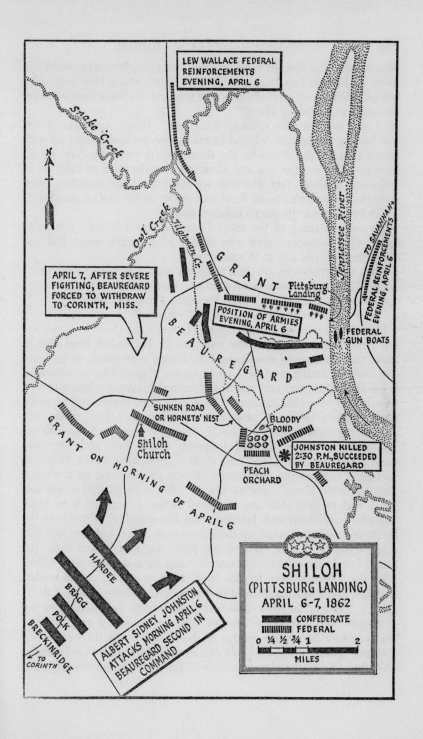

LEW WALLACE FEDERAL
REINFORCEMENTS
EVENING, APRIL 6

Snake Creek

N

Owl Creek

Tilghman Cr.

G R A N T

Pittsburg
Landing

Tennessee River

TO SAVANNAH

FEDERAL REINFORCEMENTS
EVENING, APRIL 6

APRIL 7, AFTER SEVERE
FIGHTING, BEAUREGARD
FORCED TO WITHDRAW
TO CORINTH, MISS.

POSITION OF ARMIES
EVENING, APRIL 6

FEDERAL
GUN BOATS

B E A U R E G A R D

SUNKEN ROAD
OR HORNETS' NEST

BLOODY
POND

G R A N T   O N   M O R N I N G   O F   A P R I L   6

Shiloh
Church

JOHNSTON KILLED
2:30 P.M., SUCCEEDED
BY BEAUREGARD

PEACH
ORCHARD

HARDEE

BRAGG

POLK

BRECKINRIDGE

TO
CORINTH

ALBERT SIDNEY JOHNSTON
ATTACKS MORNING APRIL 6
BEAUREGARD SECOND IN
COMMAND

SHILOH
(PITTSBURG LANDING)
APRIL 6-7, 1862

███ CONFEDERATE
▦▦▦ FEDERAL

0   ¼ ½ ¾ 1   2
MILES

Meanwhile, I've lost all track of time—except what happened from dawn to dusk on July twenty-first, 1861. That's where Doucette and I left off. Shall we all go down now and see how the turtle stew Manette promised us is coming along?"

"I can tell you, it's coming along fine," Henri reported. "I was just leaving the kitchen when I heard the uproar and caught up with Uncle Charles and René on the stairs. But it won't be done for an hour or more yet. Do you and Doucette actually need to carry on in seclusion, Father? You just said we four don't get together often enough. Why don't you let René and me in on the rest of the story?"

"Why—I think the story's finished now."

"It isn't anything of the sort," Doucette contradicted. "I want to know what happened after you routed McDowell's army. Did you chase them all the way to Washington?"

"No, unfortunately, we didn't. That's what I wanted to do, that's what General Johnston wanted to do, that's what the whole army wanted to do. But it wasn't what President Davis wanted to do."

"How could he stop you, way off in Richmond?"

"He wasn't way off in Richmond. He was right there at Manassas. He arrived very soon after the rout started. He hadn't been able to stand the suspense of wondering how things were going, so far from the scene of action, and he'd come up on a special train, secured a horse at the Junction and ridden to General Johnston's headquarters. He was still under the impression that we'd been beaten and he could hardly believe the good news that Johnston gave him, so he rode around the field to see for himself. Then the President came to my headquarters, where General Johnston joined him and they had supper together. Mr. Davis then drafted a dispatch to the War Department, announcing the victory. He was still working on it when I came in. He'd already sent an aide to tell me he wanted to see me, but I had to look after my wounded before I went back to headquarters. I sat down with Johnston and Davis and we talked over the battle and discussed what we should do next. We'd lost Bee, our first major casualty, but in spite of our grief, our morale was high. Jeb Stuart came riding back from near Centerville and urged us to follow after the Federals who, by this time, were in a state of the wildest disorder; and I heard afterward that Stonewall Jackson had said, if the Lord would send him ten thousand men, he'd be in Washington the next day. And I've got to be fair. I've got to admit that, at first, Davis would have been willing to have us pursue the retreating Yankees. In fact, he started to write an order providing that Bonham, who had the freshest troops, should get started immediately. But while he was composing his directive, someone came in and said that reports from Centerville were conflicting, that they didn't all come from reliable sources. That was enough to throw him off. He thought it would be better to wait until morning and verify every phase of the situation. I'm sorry to say that Johnston and I agreed with him. By morning, it was pouring in torrents, the muddy roads were impassable, the disorganized mob had managed to scramble back to Washington. Of course, I didn't see the rout, but from what I heard, it must have been something to behold. Political leaders, fashionable ladies, business magnates had come streaming out of Washington, all dressed for a fete, in every conceivable kind of conveyance, to watch the battle. They couldn't have been in higher spirits if they'd been going to a picnic or a ball, instead of expecting to see men—their own men, as well as ours—horribly killed and wounded. Talk about the Romans and the gladiatorial combats! They were drinking toasts to celebrate their prospective victory when suddenly wagons and more wagons thundered into sight, followed by a small band of mounted men which had once represented cavalry, and a mob of men on the run, which had once been infantry. Then a cry went up, 'We're beaten! We're pursued! Run for your lives!' and all the premature rejoicing came to a sudden and violent end, and the spectators were swept up in the rout of McDowell's army."

"You could put it a good deal more strongly than that, Father," René remarked.

"Yes, I know I could, but that isn't important. What is important is that our first great opportunity had been lost. Johnston and I have to share the blame for not pursuing McDowell immediately. But our army was almost as disorganized by victory as McDowell's was by defeat and we don't have to take the blame because fresh orders for pursuit weren't issued by President Davis when he arrived on the battlefield. After that, we were victims of the Confederate strategy of defense, aimed at European intervention. Moreover, our ranks were riddled with successive waves of illness—measles, mumps, whooping cough, chicken pox. Most of our recruits were just boys that hadn't run through these diseases before they enlisted; and the enlistments were largely for six months; some of the men, who felt they were needed at home, just took off. After all, the South had no regular army and these men still felt they were citizens before they were soldiers."

"Father, don't paint too black a picture for Doucette," René objected. "You know there were some good moments. What about breakfast on the twenty-second?"

"Yes, well, I'll concede breakfast on the twenty-second. Davis was in one of his mellower moods. While we were eating, he gave me a note, paying me numerous compliments and raising my rank from brigadier to full general. It was the last gracious thing he ever did for me."

"Well, at least he did that and it put you in the top military rank, along with General Cooper, Robert E. Lee and Joe Johnston."

"Yes, of course that's true."

"And think of all the flattering attention you received from the fair sex!" Henri reminded his father jokingly. "All those scarves and socks! All those letters begging you for your picture and a lock of your hair and a button from your coat! Think of all the babies and race horses and steamboats that were named for you and all the songs that were written about you! I've always understood Davis was jealous because you had eight songs written about you and he had only four. Numbers do count, even if some were pretty awful." Then he roared:

> "Oh! the North was evil-starred, when
> she met thee, Beauregard!
> For you fought her very hard with
> cannon and petard, Beauregard!
> Beau canon, Beauregard! Beau soldat,
> Beauregard!
> Beau sabreur! beau frappeur! Beauregard,
> Beauregard!"

"Henri, you and your brother seem determined to caricature my career!"

"No, we're not, Father. I'm only trying to brighten up the darker portions. You insist on dwelling on those, you know."

"He doesn't do anything of the sort," Doucette protested. "He's cheerful and charitable about everything until—until there isn't anything more to be cheerful and charitable about. He explains things to me, which is more than you and René ever did. You've said I wouldn't understand. Well, I understand now—at least, I understand a lot better than I did before. And I think we've got the most wonderful father in the world!" She rose to fling her arms around him with characteristic impetuosity, and slid onto his lap.

"Am I too big for you to hold me this way?" she asked fondly, nestling against him.

"You'll never be too big," he answered, a lump in his throat. "But you take an unfair advantage when you cuddle up to me like this. It distracts my thoughts. And just to prove to all of you that I don't need Henri's help in giving a light touch to the drearier parts of my career, I'll tell you about two things that happened during those months I spent at Manassas, after the battle—two things that made me very happy."

"All right. I'll sit down here at your feet and listen. What was the first thing?"

"I designed our battle flag. At Manassas, it was hard to tell the new Confederate States' flag from the old United States flag, because ours also had red and white stripes and white stars on a blue field, though, of course, not as many of each. Anyway, lots of people wanted something that would remind them of their old flag. That was all right, too, as long as it wasn't used during combat. But when Kirby Smith came up, there was confusion as to which colors the troops carried. The Confederates almost fired on their own men and the Yankees held up their fire, disastrously to them. So I made several distinctive designs and showed them to Johnston. He approved one with a red field crossed by diagonal star-studded blue bars, but suggested it would be more effective if it were square, instead of oblong. Then we asked three beautiful young ladies, the two Cary sisters from Baltimore and their cousin from Alexandria, who came quite often to visit us in camp, if they wouldn't make flags for us out of their dresses—one for me, one for Johnston and one for Earl Van Dorn. Then we would get silk for additional flags from other ladies."

"Who was Earl Van Dorn?"

"One of our generals who later went to the Western theater. Well, the flags were made and, late in November, they were formally presented to the troops in solemn ceremonies. I wrote an order which was read to each unit and reminded the men that the flag was sacred because it had been made by their wives, mothers and sweethearts. After the presentation, there were banquets at all the principal headquarters and a good many toasts were drunk—perhaps too many. Anyway, Kirby Smith, who was rather strait-laced, left one banquet —Johnston's and mine—because he thought there were. We sent an aide after him and asked him to come back and make us a speech. But he declined. He said he couldn't speak soberly to a drunken audience."

"But Papa, you hardly drink anything at all!"

"That's true, generally. But maybe the celebration was the exception that proves the rule. I'm not sure. I don't remember that part very clearly."

He looked down at her affectionately, his dark eyes twinkling in the way they seldom did any more, his lips parted in a smile. Then he spoke more gravely. "But I do remember that, afterward, I sent my flag to your stepmother in New Orleans. When the Federals took over the city in Sixty-two, she managed to get it on a foreign ship going to Havana, for safekeeping. I'm hoping that someday it will be returned to me."

"I hope so, too," Doucette said, hugging his knees. "But go on, Papa."

"Before Father leaves the subject of flags, let me tell you something he may have left out, Doucette," René interposed. "At Manassas, when the issue was still very much in doubt, he seized the colors of an Alabama regiment, shouted, 'Onward to victory and glory,' and galloped to the front. Instantly, the line swept forward."

"Yes, he did leave that out; thanks a lot, René. But now I want to hear about the second thing it makes him happy to remember."

"It had to do with the same three girls as the first, the Carys. It actually happened before the presentation of the flags, but somehow I always think of that as first. The Carys had 'run the blockade' and gone with their brother and cousin to Orange Courthouse. I'd heard of their Confederate sympathies and their efforts in behalf of our Cause in Maryland, so I invited them to come to my headquarters and sent them passes and an escort. A kinsman of theirs, a Captain Steret, provided tents for their encampment. They slept on layers of cartridge flannel and hung their hoops on a pole overhead. Our own Washington Artillery of New Orleans serenaded them and many from other units joined in the chorus. Afterward, they asked how they could express their thanks and I said, 'Just let us hear a woman's voice.' So Miss Jenny Cary stood at the opening of her tent and sang 'Maryland, My Maryland,' and presently hundreds of men were singing with her. Then a wild shout went up, 'Three cheers and a tiger for Maryland!' I don't think there was a dry eye left in the camp. . . . There, there, Doucette, I didn't mean to make you cry, too!"

He gathered her into his arms and silenced her when she reminded him, between sobs, that he said it distracted him to have her sit on his lap. "It doesn't matter, because I'm not going to tell you any more stories today, honey," he told her. "There really isn't anything else to tell. Nothing more happened at Manassas, nothing that would make a story. I spent most of my time writing letters. I wanted desperately to come back to New Orleans. Of course, I wanted to see you. I also wanted to see your stepmother, whom I loved very dearly and who wasn't well, so I worried about her. Moreover, I felt I could be of more use in my own part of the country than I was in Virginia, because I was familiar with the Mississippi River and the forts that defended it. But Davis said no, I was needed right where I was. So what did he do? He sent me to Columbus, Kentucky."

❧ 32 ❧

Melt the bells, melt the bells,
Still the tinkling on the plains
And transmute the evening chimes
Into war's resounding rhymes,
That the invader may be slain
By the bells.

Melt the bells, melt the bells
And when foes no more attack
And the lightning cloud of war
Shall roll thunderless and far
We will melt the cannon back
Into bells.

—F. Y. Rockett, Memphis *Commercial Appeal*,
March 15, 1862

❧

SUDDENLY, PIERRE REALIZED HE DID NOT WANT TO TALK ABOUT THE war any more.

He had been deeply moved when Doucette insisted that he was a hero and that he must prove it to her; gratified by the sustained interest and quick understanding she had shown all the time he was telling her about the Battle of Manassas and showing her, by means of the toy trains and villages and the lead soldiers, where the different battalions had been located, how they had been engaged. When she and her brothers and uncle had joined him in the rebel yell, he had reveled in moments of exhilaration such as he had not known for

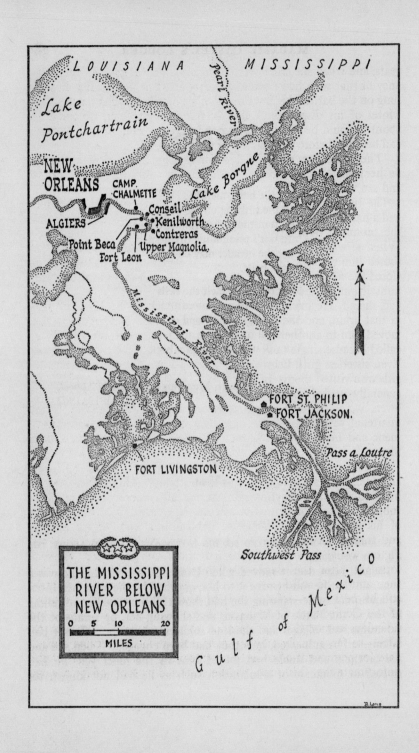

LOUISIANA · MISSISSIPPI

Pearl River

Lake Pontchartrain

Lake Borgne

NEW ORLEANS

CAMP CHALMETTE

●Conseil

ALGIERS

●Kenilworth
●Contreras
Upper Magnolia.

Point Beca
Fort Leon

Mississippi River

N

FORT ST. PHILIP
FORT JACKSON.

Pass a Loutre

FORT LIVINGSTON

Southwest Pass

Gulf of Mexico

THE MISSISSIPPI RIVER BELOW NEW ORLEANS

0   5   10   20

MILES

B. Long

years; and when she cried over "Maryland, My Maryland," the poignancy of that song had been as piercing as when he had first heard it sung on the battlefield. But now, in his narrative, he had reached "the winter of his discontent," and he felt that anything he could say about it would be painful to him and disappointing to her. Better to end his story before that happened.

"The turtle stew must be done by this time," he said, setting her on her feet. "Let us descend to the dining room, *mes chers enfants*, and see what kind of a feast awaits us."

The turtle stew was done and, like everything in which Manette had a hand, it was excellent. Hot biscuits, a salad of garden greens and the promised dewberry pie served to prolong the meal pleasantly. When it was over, Pierre announced that, because Doucette had roused him so early, he felt the need of a siesta; he went to his room, closed the door after him and, taking off his coat and shoes, stretched himself out on the bed. It was not the same bed that he and Laure had shared. He insisted, after her death, that he could never sleep in that again, and the Villerés, with sympathetic understanding, had moved him to another chamber, equipped with a "convent bed"—so-called because single beds were so rarely used, except by the religious. Even sisterless girls, before their marriage, shared their beds with the girls who visited them—and there was a great deal of visiting. Widows generally availed themselves of unmarried sisters or aunts, and widowers were apt to find almost any male member of the family quartered with them. But Pierre had managed to retain his detachment and his privacy at Upper Magnolia; both were important to him.

He had really been hopeful, when he left the rest of the family after dinner, that he might go to sleep, though it had never been his habit to nap in the daytime. But he was no sooner alone than all the subjects he had not wanted to discuss came crowding to the forefront of his consciousness. First was that burning question of supplies and transportation; if he had been given what he needed, Washington would have been occupied and Maryland freed within a fortnight after the Battle of Manassas—or so he had believed then and so he still firmly believed. But the Commissary General—still his *bête noire*—refused to heed his appeals, as did the members of the Confederate Congress whom he addressed. Then came that ridiculous rumor that he intended to run against Davis when the latter—so far, actually only a provisional President—became a candidate for permanent office in the forthcoming election. It was doubly unfortunate that this rumor had been started by some of Pierre's own

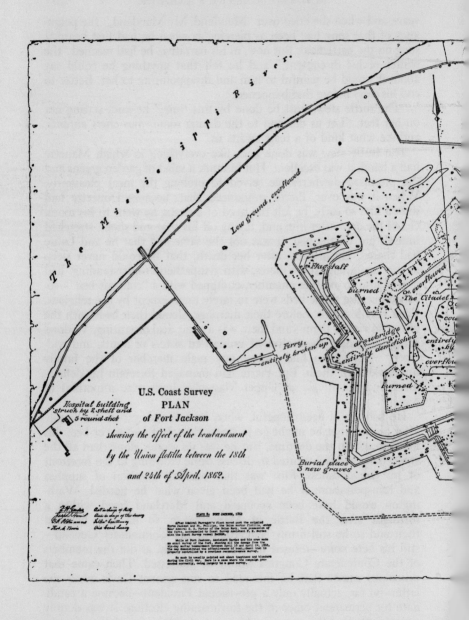

The Mississippi River.

Low ground overflowed

Flagstaff

burned

Oo. overflowed

The Citadel

cou

drawbridge
entirely demolished

entirely
by

overflow

Ferry,
entirely broken up

burned

Hospital building
struck by 2 shell and
5 round shot

U.S. Coast Survey
PLAN
of Fort Jackson

showing the effect of the bombardment

by the Union flotilla between the 18th

and 24th of April, 1862.

Burial place
3 new graves

J.H. Sands   Act in chg of Pty
Sub-Lieut.   Assis in chg of the survey
G.S. Otto un nd   Sub-Lieutenant
— Thos A. Nevin   Ass Coast Survey

PLATE 5: FORT JACKSON, 1862

After Admiral Farragut's fleet moved past the crippled
Forts Jackson and St. Phillips, the Union mortar flotilla, under
Rear Admiral D. D. Porter of the Union Navy, took possession of
the forts. Accompanied by Coast Survey Assistant F. H. Gerdes
with the Coast Survey vessel SACHEM.

While at Fort Jackson, Assistant Gerdes and his crew made
an exact survey of the fort, showing all the damage from the
six-day mortar bombardment between April 18 and April 24, 1862.
The map demonstrated the effectiveness of bombardment that is
properly controlled by a previous reconnaissance survey.

So much is usually pointed out about ineptness and blunders
during the Civil War. Here is a case where the campaign proceeded correctly, owing largely to a good survey.

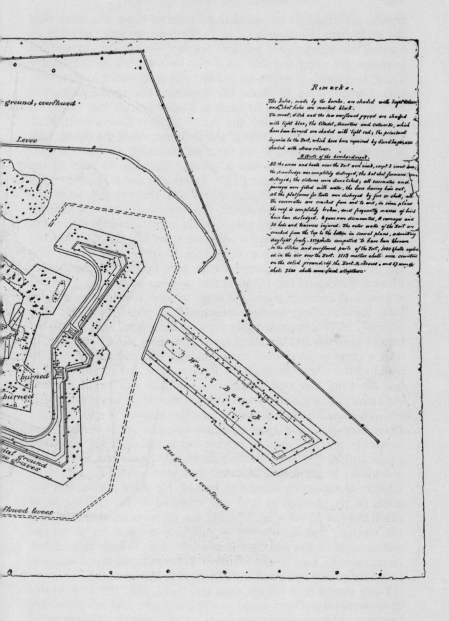

ground, overflowed.

Levee

burned

burned

ial ground
w graves

lowed levees

Water Battery

Low ground, overflowed

Remarks.

The holes, made by the bombs, are shaded with light brown and shot holes are marked black.

The moat, ditch and the low overflowed ground are shaded with light blue, the Citadel, Quarters and Culverts, which have been burned are shaded with light red; the principal injuries to the Fort, which have been repaired by Sand bags, are shaded with straw colour.

Effects of the bombardment.

All the scows and boats near the Fort are sunk, except 3 small ones; the drawbridge was completely destroyed, the hot shot furnace destroyed; the cisterns were demolished; all casemates and passages were filled with water, the lines having been cut, all the platforms for tents were destroyed by fire or shell, all the casemates are cracked from end to end; in some places the roof is completely broken, and frequently masses of brick have been dislodged. 8 guns were dismounted, 8 carriages and 30 beds and traverses injured. The outer walls of the Fort are cracked from the top to the bottom in several places, admitting daylight freely. 3173 shells computed to have been thrown in the ditches and overflowed parts of the Fort, 1030 shells exploded in the air over the Fort. 1113 mortar shell were counted on the solid ground of the Fort & Forces, and 27 mortar shot. 7500 shells were fired altogether.

friends, who thought he would make a better Chief Executive than the incumbent. Well, perhaps he might have, at that; but what he wanted was military, not political, prestige. As for rank, he and Joe Johnston got along together famously, *they* weren't having trouble about it—indeed, it would be a sorry sort who would have trouble with a small, quiet graybeard like Johnston, one of the pleasantest men in the world. When he came to Manassas from the Valley, his forces were suitably called the Army of the Shenandoah, while Pierre's were called the Army of the Potomac. After the battle, both commanders continued to use these names and it was not the fault of either one that there was a growing tendency to refer to the combined forces by the latter title. Practically, there were two corps in the same army and, though Pierre was, theoretically, under the command of Johnston, his senior, the junior had complete administrative powers over his own troops. So far as Johnston and Pierre were concerned, this arrangement worked out smoothly. But the President did not approve of it; he considered that it violated principles of military law, also that it impinged on his prerogatives. Correspondence between Richmond and Pierre, at first only exasperated, soon became acrimonious and then downright angry in tone. Benjamin, even more than the President, seemed determined to humiliate Pierre. The Secretary of War suggested that General Beauregard should read the laws of Congress and thereby discover that there was no provision for such a corps as he claimed to command. "You are *second* in command of the whole Army of the Potomac, not *first* in command of *half* the army," he wrote. To Pierre, the letter sounded as if it had been written to a schoolboy who had not learned his lesson thoroughly and was impudent to his teacher into the bargain. It was the more astonishing—and the more offensive—because, only a few short months earlier, Benjamin, in writing Pierre, had described himself as a poor civilian who knew nothing about military matters. Even Davis was willing to admit that Benjamin had gone beyond the bounds of courtesy in expressing himself as he had. He wrote a letter that was polite in its phraseology and was supposed to be soothing in its effect; but the gist of what he wrote was the same as what Benjamin had written: that there could be only one commander of the two concentrated armies and that it was Johnston. Wholly unmollified, Pierre answered that he and Johnston, between them, would work out a plan for unified command if that was what Davis wanted.

Pierre should have known, then and there, what the result of this letter would be. Davis could not tolerate the idea of permitting Johnston and Beauregard to work out a plan, amicably, between them.

He wanted to do all the planning himself and he wanted no interference while he was doing it. Manassas was too near Richmond for
his peace of mind—that is, if Pierre were at Manassas. The solution
of this problem was simple: Beauregard must be removed to a point
more distant. No doubt, he mused, Davis consulted the map to find
one sufficiently distant to suit his purposes. At all events, he settled
on the Western theater. Roger Pryor, a member of the Military
Affairs Committee, smilingly brought the message from the President: the situation in the West was critical. Beauregard's presence
would stimulate popular morale. He would serve under another
Johnston, Albert Sidney this time, and there was to be no question
that it was *under*. Albert Sidney Johnston was Departmental Commander in the West and Beauregard would command the left wing
of Johnston's forces in Kentucky, with headquarters at Columbus on
the Mississippi.

So now his unwelcome memories had brought him back to the
place where he had told Doucette there would be no more stories that
day and he decided that he did not want to talk about the war.
Heaven knew he did not want to think about it, either—not that
phase of it, at least. He was a sick man when he left Manassas—
physically sick as well as sick at heart. The winter was a severe one
and, whereas some of the hardier men enjoyed the comparative
novelty of snow, many of them contracted pneumonia and died.
Pierre's old plague, tonsillitis, took such a serious turn that his surgeon
insisted upon an operation. As in the case of many others pronounced
successful, the aftereffects of this one proved long and debilitating.
Pierre was not even satisfactorily convalescent when he began his
journey; and though he was warmly welcomed at every stop along the
way, nothing in the course of it corresponded to the ovations he had
received on earlier train trips. He went first to Bowling Green, where
Albert Sidney Johnston had his headquarters, and realized at once
that here was a man that he could respect and admire, even if he
were not so congenial a spirit as the more approachable Joe Johnston.
Albert Sidney was a handsome man, tall and well built; he had a fine
head and a fine carriage. His manner was grave, but uniformly courteous. His greeting left nothing to be desired.

Unfortunately, the same could not be said of the general situation.
The forces at Pierre's disposal, as revealed in immediate conference
and later inspection, were not anywhere nearly so large as he had been
led to believe before leaving Manassas. He could have augmented
them with volunteers, but there were not enough arms. (Pierre
thought bitterly of his early grievance against Davis when the Presi-

dent sent a "secret emissary" to England to buy ten thousand rifles. He himself could have easily got that many from Frazer and it was a hundred thousand that were needed, even then.) He had been promised that, if he required them, ten or twelve experienced officers from the Army of the Potomac would be sent to aid in organizing and disciplining his troops—in fact, he had made it a condition, if he accepted the transfer, these officers should come. Of course, he had also made it a condition that he should "return to the command of his own army in Virginia" as soon as it was possible to dispense with his services in the West—if practical, in time for the spring campaign; but it was soon quite evident that his services in the West would be needed considerably longer than he had anticipated. The day after he arrived at Bowling Green, Fort Henry on the Tennessee River was captured by Union naval forces, cooperating with a Federal army officer of whom Pierre had not heard very much since the Mexican War, except that he had failed at almost everything he ever attempted, and that frequently he drank more than he should. Unfortunately, this General—Ulysses S. Grant—now did seem to have a habit of staying with a job he intended to do until it was successfully finished; the next thing he did was to capture Fort Donelson on the Cumberland River. Though the Confederates had controlled the railroad from Bowling Green to Columbus, this was no longer useful to them, once Henry and Donelson had fallen. The two wings of the army were separated. If they attempted to act independently, they would almost inevitably be crushed. There was nothing for them to do but retire to a new line farther south.

Albert Sidney Johnston evacuated Bowling Green. Beauregard, who had never reached Columbus, ordered its evacuation by Lieutenant General Leonidas Polk, Episcopal Bishop of Louisiana. As the Confederate troops poured out, Union troops moved in. Nashville came next. Kentucky and Tennessee were lost, and lost without a battle.

An outcry arose against Johnston, a clamor for his removal. If he, like Beauregard, had been at odds with Davis, there was no question that it would have taken place, Pierre reflected bitterly. But Johnston and Davis were friends, and Davis took no action beyond urging Johnston to defend himself publicly, a course the General considered beneath his dignity. But though he declined to answer his critics, it was evident to Pierre that he suffered intensely under their attacks; he feared he had lost the confidence of his men. Both wings of the army had retreated to Corinth, Mississippi, where Beauregard was already encamped when Johnston reached there a month after the fall of Donelson. Albert Sidney Johnston urged Pierre to take over the command of the army while he devoted himself to the duties of Departmental Commander. Pierre declined, but agreed to draw up a plan for the organization of their forces and, as second-in-command, to supervise the task of organization. Johnston owed it to himself and the country not to take secondary place. One victory and all his critics would be silenced. After that, he could do as he pleased. Now that the two armies had met, now that there was at last concentration, they could, together, strike a mighty blow.

"I did give one wholly independent order, while I was waiting for you to arrive," Pierre had told Albert Sidney. "I reminded Southerners that, in times past, people had often sacrificed their church bells for the defense of liberty. I wasn't asking ours to do that—yet. But I called on all the planters to send their bells to the nearest railroad depot, subject to my order, to be melted into cannon for the defense of their property. I knew, in doing this, I was asking a great deal of them. I realized, for instance, how much the old plantation bell at Belle Pointe, put into place by Jacques Deslonde in 1792, means to all his descendants, not to mention the similar feeling about the bells at Contreras and Upper Magnolia. We always call them the voice of the plantation. But compliance to the order was immediate and universal. Go out in the country and listen. You won't hear a single bell."

"You seem to have touched a responsive chord, even if you have silenced the bells," Albert Sidney told him, making a mild jest. It was evident that he was touched and pleased by Pierre's refusal to assume command and, briefly, his somber face brightened. "Well, perhaps you're right, perhaps with you to help me. . . ."

Had this insistence that Albert Sidney should keep the command been another mistake, added to the many Pierre had made already? If Pierre had been in command from the promising beginning to the tragic end of the battle at Pittsburg Landing, twenty miles from Corinth, where the Federals were encamped, would the outcome have been any different? Would Shiloh still mean nothing but the name of a small Methodist Meeting House near there? Sometimes he allowed himself to think so. But when the choice was his to make, he was still smarting at the injustice of the accusation that he had tried to usurp the power of the first Johnston. How could he have risked such an accusation a second time? He would not allow himself to think of it now—of that or of anything else in connection with Shiloh. He had come to his room and lain down on his convent bed hoping to sleep, hoping to forget about the war. And instead, though he had not talked about it any more after he said he did not wish to do so, he had not been able to dismiss it from his mind for a single instant.

He sat up, put on his shoes, reached for his coat. Then, before he put it on, he went over to the washstand and bathed his face and hands. The cool water was refreshing. And perhaps it would be possible to get a cold drink downstairs, a really cold drink, not a beverage dependent on jangling napkin rings to give an illusion of one. But there was no one around, either in the drawing room or in the kitchen and, after calling once or twice without getting any answer, he concluded that Mme Villeré must still be taking a siesta, and that the other members of the family must have gone off on an excursion of some sort, a fishing trip perhaps. He did not resent their absence. He had made it plain that he wanted to be alone and they had taken him at his word, that was all. But in this brooding silence he was filled with sudden restlessness. True, he had intended to stay at Upper Magnolia several days. True, he had been made welcome, joyously received, abundantly fed, given the feeling that he was wanted. Yet, somehow, he felt impelled to get back to New Orleans. He went into the library, scribbled a brief note to his mother-in-law, thanking her for her never-failing hospitality, and another to Doucette, saying he would be back soon. Then he proceeded to the stables, still without meeting anyone, saddled his horse and rode slowly down the driveway, quickening his pace only after he reached the river road.

It was not until then that he recognized, and not without reluctance, the reason for his restlessness. He missed Simone, he wanted to see her again. She would be taken by surprise at his return, she would have nothing ready for him; but he did not need a real supper, after the big dinner he had eaten; he could always get a cup of coffee at the French Market—that is, if he still had a nickel in his pocket! Reassured on that score, he permitted himself to dwell on the pleasure Simone would show at seeing him again. He was sure it would be pleasure. They would sit for a while on the rear gallery, chatting of this and that, and then he would go back to his japanned boxes. There were several papers which had to do with the story he had told Doucette; he would get them out and set them aside to show her the next time he went to Upper Magnolia which, of course, should be soon. To be sure, she had said she did not care about those old papers, that all she wanted was a story in his own words. But she ought to see them. And meanwhile, he would show them to Simone, who would be really interested. He did not believe, after all, that Mme Cougot was seriously disturbed because he and Simone spent so much time together and found each other's company so congenial. He had allowed his imagination to run away with him the day before.

He returned his horse to Preval's, asked the boy who took it from him to enter the amount he owed on his account and walked the short distance from the stables to the house. He decided against the French Market, after all. He still had some of the wine Elodie had given him, and Simone was sure to have a bite in the house that would taste good with it. It was now quite dark and he was faintly surprised that she had left no light for him, until he remembered that, of course, she would not have done so, as she had not been expecting him back for several days. But usually there was one in the pantry which served as a kitchen, or somewhere else in the rear of the house, until later than this. Simone frequently prepared a *tisane* for her mother to drink before she settled down for the night, and sat for a few minutes on the rear gallery to enjoy the comparative coolness of the evening air. Momentarily he hesitated, wondering if a visit from him would be inopportune. Then he realized that, if the ladies had retired for the night, the lights would not be on in the front rooms, either. He mounted the steps, crossed the gallery, and called from the open doorway which led into the long hall.

"Simone! Madame Cougot! It's Pierre! I've returned sooner than I expected. Is it all right for me to come in?"

Another door opened, one at the front of the house, and Simone came swiftly toward him. She had not brought a candle and, with only the dim light that came from the room she had left, he could not see her clearly. But he instantly realized that something was wrong, very wrong indeed, even before he heard the stifled way in which she spoke.

"Oh, I'm so thankful you've come! *Maman* is worse, much worse! I'm afraid she's dying!"

"Steady there," he said, putting a reassuring hand under her elbow. "What makes you think so? Have you sent for a doctor?"

"Yes, I remembered what you said—that you believed Dr. Turpin would be glad to come at any time. So yesterday I sent Bette to get him, about the middle of the afternoon. That was when the change began. She didn't seem to be entirely unconscious, but she lay in a sort of stupor and I couldn't rouse her, except once in a while, and then only for a moment. Dr. Turpin came at once and he was very kind, just as you said he would be. But he told me that he couldn't find anything the matter with her, except that she didn't seem to have the will to live and was just gradually sinking. I said she'd seemed unusually cheerful and well just that morning, and this didn't seem to surprise him, either—it seems there's often a brief temporary improvement just before the end. He said he'd come back later and he did, only to say the same thing. He couldn't stay long, because there were people who needed him more, people he could do something for. He couldn't do anything for her. But his wife came and stayed all night, so that I wouldn't be alone—such a lovely lady! And they've both been back today. But, you see, there are so many sick people and I'm afraid it's just as he said—she's lost the will to live."

While Simone was talking, she and Pierre had gone down the corridor together and, as she sobbed out the last words, they came to the threshold of Mme Cougot's room. Pierre stepped inside and looked down at the sick woman. As Simone said, there had been a great and sudden change. Her slight form seemed to have shrunk to almost wraithlike proportions; her thin face, almost as white as her hair, had the pinched look of approaching death; and her hands, lying inert at her sides, had undergone that strange transformation Pierre had seen, more than once, when life had almost ebbed away. He sat down beside her, spoke her name, lifted one of the pallid hands and held it in his own, while Simone stood close to the bed, gazing down at her mother with a stricken face. Mme Cougot gave no sign that she was aware of their presence. Minutes passed and the ticking of the clock, which seemed to be getting louder and louder, was the only sound in the hushed room. Pierre shook his head and looked up at Simone.

"Charles said he'd be back?"

"Yes, as soon as he could."

"Then there's nothing we can do, I'm afraid, but wait for him. That is, unless he left some directions. . . ."

"No, I told you, he said there wasn't anything."

"Perhaps you'd better put a light on the front gallery. It's dark, going up all those steps."

"Yes, you're right."

She went out, placed a hurricane lamp near the entrance, left the front door ajar. Then she came back and seated herself, facing Pierre, beside her mother's bed. He tried to think of something he could say, but no consoling words came to him. The only comfort he could give her was that of his presence. He would stay there with her until the end and he did not believe that could be far off. And afterward . . . what would happen afterward? In spite of himself, his thoughts drifted off into the future. If he and Simone were left by themselves in this great shrouded house, what then? Could they help each other? Would they destroy each other? Should he leave her, go back to

Upper Magnolia, let her face the world alone, decline to face it himself? Or what. . . .

"Listen!" Simone whispered suddenly. He raised his head. Yes, certainly there was someone moving about at the foot of the stairway, as if uncertain whether to mount it or not. But Charles had done so before; there was no reason for him to hesitate. And certainly the hurricane lamp gave enough light to see by. Yet the uncertain movements went on.

"I'll go down," Pierre whispered. "Someone's lost his way, is trying to find out whether or not this is the right house. I'll set him straight."

"No, no! Wait a minute! Don't stir. Just wait."

The hesitating movements had stopped. Someone was coming up the steps, coming slowly, with curiously dragging footsteps, but getting steadily closer and closer to the top. And suddenly, unbelievably, the dying woman roused and sat up straight.

"Lance!" she cried. "Oh, Lance, my darling, you've come home after all!"

33

TODAY BEAUREGARD'S DECISION SEEMS AS RIGHT AS IT DID TO him on the evening of that hard-fought Sunday. He did not know, of course, of the new factor in the battle, the arrival of Buell's troops, that changed the entire situation. Nor, apparently, had he been apprised that the Federal division from Crump's Landing was approaching the field. But he did know that his own men were tired, hungry, and spiritless after thirteen hours of fighting, too exhausted even to cheer when told they had won a victory. He knew that many of the units were scattered, disorganized, and out of control and that the latest attacks had been feebly delivered. These things he had learned from the reports of his aides and other officers; some of them he had seen with his own eyes. As he rode over the rear area of the field he saw groups of men resting on their arms, too weary to move; he saw hordes of stragglers plundering the enemy camps. He saw also the sun going down. He wanted to get his army in hand before darkness. As a matter of fact, with the approach of night, as the reports of the brigade and regimental commanders show, many units were retiring from the line without orders. The withdrawal directive merely recognized an action partially in process of execution. Even with an early start, the disorganization of the Confederate forces was so great that some units did not reach their bivouac until eight o'clock. When all the elements in the situation are weighed, it seems obvious that Beauregard had no recourse but to assemble his army for another attempt the next day.

—T. Harry Williams, *P. G. T. Beauregard: Napoleon in Gray*
(Louisiana State University Press)

BEAUREGARD'S MYSTERY TRAIN

❦

SIMONE RUSHED FROM THE ROOM AND, THROUGH ITS OPEN DOOR, Pierre could see her fling wide the one leading from the corridor to the gallery and throw her arms around a tall boy who seized her in his and bent his head as she raised hers to cover his face with kisses, making small smothered sounds of unbelieving joy. Mme Cougot had not fallen back among her pillows after her sudden outcry; trembling with agitation, she continued to sit upright and call to her grandson. Pierre came still closer to her and leaned over to hold her.

"Try not to exhaust yourself like this," he said soothingly. "Be patient just a minute longer—they'll be here then." As he spoke, he rearranged her pillows so that they would support her better and eased her down against them. "There!" he said. "Isn't that better? You don't need to answer, I know it is. And here they are!"

He stepped swiftly back into a corner of the shadowy room. Instinctively, he longed to leave it, to let the two women and the long-lost boy share this sacred moment of reunion without the intrusion of any alien presence. But if he attempted to leave, he would run the risk of interrupting their rapture; in order to reach the door, he would have to pass near the bed. No matter how quietly he moved, a creaking board could betray him and thrust him upon their consciousness. He preferred not to take the chance.

The only light in the room came from the candle near the bed. Therefore, without being seen himself, Pierre could see the boy fling himself on his knees beside his grandmother and hold her close, while his mother stood near him, wiping away the tears of joy that streamed down her cheeks. The boy was murmuring indistinct words of love and happiness and, presently, he raised his hand and smoothed back the white hair from his grandmother's forehead as he kissed her face. Then he rose, motioned his mother to one of the chairs beside the bed and sat down himself in the other. Instantly his grandmother reached for the hand he had released and he clasped hers again, before turning to his mother and taking hers, too. While each clung to this tangible proof of his reality, he listened to them quietly and answered their first questions.

"What can I get for you, *cher?* Tell me quickly! I know you're famished."

"I'm not even hungry. I'm just off a packet—the *Leviathan*—that was topheavy with fine food. Take a good look at me, *maman!* Can't you see I'm not even thin? Tell *grand'mère.*"

"It's true," Simone said in a wondering voice. "He isn't thin—I mean, not too thin. Of course he's lean, the way a boy ought to be, but he's wiry—you must have felt how strong his arms are! . . . What were you doing on this packet? How did you happen to get aboard it in the first place?"

"I was lucky enough to get a job as mud clerk. And I got aboard it in the first place because Colonel Fielding borrowed a rig from one of his neighbors and drove me all the way from his plantation to Memphis. In the beginning, he didn't mean to drive me any farther than Pittsburg Landing, about twenty miles; but when he found I'd have to wait forever and a day to get a boat going down the Tennessee River to the Ohio, and then find one that was going down the Ohio to Cairo and so on to New Orleans, he drove me all the way to Memphis. He felt sure I could get a boat there right away and he was bound and determined to help me reach home as soon as possible."

"God bless him for that! But who is Colonel Fielding? Why should he be taking all that interest in you? Had you been in one of his units?"

"No, he'd been with Lee's army in Virginia. He never even saw me until after the war was over. But I'd been taken to his plantation, wounded, after the Battle of Shiloh and, later, I went back there again."

"Lance, I'm completely bewildered. You'll have to explain. How did you happen to be on his plantation at all? And why didn't you let us know where you were?"

"I did write, but it was impossible to get letters through."

"I think perhaps we're asking the poor boy too many questions, Simone. Even if he isn't hungry, he must be tired to death. We shouldn't be selfish just because we want so much to hear the whole story. Now that we know he's safe and well, now that he's been restored to us, surely we can wait until morning for that. He must get to bed. Thanks to the General, his room's all ready for him."

"*The General!* What General?"

This time, it was Lance who sprang up, startled and surprised.

Pierre stepped out of the shadows and came forward. He realized, as he did so, that Simone and her mother had completely forgotten he had been with them when the boy's footsteps sounded on the stairway outside and that, therefore, it had not occurred to them to wonder whether or not he was still in the room.

"Welcome home, Lance," he said, putting out his hand. "I'm just an outsider to whom your family has been most kind, taking me in when I didn't have any other place to go and letting me live in the quarters. I didn't mean to intrude or to eavesdrop. But your mother had sent for me because your grandmother didn't seem very well, so I was in the room when you arrived and it wasn't possible after that to leave without the risk of disturbing you. But now——"

While he was speaking, Lance stared at him in bewildered fascination. Pierre could see the look on the boy's tanned sensitive face change from one of incredulity to one of amazement and then to one of unmistakable hero-worship.

"Why it's—it can't be—it *is* Old Bory!" the boy stammered. Then he drew himself up sharply and saluted. "I—I beg your pardon, Sir. But I enlisted in the first place because I hoped some time I might serve under you and then I did for one day—at Shiloh! At least, until I was wounded late in the afternoon, when it was almost dark—"

"You're sure it was almost dark?" Pierre asked eagerly.

"Oh yes, Sir. It was dark enough to see the flashes of the guns."

Pierre drew a long breath. "Thank you, Lance," he said. "You don't know how much what you've told me means to me. I hope you'll tell me more tomorrow—everything you can remember about the battle. But your grandmother's right. You ought to go to bed now, as soon as you've had a few minutes to visit alone with her and your mother; you'll want to hear—and they'll want to tell you—what's been happening to them, too." He turned to Simone. "I'll walk around the corner and tell Dr. Turpin not to come back tonight after all," he said. "Your mother doesn't need a doctor any more than I do. Then, when I've given him and his wife the good news, I'll turn in myself. But if I may, I'll join you in the morning to hear more of it."

"But not until you send for me," he added mentally and, during the night, he said the same thing to himself over and over again. He would not intrude upon this reunited family; they must be left to themselves until he was sure that an outsider would be welcome in their midst. However, he had underestimated the tremendous pride and joy which Lance felt in the knowledge that his hero and he were actually members of the same household. The boy surprised Pierre, just as Doucette had done the previous morning at Upper Magnolia, by coming to his room before he was fully awake; and Lance had further taken it upon himself to bring the General's morning coffee.

"Sir, *grand'mère's* perfectly willing to have me carry her out on the rear gallery," he said. "She doesn't weigh anything at all; I can manage as easily as if she were a baby. So we can all have breakfast together. I was told I could have anything I wanted off the *Leviathan* and I've already been down to the wharf and laid in a stock of provisions. *Maman* says it's years since she's seen so much food all at once. Well, we'll have a big breakfast and afterward I'll tell all of you what happened to me—if that's agreeable to you, Sir."

It was, of course, more than agreeable. From the moment Pierre heard those magic words, ". . . late in the afternoon when it was almost dark," and had thereby learned what he most wanted to know —that, unquestionably, the attack at Shiloh was not called off too soon—he had been almost beside himself with impatience to hear the story of the battle, as a drummer boy would tell it.

The breakfast, as Lance had predicted, was an enormous one. The amount of food he had brought up from the *Leviathan* was staggering, and Simone had done full justice to the preparation of as large a part of it as they could possibly eat at one time. Normally, they would have lingered over such a delicious and pleasant meal indefinitely. But it was only a little over an hour after they began that Lance rose, in response to his mother's pleading look, and helped her to clear the table and take the dishes to the pantry. Then, seating himself between her and his grandmother and facing Pierre, he began his story.

"I was drummer in the Orleans Guard Battalion— your company, General, the one you joined as a private. I suppose you know that, every morning after you left New Orleans, the color sergeant answered, 'Absent on duty,' when your name was called on the roll."

Pierre smiled. "My wife wrote me about that when I was in Charleston and I've heard it from others since. . . . So you were in the Orleans Guard Battalion, and your regiment was—?"

"The Crescent Regiment, under Colonel Marshal J. Brown, Pond's Brigade of Ruggles' division in General Bragg's Corps. You remember, Sir, what a great fight the Yankees put up until General Ruggles massed all those guns—I saw you, Sir, with General Ruggles—there must have been a hundred cannon."

"Sixty-two, Lance," interrupted Pierre.

"The word had just reached us that General Albert Sidney Johnston had been killed when General Ruggles opened with all his guns and the Yankees began to wilt at last. Then there was a charge—I sounded

the charge on my drum and rushed forward with the men who captured a Yankee general and a lot of soldiers."

"That was General Prentiss, Lance," put in Pierre.

"That's right, Sir, I remember his name now. Some of our men
rounded up the prisoners, but the rest moved forward, pressing mighty
close on the retreating Yankees. We were all tired, Sir, we'd been
fighting the whole day, with no let-up. And it was getting late by now.
The dusk was falling, but our pursuit continued. Then it happened
to me—about twenty-five paces from a tree stump. A Yankee soldier
lay behind it, his rifle resting on the stump and aimed right at me.
Then the gun went off and I felt a red-hot poker in my thigh—my
right thigh, the same leg I broke, *maman*, when I was a boy. I fell
down, bleeding a lot and the pain was awful. There was noise and
shouting and cursing, and one man stepped on me, not meaning to,
of course; he just didn't see me on the ground there and the pain of
that tread is the last thing I remember. When I came to again it was
night and I heard a Negro saying, 'Dis here gots life lef' in de body,
hit warm.' Then he lifted me in his arms like nothing. I remember,
in a sleepy kind of way, about how hard the muscles in his arms felt
when they touched me.

"I don't know what direction the man who was carrying me took
while he was walking. I was asleep or unconscious most of the time
and when I woke up, I only realized that my wound was bound up
and that my rescuer was still walking. Then we were on a road and a
wagon was there, with another Negro on the driver's seat and straw in
the wagon bed. The Negro who had been carrying me laid me down
and the next time I came to there was another man beside me, who
was making bubbling noises, and I heard my rescuer say to the driver,
'Massa Johnny ain' got no chance, shot in de throat like he is. But
maybe dis other one, shot in de thigh with no bones broke can make
hit.' By and by the bubbling noise stopped and in a foggy way I knew
that whoever was in the wagon with me had died."

"Did you ever find out who it was?"

"Yes, it was Pruitt Atwood Fielding, III. The Negroes buried him
in a locust grove where there were other graves; it was a family burying ground on the Fielding plantation not far from the battlefield. I
saw his tomb later on. I'm really not telling this the way I should
because some of these things I didn't find out for so long. It wasn't
just that I was out of my head and sick with fever, though I most
certainly was all of that, but even after that cleared up, I couldn't
talk to these Negroes because they didn't know any French and I

didn't know enough of their kind of English to make myself understood."

"There!" Simone said impulsively, turning to her mother. "Isn't that what the General said all along—that the reason for some of the delay was because Lance couldn't explain to people? You remember, *cher*, I warned you over and over again, if you wouldn't make more of an effort to learn English—"

"Yes, *maman*, I remember. Do you want to scold me again now or do you want me to go on with my story?" he added jestingly.

"Oh, of course I want you to go on with your story!"

"Well, it took at least a month, what with my delirium and everything, before we got so we could say even the simplest things to each other and a good deal longer before we could talk back and forth in sentences. But I will say this: no one, not even you, could have been more kind and gentle than those Negroes were in trying to take care of me all the time I couldn't walk. The bleeding stopped and I knew I didn't have any broken bones, but the wound in the thigh was infected and, for a while, it was pretty bad. The girl they called Sis Charlie—I never found out her real name—got me clean straw for my pallet every day in the world and her mother, Pollynaise, made me some nightshirts out of strips of cloth she found somewhere and pieced together. With the help of Herky—the one who carried me off the battlefield in his arms—and his brother Lige—the one who drove the wagon they'd borrowed—the women hid me in the loft of their cabin, because Yankee patrols kept coming by and these Negroes had made up their minds that, even if they hadn't been able to save their young master, they were going to save me. There must have been a good many times when they thought it would have been better if I had been the one to die instead of Johnny, but not for one minute did they ever let on by so much as a look that this was the way they felt about it."

"How did they happen to find you in the first place?"

"They came out by Shiloh, lighting their way with a piece of pitch pine they used for a torch, because they thought that's where Johnny had been fighting. Of course, they hoped all the time they wouldn't find him, because that might mean he was still safe. But they did, like I said, with a Minié ball through his throat and it was while they were looking for him that they came across me and discovered I was still living."

"Were these Negroes the only people there were on the plantation?"

"Yes, the ones I've already told you about and two or three others who were kind and helpful, too. They'd been left to look after things. When we could understand each other, they explained to me that Colonel Fielding had gone off to Virginia long before this. Then, when the Yankees came into Tennessee, Captain Fielding—that is, their Master Johnny—had joined the Army, too, after insisting that his mother and aunt and two young sisters should go and stay with their kinfolk in Memphis. They got away just in time—it wasn't more than a week or so after that that the Yankees came and pillaged the place, but didn't burn it. They didn't find the silver because the Negroes had buried that in the woods, and they had managed to hide some of the linen and furniture and china in lofts like the one where I slept, and even some bottles from the wine cellar. But there wasn't an animal left on the place, except for one cow that strayed off somewhere, that the Yankees didn't take time to look for, and some razorback hogs in the woods that they couldn't catch."

"So at least you had milk and some meat?"

"Yes, and corn and turnips and sweet potatoes had already been planted, so we had those. And Herky and Lige caught fish and we could always pick a mess of greens down in the creek bottom until cold weather came. Pollynaise would boil them to take out the poison, as she called it, and catfish and pot likker don't make bad eating. In the fall, we trapped rabbits in snares and killed squirrels and birds with slingshots. We never went hungry.

"By fall, I could move around fairly easily and then Herky made me a hideout in the woods, so that I wouldn't have to climb up into the loft every time a patrol came around. He and the others had kind of adopted me. It didn't seem to occur to them that I was itching to rejoin the Army. But of course I was and I meant to do it, if I could only find out where it was, and I tried to explain this to him. When he understood what I was driving at, Herky warned me that if I ventured off the plantation I would be picked up, sure, because Yankees were all over the state. But I was bound to get back to the Orleans Guards, or what was left of them, Sir, and so one day I started out.

"I had no idea which way to go, so I just took a chance and walked westward. I hadn't gone but a day before I realized that that was wrong, because all I saw were Yankees. I had a little food with me and I slept in the woods, or abandoned cabins. I suppose I must have wandered around for a couple of weeks before I got an old Memphis *Appeal*—it was a month old, or more—which said that General Bragg's army was at Murfreesboro, Tennessee, and so I headed for there. But I never reached our army. A Yankee patrol came on me one morning before I woke up and took me for a straggler. They roused me roughly and asked me questions about where the Confederate Army was. They wouldn't believe me when I told them I was looking for the army, too. They took me prisoner and after a few weeks I was sent to a Yankee prison at Camp Douglas in Chicago.

"For two years I was a prisoner—and *maman*, you can't know what that means, and I don't want to talk about it, but somehow I survived the cold and the exposure and prison food until the war was over. When I was released last April, I—"

"But Lance, why didn't you write, why didn't you let us know where you were? *Grand'mère* and I were beyond ourselves with grief, worrying over you—but *grand'mère* always said you'd come back."

"But, *maman*, I did write. I turned my letters over to the prison authorities, who assured me they would be delivered. They must have gone astray or got lost. I even tried sending several to the Louisiana Relief Committee in Mobile. One of the Alabama prisoners got letters from home that told him about this. But when I didn't hear from you, I thought you and *grand'mère* had left New Orleans after the Yankees came and, of course, I had no idea where you would have gone next. . . . Well, to continue, when I got out, I had no money, so I started walking home. When I was crossing Tennessee, I was famished and so tired, I decided to go to the Fielding place and get some food from Herky and some sleep in the loft where I'd hidden from the Yankees.

"When I got there, Herky and the others were so delighted to see me and raised so much noise that Colonel Fielding and his family came out to see what the fuss was about. They had all come back to the plantation—his wife and the maiden lady who was his sister and the two young ladies, one of them with a husband and a new baby. Herky told them about me in his way and I told them in mine and right away they invited me to come and stay at the Big House with them until they could manage to send me to Memphis or some other port on the river and in that way get a boat for New Orleans. They had the guest room readied for me and a place laid for me at the dinner table, which looked beautiful with all the china and silver Herky had saved for them. And after dinner, they took me out to look at their Johnny's grave, which they kept decorated with flowers. The Colonel walked back and forth in the burying ground, throwing out his shoulders as if he were proud, but with his lips twitching under his mustache and his steps slow and dragging. And his wife was crying and so, of course, were Miss Selena, the maiden lady, and the

young ladies. And then Mrs. Fielding straightened up and said if they
felt that way about their boy, think how my mother must feel not
even knowing whether I was dead or alive for more than three years.
And that was when the Colonel borrowed a rig and a mule team
from one of the other planters and we drove to Pittsburg Landing."

⇜§ 34 §⇝

. . . AT 3:40 A.M. FORT JACKSON'S WATER BATTERY "THUN-
dered its greeting to the enemy."

Immediately, Fort Jackson and Fort St. Philip opened up
with roaring salvos, and Farragut's ships, their guns silent up
to now, responded with broadsides, the flashes of their guns
lighting up the river luridly and revealing more distinctly the
outlines of the attacking warships. The awesome grandeur of
the scene was a vivid memory of Captain Robertson:

> I do not believe there ever was a grander spectacle wit-
> nessed before in the world than that displayed during the
> great artillery duel which then followed. The mortar-
> shells shot upward from the mortar boats, rushed to the
> apexes of their flight, flashing the lights of their fuses as
> they revolved, paused an instant, and then descended
> upon our works like hundreds of meteors, or burst in
> mid-air, hurling their jagged fragments in every direction.
> The guns on both sides kept up a continual roar for
> nearly an hour, without a moment's intermission, and
> produced a shimmering illumination, which, though
> beautiful and grand, was illusive in its effect upon the
> eye, and made it impossible to judge accurately of the
> distance of the moving vessels from us; and this fact,
> taken in connection with their rapid and constant change
> of positions as they speeded up the river rendered it very
> difficult to hit them with our projectiles. . . .

As the battle reached its peak, Porter's mortar flotilla delivered a furious fire, filling the starlit sky with deadly shooting stars and little comets of destruction. But despite the

withering bombardment of the bummers, Fort Jackson's guns laid down a frightful barrage through which the fleet had to pass and Fort St. Philip joined valiantly in creating the fiery gantlet for Farragut to run. One of General Butler's officers, viewing the attack from a distance, wrote: "Combine all that you have heard of thunder, add to it all that you have ever seen of lightning, and you have, perhaps, a conception of the scene. . . ." An officer on the *Hartford* thought "it was like the breaking up of the universe with the moon and all the stars bursting in our midst." To Farragut himself "it was as if the artillery of heaven were playing upon the earth."

The flag officer, having climbed to the *Hartford*'s port mizzen to see above the smoke the progress of the battle, stood with his feet on the ratline and his back against the shrouds. Oblivious to the shells bursting around him, Farragut "stood there as cool and undisturbed as if leaning against a mantel in his own home." It had taken twenty-five minutes for the *Hartford* to get into position opposite Fort Jackson, during which time, by the flag officer's order, it had held its fire. But now it opened up, first with its bow guns, and then it engaged Fort Jackson with its port battery. A galling fire from Fort St. Philip sent shots crashing into the hull and spars and whistling through the rigging.

At first the forts fired high, but soon shot, shell, grape, and canister were bursting all around the *Hartford*. A shell struck the mainmast on a line where the flag officer stood in the mizzen rigging. Signal Officer Osbon hurried to Farragut and begged him to come down. Farragut brushed aside the plea.

"We can't afford to lose you, Flag Officer," argued Osbon. "They'll get you up here, sure."

Osbon had loaned Farragut a pair of small opera glasses, which were handier up there in the rigging than the flag officer's binoculars. So Osbon took another tack.

"Flag Officer, they'll break my opera glasses if you stay up here."

Farragut held out the opera glasses to Osbon, who exclaimed: "Oh, damn the glasses! It's you we want. Come down!"

In a few moments Farragut agreed to leave the perilous position, and hardly had he reached the deck again when a shell exploded and cut away much of the rigging where he had stood.

The *Hartford* steamed on steadily, but so thick was the smoke it was difficult to steer. At 4:10 A.M., the flagship was between the forts, caught up in an action at once general and terrible. Thicker and faster came shot and shell from the forts, while the *Hartford* answered with grape, canister, and shrapnel, which swept the parapets of Fort Jackson. Signal Officer Osbon painted a graphic picture of the action:

It is quite out of the question to give any idea of the fire at this time, or of the night picture we made there in the midst of flame and smoke and iron hail . . . A shell burst on our deck . . . I ran forward to see what damage had been done, when the wind of another shell carried away my cap . . . We were struck now on all sides. A shell entered our starboard beam, cut our cable, wrecked our armory and exploded at the main hatch, killing one man instantly, and wounding several others. Another entered the muzzle of a gun, breaking the lip and killing the sponger who was in the act of "ramming home." A third entered the boatswain's room destroying everything in its path, and exploding, killed a colored servant who was passing powder.

Death and destruction seemed everywhere. Men's faces were covered with powder—blacked and daubed with blood. They had become like a lot of demons in a wild inferno, working fiercely at the business of death.

—Charles L. Dufour, *The Night the War Was Lost*
Copyright © 1960 by Charles L. Dufour
Reprinted by permission of Doubleday & Co., Inc.

"The drums, the drums, the busy, busy drums,
The drums, the drums, the rattling, battling drums
The drums, the drums, the merry, merry drums."

THAT WAS THE SILLY REFRAIN EVERYONE HAD BEEN SINGING IN THE streets of New Orleans at the beginning of the Mexican War when Pierre had been straining to get into action. He had not thought of it for years. It must have been the association with Lance that brought it back to his mind. But he wished it would not ride him so. It was one thing to think of it suddenly and quite another to keep on thinking of it. That was tiresome, that was absurd; that was the sort of thing you did when you were in your dotage or delirious. Well, he was getting more and more conscious of his age; but he was not in his dotage yet by any means. Was it possible that he was a little off his head? It did not seem likely. Nevertheless—

Pierre had not been ill, really ill, in a long while and at first he had not recognized his malaise as indicating the onset of illness. A persistent headache, a disinclination to eat, a sore throat, a slight intermittent pain—what did these amount to? After all, he had been through a considerable emotional upheaval, what with the shock Mme Cougot had given him by the sudden collapse that had brought her to death's door, with the surprise of Lance's well-nigh miraculous return, with his grandmother's equally miraculous recovery and then with the sustained excitement of visualizing the Battle of Shiloh through the boy's eyes. For several nights, he had been keyed to such a high pitch that he had slept little, if at all; now the reaction had set in and he was exhausted. Possibly he had a fever. It was hard to tell, with the weather so unmercifully hot, how much discomfort was due to the surrounding temperature and how much to body heat. It was only when he became so dizzy, on attempting to get up in the morning, that the room seemed to be rocking around him that he realized he was a sick man. He lay down again and, without at-

tempting to call for help, succumbed to the waves of unconscious-
ness that swept over him.

As usual, Lance had brought him his early-morning coffee and had
then gone out, also as usual, looking for a job, and it was Lance who
found him several hours later, in a condition so alarming both to the
boy and to his mother, whom he quickly called to join him at the
General's bedside, that he next tore around the corner to Dr. Turpin's
house and returned, also at top speed, bringing the harassed physician
with him. Though he had accompanied Lance willingly enough, he
had at first been inclined to make light of the boy's fears; his snap
judgment had been much like Pierre's: too much excitement, too
little sleep, probably too little food, certainly too much exposure to
the burning sun, as the discouraged applicant for work went tramping
through the scorching streets. Complete quiet, nourishing broths and
jellies, the assurance that he was wanted and needed in the world and
the patient would be all right again. But when he took Pierre's rapid
pulse and looked searchingly down at the dark face that was so
flushed against the white pillow, he quickly revised his opinion.

"The General will need careful nursing, day and night," he told
Simone and Lance, who were standing beside him, anxiously awaiting his verdict. "I'll send my wife over. She's very experienced now,
she'll be able to help you and tell you what to do when she isn't here.
Of course, she can't stay all the time. But you may depend on her to
stay as much as possible. And you may depend on me to come frequently without being summoned. That doesn't mean you can't also
send for me if there's any radical change, but I don't believe there
will be. I think the General's high fever will make him drowsy a good
deal of the time and, possibly, delirious during the intervals when he's
awake. He may keep confusing the past with the present. If that happens, don't be alarmed. Just give him the medicine that I'm putting
on the mantelpiece with full directions; it will quiet him. I've already
given him something that ought to reduce his fever and left a second
dose, handy by the bed, for you to give him the first time he really
rouses. But don't try to wake him. The quieter he can be kept, the
better."

Dimly, Pierre was aware that Charles Turpin, slim and dapper as
ever and, of course, still wearing a neat white tie, was in the room—he
was also dimly aware of what Charles was saying, but the physician's
voice seemed to come from a great distance, and the sick man could
not be sure that he heard every word correctly; but he was by no
means oblivious of all that was going on. He might have said so,
except that it seemed to involve unnecessary effort, possibly even argu-

ment. Nothing would be so harassing as that, nothing so welcome as quietude.

Personally, he did not believe that he became delirious. But it was true that in the periods of wakefulness and semi-wakefulness that came between the blessed periods of oblivion, he seemed to be hearing drums and reliving another illness, the one that had already been on him at Shiloh, but to which he had not succumbed until afterward, though his detractors told a different story. They insisted that he had been lying in his tent, at the rear, throughout the engagement. Actually, he had slept in an ambulance on that fateful Saturday night before the battle and, in the morning, when the doctors took his pulse and found it to be a hundred, they advised him to stay in bed. But he had refused, he had been in the field all day. Lance, who had sounded the charge on his drum, Lance had seen him there with General Ruggles, Lance had not been wounded until "first evening" and it was after this that he, Pierre, had given the order for the fighting to stop. Perhaps it was a mistake, he thought with hindsight; but at the time he believed it was the right thing to do. His men had been fighting for more than twelve hours; those who had survived were exhausted and the slaughter had been terrific. He should have found some way to put new heart into them, he should have permitted the slaughter to go on; he should also have disregarded the gathering darkness. However, he had acted in accordance with his best judgment, and if his judgment in this instance had been faulty, so had that of greater men than he under similar circumstances. When he settled down to the actual writing of his book, the book for which he had been laying the groundwork when he was taken ill —ill this time—he was going to inscribe on its flyleaf a quotation from his idol, Napoleon: *Only those generals who have never commanded armies in the field have not committed errors.*

He had spent the night of Sunday, April sixth, in the tent Sherman had occupied the night before. He felt increasingly ill, but not so ill that he could not busy himself by conferring with his corps commanders regarding plans to reorganize his army for a morning attack. All the high-ranking officers whom he called into council believed that victory was already within their grasp—as he did. But there was one whom he had not summoned to his tent who was less confident—Colonel Nathan Bedford Forrest, a cavalry officer whose remarkable qualities had not yet been fully recognized either by Pierre or by much of anyone else. Forrest had sent some of his men, dressed in captured Federal coats, in through the enemy lines, and they had reported that heavy reinforcements were arriving; then he himself had ridden to the riverbank, and seen that thousands of troops were being ferried across the Tennessee at Pittsburg Landing. He reported to General Hardee, presented his information, and advised either an immediate attack or an immediate withdrawal; otherwise, he insisted vehemently, the Confederates would be "whipped like hell." Hardee did not think it would come to that—then or ever. He suggested that Colonel Forrest should report directly to General Beauregard and the cavalry officer attempted to do so. But he could not locate Beauregard's headquarters and, rather than lose time, he reported again to Hardee, who temperately advised him to "keep a vigilant watch."

Unfortunately, a good deal more than a vigilant watch was needed. General Buell's complete force had come up and General Lew Wallace's also. By the time Grant had all the Yankee reinforcements ready for action, the Confederates were outnumbered two to one. Pierre recalled that he could muster no more than twenty thousand troops when the fighting was renewed Monday morning. But this was not the worst of it. The exhausted men had not been able to rally from the shock of the surprise attack which had come when they thought victory was already in their grasp. They were not fighting like wildcats any more. In fact, some units were not fighting at all; they were simply disintegrating. Even the drummer boys had lost their zest. Twice Pierre seized the colors of faltering regiments and led them forward. He silenced protests that he was risking his life by shouting, "The order now is follow, not go!" and the tired troops cheered and obeyed. But fatigue and faintness overcame him; with the greatest difficulty he managed to keep his seat in the saddle, but he had to yield the flag to another standard-bearer. Between waves of vertigo, he heard himself telling Colonel Gordon that, in half an hour, he would retire. He rode back to Corinth, still upright in his saddle. It was after this that he collapsed.

This was as vivid to Pierre as the first day of the battle, the way that nice drummer boy—Lance, was that his name?—had described it before Pierre fell ill—ill this time. And it was while he was lying helpless and feverish in Corinth, after the retreat from Shiloh, that he heard from his old friend Mansfield Lovell, in command at New Orleans, that Farragut's Union fleet had passed Fort St. Philip and Fort Jackson.

The news caused him almost unbearable grief, but it came as no surprise; it was simply the fulfillment of sad prophecies which he had made over and over again, ever since he had first been assigned, as a young lieutenant, to the defense of these forts; and he had reiterated everything he had said before when General Lovell, shortly after his appointment to the command at New Orleans, had paid Pierre the compliment of stopping at Centerville on his way from New York to Louisiana, in the early autumn of '61: steam vessels could run past Fort Jackson and Fort St. Philip, unless the river were obstructed in a way that would hold enemy ships under the fire of the forts for a considerable time. Lovell, an experienced artillerist, had agreed with him. In the days of sailing vessels, these were an easy mark for gunners in the forts, as had been proved in the War of 1812. The bend in the river made it necessary for them to tack against a four-mile current and this increased their vulnerability. But steam-powered gunboats were something else again. The two friends had parted in mournful recognition of this fact, with the expressed hope that their superiors in rank, though not in experience, could be made to realize this.

After his arrival in New Orleans, Lovell had written Pierre a letter which revealed further discouragement on this score and puzzlement on another. It quoted a communication from the President which refused Lovell's request for command over the Confederate naval vessels maintained at the Port of New Orleans and its vicinity. Lovell had argued that a unified command was essential for the defense of the South's greatest city, but had been informed by Davis that the purposes for which the fleet was sent there or removed from there were transmitted to a different department with which Lovell had no direct communication. He asked Pierre to explain, if possible, how he could be responsible for part of the defenses and not for all of them. The question troubled him greatly and Pierre shared his anxiety. The one good piece of news Lovell had to impart was that, according to their mutual friend Wharton, the chain barrier across the Mississippi at Jackson and St. Philip was already in place. Lovell meant very soon to go and see for himself.

His next letter dealt with his first visits to various forts. Livingston and several others, he reported, were "so dilapidated in some places that they were crumbling of their own weight." He was favorably impressed with what Colonel J. K. Duncan had done to put them in a state of preparation for attack, but still found the means necessary to make a proper defense sadly lacking. The ammunition was inferior, there was a shortage of powder, and there were numerous other deficiencies. Moreover, Wharton's report had been slightly too optimistic; the installation of the all-important river obstructions was only just beginning.

These letters had come in during the latter part of '61. At about the same time, two new ironclads, the *Mississippi* and the *Louisiana*—the most powerful warships in the world—furnished the main topic. Two floating batteries, the *New Orleans* and the *Memphis,* constructed from drydocks, were being fitted out with twenty and eighteen guns respectively. Wharton gave, as his considered opinion, that "She [the *New Orleans*] and her consort will be amply sufficient to keep every Lincolnite ship out of our river." The confidence Pierre's old friend expressed was general, but he did not share it and he felt sure Lovell did not, either.

With the new year, not only Lovell's letters, but reports from the daily press intensified Pierre's anxiety: the pinch of the blockade was being felt more and more by the people of New Orleans; progress on the warships was being slowed by strikes and time was of the essence, for the Federals were mounting a tremendous fleet to attack New Orleans under David Glasgow Farragut and his foster-brother David Dixon Porter. Pierre read with increasing concern an article printed on January 29 in the *Picayune,* taken from the *Richmond Examiner* which, in turn, quoted the Washington *Star:*

> It is now publicly announced that Commander Farragut is to command the great expedition that is to operate on the western part of the gulf. It may be stated that the fleet will consist of the *Richmond, Pensacola,* and other large steam frigates, a great number of gunboats, and some twenty or thirty vessels carrying mortars and thirty-two pounders. The opinion is expressed in naval circles that few fortified places can hold out against such an expedition.

The opinion quoted in the final sentence of this dispatch was by no means confined to naval circles; it was very general and all too well founded. Pierre had no delusions on this score. St. Philip and Jackson were not among the few which might hold out, unless the barrier between them were securely in place, unless they were reinforced and unless the new ironclads were ready for action. None of this was the case when another disturbing report reached him: according to a ship's captain just arrived from Mississippi Sound, sixty-five Union naval vessels had actually reached Ship Island. It had been bad enough to know that a Federal flotilla was actually being readied; it was infinitely worse to know that one was only a dozen miles off the Mississippi coast. The companion rumor that Federal troops were already landing at Terre-aux-Boeufs was, of course, fantastic; the *True Delta* was quite right in warning its readers that they should not be too easily disposed toward panic. Just the same, while telling himself this, Pierre could not entirely dismiss from his mind the consciousness that Terre-aux-Boeufs was only ten miles below Chalmette, where Andrew Jackson had beaten the British, that it was his own countryside, where Contreras and Toutant and Kenilworth were located, and occupied by kinsfolk, close friends and faithful slaves; while on the other side of the river, almost directly opposite, were Fort Léon, Point Beca and Upper Magnolia; and not only was Doucette at Upper Magnolia with her Villeré grandparents, but Caroline frequently visited there, too, for she was always made welcome. Henri, thank God, was still at the Charleston Military Academy, as safe as anyone could be in these troublous times. Was he really safe? Pierre thought of those cadets at Chapultepec, the niños héroes, six killed, many wounded, one hundred prisoners. Was there any assurance that the same thing which had happened in Mexico City might not happen in Charleston? And René, a lieutenant in the First South Carolina Battalion of Light Artillery, was not yet in the theater of active warfare, but who could say that he might not be any moment now? At eighteen and twenty, they were already reckoned as men, according to the sad necessities of the day; they must take their chances, like other men, and he, their father, must be prepared to have them. But Doucette was a child, a girl child—his one ewe lamb, as Laure had been her parents'; Caroline was a young woman in frail health, his dearly beloved wife; and the Villerés were as prematurely aged as the boys were prematurely adult. Try as he would to tell himself that his fears for the plantations were groundless, Pierre's heart contracted.

Strangely enough, it was another rumor, even more fantastic, which gave him relief from the one which had so disquieted him. According to the story which had just reached him, he had been killed and his remains had been secretly brought to the old cemetery, San Bernardo de Nuevo Galvez in Terre-aux-Boeufs, for burial, a rite attended by members of his family and a few trusted friends. This really was in the same class as the story of the headless horse on which he triumphantly led charges at Manassas, the one about the reincarnation of Napoleon and the later report that he had been captured between Bowling Green and Columbus! He had laughed at the True Delta's recommendation that those who started the "foolish and mischievous rumor" of the capture "and similar false statements should have their ears nailed to the most conspicuous telegraph posts until they are made to repent the falsehoods they, with cruel indifference to the feeling of families, put into general circulation." Now he laughed again as he read the copy of the New York Tribune, which had

somehow been smuggled through the lines, and copies of correspondence between Lovell and Benjamin, which the former had sent
him. But his merriment did not last; he was too ill to take sustained
pleasure in such a gruesome jest. At first the reference to the old
cemetery merely recalled the day when he and Laure had gone there
together and sat quietly and contentedly talking of many things,
while René and Henri, still small boys, played happily among the
tombs, chasing the brilliant butterflies which they did not recognize
as symbols of immortality. This was a memory of nostalgia rather
than of sadness. But presently the report set Pierre thinking of all
those near and dear to him who *were* entombed in the old cemetery,
whose burials he had attended there, whose graves he had decorated
at *Toussaint*—his grandparents, his parents and lastly Laure, the
sweet spirit who had descended from heaven and returned there. He
did not doubt that they were all waiting to welcome him. Perhaps
it would have been better if the rumor were true, if he could be at
peace, as they were. But no, there was still victory ahead. There was
still Caroline alive. He must get well, he must press on. . . .

Before he succeeded in doing either came the news—no rumor this
time but terrible truth—that Farragut's entire fleet had crossed the
Mississippi bar and was anchored, poised for attack, at the head of
the passes; and that the same day—March 15—martial law was proclaimed in New Orleans.

This could mean only one thing: the situation was critical. So
why, in heaven's name, had the crossing of the bar not been challenged by the Confederates? Work on the *Louisiana* and the *Mississippi* was still lagging; had it not occurred to President Davis and
Secretary of the Navy Mallory that their one strategy should be to
upset Farragut's timetable, *not* to order navy vessels *up* the river?
Nothing was afloat at New Orleans except six river-defense vessels
that Lovell had managed to detain there; every effort of the Union
fleet from now on would be directed toward crashing the barrier in
the river and passing the blazing guns in the forts themselves. On the
fifteenth of April Pierre read, with apprehension, about the initial
exchange of shots which had taken place two days earlier between
Fort Jackson and several of Farragut's vessels, sent out on a range-
finding expedition; and this apprehension changed to deep anxiety as
the reports of the Federal mortar bombardment, which began early in
the morning of Good Friday, April 18, next reached him.

In the midst of the general panic, Lovell thought of him and
wrote to him: "The enemy has forty vessels just below Fort Jackson.
If we can manage to obstruct the river, so as to retain them thirty

minutes under our fire, I think we can cripple the fleet." Pierre recalled McGowan's test with the *Star of the West* which demonstrated that steam vessels could pass beyond the range of the forts in
twenty-five minutes and found no reassurance in Lovell's letter.
He thought that the forts could resist the flat fire of the gunboats'
broadsides, but he worried about the damage that could be done by
mortars lobbed into the central area of the forts. The wooden structures might well be set ablaze and more of the defenders' time would
be consumed in putting out fires than in manning the forts' guns.

His worst fears were realized when he learned that, early on Good
Friday, quarters in the bastion were set ablaze and burned down, that
quarters outside the fort met the same fate, and that the citadel was
on fire. This likewise seemed doomed, for though the flames were
extinguished several times, they blazed again when another shell
struck. By five in the afternoon, it was no longer possible to put the
fire out. The citadel was a burning mass and the magazines were
threatened. And still the bombardment went on and on. It had lasted
two days and nights—four days and nights—six days and nights.
Deadly comets filled the days with their noise and lighted the skies
at night. Then came a starkly worded telegram: Farragut had run his
fleet through the forts and was headed for New Orleans.

More telegrams came in, telegrams which, in a personal sense,
were reassuring. The fleet had come up the river so fast that the
plantations which lay along the way had not been molested. Farragut
was after the supreme prize—New Orleans; he was not diverted from
his purpose by the prospect of lesser prizes. Caroline, who was making one of her frequent visits to Upper Magnolia, had been among
those to wire Pierre. For some time past, he had been sending her a
daily telegram, sometimes instead of a letter, sometimes as a supplement to one. These telegrams were, of necessity, sent to her New
Orleans address; but when she was at Upper Magnolia, she came up
nearly every day to get them; if there were no boat, she rode, though
horseback riding was an effort for her; and now, despite the disorganized condition of the city, she somehow got a message through
to him just before the wires closed:

ALL MEMBERS OF OUR FAMILIES ON BOTH SIDES OF THE RIVER SAFE
AND WELL. PLEASE GET BETTER FAST. LOVE FROM EVERYONE.

Pierre kept the yellow sheet under his pillow where he could reach
for it easily and feast his eyes on it every few minutes. It was his
greatest source of comfort—indeed, almost his only source of comfort. Fresh details of New Orleans' fate kept arriving. Cotton, sugar

and rice had all gone up in flames on the levees. The mighty *Mississippi*, greatest warship in the world, was a blazing derelict. Farragut had given the city forty-eight hours in which to evacuate women and children; if it had not capitulated by then, it would be bombarded. When his troops mutinied, General Duncan's brief but ironic message, "We can stand it as long as they can," had not saved the forts, which were still flying the Confederate flag, from surrender. Each new report brought with it fresh anguish. Worst of all, Pierre's troubled mind was riddled with the horrible thought that he might have contributed to the disaster. He had sent a dispatch from Corinth to Governor Moore, saying he would accept troops for ninety days and part of his message had read, "Let the people of Louisiana understand that here is the proper place to defend Louisiana." This message had been printed in all the New Orleans newspapers and the *Daily Delta* commented, "It is thus clear that General Beauregard and the military authorities at Richmond agree in the conviction that the battle for New Orleans, for the great Mississippi, is to be fought in the West." Yes, the *land* battle. Lovell had said long before that he was capable of meeting any *land* attack the Federals could bring against him; and on the strength of this conviction, Pierre had felt justified in asking for the troops he needed badly. And the Louisianians had covered themselves with glory at Shiloh; had they not been there, who knows? Grant, not Farragut, might have reached New Orleans first. Moreover, Pierre's latest letter from Lovell reiterated what they had both believed: "Twenty thousand well-armed infantry would not have made any difference against ships of war." Surely this statement exonerated Pierre from all responsibility in the disaster. But the letter continued, "The people, not understanding this, cast censure upon me." If this were true, Pierre must share in the censure. He had become greatly attached to this trim, wiry, middle-aged man with the clear eyes, drooping mustache and sidewhiskers, whose gait was full of energy. Lovell's appearance was unremarkable; his talents were outstanding; his character unimpeachable.

Pierre's fellow officers came more and more frequently to the pleasant house which was his headquarters, when they recognized that his disquietude was retarding his recovery. Each in his own way did his best to cheer the General. But some of them did not share his deep concern; they still felt that the key to victory lay in the upper reaches of the Mississippi Valley. They could not refrain from arguing with him about this and, though the arguments were well-meant, they wearied him without doing anything to reassure him as to their validity. Those who did share his concern hesitated to tell him that they were as depressed as he was. Their silence betrayed them; so did their occasional disclosures. He appreciated their friendliness, but it tired him to talk with them; he would have preferred solitude.

Occasionally, he was moved to speak out, either to try holding his own, however unwillingly, in an argument or unburdening his soul to sympathetic hearers. In writing, Lovell had given three reasons why he thought the city had fallen: the destruction of the barrier; the lack of heavy-caliber guns; the lack of cooperation by the Confederate Navy. Pierre could think of several others; but Lovell was right, lack of troops was not among them.

What was more to the point and much worse, Pierre kept thinking of the results. First of all, it meant the eventual control of the Mississippi River by the Union; the Federals now had a naval base where they could operate from the south, for the two greatest warships in the world were destroyed; and in the long run, the permanent inability to reopen the port for trade was secondary only to its loss for defense in war. It also meant the loss to the South of the Leeds Foundry and other New Orleans machine shops, of Louisiana salt and Texas beef. It meant the division of the Confederacy, for it shut off Texas, Arkansas and most of Louisiana from the other states. It meant the Confederacy's last probable chance of recognition as an independent nation by foreign powers and hence a terrible blow to the power and prestige of John Slidell, now its Commissioner in France. And because of all this, and the lessening of confidence and courage that went with it, the effect on the morale of the South was overpowering. Had not Napoleon always maintained *"que la confiance est plus de la moitié de la victoire"*? It was true, terribly true. Never again would the Confederacy's statesmen be able to find words with which to convince their people that victory was just around the corner. Never again would its soldiers surge forward into battle with the fight already half won.

As Pierre said this to himself, having refrained from saying it to anyone else, he turned his face to the wall, and lay, through a long dreadful night, shaken by the sobs he could no longer stifle, now that he could not be shamed because he had not silenced them before his officers. And, vibrating through them, he still heard the sound of the drums.

> *"The drums, the drums, the busy, busy drums,*
> *The drums, the drums, the rattling, battling drums*
> *The drums, the drums, the merry, merry drums."*

❦ 35 ❧

. . . THE FUNDAMENTAL DIFFERENCE BETWEEN THE MEN [was] the actual reason for their feud. It was not so simple a thing as jealousy. Heredity played its part, and environment, and training. Jefferson Davis, in the precise meaning of the word, was a Southerner. Beauregard was not. The people of New Orleans and lower Louisiana, until the recent invasion of Goths and Visigoths, have always maintained a very separate and distinct Latin character. Louisiana was a part of the Confederacy, an integral part. But only because of geography, politics and sentiment. Culturally, in tradition, in civilization, it had nothing in common with the rest of the South. The South looked to England for nourishment and inspiration. Louisiana never ceased looking to France.

It was, in the case of Beauregard and Davis, a conflict of civilization and race. Beauregard, a little Frenchman, had gone to French schools. French had been his native tongue. His ancestors had been Frenchmen, helping to plant the flag of France in the new world. He had been taught French habits of thought, and had been instilled with French ideals. His supremest idol was Napoleon—of rich language, of magnificent deeds, a conqueror and an Emperor.

Opposed to him was Davis, Anglo-Saxon to the core, the product of an entirely different education. It was impossible for him to understand the Creole. Beauregard's fine language, which expressed very genuine thought and emotion, seemed to his pragmatical mind bombastic and boastful, causing him to doubt Beauregard's sincerity. The Creole's plans, conceived in the manner of Napoleon, were to the cautious, logic-loving Davis only dreams. Circumstance, carefully weighed and considered, was the motivating factor of Davis' conduct—not dreams.

And so two really sincere, really noble men quarrelled. There was much fault on either side. From then on Davis was to persecute Beauregard with a cold, unswerving vindictiveness. Beauregard was to suffer from it. He would be ordered from command to command, with no regard paid to his rank or his abilities, always where it seemed he would have nothing to do.

A lesser man would have been crushed. But Beauregard, going where he was directed, grossly neglected, fighting two enemies at once, always managed to survive . . . a lost soldier in a lost cause.

—Hamilton Basso, *Beauregard: The Great Creole*
(Scribner's)

꿍

WHILE HE WAS STILL LYING ILL, THAT IS, ILL IN CORINTH, AFTER the Battle of Shiloh and the fall of the forts and the occupation of New Orleans, Pierre decided Corinth must be evacuated.

Corinth was a fever-ridden place; encampment there was an invitation to all sorts of diseases, typhoid among them, and there seemed to be no reluctance about accepting the invitation. He was, by no means, the only sick person there, though people had a way of talking as if that were the case, as if he were thinking only of his own health when he decided to retire. Moreover, it was also unhealthful because it was too near the enemy, whose strength had grown by leaps and bounds. To be sure, the Union Army had not pursued the Confederates with the same zeal it would have shown if that puzzling, unpredictable man named Grant had continued in full command. Grant did have a disconcerting way of following through. Halleck, the Union Department Commander, had now assumed command of all Federal forces and did not move nearly so fast or so destructively as Grant. But when Halleck moved in the direction of Corinth and almost reached it, Pierre had decided it was best for him to move, too.

He was not too sick then to call for a conference of his generals. They all came: Bragg, Van Dorn, Hardee, Polk, Breckinridge, Price. They all agreed with the plan he outlined. He was not too sick to plan, either. . . .

Halleck, who had finally come within a thousand yards of Corinth, after a month's delay, saw signs of intensive activity in the Confederate camp and heard menacing sounds. Breastworks had been thrown up all around Corinth. Cheer after cheer rang out as trains, rattling and whistling, pulled into the depot. Bugles were blowing and drums beating. Everything certainly indicated that Beauregard was getting immense reinforcements. But appearances were deceptive. The bugles were, indeed, blowing, the drums were, indeed, beating, the men were, indeed, cheering—while one solitary train shuttled back and forth. It was not bringing fresh troops, but, under cover of darkness, efficiently removing the existing troops to a safer and more salubrious spot. When Halleck opened with his guns the following morning, there was no answering shot. Presently, a delegation of citizens appeared at his headquarters, waving a white flag and pleading that their town might be spared. There would really be no point in destroying it, since they were quite ready to surrender. As for Beauregard's army, that had gone. There was not a single Confederate soldier left in the city. All those guns? Logs painted black! All those cannoneers? Hastily contrived scarecrows. . . .

Shifting his position on his pillows, Pierre laughed. If only he could have seen Halleck at the moment he made his humiliating discovery! Halleck thwarted, Halleck enraged, Halleck impotent, Halleck forced to face the fact that the Confederate Army—lock, stock and barrel—had been successfully spirited away in the course of a single night! He had Corinth, but what was Corinth now? Nothing but an empty shell! With an enemy force which outnumbered the Confederates three to one only a thousand yards away, Beauregard had escaped, taking with him forty thousand men and all his supplies. He was not annihilated, he was not even damaged. He would live to fight another day and, doubtless, to work another ruse like the one he had just had the supreme effrontery to pull off!

Somewhere among the papers in his japanned boxes, Pierre had a clipping, from the Chicago *Tribune*, which had reached him through obscure channels. It was among those that he cherished most. He would rummage for it and read it again, as soon as he was rid of this tiresome enervating fever, which robbed him of all initiative and confused his mind. But part of it he remembered without rereading it and despite his confusion. It ran something like this: "The Confederate strategy, since the Battle of Shiloh has been as successful as it has been superior. . . . I cannot imagine how it could have been more eminent for perfection and success. If the attack at Shiloh was a surprise to General Grant, the evacuation of Corinth was no less a surprise to General Halleck. If the one ruined Grant, the other has laid out in pallid death the military name and fame of General Halleck."

Well, there was really no reason why Pierre should have cherished this, no reason at all. For Grant was not ruined and neither was Halleck; so, even if the rest of the article were correct, what did that signify, in the face of the errors with which it ended? Halleck became General-in-Chief of the Union Armies and kept that proud position until Grant succeeded him in it two years later. The one who was ruined, the one whose military name and fame came close to being laid out in pallid death was Pierre Gustave Toutant Beauregard.

At Corinth, his old friend Dr. Brodie, who was also his personal physician, had been urging him for some time to take advantage of a lull in military operations and leave the front for a rest. He need not be so far away that he could not be easily recalled. Dr. Choppin, who was Dr. Brodie's assistant, made the same imperative recommendation. Pierre refused, over and over again, to heed their advice. Then the time came when he did not have the strength to dictate orders any more, even from his bed, much less to write them. He knew he no longer had any choice.

It was then that the telegram came ordering Bragg, his second-in-command, to begin preparations for a transfer; he was needed elsewhere. Pierre was annoyed because the order had been sent direct to Bragg, instead of to him, the superior officer. His annoyance influenced the wording of the wire he sent in return to Adjutant-General Cooper, though it did not change the essential message: he did not feel he could spare Bragg just then. He was on the point of leaving the front, at his surgeon's insistence. He had already delayed his departure four months and felt he could not do so any longer; but at the earliest possible moment he would return and take the offensive. This telegram was followed the next day by a letter, enlarging on what he had said before and adding that he would go to the health resort at Bladen's Springs on the Tombigee River for rest and recuperation, meanwhile leaving Bragg in command. He had progressed no farther than Mobile when the answer to these communications came—not from Cooper, but from Bragg himself. It was brief and very much to the point.

I HAVE A DISPATCH, FROM THE PRESIDENT DIRECT, TO RELIEVE YOU
PERMANENTLY IN COMMAND OF THIS DEPARTMENT. I ENVY YOU AND
AM ALMOST IN DESPAIR. BRAXTON BRAGG.

He was stunned, he was overwhelmed, but somehow he gathered himself together. He had not believed the rumors that he was already "doomed" when he was removed from Manassas and sent to the West. Now he knew that he was. He did not need to hear, as he did, not long afterward, that fifty-nine members of the Confederate Congress had signed a petition, asking Davis to return him to command in the West, and that the President had replied, "If the whole world were to ask me to restore General Beauregard to the command I have already given General Bragg, I would refuse it." Pierre realized that the administration had no idea of restoring him to his former command or even assigning him to field duty elsewhere. When the orders appointing him to command the Department of South Carolina and Georgia, with headquarters in Charleston, came through they did not constitute a surprise or even a shock; he had braced himself for them. Meanwhile, he had long since replied to Bragg's telegram with more courtesy than candor.

I CANNOT CONGRATULATE YOU, BUT I AM HAPPY FOR THE CHANGE. IT WILL TAKE ME SOME TIME TO RECUPERATE. I WILL LEAVE MY STAFF WITH YOU UNTIL REQUIRED BY ME. YOU WILL FIND IT VERY USEFUL.

As one to the manner born, he could say no less. As a human being, deeply humiliated, cut to the heart, he could say no more.

The drums had stopped beating. Pierre was aware of comfortable drowsiness, unbroken by dreams, undisturbed by memories. In fact, the drowsiness was coupled with a wonderful sense of well-being. The sheets between which he was lying were so clean and cool, the pillow on which his head rested was so soft. And his head did not ache at all. Was he mistaken or had he suffered a good deal from headache lately? It seemed to him that he had. But he certainly had no headache now. And his waking thoughts, though lazy, were completely clear. Had there been a period of some slight confusion? He was not sure about that, either, but he thought so.

Though he made no effort to achieve a state of greater wakefulness, it gradually came to him unsought. He opened his eyes and, looking straight ahead, saw an open window, its muslin curtains stirred by a slight pleasant breeze, which framed the gallery and the patio beyond. He knew now where he was. This was the house where he had been staying since June, where two ladies had been so wonderfully kind to him. He turned his head and saw Simone sitting beside him.

Slight as his movement had been, it did not escape her notice. Her smile was immediate and reassuring.

"Don't try to talk, unless you feel like it," she said cheerfully and calmly. "You've been very ill, but you're better now and we're all very happy about it."

So that was it! He had been ill, obviously quite ill; otherwise, why should his improvement be a definite cause for happiness? He thought this over for a minute or two before framing an answer.

"I'm afraid I must have given you a great deal of trouble."

"Oh, no! You've been a docile patient. None of your nurses has the slightest reason for complaint."

"Nurses?"

"Yes, your sister Mrs. Proctor and your friend Mrs. Turpin and this friend, Simone Castel. We've taken turns nursing you and we're all agreed that you're the best patient we ever had. Dr. Turpin thinks so, too."

"How long has all this been going on?"

"Oh, not too long! Just long enough for *maman* to make a wonderful recovery, too, and Lance to become adjusted to New Orleans again and find a job."

"*Lance has found a job already!*"

"Yes, he's a runner for the Citizens' Bank. He's getting ten dollars a week."

"Did he—has he taken the Oath of Loyalty?"

"Yes. He realized it was the only sensible thing for him to do. Even *maman* agreed with that. And he's so well and so happy and so— oh, I don't know how to express it—attractive and affectionate and self-reliant and honorable! Everything any woman could want her son to be. *Maman* feels the same way. I mean, she thinks he's everything any woman could want her grandson to be. We're so glad and so grateful to be a family again—a united, devoted family! It takes a man to make a family."

She was so happy! She had said that twice now, once kindly and sympathetically, in speaking of Pierre's recovery from illness and, a second time, with ringing joyousness, in speaking of her long-lost son, now restored to her.

She was right. It took a man to make a family; and, in her case, this man was her son. She did not feel the need of any other male companionship, any other male support. If she had felt so for a little while—and whether or not she really had, Pierre would never really know—she did not do so any longer.

"And do you know, I think he's got a girl already. I'm not sure, but I believe so. Of course, he's too young to be thinking of marriage. . . ."

But you're thinking of it, Pierre thought. Not marriage for yourself—marriage for your son. Because that will mean grandchildren, a larger and larger family, all united, all devoted, the way you see it. Well, for your sake, I hope you're right. And, as far as I'm concerned, I must gradually retire from this family group. What's more, I must go to City Hall myself.

So he must go to City Hall, as soon as he was strong enough to walk there and, before the alien mayor, swear fealty to the United States. Both Robert E. Lee and Joe Johnston had urged him to do this, when they responded to the letters he had written long before, asking their opinion; they said that duty and patriotism required submission to the victor. But he had put off the dreaded moment again and again and now the time had come when he could not put it off any longer. And, while he was waiting to get his strength back, he had better write to Andrew Johnson, the President of the United States, giving his reasons for supporting the Confederacy. That much he was entitled to do before he promised a new allegiance; but it would be even harder than it would have been to write Abraham Lincoln. It was impossible for Pierre to feel respect for Johnson; but the more he had thought about Lincoln, the more convinced he had become that there was a great man, at whose hands the South could have expected mercy and understanding.

The next time Lance came to see him, he asked for a pen and a sheet of paper. Then, as soon as the boy had given these to him and left him, he sat up in bed and wrote his letter.

In taking up arms during the late struggle (after my native State, Louisiana, had seceded) I believed, in good faith, that I was defending the constitutional rights of the South against the encroachments of the North. Having appealed to the arbitration of the Sword, which has gone against us, I accept the decision as settling finally the questions of secessions & slavery—& I offer now my allegiance to the Govt. of the United States, which I promise, truly and faithfully, to serve & uphold hereafter, against all external or internal foes.

He signed it with a flourish. Then, defiantly, he added two words and three initials to the signature.

Late General, C.S.A.

❧ 36 ❧

Beauregard was packed off to Charleston, exiled to what appeared to be a small and inactive command. It was not Mr. Davis' fault that it furnished him with his greatest opportunity to establish his fame.

The defence of Charleston has largely been overshadowed, in the South, by Lee's tremendous campaigns in Virginia, Maryland, and Pennsylvania; and, in the North, by Grant's siege and capture of Vicksburg. It was not nearly so important as these operations but equally heroic. It belongs to the great period of the Confederacy, the high sweep and surge of the Southern spirit.

The North, ever since the first sentimental shell of the war, had felt a kind of moral obligation to capture Charleston. It was the "cradle of the Confederacy," the "nursery of treason and rebellion," and therefore, as certain Northern journals and journalists balefully insisted, it must be humiliated and destroyed.

But there were other, more prosaic reasons. In order for the Confederacy to keep alive it was necessary to maintain an unbroken line of transportation and communication between Virginia, the grand theatre of the war, and the more southerly states . . . both for a concert of action among the various armies and the furnishing of supplies to the troops in Virginia. The railroad line which traversed Tennessee was parallel to the Federal line of occupation and in constant danger of being broken. The other principal line, approaching Charleston within a few miles at Branchville, was consequently a vital necessity. If Charleston were taken it would be a fairly simple matter to march the few miles to Branchville, seize the railroad and thus further assist in the process of splitting the Confederacy into as many parts as possible.

The initial effort of the North to chastise Charleston had

taken the form of a blockading fleet outside the harbor. It was entirely ineffective, the commerce of the port in no wise diminished, and the North, determined to close the harbor . . . forever if necessary . . . sank old, stone-laden hulls, in the main channels. This inspired method failed more conspicuously than the blockade.

The Charleston tide flows in and out of the harbor with tremendous force. The current swept away the sand and silt beneath the hulls, they sank deeper and deeper, and eventually it was discovered that the North had done some extensive dredging for the South. Instead of blocking the harbor, the hulls helped to make it deeper.

The North, disappointed, left inspiration alone and returned to fundamentals. It concentrated all its efforts upon two objectives—an effectual blockade of the port and the capture of the city. The squadron was increased, it captured a blockade runner every now and then and gave chase to others which it did not capture, but vessels continued to unload at the Charleston wharves with more or less regularity.

—Hamilton Basso, *Beauregard: The Great Creole*
(Scribner's)

"It has become my solemn duty to inform the authorities and citizens of Charleston and Savannah, that the movements of the enemy's fleet indicate an early land and naval attack on one or both cities, and to urge that persons unable to take active part in the struggle shall retire. Carolinians and Georgians! The hour is at hand to prove your country's cause. Let all able-bodied men, from the seaboard to the mountains, rush to arms. Be not too exacting in the choice of weapons. Pikes and scythes will do for exterminating your enemies, spades and shovels for protecting your firesides. To arms, fellow citizens! Come to share with us our danger, our brilliant success, our glorious death."

—Joseph Hergesheimer, Beauregard's speech as quoted in
Swords and Roses (Knopf)

◆◆◆

AFTER THE LETTER WAS ACTUALLY IN THE MAIL, HE FELT BETTER. True, it had been an effort to write it, almost as much of an effort as walking to City Hall. Perhaps the day was past when words came so easily to him that they seemed almost to be tumbling over each other when he put them on paper; perhaps it was his aversion to writing these special words that made a struggle out of every syllable; or perhaps he still had not got his strength back, as Elodie and Celestine and Simone kept insisting. Whatever the reason, he returned to the quarters from the post office and lay down on his bed in utter weariness.

He heard Lance coming down the carriageway, talking to someone. The answering voice was young and fresh. Probably it belonged to the girl whom, according to Simone, Lance was already courting: a pretty little thing, also according to Simone, unusually fair for a Creole, with curly red hair and very white skin, though she did not have those rather pale, rather blank blue eyes that sometimes went with the rest of the coloring. Her eyes were hazel, with lots of light and laughter in them—perhaps her greatest claim to real beauty. The rest might have been just youth and vitality and the awakening to love. Simone had not put it quite that way, but Pierre knew this was what she meant. Hitherto, he had felt a mild curiosity to see this girl who had so quickly captured Lance's attention. But today he felt too tired.

The voices came nearer. He continued to hear them as Lance and the girl—Mignon, was that what they called her?—entered the patio, went up the steps, crossed the rear gallery and opened the door into the house. Doubtless, Mignon was staying for supper. Pierre could see her then, without extra effort. But even going to the house would be an effort. He would stay in the quarters, and Lance, without so much as being asked, would bring him an appetizing meal on a tray and hover around him, eager to be of additional service. Just the same, Lance would be somewhat hurt because his hero had not been interested in seeing his girl. He had been looking forward, proudly, to presenting them to each other. . . .

There were footsteps in the carriageway again, evidently a young man's footsteps, for whoever was approaching did so at a brisk, purposeful pace. Also, evidently, he was alone; at least there was no accompanying patter or chitchat. Then the steps stopped at the bottom of the steep flight of stairs leading up to the second floor of the quarters and Pierre recognized René's voice as his son called to him.

"Father! May I come up?"

"Of course. I'd be delighted to see you."

He swung his feet to the floor and crossed the room, reaching the door just as René opened it and embraced his father with the same spontaneity he had shown as a child. But he shook his head when Pierre suggested he sit down.

"No, I haven't come to stay, just to urge you to come home with me. I heard by chance that the *Mittie Stephens* would be going downriver this evening and by good luck, the *Algerine* was coming upstream this morning. Let me help you throw a few things into a bag; we haven't much time."

"René, I hadn't thought of coming to Upper Magnolia just now. I don't seem to be getting my strength back very fast and—"

"And no wonder. It's hotter than Tophet here in these small, low-ceilinged rooms. At Upper Magnolia, you'll at least have air and space."

"I have all the space I need. I can always go out on my balcony and there's the rear gallery of the big house and the big house itself, as far as that goes."

"Yes, of course. I know you're more than welcome and Lance worships the ground you walk on. But after all it's different, isn't it, since he came home? I mean, with a man of their own in the family, Madame Cougot and Madame Castel must feel more self-sufficient than they did before. They like you, they like you enormously, but they don't need either your help or your company. In fact, I don't suppose they need what you pay them for rent. Lance can't be earning much, but he's earning something and he'll soon be earning more. I have a feeling he's going to do well by himself and his dependents."

He was putting into words the thoughts which Pierre had still left unspoken; and, while René was talking, he was rummaging in a chest for shirts and socks. Now he pulled a dilapidated bag out of a corner and began to throw clothes into it.

"I might mention in passing that you have a family of your own, a family that's missed you very much," he said as he went on packing. "We've felt that sometimes you were inclined to overlook that lately.

Oh, I know you've had a good reason; you felt you had to search for work and so on. But you can't start searching for work again until you get stronger. And Doucette feels it's her turn to coddle you. She says she could learn to be just as good a nurse as Madame Turpin, if you only gave her a chance. You don't know how that girl adores you, Father. Talk about hero-worship! And she's your own flesh and blood. Give her a chance to show you how she feels. . . . Well, I think that's about all the clothes you're really going to need. I've got a hack outside, kept it while I came in to fetch you, so there wouldn't be any question of having one here when we wanted it. I'll dash along to the main house ahead of you and prepare the folks there for your departure. Then the farewells won't take so long."

Pierre resented René's high-handed methods, but not enough to rebel against them. It was astonishing how weak he still felt. But the boat trip was refreshing rather than tiring and, as soon as they reached Upper Magnolia, Doucette insisted that he must go to bed. She had a special treat for his supper; she had made it herself and wanted to bring it up to him herself. Manette was teaching her to cook and said she did very well, considering. Pierre had never been especially fond of custard, but he realized that Doucette not only expected praise; she merited it. For custard, her offering really was not bad at all; she had raised it to the status of a *crème caramel*.

The next morning he slept late and, even after waking, lay quiet for some time in his convent bed, quite content to be idle; then he got up and dressed in a leisurely way and went down to dinner. The rest of the day he sat on the gallery and, though he kept a book in his hand and read a few pages from time to time, for the most part he spent the afternoon almost as lazily as he had the morning. With the exception of Doucette, the various members of the family came and went, visiting with him for a few minutes and then drifting away to engage in more active occupations. But it was only during the time she spent in the kitchen, concocting eggnogs and *sirops d'orgeat* with which to tempt him that she left his side. She had brought her sewing with her and, though her father neglected to ask her what she was making, she informed him with some pride that it was going to be a dress and that she hoped to wear it a week or so later to a party. A party, he inquired. He did not realize anyone was giving parties yet. Oh yes, people were beginning to. It would not be much of a party, she supposed, compared to those he went to when he was young. But she had heard about this one, indirectly, and had found out that René and Henri were both going and that she had been asked, too, and they had told their prospective hostess that their sister was still too young for grown-up parties, which was, of course, ridiculous. So she had taken things in her own hands, in a nice way, naturally, and now she was making herself a pretty dress.

Pierre listened to her with amusement and with the pang of surprise, half-glad and half-sad, that always accompanied the realization she was growing up. He told her he was pleased she was going to a party, that it was high time she had more exhilarating company than the relatives she saw all the while. This brought about a protest. She did see *memère* and *pepère* and René and Henri and Uncle Charles all the time; she would be glad of some alien additions to that group. But she did not see Papa all the while. She hardly ever saw him, because he hardly ever came to Upper Magnolia. When he did come, she not only did not need any more exhilarating company, she did not want any. She could not remember that she had ever been so excited as when he told her about the Battle of Manassas. The lead soldiers and the toy tracks and houses were just as he had left them; she would not allow anyone to touch them. She had been hoping though, that as soon as he felt better, he would rearrange them to show her first about the siege of Charleston and then the final battles in Virginia.

René, who strolled up just then on one of his brief visits, let Doucette finish her remark without interrupting her. But before Pierre could answer, his elder son did so for him.

"This is where I come in, Sis," he said, with more authority in his tone than the occasion seemed to warrant, at least on the surface. "You apparently forgot that I was in Charleston with Father all through the siege. I was his aide-de-camp. I worked at the same desk with him, I slept in the same room with him—that is, when he would consent to go to sleep, which was never until the wee small hours of the morning. We didn't have luxurious headquarters this time, at the Charleston Hotel, the way Father did the first time he was there. We moved from house to house, further and further from the waterfront, as the bombardment went on. Our cow moved with us."

"Your *cow!* What cow?"

"I've forgotten now who gave her to us. But she was a welcome gift. Father had been ill for months before he came to Charleston—since before the Battle of Shiloh, as far as that goes. He wasn't equal to banquets any more—not that there were as many banquets as there had been in Sixty-one. But Charlestonians always seem to manage somehow to eat mighty well and they were always eager to share what they had with Father. And, as I said, rich food wasn't good for him any more. But he did need fresh milk and plenty of it. Thanks to some kind lady he always had it. The cow was the most practical gift any feminine admirer ever sent him, way ahead of all those scarves and slippers and things."

"René, please don't get started in that vein again. I told you before that I was very much gratified because Doucette was taking an intelligent interest in the war and I'd be very glad—"

"Excuse me for interrupting, Father. I'd be very glad to see you a little stronger before you start planning battles again, even toy battles. It's hot up in that nursery. It's nice and cool here on the gallery. If you want to correct me as I go along, I don't mind. But I think I have a right to tell part of the story. After all, I shared part of the experiences. I'll steer away from scarves and slippers and I won't do any joking if you don't want me to. But certainly it was all right to tell Doucette about the cow. Wasn't it?"

"Oh, Papa, please say yes! I loved hearing about the cow! Did she have a name?"

"I think so. Yes, I believe her name was Dixie—anyway, something unimaginative like that."

"Why, I think Dixie's a wonderful name for a cow! And as long as you had her, you were all right, weren't you? I mean, as far as your food was concerned."

"Yes, as far as my food was concerned."

"But it wasn't so pleasant, was it, moving from one house to another?"

"René says he wants to tell this part of the story. All right, we'll let him."

Pierre put the book, which he had so far kept in his hand, on the table beside his chair and settled back, looking at René. The young man instantly took up the challenge.

"When Father went back to Charleston in the autumn of Sixty-two," he said, "he succeeded a general by the name of Pemberton who'd had an insignificant record. As a matter of fact, at that time he'd never fought a battle, he'd abandoned the coast defenses Father had built in the spring of Sixty-one and, though he'd never been under dangerous attack, he was ready to throw in the sponge. Of course, none of this was calculated to impress the Charlestonians, and when he proclaimed martial law, Governor Pickens asked the War Department to remove him. You might almost say that Governor Pickens made a habit of asking the War Department to remove someone in order to get Father."

"René, I cannot let you go on unless you stick to facts. Governor

Pickens did not ask to have either Whiting or Pemberton removed in order to get *me*. He simply asked to have them removed and supplanted by somebody else."

"All right, have it your way. Anyhow, he was very pleased to get you both times—just as much the second time as the first. And so was everyone else in Charleston. There were the usual tears and cheers, the usual kisses and bouquets."

"René!"

"Father was naturally much gratified," René continued calmly. "And something else happened that I think I ought to tell you, just to show you that the devil isn't ever quite as black as he's painted. We had a wonderful surprise: Uncle Richard and Aunt Elodie came for a visit."

"I thought no one could get through the lines by that time!"

"They couldn't, normally. But the Proctors had actually been *sent* through and you'd never guess by whom."

"No, tell me quickly!"

"By Butler."

"You don't mean the man that stole silver spoons and—did all sorts of other dreadful things?"

"Yes, that's exactly whom I mean. Butler sent the Proctors to Father with a letter of sympathy and an offer for a pass and a safe conduct in case he wanted to come to New Orleans and see our stepmother, who was very ill."

"But Papa, why didn't you come? I know you didn't, because I'd have seen you if you had."

"No, I didn't come. I don't need to tell you that I wanted to very much, that I longed to see your stepmother and give her what comfort I could in what I knew must be very serious illness—what I feared might be a fatal illness, as it was. Even so, I couldn't bring myself to be under obligation to that man Butler, and I couldn't run the risk of leaving my command for any reason whatsoever. I'd been humiliated—publicly disgraced—because I'd left it once, under doctor's orders, when I was very ill myself. I knew that, if I left it a second time, giving my wife's illness as a reason, even if she were dying, I'd be accused of falsehood, I'd be shorn of what dignity remained to me. So I stayed in Charleston—with an aching heart."

"Which didn't prevent him from starting right in to show that he appreciated and deserved the affection and confidence of the Charlestonians," René said emphatically. "He worked sixteen hours a day or more, repairing and improving Charleston's defenses. He didn't have any navy yard on which to draw, but he managed to get constructed two ironclad rams, the *Palmetto State* and the *Chicora*."

"What's an ironclad ram?"

"A ram is a gunboat provided with an underwater prow, which could drive a hole into the wooden vessels of the enemy. The idea was to steam full speed into the enemy ship, hoping that the momentum and the underwater ram would cause her to sink. It was called ironclad if its surface was covered with sheets of iron or railroad iron. As soon as these rams were finished—that would have been in January of Sixty-three, wouldn't it, Father?"

"Yes, the very end of January."

"As soon as they were finished, Father decided on a night attack against the Federal fleet guarding the harbor. The *Palmetto State* disabled the Yankee *Mercedita* and two other steamboats ran out of range. The *Chicora* disabled the *Keystone State* and fired on the *Keystone City*. The same night Father captured a Federal gunboat, the *Isaac P. Smith*, in a trap he had carefully laid for her. When she anchored in the river, masked shore batteries opened on her so furiously that she surrendered. The next morning, Father and Commodore Ingraham, who had done the planning with him and led the attack from the *Palmetto State* as his flagship, declared that the blockade was raised. Perhaps it wasn't, actually, though it's true that when they made the pronouncement, none of the Federal ships was at its usual anchoring place—all but one had been disabled or gone out of range and that one had been captured. So the French and Spanish consuls in the city, who were invited to come and look over the situation, held a formal meeting and agreed that, legally, the blockade *had* been raised. Of course later the blockaders—those that still could—limped back into position again. So the attack wasn't a lasting success and, to all intents and purposes, the blockade still existed. But the effect of the night attack was excellent for Southern morale, military and civilian both. It helped us get ready for a bigger and better naval battle.

"This one began on a Sunday in April. Father rather specialized in Sundays. There was Manassas, there was Shiloh, and now along came the Yankees' invincible armada on another Sunday and, what's more, it was the first anniversary of Shiloh. Well, the Yankees had just about as much reason to believe their fleet was invincible as the Spaniards had when they designated theirs that way. It started to move into the harbor around noon—a beautiful bright sunny day. At half-past four in the afternoon what was left of it was scurrying away.

"Of course, the victory was spectacular enough in itself. But it wasn't only spectacular; it was convincing."

"Convincing to whom? Convincing of what?"

"Convincing to the Yankees that it was impossible to take Charleston away from us by a sea attack alone. They would have to attack by land as well. That was fine. But it also convinced President Davis that if Father could do so well with the forces at his disposal, he could spare a few troops here and there. That was unfortunate. Father knew that as soon as the Yankees got through licking their wounds, they'd be back, acting on their conviction. He asked for torpedo rams to destroy blockading monitors."

"What's a torpedo ram?"

"I've already told you what a ram is. A torpedo ram carries explosives, usually suspended from a pole in the bow. Its purpose is to strike the enemy ship with the torpedo which, on exploding, could do quite a lot of damage and perhaps even sink the ship. A monitor was a type of Yankee ironclad, modeled on the original *Monitor*, which fought the great battle with the *Merrimac* in Hampton Roads. They called it the cheese box on a raft and the tin can on a shingle."

"I'm not quite sure I understand how they work."

"Well, it doesn't really matter whether you do or not, because Father couldn't persuade anyone in Richmond that they would work at all. He said he felt just as Columbus must have, when he was trying to persuade Spanish royalty the world was round. Instead of sending him the torpedo rams, they made him send five thousand men to Vicksburg. They told him the Mississippi Line was essential to the defense of the Confederacy. Of course that's what he'd been telling them for years, while he was trying to get them to strengthen the defenses of Jackson and St. Philip. But they wouldn't listen, so Jackson and St. Philip had fallen under fire from Farragut's fleet and New Orleans was occupied by the enemy. After that, it didn't seem to Father to matter so much what happened to Vicksburg. He thought it was more important to safeguard Charleston. But no one in Richmond, neither President Davis nor his advisers, cared what Father thought. He had a good plan for the campaign in the West, too. But he couldn't get anyone to listen to that, either. Father felt more and more like Columbus all the time."

"Just the same, he kept right on holding Charleston, didn't he?"

"Yes, he kept right on holding Charleston. They tried to pry him loose and send him to Mobile, but he sat tight, bracing himself for that combined land-and-sea attack he knew was bound to come. A very able Yankee general, Quincy Gillmore, had been called upon to express an opinion as to how Sumter could be destroyed and the city taken and, in Washington, President Lincoln and his advisers were willing to listen when an experienced general said something. He recommended that the Union Army should try to get a foothold on Morris Island and reduce the Confederate batteries there; then mount heavy guns and destroy Sumter. After that, the Union fleet, commanded by Admiral Dahlgren, would have no trouble, according to Gillmore, in entering the harbor and, supported by army fire, in forcing the surrender of the city."

"But it didn't work out that way!"

"It very nearly did. The Yankees already held several islands. One of these was Folly, which Father had always insisted was well named. It was very close to Morris and it had a lot of sand hills and underbrush on it, which would help to conceal any sort of unusual activity. Gillmore figured that if he could get a sufficient force on it unobtrusively, he could then easily cross to Morris and, once there, surprise and overpower its defenders. Father realized that something was afoot, but he didn't have enough men or enough ammunition to defend all the places he wanted to protect and he thought he ought to concentrate on those that were the most important for the defense of the city. He hadn't visualized an attack on Charleston from Morris because he hadn't realized that guns powerful enough to fire as far as Charleston and damage it could be mounted there. He thought the approach would be made by James Island or Sullivan Island. He had never heard of a Swamp Angel."

"Neither have I. What kind of an angel is that?"

"It isn't any kind of an angel. It was an immense mounted rifle gun, so heavy that piling had to be sunk before a platform could be built to support it. It fired shells, filled with an inflammable liquid called Greek fire, and it had a range that permitted it to fire all the way into Charleston, five miles away. And that's what Gillmore eventually did with it. The Yankees had been having some pretty bad luck. Even after they succeeded in landing on Morris and occupying three-fourths of it, they still had Battery Wagner and Battery Gregg at the tip of the island, which they didn't occupy, between them and Sumter. They tried twice to take Wagner, and both times were repulsed with terrifically heavy losses. But meanwhile Gillmore had been getting more and more powerful guns into place, guns that would fire projectiles twice as heavy and capable of going twice as far as any that had ever been used before. They were all 'angels' as far as the Yankees were concerned, but the special one they called the Swamp Angel was the archangel, so to speak.

"When it was all set up and ready to use, Gillmore wrote to Father and said that if he didn't evacuate Sumter and Morris, he—Gillmore —would fire on Charleston. But he forgot to sign the letter and, when it came, Father was out on an inspection tour. The officer who received it at headquarters, after some hesitation, decided that the letter had better be sent back for the official signature; but, before dispatching it a second time, duly signed, Gillmore opened fire on the city.

"I've seen Father angry a good many times, but never as angry as he was that time. I don't know whether or not he remembers what he wrote to Gillmore—"

"*Of course* I remember: 'It would appear, sir, that despairing of reducing these works'—by 'these works' I meant Sumter and Wagner —'you now resort to the novel measure of turning your guns against the old men, the women and children and the hospitals of a sleeping city—an act of inexcusable barbarity.' "

"Did he answer, Papa?" Doucette asked.

"This is still René's story, honey. I didn't mean to break in. Go ahead, Captain Beauregard."

"He answered by doing what he had threatened. A shell hit a warehouse near the Charleston Hotel and set it afire. People who lived nearby fled for their lives, many of them shouting and screaming and, for a while, there was general pandemonium. But it didn't last long. Some houses were struck, but the shells sometimes failed to explode and the fire department was very much on the alert; most of the flames were put out quickly. The banks removed their valuables to safety, the hospitals were evacuated and a good many people moved to the rear of the town."

"Was this one of the times you moved?"

"Yes, because the house where we'd had our headquarters was one of those that got hit."

"But Dixie wasn't hurt, was she?"

"No, she wasn't hurt and, fortunately, she was a very placid cow. Of course we took her along with us and she settled down in another back yard as calmly as if she'd always lived there."

"And what happened next?"

"Well, the Swamp Angel continued its ministrations until it had fired thirty-six shells into the city. Then it burst. So it didn't do as much damage as Gillmore had hoped it would, after all. We were having disappointments of our own about that time. We were experimenting with an underwater ship—a submarine, it was called—and had several setbacks; in fact, the experiment wasn't successful until the following spring, when the *Hunley* sank the *Housatonic*—and that wasn't too successful because the *Hunley* sank also; but, meanwhile, some of Gillmore's lesser angels went right on with their evil work, not in the city, but in the forts. Gillmore had started his campaign of destruction in June, and by December he had complete possession of Morris Island. However, when he charged Battery Wagner with his infantry, after two days of bombardment, there wasn't a single Confederate left in it. We had held it for fifty-eight days and had finally abandoned it the night before. Battery Gregg was also abandoned—guns were spiked, implements destroyed, equipment carried away. Father had pulled the same kind of a ruse that he did at Corinth, and Gillmore must have been mad enough to chew nails—especially as, while he had been trying to blast nine hundred men, who eventually eluded him, out of Battery Wagner, Father had been busy strengthening the batteries on James and Sullivan and building a new line of inner defenses around the city—what he liked to call 'a circle of fire.' Gillmore must have concluded that throwing more shells into the city was a waste of time unless and until he could find some way of penetrating Charleston Harbor at the same time. And, as for Sumter——"

"What about Sumter, René?"

René laughed. "Well, to be sure, there wasn't much left of Sumter, after it had been bombarded twice. It had only one gun left, which was used to salute the battle flag—the flag Father designed after Manassas. The ruin was commanded by a man named Elliott, Major Stephen Elliott. Now that Gillmore had Morris Island, he went around saying that, presently, Sumter would be reduced; Dahlgren would attend to that. Dahlgren readily accepted the dare and demanded the surrender of Sumter. Major Elliott passed on the demand to Father."

"And Papa said?"

"'Tell Dahlgren to come and get it.'"

"So then——"

"Then Dahlgren and Gillmore joined forces. Four hundred men or more were sent out in barges and, from the crumbling parapet, Elliott watched them coming. He ordered his men not to fire until the Yankees attempted to land. As a matter of fact, they didn't have much to fire with, just a few muskets; but at the right moment they pelted the Yankees with hand grenades and anything else they could lay their hands on—mostly brickbats—and Father still had the batteries on James Island and Sullivan Island and they opened fire, too. So did the good old ram *Chicora*, a veteran of the first naval battle I told you about. It wasn't long before the attackers decided they'd had enough. They raced back to their barges and got away as quickly as they could."

"And didn't try to return?"

"No, as I just said, they decided they'd had enough." René rose and stretched himself. "Whatever else you forget about this war, Sis," he said, "remember that as long as Father was in command at Charleston, the city continued to hold out and our flag still floated over Sumter. Also, that when he left for Virginia, he saved Richmond."

ᦞ 37 ᦞ

December 31, 1861: Governor Pickens to General Lee:

Ferguson and Beauregard were appointed, supposing they had a company ready to bring right into the Battalion of Artillery, and their Commissions are not to be presented unless this is done first. There is great difficulty in enlisting regulars now, and as a large portion of a company was already enlisted for young Beauregard in New Orleans, I thought it was well to secure a company for our services, and besides I thought it would be very agreeable to all to appoint a son of General Beauregard.

–O. R. I, VI, 363–64

May 5, 1863: General G. T. Beauregard (Charleston) to General Pemberton:

In obedience to instructions from the War Department, I have sent you two brigades of my troops (about 5,000 men), having selected the best that could be spared, under two of my ablest generals—S. R. Gist and W. H. T. Walker; also two excellent batteries, in one of which is my son, Lieutenant René. . . .

–O. R. I, XXIV, pt. iii, 883

January 6, 1864: General Beauregard (Charleston) to Charles Villeré:

I send you herewith a letter from your mother to Henri, of the 18th of November. My latest from New Orleans is of the

4th of December. All were well then. Doucette wrote me on the 19th of November. I sent her letter to René; send him your mother's also. His address is Walker's Division, Hardee's Cross, Dalton, Georgia.

—O. R. I, LIII, 305

December 15–16, 1864: Major-General W. B. Bate's Report of Battle of Nashville:

Captain Beauregard, commanding my artillery, showed merit beyond his years, and managed the battalion not only to my satisfaction, but to the good of the service and to his own credit.

—O. R. I, XLV, pt. i

Few military engagements in all history can compare with the Battle of the Crater. From start to finish it is a study in crises and contrasts, beginning with the extraordinary success of the Union army in excavating a tunnel of unprecedented length and effectively setting off a mine blast, and ending with dismal failure and appalling loss of life. In between these extremes of success and failure were crowded events that reflected their own extremes of brilliant leadership and colossal blundering, heroism and cowardice, timidity and aggressiveness, sound judgment and inexcusable error, generosity and selfishness, humility and conceit, noble impartiality and petty jealousy, love and hate, prudence and stupidity. All these and more were stirred in the hot cauldron of combat on that hot July morning—and what came to the surface was tragedy.

Paradoxically, in the midst of many explanations, the tragedy was inexplicable. Everyone could ascribe a reason, and none of the reasons was satisfactory. Throughout both North and South the news was shocking and puzzling. The man in the street was unable to understand what had happened, and the newspaper he read didn't give much help. The whole thing made no more sense to the citizens of New York and Boston than it did to the citizens of Raleigh and Savannah. And in Washington, as in Richmond, there were not enough answers to go around.

—Henry Pleasants, Jr., and George H. Straley,
Inferno at Petersburg (Chilton)

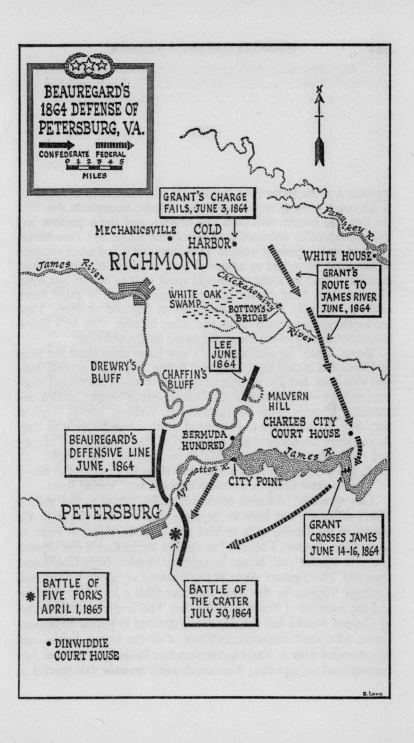

BEAUREGARD'S
1864 DEFENSE OF
PETERSBURG, VA.

CONFEDERATE FEDERAL
0 1 2 3 4 5
MILES

GRANT'S CHARGE
FAILS, JUNE 3, 1864

MECHANICSVILLE   COLD
HARBOR

RICHMOND

WHITE HOUSE

GRANT'S
ROUTE TO
JAMES RIVER
JUNE, 1864

WHITE OAK
SWAMP

BOTTOM'S
BRIDGE

LEE
JUNE
1864

DREWRY'S
BLUFF

CHAFFIN'S
BLUFF

MALVERN
HILL

CHARLES CITY
COURT HOUSE

BEAUREGARD'S
DEFENSIVE LINE
JUNE, 1864

BERMUDA
HUNDRED

James R.

CITY POINT

GRANT
CROSSES JAMES
JUNE 14-16, 1864

PETERSBURG

BATTLE OF
FIVE FORKS
APRIL 1, 1865

BATTLE OF
THE CRATER
JULY 30, 1864

DINWIDDIE
COURT HOUSE

James River

Chickahominy

River

Pamunkey R.

Appomattox R.

2. Long

❦

PIERRE WAS TREMENDOUSLY MOVED. HE HAD ALWAYS BEEN PROUD OF his son's military record, and with reason; throughout the War the boy had fought with dash and bravery, and these qualities had become especially noteworthy at Missionary Ridge and Pine Mountain and on the fields of western Tennessee; but it had never occurred to him that René had so treasured every moment of their military association that he could and would speak of it as he had just done. Pierre put his hand on his tall son's shoulder and it rested there, easily but proudly. For a few moments no one said anything. Then the soothing silence came to an end when Charles, who, with Henri, had unobtrusively joined the group, spoke for the first time.

"Bravo, René!" he said heartily. "I now know more about the Siege of Charleston myself than I ever did before. I couldn't possibly have told that story, but I've got one of my own. I was in Richmond when your father took command of the Department of North Carolina and southern Virginia, with headquarters at Weldon, late in April of Sixty-four. In fact, I was in Richmond nearly a year longer than that. As you know, Doucette, I was a member of the Confederate Congress and that didn't adjourn until March of Sixty-five. Meanwhile. . . . Well, I'm afraid I can't tell a story as well as René, it isn't in me—"

"That's a great thing for a famous orator to say!" scoffed René.

"Oh—speeches!" Charles countered airily. "Plays to the gallery! That's different. You have to be more careful when you're in the bosom of the family, with at least two listeners able and eager to correct you. Anyway, I believe I'm right in saying that it was General Lee who wanted your father brought to Weldon from Charleston, Doucette. The Yankees' Army of the Potomac was pretty well all over northern Virginia by this time and controlled a lot of its coastline and the coastline of North Carolina, too. This army was commanded by General Meade, but actually it was directed in person by General Grant, who was Commander-in-Chief of *all* the Union Armies, and who traveled with it. Early in the war, the Yankees in the East had concentrated on capturing Richmond, partly because they wanted to deprive us of our Confederate capital, but mainly because the only great machine shop and foundry the South had left after we lost Leeds in New Orleans—the Tredegar Works—which they wanted to capture, were located there. But, by the time Grant took over as Union commander, the capture of Richmond was important largely because, if that fell, Lee's hard-pressed army couldn't last much longer. So Grant tried to whittle that down by sheer weight of numbers. But Lee still had a defensive mission—to keep the Tredegar Works for the Confederacy if he could; and his chief strategy was to place his army between the Yankees and the city. This meant that, in order to reach it, the Yankees might have to approach it by a roundabout route. Your father thought this would be via Petersburg and so informed General Bragg, who was now President Davis' official military adviser. But they paid no attention to the message, although your father's mission was to hold the southern approaches to Richmond.

"The Federal advance began with the seizure of City Point on the south side of the James River, only a few miles from Petersburg, which was important to defend, because it was a railroad center."

"Like Manassas?"

"Much bigger than Manassas. City Point was an ideal place from which to launch a Federal attack. Fortunately, Butler, who was in command of their troops—"

"The silver-spoon man? The one who sent Uncle Richard and Aunt Elodie to Charleston?"

"The same. He didn't seem to realize how well off he was there. He landed most of his troops on a peninsula called Bermuda Hundred, which lies in a fork of two rivers, the James and the Appomattox, and had a strong line of fortifications. In order to reach Petersburg, the Yankees would have to cross the Appomattox and a stream called Swift's Creek. Meanwhile, your father's command had been extended to include all the defenses south of the James, and he set up headquarters at Drewry's Bluff. He had come hurrying up from Weldon with nothing but ragtag and bobtail for an army, for, as usual, he had been denied reinforcements. But in spite of this, he 'matured a plan of battle in an instant, struck Butler in the front, and achieved a brilliant victory.' That's the way the Richmond *Examiner* described what he did—and he accomplished all of that and more. Butler was now in a bottleneck, his troops unavailable to Grant, and Richmond was relieved of its immediate danger.

"Of course, the relief didn't last long. It couldn't have been expected to. Grant attacked Lee at Cold Harbor, only six miles north of

Richmond, and lost seven thousand men in one hour. That was too many, even for him, and no commander ever appeared to care less how many he sacrificed, if he could gain his objective. But, by now, it was clear he wasn't going to gain it this way. So he decided to do what Butler had tried to do and what your father had predicted all along would be done—he decided to approach Richmond via Petersburg. That is where your father was by this time. He had only a little more than two thousand men with him, because he'd left his remaining three thousand at Bermuda Hundred, which Grant's forces were approaching fast. As usual, all your father's appeals went unanswered. What was worse, he couldn't convince even General Lee that Grant's army was actually at the very gates of Petersburg. Some messages went undelivered, some were disregarded. There seemed to be only one thing to do—withdraw from Bermuda Hundred, strengthen his force at Petersburg and thereby, if possible, save Richmond. That was what he did—I mean, he did both. Then he was blamed because he had withdrawn from Bermuda Hundred.

"In June, General Lee had established his defense line around Petersburg and the long siege—it lasted ten months, you know—began. During this siege there was one of the most dramatic moments of the war: the Battle of the Crater. The Yankees had actually dug a tunnel from their lines to a point under our lines and had exploded a lot of dynamite. It blew a tremendous hole or crater in the ground and killed and wounded hundreds of our men. The Yankees poured out of their trenches and swarmed into this crater, breaching our lines. If we could not wipe them out in a hurry, we would lose thousands more. But we did wipe them out. It was a remarkable feat. If your father won't talk about it now, get him to do so some other time. He and General Lee watched the holocaust together."

Charles paused, waiting for his brother-in-law to break in. But Pierre shook his head, putting his hand over his eyes, as if to shut out the memory of the awful sight. There had been so much blood spilled, so much carnage and slaughter. He had lived four years among the dying and the dead and now the memory of the Crater at Petersburg seemed to sum up all the tragedy and futility of the bitter struggle. Again, he seemed to feel the earth tremble and hear the mighty explosion, the cries of the maimed and wounded, the hideous whine of dying horses. He had been five hundred yards away, standing beside Lee in a window of the Gee house, when the furious fight that followed the explosion began and had focused his glass on the Crater. It was thus that he had seen the Federals, who had rushed forward with the blast, taking refuge in the deep pit. He remembered, all too vividly, how General Mahone's division had charged in to engage the Yankees in hand-to-hand combat and how, under withering fire from the Crater, Mahone's men fell like leaves from a tree, but still pushed forward. They fired their rifles, swung them as clubs and rammed home their bayonets; the battle had become wholesale murder, nonetheless terrible because it was lawful murder. When Pierre finally saw a white flag fluttering over the heaps of dead and dying, he had wondered briefly why the Federals had not supported the group which seized the Crater and thanked God that they had failed to do so. But wonder was not his main sensation; it was horror.

Later, he had gone into the Crater, now in Confederate hands, and found the dead piled up on each other so deep that he could walk across the wide pit without touching the ground. No, he could not talk about this to his children, now or ever.

Looking at him with pity and understanding, Charles went on with his story, making a special effort to speak not only clearly but dispassionately. "In September of Sixty-four, when Atlanta fell to General Sherman—your brothers' old teacher at the Louisiana State Seminary of Learning—this assured the re-election of President Lincoln and served as a tonic for any war-weariness that existed in the North. The last hope of the South was gone. A few weeks after the Battle of the Crater, your father was transferred again, this time to the military command of the West, with headquarters in Columbia, South Carolina. General Sherman completed his march across Georgia to the sea and, inevitably, next turned his attention to South Carolina. Disasters were piled on top of each other fast. Columbia was first pillaged and then burned. While it was still smoking, Charleston was evacuated. Anderson returned to Sumter and raised the same flag he had lowered four years before. Lee became Commander-in-Chief of all the Confederate Armies, a position which Davis, who still considered himself a great military leader, had insisted on holding himself, declining to disassociate himself from his own office until our Congressional pressure became so great that he could no longer withstand it. René told you a little while ago, Doucette, that whatever else you forget about the war, you must remember that, as long as your father was in command, our battle flag continued to float over Sumter and that Charleston was never evacuated. There are two more things I'd like you to remember: first, that General Lee didn't become Commander-in-Chief of the Army until the last year of the war—lots of people, even a lot of Southerners, think he had supreme command from the beginning. The fact that he didn't, that it was Davis who exercised it, made a lot of difference. The other thing isn't exactly germane to the subject we're discussing right now, but it's another about which there's been too much confusion. The idea of secession didn't start with South Carolina. It started with Massachusetts."

"*Massachusetts!*"

"Yes, way back in 1812, before South Carolina even thought of such a thing. Massachusetts threatened to withdraw from the Union if Louisiana were admitted as a state. One of its leading orators, Josiah Quincy, made some fiery speeches on the subject. But eventually he was silenced; Louisiana got into the Union all right, and the whole thing was hushed up and has stayed hushed up ever since. I understand that the best way to send a Yankee into a towering rage is to mention it."

"I'm not likely to see any Yankees here, am I?"

"No, not at Upper Magnolia. But mind you don't forget what I've told you."

"I won't, Uncle Charles. Please go on."

"Well, one of the first things Lee did was to restore Johnston to the command from which he'd been removed in favor of Hood, who had first destroyed the Army of Tennessee and then demolished himself as a leader. General Johnston, who had sent your father to Raleigh, for the purpose of raising troops if possible, gained the final victory of the war in that sector, at Bentonville, North Carolina, but suffered such heavy losses, in repeatedly repulsing Sherman, that he was obliged to retire."

There was another long silence on the gallery, not a soothing one this time, but a sad one. The soft light of first evening was fading into dimness. As it grew darker, Charles Villeré turned to his younger nephew.

"Henri, we haven't heard from you yet; why don't you take over this time, instead of René?" he asked. "I'd lost my observation post at Richmond by that time. The Confederate Congress had 'adjourned'— or, to put it more bluntly and more truthfully, had ceased to exist. But you and René were both with your father when the train pulled into Greensboro, that 'official military train' in which he'd been going frantically from place to place as long as there was any chance of raising troops to oppose Sherman. Do you remember what it looked like?"

"Yes, there were three boxcars," Henri answered promptly. "One was Father's office and also served as his bedroom and a dining car. One was the staff car where René and I slept with other members of the personal staff and the general staff. The third was a car for the horses. We'd all come to Greensboro because Father was ordered to meet President Davis there. That's correct, isn't it, Father?"

"Yes, it's correct," Pierre said wearily. "But I don't think we need to drag out this last chapter any further. Some day Doucette can read all the details of what happened at Greensboro. I'm going to write them in that book I've been gathering material for all summer. I know it's hard for you to talk about this, Henri, and your uncle Charles and René have said quite enough already."

"I don't mind talking about it at all," Henri said, surprisingly. It had not previously occurred to Pierre that the boy might, up to then, have been feeling that he was left out of an important discussion, and that he welcomed an opportunity of showing this was a mistake. After all, though Henri had been obliged to wait for two years before he was allowed to enlist, he had served under General Hardee and for some time had been on his father's personal staff. Quite possibly he felt that his praiseworthy record had been obscured by his elder brother's more brilliant one and was faintly jealous.

"Oh, all right then!" Pierre said cordially, trying to keep the weariness from his voice. "Go on and tell us about Greensboro, the way you remember it."

"Well, you went there, Father, as you'd been ordered to do, and so did General Johnston, as he'd been ordered to, and the President came to your headquarters. He had three members of his cabinet with him—Mr. Mallory, the Secretary of the Navy; Mr. Reagan, the Secretary of the Treasury; and Mr. Benjamin, the Secretary of State. Mr. Benjamin was smiling. He smiled all the time. I got the feeling that man must grin in his sleep. Everyone else looked pretty sober."

"There was plenty to look sober about," René interposed.

"Yes, I suppose so. Well, there weren't enough chairs in the boxcar for everyone to sit down, so everyone stood, Mr. Davis in the center. He made a very long speech. The gist of it seemed to be that he thought the war could go on a while longer, though Richmond had fallen and Lee had surrendered to Grant at Appomattox. He said he was sure that, in a few weeks, he could raise a powerful army again, that volunteers would come flocking back to the Confederate colors. General Johnston told him they would do no such thing; the South was exhausted and beaten and knew it. All of us in the army knew it, too, and I wanted to blurt that out. But Mr. Davis went on persisting and finally the meeting broke up without settling anything. Everyone in the staff car went to bed, but Father and General Johnston talked all night and the next morning Mr. Davis called another meeting and continued to insist that the war could go on. Eventually,

General Johnston began to quote figures. He said he still had seventeen thousand men under him and the enemy had more than three hundred thousand. Then Father spoke up mighty sternly. He told the President that, to continue the war under those circumstances would be the greatest of human crimes, that we could only fight as robbers or guerrillas. And General Johnston also spoke sternly right to the President's face. He said, 'You must open negotiations for peace.' Isn't that the way it was, Father?"

"Yes, that's just the way it was, Henri. Go on, you're doing fine."

"The President didn't like to have anyone say 'you must' to him. He flared up and refused to do what Johnston asked. He said it would be futile for him to treat with President Lincoln anyhow, because Lincoln didn't recognize his authority. General Johnston was very kind and polite. He tried to soothe Mr. Davis by saying that, if he felt that way, a truce could be arranged between military leaders, instead of between presidents. He said, with Mr. Davis' permission, he'd treat with General Sherman.

"Mr. Davis wouldn't hear of that, either, and the conference broke up. A few days afterward, there was another one. Some more military leaders had come along by that time; General Bragg was there and General Breckenridge. Mr. Davis appealed to them; he insisted that, if they would stand firm, the Cause wouldn't be lost. Even if they didn't have more than twenty-five hundred men among them, volunteers would soon join them and they could still prevail. Then he asked the brigade commanders, one by one, to assure him that his confidence was not misplaced, that his judgment was sound. Not one of them gave him the answer he wanted and he lost his temper again. Then he collapsed and that was the end."

Henri drew a long breath and stopped.

"You're almost as good a storyteller as your uncle and your brother," Pierre said warmly, after a moment's silence. "But it wasn't quite the end, after all. We didn't stay in Greensboro the rest of our lives. Go on. What happened next?"

"General Johnston left the next day to confer with General Sherman and Father stayed with the troops. It took about a fortnight to complete negotiations. Then Father was free to start home. But we had a slight handicap. None of us had any money; that is, we each had $1.15 in Mexican silver—the sum paid to each of the soldiers in the Army. But it didn't look as if that would take us far. So Colonel Chisolm, who'd been one of Father's aides from the very beginning, had an idea that he thought might help out. He suggested that we should get an army wagon from the Quartermaster, stock it with stores—tobacco, nails, yarn, twine, thread and whatever else we could pick up from the army supplies—that the people along our route were likely to need and that these articles should be used in lieu of money. Then we could trade these for food as we went along. Father thought that was a fine idea. He collected all the Louisiana soldiers he could find still hanging around on detached duty. There were about twenty of them in all. He invited them to come along and they were mighty glad to. They climbed into the wagon with us and the long homeward journey began."

≼§ 38 §≽

Headquarters, etc., etc.,
Greensboro, N. C., April 27th, 1865.

To my Personal and General Staff,—Events having brought to an end the struggle for the independence of our country, in which we have been engaged together, now for four years, my relations with my staff must also terminate. The hour is at hand when I must bid each and all of you farewell, and a Godspeed to your homes.

The day was, when I was confident that this parting would be under far different and the most auspicious circumstances—at a moment when a happy and independent people would be ready, on all sides, to welcome you to your respective communities—but circumstances, which neither the courage, the endurance, nor the patriotism of our armies could overcome, have turned my brightest anticipations, my highest hopes, into bitter disappointment, in which you must all share.

You have served me, personally, with unvarying zeal, and, officially, with intelligence, and advantage to the public service.

I go from among you with profound regret. My good wishes will ever attend you, and your future careers will always be of interest to me.

—Beauregard's farewell, quoted in Alfred Roman, *The Military Operations of General Beauregard* (Harper & Row)

EXCEPT FOR THE MOONLIGHT FILTERING IN THROUGH THE DENSE foliage of the live oaks, the gallery was now in darkness. Evening had merged quietly into night while the closely knit group had been absorbed in the last chapter of the War, and no one had noticed the change until the sounds that did not come until day was finally over began to penetrate the stillness—the murmur of turtledoves nestling in the eaves, the hoot of small owls perched in the trees. A slight breeze was stirring, enough to waft the fragrance of mint and roses in the garden toward the house. The place seemed pervaded with peace.

"But it ended."

Somehow the words, gently as they had been spoken, were startling to Pierre, as well as confusing. With a sudden shift of position, he sat bolt upright and answered his daughter in a bewildered way.

"What ended, honey? It's so long since anyone has spoken, I'm afraid I don't quite follow you."

"That long homeward journey which began in Greensboro. You *got* home. You're home *now*. With your own kinfolk, who love you. Isn't that what matters most?"

He rose slowly and put his arm around her. "Of course it is, Doucette," he said. "I'm afraid I lose sight of that, sometimes, but I shouldn't. As long as I have you and your brothers, and your uncle Charles, who's been my faithful friend ever since we were both boys . . . as long as you all think well of me——"

He did not finish the sentence; he did not need to. But as he spoke, he remembered that, besides these four, who were nearest and dearest to him, there was that other family with whom his life had become so unexpectedly interwoven, and whose affection and admiration would be lasting, too, even though the nature of his relationship with them was changing, now that Lance had returned. And Lance's feeling for him, as he very well knew, went far beyond mere admiration and affection. To Lance he was and always would be, not only "Old Bory," but *"Beau soldat, beau sabreur, beau frappeur,* Beauregard!"

Moreover, in Lance were embodied dozens of other drummer boys and private soldiers, many young officers who, one time or another, had served on his staff, perhaps even a few of those older officers under whom he had served himself. Lee—who had called him "Dearest Beaury" when they were younger—had felt confidence in him and had loved him to the end. These were the things he should remember; not that Bragg had superseded him, not that Hood had flouted his authority, not that Joe Johnston's warm feeling for him had cooled, not that Davis had misprized and hated him. From now on, he *would* remember. What difference did it make whether or not, a hundred years later, he were numbered among the immortals? What counted was now. . . .

"It's been a wonderful evening, a wonderful night," he said. "I can't thank you all enough for making it one of the best in my life. But I do seem to be a little tired. As René keeps reminding me, I'm not as young as I once was and—"

"I haven't done anything of the sort," protested René. "I've said you haven't got your strength back after a long illness. When you do, you'll be able to lick your weight in wildcats, just as you always were."

"Well, we won't start an argument at this hour. We'll end on the note that it's been a wonderful evening and let it go at that," Pierre said lightly. "But I started to say, when I was so rudely interrupted by this insubordinate young officer who has no respect for rank, that I'm a little tired, that I think perhaps I'd better go to bed. No, I don't want anyone to come with me. I just want to go quietly to my room and get to sleep."

He kissed Doucette, who was still standing encircled by his arm and closely pressed to his side. Then, releasing her, he embraced each of the others in turn and walked slowly into the house without looking back. It was too dark for him to see the expressions on their faces, in any case. But he knew that, in the dimness, they were following him with eyes of love.

He slept long and peacefully. When he woke, the sun was streaming into the room and, in a straight-back chair, drawn near enough to the bed to permit close observation of its occupant, Lance Castel was sitting, upright and motionless, holding in his hand a long white envelope. Instantly the boy rose and saluted.

"I hope I'm not intruding or presuming, Sir," he said respectfully. "Major Villeré and Captain Beauregard thought it would be all right for me to come here—in fact, Captain Beauregard showed me the way to your room himself. When this letter was delivered to the house yesterday afternoon, I noticed it was marked urgent; so, as today is Sunday and I'm not on duty at the bank, I rode down here this morning to bring it to you. You didn't say when you were coming back to New Orleans, Sir, and I thought there might be something in the letter that required your attention."

"You're right, there might be. My son René has reminded me that Sunday is often a significant day for me. It was kind and thoughtful of you to bring the letter."

He took the long envelope from Lance and glanced at the return address. It bore the name of a famous New York firm—the firm, if he were not mistaken, with which Derek Vanderveer had some important connection. As he tore the envelope open, the impression was confirmed by the sight of Derek's well-remembered handwriting. He read eagerly and quickly.

Dear Beau—

Here I am back in the United States at last and thankful of it. My mission to Paris was a success and Paris is great for a while, but for a steady diet give me New York City any time.

I'm sorry to say that none of the feelers I put out for your drummer boy got me anywhere. However, I wouldn't give up hope, if I were you, or let his mother and grandmother do so. I don't need to tell you that there've been a number of irregular forces roaming around in the South since Appomattox, and that when Kirby Smith finally surrendered, a month or so later, and went off to Mexico, some of his officers and men went with him. Your boy may be there. I've heard of several cases where a soldier given up for dead turned up safe and well one day without having been able to give his family any warning, transportation and communication still being so far from normal. Perhaps that's what has already happened in the case you're interested in. Let me know. If it hasn't, of course I'll continue investigations.

"So far, the letter is about you, Lance," Pierre said, glancing up. "The writer of it, Mr. Derek Vanderveer of New York, is one of several old friends to whom I wrote, hoping that he might help us to trace you. He's regretful that he hasn't had any luck. Remind me to write him that he needn't continue his search. I must write to General Sherman and General McClellan to the same effect. They have tried to be helpful, too."

"Yes, Sir," Lance said. If he felt any surprise he did not show it. Pierre resumed his reading.

Meanwhile, I've something else on my mind. News does still get around, often through the most unexpected channels, and I heard a few days ago that Captain T. S. Williams, General Superintendent of the New Orleans, Jackson and Great Northern Railroad, was about to resign. Of course, it was a good deal of a wreck when the Federal Government finally surrendered its control to the old directors last spring; but the new president, Mr. C. C. Shackleford of Canton, Mississippi, is the right man to see that it gets back into shape. He can do it if he has help in the form of an honest experienced engineering expert as superintendent. I don't know whether or not a position like that would interest you, but I've taken the liberty of mentioning your name where I thought it would do the most good, and I think you'll be hearing from Shackleford almost any day now. In fact, I'm sure a representative of his will call on you. The salary offered will probably be around thirty-five hundred a year, but I think that can be pushed up to five thousand after things get going. Incidentally, I believe Shackleford wants to hold office only long enough to get order out of chaos, and if you took over the engineering work and made a go of it, you'd be in line for the presidency yourself.

Well, as I said before, this may not appeal to you at all and don't think for a minute that I'll be offended or embarrassed if you refuse to take the position. But I somehow gathered from the letter I received in Paris that you were quite eager to get going again and this might be a stopgap until something better comes along. I hope to see you in the not too distant future. Probably you will need to come to New York, possibly even to go abroad, in connection with your railroading, if you decide to undertake it. Meanwhile, perhaps I can get away from the office long enough to come to New Orleans. The place doesn't matter if we can get together. I've missed seeing you.

Yours ever,
Derek

"It isn't bad news, is it, Sir?" Lance asked anxiously, as Pierre put the letter back in the envelope. His fingers were trembling; he could not help it, and he was afraid in a minute his face would betray still more unmistakable signs of emotion. He tried to speak and found that he could not, but he looked at Lance and shook his head, summoning a tremulous smile.

"Are you feeling ill, Sir? Shall I call Captain Beauregard?"

Again Pierre shook his head. He still could not speak and he realized that his vision was blurred. But however indistinct this might be, in his mind's eye he could still see those dazzling figures—thirty-five hundred pushed up to five thousand! Money enough to bring René to New Orleans at last and provide for his legal education; money enough to give similar advantages to Henri and Doucette; money enough to help Charles meet his most pressing financial problems; money enough to send for Mamie; money enough to establish a simple but suitable design for living, proper for the superintendent—proper for the president—of a railroad. With such a sum at his disposal, he could no longer be classified as a vagrant on a park bench—as a pensioner on a woman's bounty—as an object of charity to friends. He would hold an honorable position, a position requiring experience and talent and knowledge, a position of responsibility and prestige. He was about to rise triumphant from the depths of discouragement and humiliation which had engulfed him. He was about to resume his predestined place among his peers. . . .

He found his voice. "You say you rode down, Lance?"

"Yes, Sir."

"There are still two or three horses left on the place. Please go and tell Major Villeré I need to borrow one—whichever he can best spare. I'll see it's returned to him promptly. As soon as I've taken temporary leave of my family and told them my *good* news, I'll be riding back to New Orleans with you to keep an important business appointment."

"Yes, Sir."

"And, Lance. You're not the only wage-earner any longer. I've got a job, too!"

THE END

Beauregard House
January 1944–July 1962

AUTHOR'S NOTE

MY ORIGINAL TENANCY OF BEAUREGARD HOUSE WAS APPARENTLY A happy accident. I stumbled on it when I was searching for temporary headquarters and nothing else seemed to be available. But I have long since ceased to believe that such occurrences are accidental; I am convinced that they are part of a pattern in which a Power higher than ours has had a Hand.

It began in this way: in 1944, when I was writing *The River Road*, I lived at the so-called Cottage—a twenty-room ante-bellum house situated on that road about eight miles south of Baton Rouge. Despite its comparative proximity to the capital of Louisiana, the Cottage seemed much more isolated than any other place I had ever lived. We had no telephone, no mail service, no drinking water and no delivery of any staple commodity; our groceries and water were brought out from Baton Rouge, our milk picked up at a dairy along the way. My secretary did these errands and went to the post office before she came to work in the morning; our wartime gasoline allowance was just large enough for her to make the trip six times a week. I seldom went anywhere.

Then it was discovered that I would simply have to come to New Orleans occasionally for research, editorial conferences and medical treatment. The members of the rationing board were reasonable; they agreed to allow me sufficient extra gas to get here once a month; more than that they said they could not do, and I recognized the difficulty of their position. But, at that time, a stay in a hotel was limited to five days; if I could not get in all the research, all the editorial conferences and all the medical treatments necessary in that length of time, it was just too bad; they would have to be put off another month and the book, not to mention my somewhat precarious health, would suffer. Besides, even five days at a hotel ran into tall money, what with a sitting room in which to hold the editorial conferences and garage space for a car. Room service was limited, to say the least, and meals in the dining room consumed too much time, always provided the dining room was open when I wanted or needed to eat. I went to bed hungry a good many nights because, after the conferences were over, I was too tired to go out in search of food and there was none to be had at the hotel. All in all, the arrangement seemed very unsatisfactory and I decided that the solution might be a small apartment which I could use as a *pied-à-terre*. Such accommodations were admittedly hard to come by; there was always that reminder, "Don't you know there's a war on?" But the undertaking seemed worth a try. I could not believe that there was not some sort of shelter in New Orleans which would cost less than five hundred dollars a month and that was what I was spending at the hotel. I started making inquiries. At first, I encountered only sad shakings of the head. Then someone said to me, "Well, there's the old Beauregard House."

"The Beauregard House?" I repeated with perplexity.

"Yes, it's always called that. General Beauregard never owned it and he lived there only two years, but they were important years. The house was built by a Spanish architect for a French auctioneer, who was the grandfather of Paul Morphy—you know, the great chess player. It was a beautiful house once; it still is, architecturally, and of course historically it's noteworthy. But it fell into disrepair after the Civil War and a few years ago it was slated for destruction, to make way for a macaroni factory. A small group of patriotic women banded together and saved it; they call themselves Beauregard House, Inc. They've done some patching up and divided the main house into two apartments. Nothing's been done to the quarters or the patio and the land where the side garden was has been sold off separately. There's a hideous chemical warehouse on it now and, of course, the neighborhood's terribly run down. But if you're really desperate for someplace to live in New Orleans . . . I understand one of the apartments has just been vacated because the tenant was dissatisfied and the tenant in the other one wants to move, too. You might at least go and have a look at the place."

Such was my introduction to Beauregard House. A week later, I moved into half of it (which, meantime, I had subjected to a very thorough housecleaning); a week after that, I extended my occupancy to the other half. And, almost before I realized what had happened, I began to dream of restoring it, if not to its erstwhile grandeur, at least to some semblance of its original dignity and symmetry. It was a very daring dream, for I knew that such improvements should include the patio and the slave quarters at least and, if possible, the separate section of the property which had once been a garden. I also realized this would have to be done very slowly, because it would be an expensive process and I could not earn money enough to do it quickly; and I further realized that my other commitments, not to mention my attachment to my own home, would keep me away from it a great deal. But I had begun to sense that, for a long while, this was where I would want to work and live during the winter, or at least part of every winter because, despite all the other work I would be doing and all the other places I would be going, I would be laying the foundations for a story about the greatest tenant the house has ever had—Pierre Gustave Toutant Beauregard.

It took nearly eighteen years to lay these foundations because, meanwhile, I have written eighteen books on other subjects; I have been three times to South America and twelve times to Europe on varied assignments; and I have always managed to squeeze out a few weeks at home—the upper Connecticut Valley—and a few weeks in Washington every year. But with all these different activities, the book we are now calling *Madame Castel's Lodger* has been my ultimate objective, because I have felt, as Hamilton Basso says in *The Great Creole*, his inspired biography of Beauregard, "I wanted, as far as I was able, to capture the feeling of a time and the spirit of a man— a man I believe to have been one of the very considerable figures of the Civil War. I claim for him no enormous greatness. He had, however, his moments of real genius and he has not been given his just due."

In attempting this "capture," the center I obtained for my work has been, from the beginning, a tremendous source of inspiration. Every year Beauregard House has returned a bit nearer its original state. When my first short lease approached its termination, I was able to sign a longer one, on condition that I would continue and expand the work of restoration that Beauregard House, Inc., had begun. Then, as the patriotic but elderly ladies who had made up that organization scattered, lost interest or died, I was enabled to secure a transfer of the property to the Keyes Foundation. The lot which had originally been the side garden and which had been pre-empted by the ugly chemical warehouse—now condemned as a fire hazard—was reclaimed, the building demolished and a garden, following as closely as possible the lines of the original one, was laid out. When this was done, I began to feel that I had realized the first part of my objective; with the improvements already made in the rest of the property, it was now restored to a semblance of its original dignity and symmetry. I could not possibly ask for a more suitable setting in which to write the book for which I had been so long laying the foundations. And, with the exception of one chapter drafted in Lima, Peru, every word of *Madame Castel's Lodger* has been written where Pierre Gustave Toutant Beauregard began his memoirs.

To the best of my knowledge and belief, no liberties have been taken with the known facts of history. Pierre's letter to Laure about Mango de Clavo is fictional, but the substance of it is not; the same is true of Caroline's letters to Pierre. Conversations are, of course, imaginary; but in every case they are based either on real situations or on situations which are typical of time, place and condition. The characters of Mme Cougot, Simone Castel, Lance Castel and Derek Vanderveer and his parents are fictional. There is no record—at least I have been unable to find one and neither has anyone I have consulted—of the identity of the caretaker at what we now call Beauregard House while it was owned successively by Mme L. A. Garidel and Dominique Lanata; but we do know that they did not live here themselves and that the property was considered valuable enough to require supervision. Neither has it been possible to get a complete list of the pupils at the Peugnets' school in New York; but it is a known fact that Beauregard made many Northern friends there and that these friendships were valuable to him in later life. The Fieldings and the Negroes who befriended Lance after he was wounded are also fictional; but his experiences following the Battle of Shiloh— after which 959 Confederates were reported missing, in addition to the many more killed and wounded—are typical of several I have been able to trace. The military personnel at Fort Jackson; Mme Castel's maid Bette and some of the plantation Negroes have also been given fictional names and the cook at Contreras has been christened Edné, in honor of the incomparable *cuisinière* by that name who presides over the kitchen of my friends, the Frederick J. Nehrbasses, in Lafayette; but Placide and Tombie are mentioned in Hamilton Basso's *The Great Creole*; Louison, Theophilus and Manette in René Beauregard's *Reminiscences of Upper Magnolia*; and Mamie was a famous character and featured as such in an excellent article published in the New Orleans *Times-Democrat* September 10, 1882.

Aside from these, none of the characters in the book is imaginary; and though, of course, the story has been told from Pierre's viewpoint—which is not necessarily always that of the author—a sincere effort has been made not to "slant" any reference in favor of the hero and his record, to show his weaknesses as well as his strength and his faults as well as his virtues. Official documents have been consulted wherever these were available; so have family papers, reliable diaries and, of course, standard works of history. In the case where the latter have been out of print, a conscientious search has been made for them and this has generally been rewarded.

As usual, I have had able assistance in this work of research and verification from numerous persons, functioning in numerous ways. At the very head of the list unquestionably belongs Charles L. Dufour, generally known as "Pie" to perpetuate a childhood nickname: a man of such varied talents and vocations that I shall undoubtedly omit several in endeavoring to enumerate them. Having begun his newspaper career as a sports writer, he enlarged his field to include frequent reviews of musical and dramatic performances. These reviews are dashed off in addition to the daily column, "Pie Dufour's A La Mode," which is one of the leading features in the New Orleans *States-Item*. This column, like that of his friend and associate, Hermann B. Deutsch, covers all sorts of subjects; but in Pie's case, whenever there is any logical way of connecting it with Civil War history, this is what happens, for the Civil War is not only his specialty but also his passion. He lectures on it at Tulane University. He has written two books about it already and has two more in the process of construction. When he goes on a trip it is to visit and revisit a battlefield or, better yet, several battlefields. When he reads for pleasure, it is about some phase of the war or some theory connected with it. As a conscientious journalist, he scrupulously fulfills every requirement of his newspaper. As a highly esteemed member of society, he mingles with his friends. But when all this is done, the rest of his time belongs to his teen-age daughter and the Civil War.

Somehow—and this seems to me a minor miracle—Pie Dufour has managed to wedge in enough spare hours to guide my faltering footsteps through the Battles of Manassas, Shiloh and the Crater, clarify the siege of Charleston and the fall of the Mississippi River forts and help me to sum up all the resultant situations. And though, as I have tried to indicate, the Civil War is his favorite subject, he is almost equally familiar with the Mexican War. Having survived (in a literary sense), Manassas, Shiloh and other major conflicts of 1861–1865, I turned the calendar back to 1847 and soon had Pie Dufour's support as I went limping over the Pedregal where, as Douglas Southall Freeman put it, both Lee and Beauregard won "laurels on a lava field."

It is hardly necessary to state that alligators are not among the creatures of field, forest and stream with which I am most familiar; but the brief account in René Beauregard's delightful diary of a female alligator and her nest so intrigued me that I persuaded Hermann Deutsch, long one of my best editorial advisers, to help me describe such an adventure in detail. In the course of doing so, a question which had nothing to do with hunting, but a good deal to do with idiom, arose to plague me. We know that Pierre Beauregard spoke nothing but French until he went to school in New York; Placide and Tombie, his companions in the forest, also spoke nothing but French—their own peculiar form of so-called gumbo French, comprehensible to their fellow slaves and their masters, but to very few outsiders. To be realistic, this is the sort of dialect I should have used in the alligator scene; but it would have been almost sure to baffle and very possibly to annoy nearly all my readers. We experimented, with the help of Mrs. Frederick J. Nehrbass of Lafayette—who, as the former Marie Mouton, was thoroughly familiar with the gumbo French spoken by the Negroes on her father's plantation—and put Mamie's conversation with Pierre, after Laure's death, into such patois. The result has been carefully preserved and can be shown to any reader upon request. But it was enough to convince all of us here that the correlative conversation on the alligator hunt must be changed to something more readable. Admittedly, present-day Negro rural dialect in southern Louisiana is an unsatisfactory substitute, but it seemed the best compromise.

To return to Hermann Deutsch for a moment, it was he who brought to my slave quarters the eminent civil engineer, Mr. Rudolph Hirschberg, Chief of the Engineering Department of the Levee Section, so that among us we could work out plausible details of a flood condition sufficiently serious to summon Pierre Beauregard to Fort Jackson at a time when he would normally have been properly loath to leave home. Subsequent conversations with Mr. Deutsch, Mr. Hirschberg and Mr. George Hero, Commissioner of Public Utilities for Plaquemines Parish, enabled me to describe the accident at Fort St. Philip, which came so near to being fatal to Beauregard because of climatic conditions. Mr. Deutsch also made helpful suggestions about other aspects of climatic conditions, about the earlier part of the Mexican War, and about plausible explanations for long periods of absence on the part of those missing in action after Shiloh.

Leonard V. Huber, director and co-owner with his brother of Hope Mausoleum, President of the Orleans Parish Landmarks Commission and past President of the Louisiana Landmarks Society, is also what is known as a "postal historian." He specializes in certain aspects of the Civil War, particularly those affecting transportation and communication; he has written several books on these and allied subjects and has assembled volumes of correspondence carried on early railroads and steamboats. He is, moreover, an avid amateur of prints and has one of the finest collections in the South. Is it necessary, for fictional purposes, to find out how often a steamboat plied between various obscure points and the name of such a steamer? Leonard

Huber has the information at his fingertips. Is the description of a black-bordered mourning notice, posted on trees and telegraph poles to bid friends and relatives to a funeral, so baffling to an outsider that she sees no way of making it clear to anyone else? Leonard Huber has a raft of such notices. He will gladly lend a few and anything else along the same lines that the struggling author would like to look over. He will get them to you tomorrow morning, or this very evening, if you really need them that soon.

For help with genealogical material, I am especially indebted to Mr. Sidney L. Villeré, Laure Villeré Beauregard's third cousin and great-grandson of Caliste Villeré, owner of Point Beca Plantation, who has made a thorough study of this and delights in its details, as well as in all details of plantation life. He has kindly allowed me the poetic license of describing the story of Quabinen as taking place at Upper Magnolia, whereas it actually occurred at Point Beca; the description of the beautiful door with the ogive arch and the panels of varicolored glass belongs to one plantation as much as to the other; the same is true of the menus used incidentally in several places and of the ancestral recipes which form part of the introductory material for Chapter 8.

For further help with genealogical material, I am indebted to Mrs. C. G. Alba, Mrs. R. M. Boland and Mrs. Herbert H. Bleuler, the granddaughters of Charles and Celestine Turpin and, hence, Caroline Deslonde Beauregard's cousins twice removed; to Mrs. George W. Davis, a great-great-great-granddaughter of Pierre de la Ronde, whose grandson, Pierre Adolphe Ducros, was a cousin and contemporary of Pierre Beauregard (Mrs. Davis began her services by supplying me with the de la Ronde family tree and went on to more expansive genealogical research in my behalf); to the Rev. Girard J. Pelletier, who made a thorough search of the records of St. John the Baptist Church in Edgard for statistics about the Deslonde family; and to Catherine Tomsyck who, with infinite patience, simplified the intricate genealogical charts of the Beauregard, Villeré and Deslonde families, so that they would be readily comprehensible.

The diary of Thomas K. Wharton, a prominent architect who was also a professional associate of Beauregard, and which is a treasure trove of information, was first called to my attention by Samuel Wilson, Jr., and later by Pie Dufour and has been freely consulted; so have Jules Villeré's account book, a copy of which was loaned me by Sidney L. Villeré; so have the reminiscences of General Beauregard's elder son, René. The monograph entitled "Magnolia," divided into eight chapters and supplemented with copious notes, is especially valuable. The Master's thesis on the Mississippi River forts written by Ernest A. Landry, now Supervisor of the Lafayette Parish Schools and previously on the faculty of the University of Southwestern Louisiana, when he was principal of the Buras High School and studying for his Master's Degree in History, is a scholarly and informative document which I have found a mine of useful information. John Adams of Boston—age ten!—furnished an interesting item about Manassas.

General source material has come to me from various individuals and institutions. Mr. Stanley F. Horn, whose *The Army of Tennessee* is a "must" on any Civil War reading list, supplied me with several well-authenticated stories of soldiers missing after the Battle of Shiloh. A scrapbook loaned me by Mr. Cuthbert Baldwin, whose grandmother, Julia Deslonde Seixas, was a sister of Caroline Deslonde Beauregard, specializes in necrologies and sheds much information on family history. Mrs. W. B. Parks (the daughter of Samuel Douglas McEnery, who was successively Lieutenant Governor and Governor of Louisiana and United States Senator from Louisiana) sent me a list of the New Orleans street cries most current in her youth and in the period immediately before that. Mrs. Edward Keating, a graduate of Visitation Convent in Georgetown, gave me the booklet issued by that institution, entitled "The Founding of a Young Ladies' Academy" and put me in touch with the current historian of the Convent, who supplemented the booklet's information about Virginia Scott and Caroline Deslonde in connection with Visitation. Mrs. Beverly Middleton, in whose historic Victorian house I discovered the wonderful print which, with her permission and her husband's, we are using for endpapers, told me the delightful story about General Beauregard's cow. Dr. Milby Burton, Director of the Charleston Museum, facilitated the acquisition of important photographs. Leon Maggiore's collection of old post cards provided helpful source material for details in the jacket and incidental illustrations. Mrs. Elizabeth G. Van Exem of Cedar Tree Plantation, Ridgeway, S.C., gave me helpful introductions.

I am very grateful to all these persons for their contributions; each one has been valuable in its way. But just as I feel Pie Dufour's name should lead all the rest when it comes to editorial and statistical assistance, so do I feel that John B. Gravelle's name should lead all the rest when it comes to cooperation with general source material. I was referred to him as the owner and restorer of Franklin Pierce's house in Concord, New Hampshire, where he and his wife now live; he might, my informer said, have something of value to tell me about the Mexican War, regarding which I was having a good deal of difficulty so far as suitable source material was concerned; he not only possessed a library well stocked with books about the Mexican War in general and Franklin Pierce (of whose life he had made a special study) in particular; he had become so deeply interested in the subject that he had gone over the entire route traversed by General Pierce and his army from Vera Cruz to Mexico City, and had recorded his impressions of the altitude, the desert and the lava beds. I hastened to write Mr. Gravelle and his response to my inquiries was both prompt and generous. His letters contained much valuable information and he *gave*—not loaned—me three rare out-of-print books: *The Mexican War* by Edward D. Mansfield, *The Life of General Franklin Pierce* by D. W. Bartlett, and *The Life of Franklin Pierce* by Nathaniel Hawthorne. I had not previously known that Nathaniel Hawthorne, whom I had hitherto associated entirely with his novels, ever wrote a biography of our New Hampshire President, who was such a good friend of the South, and my knowledge of American literature, as well as my knowledge of American history, was enriched by this gift. And, as Mr. Gravelle became better acquainted, through correspondence, with my present project, he added a fourth book, for which I had long combed secondhand bookstores in vain: *Swords and Roses* by Joseph Hergesheimer.

My strong feeling that if it is humanly possible I must see for myself any place with which I am not familiar and which I am attempting to describe, naturally led to a strong desire to see the forts which played so large a part in my hero's history. St. Philip is, alas! inaccessible, except by air, and the semi-promise of a visit by helicopter never materialized. A year ago, Fort Jackson would also have been inaccessible. Now, thanks to the Plaquemines Parish Fort Jackson Centennial Commission, it has been superbly restored; and in April, I spent there one of the most delightful and illuminating days that I have ever passed in Louisiana, with Mr. Luke Petrovich, Commissioner of Public Safety for Plaquemines Parish, acting as my guide. My friend Mrs. Kenneth T. Price, whose late husband was for many years District Manager of the Freeport Sulphur Company at Port Sulphur and was therefore a long-time resident of Plaquemines Parish, who was also fully familiar with this work, made the arrangements for the visit and took me to Fort Jackson in her car, with a stop for lunch at the Freeport Sulphur guest house, long one of my favorite haunts; the oyster pies, corn puddings and steak with "rusty" gravy made by its dusky presiding deity, Buster, are something to dream about. (The Guide Michelin would give them three stars and pronounced them "worthy of a detour!")

This excursion was so delightful and so successful that, a week or so later, Mrs. Price and I undertook the trip to the even more isolated Fort Livingston on Grande Terre Island and toured this under the direction of Dr. L. S. St. Amant, Chief Marine Biologist of the Louisiana State Wild Life and Fisheries Commission. This outing proved equally informative and equally enjoyable; and Dr. St. Amant was kind enough to read that part of my script which dealt with the fort and, in the course of a visit to me in my well-named slave quarters, to make valuable suggestions in regard to it.

I am grateful for the courtesy and co-operation shown me by Mr. V. L. Bedsole, Miss Marcelle F. Schertz and Mrs. Elsa B. Meier of the Department of Archives and to Mrs. Marguerite D. Broussard, Chief Circulation Librarian of Louisiana State University; to Mr. Sidney Forman, Librarian, and Mr. Joseph M. O'Connell of the Archives and History Division of the United States Military Academy at West Point in furnishing me with needed documents.

Several of General Beauregard's descendants have been very helpful. Among these are Mrs. Kenneth G. B. Ketchum (Esther Toutant Beauregard) of Waterdown, Ontario, a great-niece of the General, who has supplied general information; Mrs. Porter F. Bedell (Elizabeth Toutant Beauregard) a great-grandniece of the General, whose husband is commanding officer of the Pensacola Naval Air Station and who owns the wonderful portraits of the General's parents and grandparents, his parents' epergne and his niece's wedding china, and kindly had all these photographed for me, so I could include them in "Pierre's family album"; Mr. Alexander Morse, a great-grandson, who gave me a trunk which had belonged to the General and supplied me with the photostat of the invaluable letter, which he owns, from Lee to Beauregard concerning the Superintendency at West Point; and Miss Laure Beauregard Larendon, who loaned me the charming daguerreotype of her mother, the General's beloved daughter Doucette, and the equally charming photograph of her stepmother, Caroline Deslonde, reproduction of which form two of the chief ornaments in the family album.

Inevitably, part of the burden with which the creation of a book weighs me down is carried by my secretarial and domestic staff. The sudden and tragic death of my junior secretary, Veronica Hornblower, when *Madame Castel's Lodger* was less than half finished, has made the load even heavier than usual, both for me and for my senior secretary, Geraldine Bullock. As one of my granddaughters said, all too truthfully, "Ronnie will be difficult to replace professionally and impossible to replace personally." So far, we have not sufficiently recovered from the shock and grief of her loss to attempt any permanent arrangement for someone else to do her work; but Deanie and I have had intermittent help, for which we are very grateful, from Roberta Guillory and Catherine Tomsyck. In the domestic department, Carroll Fuller, Leona Pfister and all the latter's family are outstanding among those who have stood by; we are very grateful to them, too.

F. P. K.

BIBLIOGRAPHY

Bartlett, D. W., *The Life of Gen. Franklin Pierce*. Auburn, New York: Derby & Miller.

Basso, Hamilton, *Beauregard: The Great Creole*. New York: Charles Scribner's Sons.

Dowdey, Clifford, *Lee's Last Campaign*. Boston: Little, Brown and Company.

Dufour, Charles L., *Gentle Tiger, The Gallant Life of Roberdeau Wheat*. Baton Rouge, Louisiana: Louisiana State University Press.

Freeman, Douglas Southall, *Lee's Lieutenants: A Study in Command* (4 vols.). New York: Charles Scribner's Sons.

——, *R. E. Lee: A Biography* (4 vols.). New York: Charles Scribner's Sons.

Hanighen, Frank C., *Santa Anna, the Napoleon of the West*. New York: Coward-McCann, Inc.

Hawthorne, Nathaniel, *Life of Franklin Pierce*. Boston: Ticknor, Reed and Fields.

Meade, Robert Douthat, *Judah P. Benjamin, Confederate Statesman*. New York: Oxford University Press.

Roman, Alfred, *The Military Operations of General Beauregard* (2 vols.). New York: Harper & Brothers.

Sears, Louis Martin, *John Slidell*. Durham, N. C.: Duke University Press.

Smith, Arthur D. Howden, *Old Fuss and Feathers, The Life and Exploits of Lt.-General Winfield Scott*. New York: The Greystone Press.

Werlich, Robert, *"Beast" Butler*. Washington, D. C.: Quaker Press.

Williams, T. Harry, *P. G. T. Beauregard: Napoleon in Gray*. Baton Rouge, Louisiana: Louisiana State University Press.

——, *With Beauregard in Mexico*. Baton Rouge, Louisiana: Louisiana State University Press.

Willson, Beckles, *John Slidell and the Confederates in Paris (1862–65)*. New York: Minton, Balch & Company.

Beauregard, Gen. G. T., *Battle of Manassas*. New York: G. P. Putnam's Sons.

Catton, Bruce, *The Coming Fury*. Garden City, N. Y.: Doubleday & Company, Inc.

Downey, Fairfax, in consultation with Paul M. Angle, *Texas and the War with Mexico.* New York: American Heritage Publishing Co., Inc.

Dufour, Charles L., *The Night the War Was Lost.* Garden City, N. Y.: Doubleday & Company, Inc.

Eliot, Ellsworth, Jr., *West Point in the Confederacy.* New York: G. A. Baker & Co., Inc.

Farley, Joseph Pearson, *West Point in the Early Sixties with Incidents of the War.* Troy, N. Y.: Pafraets Book Company.

Hanson, Joseph Mills, *Bull Run Remembers . . .* Manassas, Virginia: National Capitol Publishers, Inc.

Hergesheimer, Joseph, *Swords and Roses.* New York: Alfred A. Knopf.

Horn, Stanley F., *The Army of Tennessee.* Norman, Oklahoma: University of Oklahoma Press.

Jones, Archer, *Confederate Strategy from Shiloh to Vicksburg.* Baton Rouge, Louisiana: Louisiana State University Press.

Manchester, Harland, *The Saga of Chapultepec.* Floral Park, N. Y.: *Travel* Magazine (June, 1962).

Mansfield, Edward D., *The Mexican War: A History of its Origin.* New York: A. S. Barnes & Co.

Pleasants, Henry Jr. and Straley, George H., *Inferno at Petersburg.* Philadelphia and New York: Chilton Company.

Schaff, Morris, *The Spirit of Old West Point 1858–1862.* Boston: Houghton Mifflin Company.

Swanberg, W. A., *First Blood: The Story of Fort Sumter.* New York: Charles Scribner's Sons.

Smith, Justin H., *The War with Mexico* (Vol. II). New York: The Macmillan Company.

Bourne, Peter, *Flames of Empire.* New York: G. P. Putnam's Sons.

Delmar, Viña, *Beloved.* New York: Harcourt, Brace and Company.

———, *The Big Family.* New York: Harcourt, Brace and Company.

Williams, Ben Ames, *House Divided.* Boston: Houghton Mifflin Company.

Gayarré, Charles, *History of Louisiana: The Spanish Domination.* New York: Redfield.

Grandjean, Léon H., *Crayon Reproductions of Leon J. Fremaux's New Orleans Characters and Additional Sketches.* New Orleans: Produced by Alfred F. Bayhi.

King, Grace, *Creole Families of New Orleans.* New York: The Macmillan Company.

Seebold, Herman de Bachellé, Dr., *Old Louisiana Plantation Homes and Family Trees* (2 vols.). Published privately.

Workers of the Writers' Program of the Work Projects Administration